KU-084-932

THE FIVE WINDS

Also by Patricia Shaw

Valley of Lagoons
River of the Sun
The Feather and the Stone
Where the Willows Weep
Cry of the Rain Bird
Fires of Fortune
The Opal Seekers
The Glittering Fields
A Cross of Stars
Orchid Bay
Waiting for the Thunder
The Dream Seekers
On Emerald Downs

THE FIVE WINDS

Patricia Shaw

headline

Copyright © 2003 Patricia Shaw

The right of Patricia Shaw to be identified as the Author of
the Work has been asserted by her in accordance with
the Copyright, Designs and Patents Act 1988.

First published in 2003
by HEADLINE BOOK PUBLISHING

10 9 8 7 6 5 4 3 2 1

All rights reserved. No part of this publication may be
reproduced, stored in a retrieval system, or transmitted,
in any form or by any means without the prior written
permission of the publisher, nor be otherwise circulated
in any form of binding or cover other than that in which
it is published and without a similar condition being
imposed on the subsequent purchaser.

All characters in this publication are fictitious and any
resemblance to real persons, living or dead, is purely coincidental.

Cataloguing in Publication Data is available from the British Library

ISBN 0 7553 0372 5 (hardback)
ISBN 0 7553 0374 1 (trade paperback)

Typeset in Times New Roman by
Avon DataSet Ltd, Bidford-on-Avon, Warks

Printed and bound in Great Britain by
Clays Ltd, St Ives plc, Bungay, Suffolk

HEADLINE BOOK PUBLISHING
A division of Hodder Headline
338 Euston Road
London NW1 3BH

www.headline.co.uk
www.hodderheadline.com

Fond memories of teachers and friends
at Star of the Sea College, Gardenvale,
including Alma Corby, Irene Mountford,
and Eileen Rushford

MORAY COUNCIL
LIBRARIES &
INFO.SERVICES

20 11 66 07

Askews

F

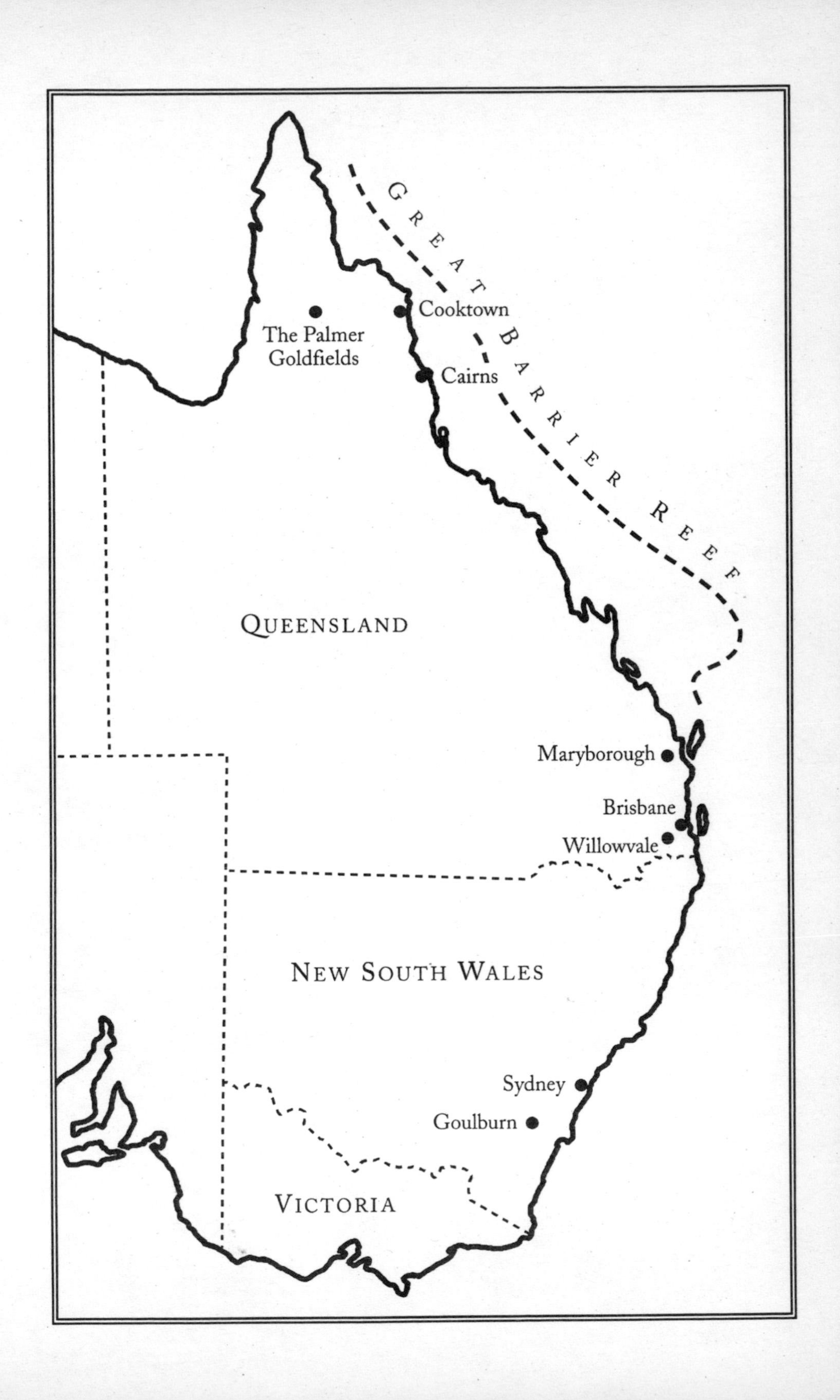
GREAT BARRIER REEF
Cooktown
The Palmer Goldfields
Cairns
QUEENSLAND
Maryborough
Brisbane
Willowvale
NEW SOUTH WALES
Sydney
Goulburn
VICTORIA

Chapter One

1873

The neat packet ship, out of Hong Kong, sailed smoothly into the long sea passage between the Great Barrier Reef and the Queensland coast, a mild breeze echoing the captain's sigh of relief. Though these waters, with their myriad islands and smaller unchartered reefs, could be hazardous, they were a haven compared to the dangerous seas the *China Belle* had encountered. It had been the worst run of bad weather Captain Judd Loveridge had ever encountered on this route, and he thanked the Lord he'd had an auxiliary engine to fall back on.

After the battering his ship had taken in the South China Sea, the captain had held over in Singapore for a few extra days to carry out repairs and find a replacement for First Officer Barrett, who had suffered a broken leg in a vain attempt to contain listing cargo. He had managed to locate a new fellow, an Australian, Jake Tussup, who had been second officer on SS *Meridian*, which had run aground in the Straits. Tussup was not exactly the type he would have chosen, given the choice, but Loveridge knew he'd be hard put to find anyone who could fill Barrett's shoes.

At least, though, the enforced delay in port had given his passengers some respite. Had Singapore been a more salubrious town he wouldn't have been surprised if most of his passengers had struggled ashore and stayed there until they'd properly recovered from the debilitating effects of sustained seasickness. But as Lyle Horwood had said: 'I'm sure we're over the worst, Captain. We're all agreed to press on.'

The captain smiled. Horwood's wife had endured dreadful seasickness, but her elderly husband had ridden out the storms like an old salt. He and the young fellow, Willoughby, had presented for all meals and as they whiled away the time in the lurching saloon playing cards, they had struck up quite a friendship – though, from Loveridge's viewpoint, they were worlds apart. Horwood was a distinguished gentleman, a director of the Oriental Shipping Line, while Willoughby was more of a rough diamond. It seemed to the captain that this tall, loose-limbed fellow with an angelic smile would be more at home on a horse than ambling about the decks of his ship.

China Belle was his favourite of the Oriental Line. She carried a substantial cargo of rice and tea, but few passengers. There were only six cabins, all first class, catering to an exclusive and wealthy clientele. Loveridge hoped he'd never have to go back to crowded passenger ships after the luxury of his beloved *China Belle*.

He sighed, squinting across at yet another green island surrounded by a white shoreline and a spread of paler waters indicating a shallow reef, and turned the wheel to keep well clear.

'Do you know these waters?' he asked Tussup.

'Not too well, sir. They're tricky with all these reefs scattered about like confetti.'

'Yes, it's hard enough trying to keep clear of the big reef without having to dodge these hazards. Sometimes I think it would be smarter to go round, stick to the open ocean altogether.'

Tussup looked up, surprised. 'You couldn't do that! It would take us right off course. This is the accepted shipping lane!'

'I know. It's just a whim. To be on the safe side we could do with a man up top. Tell the bosun to get someone up there to watch for these damn reefs – one of the Malays.'

His crew, apart from the two officers and bosun, consisted of Malayamen and Chinese, the latter working as cooks and stewards – in all twenty-two seamen, some of whom Loveridge was considering replacing in Brisbane. Admittedly, the ship had pitched about a great deal when confronted with mountainous seas during the storms, but that was no reason for the resentment and ill-temper that permeated attitudes now, as if he'd deliberately placed them in harm's way. Truth be told, even if he'd had to lash them, and shout and bully the panic out of them, he'd brought them through safely, where other skippers might have failed. He'd spoken to the bosun about the moodiness that still hung like a pall over the ship . . .

'What the hell's the matter with them? Make them buck up! The sun's shining so we'll have a good run down to Brisbane now.'

'I don't know. They're still rattled after those China seas, playing the doomed card I think, certain the gods are going to pile us up on a hidden reef. Superstitious mob, they are.'

'Then tell Tom to keep after them. Cut their rations if need be.'

While the bosun had nodded agreement, Loveridge knew that telling Tom Ingleby, his second officer, to whip the crew into shape was a futile order. Tom was a good seaman but a weak fellow. Not much of a disciplinarian. It would be up to Matt Flesser, the bosun, to lower the boom on the miserable whining wretches who couldn't see the bad joss was over.

Nevertheless, with important passengers on board, Loveridge couldn't have a surly crew, so he decided to please everyone by announcing there'd be no night sailing. During the hours of darkness the ship would remain at anchor, safe from the sharp claws of the coral beasts that lay in wait for the unwary.

Loveridge felt better too. The nightmare of the *Atlanta* disaster would remain with him until his dying day. He'd been only seventeen, a deckhand, when she was wrecked, her captain ignoring advice not to take on Bass Strait at night . . . Judd could still hear the racket of smashing timbers as she struck the rocks; the screams and shouts and the violent rush of water, as if they were passing through a pitch-black tunnel, with people being tossed about like stones.

He'd fought his way from the depths to gulp air, grateful for that much, and then struck out, blindly, to keep his head above the relentless surge of waves, not knowing whether he was swimming to, or away from, a shore, but strangely, not caring. Had he been on dry land he'd have been running, racing away in sheer fright from a force that was threatening his young life. Distancing himself.

Judd Loveridge was one of only four survivors of the shipwreck that stole thirty-two lives. His father, Captain Arnold Loveridge, had gone down with his ship.

Not all the passengers were happy with the new arrangement. Horwood had come up to complain about time lost.

'I think you are overreacting, Captain. I demand that this ship keeps moving tonight and every night, on this voyage. It's unthinkable to wallow in such placid seas.'

The captain let Horwood talk himself out, gave no specific response and shrugged when he stormed away. The reefs and islands off this coastline had not yet been precisely chartered, and he considered himself lucky that they'd come down this far without incident. Ever since they'd entered these waters from the Torres Strait, he'd been expecting any minute to hear the fearful scrape and grind of disaster, but now that he'd made the decision he experienced a surge of relief, and allowed himself to appreciate the magnificent scenery. To him the little islands resembled jewels set in a sapphire sea and he reminded himself to place that description in his log.

It was to be the last entry in his log, of the southern voyage of the *China Belle*.

As they dressed for dinner, Lyle Horwood was in a bad mood, fussing with his tie and complaining that his shirt was too stiff.

'Why don't you check them when the washboy brings them back?' he snapped at his wife. 'Surely that's not too much to ask. And what's that rag you've got on? It's bloody dowdy.'

Constance glanced at the wall mirror. She was fond of this gown, a soft floral georgette in muted autumn colours. It was superbly cut and ideal for these warm nights.

'It's not a rag, darling,' she smiled, to mollify him. 'It cost a peg or two, as you know. And it's subdued enough to wear tonight. I don't want to overdress in this small circle.'

'Are you insinuating I lack taste? Let me tell you, I was dining in the right circles before you learned which knife to use. Now put on something better.'

Constance turned back to him. 'What does it matter, Lyle? Goodness me, I don't think we have any need to impress. And this dress is . . .'

Furiously, he reached out, grabbed the dress and just as she was turning away, ripped it at the waistline. 'Now look what you've done!' he snapped. 'Get changed. I'm going up.'

Shaken, she looked down at the torn dress, and slowly stepped out of it, wondering what had brought on this tantrum, while Lyle took up his silver monogrammed brushes and ran them quickly over his thick white hair.

He was very proud of his 'mane' of hair, she reflected contemptuously, in an effort to fight back tears. Oh yes, and he was a fine man too . . . 'very successful. Wealthy. Highly thought of. A real gentlemen. And a widower!'

These were some of the accolades her father, Percy Feltham, had heaped on the reputation of Horwood, when he came home with the grand news for his daughter that he'd met an old friend.

'I must introduce you. You'll love him . . .'

'Why? What does he look like? Please don't embarrass me, Father, by trotting me out to be viewed by some old dodderer. I'm not in any rush to get married.'

'My darling, you're twenty-five, almost on the shelf. Although I have to say I'm glad now you decided to call off your engagement to Reggie. He wouldn't have been suitable at all, but believe me, Lyle Horwood is.'

'What does he look like?' Constance insisted suspiciously.

'He's a fine upstanding fellow! Tall, distinguished. You'll look well beside him. And a beauty like you – he won't be able to resist.'

Despite her mistrust of her father's enthusiasm and her own lack of interest in men of his age, Constance was surprised to find herself attracted to Lyle Horwood, and impressed by his generosity. In their courting days, she reminded herself bitterly, as she slid a hand along the rack, seeking another dress, he was the sweetest, most charming man she'd ever met, and within a few months they were engaged.

After the wedding, in a whirl of excitement, they boarded an Oriental Line ship for Hong Kong, and her new home, the Horwood mansion, overlooking the harbour.

Constance sighed, turning back to the matter at hand and reluctantly chose a red satin gown with a nipped-in waist and a softly draped skirt. It was very low cut, so it should please her husband. Then, since it needed something, she took out a delicate diamond necklace.

It might as well be his necklace, she mused angrily, since he decided when and where she should wear it. He kept it in the bank along with the rest of her jewellery. To be able to wear any of the expensive pieces he'd given her, she had to give him advance notice, and that annoyed her so much that at times she couldn't be bothered asking for them.

The necklace, a wedding present, had stunned her and sent Percy Feltham off into raptures, certain his daughter was headed for a blissful life with his hugely wealthy friend. And at first it was bliss, Constance recalled. Lyle delighted in showing her off, his lovely young bride. He even had her portrait painted and placed in the library of their home. Constance thought it flattered her, the eyes bluer, the hair blonder than the original, but gallantly, Lyle claimed, and his friends agreed, it did not do her justice.

They had a busy social life in Hong Kong, and her husband bought her clothes and accessories, sending clothiers to the house with baskets of fabrics so that she could make a choice. He loved to surprise her with jewellery: diamond and sapphire rings and earrings, pearls, a ruby and pearl brooch, a diamond pin – any occasion would do as long as there was an audience to applaud and share her joy. It took a while for Constance to wake up to that – to his need for company at these personal presentations – but she really didn't mind. They fed his ego and kept him in a good mood, at least for a while. Of late his temper had been worse than usual, probably fuelled by his irritation with this plan to relocate, temporarily, to safer shores in Australia.

She was deliberately stalling now, in no rush to join the pre-dinner socialising, feeling stupid as she clipped on the diamond drop earrings that matched the necklace, knowing how out of place she would look in the small dining saloon.

She sat at the dressing table, fiddling with the loose strands of fair hair that slipped from the combs holding a graceful chignon in place, revealing her long, slim neck, a perfect setting for the necklace. A necklace that had belonged to Fannie!

Constance still shuddered with embarrassment when she recalled the conversation she'd overheard at the New Year's Ball . . .

'Of course that necklace she's wearing was Fannie's,' the woman was saying. 'His first wife. Every piece of jewellery he doles out to this wife belonged to Fannie. Her mother, a German countess, left it all to her. It's not as if Lyle bought any of it.'

The other woman laughed. 'I wouldn't mind hand-me-down jewellery like that. I mean, it doesn't wear out.'

'A bit dated, though, don't you think? I'd have it all reset . . .'

The voices trailed away, and Constance was left standing in the doorway, hurt and confused. Shouldn't he have told her? At least let her know the history of the jewellery? Maybe not, she thought at the time, making excuses for him, excuses that became weaker and faded away altogether when she accepted that she was married to the type of man oft referred to as a street angel. Because he was no angel at home.

Out of sight of his friends and associates, he was a bad-tempered man who treated his wife with wilful disregard. His attitude was made even worse by his inconsistencies. Sometimes he could be courteous, especially when he needed a companion, someone to talk to, but he could turn, without warning, into the household persecutor, sending the servants scurrying and his wife into a state of nerves.

She had spoken to her father only recently, when he'd come to Hong Kong to celebrate her thirtieth birthday, but Feltham was so impressed by the opulence of their home and gardens, and the lifestyle that his daughter had achieved, that he wouldn't hear a word of complaint.

'Does he beat you?'

'No, but he beats the servants quite cruelly and I can't—'

'Oh, come on now, Connie. They probably deserve it. You don't understand oriental servants, he does.'

'But, Father, he has a very nasty temper.'

'Good Lord, Connie, what next? Don't aggravate the man then. I mean to say, my dear, any amount of women would sell their souls to be in your place. The man spoils you – look at those pearls; they're magnificent – and it pains me that you are so ungrateful.'

Before he left she tried again. 'Could I come back to London with you, Father? Just for a short time? I get quite homesick for London.'

He brushed off her request. 'I wish you would settle down, Connie. You seem to do nothing but complain. If your mother were alive she'd be thrilled to see how well you've done. You've got everything money can buy. Do try to be a little less critical of your husband, my dear. We all have our faults you know.' He kissed her on the cheek. 'I'll pray for you.'

'Got everything?' she asked the mirror bitterly. 'I've got nothing. I own nothing. I never have more than a few pounds, my pocket money, like a schoolgirl. He pays all the bills; my jewellery is locked away, only brought out when it pleases him . . .'

She rose and went to the cabin door, the rich gown rustling like the soft hush of the waves, as the ship swung at anchor, but then she hesitated.

'I look like a damn Christmas tree,' she muttered, 'all wrong for tonight. And I refuse to be made a fool of. What's wrong with me that I let him get away with things like this?'

In an instant, she removed the offending jewellery, placed it back in one of the velvet bags that held the various pieces, and then locked her jewel case, and slipped the key on its tiny silver chain into a pocket hidden in an underskirt . . .

She managed a nervous laugh as she left the cabin. Maybe he wouldn't notice that the gown looked a bit odd unadorned.

He never thought of himself as Lyle Horwood now, only as Sir Lyle, as if the two words were one day destined to be wedded, when, he hoped, the good Queen would bless their union, knighting him for services to the Crown, and the colony of Hong Kong. So it had only added to his irritation that the upstart Neville Caporn should call him Lyle as he entered the saloon.

'Here's a starter at last,' Caporn said to his wife. And to the newcomer, with a wave of his sherry glass, 'Thought we'd be dining alone. Where is everybody, Lyle?'

'I've no idea, Mr Caporn,' he responded stiffly.

'Oh, well. Is your lovely wife joining us?'

'Of course!' Horwood noted that Mrs Caporn, an attractive redhead, had made an attempt at formality in a purple silk gown, but Constance would overshadow her on every front.

'How very nice,' the woman was saying. 'After the pounding we took *en route* from Hong Kong, it is so nice for us to be able to enjoy company again. And to think, Lyle,' she giggled, 'people warned us about pirates but not of such fearsome seas.'

'Pirates?' he snapped. 'They'd never attack a ship like this. Cowardly lot, they only go after the smaller craft.'

'Then we should feel safe from them? I do hope so.'

Her husband groaned. 'Esme, pirates would never venture so far south. I wish you'd stop worrying about them.'

Lyle looked towards the door as it opened, expecting his wife, but it was his first wife's cousin Eleanor. Now Eleanor Plummer. He'd caught a glimpse of her this evening, just before he'd gone down to dress for dinner, and couldn't believe that the bitch was on board. He'd known a woman called Mrs Plummer had joined the ship in Singapore, taking cabin six, but he'd no idea it was her. She must have remarried. And if so, where was the husband?

'The lady in six,' he'd asked the cabin steward, 'is she a German lady?'

'Yes, sir. Velly much not always English to talking.'

'It's a wonder I haven't seen her before this. Is she taking all her meals in her cabin?'

'Lady bin indisposed,' the steward said heavily. 'Sick! Better now but. Coming out to dinner with all passengers this night. Good, eh?'

'Bloody hell,' Lyle had muttered, charging back to his cabin. If he'd known that troublemaker would be joining them he'd have taken Constance and left the ship in Singapore.

But now she was here, large as life, wearing a tailored white silk with a navy trim and a neatly draped bustle. Worth of Paris, he judged, without needing a second glance . . . no jewellery except for the large diamond ring that matched the one he'd given to Constance when they announced their engagement. Twin rings, in fact, he fumed. Gifts for his first wife Fannie, now deceased, and Eleanor from their maternal grandmother, who had been very fond of her two granddaughters.

'How are you, Lyle?' Mrs Plummer said coldly, after greeting the others.

'Couldn't be better, my dear. Lost a husband, have you? Travelling alone?'

'No. I know where he is. I believe you're moving to Brisbane?'

'Possibly,' he said with studied disinterest.

'Very sensible,' she drawled. 'I think the English contingent in Hong Kong make rather too much of themselves, poor things.'

'So, to which English contingent does Mr Plummer aspire?'

'None. He's an American. Oh . . . here's your young wife. What a lovely ball gown!'

A steward held the door open as Constance stepped inside, accompanied by the captain, and now, in the wake of Eleanor's sarcasm, Lyle was sorry he'd made her change from that other dress. The red satin *was* a bit much for the small gathering. But at least she wasn't wearing the necklace that usually accompanied it.

'Thank God for that,' he murmured to himself as he went to greet her and steer her to the other side of the wide saloon.

'Who is that woman?' she whispered, peering over her shoulder as he led her towards the Caporns. 'I've seen her somewhere before. She's very grand, isn't she?'

'Mrs Plummer? That old tart! I hardly think so. Here comes Lewis. I wanted a word with him.'

But Lewis ignored his signal, choosing to stay with the lady he'd just escorted into the saloon, Willoughby's wife. Yet another irritation he'd have to bear on this cursed voyage.

Lyle had found Willoughby an easy-going fellow, pleasant enough company, when one had no choice, but he'd been shocked to find the man had a Chinese wife. Definitely beyond the pale in Horwood circles, but having befriended the husband he was now stuck with them both.

Constance blinked, amused. He was still in a cranky mood, although no longer interested in what she was wearing, which was a relief, but to call that striking-looking woman an old tart was ridiculous. Mrs Plummer may be grey-haired, the hair softly waved to frame her face, but she was quite beautiful, and easily a lot younger than Lyle.

He can talk, she mused, and turned to listen to Esme Caporn, who had collared a menu and was reading out the evening's offerings.

'Captain, who is the exquisite Chinese lady?' Eleanor Plummer asked.

'Ah,' he smiled. 'That is Mrs Willoughby.'

'Of course. It would have to be . . . I saw her husband on deck earlier. One couldn't help noticing such beauty in a man.'

'And so they match well,' he agreed.

'Then what is their story?'

'I don't know very much, except they were brought aboard in fine style by lackeys of the Xiu family.'

'The Xiu family indeed! Very high-ranking. Maybe Mr Willoughby is taking his lady to reside in the southern land.'

'It seems so.'

'Then I will find out, because they are beautiful people and I love them already.'

The captain laughed. 'Excellent, but I wish the young gentleman would get in here. He's holding up dinner. Would you care for a glass, Mrs Plummer?'

'Thank you I would. Champagne. It is such a lovely night, I'm so glad you allowed us to enjoy the voyage at our leisure. Now you must introduce me to Mrs Willoughby.'

His name was Mal Willoughby, but his friends called him Sonny. Friends who might remember him, that is, after his four years' absence from the country. He was really looking forward to going home now, home being no place in particular yet, just the bush, the smell of the eucalypts, the familiar voices, the strong birdsongs – 'and,' he said to himself, 'the space.'

China had plenty of space; she was a huge country, no doubt about that. Since he'd grown up in the Australian outback, space didn't intimidate him, but in China there were so many people! So much clatter and chatter everywhere! People! His wife, Jun Lien, could hardly believe that in his country you could travel for days and days and never see a soul. Weeks if you were mad enough, until you ran into Aborigines who have no sense of humour about strangers.

'And there aren't so many people in the towns either,' he'd told her, but she'd laughed at him.

'Oh, tish tosh! How can that be? Your country is as big as China; you must have the population.'

He took her arm lightly as they approached the dining saloon. 'Here comes Mr Lewis. You go on in with him. I want to make one last circuit of the decks before dinner. I still think something's up.'

'You're imagining things,' she told him. 'There's nothing wrong on this ship. I think all the troubles our family has had the last few years have left you jumpy. But it's over now, my love, all that's behind us . . .'

'Go on in,' he said. 'I won't be long.'

He walked quietly along the deck, as quietly as he could in formal pump shoes, wishing he could discard them. He dropped down a few steps to the cabin level and prowled along to the end of the corridor, turning left to the bathrooms, which he checked and found empty.

On the way back he slipped into his cabin and strapped a knife on to his leg, the weapon being a veteran of many unpleasant encounters in China.

Passage on this ship was expensive, he pondered, in which case you'd think the stewards would be faultless. To a certain extent they were, when it came to serving the passengers, but he had noticed much muttering among the Chinese, too many sullen stares and several below-decks meetings between the Horwoods' steward and the Malayamen. It just didn't fit. The steward, Sam Lum, was too prissy to be associating with gorillas like Bartie Lee, Mushi Rana or any of their mob, so what did they have to talk about?

Mal found shipboard life confining. It was normal for him to wander about talking to the crew, even give them a hand with the sails just for something to do, and he couldn't help noticing that there was tension in the air. Some sort of trouble between the Malayamen and the Chinese, maybe. That could easily happen and those fights could turn nasty. It worried him.

He had spent the years in China as an associate of Xiu Tan Lan, patriarch of the Xiu family, who was always on his guard against conspirators and assassins, even on the Queensland goldfields, where they'd first met. Mal had been intrigued by the Chinese gentleman who travelled in great style, with servants and more than fifty coolies, and who was always amazingly well informed about the area he travelled. He owned a huge, comfortable junk, which he kept moored in the Mary River, and when he decided to return to China with a fortune in gold, Mal, who hadn't done too badly himself, went with him, delighted at the prospect of travel to strange countries.

Only then did he find out that Mr Xiu's fears of enemies within the ranks of the Chinese were well founded.

'Though you did not seem to notice,' Xiu told him, 'there are two times as many China people in this north of Australia than European people. My family is Manchu, and we have the honour to be greatly favoured by the Imperial Family. But we have many enemies, secret societies with anti-Manchu purposes, and illegal opium traders, who finance gangsters and pirates. There are spies everywhere, this is why we are always well armed.'

The same air of alertness pervaded life in the great Xiu households, and at first Mal thought they were all a sinister lot, especially when there were stories that someone had been knifed, or uprisings caused real street battles, but gradually he became accustomed to 'China life', as he called it, travelling about the provinces with Mr Xiu, first as a tourist, then as an armed companion, and eventually as a fur trader. Xiu himself insisted he learn this lucrative business so that his travels would result in 'an achievement'.

'When you go home, you could import good furs, continue in the business. Then you have not wasted your time here.'

Back on deck, still uneasy, Mal went forward to look in at the wheelhouse, where he thought he heard two officers arguing. Normally he wouldn't have intruded but on this night everything seemed out of kilter, so he strolled in the open doorway and found them poring over charts.

'I hear we're anchored for the night.'

Surprised, they looked back at him, and then Tussup grinned. 'Yes, we might as well. It'll only be for a couple of nights.'

Mal nodded towards the chart desk. 'What's up?' he teased. 'Can't you make up your minds where we are?'

Tom Ingleby looked decidedly guilty, but Tussup wasn't concerned. 'Slight difference of opinion, Mr Willoughby.' He grinned again. 'On my reckoning we're due east of Endeavour Bay but Tom here reckons we're well north yet.'

'What's at Endeavour Bay?'

'Nothing now. It was where Captain Cook's ship *Endeavour* had to pull in for repairs, so he named it.'

'I don't think any of the country along this coast has been explored,' Tom said quickly. 'It's all just jungle.'

'I suppose so,' Mal said vaguely, feeling a little foolish as they turned back to study the large chart and take measurements with their instruments, still disagreeing, though in a less forceful manner.

He drifted away, leaving them to it; walked back along the deck, looking towards the shadowy coastline.

'But they're wrong about that,' he said to himself. Nothing was 'just jungle'. He'd been staring at the green-clad mountains over there for days, ever since they left the little settlement of Somerset on the very tip of the continent. That country would be a wonderland of forests and strange plants and wildlife. And beyond those mountains? What was out there? That was how Mal had come to know so much about New South Wales and southeast Queensland: he'd always had to find out what was over the next hill. And it was in those travels, taking odd jobs as a drover or a station-hand that he'd stumbled into the Gympie hills, and the astonishing craziness of the goldfields.

He rounded the deck again without incident and stood at the ship's rail, looking out over the tranquil waters, recalling again the voyage north on the junk. Unlike this ship, Xiu's junk had to call at each of the few ports along this coast, for water and supplies, Trinity Bay being the last before they tackled the hundreds of miles on to Somerset.

Mr Horwood had said that the Trinity Bay settlement was now a port called Cairns, and Mal was sorry that the *China Belle* wasn't calling there so that he could show Jun Lien the picturesque bay that had almost set his life on a different course.

'I saw that bay with the great mysterious mountains beyond,' he told Horwood, 'and I almost gave up on the China idea. Almost went ashore there, to have a look around. Thought I'd buy a horse and do some exploring, but in the end the China plan sounded a bigger adventure.'

But it was homesickness for the bush that had begun to creep up on him after a couple of years in the provinces, and he'd been preparing to head back to Australia when he'd been introduced to Mr Xiu's granddaughter, Jun Lien, and fallen hopelessly in love with her. Then he'd become involved in the high intrigue of the family when it was whispered to him that Jun Lien found him handsome. And lovable. He still blushed at the revelation.

It had taken him four months, he remembered fondly, to obtain permission for them to meet openly, though in the company of various aunties. It had taken him months of formal courtship to seek her hand in marriage, and that caused all sorts of rows and upsets, but eventually Mr Xiu himself made the decision to approve, with a proviso that stunned Mal.

'She loves you deeply and I see that you are dedicated to Jun Lien, and so the marriage will happen. You will live in the Wong household in Peking with her family to set her parents' hearts at ease about the wisdom of such a match, and then after six months, you will pack up and take your wife to live in Australia.'

'What?' Mal had hoped one day that might come about, but had not dared make such a suggestion. It had been hard enough gaining permission for Jun Lien to marry an outsider.

'There are bad times ahead,' Mr Xiu said. 'Serious troubles. It would settle my heart to know you will have Jun Lien safe in your country. I have discussed the matter with her father and he is agreed. He will be packing up his household after that and retiring to their country estates where he hopes they might escape the worst of it, but we are not optimistic.'

Jun's mother, Xiu Ling Lu, a proud strong woman, was harder to convince, but when Mal insisted they would not leave without her blessing, she capitulated, making him promise to guard her daughter with his life.

Mal smiled now, remembering that Ling Lu had been surprised and very pleased to hear that Mal could not, and would not, consider taking another wife or a concubine. And as Jun said, that had won her over.

Now he supposed he'd better get in to dinner, but as he turned he heard something, like a flutter of leaves, like movements in the bush, but of course there was no bush, only the bare lines of the empty timbered deck, and not a soul in sight.

Mal shuddered. Jun Lien was the love of his life. He adored her. He counted himself the luckiest man in the world to have found and married this sweet, beautiful girl, and so he should be happy. Deliriously happy, not stumping about on the prowl all the time. Maybe Jun Lien was right. Too much drama and intrigue in China, especially in the weeks before they left, had him jumping at shadows.

He recalled the first time they managed to slip away from the ever-watchful eyes and meet in a secluded orange grove – and his joy to find her in his arms at last. But he'd been unprepared for the wonder of her response, hardly able to believe that she cared so deeply for him, afraid that this was just a dream set in the mists of strange and colourful surrounds.

Later, when protocol permitted, they used to sit in the Moon courtyard, laughing as Jun pretended to read classic Chinese poems to him, when in fact they were planning their idyllic life in Australia. Mal liked to see the stars in her eyes when he told her of the large sheep farm he hoped to buy, where she would be the mistress of all she surveyed, including her adoring husband.

Mal smiled, he loved the way she giggled at these stories.

Typical of Mal, his wife thought nervously. He had to make sure that everything was just right before he'd allow himself to relax, but he didn't seem to understand that she wasn't at ease among English people yet. Not when there were no other Chinese people for moral support.

Like her mother, Jun Lien was normally very self-assured. She was well educated in cultural subjects and spoke English fluently. She had been protected by Xiu Tan Lan's strong will from the tortures of bound feet and the practice of marriage contracts as a small child, and, to her father's despair, was always permitted to speak her mind at family and business conferences, but here, on this ship in a room with English people, she was miserably shy, looking longingly at the door to the deck. To take her mind off the problem she tried to work out who was who of these people, deferring to Mal's insistence that they were not all English.

'I'm Australian,' he'd reminded her. 'So is Mr Lewis – Mr Raymond Lewis. He is a member of the Queensland Parliament. All the rest are English, I think.'

Mrs Plummer had come forward to talk to her – to rescue her, Jun Lien felt, after the introductions.

'You speak so softly,' the older woman said. 'It is a pleasure to listen to your voice. So don't be intimidated by noisy English voices.'

'Forgive me for perhaps my curiosity, Mrs Plummer, but I am learning to distinguish the accents. You are speaking English but then different from the others here.'

'That is because English is not my native language. I am German born.'

'Oh! I understand. I believe that is a very beautiful country.'

'Indeed it is. But you must tell me, where are you bound? It is unusual to see a young Chinese lady travelling so far from home . . .'

* * *

When Willoughby left, Tom was worried. 'Do you think he heard?'

'Heard what? That we're at odds over our current position? But I think you're right. We'll have to get moving again, I reckon we could make it well before dawn.'

'I still think Willoughby is on to us. He's always snooping about.'

'No he isn't. It's your guilty conscience . . . shows up like a woman's petticoat. Willoughby's a bushie, if you know what that means. He's used to roaming about the bush, he'd know every leaf and creek in his territory, and do you know why, you simple sod?'

'No.'

'Because there's nothing else to do in the bush!' Tussup guffawed. 'That's what's wrong with him here. Nothing to do, so he's wandering about like a caged lion.'

'Well, I wish he'd stick to passenger decks. He worries me. Did you talk to the bosun?'

'Yes. And it's no use. He's agin us.'

'What?' Tom yelped. 'You said he'd leap at it because he's always grousing about the lousy wages Oriental pays.'

'Well, I was wrong.'

'Jesus! What now? How can you stand there—'

'Ah, calm down. I locked him in the empty cabin.'

Tom jerked away, ready to race for the door. 'You did what? He'll batter the door down. You're mad, Tussup.'

'For Christ's sake! I'm not that mad. I fixed him, he won't make a sound.'

'What do you mean? You said there'd be no violence.'

Frustrated with this weak fool, Tussup sighed. 'He's bound and gagged. No one will miss him until we're good and ready, so settle down. This little plan will go like clockwork. It can't miss. Everything's set except for stupid bloody Loveridge deciding to weigh anchor overnight and slow us up. I was nearly going to argue with him over that.'

'Just as well you didn't. He takes on a real treat if any of the crew question his orders.'

'Does he now?' the Australian laughed. 'Then he's about to get the treat of his life.'

Jake Tussup was born in the bush himself, thirty years ago, on a bleak, windswept farm in the hills behind Goulburn. His parents, both factory workers, had been brought to Australia under an immigration scheme funded by the Anglican Church. They dreamed of endless sunny days, of their own little farm, of being their own bosses, of plump rosy children running free, of orchards overloaded with fruit, oranges and lemons, even bananas and, most exotic of all, pineapples. The dream sustained them during the long, wretched voyage across the oceans, and the more they talked and enthused about the life ahead of them the more detailed the dream became. They designed their house: brick with mullioned windows and ivy growing on the walls, a gate in the hedge that creaked to warn of visitors . . . and they laughed so much, trying to work out how to make a gate creak.

The reality hit hard. Neither of them could read or write but they had willingly signed with their crosses to the contract that afforded them free passage, for was it not true that free settlers would be offered grants of land? Hard to believe, but it was true, Tessie and Ted Tussup were told. You got land just for turning up because there was all this space and not enough people to put in it to keep out the Frenchies. And you got something like forty acres, they'd heard, though they had no idea what an acre was, but just as long as it was big enough to put a house on and have a couple of fields, they'd take it. Too right they would!

'Try and stop us,' Tessie said stoutly.

The contract contained another clause – that Ted had to complete two years of employment at a specified workplace, or else.

'Or else we have to pay back the sea passages,' Ted wailed, when he broke the news to his wife on their third day in Sydney.

They had temporary digs in a migrant shelter near the port, which wasn't so bad, Tessie reflected optimistically. At least they'd been right about the sunny days. Sydney was warm as toast and it was real nice walking about the streets without getting jostled, and looking at all the scrumptious food in them markets.

Soon the workplace was decided upon. Edward Tussup was instructed to report to the Darlinghurst Gaol for employment as a warder.

Anxious to do the right thing, the Tussups rushed straight out there to confirm the appointment, and were duly advised that Edward Tussup had been assigned to the Goulburn Gaol.

'And where would that be, sir?' cap in hand, Ted asked the clerk.

'Over the hills and far away, mate. Be here Saturday mornin' at six o'clock to board the lorry.'

'And Mrs Tussup here, sir. Would there be work for her too at this gaol, cookin' or cleanin' or somethin' regular, like?'

The clerk looked at Mrs Tussup's swollen belly. 'Not in her condition.'

'But she can still come with me? On the lorry?'

'Yeah, if she can take the bumping about, but you'll have to find her somewhere to live out there.'

'Well, we've got a start anyway,' Ted consoled Tessie. 'A job right off isn't so bad. We can save for our farm.'

'Yes. It's me as reckons this is better, Ted. Startin' a farm without any money would be hard. I'll find us digs in the town and when the baby comes I'll get a job.'

On the all-important Saturday morning, Tessie sat on a rock outside the gaol while Ted was escorted inside to be interviewed by a Sergeant Skorn, and formally registered as a warder to be stationed at HM Gaol at Goulburn in the Colony of New South Wales. He was then treated to a lecture about his duties and a discourse about the district of Goulburn, which Skorn explained was a centre of wealth gained from wool and stockbreeding.

The sergeant was apt to ramble on a bit, Ted thought, but as he told Tessie, 'I kept my politeness, though the seat was getting hard.'

It seemed to him too that Skorn had a bee in his bonnet about who was who in the gaoler's world, insisting he remember that, once in Goulburn, he was to have nothing to do with the Towrang mob. Apparently that was a penal settlement, a convict construction camp guarded by a regiment garrisoned at Goulburn.

'And you stay clear of the police too. The Goulburn district and them hills around the place are a hotbed of bushrangers, a lot of them convicts escaped from the camp, see?'

Ted nodded.

'That's why there's a big force of police there. Mounted police mainly. They got a courthouse and a lockup, their own huts and cottages, and you'll see police paddocks for their spare mounts. Looked after like princes they are, those soldiers and coppers, but we don't have nothing to do with them. You got me?'

'Yes, sir.'

'You don't mix with them. What goes on in our gaols is nothing to do with them. We got ordinary prisoners in our gaols; we don't have them convicts. If I had my way I'd drown them all before they get here. Chuck 'em overboard. Now sign here . . .'

It wasn't long before Ted heard the joke that both of Skorn's grandparents had been convicts, though he'd never admit to it. They were seven-year folk who'd done their time and settled down as dairy farmers on the outskirts of Sydney.

The lorry, drawn by four horses, had high slatted sides as some sort of protection for the passengers, who were perched atop, and around bags of sugar and flour. Being the only woman on this journey, Tessie was permitted to sit up front with the driver, which was just as well, she thought nervously, since there was tension between the other passengers. Apparently the prison warder, who was accompanying Ted, objected to having to travel with 'iron gangs' – convicts in leg irons – and their police escort, but he was outnumbered.

'And outclassed,' the driver explained to Tessie. 'Police rank higher than warders.'

She looked back to see six men in the convict yellow and black garb climbing clumsily on board, under the watchful eyes and truncheons of four policemen, and eventually, when everyone was in place they set off.

'Where exactly is Goulburn?' she asked the driver.

'Down the Great South Road it is, missus. About a hundred and twenty miles, if a bloke's lucky.'

'Never!' she breathed. 'We didn't know 'twas on t'other side of the country. My Ted didna know that!'

She twisted about to try to catch his eye but he was hidden by the broad back of a convict.

'Oh Gawd,' she said.

'Ain't so bad, missus. You get to see the country. Pretty, it is. Them convicts, they won't bother you. Poor buggers, begging your pardon, it's like a holiday for them, even if they do stay in irons. They're being brought out to build the roads and bridges. Dunno what we'd do without them.'

'But it'll be dark by the time we get there.'

He laughed. 'No, I see to it the last day is only a run-in by midday.'

'The last day of what?'

'As long as we don't get any more rain – the road can get so sloppy at times, it'd bog a duck – we'll have a good run. We stop overnights at public inns or coach houses. The warders get an allowance for night stays so don't be worrying. You just sit back and have a good time.'

'Good time,' she gasped to herself many times on that trek as they sped along sandy roads, through dense bush, forded creeks and wound around hills. At times she climbed down to stretch her legs and trudge up sharp hills while the men pushed, and then they all stood back on steep downhill runs with logs roped to the lorry to stop it hurtling after the horses.

Even with her bonnet on, her face became sunburned, and her only good suit a bag of dust, but their travelling companions were cheerful, especially the convicts, as the driver had predicted, and by the time they rolled into the main street of Goulburn, they were a jolly lot, these travellers.

When they came to a halt, beside yet another bullock train, so called because bullock teams carting supplies and merchandise joined up together for protection from bushrangers, the convicts jeered at the bullock drivers, calling them yellow, afraid of their shadows, and worse. Their guards laughed.

The Tussups found lodgings in a shed behind the flour mill, where Tessie worked after Jake was born, but they were disappointed that, come winter, Goulburn was bitterly cold. It even snowed. The shed was freezing and the baby suffered one cold after another.

Before their second winter, Ted submitted an application for a land grant, only to learn that the practice had been terminated, and blocks of government land were now being auctioned.

By the time Jake was five they'd saved enough to buy a large block of land on the side of a hill, several miles out of town. They found that the rule forbidding warders from associating with soldiers and police was workable, but the general rule forbidding the populace from engaging in personal exchanges with convicts was ignored. These men were everywhere you went, slogging away with their picks and shovels, and it was inevitable that people would get to know them by name, passing by them day after day.

Ted would always say g'day to them in the local manner and began to learn more about them. The seven-year men, on 'light' sentences for anything from stealing a loaf of bread to assault, were not required to wear irons. They minded the horses, felled trees and carted supplies. The iron gangs had more severe sentences and some of them were dangerous, but a lot were in fact exiles, disposed of by magistrates who considered that political stirrers, incorrigible dissidents and the like were taking up too much space in already crowded gaols. But now, transported across the world if they couldn't escape, these convicts took great delight in confounding authority. Bucking the system was endemic throughout the convict fraternity and, as Ted became aware of this, he realised why local criminals were kept separate from the transportees.

At the same time their 'agin the gov'mint activities', as they were called, were a source of amusement among local communities, and tales of their daring, sometimes true, often exaggerated, abounded.

When he began to build his house Ted found that it was possible to buy cheap bricks made by convicts, and that convicts, passing by, took an interest in his amateurish efforts. They offered advice, drew mud maps for him, showed him how to build the brick chimney, use wattle and daub for the house and even how to make cheap furniture. Their guards, if offered bread and cheese and a billy of tea, looked upon the mild diversions with some interest, so that the building of the two-roomed Tussup cottage proceeded amiably and was completed within weeks.

It was hot in summer, so they learned to sleep outside under an awning, and an oven in winter with the fire going, but the Tussups were happy. Ted had acquired a retired stock horse to ride to work each day, and Tessie set about planting a vegetable garden and orchard with advice from everyone she met, since the convict workmen had moved on. And of an evening, when Ted was home, all three Tussups would sit by their front door gazing out over the valley below them, pleased at last to be settled in the growing township.

Nevertheless Ted did his best to keep away from soldiers and policemen, a warning reiterated by the chief warden at the gaol.

'And well he might,' Ted would tell his wife. 'Some of the cheating antics he gets up to could do well with a copper's look-see. He skims the prisoners' rations, and any lag can get parole if he can pay for it. Whores too, if they've got the cash.'

On first hearing of this, Tessie wasn't shocked, only worried. 'What do the other warders say?'

'They're in it too if they know what's good for them.'

'And where does that leave you?'

‘Between the devil and God-help-us, love. I ought to try for a transfer but we’ve got our cottage . . .’

Several years later, when police were called to investigate corruption in the gaol, in response to a revengeful letter left by an inmate who was hanged in HM Gaol at Goulburn, the chief warden was arrested and several of his staff, having been caught in the same net, were brought before the magistrate. Most of them, including the chief warden, were given prison sentences, to be served in Sydney.

Ted faced minor charges which, in the end, were dismissed, but he lost his job and was forced to throw himself on the mercy of the townspeople, already in the throes of a depression, as an odd-job man.

Young Jake was no stranger to hard work as the Tussups struggled on, but his parents insisted he attend the local government school, making certain he never missed a day.

Despite their setbacks they were a close-knit trio, and Jake looked forward to Sundays when he and his dad would go on shooting expeditions, bagging rabbits and wild ducks or quail. The catch afforded them at least one good feed before they had to relinquish the rest to Tessie. She’d prepare the meat and Jake would sell it in the town on the way to school. By the time he was thirteen he was known to be a good shot and had won a few competitions, scoring a trophy cup, which he promptly sold to another lad.

It was about this time that things started to look up for them. Ted managed to find a job as a bricklayer and Jake was apprenticed to a baker.

Tessie’s market garden was coming along, and she was working among her tomatoes one day when a horseman came by, asking if she could spare a little grub.

‘I’m right hungry, missus. I can’t be affordin’ to pay you naught right this day, but I always pay me debts.’

She wiped her hands on her apron. ‘No need for that. You look all in. Sit yourself in the shade over there by the water tank and I’ll get you some tea and see what’s in my larder.’

He didn’t give his name and Tessie didn’t ask. She let him drink his tea and eat a cheese bun in peace, because he did look worn out. Then, to her surprise, he fell asleep, slumped in the long grass, so she took his horse, an animal that looked better fed than its owner, and led it over to the horse trough where it drank greedily, hitched it to the nearby post and went back to work.

An hour later the stranger came over to her so quietly Tessie jumped, but he only wanted to thank her and be on his way.

‘Here,’ she said. ‘Put some of my tomatoes in your pocket, sir. They’re good eating.’

‘Terrible kind of you, missus,’ he said, accepting.

At the gate he turned and waved to her, and Tessie breathed a sigh of relief. She'd seen the scars on his ankles left by leg irons, and she knew him to be a convict, but whether he'd done his time and been freed, or he'd fled the stockade she couldn't say.

'Nothin' to do with me, though,' she said to herself. But she did wonder who he was.

Ted knew, and when he told his wife, Jake was bursting with excitement.

'He was here, Ma? Dinny Delaney?'

'Sounds like it by what your dad said. He was an Irishman, big fellow with black hair and a black beard, both showing the pepper and salt of going to grey.'

'He's famous! A bushranger. Got his own gang back in the hills.'

Tessie shrugged. 'Don't know what he was doing here then. And he didn't seem to be making much of a job of bushranging. Hungry as a horse, he was.'

'He was in town, Mother,' Ted explained. 'Came in to see a ladylove, from what they say. But someone gave him up and Sergeant Hawthorne nearly caught him. He got his horse, though, which left Delaney on the run on foot. They've been searching for him for days, so he must have been hiding out.'

'That's right,' Jake cried. 'He'd have been hiding out, and getting hungrier until he got the chance to steal a horse.'

'The horse was stolen?' Tessie asked.

'Yes. From Porky Grimwade's stables. Did Delaney say where he was going?'

'Listen now,' Ted said sternly. 'He was never here, isn't that right, Mother? You never saw any strangers at all.'

'Never a soul,' she said, frowning at Jake. 'We never see people on this track since the new road went in. And you remember that! Don't go boasting to your mates, and get me into trouble. It probably wasn't him, anyway.'

Jake nodded, grinning. He wouldn't have told his mates, because Dinny Delaney had said he'd be back to pay for the food. And Jake bet he would. Be back, like. He could hardly wait.

And he was right. Delaney rode in early one Saturday morning, coming up the hill through the fog like a scary spectre, Jake thought, as he ran out to meet him.

'Would your dad be home?' the bushranger asked.

'Me dad? Yes.' Jake tore inside but Ted was already on his way out, rifle in hand.

'Jeez; Dad, you're never gonna shoot him!' Jake cried.

Ted pushed past him. 'Settle down. I'm just making sure he doesn't shoot me.'

'Don't shoot,' Delaney called. 'I've just brought some goods here for your missus. Just some bits for her kindness to a stranger and two shillin's for me lunch.'

Ted thought he looked for all the world like a squatter, more than he did a bushranger, with his sheepskin jacket and neat clipped beard under a wide leather hat. 'You'd be Delaney?' he asked nervously.

'At your service, sorr,' the stranger replied, swinging easily down from his saddle and unbuckling a saddlebag. 'Here's some bush honey and a tin of coffee beans, and the two shillin's.'

He handed them over and, to take the offerings, Ted put down his gun, placing it carefully against the wall by his front door.

'And I wondered if I could have a word with you, sorr?' Delaney asked.

'What about?'

'It's business. Could I come inside? I'd be causing you no bother.'

'I suppose so.' Right off Ted liked Delaney. He was a nice feller; polite too.

He turned to Jake, who was jigging about them to get an earful. 'You stay here.'

Delaney saw Jake's disappointment and laughed. 'I'd be grateful if you could keep an eye out, lad.'

Tessie thanked him, and put the kettle on. Like Ted, she had no quarrel with the man; that was up to the law, which wasn't held in too grand respect in these parts anyway.

They talked about the weather, and the sheep dotted over the undulating countryside.

'Never seen so many sheep in me life,' said Delaney.

'Me neither,' said Ted. 'They say that squatter Grimwade's got more'n a thousand on that big property of his.'

'Does he now? It's a lot, is it not?'

Ted nodded. Tessie put three cups on the table, and the sugar pot and spoon. And the small jug. And a plate of biscuits. Delaney nodded and reached for one with a smile of thanks.

'It's like this,' he said to Ted. 'I've got a mate here in town who buys supplies for me, there not being much in the way of shops where I live. So I was wonderin' if he could leave them in your shed . . . because I'm after trusting you folk, see. I'd only be needing you to look the other way and I'd be making it worth your while – five bob every time . . .'

'That might be a worry for my missus,' Ted tried.

'Not from my lads. There'd be none giving you any trouble, missus, believe me. You wouldn't hardly be knowing. My mate puts the stuff in your shed by night. One of my lads comes down by night and takes it away. All you'd see would be the coins lying in the space, no bother at all.'

Tessie poured the boiling water into the teapot after the tea, put it on the table to draw, and looked blankly at her husband, unable to know what to make of such a request.

Outside, Jake picked up his father's loaded gun and prowled round the house, keeping nit. The fog was lifting down in the valley but a mist still hung about the farm, dimming the green of the orchard and the tea tree hedge that ran from the side of the house down to the shed. He was almost beside himself with curiosity about what was going on in there, and edged over to the back window to see if he could eavesdrop, but it was closed. He turned about and trudged up to the gate in the hedge, meaning to go round and station himself by the open door where he might hear a bit. He'd been out here long enough . . .

As luck would have it, Sergeant Hawthorne was returning from the Doncaster sheep station where there'd been a shootout between Boss Doncaster and his sons, and a gang of bushrangers. One of the bushrangers had been killed and young James Doncaster shot in the shoulder, but still the bushrangers had made off with twenty stock horses, leaving the Doncasters to bury the thieves' comrade.

By the time Hawthorne had ridden the forty miles to investigate the incident, there was little he could do but investigate, which didn't suit Boss Doncaster at all. He'd given the sergeant a right royal ear-bashing about prevailing lawlessness, about the lack of police, and in particular the uselessness of the local police to make any headway at all in dealing with bushrangers, who seemed to be able to rob homesteads and hold up travellers at will.

In the end, fed up with Doncaster's abuse, Hawthorne hit back. He pointed out that he was not personally responsible for these raids and that Doncaster could afford to fence the homestead and stables, and pay boundary riders to protect domestic stock and so on, until Mrs Doncaster put a stop to the shouting match. Her husband then ordered Hawthorne off the property, claiming he was in league with the bushrangers.

'I'd be a bloody sight better off if I was,' the sergeant muttered to himself as he rode back via Grimwade's station to see how they were faring.

The family there had heard about the raid but were not interested in Hawthorne's inquiries because they were busy organising a foxhunt. The animals had only recently been introduced to the district for this very purpose and there was great excitement in their camp.

Intrigued by this activity, which was new to him, Hawthorne stayed overnight to hear more of the plans, but was on his way before dawn the next morning.

Travelling cross-country, he came over the hill at the rear of the Tussup farm and, looking down, saw a saddled horse in the yard, a fine-looking mount too, better than the stock horses that Ted and his son rode.

He wouldn't have taken more than passing interest in the matter had he not noticed young Jake creeping round the cottage with a gun.

'What the hell's he up to?' Hawthorne muttered, taking his horse down by a row of pine trees to get a better look.

He thought there might be a dingo about, raiding the chook house maybe . . .

Maybe not too. He wouldn't want to be blasting away with that good horse nearby. It was then that Hawthorne's instincts took over and he realised something was up here. The kid seemed to be more on guard than looking for a dingo. And why would that be? Who was the visitor?

Hawthorne dismounted, unstrapped his pistol, and crept down along the tea tree fence to catch the kid out.

As soon as the gate opened he spoke quietly. 'All right, Jake, I've got you covered here. Now put the gun down and—'

Shocked, Jake whirled round, desperate that he'd failed Dinny Delaney. As he turned he fired the rifle and the bullet tore into Hawthorne's stomach, his pistol thrown into the air as he was flung back.

They came running.

'Jesus!' Delaney shouted. 'It's a copper! It's Hawthorne. He's shot the poor bugger.'

Ted snatched the gun from Jake and stood petrified, staring at the gaping face of the man he'd known for years, as Delaney kneeled to aid the wounded man.

Tessie was screaming. She fell down beside Delaney, who looked back at them. 'He's dead! Christ Almighty!'

Delaney leaped up. He shook his head at the bloodied body, almost disbelieving. 'God rest his soul,' he said. 'But I have to get out of here or I'll get the blame for sure.'

Tessie stopped screaming. Sharply. Creating a void. A well. And from its depth came the smell of death and then fear.

It was Delaney who helped her up before he turned and ran back through the gate and across the wide yard, his heavy boots thumping like muffled drums. Ted's voice was caught somewhere deep in his throat. He could only groan, while in the background he could hear his son whimpering. Tessie's tears came pouring out now in a welter of misery and lamentation, because already the enormity of this calamitous event was beginning to reach her.

Ted backed away from the dead man and faced his son. 'What have you done?' he croaked. 'For God's sake, what have you done?'

'I didn't mean to,' Jake whined. 'I didn't. He came up behind me. I thought he was gonna shoot me.'

Ted seemed not to have heard him. 'The gun. What were you doing with the gun?'

'I was keeping nit. That's what you wanted me to do while you were in there talking to the outlaw. He's your mate; I was only trying to help.'

'How? By shooting the first person who came along? You haven't got a brain in your bloody head. Now what are we going to do?'

'Don't shout at him,' Tessie cried. 'Isn't it bad enough for the lad? He didn't mean to shoot Mr Hawthorne. He'd never do that. Never. He's a good lad is our Jake.'

They wrapped the body in a sheet and placed it in the little brick creamery shaped like a beehive, which Ted had built. That never, Tessie thought, should ever have to be used for such a horrible purpose. While they argued about what was best to do, she vowed to herself that the desecrated creamery could only be used to store firewood from now on.

Though the day had warmed, the men stood shivering by the fire as Tessie made tea.

'There's naught for it,' said Ted eventually. 'I'll have to go into town, find the superintendent of police and tell him there's been an accident.'

'You'll tell him Jake shot a policeman?' Tessie shrieked. 'They'll never believe it was an accident.'

'Yes they will,' Ted said quietly. 'Because it was an accident.'

'I don't trust them. No, you can't do that. They'll hang our boy.'

With that Jake screamed, 'Ma's right. You can't throw me to the dogs. We could bury him down the paddock and no one will ever know.'

'A copper? That'd be madness. They'll be looking for him. They'll have every soldier, copper and convict on the search. They'd find the grave and then we'd all swing.'

'Even if we hide it carefully?' Tessie worried.

'Mother, they've got black trackers,' he said sadly. 'I wish it was as easy as that. And what about his horse? With a police brand? What do we do with the horse?'

'We just let it go,' his son said. 'Nothing to do with us.'

But Ted was trying to anticipate questions.

'They'll want to know what he was doing here. He's never called in on us before. And left his horse up by the pines.'

Jake had an answer for that. 'He rode in, that's all. We can say he just rode in.'

'Yeah? And when he got down off his horse you got such a surprise you shot him. No, give me my hat, Mother. I'll go into town now. Get it over with.'

'You can't!' Jake screamed. 'They'll put me in gaol!'

First there was shock in the Goulburn police station, then disbelief. And then the talk.

'He reckons his son shot poor Roy Hawthorne by accident? That's a good one. What was Roy doing there? How come he let himself get shot by a kid? And why? That's the real question. No accident this. Why did he shoot Roy?

What was going on out there? What did Roy know that he had to be shot? A lot of those blokes on them isolated farms shelter bushrangers for a few shillings here and there. Who else was there?'

The police station buzzed with the talk. Superintendent Carl Muller and four policeman, as well as two of their best black trackers, escorted Ted back to his farm, followed not long after by the mortuary cart.

Muller left his men to guard the Tussups while he went with the black trackers to watch and listen. He was devastated at the loss of Hawthorne, who was not only a very reliable police officer, but his brother-in-law. He had postponed breaking the bad news to his young sister until he'd identified the body.

The Aborigines examined the spot where Roy was killed, the blood still fresh enough to have flies buzzing, but they didn't take long to bust Ted's story. They followed Roy's footprints in the soft grass up to the pines where, they said, his horse had been tethered, though it was now out the front of the house.

They came back to the spot where the body had lain, pointing and nodding agreement until their spokesman, known as Deadeye, began to explain their findings.

'Four peoples here, not three. Big boots see, them fambly they all wear home-made like strap shoes, what you call 'em?'

'Sandals,' Carl said. 'Yes, they all wear sandals.'

'Who wear dem big boots?'

'Who indeed?'

'So den you come see here. Keepin' back. Big boots come from de house, running. See light marks . . .'

Carl couldn't exactly, but he knew this pair could spot a bent blade of grass at twenty paces.

'Now this time goin' back to a horse, waiting here. Horse he upset alri'. Reckon he heard em gun go off, and he got big bloody fright. Look here, boss. Dig in hooves, jump about. And looking from gate all way over to this here horse, him that was tied up here, see blood on dem boots. Not run this time, just walk heavy . . . like this, see.'

The other tracker watched approvingly as Deadeye strode out to demonstrate.

'So you think the stranger shot our sergeant?'

Deadeye shrugged. 'That your job, boss.'

For hours the superintendent and a senior officer grilled the Tussups until they gave in and admitted it was Dinny Delaney, and that made the situation worse, as Ted had known it would. He hadn't counted on black trackers being used when the police had been told what had happened. But now they were involved in the serious matter of harbouring a known criminal.

'So it was Delaney who killed Sergeant Hawthorne?' he shot at them.
'No!' Ted said, as Jake called: 'Yes!'

The woman, Mrs Tussup, wept and wept. They asked her the same question. To clarify. She would not answer the question.

The more they quizzed the family in their angry, accusing way, the more fearful Jake became. The noise, the voices were all around him, locking him in, and he could hear the bitter mutterings, the constant calls of 'Shame!'

A rock smashed through the front window, but none of the lawmen inside took any notice.

Jake looked out and saw a crowd had gathered, and more people were straggling up the hill. Seeing him at the window, they shouted abuse at him, hurling clods of dirt at the cottage, making such a commotion it was a while before he realised that they were demanding a hanging.

'Hang him!' they were shouting. 'String up the bastard,' and beside him, by the window, he heard two policemen agreeing. Agreeing! All along he'd realised that they didn't want to know about the accident, any of them, they just wanted their revenge, but his knees almost caved under him when he truly understood they would hang him. They'd hanged blokes in that big gaol before, after the judge put the black cloth on his head.

'Take him outside,' Muller said, and a constable grabbed his arm, propelling him out the door and pushing him into the yard.

Jake's legs were jelly. He crumpled to the ground but there was no helping hand, just a kick in the ribs, and he was left to pull himself up, holding on to a slip rail.

Soon Muller came out, standing by the back door to light his pipe, taking his time, before he walked over, to puff on that pipe and look at Jake, terrifying him. He could already feel the jerk of that rope and hear the cheers of those bastards outside the gaol when he was choking, the same people who were now moving about on the other side of the fence like hobgoblins, waiting to tear him apart.

A woman screamed and Jake jumped.

'Who was that?' he asked Muller, an involuntary response.

'Mrs Hawthorne, I'd say. Roy's widow. She's got four kids to bring up now, and no dad to help her along.'

Jake knew that. He also knew Charlie Hawthorne, who was a year older than him, a ton bigger, and a bloody brute who'd bash anyone who got in his way. Jake had always been scared of him. Quaking, he blurted out: 'You can't blame me. It wasn't my fault. I didn't do it.'

Squinting into the sun squared off behind Muller, he saw the boss copper turn to the constable and nod his head.

'Now we're getting somewhere.' Muller turned back to Jake. 'I never thought you did. It's the matter of the gun, see. It wasn't your gun that got fired, it was your father's. Isn't that right?'

'Yes.' Jake looked down at his dusty boots.

'Did Delaney have a gun? Yes, of course he did. We've been all over that. But you said yourself you didn't know what it was, because it was in his saddle holster and he never took it out.'

'That he did,' the constable said. 'I heard him meself. Stickynose kids see, but he wouldna have been game to tinker with Delaney's rifle. Would ya?'

'No.' Jake was eager to agree on anything, and Muller's head was nodding up and down like it was suddenly loose.

'And your own old gun, that didn't come out of the laundry where we found it, and it never got fired, isn't that right, Jake?'

'Yes.'

'So we're back to the gun that killed Police Sergeant Roy Hawthorne, a fine upstanding fellow, who was coming down to see who was visiting Ted Tussup, and who was suspicious, so he had his pistol out, but before he got to say his piece, he was shot by your dad's gun, by your Dad, isn't that right? Isn't it, Jake? We don't want any more lying now. We have to get this over with before that mob out there gets any nastier and burns down the farm.'

'Yes.'

Muller jerked his head to the constable. 'See, I was right all along.'

'I'd say you were. These bastards have been trying to pull the wool all day, switching and changing their stories.'

'Well, it's over now. We'll take Tussup in, and you, lad, you get a hold of yourself and stick to the truth or we'll run you in too. I should run you in for being in cahoots with an outlaw anyway, but I'll see how you behave . . .'

When he had to go to court and point the finger at his father, his mother took a stroke and was rushed off to hospital. She died a month later.

Not once did Ted contradict his son. Nor would he speak up in his own defence.

'I should never have let Delaney into my house,' he told his solicitor wanly. 'That was the beginning of it.'

Doing the best for his client, the solicitor managed to get a message to Delaney asking him for information, because some still claimed it was the son shot Hawthorne, not the father.

He did receive a response from the bushranger, word of mouth, in the form of simple comment: 'It's a Tussup family matter.'

That did make the solicitor uneasy, but Ted reiterated his confession so that was that.

Two months later he was hanged in Goulburn Gaol, but Jake was long gone by then. When his mother died he ran away rather than face the predictable last days of the trial.

Eventually he read about the hanging, furtively turning pages in the Sydney Library, then he went down and signed on as a deckhand on *Seattle Star*, an American clipper ship.

Jake Tussup never allowed himself to think about what happened ever again. He fought his conscience battles in nightmares for a while, and in the end he won. The story faded, and Jake emerged a hard man with his own set of rules for survival.

Chapter Two

Raymond Lewis was a mild man, industrious in every facet of his life – a Member of the Parliament of the Colony of Queensland, a busy lawyer with a practice in Brisbane, and an elder of the Anglican Church – and he was also a widower, having lost his dear wife some time back to the scourge of influenza. As he stood with the two ladies, Mrs Willoughby and Mrs Plummer, he ventured his opinion about the captain's decision to defer any further sailing until first light.

'Jolly good,' he said. 'Very sensible'.

'Damn time-wasting, if you ask me,' Horwood snapped.

'Better sure than sorry,' Mrs Plummer commented, and Raymond was pleased she'd taken his side. She was an elegant woman, in her fifties he guessed, somewhere about the same age as his sister Lavinia. Not carrying as much avoirdupois as Lavinia though, he noticed, with a glimmer of guilt.

'Did you have a mission in your China visit, Mr Lewis?' she asked him. 'Or were you simply touring?'

'Oh! A mission. Yes, indeed, dear lady. I had appointments with government people – mainly trade discussions, which fortunately I believe were successful. I found all the personnel assigned to me were most helpful.

'As, of course, one would expect,' he added, turning to the pretty little Chinese lady. 'I am pleased to tell you, Mrs Willoughby, I greatly enjoyed my visit to your country, and hope to return one day. May I ask, will you be staying in Brisbane?'

She smiled at him, the sweetest smile. It made his toes tingle to witness it. 'For a little while, Mr Lewis. My husband is more inclined to country living.'

'Ah yes. The country life, eh? But while you are in Brisbane you and your husband must allow me to show you around. You too, Mrs Plummer.'

'I should be delighted,' the German lady said. 'I hear it is a very pleasant town.'

But then the Caporns came over to join them and Raymond's thoughts drifted back to his wife. She'd loved to travel. They'd voyaged to several islands in the Pacific and also to Singapore, but it had always been their dream to go to China. How sad, he reflected, that she'd never achieved the dream, and he'd been sent on an official tour, all expenses paid.

Some time after Beatrice passed away, his spinster sister had come to live with him in the capacity of housekeeper. He corrected himself. Lavinia saw her role as his hostess and revelled in it. He and Beatrice were never much for entertaining; they preferred a quiet life. Not so Lavinia.

'You're comfortably placed,' she'd told him, 'and you have this huge house. It's ideal for garden parties and dinner parties. I never understood why you two didn't entertain more. A man in your position, you should be looking to your career, be more hospitable where the right people are concerned.'

He sighed. The matter had been taken out of his hands. Lavinia went ahead arranging all sorts of functions – 'to further his career' she said – and Raymond's life became even busier.

His partner in the legal office, Gordon McLeish, was amused. 'You and Lavinia have the social scene tied up these days. That was a jolly good musical evening you put on last night. You even roped in a couple of judges, and the Treasurer. You looking for a ministry, old chap?'

'I'm looking for some peace and quiet,' Raymond groaned. 'Lavinia's turning my home into a reception house.'

'All for a good cause.' Gordon was unsympathetic.

Raymond felt let down. He knew he had more to offer as a responsible advocate and serious parliamentarian, and resented having to stoop to jollying constituents and politicians. He solved the situation as best he could by working on his studies and speeches late at night, and arranging meetings with agriculturalists, businessmen and trade unionists at Parliament House, so as not to upset Lavinia's routine at his own house. This meant, of course, that he was always running late for social functions, no matter how he tried. No, he thought, looking around the small gathering in *China Belle*'s dining saloon, that's not true. My heart just isn't in socialising. The word gave him a small jolt, reminding him of that other denominator, socialism. Though he'd begun as a Conservative, Raymond was moving closer to the concept of socialism all the time, finding he understood the aims of the trade unionists these days, and was sympathetic. Fortunately Lavinia hadn't noticed, though Gordon had become concerned.

'Your speeches, old chap. They're sounding lefty. I hear the bosses in the house are getting tetchy about you, so don't be surprised if you get carpeted by the Premier.'

Raymond didn't particularly care. He had studied these matters and preferred fairness to popularity. Besides, both the trade unionists and the conservatives were in accord when it came to introducing a ten-pound tax on

Chinese immigrants, a tax that had already been imposed in the other colonies, commencing in Victoria, where there were estimated to be forty-two thousand on the goldfields. Now that gold had been discovered in Queensland at Crocodile Creek and several other areas, including the massive finds in Charters Towers, Chinese diggers were already flooding in. Of course, the trade unions wanted to go a step further, restricting Chinese immigration to save their jobs and wage standards, but that would require a lot more discussion. And diplomacy.

In one of his meetings with Chinese dignitaries in Peking, Raymond had been nonplussed when a gentleman raised these questions – delicately, of course, but they were on the table in front of him like dead fish, he had written in his report, just lying there stinking up the room while he was trying to sell them wool and wheat.

He'd responded with a humble explanation that his colony of Queensland was so very young, not more than fifteen years since it had been founded, the residents were only feeling their way in the world, as it were . . . doing their best to set standards, having in fact no peasantry, no coolie class, so, you see, one has to find a place for the gold diggers and when the goldfields close, problems arose, as one could imagine . . .

The translator tried to keep up as Raymond rambled on, deliberately for a change, trying to extricate himself from the situation, and in the end his argument seemed to fade. Those gentlemen probably knew perfectly well that the Chinese tax had been in force in the southern colonies for twenty years.

Apart from that incident, Raymond had thoroughly enjoyed his visit to China and had already begun a study of its history and culture, which, he knew, would take him years. He was so excited about this new project, he had wanted to discuss it with the Willoughby couple, but he'd been too shy to broach the subject.

'I wanted a word with you,' Mr Caporn said, taking him aside. 'Is it true that your government intends to ban South Sea Islanders from your cane fields? Because I mean to say, one would not wish to invest in a tea plantation there without a certainty of native labour.'

Raymond sighed. This was another touchy subject. 'It's under discussion,' he murmured. 'I'm a mite out of touch. Perhaps you could come to my office at Parliament House when we're on solid ground again and we can have a talk.'

'Jolly good. I have recently sold all three of my Malay plantations; need a change, you see. Esme would like to be back in an English environment again, but she didn't want to leave the plantation. It's a pleasant life style.'

'I'm sure it is,' Raymond said politely.

'So when we found that Queensland is also suitable for growing tea we were chuffed.'

Raymond saw the captain bend over to speak to Mrs Willoughby, obviously wondering where her husband was, and her dainty hands fluttered apologies as she looked anxiously to the door. The captain smiled, reassuring her, and signalled to the passengers.

'Ladies and gentlemen, would you join me for dinner?'

The stewards stepped forward to see them all seated and Captain Loveridge began: 'I hope you all had a pleasant day. Did you see the dolphins, Mrs Caporn?'

'No, I missed them. I'm so disappointed.'

As the small talk progressed, Raymond seated himself at the end of the table beside Mrs Plummer, who, for the present, had an empty chair at her right side. She was in good spirits and was telling him an amusing story about a Singapore club, when he noticed that the captain seemed concerned, occasionally looking back towards the galley.

The stewards were slow this evening, Raymond thought. They seemed to be floundering, bumping into each other as they placed serving dishes on the table. The soup tureen had no ladle, and dinner plates were presented instead of soup plates. The cutlery, he noticed, was all wrong too, and he laughed when Mrs Plummer whispered: 'I think there's confusion in our kitchen.'

Mrs Caporn looked along the table. 'Do we take soup or study it, Captain?'

He frowned, but just then a warm breeze floated in with Mr Willoughby, who apologised as he hurried over, kissed his wife on the cheek and took his place between her and Mrs Plummer. Then he glanced about him with a cheerful smile.

'Oh good! I'm not late after all. What's for dinner?'

Mrs Plummer beamed. 'We're to start with green pease soup, then lemon fish, and after that lamb pie with currants, and I forget what the menu promised for the main course.'

As he turned to explain these dishes to his wife, Mrs Plummer sighed. Ah to be young again and in love, and, she reminded herself, with a man as handsome as Mr Willoughby. Like her beloved Ernst, her late husband. This young man reminded her so much of Ernst – tall, fair-haired, confident in a carefree sort of way. She thought Mr Willoughby would look much better with a moustache . . . more dignified.

Lyle Horwood was speaking to the captain. Complaining, of course – about spilled soup, now that a ladle had been located. How she disliked that man! He'd made Fannie's life a perfect misery, bullying her all the time, even in public, and then in her last days he rarely visited her sick room, spending more and more time at his club, until a servant came to inform him that his wife had passed away. Fannie had died alone, Horwood refusing to admit her friends, claiming she wasn't well enough to be disturbed.

Had she been there, Eleanor would have insisted on being with her dear cousin, but by the time she returned to Hong Kong from a visit to Germany it was all over, even to a private interment. Everyone was saddened by the loss of Fannie and hurt that they were not given the opportunity to say farewell, so Eleanor had arranged a memorial service for her at St Mary's Church in Junction Street. Lyle had not attended. He'd sailed for London the week before. But, it was agreed, no one missed him.

The stewards stumbled on. One dropped a tray of glasses – not that anyone but the captain seemed to care about this, because the wines were flowing freely. Eleanor noticed Mr Willoughby ordered hock while Mrs Willoughby favoured a light Chinese wine.

Eleanor's second husband was a teetotaller, but he never objected to Eleanor's fondness for a glass. In fact he was a great host at parties.

Plummer had lacked Ernst's good looks but he'd swept her off her feet with his thoughtfulness, and American 'know-how', as he called it. He was at her beck and call from the minute they were introduced, and there was nothing he wouldn't do for her. Page Plummer had made up his mind to marry Eleanor, and set about wooing her with flowers and romantic cards.

He helped her renovate her house, he painted her carriage himself, had her stables enlarged to house the two fine horses he'd purchased for her, and happily escorted her to every social function she chose to attend. Eleanor really appreciated the latter, since she still missed Ernst terribly after three years, and she'd realised that a widow could be very lonely in Hong Kong without the support of a gentleman acceptable to high society.

And he was all of that, she mused, noticing the captain's face was turning crimson with irritation at the slovenly service. Plummer had been a stickler for correctness too. When they'd married, he'd organised a huge reception at the Victoria Hotel, which Eleanor had simply adored. It was a fabulous evening of music and dancing and gaiety, much talked about in society for months afterwards.

Looking back now, she wondered how she could have been so foolish. Even when he tried to borrow money from her to pay for their wedding reception, she'd brushed the idea away with her fan.

'Heavens no . . . allow me. After all, the expenses should be a matter for the bride's family, should they not?'

Gradually it dawned on Eleanor that Plummer was taking liberties where their finances were concerned. All the bills seemed to land on her lap – even for his apparel and jewellery items, such as expensive cufflinks and tiepins – so she'd had to make mention of these matters, which were troubling her.

But Page always had an answer. 'My dear, the cufflinks! Are they too expensive? I mean, if we can't afford them I'll take them back.'

'It's not a matter of affording—'

'That's a relief. I'd hate to cause my darling any concern.'

In the end Eleanor let it go. It was embarrassing to be quizzing her husband about money.

But really, she worried, a gentleman should take care of the finances. After all, before they were married he'd given her the impression that he was well off, if not necessarily a very wealthy man, so she'd not enquired further. And he'd spent freely on gifts for her, gifts that a poor man couldn't, and surely wouldn't afford.

It bothered her that she may be moving in the same direction as many other rich widows, allowing charming gentlemen into their lives – or rather, so-called gentlemen, who ransacked their coffers. But Page was such a wonderful husband and companion that she put away her misgivings, labelling them nit-picking, even disloyal. And, surreptitiously, as her concerns grew, she even consoled herself that she could afford his little extravagances. Until a friend, George Hollister, called with some unsettling news.

Apparently, with Eleanor's interests at heart, he'd agreed to Page's request to nominate him for membership of the exclusive Gentlemen's Club, but the application was not successful.

Eleanor was furious. 'Why was he rejected? How dare they? Ernst was a founding member.'

'But this is not Ernst, my dear. To spare you, the application wasn't formally rejected, it was simply removed, as if I'd never mentioned the nomination.'

'Why, though?'

'Ah, now, you know reasons are never given in these matters.'

'But you know, George, and you must tell me. You can't leave me like this. I'm already in an anxious state. For heaven's sake, was it because he's American? Because I'll have something to say about that. I know several members or their wives are American—'

'No, no, Eleanor. That's not it.' He took out a handkerchief and mopped his brow. 'I don't know what to say. You've got me in a state now.'

'Then just speak up quickly. Come on, George, we're old pals . . .'

'Very well, it was our American members who queried the captain. I mean his credentials, not him. It appeared they've been suspicious of him —'

'How dare they? What cheek!'

'Since I must tell you, do let me finish. They did some checking and there is no record of a Captain Page Plummer, retired, in the American army records, or the marines.'

'They're wrong, of course . . .'

'I hope they are, my dear. But that revelation produced others, that people were loath to mention in society.'

'And I hope you're not saying "to spare me", for God's sake! Get on with it, George.'

'Page owes money to several of your friends . . .'

He sat silently, blinking and ducking his head a little, and Eleanor noticed how much hair he seemed to have lost lately.

'Oh dear,' she said, patting his hand. 'We're all in a pickle, aren't we, George? Thank you for telling me. And don't worry, it's all right.'

To make sure, Eleanor made a few enquiries of her own. Overcoming her embarrassment, she slipped out of the house one day, her husband's papers in her handbag, and met privately with the American Consul, who confirmed that the papers were forged.

Outraged to discover that her husband was a liar and a fraud, Eleanor began making her own arrangements.

The last thing she wanted was to be the centre of a scandal, so she went quietly about rectifying the situation. First she wrote to friends in Singapore, suggesting she might visit, and, at the same time, to another friend, Gertrude Kriedmann, whose husband, a wholesale jeweller, had relocated to Brisbane, Australia, for proximity to valuable gem fields.

Having arranged a quiet exit, Eleanor sold all the property in Hong Kong, including the furnished house she still occupied with her charming husband.

On the day the new owners were to take possession of her house, Eleanor sailed for Singapore without a word to Page. On the same day, divorce papers were served on him.

She relocated her funds to the Bank of Hong Kong in Singapore and placed most of her jewellery, investment papers, and title deeds to property in Germany, in that bank for safekeeping. Then, after a few months, she boarded *China Belle*, bound for Brisbane. By this time she'd heard that Plummer had been arrested for forging share scrips.

'And well he might,' she'd murmured to herself. 'He'd have to think of something to cover all of his debts with my door closed.' Eleanor never wanted to see him again, nor did she want him to find her.

She was tiring of the East by now, and considering residency in Australia, thanks to Gertrude's glowing reports, but first she had to see the place for herself. Then if she found the town of Brisbane appealing, she might move there permanently, by which time the paperwork she had commenced in Singapore would restore her to her maiden name of Von Leibinger.

'With apologies to Ernst,' she murmured, and her neighbour, Mr Lewis, leaned over.

'I beg your pardon?'

'Nothing,' she smiled.

The soup was served but it was cold. Around the table people were sipping, looking up, questioning.

'It's cold,' Mrs Caporn snapped.

'I thought it was supposed to be,' Willoughby remarked, and went right on taking his soup with obvious enjoyment. His wife followed suit.

The captain thumped the table and snapped to a steward to get the chef. The man sped away and the table was suddenly quiet. Caporn motioned another steward to pour him some wine.

They waited, and finally the chef emerged from the galley, crimson-faced.

'Ah Koo,' the captain said angrily, but he stopped. Lining up behind Ah Koo were three crewmen with guns trained on the diners.

'What the hell . . .?' Captain Loveridge shouted, jumping up so quickly his heavy timber chair was knocked aside. 'What's going on here?' He turned on the first man, a Malayaman. 'You, Bartie Lee! What do you think you're doing?'

Lee smiled a smug, oily smile. 'You sit down, Captain, and keep close mouth. You all stay here. Do nothin'.' He motioned to the two others, both Chinese, to come closer with their weapons, and the captain began shouting again. He had recognised the modern Winchester rifles held by a steward called Tommy Wong and the other fellow. Bartie Lee held a Colt revolver.

'They're the ship's guns! You've broken into my armoury!'

'Listen here,' Horwood rasped. 'Is this a joke of some sort? Get those thugs out of here!'

'Ah Koo, get Mr Tussup right away,' Loveridge thundered, and the chef scampered back to his galley. 'Now we'll see about this,' he added.

'Yes, you see,' Bartie Lee said, waving at the women. 'You sit down now, see, or we kill one of them.'

'You'll what?' Horwood and the captain shouted in unison, but the captain recovered first.

'You lay a finger on any of these people and you'll hang, Lee. I'll see to that myself.'

Bartie Lee wiped a finger across his thin moustache and pointed to Mrs Plummer. 'The old woman. Get her.'

Tommy Wong moved towards her, but Willoughby pulled her back and stood confronting Wong: 'Oh no you don't, you get away from her.'

Taken aback, Wong looked to Bartie Lee, who shrugged. 'Orright, her.'

With that he reached forward, grabbed Mrs Caporn and pulled her to him. He moved so quickly that no one else had a chance to intervene, their attention still on Mrs Plummer.

The Malayaman whistled and a crewman the captain recognised as Mushi Rana came in to help Lee, dragging the woman roughly towards the exit. They didn't seem to care about the noise – Mrs Caporn's screams and passengers shouting their objections – and Loveridge knew that was a bad sign. His officers must have heard. Where were they?

Suddenly Mushi clouted Mrs Caporn across the face and the screaming stopped abruptly.

Bartie Lee nodded. 'Now you all be quiet or she goes overboard. You hear that, boss? She go for a swim, eh?'

There was stunned silence for a few moments and then the captain asked softly, 'What is it, Lee? What do you want?'

But Bartie Lee ignored him. He backed away, glancing towards a porthole.

Outside, Mrs Caporn was screaming again and Mr Lewis groaned. Willoughby looked as if he might leap to his feet any minute but the captain cautioned him to be still, acknowledging Neville Caporn's distress since his face was contorted to an almost apoplectic state.

'Could Mr Caporn have water?' he asked Tommy Wong, the nearest steward, who nodded but didn't move, so Constance Horwood poured a glass and helped him to drink.

It was then they felt the engines beginning to turn over, and the captain shouted: 'No! Christ, no! Someone's started the engines.'

'Sail too bloody slow,' Lee grinned. 'We get goin' now.'

'You can't!' Willoughby yelled. 'You'll pile us up on a reef.'

Devastated, the captain stared at Lee. 'Why? For God's sake! What do you bastards think you're doing? And where are my officers?'

The Malayaman laughed. 'They drivin' the ship. What else you tink they doin'?'

At that, several other crewmen came in armed with knives and clubs. The men, including the captain, were ordered up from the table, one by one, and told to sit cross-legged on the floor, facing the wall. The three women were then ordered outside but that brought a shout from the men so Bartie Lee called to his guards.

'Orright. Leave them sit. You wait here, keep tight watch on them all.'

His comrades responded by jeering at the captives and menacing them with their weapons. By this time, the five white men were outnumbered.

The mutineers' leader, Bartie Lee, disappeared out on to the deck for a few minutes and then they heard Mrs Caporn howling in pain. After interminable minutes she was shoved back into the dining saloon.

Mrs Horwood screamed and the men jerked back, shocked to see Esme Caporn's dress torn, her face bruised and bloodied and her long hair hacked off in patches. She had lost her jewellery, including her wedding ring, and she was barefoot. She slumped to the floor and vomited on the carpet.

Jun Lien grabbed a cloth and a jug of water and ran to her, but Lee didn't object.

'Now you see. Be bad, women get that. Or worser. Be good all, nothin' happen. See?'

'Nothing bad, you fool?' the captain shouted. 'The ship is in danger from reefs.'

'You don't listen,' Lee shrugged. Deliberately he strode forward, gave his gun to another man to hold, pulled Mrs Horwood away from her chair and struck her across the face, first one side and then the other, slamming her against the wall and then strutting away, leaving her to slip down to the floor, sobbing.

'You filth!' Eleanor yelled at him but, unperturbed, he retrieved his gun and took his place in the captain's seat. Then he ordered Ah Koo to bring him some food.

As the engine surged into life, Ingleby was nervous. 'Are you sure you know what you're doing, Jake? Maybe we should have waited until daylight.'

'No, this is the only time we could guarantee the captain and his passengers would all be in the same place. And there's no need to panic, I'm following a channel. I've studied it and I've got it straight in my head. I reckon we'll be off the Endeavour River by midnight, and that'll be the time to head ashore.'

'You hope. We don't want to be rowing to an empty coastline.'

'Jesus, Tom, quit your whining. We can't miss that river. We're not the first, so we'll see the lights of their camps. By what Mushi Rana says, his mate Bartie Lee has got the mob in the saloon under control, but take a look anyway. Go through the galley – no need to have them spot either of us yet. So far they'll be thinking the Asians have grabbed the ship. Then go down and check on the bosun. You can take the gag off him now, but keep him tied up. He can shout all he likes, no one to care any more.'

When Tom left, Jake peered over the moonlit waters, whistling to keep himself calm. His plan was working like a dream. The Chinks and the Malays, all mad gamblers, had jumped at the chance to be among the first to land near the latest fabulous goldfield called Palmer River.

Jake had heard about it in Singapore from a mate working in the telegraph office, and at first hadn't taken much notice, but then his mate had been groaning into his cups about always missing out on the big one, since only three months ago he had been in Cairns, within striking distance of a river of gold.

Cairns? Jake knew where that was: on the Queensland coast. 'Is this river near Cairns?'

'About a hundred miles north, that's all. Easy trip by sea,' he groaned. 'You could do it in a longboat along that sheltered coast. Just go north to the mouth of the Endeavour River and head in that way.'

'Why don't we go then? Come with me.'

'By the time the *China Belle* dumps you in Brisbane and you figure out how to get back up the coast almost to where you started from, it'd be all over, mate.'

Nothing would persuade his mate to change his mind, so in the end Jake gave up. 'You're just a bloody whinger, that's all. You're always whingeing about your bad luck. If the bloody gold was next door, you'd still find something to groan about. I'm sick of bloody listening to you.'

He'd lurched out into the night and stumbled down to the wharf, staring drunkenly at *China Belle*.

'Gawd,' he'd muttered. 'The chance of a lifetime. We're going right past the bloody door.'

In the morning, with the ship still at anchor, Jake studied the charts, planting a stubby finger on the very spot where he'd need to be put ashore. As if Loveridge would agree to that! No bloody fear.

Maybe he could jump ship.

He examined the longboats. Not a chance in hell of taking one of them single-handed. He'd be placed in irons within an hour.

And that was when the idea hit him. Get the crew on side. Get offshore from the goldfields and abandon ship. Row to shore and every man for himself.

Of course the plan was refined as the days passed. Now, with Bartie Lee keeping the passengers under control, Ah Koo would already be packing stores into the two longboats. The hardest thing so far had been to keep the Asians quiet, trying to make sure they gave no hint that anything out of the ordinary was going on. They'd been performing as if they were part of a conspiracy to capture royalty, and the only way he could cool them down was to threaten to tie up individuals and leave them behind.

They were starting to make good time now, the engine chugging along, and he was hungry. As soon as Tom came back he'd send him—

'Jake!' The second officer stumbled into the wheelhouse. 'You gotta get down there. Bartie Lee's gone mad. Matt Flesser's dead!'

'What?'

'Matt Flesser. The bosun.'

'He can't be dead! I only—'

'They cut his throat. Apparently he got the gag off and started shouting.'

'Who did that?' Jake yelled. 'Who did it?'

'They won't say. But they've beaten a couple of the women. Mushi says it's the only way to keep their men quiet.'

Jake digested all this, keeping in mind that he dare not let Tom or anyone else take the wheel. Every minute he was listening for scrapes, knowing that if he must he could abandon ship sooner rather than later and put plenty of hands to the oars, but he loved the sound of that engine!

'I'm sorry about Flesser,' he groaned.

'You're sorry? Is that all you can say?' Ingleby screamed hysterically. 'You're sorry?'

'What can I do?'

'You can go down there and take charge. Take the weapons from those bastards. Call this whole thing off.'

'I can't, it's too late. There's some whisky in the press. Get yourself a snort, drink as much as you like but get a hold of yourself. I can't stop them now; it's too late. We just have to look after ourselves, Tom, so don't turn your back on them. Here,' he handed Tom a gun, 'keep that on you. I've kept most of the ammo hidden in one of the sail boxes.'

He watched as Tom glugged the whisky, reached out and took a few snorts himself. 'Now go back. Don't even raise an eyebrow, no matter what they get up to. Just make certain the stores are in the longboats, and anything else we need, and they're ready to go. As soon as we spot those lights it'll be drop anchor and get both of the longboats into the water.'

Caporn was terrified when Bartie Lee gave the order to tie the men up, shouting at the captain, 'Why don't you do something? They can't get away with this. Where are the officers?'

'Yes, where are they?' Lyle cried out as he was being trussed to a chair. 'I tell you, Captain, you'll never get a ship again after this débâcle. What possessed you to employ a gang of thugs like this? You'll be held responsible for this outrage.'

When it was his turn, Loveridge appealed to Bartie Lee: 'We shouldn't be going at such a rate with so many reefs round here. Tell whoever's up there to weigh anchor or the ship will be wrecked.'

Bartie Lee, his gun still trained on them, took no notice.

Caporn called out to him, 'If it's money you want, I can pay you. I have money. Just let me go back to my cabin. I won't interfere with anything, I promise you. Here, I've got a gold fob watch, very expensive, you want it?'

His captor grinned, took the watch and then nodded to his men, who began to search them all, taking money and valuables. He kicked Caporn aside contemptuously.

Mal Willoughby felt as if his bones were on fire, the rage inside him contained only by force of will, which did not stop his body reacting with anguish. His limbs seemed brittle with the pain, as if they might crumble as he fought to stay calm. Jun Lien and those other ladies now huddled in the corner were in grave danger from these mongrels. There'd been no mention of tying them up, so . . . what? he wondered frantically.

'Hey, Bartie,' he called casually. 'You the boss now?'

The question took Bartie by surprise, but he liked it. 'Yeah,' he smiled through blackened teeth. 'Yeah, I'm boss.' He kicked Caporn, harder this time, amused by his scream. 'You hear that, rich man?'

'So what's the plan?' Mal asked genially. 'It's a mad place for a mutiny.

China Belle's trapped in these waters. Only two ways out: south and north channels. You know that, don't you?'

'Sure I know. Don't matter, Mr Willoughby.'

'Well, you got me beat, mate. I can't figure this out at all.'

Bartie jigged about with glee. 'Soon you know.'

'No, tell me now.'

'Aha. Can't do that.'

'Well, listen. I wish you'd be nice to the ladies. Us blokes here, we've got the message now. Be good, so they don't get hurt, eh? They don't mind giving you their jewellery.'

He noticed Mrs Plummer took the hint, hurriedly taking off her rings and earrings and placing them on the carpet in front of her. The others did the same, except poor Mrs Capron, who suddenly leaned forward as her nose began to bleed heavily. Mrs Horwood jumped up and grabbed table linen to stanch the blood, and Mrs Plummer ran to the table for a pitcher of water. The captain and Neville Caporn were so distressed they began shouting at Bartie Lee, who simply turned to Mal again.

'See, not good at all.' He sighed and turned to Mushi. 'Get her out.'

With that, all the women objected noisily but he soon put a stop to the commotion.

'Get them all out.'

As the women were shoved out on to the deck, it was too much for Mal. He jerked his chair about and shouted at Bartie Lee: 'You lay a hand on my wife, Bartie, I'll come after you. I'll find you and I'll kill you!'

Bartie shrugged, instructed two armed men to stand guard over the captives and followed the women out on to the deck.

'Down to the captain's cabin,' he said, as Mushi shoved them ahead of him.

As soon as they were locked in there, he and Mushi made straight for the Horwood cabin, since the stewards had gossiped about her jewellery. They found the steel box, rattled it, pleased to hear the thud of the contents, and, after searching the cabin and pocketing money found in a leather wallet, they set off to find something to smash the jewellery box open, but as they emerged they ran into Ingleby.

'What have you got there?' he asked, as if he were still a boss.

'Our business,' Bartie said belligerently, and Mushi was impressed.

'Yeah,' he said. 'Bartie the boss now.'

Ingleby only nodded. 'Where are the women?'

'In the captain's cabin, crying like babies,' Bartie told him. 'They all right.'

'We need more canvas in the longboats. Get your men to load more.'

Bartie was full of his own importance. 'No need for more canvas. My men rowing, not sail.'

'We'll need canvas for tents, for shelter. It's only bush where we're going. Nowhere to buy supplies of any sort.'

'Orright, you see Jake steer straight. Captain reckons we bang up on a reef.'

'Only an hour or so to go . . . we're nearly there. Watch for the camp lights. We're as close to the coast as we dare.'

They watched him head up top and Mushi said 'Do you think he know about Flesser yet?'

'Who cares?'

'Why don't we get rid of them too?'

'Because I'm not stupid like you. We're going into English place, we need them officers to talk for us. We get no questionings that way.' He punched Mushi in the arm. 'Officer lies better than ours, see?'

'Too right,' Mushi enthused. 'We just leave them women locked in, Bartie?'

'Yeah, I gotta talk to Jake.'

By this time, Mal had slid the knife into his right hand, and cut the ropes, but he had to hold them in place because there were two men either side of the saloon with guns trained on them. He moved his chair so that he had a clear view of both of them and took no part in the bitter comments coming from the other captives. He had to concentrate, knowing he'd only have one chance to achieve anything once he broke loose.

'How're you going?' Jake asked Bartie Lee cheerfully when he came into the wheelhouse.

'Orright, mate. Don't you put us up on no rocks, mate.'

Jake heard the insolence in 'mate' only as a warning. He didn't care what this sweaty Malay called him. He touched the overhead lantern as if to gain more light on the chart spread out beside him, and pretended to be absorbed in it.

'Gotta watch the map, eh?' Bartie asked.

'Yes.' Jake steadied the wheel, peering ahead over the moon-tipped waters. 'Can you see any lights to starboard?'

'No, I'll go get a better look-see. My eyes plenty sharp.'

He padded along the bow of the ship, looked to the land, saw nothing and took the time to peer nervously over the bow, watching for the much-feared coral, but the waters seemed deep and clear. He then collared a young deckhand and sent him shinnying up to the crow's nest.

Next thing there was a shout: 'Lights!' and the boy could be seen waving his arms about.

Bartie got him down. 'You sure they land lights? Not ship lights? Ship might be stopped.'

'Them land lights, Bartie. Too many for a ship.'

Bartie sprinted up to tell Jake.

'I knew it,' Jake said excitedly. 'I knew it. We'll get there before daylight.'

'What's it matter? Day, night, who cares?'

'I do. I want us to slide in there under cover of darkness, so we don't have to explain the longboats. We'll land to the north of the river camp, shove the boats into the bush and just appear like we been there a while.'

'Yeah, you told me that before,' Bartie said. 'The boats are ready but I reckon we make a bit more money still.'

'How?'

'That Chinese woman. She from a big rich family. They pay to get her back.'

'Oh, Jesus, no! Leave her alone! No women, Bartie, bad luck.'

'But easy lotta money. And big boss's woman, Mrs Horwood. Her man, he got millions too. He owns the whole shipping line.'

'He's only a director. Listen to me. Just do your job and leave the women out of it! Now get going!'

The captain felt it before anyone: the sudden slowing, then the shudder and the long scraping sound he'd dreaded hearing again, but the engine was still powering and the ship kept moving, waters slapping softly on the timbers.

'Cripes, we've hit a reef,' Mal said to the nearest mutineer. 'You better get out of here before you drown.'

The man looked over to the other crewman, who shook his head. 'That only a scratch. We still going.'

Not for long. A few minutes later the *China Belle* ploughed into the next tier of coral with a deafening crash. All the prisoners and their chairs toppled over and slid to the rear. Unfortunately, the experienced sailors managed to stay on their feet, their guns still threatening as they backed towards the exit, but Mal took the chance. He dived for the nearest gunman, who frantically tried to shoot him, but couldn't make the revolver work before Mal had knocked him to the floor, grabbing for the gun, too late. The other man kicked it away, raised his gun to shoot Mal but the ship listed and the bullet went astray just as Caporn climbed to his feet, demanding to be untied.

'You can't let us drown,' he begged, lurching towards the exit. 'We'll pay you. Cut us loose.'

The next bullet hit Caporn, who went down with a crash.

Mal was embroiled in a vicious fight with the first crewman when the other man with the gun ran out of the door, and suddenly Mal's knife was in his hand. He heard the captain calling to him to look out, but he was winning. All he could think of was Jun Lien: he had to get to her. He plunged the knife into the crewman's chest and was climbing swiftly to his feet when his head seemed to explode.

* * *

Tommy Wong raced into the dining saloon, saw Willoughby attack Sam Lum, so he bashed his head with the cosh he always carried. The passenger went down like a log, but Tommy saw that Sam was too far gone for any help, his eyes caught in last sight. He grabbed the knife from the killer's hand and ran out on to the deck, taking no notice of the cries and pleadings of the male passengers trussed and bundled together in a corner.

Already men were racing for the two longboats, Tommy remembering he was allotted a place in Jake's boat, and that pleased him. He liked Jake, a real wild man that fellow. He'd known him years ago in Singapore.

Ingleby's boat wasn't being lowered as cleanly as it should but that wasn't Tommy's worry. He ran past, only to be delayed by Bartie Lee and Mushi, who were dragging two of the women with them.

By the time they reached Jake's boat it was ready to go, with about ten men aboard, and Jake was shouting at them to hurry, but when he saw the two women he bellowed, 'No women. I told you, Bartie. No bloody women!'

But Bartie gave his greasy grin. 'We're saving them, mate. Saving the women from drowning. Get plenty money for that.' He pulled a gun out of his belt. 'I say no time for argue.'

So do I, Tommy thought, jumping into the boat beside the woman of the Xiu family who'd married the white man. She was weeping, frantically clutching the side of the longboat as it hit the water, and the oarsmen set to work.

The other woman, Mrs Horwood, seemed to be in shock. She was quiet, but Xiu wailed and shrieked as the boat pulled away from the ship. Tommy saw the second longboat come down with a great splash and overturn, and saw the fools fighting to right it, but they were away now; there was no turning back. They'd earned the chance to get straight to the rich goldfields and that was all that mattered.

But now the Chinese woman was yelling and fighting, trying to get out of the boat. She bit Bartie Lee, who belted her across the face, and she scratched at Tommy, trying to get past him. She was all arms and legs, wriggling like a little octopus, squirming away from them. Bartie yanked her back by the hair but she broke loose and clambered across Tommy's back. He swung round to grab her, but she was slippery with sweat, hers or theirs, he didn't know, couldn't think, because suddenly in the darkness, she'd disappeared.

As he came to, Mal heard her, and he was up and running, shouting to her to hold on, wishing he had a gun and realising, as he saw the longboats were missing, that a gun would be useless even if they were in range. Jun Lien was still screaming and he shouted to her to keep it up so he could locate the boat she was in. He'd find her, he vowed, he'd get her even if he had to tip all of them out. Without a thought that they were armed, he climbed over the rail of the ship and dived, a long dive to take him as far as possible towards her voice.

He was swimming, going after them, when he heard the screams and shouts, and Jake Tussup's voice yelling: 'Watch out, Bartie, for Christ's sake! She'll fall in.'

Then another voice, clear as a bell across the calm water: 'She overboard, boss.'

'No!' Mal shrieked at them. 'No!' His arms tore through the water, tore towards her screams, and he shouted, 'Have you got her, Jake? Have you got her?' His voice seemed to bounce off the surface of the water in sync with the thud of the oars.

'No!'

He could feel that thud in the waters, anguished that it hadn't lost a beat, hadn't slowed. Uncaring, it was pulling further away from him, but the 'No!' was still pounding in his head. Except for the steady swish of the oars fading into the distance there was a terrifying silence and he shouted her name, screamed her name. And suddenly there she was. For an instant he saw her struggling. Saw her hair streaming and the whiteness of her face against the dark, rippling surface, and struck out towards her but then she was gone. Frantically Mal dived, over and over, down and down. He would have kept on diving, searching for her until he used up his last breath rather than leave his lovely Jun Lien to face the savagery of the deep alone. But his hands found her, clutched her, dragged her up to the surface, a long way, a long long way, his lungs bursting, until they plunged through the surface and he gulped air.

Jun Lien was heavy in his arms, and limp. Too limp. He blew air into her mouth, forced air into her and swam for her life towards the ship. A man called for help, a faint sound, somewhere out there but he would not stop, could not stop, gripping Jun with one arm, long, strong legs powering them along.

Without the guards, the captain and Horwood managed to drag themselves across the room and claim table knives to saw through all their bonds. Then they rushed outside, leaving Lewis to attend to Caporn, who was barely conscious, the graze above his left ear still seeping blood. They were quick to respond to the screams of the women locked in the captain's cabin, and shocked to find Constance Horwood and Mrs Willoughby missing.

'Where are they?' Loveridge shouted. 'In God's name, where are they?'

'I don't know,' Mrs Plummer said fearfully, and then Mrs Caporn, who had been resting on the bunk, began to scream hysterically. 'Where's my husband? Have those monsters taken him too?'

'No,' Horwood said, 'he's all right. He'll be all right. I'll see to him in a minute. But they surely haven't taken the ladies. They must be locked in somewhere else.'

He and Loveridge searched the cabins, both men almost collapsing in shock when they discovered Bosun Flesser's body.

'Oh, God help us!' Loveridge cried. 'What have they done with the other officers?'

They ran back up to the deck to begin a full search for them and for the two women, convinced they were looking for bodies, after seeing the fate of the bosun.

'Both longboats are gone,' Horwood called. 'How will we get off this ship?'

Loveridge, frantic now, refused to answer. That was the least of his concerns.

The sky was a hurrah of vivid pink rays that began to spread across the sea as dawn approached, and the captain wept as he looked towards the land, with no sign of the mutineers, but then he heard Willoughby shouting for help. He'd forgotten Willoughby, he realised with a twinge of shame, but there he was in the water.

'God Almighty!' he shouted. 'Horwood, get up here and give me a hand. It's Willoughby, and his wife.'

Eleanor tried to comfort Mr Willoughby. She wrapped her arms round his shoulders and whispered: 'I'm so sorry, my dear. So very sorry, she was such a beautiful person.'

He nodded, his face wet with tears, holding Jun Lien to him, nursing her in his arms as he slid to the deck, his legs unable to support him any longer.

'Perhaps we should take Jun Lien now,' she said softly. 'The captain will carry her and I will look after her. Do her hair, make her look nice.'

But he wouldn't be persuaded, his grief too overwhelming to allow him to part with his beloved wife yet.

Then Esme Caporn burst out of the saloon, shouting at the captain, 'What are you doing here? My husband needs help! You didn't tell me he was shot. Why aren't you looking after him—' She stopped suddenly, staring at the man on the floor and the woman in his arms. 'What happened?' she screamed. 'Oh my God, what happened to that girl? Is she dead? Oh my God!'

Willoughby spoke, his voice low. 'You should see to him, Captain. We'll be all right here, just the two of us. I'd like to be alone with Jun Lien for a while.'

Loveridge found the medical kit and dressed Caporn's wound quickly, then gave him a dose of laudanum.

Mrs Plummer suggested a few drops for Esme Caporn too, which he administered right away, so that he could join Lyle Horwood, who was desperately searching the ship again.

'There's no sign of her,' he moaned. 'I think they've drowned her, Captain. They've drowned her! Remember that thug said he would.'

'No, you're wrong. It looks to me as if they've kidnapped the ladies. Two wealthy women.'

'Constance isn't wealthy. And they stole her jewel case from my cabin. All her jewellery has gone.'

Loveridge sighed. 'That's it. The mutiny was plain robbery, and they took the two ladies for ransom, I'm afraid. Kidnapping! Sadly it went wrong for poor Mrs Willoughby.'

'And did they kidnap your officers too?' Horwood asked.

'They must have.'

'Don't give me that, Loveridge. The women, yes, maybe, but why the officers? No ransom there! They're worth nothing. I say they've been murdered along with my wife. So get this crate going. We'll head for the closest port—'

'We can't do that. The engine has been deliberately wrecked and sails slashed, though they needn't have bothered. We're stuck fast on a reef.'

'Oh God, will we sink?'

Loveridge scratched the back of his neck. He was tired and nauseous, realising that if and when they managed to get off this ship, he'd have a barrage of questions to face, and they'd be far worse than this interrogation.

'No.' *Not unless a storm blows in.*

'The tide will probably float us again.'

'Yes, I suppose.' *Then we will sink with a hole in the hull and no reef to support us.*

'The Chinese woman – Willoughby's wife – should we have a burial at sea? You could read the service.'

'I'll ask him.'

When they finally persuaded Willoughby to allow Mrs Plummer, who'd insisted they call her Eleanor, to lay out his wife's body and wrap it with the utmost care in the finest damask from the saloon, the captain put the question to him as kindly as he could, but Willoughby was appalled.

'No! Definitely not! I won't have that. She's not going to be chucked into the sea like garbage. She's my wife. And a proud Chinese lady. I am taking her back to China to be buried with her ancestors.'

Horwood and Loveridge scavenged about the ship for liquids to supplement the short supply of water, while Eleanor made the company a meal of leftovers in the galley, mainly soup, cold meat and rice.

In the still of a blazing afternoon the captain sweltered on deck, watching for a passing ship, while the others took refuge below, and it wasn't until close on sunset that Willoughby came up to join him.

'They said you're still on watch, Captain,' he said, 'so I thought you'd need a break.'

'I would. Are you sure you're all right, Mr Willoughby?'

'Mal.'

'Yes . . . Mal. If you're up to it.'

'I'm not sick, Captain. Hard to say how I am. My heart's broke, that's about it, I suppose.'

'I'm sorry.'

'Yeah,' he sighed, peering down at the coral now visible beneath them and leaning out further to get a better estimate of the size of the reef. 'What's that out there?' he pointed over the channel.

'Where?'

'Back there. I think it's a water tank, and, wait on . . . there's someone hanging on to it.'

The someone turned out to be Tom Ingleby, his fair freckled skin severely sunburned, adding to his sufferings from dehydration and exposure. By the time they hauled him aboard and took him down to a cabin, he was babbling incoherently, something about the longboats and sharks.

Loveridge went off to find his medical kit again, and Mal stayed with Ingleby, listening to every word.

'Where's Mrs Horwood?' he asked, jerking Tom's arm. 'Where's Mrs Horwood?'

'I don't know.'

'Yes, you do,' Mal insisted. 'Where is she?'

'She was in Jake's boat.'

'With the Chinese woman?'

'Yes. There are sharks in that water, dozens of them!' Tom started screaming, 'Save me! I can't reach the boat! Come back! Look out, lad, behind you! Oh Lord, save me!'

'You're saved,' Mal said drily, stepping aside to allow the captain, who had rushed back, to apply sunburn salve.

'Poor fellow,' Loveridge said, 'he's had a terrible time.'

He gave Tom more water. 'There's no doubt that those wretches kidnapped Jake and Tom as well as . . . as the ladies. I think the longboat must have overturned and some of the crew righted it in the night, but kept on going, not bothering to pick up any survivors. Typical! Criminals, the lot of them!'

Horwood was at the door. 'I was trying to sleep and heard all this ruckus. Mrs Plummer told me Tom had been rescued, and I'm glad of that, but to hear you calling your own crew criminals says little for your judgement, Captain, and Mal is here as witness.'

'I didn't hear a bloody thing,' Willoughby said, but Loveridge wasn't concerned about Horwood.

'We should let Tom here get some rest,' the captain said. 'Let him settle down, he'll be all right.'

Mal took his turn on watch, pacing round the deck restlessly, hoping to see a ship. Then he talked Mr Lewis into taking over from him, while he found the captain and asked to be shown the current charts.

'I heard Jake and Tom arguing just before dinner last night,' he said to Loveridge. 'Things seemed peculiar to me. I didn't know exactly what, not knowing much about ships, that's why I was nosing about. I came up with naught, even when I barged in and asked the officers what was up. Turned out they were disagreeing about how far we were from . . . hang on, it was this chart . . . from this place. Here. The mouth of the Endeavour River.'

'Why?' Loveridge said. 'Let me look again.' He peered at the coastal chart. 'I don't know why they'd be interested in that spot. There's nothing there but jungle.'

'So they said. But tell me, where are we now?'

'Stuck on a reef about here,' the captain said angrily, stubbing his finger hard on to a spot well away from the coast.

'And where would the mouth of the Endeavour River be from here?'

'Almost due west.'

'Then I reckon that's where they've gone, led by your officers.'

Loveridge reacted angrily. 'That's an outrageous thing to say! You mustn't take on so, Mal. I know you're suffering severely at present but it doesn't help to defame two good men who, I believe, were taken as hostages.'

'Why? So we couldn't set sail after them without a craft of any sort?' Mal said bitterly.

He grabbed the coastal chart and stormed out of the wheelhouse, sprinting round the deck until he found Horwood.

'I want you to look at this, sir. Take a good look at this chart.' He spread it across a sail box. 'Now this place, Endeavour River, you heard of that?'

'Yes, of course.'

'Where's the nearest town?'

'A long way, down here at Trinity Bay . . . a town called Cairns.'

'Yes, I know about that, but what about in between? What's in between?'

'Nothing.'

'And there's no town at the Endeavour River?'

'I believe it was explored recently and a site selected for settlement. Maybe it's gone ahead – I don't know. Very much out of the way, you know. And dangerous. Countless savage tribes in that country.'

'Well, I bet that's where the crew have gone! Over there!' He pointed to the coast. 'With Mrs Horwood. Don't give up, sir. I think she's safe.'

He saw Horwood stagger, almost fainting, and took his arm. 'Come on. You'd better have a lie-down.'

* * *

Willoughby went back to see the captain. 'What did you do with Bosun Flesser's body?'

'I'm sorry, Mal, we didn't want to upset you. We buried him at sea after a short service, while you were with Jun Lien.'

'I thought as much. But don't even think of doing such a thing with my wife.'

'No. We wouldn't.'

'Well, be warned. See you don't. Can I take a break from the watch?'

'Yes. I'll keep a lookout.'

Mal went below, quietly slid into the cabin where Tom was sleeping and sat by him, waiting.

An hour passed before Tom showed signs of waking, but Mal was patient. He kept vigil, needing to have the man awake, refreshed, rid of the hysteria.

Eventually Tom became restless and cried out, but Mal soothed him. 'It's all right, you're safe now. No need to worry.'

'Oh, thank God,' the officer said. 'I was having a nightmare that I was back in the sea again. It was frightful.'

'We guessed the longboat overturned.'

'Yes it did. They righted it but they wouldn't come back and pick any of us up. They just rowed away and left us behind. It was terrible . . . I saw men taken by sharks.'

'Never mind about that now. Why did the mutineers take you with them?'

He saw Tom's eyes flicker nervously. 'They didn't say. They just herded us on board.'

'You and Jake?'

'Yes.'

'And the women? My wife?'

'Yes.'

'You're lying, Tom. My wife is dead. She drowned out there.'

'Oh God, no. We didn't . . . I didn't know. I'm so sorry, Mal.'

'You're going to be a lot sorrier, Tom, because I'm going to chuck you back into the sea. And I might cut you first just to make certain the sharks don't miss you.'

'You can't do that. You can't.' His voice rose to a scream but Mal clapped a hand over his mouth.

'I can. And I will. You were in charge of your boat and Jake was in charge of the other.'

'How do you know that?' Tom whispered.

Mal took him by the ears and lied. 'Because you're not the only survivor, you bloody fool. Now you give me the truth or you'll be dead before the night's out.'

* * *

'You'd better go down and talk to your second officer,' Mal said bitterly. 'Protect him, Captain, before I kill him. It was Jake Tussup's plan all along, so they could get to the goldfields over there. Taking rich women for ransom was Bartie Lee's idea, but that bastard down there went along with it all. He's a yes man, just as bloody bad as the rest of them.'

'He told you all this?'

'Yeah. Confession is good for the soul.'

By the third day Captain Loveridge was beginning to think they'd be forced to build a raft and abandon ship if they had to wait much longer. They couldn't ignore the rising waters that were winning the fight against the bilge pumps, and the dark storm cloud that squatted on the horizon. *China Belle*, already stricken, would be no match for wild ocean surges. He prayed to God that they'd be spared any more disasters, went down on his knees and begged the Lord to come to their aid, and for once, 'for once,' he muttered unkindly, his prayers were answered. SS *Clarissa*, a coastal steamer plying between Darwin and the eastern ports, sighted them late in the afternoon and sent a longboat to take off the survivors.

Captain Kobeloff, a burly Russian with a voice like a foghorn, was far from impressed with the motley lot of survivors. Too impatient to listen to explanations, he couldn't understand why Loveridge hadn't shot the mutineers. He balked at bringing the body of a dead woman on board, but was shouted down by Willoughby. He had Tom Ingleby clapped in irons immediately, and the Caporns sent to the ship's sick bay, before he'd listen to Horwood's carping.

Only Mrs Plummer, immaculate in a neat grey travelling suit under a white dustcoat, and a soft pink alpaca hat, managed to soften his attitude.

'Dear lady,' he said with a sweeping bow. 'Come. We will take tea, then I see about these people.'

Without further ado, SS *Clarissa* was on the move again. Despite the pleas of Loveridge and Willoughby, Kobeloff flatly refused to go near the Endeavour River.

'You think I'm mad? You saw the madness gold brings. That place, now called Cooktown, is a port. Overnight she a filthy port, with hordes of men of all breeds getting in there like a plague of rats. All after the Palmer River gold. They get their heads bashed in by blackfellows more like it.'

'I have to report the kidnapping of Mrs Horwood,' Loveridge insisted. 'I must do this as soon as possible. We have to find the poor woman. And I have to report the mutiny.'

'Who you report to there? Outlaws? Chinamen? Gang bosses? No. I put you in Cairns.'

'But we have to find my wife . . .' Lyle Horwood had aged in the last few days. He was stooped, his skin grey and dry, and his self-confidence replaced by bewilderment, leaving him shaken and shrill.

The Russian guffawed. 'You old man want to get ashore on Cooktown? The madmen in that place will eat you up! Better you sit down and be quiet and I give you a bottle of vodka for company.'

As for Raymond Lewis, MP, no one took much notice of him. He assisted Mrs Caporn where he could, appalled that a lady should have had to suffer such a beating. He stood stolidly by Mal Willoughby during his confrontation with Kobeloff, and then drifted away in search of newspapers.

Chapter Three

Jesse Field liked Cairns, with its lofty green backdrop and majestic bay. He liked to stroll along bush tracks overgrown with palms, and examine the myriad exotic plants he found in his wanderings, and often said that one day he would write a book on the subject. The trouble was that, as a reporter with the *Cairns Post*, and as a man much drawn to the conviviality of Dooley's Pub, he never seemed to be able to find the time. In fact, it was said in the town that if Jesse hadn't spent so much time at Dooley's he'd have been editor of that paper by now and, they added, would do a damn sight better job. But then, Jesse was happy. In his element, you could say. He'd come to Cairns to foil the onslaught of middle-age arthritis, to sun his bones under northern skies and cast aside the nattiness of city attire.

The Field House, as it was known, was difficult to find. He built a house in the centre of a half-acre block with wide verandas and a winding track to the road, and left his 'garden' in a natural state, refusing to trim so much as a leaf in his tropical surrounds. It seemed a gloomy place but to Jesse it was a joy. He had his books and papers, and his jangling piano – which he claimed was so tuneless it put the butcherbirds' teeth on edge – and a temperamental Chinese housekeeper called Lulu.

On this Sunday morning she woke him early, by banging a saucepan at his door, to tell him there was excitement at the port. After a heavy night at Dooley's, this awakening was not appreciated, but a few minutes later curiosity killed any attempt to recapture sleep.

'What sort of excitement?' he yelled.

'Ship sink. *China Belle* sink.'

'What?' Jesse was out of bed, standing under the home-made shower on the side veranda within seconds. *China Belle*? No! She couldn't have sunk. She was the swishest little ship that he'd ever seen, the pride of the Oriental Line, or rather of the wealthy directors and their ilk, they being the only ones willing to cough up the overpriced fares for the privilege of sailing in her.

Jesse pulled on white duck trousers, a black shirt and canvas plimsolls, and jammed his battered panama hat on thinning wet hair, but he was careful to pocket a new notebook and two good pencils before he raced down his front steps.

'*China Belle*!' he whistled. The passenger list on its own would be rolled-gold news. Stories galore. He wondered who they were, and if they'd survived.

Crowds were already gathering at the wharf as he dodged through, picking up scraps of information from their conversations.

'The survivors are on SS *Clarissa* down there.'

'Someone said it was a mutiny. There was a fight on board.'

'Is Kobeloff still skipper of *Clarissa*?'

Jesse hoped he was. Kobeloff was a mate of his. He ran the rest of the way, tearing up the gangplank to be confronted by Dan Connor, the local police sergeant, who was escorting a prisoner ashore . . . none other than Tom Ingleby, second officer from *China Belle*.

'What's going on?' Jesse asked, astonished.

Dan shoved Ingleby ahead of him. 'A terrible business, Jesse, and this here traitor a ringleader, he was.'

'A mutiny?'

'Aye, the whole crew abandoned ship, left the passengers and, what's more, kidnapped two ladies. Oh, it's a terrible business. It'll take some sorting out, let me tell you.'

'I had nothing to do with the kidnapping,' Ingleby moaned, but Connor clouted him over the head and pushed him down the gangplank.

'You can talk to him later,' he told Jesse, who then began intercepting groups of disembarking passengers to ascertain which ship they were from, and soon came across a survivor from *China Belle*, who agreed to step back into the lounge for an interview.

To Jesse's relief, this man turned out to be Raymond Lewis, a parliamentarian and exactly the right person to give him a sober and sensible account of the tragedies that had befallen the ship and its company. Which Mr Lewis did willingly.

Jesse went back over his notes. 'I want to get the passenger list right, Mr Lewis. I can't afford to publish any mistakes in an awful situation like this.' He read it out again and Lewis nodded.

'That is correct.'

'The woman who was kidnapped and is still missing is an Englishwoman, Constance Horwood, wife of Mr Lyle Horwood?'

'Yes.'

'And the woman who drowned was Chinese, Mrs Jun Lien Willoughby.'

'As I understand it, yes.'

'And her husband. Who is he?'

'A young fellow. I don't know his Christian name, or anything much about him except they came from China somewhere. But there's Mr Horwood; he knew the young chap better than I.' He beckoned as an elderly man came into the lounge.

'I say,' he called. 'Could you join us? This gentleman is from the press.'

Jesse stood and introduced himself as Horwood began with a tirade against Captain Loveridge.

'He's back there with the captain of this ship,' he snapped. 'Probably working out a story to cover himself, but he won't get away with it! I want a government inquiry! Lewis, you see to it! Did you know, sir,' he asked Jesse, 'that my wife has been kidnapped? My wife!'

It seemed to Jesse if the old man carried on like this much longer he'd give himself a heart attack.

'I am very sorry, sir, very sorry to hear that, and you can rest assured that this outrage is already causing concern in our town, concern at the very highest level. But I was wondering what you know about Mr Willoughby, whose wife drowned.'

'The little Chinese lady,' Lewis prompted.

'Willoughby?' Horwood said, quieter now. 'Oh Lord, yes. His wife, poor fellow, he's broken-hearted. He's the only one who understands what I'm going through.'

'Where is he from?'

'He's an Australian, country sort of fellow, been living in China for some years, I gather. Name of Malcolm, I suppose – he called himself Mal.'

'Mal Willoughby?' Jesse asked, astonished. 'Tall chap, thick blond hair, in his late twenties?'

'Yes, that'd be him.'

'He seemed younger to me,' Lewis said.

'That's only his looks,' Horwood sniffed. 'You should have seen him tear into Loveridge when he wanted to throw his poor dead wife overboard as well.'

'As well?' Jesse asked.

Lewis apologised. 'I'm sorry, it is inexcusable of me. I forgot to tell you that the bosun, a Mr Flesser, was murdered by the mutineers. Obviously he wouldn't go along with them. And a crew man, Sam Lum, was killed in an affray with Mr Willoughby.'

'Mr Field,' Horwood interrupted. 'I wish to leave this ship immediately. Mr Lewis and I wish to find a decent hotel. Would you be good enough to escort us? Then we will need a meeting with the authorities. And I want a doctor to call on me; I need medication for I doubt I'll ever sleep soundly again. And please require that my luggage, or what remains of it – I was robbed, you know – be taken to the hotel immediately . . .'

Jesse was happy to oblige, to keep a hold on every aspect of this story, but he was keen to find Mal Willoughby first.

'Mal!' he murmured to himself. 'Is that where you got to?'

He called a steward. 'Could you find Mr Willoughby for me?'

'No, sir. He left the ship the minute we berthed. Took the coffin with him.'

'Coffin?'

Lewis tapped Jesse on the shoulder. 'Mr Willoughby made a coffin for his wife while we were still on *China Belle*.'

Jesse found him leaning against the side wall of the funeral parlour, a desolate, lonely figure almost obscured by the shadow of the next building. He was spruced up in a dark suit, stiff shirt, black satin cravat and shiny boots, and that wasn't how Jesse remembered Mal, but then the lad was always respectful and, of all days, this one warranted . . . respect.

'How're you going Willoughby?' Jesse asked.

Surprised, he jerked his head up, blinked, and then managed a smile. 'Hello, Jesse. What are you doing here?'

'I live here. I heard about your late wife and wanted to tell you how sorry I am.'

Sonny nodded, mute.

'I thought, if you like, you could stay at my place. You won't have people bothering you there. The whole town's in uproar over these terrible happenings.'

'All right. But would you do me a favour, Jesse? I told them in there I want Jun Lien cremated like the Chinese do, so I can take her home. I left her there early this morning, now I don't know what to do. I've been standing here waiting . . .'

'Sure. I'll see what the procedure is.'

He went into the ugly building that also doubled as the morgue, spoke to the undertaker and returned to tell Sonny that he could pick up the ashes in the morning.

'Thanks.' It didn't bother him that he'd waited all day for that information, he just seemed grateful to have a decision made for him. 'I suppose I'd better move on. I have to get my stuff off the ship.'

'I'll come with you, then we can go over to my house. It's not far.'

'All right,' Sonny sighed. 'You still a newspaperman?'

'Yes.'

Under different circumstances Jesse would have said: 'And you're still a headliner, eh?' It was Mal, known then as 'Sonny' Willoughby, who'd given him the best story of his career, and the impetus to leave a dreary job in an outback town and make a name for himself. Now Jesse Field could pick and choose where he worked and, contrarily, he smiled to himself, he seemed to have picked another backwater. But here was Sonny Willoughby, striding down the sandy road with him, guaranteeing another headline. Some people, he thought, seemed to attract attention no matter how harmless, even uninteresting, they appeared to be. And Sonny was one of those people.

Willoughby had been pottering about the Gympie goldfields, not too interested in the scene at all, made a few pounds and prepared to leave, only to get mixed up in the robbery of a gold shipment and murder of the guards on the road to Maryborough. It had all been planned by the Gold Commissioner himself, who saw to it that Sonny Willoughby was nicely framed for the job.

But when he was arrested, Sonny escaped the first chance he got, and was on the run for months, until an uncle gave him up for the reward. The old coot knew Sonny was innocent but the thought of the reward had him riding full pelt to the nearest police station, hands out.

That was about the time that Jesse Field took an active interest in the story. There had been so much publicity about this young outlaw, who could travel hundreds of miles through the bush, moving from one district to another, giving police the slip every time, that the public began to cheer him on. When his photograph was printed in newspapers and on 'WANTED' posters, women rallied to his side. They wrote letters offering him refuge, support, money, even love, none of which the wanted man saw, but Jesse came across a few of them and was intrigued.

When he heard that Willoughby had been caught right there in Jesse's hometown of Chinchilla, thanks to a tip-off from Sonny's uncle, Silver Jeffries, he shot out to interview the man. Eventually, after ten shillings had crossed the table, adding to the Judas pile, the old man agreed to talk to Jesse about his nephew. Jesse was amazed that Silver spoke so proudly of Willoughby.

'You give the impression you think he's innocent?'

Silver nodded. 'Yeah, he's innocent all right. He told me the whole story. Sonny wouldn't lie to me.'

Jessie was incensed. 'And yet you gave him up, you bastard!'

'It wasna' like that,' Silver whined. 'I reckoned he'd be all right, soon as he got to tell them his side of the story.'

'Meanwhile you got the reward!'

Silver's eyes glinted with glee. 'Yeah, and I spent it right bloody quick afore they could get it back off me.'

'But your nephew's in gaol. They've got him on a murder charge now.'

Silver only shrugged. 'Well, they're wrong, aren't they?'

Jesse managed an interview with the prisoner, convinced then that he was innocent, and began writing articles outlining the story from the very beginning. Sonny was transferred to Brisbane, his case now famous. Robbery and murder, and a missing cache of gold, as well as the persona of the lad himself, had caught the fancy of newspaper editors in the other capital cities, and Jesse was in demand to provide more copy. He was offered a job with the prestigious *Brisbane Courier*, said his farewells to Chinchilla and moved to the metropolis. He interviewed anyone even remotely connected with the gold shipment robbery, even Willoughby's girlfriend, Miss Emilie Tissington, but he couldn't seem to break through to the truth, although he and Pollock, a police officer from Maryborough, were convinced that the Gold Commissioner himself had set the whole thing up.

When it seemed that all was lost, that Willoughby would hang, he stumbled on a way out himself. He heard another prisoner, Baldy Perry, who had been arrested for assault, boasting about being rich, though no one took notice of the known liar except Willoughby. Talking to him, Sonny realised that this man had been in Maryborough at the time, and alerted Pollock.

They instituted a simple, often-used trap of pitting that man's information against the Commissioner, giving the impression that each man had informed on the other . . . and it was all over. Confessions ensued. Sonny was released. The gold was never found. It had not been hidden where the Commissioner had instructed it to be, because his partner didn't trust him. And because he was due to hang, Baldy would never reveal where the gold was hidden. He had his last wish, to die a rich man.

Released, free, Sonny's confidence had deserted him. The degradation of being branded a criminal for such a long time had taken its toll, and he simply disappeared.

Jesse had thought he'd go back to Maryborough, to Emilie, but then he heard that she was engaged to marry an English businessman. One of her own, he supposed, rather than the footloose Australian. A sensible choice perhaps. But one that would have been yet another blow to Sonny's already battered self-image.

'I always wondered where you got to,' Jesse murmured now as they tramped along the sandy street.

'Yeah.'

Mal was aware of everything around him, especially the voices, the accent. He'd been so long in China he'd forgotten his own sound. When passers-by spoke, they sounded so familiar, as if known to him, that several times he jerked about to check.

'You all right?' Jesse asked him.

He nodded. The heavy perfumes of this tropical town were familiar too, and the heat had a thickness about it, moulded through with jasmine and eucalypt and frangipani and all the rest of the clamourers, that he had missed. Yes, he was very aware of them now, and of the littleness of this town, and of all the little bush towns he'd known and loved.

A sob escaped him. Jesse pretended not to notice. Mal was aware of even that, and yet his head was foggy, his brain wasn't working too well, he couldn't think. He still couldn't believe Jun Lien was gone – wouldn't believe. Didn't want to have to think of time without her, what to do without her. Men raised their hats to him as they passed.

'What's the matter with them?' he growled.
'They know who you are. Your clothes. They're offering condolences.'
'Should I get rid of these clothes now?'
'You can.'
'What about tomorrow, when I have to . . .'
'I'll go. I'll collect Jun Lien's ashes for you if you'd like me to.'
Mal sighed. 'If it's all right, I would, Jesse. I would.'

Two days later, Mal was sitting on Jesse's veranda, poring over newspapers, when Lyle Horwood and Raymond Lewis came to see him.

The two men offered their condolences again, and enquired after a funeral service, 'which we would be honoured to attend,' Lewis said.

'I appreciate that,' Mal said, 'but she'll have a family service later.'

'Captain Loveridge is organising a memorial service for Mr Flesser, to be held tomorrow at the Anglican church. It seems the whole town will be attending, they're so shocked.'

'So they should be,' Mal growled. 'Any word of Mrs Horwood?'

Lyle Horwood shook his head angrily. 'No. Nothing at all.'

'There's no telegraph to that place,' Lewis said. 'No communication except by ship, so the police can't tell us anything yet. They've commandeered a schooner to take some deputies to Cooktown, leaving in the morning. That's the only way they can alert what passes for the authorities there. I believe there are only two policemen.'

'And this is what I wanted to talk to you about,' Horwood said as he lowered himself wearily into a cane chair. 'I want you to lead the deputation, Mal. Find Constance. God knows what she's going through in the hands of those thugs.'

'We thought you'd be able to recognise the men quickly,' Lewis added. 'Point them out to the deputies, and find Mrs Horwood. But, you know, I think they'll already have let her go. After the tragedy with . . . with Mrs Willoughby, they might be scared now. She could be safe with the police by this time.'

'And if she's not?' Horwood snapped. 'If she's not? If they've still got her? Mal, I beg you. You understand the bush . . . you could search for her faster than these deputies; they don't seem to know what they're talking about.'

Lewis took his arm gently. 'They were only trying to explain that there is no town, no amenities, so to speak, all rather scattered.'

Mal pushed the papers aside. 'I'd like to help but I can't. I'm taking my wife back to China, back to her parents, so I'll be on the first ship out of here.'

'Couldn't you postpone that sad journey for a while?' Horwood asked plaintively, but Mal's resolve was firm.

'No, I'm sorry. No.'

'I'd go myself, but my heart, it's not up to it. I couldn't survive those conditions. I'd be willing to pay you, Mal. I'd pay you handsomely.'

'It's not the money, sir. I'm obligated. And if I were you I wouldn't think of setting foot in Cooktown. The papers say it's rough going, marshy and alive with mosquitoes.'

'Then I'll go,' Lewis said suddenly.

'You?' Mal and Horwood stared at the dapper gentleman.

'Yes. I'm not so old. I'm only forty. I might be rather round of girth but I ride jolly well, you know. The captain can't go. He's not only tied up with legal and police matters, he's not too good himself. Rheumatics, I think, or shock more like it, losing his ship and all . . .' His voice trailed off as he realised what 'and all' meant to these two devastated men. 'I mean, Caporn's injured, that leaves me. Don't you see, I have to go, I can recognise those men, I can spot them, point them out to the police.'

'What about the Parliament?' Lyle asked.

'It will have to wait. I thought perhaps, Mal, if I may call you so, that you might give me some pointers on what to pack?'

'Yes, I will,' Mal said grimly. His first thoughts were for guns and rat poison but he started his list with fresh water and antiseptics, before the usual bushman's fare of tea, flour and sugar.

'I thought you might know some native foods,' Lewis said, 'in case of a shortage.'

'I do, but it's no use trying to describe them. You could get very sick if you tried the wrong thing. Stick to what you know.'

Mal and Jesse and Lyle were at the wharf the next morning to see Lewis leave with the deputies, and were enraged to be shoved and jostled by crowds of prospectors, some with their families, desperate for transport to Cooktown, to the goldfields. When the skipper refused there was a riot, and mounted police had to clear the area.

Mal pushed through to Lewis in time to hand him a new check saddlecloth. 'When the horse isn't using it, you might,' he called, but he wasn't smiling. 'Good luck,' he added, and turned away.

The mutiny on the famous ship *China Belle* had all the residents of the coastal ports fascinated and none more so than the people of Maryborough, who had almost hanged an innocent man, one Sonny Willoughby. Now he was in the news again and curious faces turned to Mrs Clive Hillier, known to have been a friend of that fellow. More than a friend, they whispered, nudging each other, before she married Clive. And anyway, what's more, they whispered, who's to say that Willoughby wasn't in on that hold-up? The gold was never found. Maybe he had it all along and he gave it to her. That store the Hilliers opened, a gentlemen's outfitters, had grown fast into an emporium selling women's clothing as well. That must have taken extra cash. Well, who's to say where that came from? the voices asked, and answered . . . judges and juries, speculating. And what was Willoughby doing with a Chinese wife, anyway? Wait till Emilie hears about that. Some say he threw her over for the Chinese woman, broke her heart. She married Clive on the rebound. Where is Clive anyway? No one's seen him around lately.

As it happened, Clive was in Cairns on business. He was aware now of how fast these ports could grow, aided by gold rushes, and then when the diggers left for more fertile fields, real towns grew in their wake. This time he wanted to be in on the ground floor – though not in the search for gold; he'd tried that and would never make such a mistake again. No, he bought four blocks of land in the Cairns town centre and began building four shops, two for lease and two to accommodate a new Hillier clothing store, to be called Hillier's His and Hers.

He wrote to Emilie, who was managing the Maryborough store, that he was certain Cairns would overtake Maryborough in a very short time, because this was no up-river port. 'Cairns,' he wrote, 'has a spectacular harbour and provides easy access to the huge Far East markets.' Indeed his enthusiasm for the new venture had him writing page after page, ending with the instruction to prepare to sell their present premises. But not once on those pages, which also contained news of the town of Cairns and people he had met, who were most hospitable – not once did he mention that Sonny Willoughby was in town. That Sonny Willoughby, her former admirer, was a survivor of the *China Belle*.

Clive had seen Willoughby in town twice, in fact, but he made no effort to address him or communicate with him in any way, even though Sonny had been his friend in the first place. It had been Sonny who had introduced him to Emilie, the English governess, now his wife.

Clive was convinced that Emilie was still in love with Sonny, despite her protestations. He would taunt her with it, remind her that the country bumpkin had dumped her, claim she'd only married him on the rebound, and warn her against daring even to think about Sonny, or any other man, for that matter.

Emilie had read his letter with sadness in her heart, convinced that Clive would never change now. The news of Cairns was interesting, but had he forgotten that Maryborough had newspapers too? He'd made no mention of the *China Belle*, though it was all people seemed to talk about this week. And Sonny, of course.

She sighed. It had been a rather trying week. She'd been thrilled to read of Sonny, and know that he was in good health, and then genuinely upset to learn that he'd lost his wife in such heart-rending circumstances.

Poor Sonny, she thought. He's had such a sad life. What else can happen to him? He's a good man, he doesn't deserve these miseries. And as for Clive . . . come to think of it, he would know we'd read about the mutiny here. Maryborough isn't that much of a backblock. Yes, he'd know, but he's making a point with me. By not mentioning the mutiny or Sonny, he's harping on his old jealousies. Fuel to the fire. Another excuse to make my life a misery.

Emilie had never realised that such raging jealousies existed. It wasn't just about Sonny; it was about every other man who even smiled at her.

She remembered when he'd started teasing her about being dumped by Willoughby, calling him a country bumpkin, a local lad, intellectually inferior to the English-born and educated Hilliers.

For a while, embarrassed, Emilie had let the teasing pass, but when it turned into taunts, she'd pointed out that it had been the other way round.

'I chose you, Clive, not Sonny. I wish you'd stop this. I love you. I told him that.'

'Are you saying he made you choose?'

'Well, I had to make the decision.'

'When was this? When you were in bed with him?' Clive snarled. 'You must have been bloody close for him to want to marry you.'

'No. It wasn't like that at all!'

'You're a liar! Sonny wouldn't have dared put a finger near you if you hadn't led him on.'

'That's unfair! Please, Clive, be reasonable.'

And that was the first time he had struck her, slapped her so hard across the face that she'd had to stay hidden in her room until the swelling died down.

Emilie put down his letter and walked to the window of the parlour, looking out over the moonlit garden, trying not to think of Clive. Of his rages. Of the beatings. Of the times that he took her in his arms, explaining that he loved her.

'Can't you understand that you upset me when you flirt?' he'd ask. But Emilie had long since argued that she never flirted, not even in her single days. It was simply not in her nature.

Besides, she knew by this time that none of it had to do with loving or flirting. It was possession. The man was possessive of her and he was also a wife-beater. As plain as that. She wasn't one to mince words when talking to herself, but she'd learned to be very, very careful when in the presence of her husband.

A year ago, almost to the day, she recalled, she had sat Clive down and talked quietly to him about the situation, telling him, respectfully, that he shouldn't expect this to go on.

'A wife isn't a punching bag. You've got to think about what you're doing, Clive. Surely you don't get pleasure from injuring me.'

Emilie sighed again, with an involuntary hand to her throat. It was a question that had seriously interested her, as she struggled to deal with his violence, but one that she never put to him a second time. He'd been so offended by her temerity that he'd almost strangled her with the scarf she'd been wearing.

'It's not to go on, though,' she said loudly, and forcefully, to the empty room, to the blessedly empty house. 'I have to leave him. To get away from him.'

Emilie had owned a small cottage in Maryborough before they were married but after a few months Clive had insisted she sell it. The money was used as a deposit on a bigger house right here in town.

They had done well with the shop, now called Hillier's Emporium, and would probably do even better in the next town, having learned from their successes and their mistakes the ins and outs of starting a new business in a new town.

'What can I do?' she asked herself. 'I have to leave him, but how? I have no family in this country, and only my sister, Ruth, back home, and we don't get on. And what about money? Our money is in the business. I take two pounds a week for housekeeping, which is generous, but I could hardly save anything from that source.'

Emilie occasionally put a few shillings into a chocolate box but they never amounted to much, because she couldn't see past her front door. The world out there was blank – it was like peering into a fog. How could she make her way on her own, with no money?

In the morning, though, she had better do as requested and see Mackenzie, the local real estate agent, about selling the Emporium. Maybe she and Clive could make a new start. But then she shuddered. With Sonny Willoughby in town?

Chapter Four

The Chinese girl got away. She fought them off! They were grabbing at her from all directions but she got away, jumped overboard, and her husband was there to save her. Oh God, help me, why didn't I jump when I had the chance? They wouldn't have turned back for me; they didn't turn back for Jun Lien, more interested in getting to shore. That officer, Tussup, hadn't wanted the thugs to drag us along. I wish I knew what was going on. Maybe they've got the other women in that second longboat. I feel sick, sitting here being jostled and shoved about by these filthy men; my dress is wet, ruined, not that I care about the damned dress, but I'll look a sight when we get ashore. The one they call Bartie Lee keeps leering at me, asking if I'm 'orri', but I won't answer, I won't talk to them at all. It's the only way I can keep control of myself, just hang on, try not to let them know I'm scared stiff. As if they'd care whether I am or not. I'm hungry and I'm feeling light-headed – hysteria, probably, because I'm not thinking straight, I know. Too confused. All the more reason to shut up, say nothing, just listen to the plod of the oars. What's happening back on the ship? There'll be terrible trouble over this. They hang mutineers, I think. I hope they do, anyway. There's water in the bottom of the boat. I've lost my shoes and my stockings feel grimy. They'll hang Tussup too. He has glanced back at me a few times, his expression a lump of granite, not one word of help or encouragement. I think I must have been in a daze for some time, my neck is sore and I'm so cold my feet are like ice.

We're getting close to shore; these wretches are all excited, chattering like monkeys, wanting to pull in. I can see the glimmer of lights way ahead. Please God the people there will come to my aid when they see me like this. These men won't get away with dragging a white woman ashore. What is it all about anyway? Why are they all so damned pleased with themselves? All they've managed so far is to desert a good ship and row to a lonely shore. Maybe they're smugglers.

Oh no! The lights are gone, lost behind a dark headland. Tussup is pointing to a beach, white in the moonlight, and they're making for it now, rowing like madmen, cheering and punching each other with Tussup ordering quiet. I hope they yell and scream, alert the residents. I knew they were rowing too fast; we've hit the beach, ploughing into the sand, everyone tumbling out. I have to get myself out, not a hand offered, clambering over the side of the boat, wading ashore, the water surprisingly warm, stumping up the beach, my stockings filled with grit, and I can't stop crying. I'm tired and wet and sick and hungry and I'm so confused I don't know what to do. And I hate these people. I'd kill every one of them if I had the means.

They're ignoring me, dragging the boat up into the matted forest bordering the beach, hiding it, all busy now, unpacking and setting up a camp with Tussup striding about like a tin god. I should run away while I can, but first I have to slip into the shadows and get these stockings off.

'Where you think you're going, lady?'

It's that horrible Bartie Lee, but I won't talk to him, won't acknowledge him at all. I'm sitting at his feet and, *voilà*! My stockings are off in a flash.

'Ah Kee!' he yells. 'You mind the woman. Tie her hands, put her in a tent. Keep her out of sight.'

Ah Kee comes running. He's the ship's cook, a better type than these thugs. Surely he'll have pity on me, but no, he grabs me by the left wrist and hauls me across the sand as if I were a small wayward child. I feel like screaming at him but I can't, I won't speak. Instead I go for him, whacking and kicking the traitor.

Oh God, my nose is bleeding. He struck me, punched me in the face and the pain has started all over again. My whole head is agony and I must be a mess of bruises by now. I have to use my skirt to sop up the blood. He'll be sorry he did this. I won't forget him in a hurry. Any of them. They've made shelters of canvas, lit a fire, food. The very thought of it makes me sick.

My hands are tied with cord; I couldn't get to the plate of mush they left for me even if I wanted it. Though I suppose I could tip the plate to my mouth. It isn't a real tent, just a shelter, no walls, and all around this place is matted greenery, thick bushes with huge leaves, and ivy thick as ropes trailing and curling everywhere. They had to use machetes to clear some space on the ground and even though the sun is up now it's dark and steamy in this jungle, with the trees forming a canopy overhead.

A Malayaman sidled up and grabbed my food. He ate it, licked the plate and put it back by my side, and I don't know why I'm upset. I wasn't about to touch it anyway. But I am shockingly upset, my jaw is aching from the blows and from forcing myself not to talk. Or to cry. I will not cry any more. What are they doing here anyway? Maybe they're smuggling tea, though that doesn't seem worthwhile. I can't see much else here but supplies. I wonder where the other boat is. With Mrs Plummer and Mrs Caporn. Why couldn't they have put us in the same boat? I wish I could scream at them, tell them to bring Tussup here immediately because I want to know what's happening. Now! Immediately. My eyes are wet with tears but it's not my fault. It's not. I couldn't hold out any longer.

Jake saw her sitting on the grass under a small tarpaulin. She looked awful, her face blotchy and swollen from the blows she'd received from one of the Malays last night. He'd warned Bartie Lee since then that the woman had to be treated properly or he'd have to step in.

Now that they were ashore he was feeling stronger, freed from the creepy feeling he'd had in the boat that some of the Asians were plotting to throw the white boss overboard. He strode out on to the deserted beach. There was no sign of any survivors from the other longboat, but then they could have been washed up on one of the islands anywhere along the coast. He shrugged. Every man for himself on this tour.

As he strode back to find Bartie Lee, he noticed that Mrs Horwood had eaten her porridge, and nodded to her. Very sensible; she had to keep her strength up until he could find a way to prise her free of these jackals. It was a damn nuisance, though. Once they'd stepped on to firm ground he'd realised that his dream of arriving at the goldfields with his own workforce of coolies had been usurped by Bartie Lee, so he might as well take off on his own, without even Tom Ingleby as a partner, wherever the hell he'd got to.

'I'll climb that headland,' he said, 'and get our bearings.'

'Me too,' Bartie Lee said, pulling on a shirt.

'First you tell the men to keep their hands off the woman while we're gone, or I'll put a bullet in them.'

Bartie Lee laughed. 'She not so pretty today, eh?'

'Tell them! Especially your pig mate Mushi Rani.'

Lee yelled his instructions and eyed Jake as he tucked a pistol into his belt. 'I got a gun too.'

The headland overlooked a mangrove swamp on the immediate coastline, and a jungle-clad landscape but in the distance was the silvery outline of a wide river.

'There she is!' Lee shouted excitedly. 'Our gold river.'

'We're further away than I thought. But it'd have been tough landing in those mangroves. We'll have to hike to the river.'

'To our goldfield! Come on, we get them pack up now and move camp.'

Jake packed his supplies and weapons carefully. Then he sent Ah Kee to find some footwear for Mrs Horwood, but when he returned with a pair of Chinese slippers, the same as they all wore, she shook her head, refusing them.

'Put them on,' he ordered. 'We're walking now. You'll need some protection or your feet will be cut to pieces. Even the grass is sharp.

'Get her something to tie her hair back too,' he told the Chinaman, 'or she'll be stumbling along blind, and holding me up. She'll walk behind me and you follow right after her. You got me? If she falls you pick her up fast.'

He looked at her as she thrust her feet into the slippers and stood up, facing him without a word, but the contempt in her face was easy to read. He shrugged that off, turning his attention to her long red dress. It was still damp and clinging to her, the skirt more of a hobble than a help, so he leaned over and slit it from knee to hem with his knife.

She screamed, pulling away, but the dress had been fixed.

'Now wear this,' he said, giving her one of his shirts. 'You'll get insect bites with so much skin showing. Besides, you have to keep covered with these bastards around.'

He was surprised she had nothing to say, but she blushed the same colour as her dress, so he guessed she got the message.

The crew had turned into a line of coolies, carrying their supplies, while the leaders forged a path through the scrub with their machetes. Jake and his small party followed in their wake but their progress was slow. From the headland the terrain had looked like a massive green carpet, but down here at ground level the land was scored with hills and deep gullies. Mrs Horwood was fortunate, he thought, that the trek was slow or she'd have been a real problem, but after a bad start, slipping and tripping every few yards, she managed to stay on her feet.

At noon they rested. Jake was sore already from ducking and weaving along the greasy track, so he turned to her.

'You all right, Mrs Horwood?'

No answer.

Stuck-up bitch, he thought, but felt better for the snub. It allowed him to care less.

The galley staff served tea and meatballs with rice, but when Ah Kee handed Mrs Horwood her lunch she threw it on the ground.

Jake had to move fast to grab Ah Kee's arm and prevent him from striking her, and Bartie Lee leaped to his feet, watching.

'Don't you ever touch her,' Jake shouted at Ah Kee. 'If you do I'll break your arm. Now go get her another serve.

'And you!' he rounded on her. 'You stupid bloody woman! You eat, you do every single thing you're told or you'll be in the worst sort of trouble you could ever imagine. Do you hear me?'

She nodded, and when Ah Kee came back, took the plate.

'Say thank you,' Jake snapped, and she mouthed the words but nothing came out, so he supposed that would do. He dismissed Ah Kee and noticed Bartie Lee, mollified, sink back to the ground to drink his tea.

They pushed on and by late afternoon they had climbed the last ridge where they were stunned at the scene before them. Below them, by a river crowded with all manner of small vessels, were some tents, but on the other side of the river a canvas town was spread out before them. Hundreds and hundreds of tents jostled for space among tall trees and a flourish of tropical blooms. Lanes between the tents were haphazard, with no order about them; clothes fluttered on makeshift lines or on tree branches, fires smouldered, and the residents seemed to be wandering aimlessly about.

'Is that the goldfield?' Bartie asked incredulously.

'No, it must be beyond that wall of trees,' Jake told him. 'I say we camp near the base of this hill now. Tell the bearers to get on down.'

The bearers were only too pleased to find themselves at the end of this hard trek, so they made short work of the descent, dumping the supplies on the banks of a small creek and splashing into the water to quench their thirst.

Jake and Ah Kee helped Mrs Horwood to follow them down the steep, slippery track.

'You can have a rest now,' he said, not bothering to tell her that she looked exhausted, since he was sure she was well aware of that. 'Just stay here and I'll see what I can do.'

He gave Ah Kee instructions to get her tea, then make a tent for her. A private tent so that she could sleep. At least for a little while, he thought.

Constance fell down into the grass and let the Chinese cook set up a tent around her. She was convinced now that she was going mad, that the terror of this situation had affected her wits. And her speech. She remembered making a decision not to talk to any of them, to keep herself totally aloof, but when she needed to speak, when Tussup yelled at her, she couldn't make a sound. Her throat had somehow constricted, though it wasn't sore. And since Tussup had tamed Ah Kee by threatening him, the man had been quite helpful, assisting her without being asked on that arduous trek. That had given her the courage to ask him where they were taking her, but the words wouldn't form. They came out in such a whisper that embarrassment followed. He misinterpreted the whisper.

'You want go, lady? Go there, in behind there.'

He stood aside to offer her privacy behind dense bush, causing Constance to blush scarlet, but then nature nudged and she took advantage of the opportunity. She also considered running away, but this jungle was frightening; one man had already been bitten by a snake. Unfortunately, she mused as she tramped on, it had not been a venomous snake. That would have been one thug less.

It bothered her too that when they reached the ridge she was feeling pleased with herself. Further proof that she was going off her head. There was nothing to be pleased about except that she'd survived this afternoon's wretched trek, considering her fears and her lack of decent walking shoes. But she'd soon learned to step firmly, to trust overhead vines and branches to steady herself, and so avoid the snags of thick roots and rutted earth beneath her feet, and the slimy green rocks that had been the downfall of several bearers. A cheering sight. In fact, she told herself, examining the blisters on her hands, she'd practically swung along that track like a monkey. And she'd kept her mind off her troubles by listening to the clatter of birds and watching the uneven ground.

Tussup had looked back to her several times, asking if she was all right, but she had not bothered even to try to answer him, and she took the walking stick Ah Kee gave her to help herself along as they waded across a stony creek.

That was another joy, she thought as they began the steep descent to a large camp – that creek water. It had been crystal clear, and had tasted so delicious to her parched mouth that she was sure she'd never forget it. Never had water tasted so marvellous.

She'd heard the men talking about gold. This apparently was their destination, this sea of tents by a big river. Goldfields! It couldn't be anything else. Constance still had no idea where she was, but down there were people, a lot of people living in a scruffy settlement, and she was now in sight of help. In fact she could probably sneak away through the bush as soon as darkness overtook Tussup's camp. I'd have to be damned stupid not to find my way down to that river, she gloated.

What do they want with us anyway? she kept asking herself. Why would they burden themselves with women? Surely they're not after ransom? The question intrigued her. After all, she had heard of white slavers. What would Lyle pay to retrieve his wife, she wondered. What indeed? That thought gave her a jolt; sent a rush of trepidation through her system. Ah Kee brought her tea and a comb. I am feeling very giddy, she worried as she sipped the hot, weak tea from an enamel mug. I'm so hot and dirty, I'd love to go down and throw myself in that river. I would if they'd let me, I really would.

It was agreed that after they'd eaten, Jake and Bartie Lee would find someone to ferry them across the river to the main settlement, so that they could explore the place and ascertain the whereabouts of the goldfield.

Though no one had approached their camp so far, they told Mushi and the other seven crew members never to mention *China Belle*. They were to stick to the story that they'd come here in the schooner *Lagos*, having boarded in Kupang.

'We'll have to take the woman with us,' Jake said, but Bartie Lee objected.

'Why? You want her to get away, eh? She my business, Jake. I see to her.'

'She's your business all right, and it's madness. If you're smart you'll let her go. We can say we tried to save the women.'

'Then she run off to the police pointing fingers at us. We be in gaol before sunset.'

Unfortunately it was true. 'Jesus, you sure have messed up a simple operation, Bartie. There's no law against jumping ship – that's all it was to be . . .'

'Until you run her on to a reef, Mr Smart Officer. Leave the woman to me.'

Until you or Mushi murdered the bosun, Jake recalled, but it was no use going into that now. 'We can't leave her,' he said. 'I don't reckon she's safe with Mushi in charge.'

They argued about that until Bartie Lee called the men together and harangued them at length about leaving the woman alone, and being quiet, not to draw attention to themselves.

While he waited Jake realised that Bartie liked jabbering on at them, enjoyed being boss, and he hoped they would obey him. He considered giving Mrs Horwood a gun to protect herself in his absence, but he knew it was a stupid idea. Instead he promised to pay Ah Kee two pounds, a fortune in any of their terms, to see she came to no harm. It was the best he could do.

'We have to sort out our monies first,' Bartie Lee said, as Mushi tipped a bag of spoils on to a canvas. Not that this surprised Jake – he'd known they'd grab all the jewellery and cash they could before leaving the ship.

'This ours,' Mushi said belligerently, glaring at Jake. 'Our men find these stuffs.'

'Do what you like,' Jake snapped, 'just get a move on.'

The cash divided, they collected the jewellery, including some more expensive pieces they took from a battered steel jewel case, and dropped them on to a coloured headscarf, which Bartie Lee knotted into a bag and strung on a cord looped around his neck.

'You bringing that stuff now?' Jake wanted to know.

'Yeah, sell quick, get real money quick. Then we find the gold.'

This tent city was as confused as an Asian market and just as noisy. Men and women were preparing their evening meals over open campfires, while raucous drunks hung about makeshift taverns that were doing a roaring trade. To Jake that was a very good sign. Gold was still here for the finding.

As usual at this latitude, the sun slid quickly out of sight, leaving distant hills to soak up the last of the golden rays. Lanterns were lit and candles wavered as the men picked their way carefully through the tents, finally coming upon what seemed to be the centre: a strange retail area, all under canvas, of stores, butchers, fettlers, inns, jewellers and assayers, stables and more rollicking taverns.

Not wanting to be part of Bartie Lee's operation, Jake bought a bottle of beer and sat under a tree to wait for him and watch the passing parade. It was a relief just to be sitting there, alone, to not have to think about anything.

He finished that bottle in no time and bought another. As he walked back to the designated meeting spot, he asked an elderly man about the goldfields.

'Are they still going strong?'

'Yes, mate. Plenty of gold there yet, they say.'

'Where are they – the goldfields?'

'Over them hills back there. You new?'

'Yes. Over the hills? That looks a fair way.'

'That it is. A hundred and fifty miles or so to the Palmer River. Bloody horrible track it is too.'

Jake was stunned! 'I thought the Palmer River was here somewhere, a tributary of this river.'

'No. This is the Endeavour River. The mouth is just the nearest port, or what's come to be a port. The gold's out at the Palmer.'

'Cripes,' Jake breathed as he sat down with his bottle. 'This is bloody lovely! We're nowhere near the goldfields. So what now?'

In the end he had to go in search of Bartie, and found him exiting drunkenly from a flophouse with a couple of elderly whores on his arm.

'Ah, there!' he called. 'My fren'. Partner. I got a lady here for you.'

Angrily, Jake ordered the whores to disappear but they wouldn't budge until Bartie paid them ten shillings, which he did, happily displaying a wad of notes.

'Got plenty here,' he boasted to Jake. 'Them jewellers crooks, but a boss Chinaman, he pay me a hundred pound. What you say about that?'

'Good,' Jake said, though he knew the jewellery had been worth a great deal more. 'But we'd better go back before you get mugged. We're gonna need that cash.'

'Whaffor?'

'Horses.'

'No horses. No!'

'Do you see any goldfields round here?'

Bartie staggered along beside him. 'Here's another good grog shop. We get a drink here, eh?'

'No, we get a boat back to camp.'

The ferryman had charged them a shilling to cross the river. The return boat trip cost three shillings. Remembering that the bottles of beer had been expensive, but so welcome he hadn't cared, Jake realised that gross overcharging was the name of the game in this remote location. And he wondered what horses cost, because sure as hell he wouldn't be hoofing it over those gloomy mountains.

The camp was quiet. Ah Kee, sleeping outside Mrs Horwood's hut, smelled of booze. Jake looked in on her with his lantern and saw someone had taken the precaution of tying her hands behind her back.

'What brought this on?' he asked, slicing the cords with a knife. 'You try to get away?'

'Yes,' she whispered furiously. 'They were all drunk but your watchdog there caught me.'

'They didn't hurt you?'

'Oh no! Being trussed up and thrown back in the tent, that didn't hurt me.' The whisper was disappearing. She'd found her voice now, just when he didn't need it.

'Shut up,' he said quickly. 'Be quiet, I'll be back in a minute.'

He stole quietly past Bartie Lee, who was snoring under a tree, the bag of cash still bulging in the pocket of his grubby jacket.

I could grab it now, Jake thought, take the money and the woman and get the hell out of here. I could let her loose in the settlement. But they'd come after us, both of us. They'd follow me right out to the goldfields. I'd always have them breathing down my neck. If they found her anywhere over there, even after she went to the police, they'd kill her out of sheer bastardry. They'd be after her before she had a chance to find police anyway . . . Come to think of it, I didn't sight any police, though I suppose there'd be coppers around some place. But she looks in a worse state than those old whores. At least they were wearing clothes, not rags. She'd get short shrift from strangers this hour of night if I left her. Or she'd be attacked. There's a heap of low-life prowling that tent town.

He knew that the only real solution to this problem was to take her and go in the other direction. Give up his plan to find gold. Jake groaned at the thought of all that planning and effort ending up a total waste of time. But it would never occur to Bartie Lee that he would ditch the goldfield plan altogether. Never. He and his mates would tear the place apart searching for them. No. He'd have to run, and take this bloody nuisance of a woman with him. She was like a goddamned albatross around his neck. He'd get on a boat to any port he could find. Then he'd be rid of her. It was the only way out. And if he didn't make a move soon, they'd have a pack of Asians baying after them.

Only if I took their prize, the wealthy woman, though, he thought. If I let Bartie Lee keep her, they wouldn't bother coming after me.

Why don't I just go? Leave them all to it. I've got my own funds, kept well out of sight in my pistol holster. I could probably steal a horse to save a few quid.

Jake looked down at Bartie Lee, snoring, heaving, and resisted the urge to kick his rump, before turning away.

'Come on!' he said to Constance Horwood, grabbing her arm. 'We're going.'

'Where?'

'Move!' He slung his swag over his shoulder and crept round Ah Kee, his hand on a lump of wood ready to silence him if he woke, then crept through the bush towards the river. He glanced back, not sure whether to be pleased or sorry that she was right behind him, and grimaced at her clownish appearance in the dirty shirt, torn skirt and slippers. She won't be any help, he thought, in charming us into a strange boat, if there's one around.

He skirted the other camps and marched along the riverbank until he saw some folk sitting by a fire.

'Sit down here,' he said to her, 'and listen to me. We're not clear yet, they'll come after us and kill us if we're not very careful.'

She was terrified. She screamed at him, 'I'm going straight to those people and demand they get the police.'

'Then what? You sit here with them? Wait for those thugs? The Asians are well armed. Besides, this is no ordinary town. It's little hell; they won't give a damn about you . . .'

But she wouldn't listen. She broke away from him and ran towards the camp, where several men were playing cards.

'Help!' she cried. 'I need help!'

'You sure do, missus,' one man said. 'You been partying, eh?'

'No, no! I've been kidnapped. From the *China Belle*.'

They laughed, angering her, and she began screaming at them, until a woman came out of a tent, calling her a hussy, telling her to 'get out of it', while the men urged her to go and get this 'Chinese belle'.

When Jake came for her she was on her knees, begging them to help but the men had shrugged her off as mad, and returned to their cards, and the woman was standing over her with folded arms.

'She's distraught,' he explained. 'Been through a bad time. We've lost our belongings.'

'Nothin' new about that in this place. Robbed, were you?'

'Yes,' Jake said. 'Do you reckon you could sell me some sort of a dress for her?'

'Cost you,' the woman said warily.

'I know, but she needs something.'

'I'll see.'

She disappeared into the tent and came back with a cotton blouse and a rough plaid skirt. 'Best I can do. That'll be two pounds.'

'Two pounds!' Mrs Horwood cried. 'They're not worth two pounds. I haven't got two pounds.'

'They'll do,' Jake said quickly, handing over the notes, which the woman took into the lamplight to examine before she gave him the clothes.

'Reckon your missus needs her head examined,' she sniffed as she tucked the notes between her breasts.

'They'll have listened to me if you'd given me time,' Mrs Horwood insisted as Jake dragged her away.

'Don't you understand yet?' he snarled at her. 'You haven't got the bloody time. Bartie Lee will be after you. If they can't get you back, you'll be dead before you get anywhere near the police. They can't have you reporting them, not yet, not before they've had a chance to lose themselves on the goldfields.

She ran into the scrub and came back within minutes, dressed soberly and looking more sane, he thought, but she definitely wasn't thinking clearly.

'I will get across the river somehow . . .' she began.

'And lead yourself into a heap of trouble.'

'You don't seem to realise who I am,' she wept. 'My husband is a director—'

'Lot of good that will do here unless you can produce plenty of cash to back it up. Then you'd be in business.'

'You're wrong. As soon as I tell them I'm from the *China Belle*—'

'Like you did a while ago. No one here would know or care about *China Belle*. Not yet.' That was the beauty of my plan, he recalled angrily, no one would have heard she was stuck on a reef yet. It's too soon. 'In the meantime I'll have to buy our way out of here.'

'Our way? I don't want anything to do with you!'

'Then I hope you can walk on water. The ferrymen have to be paid.'

In the end he took her down to the ferry, paid her fare, and at the last minute jumped aboard as well.

He heard her telling her story to the ferryman as he rowed them across, and then she called back to him, 'Mr Tussup, this gentleman has promised not to tell that fellow Lee or any of his men that we have crossed the river. But he needs some incentive. Please give him two shillings.'

Jake ignored them both. Two bob would buy silence until Bartie Lee arrived with a better offer.

Constance was appalled that this criminal was still with her when she stepped off the boat, and was walking up the jetty.

The canvas town was a surprise. It had to be well after midnight, but the place was very much alive with gaiety. The tents were lit with myriad lamps and candles, and Chinese lanterns were strung across the entrance to several large tents, adding colour to the night. It was a rowdy place too, men and women bustling about, their voices competing with street minstrels and the jangle of a hurdy-gurdy belting out music-hall tunes.

She turned back to him. 'I'm grateful to you for helping me to get away from those other men, but I'm going straight to the police station now. The ferryman gave me directions. Obviously it is not a place for a person like you, unless you intend to give yourself up. So you may go.'

'Whatever you say, madam.' He tipped his white officer's cap further back on his head, gave her a stage bow and strode away.

Constance gave a sigh of relief. She was rid of them at last. Free! She felt like singing along with the street serenader as she began to make her way through the maze.

The directions were no help at all, and when she admitted to herself that she had strayed beyond the well-lit area into a dark dormitory of tents, she couldn't find anyone to ask the way, except for some hideous drunks, who cursed her in the most frightful manner as she stumbled away from them. And stumbling seemed to be all she was doing in this search, with so many obstacles lurking underfoot. She tripped on tent ropes and pegs, fell into the ashes of a campfire, blundered right into a tent and was screamed at by the occupants, and finally slipped down a gully, injuring her ankle.

And there she stayed. She felt safe there, hidden by bush. Even though the place stunk, it would have to be her refuge until daylight.

Constance found the police tent later the next morning. It was behind a row of timber buildings under construction, but the flap was tightly secured and carried a sign that read 'NO ENTRY'.

Not to be deterred, she asked the carpenters working nearby where she might find a policeman, but they had no idea.

'Try the hospital,' one man offered. 'Follow the wagon track up the hill.'

Suddenly Constance realised that Bartie Lee and his men would be searching for her now, so she ran, limping painfully, for the sanctuary of the hospital.

This, she found with relief, had evolved from canvas to a long rough structure with a thatched roof, the thatch made of leaves from palm trees. But the canvas hadn't been wasted, held up by poles it provided a roof for scores of people who seemed content to rest on the ground in its shade.

The hospital had a simple layout. Men's ward to the left, women's to the right, and beyond the narrow lobby was a sign: 'NO ENTRY'.

Constance waited until a nurse came from a ward and asked her where she might find a policeman.

'Police station down there.' The woman pointed and rushed away.

Constance waylaid several women after that, but they all seemed too busy to listen to her, except for one, who had noticed she was limping.

'If you want treatment for your foot, miss, you'll have to get in line out there.'

Only then did Constance realise that the scores of people sitting patiently in the shade were in need of treatment.

'No, no,' she cried. 'You don't understand. I was kidnapped from the *China Belle* . . .' She saw the woman's eyes waver as if she were already trying to disconnect from this conversation. 'Please,' she entreated. 'I'm English. I shouldn't be here. I'm destitute. I need help. Please could you let me stay here until the police get back?' She was hanging on to the woman's pinafore. 'Please. I'll pay you well as soon as I can, whatever you ask. If only you'll help me. My husband is very rich.'

'Yes, dear.' The woman undid Constance's fingers. 'Settle down now. Go and sit out there, and keep out of the sun. Stay there and Doctor will see you. The charity ladies will be along soon with the tea. Hurry on now or you'll miss out.'

The tea and buns distributed by the 'charity ladies' were a godsend, and Constance took her share gladly, then she lay on her side to rest, copying the patients surrounding her. The air was heavy, humid, and everyone was quiet, some dozing. This day seemed so different from the Babel of the previous night that she began to wonder if she'd imagined it.

'One thing for sure, though,' she told herself, 'those crewmen won't dare try to hurt me or pull me out of this crowd. There must be a hundred people here.'

Mrs Horwood smiled as she dozed, taking credit for her cunning in finding this hiding place.

'Who is she?' said Dr Madison as two volunteers carried her in on a stretcher.

'No one knows,' the matron said. 'People thought she was just asleep out there, but when it came to her turn they couldn't wake her.'

'Her temperature's high. We'd better get her cooled down right away. Do it quickly, I think she's coming round now.'

Their patient groaned, tried to raise herself but was whisked away by two nurses, who placed her on a bed and proceeded to undress her.

As they set to work with sponges and towels, Matron raised an eyebrow at the fine crêpe de Chine undergarments her nurses had dropped on a nearby chair, but then she hurried away. She had no time in this overcrowded and undermanned infirmary to do more than notice.

Jake changed his mind and went back to keep an eye on her, but she'd disappeared into the crowds.

'I'd better get moving then,' he told himself. 'She'll have the police on the job by now.'

Though he had decided to board a ship and get out of this place while the going was good, he was still loath to give up on his original plan. The gold was within reach, goddammit. He cursed Bartie Lee for ruining everything, and Tom Ingleby for not keeping control of the Malays as Flesser would have done. He wondered if the silly bastard had drowned. He should have overseen the loading of that longboat; got it right. That surely wasn't too much to ask of the fool. And he cursed the woman, Mrs Horwood. She was the bad joss in the end, the last bloody straw.

He glared at the scene in front of him, this river settlement, this impostor, luring men to its shores with the promise of riches, then revealing the prize was out of reach. He wondered how many had gone on into the wilderness and how many hadn't got any further than here.

'You've been too long at sea,' he muttered. 'Feeling sorry for yourself.' So the goldfields were a hundred and fifty miles away, he reasoned. Hadn't he walked from Goulburn to Sydney as a kid? Hoofed it all the way on his own with only a few pence in his pocket. This time he'd have a horse and supplies.

'So get on with it,' he told himself.

His first stop was at a brothel where his choice, a cheeky girl called Madeleine, was only too pleased to look after the handsome seaman for some hours, as he'd requested. And as he had told her after the first hour, she was the best thing that had happened to him for many a day, but now he had other plans for her.

'Don't be nervous,' he laughed. 'I just want you to cut my hair.'

'Cut your lovely curly hair? No!'

'Has to be. It'll be cooler. And while you're about it, what can you tell me about the track out to the goldfields?'

When his hair was cropped she gazed dismally at him. 'You've got a convict cut now. And it looks mad with that nice beard.'

'I know. Now I need a shave. I've decided to get rid of the lot. Can you give me a shave or will I go find a barber?'

'I'll do it,' she said quickly, not eager to part with the chance to earn more. 'I'm more fun than a barber.'

'You certainly are,' he slapped her soft bottom as she went off to find a razor. Barbers, he mused, are notorious bigmouths. Whores, on the other hand, are secretive, especially when sweet-talked and well paid. Jake didn't need anyone identifying him if the police or Bartie Lee began asking about.

When he left, clean-shaven and almost bald, he paid more than she asked and promised to call on her again when he could.

'What's your name?' she asked.

'Rory. Rory Moore,' he said, a new name, quick to the fore from habit.

'Oh! That's a nice name. It suits you! Good luck!'

* * *

His peaked cap went to the bottom of a rubbish heap when he bought a straw hat from a stall. Then he began to acquire provisions and equipment, the bare necessities, hauling them back to the scrub on the outskirts of town. It was still very early and he had to keep out of sight, so he hid his belongings and went in search of a meal, whatever was on offer. Within minutes he found a woman cooking fish and potatoes over a campfire, and bought a share from her.

After that he preferred not to show his face, so he stretched out under a tall gum tree to sleep the day away, though his mind was in turmoil. He tried to shut out the sounds of raised voices, barking dogs, the clump of horses and rumbling wagons – the familiar country sounds. So familiar, like the pungent smell of eucalypts that filled the air, cleansing it, he dreamed he was back in the spring freshness of Goulburn, with its orderly streets and mannered folk, until he awoke with a sob.

It was a long day, just lying there, unable to sleep now, refusing to sleep . . . cursing the bloody gum trees for dragging memories to the surface, memories he thought he'd buried long ago.

But at dusk he was wide awake, prowling about looking for a horse, watching drunks, hunched over, following them as they lurched in and out of grog shops and brothels, eyeing their mounts. Eventually one came to him more like a gift than theft, he grinned as he rode down to collect his gear. The drunk had stumbled off his horse, fallen down, picked himself up, and handed the reins to Jake.

'Hold me horse, will you, mate?' and he'd staggered a few yards away to relieve himself. But that effort was too much. He'd crumpled into the urine and passed out.

Within an hour Jake was well out along the inland track, riding steadily through the gloomy bush, a rifle in a saddle holster and a pistol stuck in his belt. While he knew that the long ride wouldn't bother him he had to be on the lookout for the known enemy, his shipmates, and the unknown as well. Madeleine had found plenty to tell him about the Palmer River goldfields . . . a little too much, he feared.

The goldfields were still paying handsomely, even though the population out there in the wilderness had grown alarmingly, she'd said. Men were coming back millionaires after only a few days at the digs, but it was hard, rough living.

'Worse than here?' he'd joked.

'Well, they reckon anyone who takes on the Palmer has to be real brave, real mad or real desperate.'

'Why's that?'

'Because it's only for winners and losers. No side bets. Losers get sick and die, or they starve to death – that's if the savages don't get them.'

'What savages?'

'The blackfellers, of course. It's their country, and they don't like all these mobs tracking on to their land, so they're on the warpath. They've killed hundreds of diggers,' she told him, wide-eyed over the horror of it. 'Speared them, hanged them from trees, scalped them, chopped them up and left the bits on the tracks for dingoes to fight over. Real sickening, it is.'

Recalling her tale, Jake glanced nervously about him. He'd forgotten about the Aborigines . . . if he'd ever thought about them at all. He supposed it would be right, though: there would be tribes who'd lived in this country undisturbed for centuries. And an invasion of diggers would guarantee war.

'Jesus!' he whispered as a shudder slid down his back, his vulnerable back. 'I'm bloody sure I'm not one of the brave ones in this game. Mad, more like it.'

He wondered if it would be smarter – safer – to travel at night rather than be exposed to spears in daylight, but dismissed that idea, realising a man sleeping in the bush in broad daylight would be easy prey. He would just have to get this journey over as quickly as he could.

Mushi killed Ah Kee with his machete for letting the woman get away, though by this time Bartie Lee didn't much care one way or another. He hadn't told Mushi that he didn't know how to collect the money from her rich husband. Couldn't figure it out. And it would take time. This wasn't the goldfields, after all. Stupid Tussup had got it all wrong. To try to ransom her they would have to stay holed up here in the river settlement while everyone else was digging up gold by the spadeful on the other side of the mountains. The very thought of what he was missing out on was breaking his heart. And that brought him back to the woman herself. She'd become a burden, they'd have been better off killing her than Ah Kee, and hiding her body deep in the bush. At least Ah Kee was a good cook. Now he was buried in the bush and she was down there screaming her silly head off to the police.

And where was Jake? 'Not there,' he grinned. 'He's not at a police place. I reckon he gone after the gold.'

He and Mushi headed into the town, bought some good Chinese clothes so that they could mingle with them and went looking for the woman. They found the police tent, and kept it under observation for a while, but it remained deserted.

'I say the police have taken the woman to a boat,' Mushi decided. 'She a boss woman, she'll make them send her home.'

Bartie decided that explanation would do, so the pair of them decided to celebrate by getting gloriously drunk.

'Because tomorrow we march,' Mushi intoned.

'Yes, tomorrow we pack up everyone, get more provisions and digging tools and we go get our gold.'

'What about Jake?'

'We see him another day.'

The schooner *Torrens* followed the coast northwards from Cairns until they came to Cooktown, and Raymond remembered *China Belle* out there, stranded on a reef, waiting for the inevitable. Sooner or later the ocean beyond the reef would come to claim her.

He felt pity for her, such a splendid ship, to have to face destruction so early in her years. He would have liked the skipper of this boat to take them out there to see how she was faring, but of course that was impossible. They had an imperative duty to rescue Mrs Horwood, and then find and arrest the mutineers. In the meantime Constance Horwood had become the chief topic of discussion among the deputies and the crew, and Raymond was horrified to hear their opinions. They seemed to think that if she were not already dead, she might as well be, in the hands of those thugs.

'I disagree, gentlemen. They would have no reason to injure Mrs Horwood. Rather the opposite if they are to claim ransom. I imagine they would need to take care of her.'

They'd laughed at him, coarse in their observations of the treatment she could expect, if she were still alive.

Even the deputies, Trooper Bill Poole and Hector Snowbridge, formerly a farmhand, were pessimistic about her fate, disallowing any suggestion that this gang of murderers (not forgetting the late Bosun Flesser) would treat a white woman with any regard.

Raymond recalled Esme Caporn's screams and the battering Mrs Horwood had already taken in the dining saloon, and quaked with fear for her.

As a kind of penance, or maybe an offering to the gods on her behalf, he refrained from making any complaint about the horrible conditions on this boat. There was only one long cabin that carried an overpowering stench of mould. It housed a grease-spattered galley, several bunks covered with blankets stiff with salt and grime, and at the far end, in full view of all who entered, was the lavatory, a hole in the deck. Raymond, a modest man, did not care to investigate it too closely and delayed using it until nature forced his capitulation.

The food slopped to them was disgusting, but to his surprise no one complained, all of the others going at the stews with gusto, washing them down with firewater which, he was assured, was the very best local rum.

'Overproof,' they told him, the word meaning little to him, as he drank manfully, desperate to show them that he was adequate to his surrounds.

They were surprised, he thought suspiciously, that he managed to stay sober after drinking with them, but in the morning his head felt as if it had been attacked with an axe, so he took a book and hid on deck to endure the torture in silence.

When they finally came upon the mouth of the Endeavour River, he could have fallen on his knees in gratitude that the nightmare was over, only to discover that it was just the beginning.

The skipper manoeuvred his boat upriver, passing Chinese junks and an assemblage of decorated Asian craft, and hundreds of less exotic boats, from tubs, lighters and ketches to sailing ships that had obviously drawn in packed with passengers.

All on board were newcomers to this gold-rush transit camp, but they'd heard enough about it not to be concerned by the disorder. Their first task was to keep their eyes peeled for *China Belle*'s longboat, which they hoped they could spot somewhere along the riverbank, and though they sailed upriver as far as they could, taking the time to examine the longboats on shore, there was no sign of it.

'They've probably got it hidden in the scrub,' Trooper Poole said, and Raymond wondered about that.

'Might they not be better off to destroy it, use it for firewood?' he suggested, but Poole shook his head.

'A good longboat's worth money.'

Raymond didn't wish to be impolite, and question the trooper's reasoning, but he did ask himself: 'To whom?' After all, the skipper had just said that the prospectors didn't use the river for transport; they had mountains to cross. And on their return they'd hardly set to sea in a longboat with such distances to cover.

Eventually the schooner was moored and Raymond accompanied the deputies ashore, interested to see a wharf under construction, and labourers clearing tree stumps through the centre of the squalid settlement to form a main street.

'Looks like it'll be a real town soon,' Hector remarked, and the trooper agreed.

'For a while. But I don't know why your gov'mint is wasting money on the place, Mr Lewis. When the gold runs out it'll be a ghost town.'

'Could you ask directions to the police station?' Raymond said, looking anxiously about him for an inn or lodging house. He had to get off that stinking boat.

Hector called out to him, 'You keeping a lookout, Mr Lewis? There's enough Chinks here to sink a ship.'

'Yes of course,' Raymond replied hurriedly, mortified that he had already forgotten his role. He began peering at the crowds as they entered a maze of tents and lean-tos, searching Asian faces for the mutineers, and staring at bearded white men in the hope of finding Officer Tussup, the ringleader, but soon it began to rain, so his efforts were curtailed for the time being.

Sergeant Gooding, a tall rangy man with red hair and a short temper, gave them shelter in his tent while he listened to their story.

'They what?' he exploded. 'They mutinied and took a woman with them! What the hell were her husband and the rest of the passengers doing?'

'We were few in number and overcome by their weapons,' Raymond explained patiently. 'We are concerned for the lady . . .'

'Bit late. And you reckon they're here somewhere? With her?'

'Yes.'

'If they haven't done away with her,' Trooper Poole said.

'Probably have, the bastards,' Gooding agreed.

'We will nevertheless proceed on the premise that the lady is here, and must be found,' Raymond said firmly. 'Where will you start, Sergeant?'

Gooding gave a long, frustrated sigh. 'I've been away for weeks. I just got back from the Palmer this morning. I had a quick look round this hellhole today and I reckon there could be another thousand diggers turned up here since I left. It's a floating population. The diggers I did know have gone on up the track by this time, and the only folk I can recognise are the sly-groggers and the whores and the few smart ones setting up shop. You tell me where I can start, mate.'

Raymond, unused to this tone from subordinates, was taken aback.

'What's more,' Gooding continued, 'I now hear my off-sider, Constable Colman, has quit the job and taken himself off to the goldfields. It's a bloody good job you lot turned up. Trooper Poole, consider yourself seconded to this here station.'

'I can't do that, I'm already on duty.'

'You can do that duty as well, and if you don't jump to it I'll lock you up. We've got a morgue over past the hospital. It's a wattle-and-daub building with a shingle roof. Get over there and get the details of any new customers since I left. I have to try to keep some records.'

He turned to Raymond. 'I reckon your best bet is to take this deputy with you,' he said, nodding at Hector, 'and go through the place yard by yard, making your own enquiries. Tell them you're acting on my orders. In the meantime I'll have my ears open. Right now I have to go. There's a private war going on between Chink mobs camped by Billygoat Creek. Make yourself at home here if you can find any space.'

Raymond looked about him. The large tent was more of a store room than an office, with rows of trunks and boxes stacked on timber blocks in and around a bunk and a tall clerk's desk. A lantern hung overhead and a lump of linoleum provided a little comfort in front of a hard wooden chair.

'I was wondering if there were any lodgings hereabouts,' Raymond asked quickly, and the sergeant gave this some thought, frowning as he buckled on a gun belt.

'Dunno. They're building a hotel down by the river. Go back to the wharf and head west. It could be finished by this time. One of many, they say. By the sound of things we'll have more pubs than people if the gold holds out.'

'Thank you,' Raymond said. 'We'll go there right away.'

'Yeah, worth a try. What's the name of the boat you came on so I know where to find you if I hear anything?'

'It's a schooner called *Torrens*.'

'Righto. And listen, I'm bloody sorry about your Mrs Horwood, but I can't see how a mixed crew of Chinks and Malayamen could drag a white lady round this crowded neighbourhood. They'd be spotted first up. It'd cause a riot. If you want my opinion, I'd say she's not here.'

'But the crew are,' Hector insisted. 'If Mr Lewis can point out even one of them we've got a start.'

'Yeah? If you do see one of them, don't wait on the niceties. Just grab him. Yell thief, then folk will help you. Truss him up, tie him to a tree, and send someone for me. Now I have to get going.'

He ran his hand through hair clogged with dust, set a wide-brimmed leather hat on his head, patted the revolver at his hip, picked up a rifle and walked out into the teeming rain.

They'd said this was a hospital but it was a terrible place. Her bed was only a low bunk among the dozen in a row along the wall. The smell was dreadful and women moaned and groaned all night. Constance couldn't wait for morning to make her escape.

When the dawn finally did creep through a fog of steady rain, a; doctor came by and spoke to her.

'Why! You're awake. This is a nice surprise.' He felt her forehead, took her pulse, put his watch back in his pocket and nodded.

'You're a lot better. You had us worried a few days ago.'

'A few days ago?' she echoed.

'Yes, you had a fever and passed out on us, miss. What is your name? The nurses have you down as Miss X.'

'Horwood. Constance Horwood.'

'Good. And you're from?'

'Hong Kong. I was kidnapped. I was on the *China Belle* . . .' She could feel the heat in her face, embarrassment, because his eyes seemed to flatten, to look at her person as a horse sometimes does, watching rather than listening. But she couldn't stop, she was babbling. 'You have to help me. They're after me, the men from the crew, they'll kill me, they're Chinamen and Malays, I want them arrested.'

She grabbed his white coat. 'Could you lend me some money so that I can leave here, Doctor, please?'

He took her hand and put it under a thin blanket. 'Don't be worrying. You're all right here, Miss Horwood. Now I want you to rest. You've still got a temperature, so you'll have to stay a few more days. But you can have a little soup, and plenty of water to keep cool.'

A young nurse hurried over to join him and Constance heard him giving her whispered instructions. But this woman queried him.

'I remember she came in with a sprained ankle and she had a lot of cuts and bruises, Doctor. Look at her face, that's bruised too. I don't think she's bats, I think she is in some sort of trouble.'

'The sort of trouble we don't need,' he said crossly. 'The boyfriend probably beat her up. I don't want him barging in here.'

Constance struggled to hear more of the conversation but unfortunately they both moved on to other patients and she had no choice but to remain in the bed. She had just realised they had taken her clothes and put her in a cheap cotton nightgown, hospital issue. Tears welled in her eyes again as depression set in, far worse than her miseries with her captors. With them, she'd been continually plotting, both escape and revenge that kept her spirits up, but now she was exhausted, too tired to fight these people. She was angry with them. She couldn't believe that they would ignore her situation, treat her as if she were . . . what had she heard? Bats! They thought she was bats. And, Constance wept, they kept calling her Miss Horwood. How dare they be so offhand with a respectable married lady! She looked down at her left hand, and shrieked. Her rings were gone.

A nurse came running, another plump, middle-aged woman. 'What's up, miss?' she called.

'Nothing,' Constance said, turning away. She'd just remembered they'd stolen her rings on the ship. They'd taken all the passengers' jewellery.

'Well, you better not go making a noise like that again. You near gave me a heart attack, not to mention upsetting all the other patients. You be quiet, miss, and I'll bring you a cuppa tea as soon as I can.'

The hotel wasn't completed but Raymond was determined not to stay on the schooner any longer than necessary. He produced his credentials as a Member of Parliament and persuaded the owner to allow him to occupy an unfurnished ground-floor bedroom, at a rate of two-and-six per day.

'Why would a gentleman like you want to sleep on bare boards?' the owner/builder, one Shamus Flynn, wanted to know.

'Necessity, sir, necessity. I shall purchase some blankets for bedding, and be most grateful to you.'

So by midday, with Hector's help, he'd removed his luggage to the shell of the Criterion Hotel and set himself up grandly, finding the scent of new timbers refreshing.

Raymond always travelled with a portable desk and plenty of writing materials, so now he found a box for a chair and began a plan of attack. Flynn drew a general map of the town for him, and Raymond divided it into sections so that a thorough search could begin.

By nightfall, slogging through the rain and mud, Raymond and Hector had interviewed hundreds of people, finding that repeating the story of Mrs Horwood and *China Belle* gained immediate attention, as well as a large number of volunteer searchers who had no inhibitions about diving into occupied tents in search of the missing woman.

Trooper Poole came by to tell them that at least Mrs Horwood wasn't in the morgue, and stayed to dine with them at Flynn's eatery next door, where Mr Lewis became the centre of attention, as more folk crowded in to hear the tale at first-hand. Flynn was delighted that his lodger was attracting so many customers, and shouted him a bottle of surprisingly excellent claret.

When he bundled down in his blankets that night, Raymond felt guilty that he'd had a very enjoyable evening among all these plain folk, while poor Mrs Horwood was still missing. God knows where. Surely, he thought, this whole settlement will know about her by tomorrow.

He was right. Next morning, a deputation of eight white men came to the hotel to express their horror that a white woman might be in the clutches of Asians in this very town, and offered to help.

Naively, Raymond agreed.

His unauthorised posse then rode wildly through the Chinese sectors, firing guns, dragging down tents and scattering their contents while the occupants ran for cover. But not for long. Several hours later the Chinese retaliated, setting fire to rows of tents and beating up any white men who ran to put them out. That night, more fires broke out and an angry Sergeant Gooding blamed the Member of Parliament for causing riots, and organising illegal posses. He ordered Mr Raymond Lewis and Mr Hector Snowbridge to 'get the hell out of my town'.

Lottie Jensen had been working at the hospital for only a few weeks. An apprentice nurse, they said she was, and a horrible job it turned out to be. She'd rather be an apprentice laundress, or a cowhand, or an apprentice street-sweeper than this mucky job. All she seemed to do was clean up spews and poos, and change smelly beds, and even then you never got treated nice. The real nurses ordered you around like you were their lackey and as for that Dr Madison, well, he was royalty, he wouldn't spit on you.

But he was wrong about that woman. To him, she was just another tart fallen on hard times, and they were aplenty in this poverty trap. He didn't have to listen to the likes of her, even if she did speak nice. He heard only a couple of words and decided she was bats. Lottie heard him telling Matron that this wasn't a mental hospital, and to discharge Miss Horwood in the morning and let her own people take care of her.

He also, Lottie recalled, told on her, and got her into trouble for daring to contradict him.

'Doctor Madison diagnoses the patient,' Matron snapped at her. 'Don't you ever dare contradict him again or you'll be dismissed on the spot. It's a wonder he didn't sack you himself.'

Yeah, well, Lottie thought. I might just beat him to the punch.

But that night she awoke with a start. 'Oh Jesus,' she wailed. 'Miss Horwood!'

Her brother, curled up in the other bunk, stirred, and muttered: 'Whassamatter?'

'Nothing,' she said quickly. 'Nothing. Go back to sleep.'

Then she lay there, listening to the hiss of misty rain that enveloped their camp, praying for dawn, praying that Miss Horwood was still in her bed. She would have run all the way over to the hospital right now if she weren't too scared of being out there in the dark. Bart, her brother Bart, always came to collect her after the night shift. He wouldn't have any sister of his walking about Cooktown unprotected. Soon they'd be out of here though, as soon as they'd saved enough money to push on to the goldfields.

Sleep had deserted her but she had to stay in bed, nursing her impatience for another hour before the warm golden rays touched the tent and set her free. There was purpose in her swift movements now. Though she wasn't due on until six she had to get to the hospital as quickly as she could. She pulled on her long black dress and black stockings, and slipped into her worn shoes, relieved that the rain had stopped, grabbed her shawl and began to run to work.

Last night Bart and his friends were all talking about the important people who'd come to town searching for a gang of Asian murderers who'd robbed and sunk a ship, slit the throats of the male passengers and made off with their women. White women. Brought them here to Cooktown!

Lottie realised that she'd been so absorbed by this grisly tale and the plight of women kidnapped by white slavers that she hadn't been thinking right.

'Damn fool,' she muttered as she sped across a horse paddock and leaped over a small stream to come up beside the place they were building for the policemen. 'What if they've found her already? Damn bloody fool you are. "Kidnapped" that woman said, plain as day. And Madison said she was bats. Well, we'll see who's bats.'

'Talking to yourself, little lady?' a man asked, laughing at her as he passed by, leading his horse. 'If it's company you want, I'm available.'

'No, thanks,' she said grimly, her mind, her whole being, focused on the woman in the fourth bed from the door. God! What if she's gone? Lottie screwed her face up in pained apprehension. I'll scream. I'll sit down and scream if she's not there.

She galloped round to the back door and flung in through the kitchen, where she came to a sudden halt, reminding herself to take it quiet, and slow. No one was awake yet, the nurse on duty was dozing on the old sofa by the front door. Lottie looked at the large clock in the passageway. Only five o'clock. Good.

Constance was stiff and sore from the hard bed, and she had a terrible thirst. When the nurse approached she grabbed her arm gratefully. 'Could I please have some water? I'm so thirsty.'

'Yes, I'll get you some, Miss Horwood. Come with me. I'm Lottie.'

Dutifully Constance climbed out of bed and tried to stand, but she felt a little giddy and her ankle hurt.

'Here, I'll help you,' the kind nurse said. She was strong too. She put Constance's arm over her shoulder and half-carried her along the narrow aisle, out into the passage that had rough coir matting on the floor, leading Constance to believe she was right in the first place. This wasn't a real hospital at all.

The nurse sat her on a chair in a large kitchen that smelled of onions. 'Now, Miss Horwood. My name's Lottie and I want to help you . . .'

'I need a glass of water.'

'Yes. In a minute.'

'Now. I'm very thirsty and very tired. I've been running for days.'

Lottie wondered about that comment as she brought the water. 'Miss Horwood, you were kidnapped, weren't you?'

'Yes, I've told you that before.'

'From a ship.'

'Yes. They beat us. Mrs Caporn and me.'

'Good. I mean, I'm sorry. What was the name of the ship?'

'I'll never forget it. *China Belle*.'

'Right! Drink your water. You shouldn't be in a horrible old hospital like this. I'm taking you to your friends right away. They're waiting for you.'

'I can't go out like this. In a nightgown! Where are my clothes?'

The nurse rushed away and came back with a skirt and blouse that Constance didn't recognise, but she claimed them as hers – anything to get out of this place. She provided some dirty Chinese slippers as well.

'I don't think you had anything else with you,' the nurse apologised.

'Never mind. I look a wreck so you must take me to a good hotel where I can get cleaned up, and send out for some decent clothes.'

She began to weep. 'Lottie, I'm so thankful for your kindness. You'll be rewarded, I promise you.'

'I expect so,' the nurse told her. 'Your friends were offering a reward.'

The workmen were only just arriving at the site of the Criterion Hotel when Lottie approached, shocked to have found it only partly constructed. She was sure Bart and his friends had said the important people looking for Miss Horwood were staying here.

She looked back at Miss Horwood, whom she'd planted on a box by a huge bush with scarlet blooms. The woman was rather vague, she'd had to admit to herself as they stumbled all this way from the hospital, but she was content to stay there for the minute with Lottie's bonnet plonked on her head for shade.

'Hey!' she called to a carpenter. 'I thought those blokes looking for . . . for the Chinks that did the mutiny were stayin' at this here pub, and it's no pub at all. Where do you reckon they got to?'

'They're still here,' he said cheerfully. 'One of them anyway. Go in that way and along a passage, and bang on doors. He's in one of them.'

The carpenters were already making so much racket that Raymond was up and dressed, still shocked that he'd been ordered to leave Cooktown.

Perhaps today the sergeant will be in a calmer state of mind, he hoped, and relent. After all, as Flynn had told him, the man had good reason to be fed up with any authoritarian from Brisbane.

'Hasn't he been begging Brisbane for more lawmen, but what do they send? Customs officers, and the wherewithal to build a fine customs house by the river.' He laughed. 'No offence, sorr, but is it not just like a gov'mint to be going after the money first? They're getting a pretty penny from the gold tax.'

Remembering that information made Raymond even testier this morning, and he vowed to see the Premier about the matter as soon as he returned, but for now he couldn't allow himself to be ejected from this place. He'd be a laughing stock back in Brisbane. What headlines that would make!

He heard a timid knock on his door and found himself looking down at a young woman standing there, hatless.

'What can I do for you, miss?' he asked, curious about this early intrusion.

She was nervous. 'Can I speak to you, Your Honour?' she whispered.

'Yes?'

'Like about that ship and the Chinks and the women.'

'The *China Belle*? Have you heard anything?'

'They say there's a reward. What's it for?'

Now she was overcoming her nervousness and was watching him with a glint of excitement in her eyes.

'I haven't heard of a reward but I'm sure if you have any information leading to locating Mrs Horwood, you will be well recompensed.'

She seemed to back away. 'Oh Jeez. I dunno about that. How do I know I'll get recommenced?'

'If you can help us, miss, you must. And I will consider it my duty to see that you are well rewarded.'

'Ah, but can I trust you?'

'You certainly can. My name is Raymond Lewis. I am a Member of the Queensland Parliament.'

She still wasn't sure. 'Tell you what,' she said. 'You write that down for me – about the recommenced – and sign it with your name.'

'Very well,' he sighed, thinking this was probably another waste of time, but every chink of light had to be examined. 'What is your name, miss?'

'Lottie Jensen. I'm here with my brother. I'm a . . . nurse, so don't go thinking I'm not respectable like most of the trollops in this place.'

'I wouldn't dream of it,' he murmured as he took pen and paper and wrote: 'To whom it may concern . . .' promising her recompense for her assistance.

She regarded the page suspiciously. 'This won't do. Who do I give it to? The local bank manager? I'd get thrown out on me ear. And you don't reckon Sergeant Gooding would have spare quids in his pocket. This won't do at all. You have to say who I give it to.'

Raymond sighed, convinced now that this person was trying to elicit money from him under false pretences.

'Very well! Give me back the note and if you do have correct information regarding Mrs Horwood, I shall go to the bank and obtain enough to pay you myself.'

'That's better. But I think I'll hang on to the note if you're not minding, sir. Until I'm paid the reward, like. And how much would that be?'

'Goodness me, Miss Jensen, I don't know what it would be. Fifty pounds maybe, or a hundred. I've really no idea.'

'A hundred will do, sir. The round hundred. Now you come with me, quick, quick . . .'

She was jigging about with excitement, actually pulling him by the arm into the bare hallway.

'Hold on, miss. Hold on. I'll get my hat!'

'You don't need a hat, sir. You don't! Come on, please! I don't want her wandering off!'

'What?'

At that, he rushed through the building, dodging ladders, and ran out on to the cleared building site.

'There,' she said. 'Over there. Is that your Miss Horwood?'

'Mrs,' he corrected absently. 'That woman?' He peered at the shabby woman sitting listlessly by a tall hedge of bougainvillaea, her faded brown clothes in stark contrast to the flashy scarlet blooms glowing all round her.

He was embarrassed, encroaching on the woman's privacy in such a manner but he had to get a better look at her. Then, as he crunched over the caked mud of the yard, she looked up.

'Oh, Mr Lewis! Thank God you've come!' She began to weep. 'Where are we? I'm lost. Mr Lewis, would you please take me back to the ship?'

He took her in his arms, comforting her, and smiled at Lottie's triumphant face, nodding as she held up her precious page.

'I found her!' the girl yelled. 'Me! I found her. I get the reward! A hundred pounds!'

Chapter Five

Funeral processions were not rare on the cold, windy Peking roads but this one caused clusters of pedestrians to shuffle aside and whisper and stare.

The beautiful silver urn containing the ashes was set on a flowered stand within an ornate glass-windowed palanquin, which was borne by four coolies, in the manner of a sedan chair. The people knew that to be travelling in such opulence, the Departed must have been a person of importance, so they folded their hands and drew back respectfully as they took note of the vehicle's elegance of line and its decorations of gold leaf over black enamel. The curtains bordering the small windows were much admired, being of expensive embroidered cloth with black tassels, but the gorgeous sea of fresh flowers that covered the floor around the central stand brought gasps of delight. Those close enough observed that the colour of the blooms, reflected in the shining silver of the urn, seemed to dance about with the movement of the bearers, and they wept, entranced by the beauty they were witnessing.

But this was a strange affair, they had to agree, because you would think a rich personage would have a much grander cortège, but instead it was the bare minimum.

Two gentlemen, heavily clad in leather and furs, their faces pasty with dust, rode ahead on fine horses, the mounts' funeral regalia fittingly splendid also, and at the rear were two armed guards, their swords clanking as if in warning.

The horsemen turned into a narrow alley, now forced to travel single file, and the coolies padded after them, negotiating their burden round corners until they were instructed to stop at a gate near the Heavenly Fountain . . . though the fountain hadn't worked in living memory.

Soon the gate swung open and the cortège entered the courtyard of a house owned by Xiu Tan Lan. The stallholders watching could have told them that Mr Xiu had not lived there since the last street battles, and only his old housekeeper, Zina, was in residence with his servants, but they'd disappeared from view now, swallowed up by the high wall.

* * *

Mal remained seated on his horse, waiting for Chang, his major-domo, to seek permission of the housekeeper to rest here overnight.

When he had reached the Chinese port of Tientsin, after difficult voyages via Manila and Hong Kong, he had engaged the services of a superior major-domo who spoke English to guide him through the intricacies of protocol, which he knew would be of paramount importance, not only for the journey ahead, but for the sad duty he had yet to perform.

Chang was a tall, handsome man, in his forties, Mal guessed, and rather effeminate in his manner. His hair was pomaded into a topknot and he had a thin moustache like a sliver of black over a wide upper lip. It was so thin, Mal wondered if it were pencilled on. Not that it mattered to him, as long as this fellow could do the job. He'd been highly recommended by a priest at the main temple.

'This is a very sensitive situation, sir,' Chang told Mal at their first meeting. 'The family Xiu have connections to our Dowager Empress Cixi. Are they aware of this terrible tragedy?'

'Yes. I wrote to them from Queensland. That's in the great south continent.'

'You wrote? Oh dear, sir. You should have sent an emissary with such important news. Oh my!'

'I did the best I could. I had a learned Chinaman living in that town compose the letter for me, because I believed the family needed to know what happened as soon as possible. He also mentioned an emissary, but such a person couldn't get here any sooner than I have.'

'Do you wish me to go ahead as your emissary now? Inform them that you have brought home their dear lady's ashes, and wish an audience?'

'No. I will go directly myself, but I'd like you to help me arrange proper transportation of my wife's remains, and accompany me on the journey because I will need your advice.'

'You surely will,' Chang said. He sat back in a large cushioned chair and studied his buffed and pointed fingernails.

'Mr Willoughby, you do understand that gentlemen of my calling do not come cheap?'

'I didn't suppose you would. I want the very best for my wife, and I don't want to let her family down. If you have any qualms about my ability to pay, then you may check at the Bank of Hong Kong.'

Chang smiled. 'I already have. But one has to make sure that the client is willing to pay for what is required. Some are inclined to want to bargain after the event, so to speak, and I won't tolerate that.'

He sat forward. 'I do wish you'd be seated, Mr Willoughby, I can't think with you pacing about the room. It seems to me your nerves are in a bad state. Now you must take tea with me, and tell me quietly exactly what happened to your dear wife . . . and then we'll see what's best to do.'

Chang proved his worth. He organised a suitable conveyance to be built to carry Jun Lien's ashes. He made enquiries about the whereabouts of her parents, hired the necessary staff, and as Mal noticed during their progress along the road to Peking, had his coolies find fresh flowers every day. He believed that the cornucopia of blooms surrounding the silver urn should reflect the youth and beauty of the Departed, but would also be a comfort to her broken-hearted husband.

He was right about that, Mal thought as he waited. The flowers were so beautiful, so extravagantly massed in that small rectangle behind the windows, that they made him smile. Jun Lien, he felt, would have loved them.

Zina came out cautiously, standing in the doorway under the coloured bamboo canopy that Mal knew so well, but he still did not dismount. He had visited this house on many occasions, but Chang had warned him that his circumstances had changed. He must wait for permission to dismount, even from a housekeeper, because Zina in her young days had been a favoured concubine of both Mr Xiu and his elder brother.

She beckoned him to dismount, and Mal did so, bowing humbly from his distress, and Zina, no longer able to contain her emotions, ran forward and fell to the ground at his feet, weeping profusely.

Mal lifted her up and stood with her in the chilly courtyard, his own tears overwhelming them both, because this was the first encounter since Jun Lien's death with anyone who had known and loved her. It seemed to unlock the dam of his emotions so much that he dreaded going on, dreaded the misery ahead.

Zina gave them directions to the mansions where Jun Lien's family were living at present, more than a hundred miles away in mountainous country, where they could more easily defend themselves from attack, but Mal wasn't fazed.

'We will go on,' he told Chang. 'It's really much closer than I thought it would be.'

The housekeeper arranged for Chang, the coolies and their guards to be fed and quartered according to their status, and escorted Mal to one of the larger bedrooms on the first floor.

He was relieved to be able to divest himself of the layers of clothing that he'd always found irksome but necessary in the cold climate, and wrapped himself in a blanket to take a nap, just as a servant entered the room. Taking no notice of him, she gathered up all his clothes, including those he had in his saddle pack, and disappeared with them.

Mal smiled. He'd forgotten that ritual. Some would be washed and pressed, some thoroughly dusted, according to the material. Buttons would be replaced, tears stitched. He appreciated it more than he had before, because

Chang had chosen his new Chinese clothes, insisting he would have to look his best for an audience with Jun Lien's family. As he had expected, his linen underclothes, and his jerkins and trousers were of the best quality – very expensive! The fur-lined leather coat and high boots, and the fur hat with earmuffs were bought on the same day, at the same shop where Chang obviously received a commission, so he was delighted.

'Our excellent clothes suit you far better than Western wear,' he enthused. 'And the hat is very grand.'

'You think so?' Mal asked.

'Yes, I do indeed.'

'It is much finer and sturdier than yours.'

'Ah yes. That is true.'

'Well then, we'll buy one for you as well.'

'Sir, I couldn't!'

'Why not? We'll take two.'

Mal wasn't very good with words at the best of times, and clumsy in another language. He didn't know how to say to Chang that he was grateful for his help, and for his company. He hoped the gift would suffice.

Then he saw that it had. Chang sold his own hat to a street vendor and wore the new one with great pride.

Another servant came with a warm wrap for him and escorted him to the bathroom, where he took over, dismissing her. He'd never been comfortable being bathed by female servants, though Jun Lien had thought his modesty amusing. Everything still revolves around my darling Jun, he consoled himself, as he stepped down into the warm tiled bath. I'll always have her in my heart.

Dinner was brought to his room: tureens of chicken soup with dumplings, spiced pork, cabbage and beef rolls . . . more tea. And not long after he'd finished his second cup of tea and polished off the last of the beef rolls, Mal was fast asleep.

In the morning, his clothes were all returned, so he dressed quickly and went in search of Zina but just as he reached the bottom of the staircase, he heard a banging on the heavy gate.

He saw Zina's manservant open the small door set in the gate, speak to whoever was outside and return to report that the visitor wished to speak to Mr Willoughby.

'All right,' Mal said, and set off across the courtyard, only to be intercepted by Chang.

'Who is it?' he asked Mal.

'I don't know. I'm just going to find out.'

'No. You stay here.' Chang called to their two guards to accompany him, and went to the door.

There was a swift exchange, and Chang slammed the door shut, apparently refusing admission.

'What's going on?' Mal demanded.

'They wished to speak to you.'

'I know. Who are they?'

'They say they are retainers of the Xiu family, but I am not sure. I certainly do not believe they wish you well. Forget about them for now.'

This seemed all wrong to Mal. He was adamant that he should have spoken to those strangers himself, but Zina intervened.

'Your man is correct,' she advised. 'You should listen to him. Let him do his job.'

Later, before their departure, he noticed Zina and Chang deep in worried conversation, then they both went towards the armoury, which Mal knew was behind the first door on the right of the gates, so he sprinted after them.

'Are you looking for weapons, Chang? What's going on? I demand to know.'

Zina unlocked the armoury and Chang peered inside. 'What I told you was true,' he said to Mal. 'They probably are retainers of the family, or involved somewhere, but . . .'

'But what?' Mal followed them into the chilly room with its stone-flagged floor, and gazed at the large collection of blade weapons, from dagger to curved scimitars. He'd always found this collection extremely interesting since many of the pieces were jewelled antiques of great value.

Chang took a flat sword from its scabbard and tested the blade. 'They want to challenge you. A matter of honour, they say, for the death of Lady Xiu Jun Lien. They consider you responsible.'

'Challenge me to a fight?' Mal was bewildered.

'That is so. I think this sword will suit you if you are forced to defend yourself.'

'I wish you'd talk straight. Did you explain to them that no one is more distressed than I am at the loss of my beloved wife? So what right have they got to intrude on my mourning?'

'No point, they wouldn't listen,' Chang shrugged. 'There are hotheads in every family, and these fellows are looking to make names for themselves as preservers of family honour. You will have to arm yourself in case they insist on the challenge, so take this sword.'

'A duel? Would someone challenge me to a duel? A bloody sword fight?'

'Yes. That is so. And you would have to accept the challenge or lose face. But our guards will try to keep them at bay.'

Mal handed the sword back to Chang. 'I don't give a damn about losing face and I will not fight Jun Lien's relations.'

'You may not have a choice.'

'All right, I'll give them a choice! Bugger swords, guns are quicker. I want you to go into the town and buy me the best revolver you can find. And don't forget ammunition.'

Zina shook her head. 'May I suggest, sir, that to avoid any further sadness, you allow Chang to take our Lady Jun Lien on from here? Thus you do not lose face as you have already fulfilled more than your duty, bringing the dear one across the world.'

Chang agreed. 'I think that would be best. The guards can protect you on your return journey to the port. Zina will give me two more servants to replace them on our journey to the parental mansion.'

'No! Definitely not!' Mal said angrily. 'I have to take Jun Lien home to her parents myself. I must do this. Now you buzz off and purchase a gun for me, and if you see any of those heroes out there, tell them that in my country a challenge means shoot. No mucking about. If anyone challenges me with a sword they get shot. That should sort the men from the boys.'

Chang disapproved of Mal's attitude but he did go out and buy a gun in mint condition, before they set out on the next leg of their journey. As the gates were swung open and Mal turned to wave farewell to the sad-faced Zina, he noticed that the flowers around Jun Lien's ashes had been replaced by brilliant blooms once again, and he felt cheered by them.

He also noticed that Chang now carried the sword, and hoped he wouldn't stab himself.

They travelled northwest into the furrowed grey skies as the wind grew stronger and the coolies ploughed on, grateful that their burden wasn't too heavy. Mal tied a neckerchief across his lower face to protect himself from the swirling dust that was almost as bad as the blinding dust storms that he'd encountered back home.

'How long do these dust storms last?' he asked Chang, who was already complaining bitterly about the discomfort.

'Days, maybe weeks,' he replied crankily. 'If you please, I should go on ahead and find a respectable inn to shelter us, before all the rooms are taken.'

'Good idea.' Mal noticed that he went back to talk to the guards before he left, and one of them came forward to ride beside him. He supposed Chang had alerted them to the possibility of that ludicrous challenge. He had no doubt too that Chang had found and spoken to the so-called preservers of family honour when he went out to purchase the gun, since they seemed to have backed off.

Late in the day he caught up with Chang at a crossroads, and Chang directed him to turn in to a small village.

'They have an exceedingly pleasant inn, considering this poor district, and they are cleaning out the stables where your lady may be placed, with her bearers and guards. Come, I will show you.'

The Inn of the Five Winds overlooked a picturesque lake, and Mal wondered what the fifth wind was as Chang sent the little cavalcade on past the front entrance to empty stables, where four servants were busily sweeping and cleaning. Soon they had them orderly enough to receive Jun Lien's vehicle and its bearers.

Satisfied, Mal was riding back towards the inn with the two guards when one of them reached over and grabbed his horse's reins.

'Stop here, Master.'

Three young men were standing arguing with Chang, all speaking far too quickly for Mal to translate, so he quietly slid his gun from its holster and turned to the guard.

'What's going on?'

'They say you will not accept the challenge, so the family has appointed its own major-domo to challenge Mr Chang.'

'What? I'll put a stop to that!'

The three newcomers turned as he rode down to confront them, and spat insults at him, calling him a coward and a fraud.

'Get out of here,' Mal yelled at them, careful not to return the insults and offend anyone in Jun Lien's family. 'You do not interfere in my business.'

'Not your business any more, Master,' the guard said quietly. 'Mr Chang has accepted the challenge.'

'The hell he has! You two get in there and stand by him. That's what you're paid for.'

'Not possible,' they said. 'That is Lord Xiu Min Soo. Bad form to interfere, Master.'

'I don't care about form. This isn't his fight. He'll get killed.'

'No he won't, Master.'

'What? This is a real fight, isn't it?'

Neither of his guards responded, so Mal leaped down from his horse. 'I'll put a stop to this myself!'

But Chang wouldn't allow that.

'Stay back,' he called to Mal as he divested himself of his hat and heavy coat, calmly turned his deep cuffs back and buttoned them into place, while his challenger waited, sword drawn.

He was a burly fellow, shorter than Chang but much younger and obviously adept with the sword. He began swishing and switching it about him, grinning and showing off to his friends, while Chang unsheathed the heavy sword he'd brought from the armoury.

Suddenly he swung about, both hands wielding the sword in a wide, menacing arc.

Mal was as startled as the remaining two retainers, who found their champion now engaged in battle with a whirlwind. Chang slashed and feinted, leaped easily from a sword thrust, twisted and turned, his face expressionless, and it was all over in minutes. The challenger screamed in pain as Chang's sword slashed his upper arm and his sword clattered to the ground.

'Take him from my sight before I cut his arm off,' the victor ordered.

The challenger's arm was bleeding profusely from the savage thrust, and his friends were frantically trying to stem the bleeding as Chang walked away.

'Their challenge has failed, sir,' he said to Mal. 'They have relinquished the right to bother you again. You should retire now.'

'And you shouldn't be fighting my fights. I didn't ask you to do that.'

Chang's smile was thin. 'I enjoyed the challenge.'

'So I noticed. You're very accomplished with a sword.'

'Yes,' he sighed. 'Unfortunately I had to spare him on your behalf or I *would* have taken his arm off.'

'Anyway,' Mal asked him that evening, 'why five winds? What is that about?'

'The fifth wind always returns,' Chang said leaving Mal to ponder that information.

Two days later the cortège was within hours of the family mansions, which Chang had ascertained were well fortified behind huge walls, and permission had to be sought to enter.

This time Chang saw to it that they were accommodated in elegant rooms set in walled gardens, and instructed Mal that he should write to the bereaved parents. This took time. They composed the sad request between them and then Chang transcribed it onto fine parchment, after which he rode off to deliver the letter himself.

Mal was disappointed that his man returned without a response but Chang explained it would have been ill-mannered for him to wait.

'One wouldn't dream of giving any hint of impatience on this, the very saddest of occasions. One withdrew in the gentlest of manner. But I talked to people in the village by the main gate and they informed me that your lady Jun Lien's papa is seriously ill, but her mother, Xiu Ling Lu, though still in mourning, is in good health.'

Mal took himself off to a corner of the garden to digest the news. Ever since Jun Lien's death, he'd been rehearsing what he could, and should say at the first anguished meeting with her parents – if he could manage to speak at all, to speak of Jun Lien in the presence of people who loved her as much as he did. Often he'd woken in tears, after dreaming of this meeting, and suffered depression for days afterwards, but he'd always reminded himself that Jun Lien's parents did at least have each other for support and consolation. And he envied them because he was denied that blessing. Now, Xiu Ling Lu would feel her loss even more keenly. Perhaps, as he was doing, she was steeling herself for their meeting. She might even take days to ready her heart to mourn with him, her daughter's ashes a heartbreaking reality at last.

But then the reply came. Swiftly and unexpectedly.

Within an hour of Chang's return, a cavalcade of horsemen and foot soldiers entered the village and came to a halt before Mal's quarters.

Chang hurried out to greet the commander, an imposing man who dismounted and swaggered forward, attired extravagantly in a wide-shouldered, brocade coat with a stiffened sash, and a large hat trimmed with mink. Also, Chang noticed with a shudder, he wore a magnificent ceremonial sword.

'You are the person who delivered a letter to the Lady Xiu Ling Lu?' he barked.

'Yes, sir,' Chang acknowledged with a deep bow. 'I shall fetch my master.'

'You will remain where you are.' The commander turned and ordered the footmen to go immediately and bring forth the conveyance with the ashes of the Beloved Departed.

'I must inform my master, sir,' Chang insisted.

'Do not dare talk back to a prince of the House of Qing!'

Realising he'd been addressing a warlord, Chang dropped to his knees and bowed again, forehead to the ground.

'Forgive me, sire,' he murmured.

Hearing all this activity, Mal came out to the street, amazed to see Chang at the feet of an evil-looking, overdressed big shot of some sort, but was shocked when his coolies came running along the street bearing Jun Lien's remains, once again surrounded by fresh flowers.

'Stop!' he shouted, running after them. 'Stop!'

But he was stopped by the foot soldiers who surrounded him, grasped his arms and marched him back to their lord, taking no notice of his frantic shouts.

'You don't understand!' he yelled at this fellow. 'There must be some mistake! They're taking my wife's remains. My wife's!'

'The Lady Xiu Ling Lu had requested that her daughter's ashes be brought to her presence without delay.'

'And I will do that. It is my prerogative,' Mal shouted. 'Let me go! I demand you let me go so that I can accompany my wife on the last steps of our journey.'

The commander took out a scroll, drew a deep breath and commenced to read: 'To the foreigner known as Malachi Willoughby. You have failed in your duty to protect our beloved daughter. You gave a solemn promise that you would love and protect her if we permitted you to take her over the oceans to your land. You broke that promise.'

'I did not!' Mal shouted. 'In the name of all that's holy, I did all I could to save her!'

Too late, Chang hissed at Mal not to interrupt a public proclamation.

The commander glanced up at the nearest horseman, jerking his head at Mal, and instantly the horse leaped forward. Before Mal could retreat, the rider slashed him across the face with his whip, and would have trampled him had Mal not leaped out of the way.

Infuriated, Mal went after his attacker, grabbed his arm, yanked him from his horse and kicked him into the dirt.

With that, the horse bolted and the narrow street was chaotic as the other horses plunged nervously about. The commander screamed orders as he dodged flying hoofs, the foot soldiers were in disarray, and crowds of onlookers pressed forward to witness this excitement.

Chang mysteriously disappeared. When order was restored, Mal was overpowered, his hands bound, and he was made to kneel before the spokesman and listen to the rest of the proclamation.

'For such failure we instruct that Malachi Willoughby never speak to or approach any members of this family ever again, under pain of death. We decree that this person has two more days to remove his disagreeable presence from our district or suffer imprisonment.

'This letter,' the commander announced in an even louder voice, 'was signed by the Lady Xiu Ling Lu, by her own hand.'

He rolled up the parchment, buckled it into a leather folder and mounted his horse.

The villagers broke the silence by bursting into excited chatter as the rest of the lord's retinue fell in behind him for their return journey. Not one of the horsemen or foot soldiers gave the foreigner a second glance. He was left sitting in the dust, his hands still bound, until Chang came to cut the bonds.

Shocked at Ling Lu's cruel and unreasonable attitude, Mal couldn't believe that Chang agreed with her.

'You mustn't mind. Anger takes her mind off the grief.'

'But why take it out on me? She hasn't even allowed me to explain what happened.'

'What does it matter? Her beloved daughter is dead. She would be glad you returned her ashes.'

'A strange way of showing it.'

'Why would she have to show it, as you say? Do you want to wring thanks out of her for doing what you knew to be correct?'

'Well, anyway, I'm not leaving until I see her.'

'Why? The lady's ashes are home now. Lady Xiu Ling Lu will arrange a burial.'

'It is my right to be present, to see where my wife is buried. And I'm not going home until I can do that.'

Chang shook his head. 'You're always talking about your rights. Don't you understand you have no rights here?'

'Who says so?'

Chang gave up. He walked to the gate and found the four coolies waiting for him.

'We carried the lady's remains to the family's mansions. Our job is done, and you don't need us to search for any more flowers. Can we have our money?'

Chang nodded, took out his purse and paid them. 'You may go now. The sad master bids you farewell.'

The guards had heard the threats issued by that powerful lady and were also keen to leave as soon as possible. Their master had become a liability in their eyes.

'We can protect him from brigands,' they said, 'but we're not getting mixed up in family enmities. We should go now. Get him as far away from here as possible.'

The second day was stretching to the danger point when the guards confronted Chang again, demanding their pay.

'I agree with you,' Chang told them, 'but this master is stubborn. He refuses to leave. If you wait I may still persuade him.'

But they were so fearful of the powerful lord, they would not remain in the area. They took their pay and headed back to Peking, leaving Chang in a quandary. He and his master were well able to defend themselves from attack by brigands now they could travel faster, not hampered by the necessity to protect the lady's remains from thieves and vandals. But to remain in this village was madness. The vengeful mother-in-law could have him murdered as well as his master.

Finally Chang spoke up. 'Master, it is well past noon. We have only a couple of hours left. In one hour I shall depart. If you remain in this village you are a dead man. Therefore I place before you my accounting and humbly request payment while you are still able.'

'Good on you!' Mr Willoughby actually laughed at his request, and Chang was mystified. The situation was far from amusing. That lord's soldiers may not count the actual hours as being important. They could descend on them at any minute.

Nevertheless Mr Willoughby did pay him, and handsomely – twenty yuan above the total. Then again, he reasoned, a dead man had no use for money. He wondered if he should remain in the background, to collect Mr Willoughby's money, his horse and effects, were he to be tragically disposed of by the powerful family. Why should strangers be enriched by misdeeds?

'I want you to write another letter,' Mr Willoughby said.

'To whom, Master?'

'To the Lady Xiu Ling Lu, and don't start arguing.'

Chang's hand shook as he dutifully executed the characters required for this outrageous letter.

‘ “My dear Madame, I write to you with great affection, despite the grief that has turned your face from me. I share that grief and will do so for the rest of my life. I have been informed that you have placed me under sentence of death if I do not depart within hours. If that is how you feel, so be it. But I refuse to leave until I have stood by the burial place of my beloved wife. I need to be able to remember where she is and see it within my memories.” Then I shall sign it.’

As he came to the end of the letter, Chang suggested that he should show some humility in closing, but Mr Willoughby shook his head.

‘No fear. The time for humility is over. This business of run or I’ll kill you is hogwash. If she’s that revengeful she could have me killed anywhere, even back home. I have to get this over with right here. I’m not spending my life looking over my shoulder. And don’t look so shocked. I’ll deliver the letter myself this time.’

‘You’d better go well armed,’ Chang said, a chill in his voice.

‘Don’t worry, I’ll sit with my back to the wall and the loaded gun in my hand if that makes you feel better.’

‘I’ll only feel better when we get out of here.’

‘Then you go now, Chang. I insist.’

Their farewell was formal, Chang full of dread and his master, grim-faced, determined to stay with his lady to the very end.

Mal rode through another village before he came to the road leading to the Xiu household. He knew that his friend Mr Xiu Tan Lan was not in residence here either. Zina had told him that the gentleman had gone further north with his wife and grandchildren. Mr Xiu, possibly, could have acted as mediator, but then again maybe not, Mal thought sadly. His old friend could easily be as angry and grief-stricken as Ling Lu.

As he approached the village he could see the walls of the family mansions looming up over the crowded huts and houses of the villagers, and he felt threatened by them.

Mal acknowledged he was nervous. Brave? By no means. But he had to do this. He would see Jun Lien right through to her last resting place as he’d promised, as he’d held her in his arms on the deck of that ship. Held her poor lifeless body with the streaming wet hair . . . A sob grew within him and he brushed at his eyes. Brushed dust from his eyes. It seemed to be colder now, so he dropped down his earmuffs and buttoned the fur collar at his throat, urging the horse into a canter.

The letter handed in, he went down to one of the many street stalls crowded round the south gates, and bought a bowl of rich soup, which he demolished quickly, followed by four spicy crêpes, then he sat by the gate and waited. His gun was well hidden in his mantles of clothing but was not loaded. The scene was so peaceful, he was afraid it might cause panic if he were so brazen as to have it on view.

With time to sit and stare, he enjoyed the comings and goings of people conducting their business in the streets, or milling about eating, shopping, bargaining with vendors selling anything from silks to spices, and dodging horse carts as they struggled out of narrow alleyways. He'd always enjoyed the volume of personalities that ranged in crowded marketplaces like this, and the time went quickly as the scene changed magically to night life, different crowds, different endeavours; coloured lanterns all about in giddy array. Mal dozed.

Eventually the picture faded . . . villagers drifted away, footsteps echoed on cobbled alleys, guards hunched by the great gates, ice set hard in the horse trough, and scores of rats scuttled across the deserted square.

Mal considered taking shelter for the night at a nearby inn, and debated the idea with himself as the night wore on. He could do that and take up his vigil again first thing in the morning. It would probably be safer there since the hour of his eviction had passed, and he was facing punishment. Though, he mused, it was interesting that Ling Lu's soldier boys hadn't come thundering out to slice his head off hours ago. He had a feeling that the swarthy prince would enjoy an execution or two.

He wasn't bothered about losing face by seeking shelter for a few hours, figuring he couldn't be more unpopular than he was now, but decided against it. Instead he took himself across to a vacant stall, where he sat in a chair, under cover, facing the gates.

In full view of the guards, he lit a cheroot and settled doggedly to await a response to his request. Let her see that he meant what he'd said in the letter. Let her see he wasn't intimidated by her threats!

'Not much you're not,' he muttered, breathing in the calming aroma of his last cheroot. 'You can't stay here for ever . . . until you're old and bearded and grey . . . but you have to give it a go. If she doesn't give in after a few days, if you're still alive, then you'll have to apologise to Jun Lien, and back off. But in the meantime, Mother-in-law, I ain't goin' no place.'

No one came near him the next day. Not a soul. He was the pariah, to be stared at, gossiped about, sold food to, avoided when he walked among them, but not touched. Not even spat upon.

Mal had never been much for the drink. As a young boy he'd spent years on the road caring for his father, an itinerant farm worker who was also an alcoholic, so alcohol wasn't high on his agenda, but faced with another long afternoon, trying to stare down Ling Lu, he bought a bottle of beer to cheer himself up.

The great gates were swung open time after time, to allow entry or exit, and he couldn't help hoping it was his turn when he heard the iron bolts jerk back and the hinges creak. It became a game with him to refuse to look, to refuse to keep suffering those disappointments, to simply wait and appear calm.

So the Buddhist priest who approached him seemed to come from nowhere. Mal was still propped against the wall, in a new position beside a buttress, out of the wind, when the priest bowed and spoke to him in English.

'Mr Willoughby, my condolences at the grievous misfortune that has beset you and the family of the late Jun Lien.'

'I am also her family,' Mal corrected him gently.

'Of course. A thousand pardons. I hope you are well.'

'I still have my head.'

'Ah yes. I have heard of this difficulty and would very much like for you to join with me in prayer for your late wife's happiness, and your continuing good health, if you would be so kind.'

Mal jumped to his feet, stamping to restore the circulation. 'Thank you,' he said, wondering if he had heard correctly that bit about his health.

'Come along then,' the priest said, allowing no time for excuses, and walked towards the open gates.

Taking a deep breath and telling himself that, if he couldn't trust a priest, whom could he trust? Mal followed him into the main courtyard, which led to a tall flight of stairs at the far end. But they didn't walk that far; they turned down a lane and through the maze of apartments. Mal had become familiar with this style of wealthy Chinese mansions over the years, knowing that the various apartments and gardens were separate entities belonging to family members, but there was usually someone who lorded it over the rest. He hoped it wasn't that prince in this case, because he was beginning to feel very jittery, keeping away from shadowy corners.

But the priest walked on, and Mal kept following until he figured they must soon reach the back gate and, sure enough, there it was, but beside it was a small temple.

Mal went through the motions with the priest, kneeling, trying to pray, to concentrate, lighting candles before the ornate altar, standing patiently, head bowed when the priest was joined by two others who assisted him in the service. Their chanting seemed to give Mal a strange sense of hope, a really strong feeling that Jun Lien was nearby, and as the ceremony drew to a close, he was escorted out to a small stone crypt with the usual curved roof, draped in flowers and ribbons.

The small door was open and he was encouraged to peer in.

There on a ledge, straight in front of him, was Jun Lien's silver urn.

Mal's tears were gratitude, were happiness – a strange emotion for such a solemn occasion, he thought, but it was a beautiful grotto, and Jun Lien was home. Nothing else mattered.

He stayed for a quiet time with her, just the two of them, as it should have been for ever, and when he turned away the priest was waiting.

'We must go now,' he said.

'Yes. But I would like to see Jun Lien's parents before I leave.'

The priest drew his breath in sharply, nervously. 'I am sorry. They will not allow an audience. Only by the grace of God, and our entreaties, was this request granted.'

'Do they hate me so much?'

'It is not hate, Mr Willoughby, grief. And the shattering of your promise. But it will pass. Prayer will restore them to a more reasonable plane when they accept that Jun Lien's passing was God's will. But you brought their beloved daughter home, and though they can't admit it, especially the Lady Xiu Ling Lu, they do have respect for your kindness.'

Just then, Mal looked up and he thought he saw Jun Lien at a window, but it was her mother, just standing, watching. Surprisingly, her presence did not disturb him; rather it gave him a sense of relief. He supposed that he would never be accepted by the family again, but neither was he an enemy.

It was time to go home.

Mal thanked the priest and walked out of the main gate, not surprised to see Chang materialise from among the crowds in the square.

'I thought curiosity would get the better of you,' he grinned.

'That is true. One had to know the outcome. So are you fleeing now, sir, or heaped in honours?'

'Neither. I was permitted to see Jun Lien's last resting place, that's all. So I'm heading back to Tientsin. Are you coming with me?'

'Yes, of course, sir. One must fulfil the contract to the best of one's abilities. But there is something I wish to discuss with you. I am very much interested in your fields of gold. They sound like places of great magnificence.'

'They're not. They're ugly, terrible places. And dangerous. Gold greed sends folk mad.'

'But people dig up plentiful gold.'

'A lot do, but most of them don't. Wait here and I'll get my horse.'

They were back on the road, headed for Peking, when Chang brought up the subject again.

'So. You are returning to your homeland?'

'Yes.'

'And are you going anywhere near the fields of gold?'

'Probably. Yes, I may have to. I'll be looking for the men who were part of the mutiny. I'm sure that was their destination.'

'And you think they'll still be there?'

Mal nodded. 'Let's say that's where I'll start.'

'Then you'll need a servant on your travels, and perhaps, sir, you would employ this humble servant?'

'Thanks for the offer, Chang, but I won't need a servant.'

'I will seek very little pay.'

When Mal shook his head Chang reduced the offer. 'For no pay then? You say it is dangerous, this place. I can protect you, be your guard. Is that not a sensible arrangement?'

'No. I'm sorry. You don't want to be travelling to those miserable diggings, Chang. You have a good set-up here: you can choose your masters and you earn good money. Don't give up your life here for the chance of finding gold.'

Chang sighed. 'Games of chance have always intrigued me. Gold seeking I agree would be a great gamble. But, sir, I would dearly love to be a rich man.'

Mal had intended to retain his prosperous fur company, located in Peking, since he had an efficient manager, recommended by Jun Lien's father, and he had expected to return to China quite often.

Now, though, he decided he might as well cut ties here too, so he apologised to the manager, who was offering condolences on behalf of all the staff, and put the company up for sale.

But it seemed his manager had foreseen the owner's reaction upon the death of his Chinese wife, and was prepared to make an offer to purchase. As a mark of respect for his employer's sad loss, nothing further was said on that day, but several days later Mal received a written offer. And a handsome one at that. Far more than he'd expected to receive. It occurred to him that Xiu hands were at work here again, backing the young manager with finance, but he shrugged.

'I'm going,' he muttered to Chang. 'There's no need for them to push.'

'Should one growl at unexpected good fortune, sir? I think not. The why of it seems an unnecessary question.'

'Yes, I suppose you're right. You've been a good friend, and I very much appreciate all you have done for me.'

'Thank you. But I fear you are saying farewell. You do not wish for me to accompany you to Australia?'

'That is true. When we reach Tientsin I'll be on the first ship headed south. What say you choose a top-class eatery before I leave and I'll shout us a feast?'

'What is this "shout"?'

'Pay. I'll pay.'

'As you should when you invite a friend,' Chang retorted, 'and I shall be honoured to accept.'

Chapter Six

'It's an ill wind, old dear,' Neville told his wife, who was resting in their cabin on the good ship *Clarissa*, still bruised and battered from her ordeal. 'The doctor says some friends of his, plantation owners, are in town at present. They were very upset to hear of the terrible beating you suffered, and since they heard that we are also planters, in a spirit of camaraderie they've offered to put us up for a while.'

'Where?' she asked weakly.

'At their plantation, of course. Apparently they have a huge sugar plantation.'

'But I thought we were going on to that Brisbane place.'

'We were. But we've been dumped right in the heart of plantation country, I'm told. We ought to make the best of it. We can say we were tea planters but we are interested in growing sugar, Cairns being a promising spot. We can say we're now interested in purchasing one of these local plantations, a breeze, because we don't have to pretend we have a clue about them, we can let people explain it all.'

'Neville, you're giving me a headache with all this rigmarole. Did you speak to old Horwood about my wedding ring?'

'Yes. He's claiming that the Oriental Line will have to cover him for the loss of his wife's jewellery. He seems madder about all that than the missing wife.'

'Maybe she ran off with Officer Tussup, he's more her age and not a bad looker.'

'And the Chinese girl too? Don't be daft. He says the shipping company is insured through Lloyd's and he's determined to claim every penny. Seems he's given a description of the stolen jewellery to the police, and his next move is to claim from the company. So we'll do the same.'

'Oh yes, why not?' Esme said sarcastically. 'One plain gold wedding ring and one cheap sapphire engagement ring?'

'No, no, no. I can see you're not well, my love. Pay attention. The wedding ring had four rubies set in it; the sapphire was large and expensive. Now start dictating.'

He sat at the dressing table with pencil and paper and looked back at his wife. 'Tell me, my dear, what fabulous gems were stolen from our cabin? Ladies who could afford to travel in *China Belle* would have scads of jewellery. They'd take that for granted.'

'Oh. But of course! Now let me see . . . what about pearls? A three-roped choker of the best. And a diamond ring – two diamond rings – a gold bracelet, and what about diamond earrings?'

'Anything you like, but you'll have to describe them in more detail. You'd better work on this, and listen, when you've finished, make two copies. One for us to keep so we remember what we've claimed. And do you want to go out to that plantation? It'll save us having to pay hotel bills.'

'Tell them yes, right away. We'll need every penny until we can get something moving here, while they all think we're knee-deep in money like the rest of the passengers from the *China Belle*.'

Neville puffed grandly on his pipe. 'Not just wealthy, but famous and wealthy after all that drama. Those tickets were well spent, Esme.'

She swung her legs off the bunk. 'Just as well we could bring all of our new clothes off that damned ship. We'd have trouble posing wealthy in rags. Now run off and find our new hosts while I do this list. It'll probably take months to drag this money out of the shipping people, but it'll be worth it.'

When he left, Esme began visualising jewellery, revelling in the fantasy of quite exquisite pieces, but then she told herself she couldn't overdo it, so she started the list again with more modest items. Sadly, she found herself describing her mother's jewellery, the diamond rings, the superb pearl stomacher, the gold locket and the elaborate Indian necklace swagged with rubies . . . and the diamond pearl choker she'd worn when she was presented at court. All of them long gone, frittered away with the rest of her inheritance by profligate parents, whose fast life and reckless gambling sent them down the road to genteel poverty.

Esme recalled the humiliation she'd endured at the age of twelve when they moved from their lovely home in Surrey to an ugly apartment on Edgware Road. And the parents didn't seem to care, that was the awful part! They still drank a lot, teasing one another that wine was cheaper these days, played cards, rushed off to the races in public conveyances, and Esme hated them. She hated leaving Miss Fortune's College for Young Ladies and being dumped in the miserable school down the road, but her brother, Arthur, was devastated at having to leave Eton.

'It's not the end of the world,' her mother told Esme. 'They don't learn much there anyway.'

'Perhaps we could move to Russia. That would give him an excuse for leaving,' she suggested, sending her mother into fits of laughter.

'Dear child, going abroad is no excuse. I wish you would stop fretting. We're not entirely broke. Let's say we're just severely bent.'

'But Arthur wanted to go to Oxford. Daddy went to Oxford.'

'I know, but where did that get Daddy? He knows a lot about history and cricket and precious little else, except for horses, of course. Times have changed. Arthur has to learn how to make a living or marry a very rich lady. You'd better keep that in mind too.'

When he was sixteen Arthur was found a position as a bank clerk, which he hated. He lasted a year before he was dismissed.

'I never was much good at sums,' he told his sister miserably. But the parents, relentless now in the pursuit of a career for Arthur, roused friends to assist, and he was placed in one situation after another, none of which proved suitable, the last, behind the counter of a gentlemen's outfitters.

'They are so appallingly rude,' he told Esme.

'Who?'

'Everyone. The customers are bad enough, but the senior sales people are quite dreadful. I can't stand it much longer. I tried to join the army, you know, but they wouldn't have me. It's my lungs – rather weak, they say.'

'Oh well, cheer up. There's always the Church.'

'I wish you wouldn't make fun of me.'

'I'm not. They're starting on me now. Talking about sending me to work somewhere since I'm not pretty enough to attract the rich husband without a dowry.'

'I'm sorry, Es.'

'Don't worry, I'll survive.'

But Arthur did not.

Arthur hanged himself from a tree by the river, the day after Esme's eighteenth birthday.

And Esme met Neville Caporn, his friend from Eton schooldays, at the funeral.

Afterwards they walked away, just the two of them, Neville and Esme, and they talked. Neville was shocked that his friend would take his own life and listened sadly as Esme explained. He was a good listener. He took her to a warm coffee shop where they sat by the fire and Esme poured out all her troubles. She told him about Arthur's last job and he was so incensed that as they were leaving the coffee shop, he had a brilliant idea.

'Let's go there! Let's pay them a visit!'

They ran most of the way, strolled past the shop several times, and then marched in.

Neville was at his haughtiest best and Esme was offered a comfortable chair while he decided what to purchase. It was sheer delight for her to watch his outrageous behaviour, demanding to see the best jackets, hats, ties and stockings. Almost every drawer in the shop was opened, while the senior salesmen who had treated her brother so badly, hovered about, anxious to please.

Finally a pile of purchases were made ready for the young gentleman and Esme watched, holding her breath. She hadn't realised that Neville would actually be buying, or that he would be spending so much, but there they were, all boxed and wrapped, and the bill was being totalled.

'I say,' Neville said to Esme. 'As I recall, there's a better gentlemen's shop in Bond Street, isn't there?'

'Yes,' Esme responded, on to the game now.

'Then I think we'll go there.'

He turned to the salesman and drawled. 'I've changed my mind. I shan't be needing these articles. They're really not up to my standard.'

Esme took his arm as they sailed sedately from the store and strolled around the corner where they fell about laughing.

After that they became firm friends, spending as much time as possible together, until Esme's mother became concerned.

'That fellow, whatsisname, who is always underfoot . . . what is his situation?'

'You mean Neville. I've told you his name a hundred times. His father owns Caporn Engineering, and Neville and his brothers work at something there. It's a family business.'

'Really. Then I hope you're not entertaining any ideas about marrying the fellow.'

'Why not? The Caporns are well off. If I marry him you won't have to send me to the salt mines.'

'Try not to be droll,' her mother sighed. 'You are not good at it. And you can't marry this Neville fellow. You could do a lot better, a good-looking gel like you.'

'Good-looking?' Esme was amazed. 'You said I was ugly.'

'No I didn't. You were plain, but you have blossomed. Your father was only commenting yesterday that your hair colour seems to have deepened from that gingery shade to a nice auburn.'

She came closer and peered at her daughter. 'Yes it has, and your skin has cleared up, and your figure has rounded out nicely.'

'Stop looking me over as if I'm a horse! It's extremely rude!'

'Nonsense! We can't afford a suitable coming-out ball, so your father and I have decided we'll embark on an "Esme" expedition. It'll really be quite fun. We're taking you on a tour, visiting friends in their country houses, where you're bound to meet eligible young gentlemen.'

'I won't go!'

'Yes you will. Now come with me and we'll see what we can do about a wardrobe for you.'

Esme did meet, and charm, several eligible young gentlemen but her heart was with Neville, who worried himself into a nervous illness for the three months that she was away, and on the day she returned he rushed to the flat in Edgware Road.

'Have you fallen for some blighter?' he asked her breathlessly.

'No, silly. Of course not.'

'Then let's get married.'

'Good-oh. When?'

'I thought we should elope, and never come back. I hate working in the factory. Even when my father pops off I'll still be bossed around by my brothers.'

'Where would we go?'

'What about the Far East? That sounds as far away as you can get, wherever it is.'

'Righto.'

But the following day Esme had second thoughts. 'We can't elope. You don't have much money saved and I have none, so we have to be sensible. We should get engaged first, then have a wedding. Think of all the presents!'

'What about the Far East? Do we set off carting silver cake dishes and teapots?'

'No, we sell them. They'll be our running-away money.'

Neville grinned and pinched her chin. 'You little imp! What a good idea.'

Esme's idea served them well for a start, since Neville's father allowed them a rent free cottage near the factory for a wedding present.

As soon as the young marrieds were installed in their new home, they visited the library to study maps that could tell them something about the Far East. They decided Bombay was too close, Hong Kong too far, but Singapore was just right.

Thoroughly enjoying themselves, they enquired about passage to Singapore and bought two pith helmets, as recommended by the shipping clerk. Then they began the process of selling up everything they couldn't carry.

Eventually the day came when Mr and Mrs Caporn shut the door of the empty cottage, leaving the key under the mat, and took a cab across town to the Tudor Inn, where they stayed for three days, until the departure of SS *Pelorus* for Singapore.

Their jubilation knew no bounds that night, as they celebrated with champagne, presented to the honeymooners by the captain, toasted their triumphant escape from families and looked forward to great adventures in exotic lands.

They discovered more adventures than they'd bargained for, mainly caused by a serious lack of money, but it never occurred to them to return home. Singapore was a British crown colony so Neville was able to find a position with the Colonial Office without much effort, and they fitted well in the rarefied atmosphere of the exclusive expatriate society. As Esme wrote to a friend, they were having a simply marvellous time. She did not add that the cost of living was low, and so was Neville's wage. He was known in the Colonial Office as a good chap, a good cricketer and a good dancer, so his job was secure, but a promotion was out of the question. He and his wife were referred to, on the quiet, as being rather giddy. Irresponsible, so to speak.

It wasn't all that surprising then, that the Caporns found their own methods of making ends meet. First by buying flawed or paste jewellery and hiring an Indian to set up a stall at the port and sell their merchandise to travellers as authentic, valuable pieces, at outrageous prices, which they referred to as 'smashing bargains'.

Months turned into years. Their lives meandered along in the benign tropic setting. They treasured indolence and spent many a sultry evening in their garden, drinking gin and breathing the jasmine-soaked air. Occasionally they'd come up with another little plan to augment their income, unconcerned that all of their 'little plans' meant cheating someone. They rarely paid much rent, removing themselves to another bungalow in high dudgeon if their landlord became insistent, thereby depriving him of final payments.

Neville became adept at the clerking business, as he called it, a real whiz with paperwork. He knew the regulations and every complicated form that came with them in order for the London office to keep some vestige of control of the Far Eastern colony, and he used them to his advantage. He ordered goods that somehow found their way to his house, and pleased his superiors by rerouting liquor for the Army and Navy Club to the Cricket Club. They thought it was a hoot, and had a wonderful Christmas party that year.

A large bungalow, beautifully appointed and set in a wonderful garden had always appealed to Neville as he passed by, and when he heard the Indian couple who owned it were returning to Bombay for a while, he enquired about renting.

The owners were happy to grant the gentleman from the Colonial Office a lease of one year, and Neville drew up the papers for them to sign. He paid the rent to the manager of their trading house, for a few weeks, and then the payments ceased.

'To cut a long story short,' he told Esme, 'we don't have to pay any more. We've bought the place. What they signed was a sale document, not a lease. I don't think they quite understood that.'

'Oh, sweetness. How clever of you,' she gushed.

The sale document was foolproof. Years later they sold the fine house for a tidy sum before relocating to Hong Kong where Neville was welcomed into the Colonial Office as a whiz with forms and regulations.

* * *

In Hong Kong they managed to purchase not one but two houses, by dint of making sure the Chinese owners did not read or understand the fine print, and were doing well, absolutely loving the more sophisticated ambience of this great city, when things started to go wrong.

After only eighteen months with this Colonial Office, an efficient superior started to become suspicious. What passed as a hoot in Singapore did not amuse this gentleman. He disapproved of liquor orders being rerouted, especially when he discovered that crates were delivered to the Caporn household. And no payment could be seen. The Chinese owner, or former owner, of the house in which the Caporns now resided, complained to the First Secretary, who looked into the matter. He resolutely defended the clerk, Caporn, pointing out that the sale had been perfectly legal, thereby saving face for his department, but then he turned a thunderous visage on Neville, who was gentleman enough to quietly hand in his resignation. His attitude was appreciated.

'I'm glad you're out of there,' said his wife. 'They were all such boring people. We need to spread our wings, have a little fun now.'

'You're quite right, sweets. I think we should travel.'

'Where to? Back to England?'

'Good God, no. The European climate would be too hard on our constitutions now. We could take a ship to the Australian colonies. Have a look around there. I believe *China Belle* is sailing down to Brisbane shortly.'

Esme looked up sharply. '*China Belle*? How very grand! But could we afford it?'

'Why not? We'd be mixing with real class. You never know what might be on offer.'

Esme sucked the pencil, her list of non-existent jewellery no further advanced. 'True,' she muttered. 'You never know what might be on offer, like getting your head bashed in.' She would never agree that tickets on *China Belle* were money well spent, and she was cross with Neville for being so insensitive.

He came back to the cabin. 'Have you finished?'

'No! I'm sorry. I must have fallen asleep. It's these headaches. Ever since that bastard beat me, I can't seem to concentrate.'

He bent over and kissed her on the forehead. 'I'm sorry. You really are being a brick about the way they treated you. I've got a reporter outside who particularly wants to interview you. He knows how important you are in this story, because of your shocking ordeal. And he's willing to pay, so don't be afraid to speak up. I've already told him I, myself, looked death in the face.'

'All right. I'd better see him now. Wait until I put a hat on.'

Neville looked at her hair. 'I would leave the hat off. I mean, it would help to let him see how they hacked your beautiful hair about.'

'No! Definitely not! I look horrible without a hat now.'

'You never look horrible, darling.'

'Don't try to flatter me. I won't see anyone unless I can keep a hat on. The reporter might know a ladies' stylist who can even it up for me. I might as well have it short than live with chunks missing. The bastards!'

Esme prided herself on being game. She'd even shouted abuse at the Malay pig when she'd been struck the first time. After that it was sheer horror and humiliation. And fear. She'd heard them say they'd throw her overboard! And she'd known they would if it suited them. Instead they bashed her, tore her dress, hacked her hair! She felt perspiration dripping down her face as she talked to the reporter, and her clothes were becoming damp, which was embarrassing. She looked about to escape from the crowded lounge but all the doors were sealed shut.

'I'm sorry,' she said. 'I really can't continue this conversation. I'm a little tired.'

Tired? she asked herself. Terrified if you want to know. I'm still terrified. I have to get over this. If I could only sleep at night I'd be all right.

'Just one more question, Mrs Caporn. How did you feel when those men put their hands on you?'

Neville objected angrily. 'They did not put their hands on her as you insinuate; they beat her, viciously.'

'But you yourself said her dress was torn. They may have had other ideas. A white woman, you know . . . our Brisbane readers . . .'

'Your readers, the women especially, would also like to know about my wife's hair. She has beautiful hair, it's a lovely auburn colour, hidden under that hat. It was long, magnificent! They cut it off. Not neatly, mind you. Oh no! They hacked it off with knives. Can you imagine the terror of a poor woman, thrown to the deck of a ship and set upon by a gang of Asian thugs? In all our years managing plantations, surrounded by natives, nothing of this sort ever happened to us, not until we boarded that expensive and exclusive ship.'

Esme was frantic now. The windows were sealed up too. Other people were managing to escape but she couldn't see how. And it was becoming dark, letting the nightmare in. She clutched Neville's arm, and looked up at him but it wasn't him at all, it was her brother, Arthur, telling her to hang on, so she did hang on. She kept the scream deep inside her, the scream that had remained with her even when she knew she was safe – that they'd all gone. But the scream was an ugly, cunning thing; something horrible they'd left to torture her.

'I really have to go,' she said, mopping her face with one of Neville's handkerchiefs. 'It's so hot in here.'

'All right, my love,' Neville said. 'You run along. I'll finish the interview with this young gentleman.'

Esme wanted him to help her, to at least direct her to an exit, but he was in full flow by now, holding forth about his horrific experiences during the mutiny, and it made her angry.

'His experiences!' she muttered to Arthur as she found a locked door and hammered on it, hurrying out on to the deck as soon as a steward swooped to open it for her.

'I should think so!' she snapped at the steward over her shoulder.

'His experiences,' she muttered again. 'The bullet just grazed him. He only came off with a headache. I'm still sore all over from that bashing, when I was out on the deck with them and so frightened.'

She stood, holding the rail of their rescue ship, looking down at the busy wharfs. Then she turned back to Arthur.

'I'll be all right once I get on solid ground again. Go and tell Neville that I wish to go ashore immediately. If the plantation people who want to put us up aren't around, then it has to be a hotel. But I can't stay on a ship a moment longer.'

The stranger who'd been standing beside her, gaped at her. Then he backed away and disappeared in the crowd.

Chapter Seven

With this, her first taste of the southern continent, Eleanor Plummer was not at all dissatisfied. Cairns seemed a comely little town resting on the shores of Trinity Bay, where bosomy mountains gave the harbour depth and created glittering emerald bays. She loved strolling along the palm-lined waterfront, admiring the bay and soaking up the wondrous lack of crowds, especially at noon, when the somnolent town seemed deserted.

Though SS *Clarissa* had been a godsend to the stranded passengers, they were all greatly relieved to find themselves in one piece, on terra firma again. Eleanor had thought of voyaging on to Brisbane in *Clarissa*, but by the time they reached Cairns she had changed her mind. The Russian captain had declared his undying love for her within twenty-four hours of her boarding his ship, and she wasn't inclined to suffer his advances for the rest of the voyage. Mrs Plummer, among the first to disembark, soon found her way to the Alexandra Hotel, which she'd been told was the best in town.

She stood and surveyed the unpainted, two-storeyed timber building with wide verandas, then nodded approval. It bore no relation to the sturdy European-type hotels to which she was accustomed, but it appeared clean, so she took a chance.

As it happened, the place was new, and spotless and, better still, owned by a German couple. Frau Kassel herself escorted the lady proudly to their only suite, which was at the front of the building, with a balcony overlooking the bay. It was cool and comfortable, and later that day Eleanor sat smugly on her balcony watching Lyle Horwood march towards the front entrance with Mr Lewis and two other gentlemen. Horwood having to put up with second best?

She supposed she shouldn't be so mean, since Lyle must be frightfully worried, as they all were, about his wife. But she still wouldn't give up her pleasant surrounds. The sitting room adjoining her bedroom was a delight, with cane furnishings, cushions and rugs straight out of good Singapore stores.

'I'll be staying a while,' she told herself, 'at least until they have news of Mrs Horwood. I'll help in any way I can.'

A week later she wrote to her friends in Brisbane that she found this little tropical town, and its climate, quite delightful, and may even buy or build a house here, so that she'd always have a base to come home to after her further explorations of the other Australian cities.

'That's rather sudden,' Mr Lewis had said when she spoke to him of her intentions.

'Oh no! I'm always quick to make up my mind about things.' Then she laughed. 'Not always right, of course. But what's a house? I will have fun furnishing, and then if I get miserable, I can sell. Go someplace else.'

She was taken aback by his mild response. 'I hope you find what you're looking for.'

It didn't seem to her he was talking about a house.

Frau Kassel, an enthusiastic migrant, was anxious to conform, to fit in with everyone else in this new society, but she found their mealtimes a mystery. Until now, she hadn't dared remark on this phenomenon, but when Frau Plummer asked the question, she responded to a kindred soul at last.

'Madam,' she said to this grand lady, 'I am glad you asked. Breakfast is the normal hours but do not be surprised to see large meals being served. They like steak, eggs, bacon, liver, with bread and butter and sauces for breakfast. Midday is dinner! This I don't understand, eating three, four courses in the midday heat. Six o'clock is tea.'

'Rather late, isn't that?'

'Oh no. Tea is the evening meal. Soups, cold collations, savoury dishes and desserts.'

'Really? So we don't have tea?'

'Yes. That is known as afternoon tea, with tea and cakes. But there is morning tea before breakfast,' she began to laugh, 'morning tea after breakfast, and supper after evening tea. Though the nights are also hot, here they have a great preference for hot chocolate.'

'How very strange! But I suppose a lot of things are different here. I shall find it all most interesting.'

Frau Kassel, who was also the cook, was relieved that this lady was happy to fall in with the routine. Some foreigners – Frau Kassel, having resided in Queensland for two years, did not regard herself as a foreigner – made quite a fuss about the odd arrangements.

Mrs Plummer didn't mind conforming. She wore a neat navy suit and a satin-trimmed navy hat as she came down the stairs for dinner a little after six and made for the small dining room. Frau Kassel rushed out to greet her and ushered her straight to the table occupied by Lyle Horwood and Mr Lewis.

Both men stood, Lyle decidedly unimpressed by her arrival, but Eleanor took her place with them, rather than create a fuss,

'How good of you to join us,' Mr Lewis said.

'Unearthly damned hour to be dining,' Lyle muttered.

Over the next few days there was much to do. All of the people from *China Belle* gave statements to the police; there were constant meetings and discussions regarding Mrs Horwood; a service was held to the memory of Bosun Flesser, after which Mrs Caporn took Eleanor aside.

'I wonder if you could do me a great favour? My hair needs attention, it looks foul, but they only have a barber here. After those thugs chopped it about, I won't let a bush barber shear me. Do you think you could have a go at cutting it?'

'My dear, I shall try. Why don't you come up to my room at the hotel and we'll see what can be done?'

Neville Caporn walked them back into the town, all talk about their intended stay at the sugar cane plantation.

'Fate has thrown us on to these shores. We were headed for Brisbane, but now we are informed that these areas, much further north, are far better suited for the growing of sugar cane, which has been our intention all along. So, to be able to stay at a plantation and see the operations at first-hand before we invest is a change of luck for us, after all we've suffered.'

'I am so pleased for you. You deserve some good fortune after that dreadful experience.'

Eleanor turned back to Mrs Caporn. 'Are you feeling better in yourself now? You had a terrible time of it.'

'Oh yes, thank you, I'm much better.'

'Esme has been wonderful,' Neville said. 'Takes it all in her stride.'

'So I see. I think you're very brave.'

Eleanor did the best she could with Mrs Caporn's hair after her initial reaction to its sorry state, trying not to cut too much off, and enjoyed chatting to her. Contrary to her previous shipboard assessment, the woman seemed to Eleanor to be quite a nice person.

'Several of those English actresses wear their hair cut short and curled at the front,' she advised her 'client', 'and long at the back so they can plait it or roll it into different styles.'

Mrs Caporn shrugged. 'I've got hunks of hair missing at the back, though.'

'No one would notice once it's styled and worn up. Then you won't have to be worried about wearing hats all the time.'

'Yes, I imagine that's best.' She looked about. 'This suite is very presentable for a country town, isn't it?'

'A surprise indeed, I can tell you. This settled my decision to stay on awhile. I was telling Mr Lewis I might even buy or build a house here.'

'Good heavens! I was thinking of doing the same thing.'

'But what about the plantation?'

Mrs Capron leaned forward into the mirror as Eleanor pinned her hair in place. 'Good God! I almost look presentable.'

'You look lovely! Here, put some of this cream on your face. It has a little colour in it . . . my secret . . . to cover blemishes.'

When Mrs Caporn rubbed some of Eleanor's cream over her cheeks, she was delighted. 'It hides the last of the bruising altogether! It's amazing. Where can I buy it?'

'Oh, take the jar with you, Mrs Caporn. I make it up myself.'

'Thank you. You're so kind, but I wish you'd call me Esme. We've come through that awful experience together.'

'You more than I, my dear Esme. You may call me Eleanor if you wish.'

As they were leaving the room Esme remembered the question. 'Oh . . . I was talking about a house in the town. It's an absolute must for me, as I've always told my husband. Plantation living is very pleasant, but there are always so many workers about. I need a nice quiet house in civilised surrounds.' She burst into a laugh, an infectious laugh that engulfed Eleanor. 'Translated, that means shops and theatres,' she said, and Eleanor warmed to her.

'Of course,' she giggled. 'Of course.'

A few days later, she was disconcerted to find that Mr Lewis had gone to the gold town to search for Mrs Horwood, by now known to the trio at the hotel as Constance, and that meant sharing the table with Lyle. Awkward though it was at first, neither could desert, so they stayed together under sufferance.

They never spoke of Fannie but Eleanor often thought of her, and of the jewellery that was now gone for ever. What a strange fate for it, she mused as she sat facing Lyle. In the end she couldn't resist enquiring what the police had to say about the robberies, and then was sorry she'd asked. It was like touching a wet paint sign, she told herself: succumb to the temptation and suffer. Lyle was furious about the theft of the jewellery, livid, carrying on about it at such length that Eleanor was moved to remark that she and Mrs Caporn had also lost quite a few expensive pieces.

'Nothing like ours!' he snapped. 'Constance's jewel case was packed. I lost a quarter of a million pounds in jewellery, at the very least, and I've told the captain I will have compensation.'

'Perhaps the jewel case should have been in his safe.'

'Don't talk nonsense, woman. Tussup had the keys to the armoury and to the safe, so a lot of good that would have been.'

Eleanor listened patiently to his rantings, paying more attention to her boiled egg. She had lost only the rings she'd been wearing. Rather than bother showing off jewellery shipboard, which seemed to her to be in bad taste, considering it was such a small company, she'd sewn the best pieces into the hem of her petticoat. The rest were stuffed into the toe of a shoe and went unnoticed by the thieves. She decided it wouldn't be tactful to let Lyle into that secret but when she told Esme, the poor woman was devastated.

'I wish I'd been as sensible,' she wailed.

They were all waiting now for Mr Lewis to return with news of Constance and, they hoped, the arrest of all those mutineers.

'They'll get them,' Lyle said. 'According to Jesse Field the mutiny and the abduction of the women has caused such outrage in the south, they're sending more police up to Cooktown.'

'That's good,' Eleanor said gently.

'For a start. I said they ought to send soldiers to patrol the dangerous track over the mountains to the goldfields. They could bail up everyone coming and going, check their miners' licences. That way they could grab Tussup and his gang. They have to have licences before they can stake a claim on the goldfields.'

'Oh yes,' Eleanor's response was vague. She patted her hair in place, and for his sake, kept her own counsel. She'd already mentioned this matter to Mr Field but he'd said the goldfields attracted hundreds of underworld characters using false names to avoid authorities. The licensing inspectors had no way of checking true identities so they simply took the fees and handed out the papers.

'Unfortunately,' Field had told her, 'that means Tussup and his gang would all have assumed names by now, and would have melted into the crowd. Raymond's our best bet for the minute. He's the only person who could spot them. Until Sonny comes back from China, that is.'

'Sonny?'

'Aye. Mal Willoughby. People used to call him Sonny.'

'And you think he'll be back?'

Mr Field looked towards the door as if expecting the young man to walk in that second. 'They killed his wife,' he said ominously. 'He'll be back.'

The plantation owned by Jack and Delia Foster was a long way out of town, but that suited their guests. The Fosters were English too, having come to this corner of the earth via India, where Jack's parents owned tea plantations, and they were amiable hosts. The sandstone house was large and airy with separate guest quarters.

'I hope you'll be comfortable here,' Delia said as she ushered them past a long cool veranda. 'You're most welcome to stay until you've decided what to do next.'

'You're so kind . . .' Esme began.

'No, no, no! Not at all. You've had such a harrowing experience this is the least we can do. Besides, it's lovely to have visitors. We only started up here two years ago and this guest house has recently been completed. Just in time really!'

The four of them got along extremely well. Neville gave a hand where he could, knowing Jack would appreciate his small efforts, and Esme was adept at keeping the lady of the house amused. The two women liked to take a dip in the crystal-clear rock pool before their afternoon nap, and then dress for dinner, after which they all took their places for cards.

After a week of this idyllic lifestyle, Neville asked to go into town.

'We have to beg off for a day, old chap. Things to sort out, you know – banking and all that – and Esme is anxious to see our shipmates and find out what happened to her dear friend Mrs Horwood. Could we borrow the gig?'

Their host was only too pleased to assist, and the next morning they were on their way.

'I'm pleased Delia's cold has kept her in bed today,' Esme said as they drove towards the sandy track. 'She wanted to come with us but she's so damned gushy!'

'The poor woman's lonely. I rather think she'd pay us to stay on. Obviously there aren't too many English-born folk round here, not with any class.'

'Don't forget we have to look up their friend Mr Hillier. Clive Hillier. What's the betting he's one of us too?'

'I don't care whether he's English or Indian. He has a clothing emporium somewhere and is building a new one here. Jack said the poor fellow has rather overstretched himself, financially I mean. Could be a sound investment for us, my love. You never know, he might need a partner. I think Jack was telling us in the hope we might offer to help out.'

The gig was well sprung and the leather was soft. As they spun along the hazy track, sunlight dipped in and out of the treetops as if it were chasing them, and Esme dozed, grateful for this respite. She had become so weary lately, her nights shrill, her days spent play-acting, that if it were not for the company of her poor dead brother, Arthur, she would have collapsed. And revenge, of course: every day she prayed those thugs would be caught and punished. Preferably hanged. It was still hard to believe that men had actually bashed and battered her like that. And humiliated her so horribly. She sobbed, blinked and straightened up.

'You were having a good old rest there, sweets,' Neville smiled. 'It's nice to be off on our own again, isn't it? But what say we call on old Horwood at the hotel? He's sure to invite us to lunch.'

'Not him. He's too tight. Mr Lewis is a better bet. Do you think the mutineers will have been caught by this time?'

'Maybe. I hope so. Poor Mrs Horwood. God knows what has happened to her after what they did to you. No pity, no pity at all. They're just animals.'

Esme shuddered. 'I don't want to talk about them.'
He squeezed her knee. 'That's right. Good girl. Best thing.'

As it turned out it was Mrs Plummer who invited them to lunch, since Mr Lewis had gone up to Cooktown to see if he could help locate Mrs Horwood.
Lyle Horwood, looking wan and dispirited, was so pleased to see them he welcomed them like old friends, but though he sat at table with them he made no effort to stand them the meal. Neville smiled at Esme: you were right.
Lunch was a huge meal: roast beef with all the trimmings, which they very much enjoyed, and thanked Mrs Plummer accordingly.
After lunch they took her for a walk round the town, interested in a block of shops under construction in the street behind the Esplanade, which they learned were being built by Clive Hillier, the very person they had to see.
Mrs Plummer then took them a little further out of town to show them large cleared blocks of land.
'I wouldn't mind a house here,' she said, 'overlooking that splendid bay with its fine sea breezes.'
'Just what I was saying to Esme on the way in,' Neville agreed. 'There's the spot for your townhouse, my dear. You won't find better.'

Clive was pleased to meet this affable English couple, especially when he heard they were considering settling in the district.
'You can't go wrong here,' he told them. 'New towns are taking off like lightning in this country, thanks to the gold rushes. Now that they've found more gold inland from here, in the Hodgkinson River, this little port will blossom into a city in no time.'
'Amazing,' Mr Caporn said. 'Though we haven't yet recovered from the shock of that dreadful mutiny, we're absolutely fascinated with all the goings-on in this country. We hardly know where to look first, and we were just saying this morning as we drove into the town, we should have come here years ago.'
Clive was equally fascinated to talk to them and hear first-hand about the mutiny, and their fear that the stranded ship would break up under them.
'It was such a beautiful ship too,' Mrs Caporn said. 'The cabins were really staterooms. There were only half a dozen or so and everything was of the best quality. I doubt we'll see the like again, except on a private yacht.'
'I believe several of the passengers are staying at the Alexandra Hotel,' Clive said.
Caporn nodded. 'Only two at the minute. Poor Horwood, waiting on news of his wife, the woman who was abducted, and a German lady, who I think is so taken with the colour and vivacity of Cairns, she is considering remaining here.'
'What happened to the others?'

'Well, let me see . . . the captain is with friends. Mr Willoughby has gone, and Mr Lewis joined the search for Mrs Horwood.'

'Willoughby? He was the gentleman who lost his wife?'

'That's correct. She drowned, poor little thing.'

'And where did he go?'

'Left the country. Gone back to China, I believe.'

'It's all too sad,' Mrs Caporn said, and Clive thought she was quite lovely, something new and welcome in this town. She was an attractive redhead, dressed very smartly, but she had big sorrowful brown eyes. He felt drawn to her, saw the trust and respect in her eyes as she looked up to him, giving him her gloved hand as they were leaving.

'I hope to see you again,' he said wistfully.

'But of course,' Mrs Caporn said.

He watched them walk away, admired her shapely waist and the curve of her hips, sighed, and remembered Willoughby. Gone back to China! Good riddance. That was the best news of the day. Apart from meeting Mrs Caporn.

The news took Cairns by storm. Mrs Horwood had been found! They'd brought her back to Cairns!

People rushed into the street from their shops and houses as if they might see her ride triumphantly by, and they stayed to congregate and speculate as to the where and the how, and more importantly, the what had happened to her in the meantime. What had her captors done to her? Were they white slavers? And how had she escaped their clutches? Many and lurid were the conclusions reached, and when it was known she'd been rushed, in the dead of night, from the little ship that had borne her bravely to Cairns, the worst was thought. Some said the poor distraught woman was naked, wrapped only in a ship's blanket.

The latter was not quite true. When the ship slid silently over the moonlit waters of Trinity Bay, the woman was grateful for the blanket that Raymond wrapped around her, because the breeze had a chill in it. He recalled that morning back in Cooktown, when the surly police sergeant heard Mrs Horwood had been found, and dashed down to the wharf to see for himself. He was so happy and relieved that he almost hugged Constance when he stepped on to the boat. Instead, he shook her hand, wished her well, asked her if there was anything she needed, and if she could spare the time to talk to him about her abduction.

Raymond had to intervene, to ask that Gooding step out of the cabin for a minute. 'Sergeant,' he whispered, 'the woman is disoriented, can't you see that? She doesn't know where she is or what's happening. She's not fit to answer questions right now.'

Gooding scrutinised her. She was sitting quietly at the table, holding a mug of tea. The girl, Lottie, had gone, caught up in her own whirlwind.

'She looks all right to me,' he said.

'But she's not. I don't think anyone should question her until she understands where she is.'

'Does she know her name?'

'Yes, but that's about all. When I brought her on board I asked her what happened to her and got nowhere.'

'What do you mean?'

Raymond walked further down the deck. 'That's what she said. I was astonished. She asked me what I meant. "Nothing happened to me," she said, and she asked me to take her to a good hotel so that she could tidy up. When I said she'd have to stay here, that this boat would take her to Cairns, she became upset'

'Even I know that'd be a mistake, Lewis. I reckon you're confusing her. From what you told me yourself, she's never heard of Cairns.'

'I corrected myself,' Raymond said stiffly. 'I said we'd take her to her husband, Lyle, as soon as possible. In which case I asked the crew to prepare to sail. The deputies will stay, you need them, but I must take this woman back to her husband without delay.'

'No bloody way!' Gooding snapped. 'Let the crew take her down to Cairns. I need you here. You're the only one who can identify the mutineers, remember? Unless she stays to help.'

'Under no circumstances will I allow this sick woman to have to sail all the way down to Cairns with strange men.'

'Typical bloody politician,' Gooding growled. 'Love the limelight, don't you? Well, you're out of your depth here, mate. This ship isn't going anywhere until I've had a long chat with Mrs Horwood. Let her have a sleep now and give her something to eat – she looks half starved – and I'll be back this afternoon.'

He called to the skipper. 'If you try to take this ship out before I give you the go-ahead I'll have your ticket.'

Gooding was surprisingly gentle with her, Raymond had to admit, asking his questions in a conversational way over tea and hot scones, which he'd miraculously produced, but there didn't seem to be much to discover. She was thin and her legs and arms were scratched, from bush walking, they presumed, but otherwise she seemed well.

'They didn't beat you?' Gooding asked eventually.

'No I don't think so. They dragged me about. In a rowboat. On a beach. I had to sleep in the bush and all those men were there.'

She cringed back, wrapping her arms about herself. 'He cut my dress with a knife.'

'Who did this?'

'The officer. He bullied me. Made me run through the bush, all day. We were running all day, and I fell . . .' She began to weep, and looked to Raymond. 'Oh please, where are we, Mr Lewis? Can't we go back to *China Belle*?'

He had explained her situation to her earlier, telling her where she was and so forth, but she'd forgotten.

'It's in port now,' he lied, so as not to upset her further. 'Not too far from here and we can go there soon.'

'Why didn't you run away from those men?' Gooding asked.

'They wouldn't let me go. They would have killed me. We had to run away in the end.'

'Who's we?'

She blinked, bewildered by the question. There was a persistent dribble in the corner of her mouth. She dabbed at it with the handkerchief Raymond had given her.

'We? I don't know. Someone. My red dress was torn. I got another from a mad woman. The ferry man rowed me across and I ran.'

'I'll check on him and in camps on the other side of the river,' Gooding said to Raymond. 'They might still be there. Possibly they just let her go.'

He looked up as a shadow loomed in the doorway. 'What are you doing here, Madigan?'

'If that's the doctor, I sent for him,' Raymond said. 'I would like him to see Mrs Horwood.'

The doctor peered in and smiled. 'Ah, we meet again. This is my patient; she was in hospital with a fever. How are we feeling now?'

But Mrs Horwood didn't remember him, didn't want to be examined and it took a while to calm her down.

Raymond and Gooding waited on the deck, watching the crowds gathering on the wharf.

'What's going on here?' Gooding asked no one in particular and then shook his head. 'Ah Christ! They're here to gawk at Mrs Horwood. She'll be a sideshow from now on.'

Raymond had guessed that would happen, and a week later, when *Torrens* sailed into Trinity Bay, he asked the skipper to weigh anchor until dark, so they could bring the lady in quietly and unobtrusively.

Madigan had managed to gain her confidence and gather a little more information. 'She was treated badly but not beaten or interfered with, which is some blessing, considering the sort of men who held her captive. But when I first saw her she had a fever, she was covered in insect bites and had an injured ankle, a sprain. This is the sort of condition I'm looking at every day in this place – people who have no idea what they're doing, living like bushies, so she was nothing unusual. I had no idea who she was. But I can tell you now, she's in a bad way. The woman has been living in terror, and the terror is still with her. What they did to her, dragging her about like a coolie, frightened the hell out of her. She was certain they would kill her and thinks they're still after her.'

'How did she get to the hospital?' Gooding asked.

'She has no idea. She only remembers fragments, as you've already discovered, I don't doubt, and she doesn't want to remember too much, so you're better to leave her alone. No more questions, she's had enough.'

Lewis refrained from a righteous frown at the sergeant over that advice, but asked Madigan if he would approve her immediate transfer to Cairns, where her husband was waiting.

'Why didn't he come for her?' Madigan asked.

'I hear he's an old bloke,' Gooding grinned. 'Did well for himself, wouldn't you say?'

'May we leave when the skipper's ready?' Raymond asked, and, receiving Madigan's approval, turned to the sergeant. 'You can't force me to stay, but once I've delivered her to her husband I'll be back. I want to get those men as much as you do.'

Lyle had been dreading her return. He'd known she'd be an embarrassment. He'd seen the looks on people's faces when they asked after her, especially the men, tongues sliding across lips, leering, eyes brazen, nudging, and he knew what they were thinking. Day and night he knew what they were thinking, as his own mind prowled about her with those brown-skinned men, peeking at her, touching her, handling her lovely body, hardly believing their luck . . . sharing her! And then they'd claim ransom for her, laughing at him, get the money and kill her. Or they'd throw her back . . . damaged goods.

Trouble was, he hadn't realised how much of an embarrassment she would be.

When Kassel banged on his door all excited, waking him from a heavy sleep to tell him Mr Lewis had found his lady, Lyle was shocked. It was too sudden.

'What? What are you talking about? Don't shout, man! Where is she?'

'Here, sir!'

'Where?' Lyle clutched his nightgown and peered into the dark passage-way.

'In Cairns. Mr Lewis sent a message. He needs a vehicle to transport her.'

'Here in the town? How can that be? She can't be here in Cairns. How did she get here?'

'By boat, sir. My cellarman, he's getting the wagon ready for you. He'll drive you down to the wharf.'

'At this hour? What time is it? No, no. I must dress. Did you say Lewis is with her?'

Kassel was becoming impatient. 'Should I go? Take the wagon?'

'Yes, go. At once. I will dress. And tell your wife I should like coffee and brandy. I'm overcome with nerves.'

He hadn't asked for Mrs Kassel and Mrs Plummer to be woken to dance attendance on his wife, fussing over her in the hotel kitchen, when it was plain to see she was perfectly all right.

'Sailing down here from Cooktown helped to calm her,' Lewis told him.

'Where did she sleep?' Lyle asked.

'The skipper gave her his cabin. But as I was saying, Constance does look well now, better than when I found her, but there are problems.'

'Like what?'

'The doctor who examined her said she was still in shock from the terror of that experience.'

'Now she's back she'll get over that. What are the problems he's talking about?'

'Nerves, that sort of thing.'

'A lot of bosh, this nerves business. Don't believe in it myself. Guilty consciences most of the time, I say. People with clear consciences don't have nerves. You heard my wife, she said they didn't beat her. She got off lightly. Look at little Mrs Caporn – what they did to her. Slapped her face! Beat her! Belted her to the ground, tore out her hair. My God! What that woman went through! But she's got grit; she put her chin up and marched on. She didn't need to be molly-coddled and have some namby-pamby doctor say she's got nerves.'

He turned to the women. 'It's time my wife retired.'

'But of course,' Mrs Plummer said acidly. 'Is there anything you need, Constance?'

She shook her head.

'I unpacked some of your things,' Mrs Kassel told her. 'I'm sure you'll find everything in order. All your pretty things sitting there waiting for you. It is so wonderful to have you safe. We were all very worried. You like me to take you up?'

'Oh, yes please,' Constance said, grabbing her arm.

'It was fortunate Constance found her way to that hospital in Cooktown,' Lewis said, and Lyle was annoyed with him, playing the hero, as if he'd found her on his own, when in fact she was brought to him.

'Yes, I've been wondering about that. She's supposed to be their prisoner but she calmly takes herself off to hospital.'

'Lyle, I told you, she ran away!'

'Oh, I see. Now she can outrun a dozen men. If people would stop interfering and leave it to me, I will find out exactly what happened. And please inform the reporters and the police that my wife will not be giving interviews. I will not have people using her to further their own interests.'

'Best you tell them that yourself. And, by the way, you owe me a hundred pounds.'

'What! What for?'

'For the reward. I had to offer and pay a reward of a hundred pounds for information leading to—'

'You paid someone a hundred pounds for doing their civic duty? Are you mad, man? My God, is it any wonder this country is so backward with politicians flinging money about like that?'

'A gentleman would repay a debt like this without a quibble, Horwood.'

'Rubbish!' Lyle watched Constance walk towards the door with Mrs Kassel. She was walking quite well, nothing wrong with her at all. She was a strong young woman, healthy as a horse. He'd soon shift the 'nerves' after he'd heard the full story of what really went on with those men. From go to whoa. From the minute the men had taken her from the cabin, where she'd been imprisoned with the other women.

Was it really for money? Or was there something going on with her and Officer Tussup? One of the policemen had actually asked him how long she'd known Tussup. Made you think.

He was so wrapped in his own thoughts, he finished his brandy and left the kitchen, and the three people still in there, without a backward glance.

'You're lucky I was able to bring most of our luggage from the ship,' Lyle told her, as he hung up his dressing gown and brushed his hair. 'Why don't you get into bed?'

Constance didn't seem to be listening, so he went over to her. 'Are you intending to sit in that armchair for the rest of the night?'

She shook her head. 'I didn't talk to them. I wouldn't speak to them for a long time.'

'Why? What did they want to know?'

'I don't know.' She curled back into the armchair.

'Where did they land the longboat?'

'A beach, I think. It's hard to remember and that's where I wouldn't speak to them.'

He sat on the end of the bed, trying to get some sense out of her. Who cared if she didn't speak to them? Probably they didn't either.'

'Where did you sleep?'

'I can't think. I was tired all the time. Where is Mrs Willoughby? The Chinese lady? Is she staying here too?'

'No, she drowned. If you landed on the beach at Cooktown, what were you doing wandering through the bush, where you got all the cuts and bruises on your arms and legs?'

'They dragged me in there.'

'Why?'

'I can't remember.'

'That's convenient,' he said, suspicion nagging him. Lewis had said they got little out of her about the days of her captivity, and he wasn't faring much better. He decided to get firm with her.

'Where's your dress?' he asked sternly. 'The red dress you were wearing when they put you in the longboat?'

She looked down and fingered the nightdress Mrs Kassel had laid out for her, and seemed confused. 'My dress. I don't know. Yes, they cut it with a knife.'

'They cut it off you?' Now he was getting somewhere.

'With a knife. I got a fright. I was speaking to them then. I'm tired, Lyle. I wish you'd go away.'

'You were in the bush undressed? With all those men? What did they do to you? You can tell me, I'm your husband.'

'I don't know. I'm tired. They pulled me about. Gave me dirty slippers, treated me like a coolie woman. Did you say the Chinese girl drowned? That can't be true! You're lying to me! She got away from them.'

'Quieten down, woman. You'll wake the whole hotel. As if you haven't caused enough trouble as it is. We'll finish our talk in the morning. Get up and get into bed.'

Obediently she walked over, pulled back the sheet and went to climb into bed, but he stopped her. 'You've forgotten, I don't like you wearing nighties in bed. It's a hot night. Take it off.'

She unbuttoned the gown, took it off and dropped it on a chair, then she slipped into the bed, immediately curling up to sleep. Lyle had been missing her lovely youthful body beside him but as his hand slid over her hips and across her stomach, he felt a lurch of revulsion. Would she ever tell the truth about those nights in the bush? Could he ever be sure the Asians hadn't got at her? Or Tussup? She'd avoided mentioning him, hadn't she?'

He drew his hand away and sat up. 'What about Tussup? What was he doing all this time?'

'We ran away.'

'Who? You and Tussup?'

'Yes,' she said drowsily. 'We ran away.'

Chapter Eight

Jake may have walked all that way from Goulburn to Sydney as a kid. Walked it along sandy roads under a sunny blue sky. But this! This track over the range was a nightmare.

No sooner had he set off than drizzling rain started to fall. Not that rain bothered him – it was to be expected in the tropics – but this track through the jungle was slippery, littered with damp steaming leaves. He couldn't risk injury to the horse, so he slowed it to a walk and kept going as grey, sodden daylight emerged through the dark canopy of trees.

With the light came other travellers. Ghostly figures, hooded from the rain with blankets and oilskins, stepped out of the forest to continue the trek. There was no chat, no camaraderie. This was tense, serious business. Determination pushed, passed, shoved, as the track worsened, rising into the foothills. Men dragged handcarts laden with necessities; they marched head down with swags on their backs. Ahead Jake came across a family lodged in a wagon with a broken axle, but like the others on the track he kept going. A long line of Chinese coolies jogged along beside him, baskets balanced on their shoulders, looking neither to the left nor the right, so he urged his horse faster to be rid of them – reminding himself that Bartie Lee would be travelling like this, with servants, as he had planned, to carry and cook and dig for him.

When the sun came out, he stopped by the wayside for a quick meal. Jake was used to heat, the dry heat of his hometown and the humidity of Asian ports like Singapore or Batavia, but he was aware that heat would be the least of his problems in this torrid wilderness. Beginning with the grey snake that swished through the grass by his foot. He would have to keep his eyes open.

Soon he was riding again, moving faster on some patches of track that suddenly swept into open country, desperate to get this ride over with as soon as possible. Then he began the climb into the hills until dusk found him at a busy camping ground. It crossed his mind that he must have made only an average run of the first day, since so many others called a halt here, and he resolved to do better the next day.

Not needing to meet or talk to anyone, he set up a small camp apart from the others, and when he'd eaten he stamped out the fire and laid his bedroll between the jutting roots of an ancient tree. He was just dozing off when he heard screams and shouts coming from the nearby camp, so he remained very still, lost in the shadows. Shots were fired, a woman shrieked, feet pounded on the heavy ground, pandemonium was let loose.

Jake guessed by this what had happened. The whore, Madelene, had warned him. So he stayed low. If blackfellows were on the warpath he figured he was safer right where he was.

Sure enough, in the morning he heard that two men had been speared, killed by blacks in a sneak attack; another took a spear in his chest and wasn't expected to live, there being no doctor around to give an opinion.

'I heard shooting. Did they get any of the blacks?'

'We don't know,' he was told. 'No one's game enough to go into that dense bush to find out.'

Jake shrugged. Running this gauntlet was no joke. What would happen on the return journey, he wondered. What if you came back with gold? Blackfellows wouldn't be the only danger. Any one of these bastards, white or yellow, would cut your throat for gold. There had to be an answer to that one. He'd have to find out in time.

As he kept going on this wretched muddy route, he came across people too sick to travel, cut down by fevers or influenza; suffering snakebites, all sorts of ailments, or injured in fights that were many and frequent – first fights, gun fights, all part of this contest, this struggle to reach the gold before it disappeared. None of it interested Jake. He heard it all but trained himself not to look left or right, no matter how pitiful the sight. He pushed on and days later he had passed the Battle Camp Range and left the jungle behind him. Now he was riding through more familiar bushlands, big open country, cattle country, he guessed, headed for Maytown, the second prospectors' camp that had grown into a sort of village, not unlike the chaos of Cooktown. Further on, he heard, there was another camp called Palmerville, but this would do for now.

Exhilaration surged through him! He couldn't believe he'd finally made it to a real live goldfield, where pots of gold lay about waiting to be sifted from the riverbed or dug from the ground! He threw aside his exhaustion, broke the promise to himself that as soon as he arrived he'd throw himself in the river to cool down and clean up, and went in search of the Gold Commissioner's office where he bought a licence under the name of Rory Moore.

'Occupation?'

'Occupation?' he echoed. 'Uh . . . farmer.'

'Righto. Where you from?'

Where was he from? Jake had been away from this country for years. He plucked the first name that came into his head.

'Goulburn. Yes, sir, Goulburn.'

One of these days he'd go back there. He owned that farm now; his own property. He'd set the deeds to rights years ago.

'You want to register a claim too?' the clerk asked.

'No. Haven't picked a spot yet. Where do you reckon's a good place to start?'

The clerk shrugged. 'Buggered if I know. Here's your licence.'

Days later Bartie Lee and his squad trekked over the range in the midst of a large contingent of Chinese. If the Chinese noticed that he and some of his men were Malays, they didn't seem to care, too intent on their own progress. There were so many that they suffered the whips of horsemen for crowding the track, and threats from wagoners who were having enough difficulty hauling supplies without being slowed up by hundreds of unwanted 'Chinks'.

Bartie soon learned that the Chinese were unwilling to give way from the actual track and go up through the bush because such short cuts were too dangerous. They were soon pounced on and killed by lurking blackfellows who often tied the bodies to trees as a warning to travellers.

He had warned his men that they would have to change their names to avoid discovery.

'That's easy, see. Then we'll all be free as birds. No policemen chasing us. They too busy chasing them big bad mutiny men.'

But as they continued the climb, it wasn't so easy after all, because they kept forgetting one another's new names, Bartie himself being the worst offender. Then his three Chinese, the former stewards, disappeared in the night.

'Blackfellows got them,' Mushi said juicily. 'Chop 'em up and hang bits on trees back there. You bet.'

But their own men knew better.

'No. They don't want police after them. They say they not mutiny men if they be Chinese again. They gone with the China coolies.'

Bartie was furious but he knew he'd never find them. They'd be well hidden in the ranks of fellow countrymen.

'Ah, who needs them?' he snarled.

But that wasn't the end of his wily stewards. They were unhappy about being stuck with Bartie Lee as boss after Jake disappeared with the woman, so they entered into negotiations with a Chinese boss they met on the track, and soon the deal was struck.

He had brought his men into Cooktown legally, having registered their entry at the customs office by the wharf, so he would simply add their three (new) names to the list.

'No one will notice a few more,' he informed them sedately. 'And possibly some of my men will die before we get out of this place.'

In return for this great favour, they informed the boss that Bartie Lee was carrying a significant amount of money stolen from the ship. They knew he had twice as much as the amount he shared with them. No one had expected him to be that truthful! And having handed out the money to his crew he began charging them for daily food.

After a particularly hard day, Bartie and his team slept heavily by the track, aided by cheap whisky, while three stealthy Chinese raided his camp. They went straight for his swag, where he always hid money, and for his boots, white men's boots, where he kept the rest, being careful, and disappeared into the darkness.

It was hours into the day, when they were descending the range, before Bartie discovered the theft and began screaming at Mushi, who in turn blamed their crewmen. The money was never found and trust between them had taken a severe battering.

Bartie insisted they now pool their money, and they went in search of somewhere to start digging, very much intimidated by the goldfields, a huge landscape, recklessly pockmarked by shafts and pits. Grey tents slung among the ugly mounds of red dirt, cringed under the hard sun, and the now-famous river, meandering among all this, seemed something of an afterthought.

Bartie wanted to get as close to the river as possible but they couldn't find a space without being told to 'bugger off' by irate miners. Then they got the same reaction from Chinese, when they wandered into their camps, astonished to see Chinese were so organised, with armed guards patrolling their areas. Finally they decided to follow the river until they did find a spot, ending up more than a mile from the central point, a village called Maytown.

Miners glared at them as they sat down.

'We don't want no Chinks here,' they shouted, 'Bugger off!'

'See,' Bartie said to Mushi. 'This is why I wanted Tussup with us. He'd keep those pigs away.'

'Not Chinese, sir,' he said, bowing. 'Good Malayamen. Very clean.'

'Ah, bugger off,' came the indifferent response, so Bartie decided to ignore them. At the same time Mushi was clearing waist-high grass with practised slashes of his machete, so they could make camp. And Bartie guessed that display of sharp steel wouldn't go amiss. They would not be moved from their chosen golden ground.

He folded his arms and stood proudly on the riverbank, lord of his little domain, on the threshold of riches beyond measure.

Dawn brought clatter and a clamour of excitement for a new day. No one dallied. Never was the first flutter of sunlight received with such enthusiasm as along the banks of this river of gold. Bartie had heard that one ton of gold had already been drawn from here, and duly noted by the Gold Commissioner as he collected his excise, and that was apart from the heaps that the Chinese were spiriting out of the country. Bartie had already decided to follow the latter trend; he saw no reason why he should pay duty on the gold he found.

Instead of being Bossman, as he'd planned, standing watch over his workers, Bartie was down there with the best of them, working as hard as the others, frantic to find the precious, elusive gold. He had built a long sloping trough through which they poured buckets of water to separate gold from sand and gravel, and followed up with fine sieves to make doubly sure, while a few yards away he'd instructed Mushi to start digging. He was going at this business carefully, trying both the riverbed and a mine.

By midday they'd found a few grains of alluvial gold and he was hopping about like a flea on fire, rattling the gold in a matchbox, and plunging back into the river to dig out the soil.

'Hey, you there!'

Bartie looked up to see a man in a black uniform standing over them and his heart sank. Police! They'd caught up with them already! He was so shocked he almost reached for his machete, ready to attack anybody who tried to prise him away from his goldmine.

'You got a licence to dig here?'

'Licence, sir? No. What is this?'

'If you and your mates haven't got miners' tickets, you get out of here before I lock you up.'

'Ticket, sir? What is this?'

The officer explained they all needed tickets and they had to register this claim, insisting they hand over two pounds, which Bartie did willingly, not caring that their pool of funds was dangerously low. He would have handed over the lot if need be. He wondered what Jake called himself now, since he too would have had to give a name to comply with this unexpected law. Once he got the mining organised he'd have to look for that double-crossing son-of-a-bitch.

Soon they were back at work, keeping at it non-stop until darkness forced them to give up. Bartie allocated himself the job of searching for the gold in the sieves, squatting in the shallows, day after day, adding the specks and grains of alluvial gold to the little round matchbox, not bothering to mention he had another matchbox. This one he kept behind the bark of a tree that he leaned against when he went back into the bush to piss.

When the second matchbox was needed for the collection of shared gold, matchboxes being in great demand, he transferred his private store into a battered leather pouch he'd found on a track. It was slow going, very little result for the long hard hours, but none of them minded. This was a game, a chase, and they would not stop until the race was run. Or so they thought.

It was Mushi who caused the trouble. At night he would go off on his own, prowling the squalid alleys that were home to opium and gambling dens, sly groggers and whores, and make his own money slitting pockets and purses with a sharp knife. These earnings bought him grog, and cheap Asian whores, but he longed for a white woman like that Mrs Horwood from the ship. A woman with the smooth skin, soft boobies and fair hair.

Then one night, in the grip of the fiery liquor miners produced from potatoes, Mushi saw her. He ran stumbling after her but she disappeared behind the tea tree fence that surrounded a latrine for women.

'Better still,' he muttered. 'Better still. I get her all to myself.'

She fought him, biting and scratching, a bad thing for a lady to do, a wrong thing, proving she was no different from whores the world over, so he whacked her across the jaw to make her behave and then it was all right. He gave her good and plenty, shoving her into a muddy corner when he was finished, and she spat at him, so he yanked her hair up and hacked at it with his good sharp knife.

Violence was rife in the shanty town. Jake was hardly surprised that drunken scraps and race fights were daily events, that women mad enough to come to this roughhouse were bashed and occasionally one who hadn't learned to defend herself was raped.

He was drinking with a few blokes one night when he heard of the latest rape. Heard that the rapist had hacked her hair.

Mushi, he thought. It sounds like the handiwork of that bastard Mushi. So they're here. I wonder where?

He'd staked a claim on an old mine, already two feet deep, and begun digging, so far without any success, but it was early days. He had sold the horse and now rarely moved far from his site, pitching his tent beside the shaft. But the more he thought of Bartie Lee and his gang breathing down his neck, the more he worried.

'I'd better find them before they find me.'

Systematically he began the search, unable to ask if anyone knew them, relying on his knowledge of the night haunts that would attract them. This seemed to him to be the only safe course, since he wouldn't dare go marching about looking for them in broad daylight. Besides, he had better things to do with the daylight hours.

Night after night, with a heavy scarf draped over his head, he sat in the darkness by a sly grog shop like one of the derelicts who'd lost their way in the turmoil, watching passers-by as they stepped into the light of hanging lanterns. Eventually one of the Malay crewmen came by, confirming Jake's guess that Bartie's gang had made it to the Palmer. The man's wanderings seemed aimless, except for the foul-smelling soup he bought from a wayside vendor, but Jake followed doggedly until he was led to Bartie's camp.

The next day he hurried back, taking a risk, but he needed daylight to note the location and registration number of the claim, which they had dutifully displayed according to law. He was surprised to see that there were only Malays in the camp, none of the Chinese crewmen, and figured that they must have split up.

But it wasn't smart to hang about the vicinity so he took off, found pen and paper and wrote down Mushi's name and location. Then he headed back to the grog shop, idly asked about the woman who was raped, and whose hair had been cut by her attacker.

He paid an urchin to run to her, give her the note and tell her this was her attacker, then he went back to his mine, and more important problems. It was time to find some timber to brace the walls of the mine so that he could dig deeper. So far he'd coped on his own and though he knew partners were a much-needed safety measure for underground work, he still balked at the idea. Jake was a loner. The lad had once known the warmth of a loving family unit, but that warmth had been tragically snatched from him, sucked out of him as if there were bellows at work, so the man was cold. Indifferent. He'd always shrugged off shipboard friendships and gone his own way in port. This new life, this solitary mining job, appealed to him. He didn't have to talk to people, answer poking questions, listen to their pap, or just bloody put up with them.

He walked to the timber mill at the edge of the bush and ordered the supports he needed.

'Can't help you, mate,' the owner said. 'Can't keep up with the demand. But my loggers will bring in another load tomorrow. Come back then. I'll set some aside for you.'

Jake watched a ferry being hauled across the river, and studied the diggings on the other side.

'What's out there?' he asked. 'What's out past all these camps?'

'Nothing much. Cattle country.'

'Are there farms out there?'

'Nah, but cattlemen are moving up all the time.'

'How can they drive cattle over that range?'

'They don't. They overland them. Bring them up from the south.'

Jake was interested. 'So there's an inland road?'

The timberman laughed. 'Not so's you'd notice. But the men who explored this here country and found gold, they come up inland. Bloody long way. There's a settlement at Georgetown, a couple of hundred tough miles from here, nothing in between. But the squatters are fanning out from Georgetown now, grabbin' land by the hundred square mile,' he grinned. 'And good luck to them, I say.'

Jake was thoughtful as he strode away. He hadn't realised there was a back door to this place. It could come in handy. 'Very bloody handy,' he muttered, searching for his tobacco tin.

* * *

The girl was a butcher's daughter. Her father and his partner worked in their mine by day and in their butchery cum-sly grog shop by night. His daughter, his pride and joy, worked hard too. She cleaned and cooked for the men during the day and served in the rickety shop until midnight, when her daddy closed down. Her name was Cora.

At about eleven o'clock this night, a woman found her, the thin little thing, in a sobbing heap by the tea tree fence.

She ran across the lane to the butcher.

'It's your Cora,' she said, 'she's in trouble.'

'Where is she? We'll be closing up soon, I want her to . . . what sort of trouble?'

'Come quick!'

They swore you could hear his bellow of pain and rage clear across the settlement when he came upon Cora. He picked her up gently and carried her back to his camp behind the shop. For the sake of delicacy, he asked the woman to clean her up, wash off the dirt, and get rid of the torn clothes . . . 'and talk to her, willya? You can ask her things I can't, if you see what I mean. I want to know exact. What happened to her, and who done this, by Jesus!'

He closed the shop and waited anxiously, wringing his hands. He knew in his heart she'd been raped, but prayed it was not so. His mind ran to the consequences of rape. Cora was a timid girl. She'd had the fright of her life. And what if the animal made her pregnant?

'Oh, Jesus!' he wept.

'How long you gonna be in there?' he called.

His daughter had been beaten and viciously raped. She was incoherent with terror. She had a broken nose, two broken fingers, obviously from trying to fight him off, and, the woman guessed, a couple of busted ribs.

'I'll get her a cup of gin to calm her down,' she said, and hurried away.

The butcher took down his rifle and loaded it. He patted her on the head. 'Don't you be fearful no more. Your daddy won't let no one hurt you. I'll stay right here all night.'

It was daylight when he looked down at Cora, saw the sadly bruised face, and the ruins of her silky blonde hair . . .

He had to rush out of the tent to contain his rage, for fear of waking the poor girl.

'How is she?' his partner asked, but the butcher shook his head. 'I'll kill the bastard.'

The rape was reported. A policeman began enquiring. At the insistence of the butcher and an outraged community, two mounted police, who'd been posted to Maytown only two days ago, were instructed to ferret out the rapist. But a week had passed, there was no sign of an arrest and the butcher was calling them incompetents.

Then Cora, a large red handkerchief tied around her head, brought the note to her daddy because she could not read.

'What?' he shouted. 'What's this?'

He threw down his spade and called his partner out of the mine. Other miners gathered as they pored over this stroke of luck. Then more folk gathered, women, and kids too.

And there was a shout: 'Let's get him. Hang the bastard!'

The miners knew the layout. They soon tracked down this claim. An angry crowd led by the butcher and his unwilling, petrified daughter, converged on Bartie Lee's mine, dragging out all five Asians. They lashed the protesting men together and pushed Cora forward to look at them.

'Was it these blokes, Cora?' people called out to her. 'Was it them?'

She shook her head mournfully. 'No, it wasn't them.'

She heard a sigh of disappointment, and looked straight at Mushi. For all the darkness and the fury of that night, she knew him; she could still smell his breath and feel those coarse stubby fingers. The shape of his head was imprinted on her brain like one of those cut-out silhouettes so popular at fairs.

'It was him!' she spat, raising her hand to point at Mushi as she backed away from him, the proximity rekindling terror.

Uproar! Bartie and his men were dragged, screaming, to a tree and bound to the trunk while his camp was ransacked and his equipment wrecked. There were calls to 'hang the bastards' while a petrified Bartie Lee was shouting for a 'fair go', an Australian expression he'd picked up from Jake.

Some more moderate souls in the crowd heard him and agreed. They took advantage of the lack of suitable sturdy trees for a hanging. The mining landscape was all but shorn of trees; the one they were bound to had been stripped of its branches, so there was talk of taking them into the bush and getting the job done, until a young fellow stepped forward.

'She only pointed to one of those blokes, not all of them. Was it one or all, miss?'

'One,' she whispered, turning away in shame.

'There you go then. We've got him. We can't hold the other four.'

'You can't hold any of them!' A mounted trooper muscled his horse through the mob. 'What's going on here?'

'They gonna kill us,' Bartie wailed. 'He done it, this bloke here, Mushi, he done it, he root her and chop off her hair. We done nothing, us, we done nothing!'

The crewmen beside him chorused their innocence too, and the trooper ordered them cut loose, but the butcher grabbed Mushi.

'This is the bastard. He violated my Cora. He's gotta hang.'

'No!' Mushi screamed. 'Not me, mister. She got wrong this. It was Bartie over there. Bartie Lee.'

Too late, Bartie realised that in the heat of the moment they'd been using their real names, not the carefully learned new names.

'Shut up!' he screamed at Mushi. 'Shut your mouth. Wrong names, you bit of shit.'

Mushi didn't care, he continued jabbering his accusations but the butcher solved the problem for Bartie by smashing Mushi in the mouth with an iron fist.

The trooper dismounted and called to the crowd to disperse as he pulled Mushi to his feet, ignoring his bloodied face, and tied his hands together. He went over to the girl standing by the butcher.

'This him, Cora?' he asked kindly.

She nodded.

'I'm terribly sorry, miss. But he won't bother you again, you can count on that.'

'And you can count on me making bloody sure you're right,' her father said with a parting shove at Mushi.

The trooper was cheered as he rode through the town with his prisoner running alongside.

The four men, remnants of the mutineer party, cursed Mushi as they ran back to the ruined camp. The damage wasn't as bad as they'd first thought, so they looked to Bartie as he stood scratching his head, unable to work out what to do next.

Bartie had come to the end of his rope. He knew his job on ships, all plain routine to him, but he wasn't equipped for strategy. He did not know what to do next, any more than he'd known how to acquire blackmail money once he'd captured the rich lady. His crewmen were standing huddled together as if in a storm, looking to him for guidance. Mushi had brought this trouble down on them. They'd only been tolerated by men on neighbouring claims before this, but they could be in real danger now. They knew white men didn't need an excuse to attack them if they felt like it, and Mushi had fuelled the fire. So what to do now? Should they move? Get a claim way over the other side, out of the way where they wouldn't be so well known? But there was a trickle of gold here. Or should they leave this place while they could? Mushi and Bartie Lee, both, had shouted out their true names. The very thing they'd ordered this trio not to do, under pain of a beating. Would the police be searching for them now for abducting the woman? And what about Ah Kee? They'd have found his body by this time.

Bartie Lee was aware of these concerns; they were fogging up his brain so much he simply couldn't see what to do.

In the end he did nothing. Nothing really. He just started tidying up the camp, putting everything in place, shrugging at ripped canvas, a familiar chore there, and his men took his lead, satisfied, thinking he'd made the decision. Soon they were prospecting again. Everything was back to normal. Mushi was gone. Forgotten.

Jake soon heard the rapist had been captured, fingered by the butcher's daughter and taken down to Cooktown, despite the protests of miners who wanted the yellow bastard hung right there on the spot. He nodded, satisfied, and went back to bracing the walls of his mine with timber stays, reminded of the times he'd had to brace the timbers of leaking ships with panicky crews.

But then he put the *China Belle* and her company behind him. He'd started another life, he was a prospector, his own boss. He worked out a rigid routine and kept to it – digging and sluicing at intervals, breaking occasionally to rest his eyes, not wasting a minute of daylight.

Days turned into weeks and he was still slogging away, still keen, but he hadn't turned out even a glimpse of 'colour'. Not that he was despairing . . . Jake was thoroughly enjoying himself, the excitement was all round him. Every so often there'd be shouts of joy when someone struck gold, and he'd feel a shiver down his spine, the sort of shiver a gambler gets when he passes by a racecourse. Every time that happened, Jake promised himself he wouldn't be shouting when he found gold, he'd shut up, keep it quiet. There was no law said you would have to advertise, he'd tell himself. What he did and what he didn't do was his own business. No, he'd stay on the job until he got every speck out, until he'd made his fortune, and then he'd find another claim.

He laughed as he plunged his pick into the grey wall at the head of the narrow corridor he'd burrowed into the earth. He wasn't about to be just rich, he would be filthy rich. He wouldn't be leaving the Palmer until he was sure all the gold was taken out. So far, word had it that two tons of gold had passed through the Commissioner's office and there was still no sign of the output decreasing.

Having settled on his plans and attitudes, Jake was hard at work one morning when he saw that gleam, the one they talked about, that colour, and he shook with anxiety and anticipation as he dusted and scratched around it with his bare hands, dazzled as a lump of gold began to appear. He tore it from its ancient bed, a dusty glittering lump as big as the top of his thumb! He tore himself from his gloomy excavation and dashed into the sunlight, his planned attitude forgotten.

His neighbours grinned and cheered and clapped as Rory Moore capered about the nearby shafts and sluices, waving his prize. Several miners edged into his mine to note the spot and give him advice on where and how to proceed, but one man stayed behind to examine the walls.

'I'm Theodore Tennent,' he said, scratching and prodding, causing little landslides, worrying Jake. 'I'm from Sydney Town. I'm over the back of you here. My claim. You keep going this way and you'll meet me. Now I propose we amalgamate. We could have a reef here. I've taken out stones like that,' he pointed to the treasure Jake still held in his hand, 'so there's good reason to believe we're on to something big. I say we go partners, work together, and we can really scour the area.'

Jake climbed out of the mine and Theodore followed. 'What do you say?'

'I'll think about it.'

'Fair enough. Don't leave it too long. Quite a few claims are merging these days.'

'Yeah,' Jake rolled a cigarette, holding the paper in his mouth, and as he looked up he saw Raymond Lewis walking towards him. Raymond Lewis! From *China Belle*!

He dropped the paper and began walking to the rear of his mine. 'Round here?' he asked Theodore. 'This your mine? Let's have a look.'

The miner, a slight man with the physique of a jockey, darted forward. 'Yes. Come on. I reckon I'm working on much the same level as you so far, but I've widened the base. Been here longer.'

Jake dived into the mine and let Theodore talk, asked exactly where he'd found his gold and searched about himself, as if he might discover a reef the owner had overlooked.

When eventually they emerged, the danger seemed to have passed: there was no sign of Lewis.

'Well, what do you say?' Tennent asked again.

'I'll think about it,' Jake told him and hurried back to the safety of his mine, staying underground until the protection of darkness.

There was no need for him to wonder about Lewis's presence. He was nattily dressed like one of those explorers or big-game hunters you saw in the newspapers, white pith helmet and all.

'Bloody hell,' he spat as he stayed in his tent that night, comforting himself with a shot of rum that was originally bought and held for celebration, to mark the occasion of the first gold strike. Now the celebration was ruined. He supposed they'd found Mrs Horwood by now. Unless Bartie Lee had caught her. That set his heart thumping. What if they had? Jesus! He should have stayed with her.

'How could I?' he asked himself. 'I lost her.'

But there was no way they could have dragged the woman all the way out here, he reasoned. Impossible on that dangerous and busy track. So one way or another she must have been left in Cooktown. He thought of Mushi and the butcher's daughter, and his blood ran cold.

They had Mushi. He'd talk. Soon they'd be after the rest of them. He'd have to keep totally out of sight or leave the Palmer. Run for it, go south on that inland route. But wait on, he'd only deserted the ship, he hadn't kidnapped the women. And he'd helped Mrs Horwood. He'd kept their hands off her.

She could tell them that. She'd speak up for him. The woman hated him, that was understandable, but she wouldn't lie. Yes, he thought, feeling a little calmer, she wouldn't lie. If asked, she'd have to speak up for him. If she were still alive.

He couldn't think of a way to find out, short of collaring one of Mushi's men and questioning him. Which would set Bartie Lee on his track. And the police. He wanted to see if Bartie and his mates had been picked up yet, on Mushi's evidence, but dared not venture in that direction. In any direction, he corrected himself. I'll have to keep my head down now, with Lewis marching about. Maybe a partner will be a good idea. If I throw in my lot with Tennent, he can be my runner. Get supplies and so on, stay up there while I work underground.

Jake was truly rattled, knowing Lewis could identify him. He hated the idea of a partner, but it might be the only way to stay out of sight.

At first light, Jake shaved the stubbly beard that he'd allowed to grow. Lewis had only seen him with the mariner's full beard. But then he felt the small gold nugget in his pocket and forgot his worries. He had more important matters to think about.

Bartie fretted about that potato-head Mushi. They'd hang him, all right, but before they did, the police would know everything there was to know. He and his men worked feverishly, digging deeper and deeper into the earth, finding pebbles to add to their treasure tin, but so far, no gold stones. For fear of being attacked by the surly white men who surrounded them, they spent most of their time underground. They slept and ate in their musty lamp-lit cave, coiled into blankets like a nest of snakes.

For the life of him, Bartie couldn't think how to beat the police. Any minute he expected them to look up over his claim and arrest them all. He became so panicky he forbade his men to come out of the mine at all, in case they were recognised. It was curious how the butcher and his mates had come straight for Mushi, as if someone had fingered him. One of the Chinese crewmen? Had they seen him attack that girl? Or Jake? he asked himself, never forgetting that Jake was here somewhere.

Other miners were doing well. Some were better than others. The gold was everywhere and anywhere. So why keep on at this one? They should up and run, grab another pitch away from here. But there are four of them. The police and troopers had spies. They'd soon track four Malayamen, no matter where they camped.

'That pig Mushi,' Bartie muttered. 'I hope he's suffering in the lockup now, for causing me this trouble. I hope they flog the skin off him.'

He supposed he could bolt on his own, take the tins of gold pebbles and go, but they'd still look for him, and they'd arrest his own crewmen – weak pissy lot they were, ignorant coolies – to help them search for him. He blamed Jake for this mess. If it hadn't been for Jake's idea of deserting the ship, they wouldn't be here at all. But then he thought of all the gold lying about waiting, all these riches just waiting to be picked up, like in a dream, and he shook his head.

No. A thousand no's. He'd have killed to get here and he'd do it all again.

Killed? There was a thought. A good one. He slid down the pole into the mine and ran through the cave to the down-sloping tunnels beyond. At the end, the coolies were digging into the walls as he'd ordered them to do, making three separate alcoves, just big enough to crawl into, spreading out the search.

He kicked at each one, shouting at them to keep up, that they were too slow, that there was plenty of gold for all.

'You can't see the gold. You all dumb-blind if you can't see it like the white men. You get harder at it, use them little picks. Find the gold and we all go home rich.'

He grinned as they flung themselves at the walls, lifting their small oil-lamps to peer at the rock, and, sitting back on their dusty haunches to continue the search.

That night he kept them working until they were ready to collapse, with the promise of a bottle of overproof rum for the first one to find more colour, and though no one did, he opened the bottle anyway. They soon demolished it, and Bartie was feeling a little less despondent by the time they shared out the rice supper, so he blew out the lamp and told them to sleep.

'Get plenty sleep,' he told them. 'We all need plenty sleep. Work hard tomorrow. Me, I dig another tunnel, that way, tomorrow, I show you how to dig. Bartie go faster than any of you, I bet.'

Trooper Tim Walsh shoved Mushi into the Maytown lockup. He couldn't make sense of the Asian fellow's jabbering so he called on a Chinaman to translate.

The Chinaman said Mushi was a Malayaman, he spoke a language unknown to this connoisseur of many Chinese dialects, so he could not help. But when he left, the prisoner calmed down and startled Tim by suddenly whimpering in English.

'I do not do that bad thing, kind sir. I am a good man. You must let me go.'

'Not a chance,' Tim said. 'What's your name?'

'Why you want to know my name?'

'Because I do, for Christ's sake. Don't be bloody stupid. What's your name?'

The prisoner shuddered, shook his head. 'Can't remember.'

'You can't remember your own name? Are you mad or something? Give me your name or I'll knock your block off!'

He emphasised the threat by punching the prisoner in the head, causing him to fall to the dirt floor screaming for mercy.

Tim rubbed sore knuckles, making a mental note to use his cosh when interrogating these fellows in future, and kicked him in the ribs. 'Name? What name you, you greasy git?'

'No name, you hang me! No name, sir. Me not touch them women. All lies.'

It occurred to Tim, who was new to the north and had not actually come across Asian natives before, that they would have different practices from that of civilised folk. And for all he knew, they might not use names like we do. But . . . anyway, he didn't have time to deal with this so he gave the wretch a name. The first thing that came into his head. He called him after his favourite food; wrote in the register: 'Lam Fry. Rapist.'

There were several tracks over the range. Eager prospectors were too impatient to keep in line behind burdened climbers and slow wagons, and they resented having to pull aside to make way for downhill traffic, so they established new routes.

Sergeant Gooding sent men out to warn travellers to stick together.

'It's not called Battle Camp Range for nothing,' he told Lewis, who had come back after delivering Mrs Horwood to her husband in Cairns. 'The first miners had a helluva fight on their hands trying to get through. A camp halfway up the track was attacked by a mob of blacks. They had the miners bailed up for days, picking them off with spears, and would have wiped the whole camp out if reinforcements hadn't arrived with more ammunition to chase the buggers away.'

'I suppose the blacks are quieter now?'

'You mean now that they've found out about guns? No, they're just more careful, no more frontal attacks like that camp battle. They're more cunning, and bloody dangerous.' He pushed his hat back and scratched his head.

'It's bloody impossible to protect people on that track. Too many are getting killed, but what can I do? They just have to take their chances.'

'I still have to get to those goldfields,' Lewis said.

'What? Last night you agreed to stay in Cooktown.'

'One didn't feel up to arguing, Sergeant. It is imperative that I set out immediately. We know the mutineers will all be there. I simply have to point them out. If necessary I shall go alone.'

Gooding shrugged. 'What do you mean, "if necessary"? Were you expecting me to provide you with an escort?'

'You seem to have forgotten my deputies. They came with the specific purpose of finding and arresting the mutineers. You have had their assistance for weeks, but now that I am back I require their company. I simply hope you do not force me to go alone.'

'All right, take them, but you keep in mind they're civilians, volunteers.

They're your responsibility, Mr Lewis. You better make bloody sure they know what they're getting into.'

Hector Snowbridge was willing to accompany Raymond to the Palmer, but Trooper Poole flatly refused.

'Whoa!' he called, as Raymond was issuing his instructions. 'No fear! You know what they call that track? Blood and mud! I said I'd come here to look for your mutineers, but wild horses wouldn't get me into that blackfellow country.'

'We might pick up a bit of gold for ourselves,' Hector said slyly.

'And we might not too. More likely a boomerang in our skulls. There's gold at Charters Towers, and a good safe track out there from the coast if folk want to have a go. Only a madman would take on the Palmer!'

'Precisely,' Raymond said. 'And that's where we'll find our mutineers.'

'Not me, mate. Count me out.'

Poole turned and strode away.

'It seems, then, it's just us,' Raymond said to Hector, 'so we might as well pack up and be off. Jolly good of you to stick with me.'

They were sleeping soundly, all three of them, as Bartie slid from his blanket and crept along the tunnel in total darkness. He knew exactly where he was going, and he had to hurry. The last few hours had been sheer terror for him, time crawling past. Every little sound – a rat scratching, a loose funnel of dust sliding down the walls, a crumble from an uneven roof – brought the fear out in him, fear that he might have overdone it when he loosened the already poorly constructed slats that held the walls at bay.

He was breathing heavily, almost snorting like a horse, when he yanked the main support aside, the one at the entrance to the cavern where the men slept . . . and ran for his life ahead of the collapse, from the sudden heave of earth as the mine caved in, and the tumult of choking dust that raced after him along the narrow passage to the shaft.

Even here the stays were being dragged down, creaking as they readied to crash, so he shot up the pole like lightning, right into the clean night air, and kept on going.

All was quiet. Sleepers in the dark tents heard nothing. A dog barked fretfully at something untoward, thought better of it and went back to sleep. A flying fox flapped overhead, and Bartie ducked into the bush where he had stashed the gold, and a canvas pack. Then he was gone, walking quickly out of this area, to find a new spot, miles away.

That wasn't too hard after all, he congratulated himself as he put distance between himself and the useless mine.

'I'll get a better one now.'

No one was interested in the Asiatics who worked that mine, after the rapist was taken away. No one really saw much of them. They were a sinister-looking lot, and they stayed underground most of the time, working night and day, people reckoned, burrowing like ferrets, their mine shaft hidden by ever-growing mullock heaps.

No one noticed the depression in the ground, until a heavy shower formed a small pond.

'I seen it days ago,' a miner said. 'Seen it but didn't notice it, if you get my meaning. Didn't put it down to nothing, until today when I saw the dog going there to have a drink and yelled at him to get out of there. Them Chinks eat dogs.'

'They ain't Chinks,' a Welshman called Taffy said, as he stood staring at the abandoned mine. 'They be Asiatic. When did they go?'

'Just in time,' the miner laughed, 'by the look of this. That rain must have undermined all the supports, sunk it all in. Even the shaft's chocablock. But it was never no good, that claim, and I can't say I'm sorry they've moved on, what with my son and his wife coming to join me any day.'

Taffy wandered about the claim, hoping to pick up something useful for his camp, but the Asiatics had only left garbage, rusting pans, worn out slippers, nothing much else except a large pot of stinking rice.

He wasn't surprised, though. 'They travel light, those blokes,' he said. 'Live on the smell of an oily rag.'

Hector Snowbridge's dad, who was a postmaster, always said his son would never amount to anything, and Hector thought that was probably right 'Unless Queen Victoria needs a good stud for one of her fillies,' he would ho-ho.

Hector could always find work, when the urge was upon him. Farm work mainly – milking, fencing, cropping – but there were chores he would draw the line at. After all, he had his pride.

'I don't mind milking, or stable work,' he would inform prospective bosses, 'but I don't clean up no shit after animals. And after human beans neither. Long as we got that straight. I'm no bloody lackey.'

He was easily offended. No slight, even if only perceived, was allowed to pass. Hector took his umbrage seriously. When the Turleys' maid told him to go round to the back door for the mailbag, he quit. When someone sat in his place in the canteen over at Jack Foster's plantation, he sulked, insisting on eating outside for the rest of the week. He was, in fact, a humble man who lacked humility.

But he was on top of the heap now! A deputy – as if that weren't glory enough – but he was set to travel to the Palmer goldfields, on his own, with this important gentleman, a Member of Parliament, no less. Let those blokes back in Cairns put that in their pipes and smoke it!

When they started out along the track, Mr Lewis was leading, but Hector soon set him straight.

'If I'm to be your guard, Mr Lewis, I better be up front. You just take it easy now and follow me.'

Mr Lewis found the going very hard. His gallant little stockhorse was ideal for these conditions, but he was a bony mount and Raymond was sore and sorry by the end of the first day. Nevertheless he pitched in and helped Hector make camp that night, under conditions so dreadful he vowed never to complain about the good ship *Torrens* again. Everywhere they turned, the rainforest seemed to press in on them with its floor of mulch, sticky undergrowth and vast population of flies and stinging insects. They didn't seem to bother Hector, who, on that account, hadn't bothered to pack mosquito nets.

'I hope you're not blaming me, Mr Lewis,' he said ominously. 'It ain't really my job to do the packing.'

'No, no, no. Not at all, Hector. Foolish of me not to have seen to it,' said Raymond, who hadn't thought it was his job either. He'd provided the funds, from his own pocket, it may be remarked, and left the provedoring to Snowbridge.

The muscular, heavy deputy seemed at home squatting on his haunches in an alcove of voracious greenery and meaty vines. He managed a smoky campfire over which he cooked chopped beef and eggs in a sea of lard, while Raymond peeled potatoes to be fried in their turn.

'I'm a good cook, even if I do say so meself,' Hector said proudly, handing Raymond his exact half share of the evening meal, piled on to a tin plate.

The night was excruciating. While Hector snored, stretched out on his oilskin, Raymond's aches were aggravated by the lumpy ground and night chill. He couldn't sleep a wink, what with the mutter of passing marchers, relentless in their efforts to keep going, the thud of their boots, and his battle with the ferocious mosquitoes.

In the morning the cooking utensils were black with ants. Disgusted, Raymond tried to wash them off but Hector laughed.

'Why are you doin' that? The ants'll clean them up.'

And so they progressed. Overnight the meat went off and was discarded. They polished off all the eggs and the bread the next night and by morning the fare was bacon and tea. That night it was cheese and tea.

'Is that all we have?' Raymond asked as he dragged his weary bones into the tent.

'It's all you paid for,' Hector said angrily.

'My dear fellow, had I known more money was required, I'd have gladly paid.'

'There you go! Blaming me again!'

'I wish you would stop saying that. It's quite uncalled for. We're both in the same boat and we just have to make the best of it. Now, while the water in the billy is still hot, would you give that pan a good wash? I'm exhausted, I have to rest.'

'Why me?'

Raymond looked back, bewildered. 'I beg your pardon?'

'Why do I have to clean the frying pan? I did it last night.'

'Oh, for crying out loud! Who cares? Just clean it, please, Hector, I'm too tired to think.'

'No, you're not. You're thinking all the time. You think I'm your servant. Hector do this, and Hector do that. Hobble the horses. Light a fire . . .'

Raymond held up his hand. 'Stop. If you don't want to clean the damned thing then don't. Just stop making such a fuss.'

'I'll do more than stop making such a fuss. I'll quit! How do you like that?'

'Please yourself,' Raymond muttered as he spread out the oilskin ground sheet. He was too tired to care.

Sheer exhaustion gave him sleep and when he awoke his companion was gone. The pan, cleaned, sat outside the tent on the steaming grass. Hector had divided the remaining tea, sugar and rancid cheese into two portions and Raymond's share sat in the pan, wrapped securely in brown paper.

He could not bring himself to ask other travellers for help, so he battled on. Weakened by lack of food, he took longer each day to struggle over the range, until one evening he collapsed on the track when he dismounted from his horse. He awoke to find three women tending him. Three gorgons, he told himself, as he took in their painted, fleshy faces and realised his angels of mercy were prostitutes well past their prime.

But they fed him, cared for him, put him in their pony cart and took the Member of Queensland Parliament on the road with them, entertaining him with bawdy songs and magic tricks.

Raymond sat shivering in the pony cart, suffering, he thought, from influenza, the horse rug that Mal Willoughby had given him wrapped about his sweaty shoulders, and occasionally he slept. And then suddenly he felt better, and overwhelmingly grateful to the women, ashamed that he'd thought of them as gorgons. Embarrassed when one of them – Merle, he thought – asked what a gorgon was.

'I don't know,' he lied.

They packed up his belongings and deposited him at the Maytown office of the Gold Commissioner, a presentable timber building next door to the police station and the lockup.

'You've been very kind, ladies,' Raymond said, unhitching his horse from their cart. 'I am grateful to you.'

'Then you have to come a-calling,' they chorused, and waved him a hearty farewell.

Raymond thought he'd best introduce himself to the Gold Commissioner first, as a matter of protocol, but the clerk told him he was absent.

'Gone down to Cooktown with the gold consignment.'

'Good Lord! Does he take the gold down himself?'

'Yes. With an armed escort but. And he took the rapist, that bloke Lam Fry. You ever heard a name like that in all your born days? Lam Fry! I nearly bust my britches when I saw his papers. But them Chinks, they're a weird lot. There's one bloke here called Ah Choo!' He snorted his merriment and threw in a sneeze to make his point. Raymond backed out the door.

His next official port of call was the police station, where he met a young trooper called Tim, who advised that his superiors were out and went back to contemplating pieces of a jigsaw portraying the Queen in her coronation glory.

'Have you seen a deputy called Hector Snowbridge?'

'The new bloke? Looking for them mutineers? Yeah, he was in here. He went off scouring about, searching for them.'

'I don't see how he could find them,' Raymond sniffed, 'since he has no idea what they look like.'

'He'll do his best,' the trooper retorted, loyal to his kind.

'I'm sure he will,' Raymond muttered, bending down to scratch his legs. They were itching unmercifully from the stings of insects, and he couldn't wait to find a room and slather them in cooling salve. 'Now would you tell your sergeant that Mr Raymond Lewis was here, and wishes to speak with him?'

'Yeah, I'll do that,' Tim said, hovering over the Queen's eye with a likely piece.

'I am a Member of the Queensland Parliament, you may tell him, and should very much appreciate his assistance.'

'Right you are.' The trooper had obviously lost interest in this conversation.

'I need accommodation,' Raymond persisted. 'Could you recommend a place?'

'Depends on what you want to pay. You can get a bed in Ma Perry's dormitory tents down the bottom of the road, or in her log cabins in the paddock at the back.'

'Thank you. I shall go down there and enquire.'

As he left, Tim called after him. 'What did you say your name was?'

'Lewis,' he sighed.

'Righto, Lewis, I'll tell the boss you were here.'

Maytown was crowded. A hectic atmosphere prevailed. Cooktown seemed positively lethargic compared to the rush and dash here. Twice Raymond had almost been skittled by carts as he tramped down the road, leading his horse, to spare his aching back.

The bottom of the road was a half-mile away but Raymond's spirits soared when he saw the new cabins. What bliss to be safe from nature at last with a roof over one's head! And yes, the woman said, pointing, she did have a vacancy.

Disappointment caused his knees to buckle when he opened his door.

The cabin stunk of stale liquor and smelly socks. It contained four bunks, one presently occupied by a snoring sleeper, the others, in disarray, obviously taken.

After negotiations, he managed to obtain a cabin to himself, wherein he paid for all four beds, per week, but she provided breakfast. Satisfied, relieved, Raymond stretched out under a mosquito net and gave himself over to glorious sleep.

The goldfields were as he expected – vast, untidy – the landscape degraded by mullock heaps and ugly timber sluice constructs, and a few miserable trees left to hang disconsolately above the litter of grey tents, waiting maybe, for this misery to end. He could barely glimpse the sluggish brown river, through the widespread crush of this rabble, and felt depressed that its pristine surrounds should be so shockingly despoiled.

Every day since he'd landed in Cooktown, Raymond had been studying faces. Now many of them seemed familiar and that confused him, making his search more difficult. The crewmen and Jake Tussup were here somewhere, and he would find them. Daily he marched in and around a designated section, peering about, asking questions, hoping at least those Malayamen would stand out from the large Chinese population, but they seemed to have disappeared from the face of the earth.

By this time he'd lost a fair amount of weight, and was still feeling rather weak, but he had a job to do and he was determined to carry it out, convinced his search wouldn't take long.

'The country air must agree with me,' he lied in a letter to his sister. 'I am in good health so do not worry. Since I'm looking further and further afield, I get about on horseback. My mount, Jubal, and I, have become great mates. There's no social life here, as you can imagine, but that suits me. I tire at the end of the day, eat a meal at a kitchen-cum-café run by a Greek, read weeks' old newspapers and go to sleep. Please give my regards to the Premier and my thanks for granting me leave of absence from the Parliament.'

He didn't think it was worth mentioning that the lumpy sores on his right leg, caused by insect bites, had cleared up, but two on his left leg were weeping constantly. By the end of the week he could see they were infected so he called on an apothecary for advice.

The gentleman recommended a soap poultice to draw out the pus, and his wife kindly made one and bandaged it on to Raymond's leg, making sure it was secure.

Days later the sore was worse. The landlady noticed him limping, and after some argument, insisted Raymond let her examine the sore that would now not be contained by bandages.

She removed the poultice and shook her head. 'Gawd. You better go back and get him to lance them.'

'What will that do?'

She blinked. 'Cure them, I suppose. That's what they do with those infected sores.'

Raymond was surprised. 'Are they common here?'

'Ah yes. Lotsa folk get them. They can get real nasty.'

The sores had amalgamated and become one. An abscess, the apothecary told him. And the lancing, a painful operation, took place. But while his search for the crew continued, the abscess remained, festering away on his leg, and bleeding so much he'd had to beg clean rags from the landlady. Then a doctor hung up his shingle in Maytown, and Raymond's landlady insisted he get up there.

'A tropical ulcer,' he was told. 'And a nasty one at that.'

The doctor cleaned the wound, dusted it with curative powder and bandaged it again.

'That'll be two and six,' he said, with an eye on the queue gathering outside his tent. 'Here, you can have some of this powder. Keep the sore clean and come back if it hasn't cleared up in a few days.'

Raymond was sure he recognised one of the crewmen, a Chinaman, working by the riverbank with a row of coolies. The man denied any knowledge of the *China Belle*, and his companions ganged up like noisy miner birds to distract him, but Raymond had the trooper pull him in. If he were wrong, he explained, no harm done, but if he were right, this was the break he needed. He was tiring of this job now, his leg a constant concern.

If only he could find Tussup. He was sure the fellow was here. He even had a feeling that he'd seen him somewhere around the mines. Only an image in passing, but he hadn't realised it was him in time. Maybe it was, maybe not. He was not sleeping well any more. Dreams circled at night, disturbing dreams, not exactly nightmares, mingled with the throb of the leg. He worried that he was becoming obsessive, unable to think of anything else but conjuring up faces. Faces that he could easily have wrong by now.

The Chinaman kept insisting he never heard of the *China Belle*.

'I better send him back to his mates,' the sergeant said.

'No not yet.' Raymond stood over him. 'You a coolie, eh?'

'Yes. Coolie,' the man grinned.

'Where did you learn to speak English?'

'Home. From master family.'

'What ship did you come on? When? What day? Where did you land?

How many people? Who is your master? What sort of ship was it? Who was the captain?'

The Chinaman had to struggle to find answers to these questions, though Raymond repeated them many times. It was becoming clear to him that the coolie was lying.

'It he's a coolie,' he added.

'He's probably confused,' the sergeant offered. 'These fellows get dragged from pillar to post. They don't know where they are half the time. For all they know they could be in Africa.'

'Never mind, I'd appreciate it if you'd keep at this questioning. Pin him down to something specific, then go and ask his Chinese master the same questions. See if they tally up. Put the fear of God into the master too. Tell him you'll take away his licence if you don't get the truth. Ask the names of all his men. All of them. And double-check, one against the other. The crewmen could have changed their names,' he groaned. 'I'm sorry, sergeant, I'd do this myself but this damned leg is giving me hell. I'll have to find that doctor again.'

'Don't worry, Mr Lewis. I'll give them a good going over. A few less Chinks out here won't do any harm.'

The doctor was off on his rounds, so Raymond couldn't see him until five that afternoon.

'I'm sure it's a lot worse,' Raymond said, wincing as the bandage was removed, revealing the ugly purple mass. 'And it smells pretty badly too,' he added, embarrassed.

'Yes.' The doctor was noncommittal. He disappeared out the back and returned a while later with a jug of boiling water, and commenced to probe and clean the ulcer, while Raymond gritted his teeth to keep from crying out, because the pain was now more than he felt he should rightly be expected to bear.

'It's much bigger now, isn't it?' he breathed unsteadily, when the worst was over.

The doctor nodded. 'You look pale, Mr Lewis. Would you like a brandy?'

'Eh? A brandy?' Raymond's leg was still throbbing. 'My dear fellow, I should very much like a brandy.'

It did settle his nerves; revived him a little. 'Jolly good,' he said, handing back the glass. 'Jolly good.'

'Now, Mr Lewis, I want you to go home and go to bed. You have to keep the leg up. Here are some pills to ease the pain and help you sleep.'

Raymond took the bottle of pills. 'What are they?'

'Opium. Three grains. They should do the trick.'

'Opium? Are you sure they won't harm me? I've heard opium can send people mad.'

'No. They're perfectly safe. I've nothing else to offer you, I'm afraid. Sedatives are in short supply . . .'

'Wait a minute. That sore, the ulcer, it isn't getting any better, is it?'

The doctor shook his head. 'No, Mr Lewis, it's not. It's too close to the bone now. I'll arrange for you to be taken back to Cooktown tomorrow. You'll have to go in a wagon. I'll make you as comfortable as possible.'

'No, definitely not. I have work to do here. My mission is far from complete. I simply cannot leave yet.'

'You don't have any choice.'

'Ah, but I do. I will look after the leg, take your pills . . .'

'Mr Lewis, I didn't want to frighten you, but you leave me no choice. That ulcer is serious, you could lose your leg . . .'

'Oh, dear God. Surely not! I mean, it's just—'

'A tropical ulcer, sir. That is their *modus operandi*. They will eat the flesh and penetrate the bone if not stopped. Removed.'

'How can they be removed?'

'By an operation. As it is, you will have quite a hole in your leg. Now do I have your permission to arrange transport?'

Raymond was devastated. 'Yes, of course. Thank you.'

The sergeant of police in Maytown was ecstatic. 'I got 'em, Tim,' he whooped as he marched into the office. 'Got three Chinks from the *China Belle*! Had myself a chat with the bigwig they call master, otherwise known to locals as Maxie. You've never seen anything like his tent. Huge, it is, dark and sinister inside, but when your eyes get used to it, the bloody thing's furnished like an Arab harem. Or was. We raided it, Deputy Snowbridge and me, gave it the smasheroo when Maxie's servant said the boss did not wish to see me.'

'He's got servants?' Tim whispered, wide-eyed.

'Of course he's got bloody servants. What do you think the coolies are for? Anyway, he soon came to the party when all his flash furniture started flying around. I asked him where he'd come from and what boat he'd come on, with all these offsiders, and he told me, and I said how come his coolie, the one I had in the lockup, told a different story. I reckoned Maxie was lying through his teeth, trotted out the handcuffs, said I'd have to take him in, and he went green.

'Anyway, we put the wind up him all right and he says he employed this bloke here on the goldfield. No law against that.

'No, I says, but you're too sharp, Maxie, sitting here like Buddha, not to figure out he's an illegal. How come a coolie suddenly springs up in the middle of outback Queensland? We're on to you, Maxie. You're looking at a hefty fine for harbouring an illegal, who hasn't even got a miner's licence. Probably gaol. Unless you give me the goods on him . . . Well, Maxie soon threw him to the wolves. And his two mates. Came in on a ship called the *China Belle*, he said.'

'You got 'em!'

' "Deserters, that's all," Maxie said. "Not criminals."

' "Not as you'd notice," I says. "Just hand 'em over and we'll say no more about it. Except I hear you do a good trade in Scotch whisky, and a few bottles will make up for all the trouble you've caused me." '

'Go on!'

'Yeah, he's sending me down a case. I tell you, Tim, I showed that politician, and Sergeant Gooding, a thing or two by arresting those Chinks. This'll be a real feather in my cap. That pansy Lewis would never have found these blokes. I'm gonna have a good talk to them tonight. I could capture the whole gang up here.'

Raymond's retreat to Cooktown was memorable. The journey by wagon, in the company of three successful and well-armed miners, took more than a week, thanks to attacks by blacks and the huge landslides they initiated to destroy the tracks, forcing travellers to turn back and find another route.

At one stage, lying helplessly on the tray of the wagon as the horses dragged it over a bumpy track, Raymond saw two painted blackfellows with long spears, standing high above them, surveying the small convoy. He was surprised to be more interested in them than frightened; they looked so bold and manly.

By the time the wagon drivers delivered him to the Cooktown Hospital, their passenger was in the grip of severe fever and close to delirium.

A week later, Gooding received the three Chinese prisoners from the goldfields and, after the necessary paperwork, sent them on to the Brisbane Gaol, chained in the hold of a ship with a large batch of other lawbreakers.

Chapter Nine

From the Cairns Post:

Three Chinese sailors from the stricken ship *China Belle* have been arrested in Maytown, in the heart of the Palmer River goldfields. Authorities in Cairns are disappointed that these men have been transferred to Brisbane, since it was considered important that they be interviewed by police and Oriental's representatives in our town, so as to seek information on the ringleaders of this horrific mutiny that cost the lives of a female passenger and the ship's bosun.

Mr Lyle Horwood notifies that he will make a point of seeing these men himself, when he continues on his interrupted voyage to Brisbane shortly.

We are pleased to report that Mr Neville Caporn, a wealthy Hong Kong businessman, is so taken with our fair town that he is considering investing with us. We can assure him that he won't be sorry. Cairns has a great future as a leading port and commercial centre for the fast-growing agricultural districts of her vast hinterland.

The manager of the Bank of Australasia was delighted to oblige Mr Caporn with a temporary loan until his funds were transferred from Hong Kong. He invited him and his lovely wife to dine with him at the Alexandra Hotel, a calculated move that paid off. He knew other passengers from the luxury ship were staying at that hotel and had hoped to be introduced. They were all of the moneyed class, and Ted Pask wasn't about to let them slip away without meeting the real big fish, Lyle Horwood.

The arrangement turned out even better than expected. He wasn't just introduced to the other passengers; Horwood actually joined them, as did Mrs Plummer, a very distinguished-looking German lady. He listened avidly to all their 'ship talk', tucking away every bit of information for his bridge club, while administering a cold stare to less fortunate friends, who sidled by in the hopes of joining the illustrious company.

There was only one small disappointment: they ordered freely of the hotel's best light wines, Mrs Caporn being especially partial to champagne, and he was left with the bill for all four of them. Fortunately, Mrs Horwood did not attend.

Lyle Horwood was celebrating. He'd called for champagne under the pretence of pleasing little Mrs Caporn, because he was not supposed to tell them his secret. But to make up for it, he determined to enjoy himself on this day.

He'd only just received the news this morning, in mail forwarded on from his former office in Hong Kong. Of course everyone at Oriental was aware of the tragedy that had befallen *China Belle*, their pride and joy, so that the letter from the Governor of Hong Kong was almost lost among the many they sent with their commiserations and best wishes. But it was there! Dear God, it was there! The Governor had come good on his promise at last.

By the time the luncheon ended Horwood was a bit wobbly on his feet . . . 'Walking on clouds,' he told the excellent young host, Mr Ted something-or-other.

'A jolly good time!' he told them all, and went upstairs to have a serious talk with Constance, shortly to be Lady Horwood.

'Under the circumstances,' he said to her, 'I'll have to get Raymond Lewis to introduce me to the Governor as soon as we arrive in Brisbane. Colonial Governor is as good as the next. The Brisbane fellow can do the honours just as well as Hollis in Hong Kong.'

Then he remembered Lewis was still in Cooktown. 'Damn the fellow! When will he be back?'

His wife was silent as usual. She just sat on that sofa staring at nothing, fiddling with her hair. He was glad she hadn't come down to lunch and spoiled their good time, sitting around like a dummy. The doctor had given her medicine, that white stuff on the dresser, to settle her nerves. It did that, all right; she'd stopped her weeping, and jumping at every sound, but she was now so bloody quiet you couldn't get boo out of her.

'You'd better sharpen up before we go down to Brisbane,' he said. 'Get over this. Mrs Caporn was in for lunch, as gay as ever. Had us in fits telling us about the time she took Neville to dancing classes in Singapore.'

'Oh.'

'Yes, oh. You could take a leaf out of her book. Show a bit of grit.'

'I'm sorry.'

'You ought to be. Hardly a blink do I get from my wife when I tell her I've been offered a knighthood. It's as if you don't care.'

'Yes, it will be very nice. Have I had lunch?'

'Jesus! How do I know? Didn't you ring the bell? Well, it's too late now.'

He sat on the edge of the bed and sighed. He was to be Sir Lyle at last, and look at her! Lady Horwood, the dummy. It won't do. She'd have to smarten up before he could take her into Brisbane society. He was about to tell her to start packing when he realised he was getting ahead of himself, so eager was he to meet the Governor of Queensland. He'd have to make enquiries about shipping movements.

As he lay down on the bed he recalled the bank manager fellow telling him about a company being established here, to invest in commercial property in the centre of town. He had agreed that this port would be of major importance in due time, and so a stake in its future wouldn't go amiss. He'd told Neville to count him in. The company, though . . . what was its name? Called after a Greek god, he thought Apollo. That's it. Apollo Properties.

'Constance. Apollo, the Greek god. What was he the god of?'

She glanced up, looking bloody vacant, he thought. 'I don't know. I don't think I know,' she said and started chewing her fingernails, a new habit she'd acquired. 'Shall I ask someone?'

'No, for Christ's sake no! Go and sit on the veranda. I need to take a nap but I can't sleep with you stuck there.'

Constance went outside, picked up the cane armchair with its large soft cushion and turned it round so that it faced the hotel wall. To sit the other way meant looking out to sea, at Trinity Bay. A wonderful view, everyone said, but she hated it. The sea, even when it was calm like this, gave her butterflies in her stomach, and awful headaches. It never used to, she pondered; she had loved the voyage from England to Hong Kong, but then that had been a joyful time. The *China Belle* voyage had been a disaster from the first day . . . she began to weep, remembering she hadn't taken her medicine, didn't dare go back into the room and disturb him, wiped her eyes and sighed, trying to think what was upsetting her now.

After a while it came to her. Lyle had said they would be going to Brisbane. There were no coach routes this far north, so that meant they would have to go by ship. Terror gripped her at the thought of another sea voyage.

With cash available now that the bank had approved a substantial loan, Neville and Esme acquired a smart horse and gig suitable to their standing in the town, and bade a sad adieu to their hosts.

'We'll miss you,' Delia said. 'You won't forget to visit us, will you?'

'And don't lose that cheque,' her husband laughed. 'We don't want to miss out on shares.'

'I won't lose it, and, to make sure, I'll put it in the Apollo Properties Trust account as soon as we get to town.'

'Is it true that Lyle Horwood is to be Sir Lyle?' Delia remembered to ask.

'Yes,' Neville said. 'So we can't go wrong with him at the top of the list of shareholders. I'm really excited about the concept now that he has thrown his weight behind it and, incidentally, suggested that we enlarge the plan and build residences behind the shops. But I'm a cautious man, I'd want to look carefully at it first.'

'Of course,' Jack Foster agreed. 'You keep a weather eye on the project, Neville. Don't let him get too fancy.'

'Not on your life,' Neville said, giddyupping the horse as the gig sprang away and Esme waved, throwing kisses.

'Bye, darlings! Bye. And thank you for just everything!'

She hung on to her hat and clutched her purse. 'For heaven's sake, slow down, Neville. You'll tip us over.'

'Sorry, old thing, it's only the thrill of getting away from their clutches. They do cloy, don't they?'

She nodded. 'What's this about residences?'

''Tis true. I envisaged Apollo Properties as a row of shops. Showed the plan I drew to old Horwood, and next thing he's got a pencil and is altering it. Wants to put residences on the back of the shops. Says storekeepers like to live on the premises.'

'A lot he'd know.'

'Exactly. But who cares? We'll come out of it smiling. I pointed out to him that there's not enough space on the blocks for residences as well, but he waved the hand and told me that would be easily solved. We buy the blocks to the rear as well.'

'I haven't quite got this clear in my mind,' she said. 'You get them all to invest in Apollo Properties so that you have enough money to build the shops, and the attached quarters, I suppose, and then do you sell to the shopkeepers or lease to them?'

'What do you think?'

'I suppose leasing them long term would be best, since the properties would increase in value.'

Neville smiled. 'Whatever you think best. Now we might as well head for the hotel to keep them all in tow. And what about our Mr Hillier? We can't let him escape.'

Clive Hillier accosted him in the street. 'A word with you, sir.'

'Most certainly.'

But Neville's broad smile failed to impress Hillier. 'I had the impression you intended to invest in a plantation, Mr Caporn, and now I hear you intend to build a block of shops down the street, in direct competition to my enterprise. What have you got to say for yourself?'

'My dear fellow, one never thought to injure your enterprise. Certainly not. As a matter of fact we were looking to purchase a plantation but Lyle Horwood – you know who he is . . . from the ship – well, he convinced me that Cairns needed a strong retail centre. I pointed out to him that you were already constructing several very modern shops, but he said there was room for all.'

'That depends. You might have had the courtesy to discuss this with me first.'

'Early stages, old chap. When the time comes we'll simply sit down and work out what sort of shopkeepers we'll allow. Did you say, or did someone tell me, you're opening an emporium of clothing?'

'Yes, and I would take great offence if you leased to any other clothing retailers.'

'I will see to it that such a thing cannot happen, Mr Hillier. You can count on me. Besides, as I was saying to Lyle, we have to work together in a spirit of co-operation, not only among ourselves, Mr Hillier, but with shire councils to make certain they do their duty by the town also.'

'Well, I'd go along with you on that,' Hillier agreed. 'The swamp needs draining, it's too close to town, that's why we are plagued by so many mosquitoes.'

'Then we'll chase them up,' Neville said. 'I'll make a point of it. And how is your building coming along?'

'We're held up at the moment. Waiting on timber deliveries.'

Neville nodded sagely, though he knew that Hillier's project was suffering not from lack of supplies, but lack of cash. Jack Foster had told him that he needed the funds from the sale of his emporium in Maryborough to be able to get on with it.

'Why doesn't he take out a bridging loan?' he'd asked, and Jack was surprised.

'What's that?'

'A loan to tide him over.'

'Oh. I see. I suppose he hadn't thought of that.'

'I'd be willing to oblige him with a loan,' Neville said airily, 'but one couldn't embarrass him with an offer.'

For days Neville was busy drawing up 'official' documents. A quantity of regulations, rules, clauses and subclauses regarding Apollo Properties emerged, then an outline of needed share scrip with detailed trust account receipt forms, all verbose when they came to the small print. When finally he was satisfied with his efforts he turned to Esme.

'Here we are then. I think this is all we'll need for a start. Read these notes and see what you think.'

She went through them carefully, a finger tracing each line. 'They seem all right.'

'All right? They're a triumph, if I do say so myself. Legalese at its best. Half of that stuff makes no sense at all, while the rest is our way. Now why don't you go for a stroll somewhere while I concentrate on my calligraphy? Find some excuse to call in at a government office and pick up a piece of stationery. I need to copy the government stamp. A bit of prestige, what?'

He toiled over the stiff parchment pages, humming to himself as time flew, pacing the floor to allow the ink to dry, then standing back to admire his work. No one who knew Neville's everyday handwriting, his muscular scrawl, would think that the same person was capable of such perfection of letters as displayed here. There were no fancy flourishes, so squirls attached to the capitals, just letters completed exactly as they should be . . . evenly spaced, evenly sloped, lightness on the upstrokes and a little more strength on the down.

'A winning hand,' he liked to call his talent. And it pleased him that Esme was the only person who knew that this writing was natural to him. 'Twas the other, the rough hand that was the sham. He grinned.

His wife did not like walking the streets alone. Not any more. Once upon a time she wouldn't have given it a second thought, especially on a lovely day like this, but now the butterflies in her stomach clamoured like beetles.

Esme missed the crowded Hong Kong streets where she could drift along with the tide. Here, with so few pedestrians ambling by, she felt exposed, subjected to polite nods and raised hats. Noticed. And that was worrying. She tried to convince herself that this was nothing to be concerned about, that she was looking very smart in her plum-coloured costume and pretty little velvet hat, but she was unable to shake off what seemed to be a form of stage fright.

'Stupid,' she muttered to herself, nervously adjusting the netting on her hat so that it gave some cover to her eyes. 'It's not as if you're in any danger. Why on earth are you doing this to yourself? The way you're behaving you'd think there are bears around the next corner.'

There were no bears around the next corner but there was a hotel with an open saloon spilling on to its wide veranda, and Esme almost ran up the steps. A few minutes later, seated in the deep cool interior of the almost deserted saloon, she swallowed a brandy with a sigh of relief and ordered another.

She left the hotel with two small bottles of brandy in her smart suede handbag, feeling much better, even quite gay, when she came upon Mr Hillier, who greeted her enthusiastically.

'How wonderful to see you! I really needed brightening up today and your happy smile is just the thing.'

'You're too kind,' she responded, with a twinkle in her eyes.

'Not at all. I was admiring your ensemble as you were coming towards me. Perfect. The velvet hat really sets off the gown.'

'Thank you. I almost forgot you have a business eye for ladies' fashion. I'm pleased you like this outfit, it's a favourite of mine.'

'Did you have it made in Hong Kong?'

'Yes. A French couturier called Raoul.'

'Incredible! To be able to find such elegance at your fingertips. How fortunate you ladies must be. I'm afraid I could never aspire to stock outfits of that standard.'

'I don't see why not,' she giggled. 'You just get a good tailor, give him good materials and a French name, and *voilà*!'

He laughed. 'Is that so? I can see your advice will be invaluable when I open the ladies' store here. If and when, I mean. Delays are driving me crazy. Still, I suppose these things are sent to try us.'

Esme made no objection when he offered to walk with her, so they crossed the road to the waterfront and watched a tall ship sail into the bay.

'Oh,' she said. 'It's from Hong Kong!' with such pleasure in her voice he turned to look at her.

'I gather you're fond of that city?'

'Yes,' she said. 'I was.'

When she returned to the hotel she sat alone in the lounge, pondering their present situation. She did miss Hong Kong. She was only now realising how much she missed the place, its racy cosmopolitan atmosphere and the general air of rush and excitement. 'By contrast, this town is too quiet, for people in our business,' she murmured nervously.

Neville was certain that the easy pickings he was discovering here were only the tip of the iceberg.

'These people are so naive,' he said, 'they're practically shoving money at me. After here we'll go to the southern cities, there are only a few. Give us five years in this country, sweets, and we'll go back to the East richer than we ever dreamed. We should have come here years ago.'

That's as may be, Esme thought as she plucked a pink rosebud from a vase of flowers, but I couldn't think of anything worse than five years in this boring country. I want to go back to Hong Kong. We never should have left.

Clive had been hoping she might join him for lunch, but that was hardly possible with a husband lurking in the background, so he'd escorted her back to the hotel, and reluctantly gone on his way, returned to the depressed state from which her charming presences had lifted him. Temporarily.

She'd come upon him when he was emerging from the bank, and from yet another refusal by that dolt Ted Pask to extend his loan.

This, of course, was Emilie's fault. It shouldn't take all this time to sell the emporium in Maryborough. The business was flourishing, it was a good investment, and buyers ought to be queuing outside.

He marched crossly down to the Fish Café, sat at a long table with a newspaper, and ordered a bowl of fish kedgeree.

Ted Pask had a damned cheek to be telling him the Maryborough emporium was overpriced, that if he dropped the price he'd have his quick sale and would not need to borrow more for the new premises. What did he know? Angrily he slammed the paper on the table, only to read that weather experts were predicting a very wet summer.

'Nothing better to write about,' he snorted. 'Everyone knows the tropic summers are always wet. It's the wet bloody season, for Christ's sake!'

His office, the office of Mr Clive Hillier, Proprietor, was on the mezzanine floor of the Maryborough emporium, overlooking haberdashery. It was a tidy office; files were always swept to cover unless in use, leaving the mahogany desk to reflect the brass pen and inkstand, the pipe stand and the brass ashtray.

Emilie hurried in the door, closed it behind her and sank into Clive's swivel chair. She felt faint. All of her plans had just run headlong into disaster.

Only last week she had made the decision. She would leave him. Leave Maryborough. Go . . . not to Cairns but down to Brisbane. She would find a lawyer who could advise her on a divorce and, possibly, on how to make him give her some financial support, though she doubted Clive would let her have a penny. If necessary, she would support herself. She was twenty-six and had some experience . . . there was always teaching, and she'd proved to be an excellent shopgirl, both roles a certain improvement on her present status. She'd warned him that she wouldn't put up with his brutal treatment, and six years of it was far too much.

'I've been such a fool,' she murmured. 'I should have left him the first time it happened, but I was too concerned about what people thought. Now it's too late.'

She could not allow tears. Not now, not with all the staff about. She wished she could pick up that ashtray and hurl it through the window. Smash it! Smash something!

Emilie had been so wrapped in the idea of actually making the break, and all the contentious issues involved in such a move, that she'd forgotten to pay attention. When it dawned on her that morning nausea wasn't the result of anxiety over this outrageous plan, she began to pray.

'Please God, not now.'

But God, the benign Lord, hadn't been listening. Instead He'd blessed her with pregnancy at exactly the wrong time.

She went to the cupboard, took out the latest stock sheets and started poring over them, anything to distract herself from overwhelming self-pity. She couldn't leave now. Pregnant women couldn't get jobs. She'd starve.

'And he'd let you starve too,' she said. 'Stay with him or starve. There's a choice now!'

One of the girls knocked on the door and poked her head in.

'The mayor, Mr Manningtree, to see you.'

Mr Manningtree? Emilie wondered what he wanted. He was a nice man, rough and ready, but kind-hearted. He'd been her first employer in Maryborough, employed her as a governess to his three children. And a mixed blessing that had been. The house and grounds were delightful and everyone was very pleasant, except for his wife, an absolute harridan. Emilie had stuck out that job until scandal over Sonny Willoughby had given Mrs Manningtree the opportunity to sack her.

She went to the door to greet him. 'How nice to see you again, Mr Manningtree. Do come in. Would you like a cup of tea?'

'No thanks, Missy. How are you keeping? You're looking a bit peaky on it.'

'Oh, I'm very well, thank you. I hear Kate won first prize in the piano competition. You must be very proud of her.'

'Proud of all three kids, I am. You gave 'em good grounding, Missy, taught 'em how to learn.' He walked over to the window and peered over the lace curtain, strung across at half level. 'Business keeps steady here, doesn't it? But you know when your husband first started up his gentlemen's outfitters I wouldn't have given tuppence for it. But I think you brought him down to earth with less fancy clothes.'

'I don't know about that,' she smiled.

'Well, I do, and you know me, Missy: I never mince me words. Then you, quick smart, brought in women's clothes too. This is a real going concern now, isn't it?'

'It is. We've been fortunate.'

'Now you're leaving us?'

She sighed. 'Yes, time to move on. But I won't forget Maryborough. I'll miss our friends.'

He pulled over a high stool and perched his bulk on the edge. 'You haven't found a buyer yet?'

'No.'

'You're asking too much.'

'Clive doesn't think so.'

'I think you are. I've been waiting for you to get a bit kinder with the price.'

'You have? Are you interested?'

'Not me. The missus.'

'*Mrs* Manningtree?' Emilie gulped.

He grinned. 'Yes, that's her name last heard. Now the kids are all off at boarding school she's got her heart set on owning this store. Reckon she thinks she'll be in heaven with free dresses and a store all to herself . . .'

Emilie took all this in very carefully. Violet Manningtree, the shrew with the worst imaginable taste in clothes, wanted to own the emporium? Was he joking?

'. . . so I thought I'd come and have a chat with you. Me and Clive, we never did get along that well.'

Emilie remembered his shrug when they'd announced their engagement: 'Don't know what you see in him, Missy.'

'I reckon we could come to some arrangement,' he continued now, 'me and you. Let's have a look at the figures again. I'll buy the place for her but I'm going to put a manager in to keep control. We'll have a look at what the stock's worth again, and the annual turnover, see what we can do here.'

They went over the books together, both of them taking pencilled notes, until he suddenly looked at his watch. 'Emilie, I'm late for a meeting. Can I come back same time tomorrow? Just don't go selling to someone else or Violet will have my hide.'

At the door, he looked back. 'You ought to take more care of yourself, Missy. You look tired; go on home.'

Emilie couldn't help being excited at the prospect of a sale at last, especially when their difference was only a matter of about forty pounds or so.

Then she remembered the house had to be sold too. After that, was there no choice but to pack up the furniture and join Clive in Cairns? That was definitely not a pleasant prospect.

Settlement had been arranged for eleven this morning at the Bank of New South Wales.

Emilie was unable to quell her misgivings at what she proposed to do, but she supposed she'd better get on with it. She left the store and crossed the road to the bank, where she opened an account in her own name.

The mayor was punctual as usual and in a genial mood as he marched into the bank, not forgetting to greet the tellers and shake the hands of the bank customers, before following the manager into his office where Emilie waited.

There was plenty to chat about. Maryborough was preparing to celebrate its twenty-fifth anniversary.

'It will be a gala occasion,' Manningtree boomed. 'One whole week of celebrations beginning with horse races and sports day on the Saturday, ending with a gala ball the following Saturday night.'

'Amazing to think the town's only twenty-five years old,' the bank manager said. 'We've certainly come ahead, and that's mostly due to your good offices, Bert.'

'That's true,' the mayor agreed, and Emilie smiled, thinking that her former employer would never change.

She sat quietly, settling her nerves while they discussed street decorations, until the mayor announced they'd better get down to business.

The contract was perused and signatures were given, witnessed by the bank manager.

'Now, Missy, who do I make the cheque out to?' Manningtree asked.

'Oh. If you please, to me, E. M. Hillier. I have to draw on it to forward funds to Clive and arrange the move to Cairns.'

As he wrote the amount, he glanced up at her. 'I don't know why you're leaving. I thought you enjoyed living here, Emilie.'

'I do. Of course. But . . . well, Clive is ambitious, and he's got his heart set on another store in Cairns.'

It was all over in such a short time that she was surprised to find herself walking along the main street with no particular destination in mind. The large emporium was no longer her concern. The money was in the bank.

She didn't feel like going home yet so she stopped at the Riverside Café and treated herself to tea and scones.

So now, she thought, as she looked over the tranquil river, it is time to let Clive know where things stand. She took out a notebook and pencil and began totting up figures again. Then she nodded. 'Yes, that's fair.'

The following day Emilie called on the bank manager again.

'I have to send some money to my husband as soon as possible. How do I go about that?'

'Very simply, my dear. How much do you want to send?'

'Two thousand and fifty pounds.'

He took note of the figure. 'No problem. You sign the withdrawal from your account and I'll make the money order to Clive for that amount. It's perfectly safe to post. I'll just cross out "Bearer" to make certain it's for Clive's hands alone. He'll be pleased to know the store is sold, I'm sure.'

'Yes.'

'At least it's in good hands. Our mayor's a smart businessman.'

Emilie doubted that Violet Manningtree's hands would be much of an asset, but made no comment, waiting patiently while he fussed with pen and ink and blotter, and finally handed her a money order encased in a new brown envelope, with the bank's good wishes.

Later that day Emilie posted the money to Clive with an accompanying letter outlining the details of the sale of the emporium, and then splitting their funds into equal shares:

Your fifty per cent of the sale monies: 2,000 pounds.

Sale of Hillier residence and contents: 55 pounds.

Explanation: Since I provided the money for a deposit on the Hillier Stores, via sale of my house by the river, and have always worked with you in the business, I have decided to keep my share, and am therefore forwarding your share to you as shown.

I have bought our house myself, at a fair price, as you see, and am forwarding this amount also.

By this, please understand that I shall not be joining you in Cairns. For reasons well known to you, I wish to have nothing further to do with you, and on this account am applying for a legal separation.

When she left the post office and walked home, to *her* home now, misgivings had fled. In the end, instead of holding her back, the pregnancy had provided impetus for her decision. Now that a new life was entering her household the violence had to go.

'For the sake of the child, I can't take the risk of having Clive around any longer,' she told herself. 'I've no choice now. I'll have to begin divorce proceedings as soon as I can.'

Then she smiled. I don't have any work to go to. I've got money in the bank. My time is my own at last. I'm having a baby and feeling extremely well. And it's a glorious day!

Emilie was humming a tune as she walked in her front door.

Her maid, Nellie, glanced at her. 'You're in a good mood, Mrs Hillier.'

'And with good reason,' Emilie sighed. 'I've decided not to move to Cairns. And I'm keeping this house. So you've still got your place here if you want to stay on.'

Nellie was thrilled. 'Of course I do! Oh, thank you, that's a relief for me. But what happened? Has he decided against the place in Cairns?'

'No, I have. I won't be joining him there.'

'What?' Nellie had been working for the Hilliers for three years. She was a shy girl, but no fool. She turned away and muttered: 'About time!'

Emilie pretended not to hear. 'Mr Hillier won't be coming back, Nellie. I want you to pack his belongings. We have to ship them to him right away.'

Eleanor Plummer was feeling very much out of things, with all this talk of Apollo Properties. It was just her luck that Plummer's raids on her funds had reduced her financial situation considerably, at a time when she needed extra to invest in this excellent proposal. It was galling too that Lyle Horwood should be leading the charge. She would hate for him to discover that she couldn't afford to buy shares, so she brushed the talk aside, telling people she was much more interested in finding a decent house here in Cairns.

She wrote again to her friend Gertrude in Brisbane, to say she had a house in mind, and one of her new friends, a Mr Jesse Field was accompanying her this afternoon to have a good look at it.

'Men are better at these things,' she wrote, 'so I am grateful for his assistance. I am finding the people in this town most accommodating, and I hope that if, and when, one is able to find a suitable residence you will visit me at your earliest convenience.'

Gertrude had been concerned that Eleanor should so suddenly decide to stay in the strange town, not realising that her friend needed to show some independence after that marriage débâcle. To Eleanor, this seemed infinitely better than running and sheltering under Gertrude's wing, which had been her first reaction. And she already had several good friends in the town.

'I am the most fortunate of women,' she wrote, 'to have survived that *China Belle* ordeal and be washed up on the shores of a pretty town like this. I feel as if it is meant to be.'

The house was called Shalimar. It had been built by Jordan Kinkaid, a wealthy grazier who owned huge cattle stations out west. It was to be the family's summer house, but on their first holiday by the seaside, his wife contracted scarlet fever and died. Jordan was so devastated he gave instructions for the house to be sold, and took his family back to the bush.

'Kinkaid always insisted on the best,' Jesse told Mrs Plummer as he escorted her along the street to the gate. 'It's a fine house, but it may be a little too big to suit you.'

'Maybe,' she nodded. 'But the only other houses I've found are workers' cottages, much too small.'

She stood back and surveyed the house before her. It wasn't as imposing as she'd expected. In fact the white timber building was quite charming, with individual verandas outside the two front rooms on either side of the entrance.

'They look very romantic, don't they?' she commented.

'Yes,' Jesse smiled. 'I believe they call them Juliet verandas. And the decorative woodwork around the house is supposed to be very fashionable. What do you think, Mrs Plummer?'

'It's beautifully done. Quite splendid.'

They walked up the wide stone steps and into a tiled lobby, through stained-glass double doors to a long hallway. A door on one side revealed a comfortable parlour; on the other, a music room, complete with piano and busts of three old masters.

'But it's a lovely house!' Eleanor cried. 'Lovely! I had no idea it would be furnished. And to such perfection.'

'Yes. I have to admit, I did suggest to Jordan that he shouldn't give up on it so quickly. That he'd be better to lease it for a while, a year or so . . .'

'Goodness gracious! He didn't listen to you, did he?'

'Sadly, no. I just thought it was a pity . . .'

'It is a pity, a shame to relinquish a house that has been built with so much love and attention, but if it has sad memories then one can understand.'

They walked through the rest of the house, taking in the fine dining room, the spacious bedrooms and the softly furnished sitting room at the rear of the house.

The kitchen was very large and neat as a pin, with a wood stove and cool pantries and, beyond it, across a cobbled yard, were maids' quarters, sheds and stables.

Eventually Eleanor breathed a sigh of disappointment. 'It is just perfect, Mr Field. Too perfect. I couldn't afford a place like this. The furnishings alone are worth a fortune.'

Jesse was surprised. Neville Caporn had given him to understand that the German lady was extremely wealthy.

'Never mind.' He smiled. 'It's interesting to look through the house, isn't it? I think it will be a long time before anyone builds anything comparable in this town. Shalimar is probably before its time.'

He was walking ahead of her towards the front door, when Eleanor thought she heard movement behind her. She glanced back, stopped and looked into one of the rooms.

'Is anyone there?' she called, and Jesse turned.

'I shouldn't think so, Mrs Plummer. Did you think you heard something? Not rats surely?'

'Oh no. Goodness me, no. It must have been the wind. The breeze is strong today.'

When they returned to the lobby, Eleanor opened the front door and gazed out at the neat, ordered garden.

'I take it you know Mr Kinkaid well?'

'Yes, he's an old friend.'

'Then perhaps, if I cannot afford to purchase just yet, you might persuade him to lease. I would be an excellent tenant, Mr Field. I know I spoke otherwise a few minutes ago, but now I have to make a lease or nothing. You understand?'

'No harm in asking,' he said, and she took his arm.

'Do tell the gentleman I am an outstanding gardener also, and I would greatly care for his garden. It would be my pleasure.'

He closed the front door behind them and Eleanor took a last view of the interior of the house through a glass panel in the front door. This time she thought she saw a flash of movement, but made no mention of it in case Mr Field should think her foolish. Probably a bird, she told herself. A bird could have easily have found a way in, and now searched for a way out.

Back at the hotel she made no mention of Shalimar. She couldn't bear to think someone else might buy it. It was just a matter of waiting now, and depending on Mr Field's powers of persuasion.

Clive had already made up his mind to take Neville Caporn's advice and keep himself covered by investing in Apollo Properties, while continuing to build his own block of shops.

Neville was right. Ownership of retail properties in the town centre was obviously a sound investment. After all, it was his idea in the first place. But Apollo was a much bigger proposition, with residences attached to the shops, and would bring much greater returns.

As he'd said to Neville: 'I'll only have a flutter of a few hundred for a start, but once I get my building completed, I can turn my attention to Apollo. When will the company be registered?'

'Within the week, I'd say. Lyle is anxious to finalise matters before he sets sail for Brisbane and the honours awaiting him. We have already made an offer on the land, and he is taking our preliminary plans to council, before we go to the expense of hiring an architect.'

'An architect? Is that necessary?' Clive asked. 'I simply gave my plans to a builder and he went to work.'

'Yes, and you've done a good job, but with a company it is important to make sure everyone's views are taken into account, and we have the best possible advice.' He smiled. 'You'll see, these shops will be equal to the standard you are setting here, Clive, and I think we'll be very proud of our town centre.'

That was Friday. On Monday morning Emilie's letter arrived, admittedly with enough money to restart the building work and invest a few hundred in Apollo Properties, as he'd promised, but where was the rest? He read her letter again, couldn't grasp it at all, and rushed back to the room he was renting to sit down and sort this out.

Had she gone mad? What was she talking about? Keeping her half of the sale monies. And buying the house from him for fifty-five pounds!

'For reasons well known to you . . .' What the hell is this? he asked himself. She wants nothing further to do with me? You'd think I'm a criminal the way this stupid woman is going on. As if I'm besmirching her name. *Her* name? That's a laugh. After she chased Sonny Willoughby down to Brisbane, even hired a lawyer to get him off. A fine lot of gossip that caused. Maryborough had a field day with her goings-on. Then Willoughby dumped her. Wouldn't she love to know he'd been right here in Cairns?

He peered out the window at gathering clouds and snarled. 'I'll bet you'd be on the first boat to Cairns if you thought Willoughby was here, you bloody stupid woman!'

He sighed, stared at the bank order again. 'I might as well bank it,' he muttered, 'get the men working again, and then write to her and demand she gets herself up here, with the rest of my money. If she doesn't I'll have to go down there and drag her out. Bloody hell! I don't need this aggravation. She'd better get over her sulks and smarten up or I'll want to know why!'

By the time the money was in the bank and his immediate financial problem solved, Clive was feeling better, but then he encountered Caporn and Horwood sauntering down the street.

'Do you still wish to invest?' Neville asked him.

'Yes, of course. As a matter of fact there's nothing like the present. I could buy in right now. Two hundred, was it?'

'I'm sorry, Clive, but we've agreed to a five-hundred-pound minimum.'

Beside him, Lyle Horwood nodded and poked his walking stick at a dog sniffing a tree trunk.

Clive was shocked but couldn't afford to lose face with this pair, so he shrugged and walked into the bank to withdraw five hundred of his precious pounds.

'I shouldn't have let the buggers talk me into any of this,' he muttered to himself as he emerged, but it was too late now, so he rearranged his face into an easy smile and handed over the cash.

'Welcome aboard,' Neville said, shaking his hand. 'I'll have the receipt on your doorstep first thing in the morning.'

'Have you seen Constance?' Lyle asked them, and when both shook their heads, he groaned. 'If you see her, tell her I'll be back at the hotel. It's bloody hot now, too hot to be standing about.'

Clive excused himself and made for a pub in a backstreet where he could have a quiet drink and sort out the day's confusions. He wished he'd had the guts to tell Neville he'd changed his mind about investing in that other block of shops. One didn't have to explain one's self. And Emilie! For God's sake, what the hell was she carrying on about? Her share of the business? He'd never heard such rubbish.

He drank his whisky with a snort of rage and ordered another. What had brought this on, anyway? Which reminded him. Where was Willoughby? Was he in Maryborough? With Emilie? Was this the reason for her sluttish behaviour? Wanting nothing more to do with her own husband! He ought to go back to Maryborough right away, but there'd been enough delays. The shops had to be completed and stocked as soon as possible.

Thunder rolled in the deep hills that overlooked the little town and Clive shuddered. He was a handsome man – distinguished, people would say. Educated, confident, he had sailed through life so far without any major concerns. But now he was nervous and confused. Emilie had confused him. He couldn't think how to cope with this situation without creating a major scandal. Because if she really were talking about leaving him it would create the most horrible scandal. He felt his face flush scarlet. He would not allow her to besmirch his reputation; something would have to be done.

Chapter Ten

Cooktown Hospital was set on the side of a hill, almost hidden by stout palms and a crush of rainforest that seemed hellbent on reclaiming its territory.

Raymond liked to watch Joseph, the gardener, at work, interested in the fellow's wry comment: 'Back home in England I kept planting, hoping for the best. Here I garden with clippers, cutting back all the time.'

Every morning, rain or shine, the nurses would wheel Raymond out on to the veranda while they attended to other patients and mopped the floors, and most times they'd forget and leave him here. But he had no objection; with nothing else to do he'd become fascinated by the local flora, and this man's knowledge of botany. Whenever he could, Joseph would bring him rare and colourful specimens, which Raymond liked to press between dry pages, to begin a collection of his own.

This day, though, Joseph was working elsewhere and so missed the marvellous sight of a cloud of blue butterflies, thousands and thousands of them, moving up the valley. Raymond was so entranced, he shouted impatiently when someone stepped in front of him.

'Get out of the way! Now! Quick! Get away!'

Had he been closer he would have shoved the man aside.

'And good morning to you too,' Sergeant Gooding retorted, but Raymond leaned to the side, hoping to get a last glimpse of the gorgeous phenomena.

'Please,' he said. 'Just a minute. The butterflies . . .'

But as Gooding turned, looking in the wrong direction, they were fading into a distant fog of blue.

'What about them?'

'Never mind,' Raymond said crankily.

'All right. So how's the leg?'

'They removed the ulcer but it has left a huge hole in my leg and it's taking far too long to heal.'

'Ah no, these things take time. They can't stitch up a hole like that, they just have to keep it free of infection and let the skin heal over. But you'll be left with a lump of muscle missing there.'

'So I'm told.'

'But they're looking after you?'

'Yes, as best they can. The place is horribly overcrowded.'

'So is the town.' Gooding shrugged. 'Bloody miners pouring in here by the hundreds every day. A boat overturned on the incoming tide yesterday, a ketch, came all the way up here from Melbourne, and three passengers drowned. It was overcrowded like all the ships that come into this little seaport. By the way, did you know the Premier called a snap election?'

'What?'

'It's true. Not that anyone up here cares. We've got an electorate called Cook, and Bill Murphy's our rep. You ever meet him?'

'Yes, I met him in Brisbane. I had no idea he represents this area, but just a minute. The elections. How do you know?'

Gooding pulled a folded newspaper from his hip pocket. 'Here it is. In the *Brisbane Courier*.' He began to read: ' "Premier Douglas has called an election for 4 November to put a stop to all the strikes that threaten not only the business and agrarian communities . . ." What's agrarian?'

'Farmers,' Raymond said absently. 'Let me see.'

Gooding handed over the paper. 'The thing is, Mr Lewis, I figure we've got a population of near to ten thousand now, that's including the Palmer district, and what if they demand a vote? What am I supposed to do about that?'

Raymond stared at the date on the newspaper. 'It's more than three weeks old! This paper is weeks out of date.'

'Well, you'd hardly think we'd get yesterday's up here. We're lucky to get one at all. And did you see where the unions are lowering the boom on the Chinese now?'

Raymond wasn't listening. He thought it was a foolhardy tactic on the part of the Premier. 'The dolt,' he muttered. 'Tom McIlwraith's Ministerial Party will beat him hollow.'

Gooding was interested. 'So you reckon McIlwraith will be the next Premier?'

'Yes.'

'Are you on his side, or Douglas's?'

'Neither,' Raymond said dully. 'I've missed the nomination. I had to advise the electoral office of my intention to stand again, in writing and witnessed, by last Thursday. Time has run out.'

Gooding shrugged. 'Ah well, I guess it's not much of a job sitting in parliament listening to speeches all day.'

'It's a damned sight better than sitting here with half one's leg cut away,' Raymond snapped, frustrations spilling into anger.

'Cripes, that reminds me,' Gooding said. 'Where the hell is your deputy, Snowbridge?'

'How would I know?'

'Well, he came with you and he was supposed to be under your jurisdiction. The lads at Maytown say he's still claiming bed and board from police funds but spends half his life prospecting. What do you want me to do about him?'

'You can shoot him if you like,' Raymond said savagely, and Gooding laughed at the change in the parliamentarian's mannered demeanour.

'Ah yes, as I always say, nothing like that blood-and-mud track to knock the smooth edges off any man.'

When he left, Raymond tried to make sense of the situation. He picked up the paper again and saw the letter tucked away on the page, entitled: 'Beyond Capricorn. The badlands of the north.'

The writer, a Reverend Buck Wiley, went on to explain that the Tropic of Capricorn divided civilised Queensland from the barbarism of the northern section of the colony.

> Thousands of diggers, criminals, prostitutes, thieves and gamblers constitute the population of the Palmer goldfields, but to get there they have to run the hundred-and-fifty-mile gauntlet of murderous attacks by mobs of blacks. Last week two hundred blacks fell upon diggers at a river point known as Hell's Gate and were eventually driven off, but eight diggers died. As if that isn't enough, battles between the European and Chinese diggers add to the hazards, making it commonplace to stumble over bodies along the track.
>
> It behoves Bill Murphy, as the Member of Parliament for that appalling blot on the colony's reputation, to bring order and Christian principles to Cooktown and the Palmer districts without delay.

He urged that all heathens and black savages be rounded up by the military and placed in detention camps.

Raymond threw the paper down in disgust. Once the gold ran out, he mused, this place would probably return to jungle, and all would be quiet beyond Capricorn again. But then he realised that the struggling town of Cairns was also beyond Capricorn, and teetering on the edge of the goldfields. He wondered if the cattle stations inland would be prosperous enough to sustain that seaport when the gold was gone.

But these were matters for another time, only engaging him now to prevent self-pity encroaching. He should have heard from Lavinia about the political situation. Surely she, or his father at least, could have seen what was coming and insist he lodge the nomination in time. Officialdom of sorts did exist here. He hadn't heard from anyone in Brisbane for weeks, though he'd written to Lavinia to let her know of his predicament; that he was unable to be moved just yet. His leg had to stay rested to allow the healing to take hold, and it was bloody awful in this hospital. And, he did not add, lonely. He had never been so desperately lonely. Nor would he add that he was suffering from hideous bedsores on his rear end.

* * *

The next day, as he waited for the doctor to do his rounds, Raymond began composing a response to the outrageous views of that so-called Christian gentleman, who obviously had never understood Christ's teachings. He thought it might be a good start to describe the beauty of this area – a terrible beauty, he had to admit, thanks to man's inability to live and let live. But the forests here, he mused, are magnificent, and the wildlife astonishing. He'd seen so many unusual animals in his travels over the range . . . 'After all,' he would write, in an attempt at humour, 'how many people have been transported sick out to the Palmer River and back again?'

Very few, if any, he was sure. But the slow progress had given him the leisure to study the flora and fauna. On several occasions he'd even seen cassowaries, large birds like emus, but far more colourful. Even now, the gardener had told him, people denied that cassowaries existed.

He sighed. He could produce a most interesting letter on this subject if he put his mind to it . . . But then embarrassment engulfed him. Who would be interested in reading descriptions of rainforests written by a man who would be a laughing stock by this time? A parliamentarian who would lose his seat for the most foolish of reasons, that he had failed to nominate himself in time.

Raymond knew the press. He knew that reporters would not be interested in his reasons; the opportunity to lampoon a politician was too tempting. He groaned. Cartoonists! They'd have a field day.

As if on cue, to merge with his thoughts of Brisbane, a nurse brought him a letter.

'Looks like a lady's handwriting,' she remarked. 'Your wife, eh?'

'No. I am a widower,' he replied reluctantly.

'Ah well, good news, I hope.'

'Yes, I'm sure,' he nodded, dismissing her, pondering her assumption that a letter, like a telegram, should contain news of great import.

This letter, though, had more shock value than news. Lavinia was enraged that he was still in Cooktown, that he had missed the nomination. The Premier was furious with him for letting him down, as he desperately needed the numbers to hold office.

'He should have thought of that before calling an election,' Raymond growled.

Her attitude mystified him. Surely Lavinia should have some sympathy for him. He was shaking his head in bewilderment as she castigated him for being so irresponsible as to be plunging about goldfields, playing at being a sheriff when matters of state needed his attention.

It wasn't until he reached the last few lines that he began to understand.

'Not a word from you,' she wrote fiercely. 'Not a damned word except to say that you're going back to that place called Cooktown, which is not even to be found on a map, on a wild-goose chase after mutineers.

This, you inform me, after I sent an urgent letter to you in Cairns to warn you that you'd better hurry home because the Premier is threatening an election.'

Raymond sighed. He must have missed the letter she sent to Cairns. And obviously, none of the epistles he'd sent from the goldfields and, more recently, from his hospital bed, had reached their destination. That didn't surprise him, given the chaos of instant overpopulation here, but it didn't help to know the letters had gone astray. Or been dumped and forgotten in the hold of one of the leaky government ketches that found their way here occasionally.

His leg was throbbing. The day was already hot and clammy. Clouds hung low, turning the town into a steam bath, and all about him people cheerily talked about the wet season getting under way any day. Raymond had always found the Brisbane summers very trying, so he dreaded summer a thousand miles closer to the equator.

He saw she'd added a postscript to tell him, as if he were a lad at boarding school, that his father was disgusted with him, and had apologised to the Premier for his failure to return on schedule.

Raymond supposed he should make an effort and write to Lavinia, explaining, apologising, rehashing the problem of the ulcer, but what was the point? It hurt him that they would think that he'd deliberately neglect his duties. He was not a capricious person; he took his responsibilities seriously; he always had done. Surely they knew that of him.

Now he wondered. He had always been the good son – rather stolid, he supposed, but he meant well. So what did this wretched letter tell him – not about her, or his father, but about Raymond Lewis?

He knew the answer, and turned his head away in distress.

Raymond Lewis might have seen himself as a model citizen, but it seemed that in his own family he didn't command respect. The letter reeked of deeply founded disrespect, and he thought that was very sad.

As the days passed he couldn't bring himself to respond to Lavinia's letter, though he did make several attempts, until it dawned on him that he didn't care any more. Not about her or her opinions, nor his father's dictatorial manner, nor about the election damn them! And he was fast becoming fed up with Dr Madison's cavalier attitude.

'You said the ulcer would be healed by this time,' he charged, but Madison shook his head.

'I hoped it would. But the infection has spread again.'

'Why is that?'

'What do you mean, "why is that?" Because it has.'

'There has to be a reason. Is it not being kept properly sterilised?'

'We're doing the best we can!'

'I disagree with that. I think treatment here is very sloppy. Some days that wound is not cleansed at all.'

'That won't do any harm.'

Huffily, Madison moved on, and Raymond was taken out to the veranda as usual.

When Joseph came by to tell him that he had actually observed an army of ants defending aphids from attack by spiders, Raymond wasn't very interested.

'And do you know why they do that?' Joseph asked.

Raymond shook his head listlessly.

'Because aphids provide them with the honey they need for their babies.'

'I see,' Raymond nodded.

'I don't think you do, mate. What's up?'

'Oh . . . who knows? Everything! I apologise, Joseph, I wasn't really listening. It's this leg. I'm worried that they can't stop the infection spreading, the sores are deep, and, I fear, gangrenous though they will not admit it:

'Yeah. I don't blame you for worrying. Listen, I've got a friend who might be able to help. Can I ask him?'

'Is he a doctor?'

'No, but he's very clever. He got rid of my fever overnight.'

Rather than offend the gardener, Raymond gave his permission, but he didn't expect anything would come of it.

That afternoon, he was dozing when a tall Chinaman with a long grey beard loomed up on the veranda. He was wearing a long brocade coat and had an embroidered pillbox hat set squarely on his smooth forehead, with the usual pigtail hanging down the back.

'You are the Honourable Mr Raymond Lewis, sir?' this apparition asked, and Raymond, taken aback, could only answer yes instead of endeavouring to point out that he was only a Member of the Legislature, not a minister, and therefore was not entitled to be addressed as the Honourable.

The Chinaman bowed, clasping his hands together at the tips of his wide sleeves. 'I am Li Weng Kwan. Our mutual friend, Joseph, asked of me to visit you, but if this time is not of your convenience pray forgive me, I shall retire.'

'Mr Li, it is very kind of you to call on me but, as you see, I am in no position to receive you with courtesy.'

'Then perhaps you might consider visiting my humble house?'

'Afraid not. I'm stuck here. The leg, you see.'

Mr Li glanced at the heavily bandaged leg resting on a stool and sighed. 'You appear to be in great discomfort, Mr Lewis.'

'I am that,' Raymond groaned.

'Even crocodiles can be moved,' the Chinaman said gravely.

Raymond was startled. 'I beg your pardon?'

'There was a man-eating crocodile in the river. The people called for it to be killed but a man wanted it for his private zoo, so he called his servants to lash its mouth closed and tie it into a wagon. Therefore it was removed.'

Raymond laughed. 'I don't suppose anyone would object if I took leave for a few hours.'

'Then I shall bring some servants and a wagon.'

Within the hour, Raymond was being trundled through the town once again, only this time he was resting on a sea of gaudy cushions. Two servants held up a large umbrella to protect him from the sun, and behind him the strange Mr Li sat with the driver.

The horse pulled away from the town and plodded up the hill, which was part of the headland overlooking the mouth of the river. Then it turned down a bush track and they came upon Mr Li's residence.

It was an unusual house, built on poles to comply with the steep hill-side. There were three levels – Raymond could see that from his wagon, because to his astonishment, the house appeared not to have any walls.

'The climate calls for air,' Mr Li said as the servants carried Raymond up the steps to the first level, 'and the view of the ocean will not be denied, hence no obstacles.'

'Like walls?' Raymond asked him. 'But what if it rains?'

'Rain here is weighty. Just falls. Inside is all dry.' He chuckled. 'Come hurricane rains we all get wet. But so far not happen.'

Stretched out on a sofa, Raymond took tea with Mr Li, who asked him about the ulcer and its present condition.

'I have had some little experience with tropical ulcers,' his host said. 'If you wish I will examine it.'

Raymond agreed; he didn't suppose it would do any harm and, besides, the moving about had it throbbing again. He hoped Mr Li would have some balm for the pain.

While he waited for Li to return with whatever dressings he required, Raymond glanced about the house. The floorboards were cedar, as were the roofing timbers above him, and rugs were scattered about the floor. This level seemed to be a small lounge room, with all the furniture set to take in the view, but further back, by a staircase, was a wide bed almost hidden by a mosquito net hanging from a central canopy.

Immediately Raymond felt hard done by, sorry for himself. What wouldn't he give for a mosquito net and something to hold it in place over his bed in that insect-ridden hospital.

He lay back on the cushions, feeling more comfortable than he had for a very long time, and dozed. Mr Li seemed to be taking ages.

When he awoke Raymond was disoriented. He couldn't make out where he was until a voice spoke to him from behind a white curtain and he realised it was Joseph.

He pulled the mosquito net back. 'What the hell's going on here? Where am I?'

'I'm sorry, Mr Lewis, you're at Li's house.'

'God Almighty! Don't tell me I've been kidnapped too?'

Joseph laughed. 'No. Nothing like that. But back at the hospital I heard the nurses talking. They said you were being lined up for another operation. Dr Madison and matron said nothing more could be done.'

'About what?' Raymond said groggily.

'About your leg. They were going to cut your leg off.'

'What?'

Mr Li appeared on the other side of the bed. 'You must not upset yourself. That will not happen.'

He explained that the tea Raymond drank had put him to sleep so that he could examine the ulcer without causing him pain.

'We have cleaned the wound, bathed you and treated your bedsores.'

Raymond flushed but then his fear of amputation flooded back. 'Dear God, are you sure they're about to cut off my leg?'

'Not as long as you stay here,' Joseph said.

'But I can't do that . . .'

Mr Li helped Raymond to sit up and placed pillows behind him. 'How do you feel?'

'Quite well, actually. A little thirsty . . .'

'And the leg?'

'At the minute it isn't bothering me.'

'Infections run all about the body. One sore infects another so it was necessary to treat all. This must be done twice a day.'

'No chance of that in the hospital,' Raymond groaned.

'But Mr Li will see to it here if you stay,' Joseph put in.

Li nodded. 'You are welcome to remain here, Mr Lewis. The infections must be fought and your comfort is just as important. The pain areas have been numbed with herbal treatments, which will last until next we dress the sores.'

Raymond took a while to adjust to the situation but not before he'd learned more about the mysterious Mr Li.

Apparently he was from Tientsin and had come to Cooktown with his brother.

'And where is this gentleman now?' Raymond asked.

Li smiled. 'He has gone to the interior with many coolies to mine for gold.'

'And he left you behind? Your obvious knowledge of medical treatments would be of great assistance to the gentleman out in that dreadful place.'

'True,' Li sighed. 'But I could not fancy that long trek at my age.'

Raymond thought the arrangement quite strange and Li must have noticed his puzzlement.

'Also,' he added, 'I only agreed to accompany my brother thus far. It is Li

Wong Su's expedition. He has several gold-bearing mines operating now – most successful, he says – but he needs this peaceful house every so often to recuperate his spirit.'

'I'm sure he does,' Raymond said grimly.

In the end he wrote a letter to Dr Madison, thanking him for his services, and advising of his whereabouts should anyone enquire. Joseph volunteered to deliver the letter and collect Raymond's belongings from the hospital.

That evening Raymond enjoyed the company of his charming host and the first decent meal he'd had in weeks. His travels in China still fresh in his mind, he was extremely interested in conversing with Mr Li, who, in his turn, wanted to learn more about the Australian colonies and their political systems.

The two men became firm friends and, under Mr Li's strict regime of treatment, within a week the bedsores were disappearing and the deep leg wound was, at last, beginning to throw off the infection.

Nevertheless, Raymond hadn't forgotten his mission. He asked Mr Li to forward a description of the wanted murderers to his brother, and ask if he might keep an eye out for them.

'It's all I can think to do now,' he said miserably.

Mr Li nodded. 'You should not risk going back to the goldfields. You have not the constitution for it.'

'I know. But it's very annoying to have to give up. I feel such a failure in all directions.'

'You still have your leg.'

Raymond laughed. 'Yes, of course!'

The Midas mine, owned by a bank teller from Sydney, employed over a hundred men. The teller and his partner had panned more than six hundred ounces of gold in their first weeks on the Palmer and had progressed to a nearby gully where they dug a fortune in nuggets out of the bedrock. Both wealthy men by now, they decided to go their own ways. They shared their wealth equally, and the partner left for the coast with his gold, while the teller began to peg claims and employ more workers. He was determined to remain until he was the richest man on the goldfields, so he followed up those enterprises by building two hotels in Maytown, making the total at this time of seventeen hotels and a dozen gambling dens in the roaring shanty towns. By then three banks had opened their doors, and the gold assayer was the busiest man in the area. There were also several general stores and Chinese shops, and even a newspaper, called the *Golden Age*.

Bartie Lee's crime had gone unnoticed, the bodies still buried deep in the collapsed mine, which everyone knew wasn't a goer anyway, but his actions left him with a terror of authorities. Rather than peg out a new claim and apply for registration, Bartie took a job at the Midas mine, where he was paid and fed for his toil. This suited him for the time being, until he could figure out how to get his hands on gold. There was so much about, he'd seen so much – gold bars, gold nuggets, buckets of gold dust – that he almost wept at the thought of missing out altogether.

He'd heard that his Chinese shipmates had been captured, another reason not to be raising his head in front of inspectors of any sort, but there was always Jake Tussup. He had to find Jake. His mate Jake. Forget all the rest of them.

'Jake, he been right all the time,' Bartie muttered to himself as he jammed his pick into the rocky crevices on the western face of the Midas mine. 'By Cri' he was. Gold every-bloody-where here.'

Bartie had even dug gold-bearing quartz out himself, quartz that belonged to the boss, though. A cruel thing that. Painful to have to hand it over. And they were searched after every shift; no chance of stealing a speck. He still had his own bag of gold that he kept well hidden but it was only worth a few pounds. There had to be a way to get more.

He could make Jake his partner, then he wouldn't have to front up to any officials; Jake could do that. But where was he? Bartie made up his mind to search the area properly, inch by inch if he had to, but he'd find him.

They pegged out a bigger claim and called their mine the Duchess, and she smiled on them. Theodore Tennant had been right, they had found a reef. He and Jake, alias Rory Moore, worked every day until exhaustion forced an end to the day's work. They were paying the crusher two pounds ten shillings per ton, and the same amount for cartage. The crusher was returning them ten ounces to the ton, so at four pounds per ounce for every ton they took out of the mine, they earned thirty-five pounds. More than either of them had ever earned in a year.

Every time the crusher paid them, they'd bank their money in separate accounts and buy their own supplies, but these joyous breaks from their routine were beginning to take their toll on Theodore. He needed to celebrate, to sing of his swelling bank account, to spend a bit and be happy.

Jake had no objection. Theodore could do what he liked with his money as long as he was on the job each dawn.

His partner could do that. A hardworking, wiry little man, no matter how much he had to drink the night before, he would always have the fire going and the billy on even before Jake crawled out of their tent.

All was well until the night Theodore brought home a friend. A blowsy woman called Maisie, who stunk of gin and cheap perfume.

She was still in Theodore's bunk the next morning, so Jake shook her and told her to beat it.

'I ain't goin' no place,' she whined sleepily. 'Teddy invited me to stay here. He said I could live here with him.'

'The hell you can. Get your fat bum out of here, this is my tent too and there's no room for floozies.'

Theodore pulled back the flap of the tent. 'What's going on?'

'You brought her home last night and she thinks she's staying.'

'But she is. Maisie's my girl, aren't you, love?'

She nodded, plump face dimpling. 'He tried to throw me out.'

'Ah, you can't do that, Rory. I live here too, you know. Me and Maisie, we're getting together for permanent.'

'Oh sure, you've known her full twelve hours,' Jake said. 'Don't be so bloody stupid. She's only after your money.'

'Who are you calling stupid?' Theodore challenged, but Jake knew the whore would win this round so he started packing up his things.

'You. But you keep her if you like. I'm going back to my old camp.'

'Suit yourself.'

It was obvious that Jake's departure pleased them both, but he was still concerned. Everything had been going so well that he saw this woman's intrusion as a bad omen. To Jake, and to most gold miners, good luck was a precious possession. Great care had to be taken to see that the delicate balance was not allowed to slip the other way, so every known superstition to do with good and bad luck was taken seriously. Horse shoes, shamrocks, rabbits' feet and myriad other such talismans were treasured. Charm signs were displayed, anything or anyone deemed unlucky was studiously avoided, and lucky men had to suffer the indignity of being touched by lesser mortals hoping their good fortune would rub off.

Jake crossed his fingers behind his back every time Maisie crossed his path but it didn't help. The reef began to run out, their quartz returning less and less gold. To top that off, Maisie and Theodore began to engage in drunken rows over her spending; she couldn't resist pedlars, with their hats and scarves and trinkets, and no matter how much money her lover gave her, she always needed, or wanted more.

After a few weeks of this Jake was forced to intervene in a stand-up fight between the two of them, a ding-dong drag-out rumpus of hair-pulling and clouts and scratches and screeches and kicks and upturned skirts that brought folk racing over to watch the fun and cheer them on.

And in that audience, grinning widely, was none other than Bartie Lee, his search for Jake Tussup ended.

'I reckon this mine is just about done,' Theodore said, and Jake had to agree. 'Time we pegged another claim then, but Maisie wants it three ways. She's willing to give a hand, see, so there'll be me, Maisie and you, Rory.'

'No bloody fear. Can't you see she's cleaning you out?'

'Now you listen to me, Rory. I like Maisie: me and her, we have a good time. So what if I spend a bit extra these days? There's plenty more where that came from.'

'You're not making sense. One day you're clouting her for spending and the next you're telling me it's all right.'

'And I've told you before,' Theodore said ominously, 'you mind your business and I'll mind mine.'

'Then you keep her out of my tent. I've caught her ratting around in there a couple of times.'

'Are you calling my Maisie a thief?' Theodore was furious. He swung at Jake with a pick handle but Jake was too quick for him; he grabbed the weapon, tore it from Theodore's grip and whacked him behind the knees with it, causing him to collapse in a heap.

'Don't ever try that again,' he snarled. 'I'll give this mine one more week and that's all.'

'You can do it on your bloody own,' Theodore snivelled. 'I know when I'm not wanted. Me and Maisie are pulling up stakes today. You think you're the big boss – well, who needs you? We bloody don't.'

Jake strode off, grabbed a pick and crowbar and dropped down into the mine, where he worked for hours until he was sure he'd seen the last of them. Then he went back, turned the wick up in the lantern and studied the rock wall down at floor level.

For days he'd had an inkling there could be colour in this section, but this time there'd be no sharing with Theodore and his slut. Kneeling, he began to tap and pick at the wall with smaller implements, searching carefully, rubbing, until the familiar gleam caught his eye and he smiled, satisfied.

Within days he had re-registered this mine. He remembered the gay party they had thrown on board *China Belle* when she crossed the equator. It was so successful that Captain Loveridge had promised that they'd have another party when they crossed the Tropic of Capricorn *en route* to Brisbane. At the time, Jake had grinned, knowing most of the crew would have left the ship long before they reached Capricorn. They'd be ashore, digging for gold. But Capricorn had a good ring about it, a mysterious northern ring, and a lucky sign it had turned out to be, so the Duchess mine was no more, and Capricorn took its place.

Jake began to dig in another direction now, and that necessitated moving his tent and belongings. Only then did he discover that several things were missing: his compass, a holey dollar, a thin leather belt, two neckerchiefs and a good penknife, courtesy of the Oriental Shipping Line. It was the best one he'd ever owned, with all sorts of hidden gadgets, and it carried a *China Belle* badge. These penknives were often given to gentlemen as gifts, but the officers made sure they weren't left out. Even Loveridge treasured his penknife, with its red enamelled handle.

'Bloody bitch,' he snarled, relieved that his wallet was always well hidden. But now there was Capricorn to consider. Should he find another partner or employ a couple of diggers? In this cutthroat environment neither plan appealed to him, especially when trivial possessions weren't even safe from thieves.

Maisie was fond of showing off her penknife, especially the natty little appliances from a corkscrew to a nail file, an extra tiny knife, a pipe cleaner and a few other utensils.

'Has it got a mouth organ?' a wag in a bar asked her.

'No,' she said. 'Have you?'

He laughed. 'Let's have a look at it.'

Proudly Maisie handed it over and he weighed it in his hand. 'Good value, this.' Then he peered at the badge. 'Who is China Belle?' he asked.

'Me, of course,' she chortled, pulling her eyes into slits and sashaying across the bar. 'The belle of the bloody ball I am!'

The men roared with laughter when she turned to sashay back and tripped on the rough boards, landing flat on her flabby stomach.

It was Hector Snowbridge who stepped forward and helped her up.

'Thanks, mate,' she said. 'Can I have me penknife back?'

'Yes. Righto. It's a beauty. Where'd you get it?'

'Bought it from a bloke.'

'He got any more? I wouldn't mind one for meself.'

'Nah, he only had the one.'

'Who was he? I could ask him.'

'I told you. He don't have no more.'

A little bloke came over to her. 'What are you doing? Making a sight of yourself again?'

'I am not,' she said stoutly. 'I slipped on the damn boards and this gentleman helped me up. A gentleman, he is.'

'Then he can push off.'

'Who are you telling to push off?' Hector bristled, standing over the newcomer.

'Theodore Tennent,' he replied, shaping up. 'You want to make something of it? I been a boxer in my day. I'll make mincemeat of you, farm boy.'

Thoroughly annoyed but unwilling to suffer pain for his dignity, Hector retreated to a corner of the bar but kept an eye on them.

'Who's she?' he asked a woman sitting nearby.

'She's Tennent's whore.'

'Who's Tennent?'

'Ah, he's got the Duchess mine over by One-Tree Hill. He and his partner do all right too, but Theodore'll have nothing left by the time Maisie's finished with him. Bloody fool.'

'Who's his partner?'

'Dunno.'

Hector thought he should have a look at this Duchess mine to see who Tennent's partner was. Coming upon that *China Belle* penknife was a stroke of luck. He could always pull the whore in and get more out of her but what if this partner was from the *China Belle*? He wouldn't want to scare him off.

Excited, he trudged over to One-Tree Hill but couldn't find the Duchess mine, until someone told him it was now called Capricorn.

He soon came across that mine and called down into the shaft. There was no response but it was close to dusk and people were moving about, so he was able to keep his distance and not draw attention to himself while he waited for the partner to appear. What if he was one of the blokes from that ship? A Chinaman or the officer? What a score that would be! But could he get that lucky?

Hector had forgotten the names of the Chinese and Malays but he did remember the officer's name. One Jake Tussup. Becoming impatient, he started asking occupants of nearby tents and shops if they knew Jake Tussup.

Bartie Lee quit his job and began to keep a watch on Jake. When the skinny man and the fat woman packed up and left, Jake went back to digging on his own for a few days, then he put a cover over the shaft and walked away towards town. To fill in time Bartie went to a barber and had his head shaved bald again, and while he was there he heard this big log of a bloke asking if anyone knew Jake Tussup.

He was too smart to lift his head and reply in the busy barber shop, but he clapped on the little Japanese cap he'd taken to wearing of late, and soon caught up with the enquirer.

'Me, I'm a Jappie man,' he lied. 'My master, big rich Japanese person, wishes to know why you want Mr Tussup.'

'Because I'm the law, mate. I'm a deputy, that's why. So if you know where he is you better cough up or I'll run you in.'

'No, no. My master honourable man. If Mr Tussup a criminal then this is bad.' Bartie Lee bowed. 'My master will be pleased of this information. He will send Mr Tussup away. Never mix with criminals. Never! Thank you, sir.'

Bartie turned to leave but the deputy grabbed his arm. 'Hey, wait on! You say your master knows Tussup?'

'Never no more,' Bartie Lee replied, keeping his eyes down to cover his amusement. Typical of these white men: none of them could tell a Chink from a Jap and they wouldn't recognise a true Malayaman if they sat on one. 'My master chase him away, sir.'

'No, no! Don't do that. I'll come and meet your master, and he can point Tussup out to me. He's a criminal, believe me. Your master would be doing his civic duty in helping us arrest him. Yes, I'll come with you now. Quickly. I suppose I should go back and get the sergeant . . .'

Bartie held his humble stance. He didn't want to rush this bloke, but he had to shepherd him away from Jake's mine. And he certainly didn't want him bringing another policeman. He started to shuffle away.

'Hang on. Where are you going?' the deputy called.

'To tell my master.'

'All right, I'll come with you. Where is he?'

'He has a fine place in the Burrows.'

'Ah yes.' The deputy accepted that was where the Japanese master would be, but he wasn't too thrilled about it. The Burrows was the name given to a crowded Asian enclave.

'You not frighten on Japanese people, sir?'

'No, of course not. But why do we have to see your master? Why can't you take me to Tussup yourself?'

'It is not for me to know where he lives, sir. I am but a servant.'

'Very well. What is your master's name?'

Bartie Lee kept calm. He didn't know any Japanese names, but he knew he must not hesitate. 'Tokyo-san,' he said proudly, as he set off. 'My master a prince. Good fambly.'

The deputy ambled after him. 'A prince, you say? A real prince? Well see, you never know who turns up on these goldfields. Me, myself, I came here with a Member of Parliament, a real one too. That's about as high up as you can get in this country.'

Bartie nodded and padded on, grateful for the Japanese flip-flops he'd stolen from a wagon only days ago. They made him feel a little more authentic.

It was more than two miles to the Burrows, but walking never bothered Hector. He always said that's what feet were made for, and sneered at blokes who'd call the horse to go to the pub. Which reminded him, he'd left his horse in the yard behind the Cock and Bull pub, where he'd come upon the woman with the *China Belle* badge. That was the best clue . . . He savoured the word 'clue', feeling like one of those detectives who solved crimes.

What he would do, he decided, was get Tussup through Mr Tokyo-san, and if that turned out not to be him . . .

'But it would have to be, wouldn't it?' he muttered, keeping an eye on the swarthy Jappie trotting ahead.

'I suppose so,' he answered himself. 'But if not, the partner of that billy goat Tennent might know something. He must have seen the *China Belle* penknife. Or even sold it to her, by God!'

Enthusiasm quickened his steps as they turned down a track and on to a busy road laden with Asiatics of all shapes and sizes, and he poked the servant.

'Don't get too far ahead. I haven't come all this bloody way to lose you.'

He was glad he was wearing good boots – the track was so worn there were rocks jutting up everywhere – but then the servant beckoned him to follow him down a steep incline, which he managed, slipping and sliding in a death-defying drop to the bottom.

Angrily he shouted at his guide, but then he realised they'd taken a short cut, leaving the track to wind its own way down, and were right at the edge of the massed huts and shanties.

'Good, eh?' the servant grinned. 'Save plenty time. We go fast now.'

As they plunged into the crowded lanes, Hector poked the servant again. 'Go fast? We can't go fast here. What are all these people doing? Can't we go another way?'

Never in his life had Hector seen such crowds! They issued from every cross-lane and corner, they stood massed outside street stalls; they sat by waysides; they pushed past swinging bundles on sticks, forcing him to dodge or have an eye poked out. It was like wading against the tide, high tide. He could see the servant up ahead and shouted to him but only got a cheery wave, so he plunged on, hurrying to keep up as best he could, until he realised that he'd lost him. That he must have taken the alleyway they had just passed. He turned back and pushed into the alley, stumbling over baskets and bins, floundering into open shanties, getting caught up in beef strips strung across the alley, angrily forcing his way into another turn, into another crowded alleyway.

Hector was lost. He twisted about angrily, cursing the bloody idiot of a servant who couldn't even handle a small task like this, and he waylaid people, asking directions, wanting to know where Mr Tokyo-san lived.

Some smiled, most ignored him, but he continued to insist on directions until a woman became angry, snapping at him, shooing him away. He stood in a crowd watching a Chinaman weighing alluvial gold on shiny scales and wondered if this fellow was using cheats' weights like so many freelancers on the goldfields.

A woman was selling hot dumplings wrapped in newspaper and they smelled good, so he bought two and pushed back through the crowd to a row of square laundry baskets that would provide a seat for him while he juggled his dumplings, but someone thumped him, hard! His body jolted and he jerked about, surprised, seeing nothing out of the ordinary. He stumbled on a few steps, feeling very tired . . . giddy . . . made it to the first basket and slumped on it, relieved. He lifted up the dumplings. They almost made it as far as his chin, dripping juice, when he felt a wetness on his back, a cold trickling and while he was trying to figure that out, thinking one of the laundrymen behind him had tipped water on him, the pain struck. It came so fast and fiercely he had no time to cry out. The dumplings toppled away. Hector gaped in agony. He felt himself sliding off the basket, thought he was drowning, that he needed to keep his head up, so he clutched the wicker canes and breathed his last breath slumped over the basket.

He looked to be asleep. People glanced, kept going. Some thought he was drunk. Left him there to sleep it off. He wasn't in the way. A dog nuzzled by, gulped down the dumplings, licked the paper, investigated the man and slunk away. A sly thief rifled his pockets. Another had his boots in a matter of seconds. Eventually a woman came out of the laundry, bawled at the stinking drunk to be off with him, pushed him to show she meant business, then ran inside to tell them what she had seen, what was outside their door.

Quickly they picked him up, carried him in, placed him on a bench with a small cushion under his head. Tried to revive him, plunged a towel over the knife wound but they all knew it was too late, so they called an important man, a Chinese man of authority to ask what they should do.

The authorities in the Burrows could not afford bad publicity. The Asians, especially the Chinese, who were in the majority, had enough trouble with the white population without bringing outrage down upon themselves by a report of murder! Murder of a white man in the Chinese sector! If known, this would cause riots, aggravate hostilities, cost the death of many Asians and the usual sweep of random expulsions by immigration officers.

They buried Hector in the lonely graveyard beyond the Burrows, and gave him a headstone similar to all the others. The inscription informed the world that this was a Caucasian, thirty years, gone to his God. And like the other headstones in this particular graveyard, it was written in Chinese characters.

Bartie Lee was sitting on a battered tea chest near the entrance to the mine when Jake emerged.

'Look like you doin' orright, eh, Jake?'

'The name's Rory. Rory Moore. What are you doing here?'

'Thought we oughta have a talk.'

'Well, you thought wrong. We've got nothing to talk about.' Jake swabbed his face and hands in a bucket of water and dried them on a grey towel hanging from a nail in a timber stay.

'You look smart with no beard,' Bartie Lee observed. 'And you got your hair all shaved off like me. Reckon we both got the same idea, eh?'

He thought that was very funny but it failed to amuse Jake. 'Why don't you push off? I've got work to do.'

Bartie's dusky eyes narrowed. 'I say we talk, boss. Better for you we go over to your tent and have a yarn.' He stroked his thin wispy beard.

'What's that stupid beard about?'

'Aha. Me Jappie now. This here beard growing long. You like my black Jappie clothes?'

Jake shook his head impatiently. 'They look like pyjamas.'

'No, all true Jappie.' He jumped to his feet, chortling as he bowed, imitating Japanese courtesies. 'See, me a Jappie orright.' His black satin pillbox hat fell off but he recovered it quickly, dusted it and plonked it on his head, and Jake had to admit that to the untrained eye he might pass as a Jap.

'You speak Japanese?' he asked, but Bartie Lee only grinned and shrugged. 'You're bloody mad. How can you pretend to be a Jap when you can't even speak the language?'

'Speak English,' Bartie Lee said resentfully. 'Everyone speak English.'

Since he didn't look like moving off, Jake took him over to his tent. 'Now tell me what you want. I'm busy.'

'You and me partners now.'

'We are not. Where are your mates?'

'They all gone. Police got Mushi. Other mates run away. The Chinamen, police got them too.'

'I know. It was in the paper.'

'Did the paper say about the woman too?'

'What woman?'

Bartie Lee laughed. 'What woman? Mrs Rich Lady Whore-wood. You took her from us, gave her to the police.'

'I did not. I took her into Cooktown, that's all. Away from Mushi.'

'Man from Cooktown, I hear him say his sister got the reward. One hunnerd pound. That should be my money. You stole her!' He poked a finger at Jake. 'You got plenty. You give me a hunnerd pounds.'

'I'm not giving you a hundred pounds. It was a stupid idea to kidnap those women.'

'Could have got two hunnerd pound.'

'Shut up about the money. You'd have got hanged. Still would.'

Bartie leaned over with a sly grin. 'You too, Jake. They hang you too if I say so.'

'What?' Jake's reaction was swift. The revolver hidden under his bunk was suddenly in his hand and pointed at Bartie Lee. 'Are you threatening me?'

'Who says threat? Me, I come here to be your fren. I be your partner, see.'

'The hell you will.'

'That mine there – you doin' good. I be watching, but you need a partner . . .'

'Who won't be you.'

'Yes, we work hard, get out plenty gold. Or I tell the policemens you Jake Tussup from *China Belle*. They got the Chinamen, they get you too.'

'And you!'

'No fear. See, I got some gold. But can't do the writing things on my own. No good getting a mine on my own. Even panning need the paper tickets. Better I be your partner or I go. Then I tell the policemens. Maybe get someone write a letter, eh?' He looked dreamily about the tent. 'Not hard telling on you, Jake. Easy. They hang you for murder, and I'll be gone.'

'You bastard.' Jake looked down at the gun. 'I should have killed you when I had the chance.'

'What chance? No, you never kill me. I your fren. Tell you what. You still be boss, eh? That fair enough? You see, I work hard. Me, I worked in the big Midas mine for a long time after my boys ran away. But better here. You see, Jake, we get rich.'

'I'll think about it.'

'No. We start today. Did you know there was a law man – he said he was from the law, true – in the barbershop down there?'

'So what?'

'He was asking for Jake Tussup. Asking everyone. I could have just pointed to you, to this mine.'

'You're a liar!'

'Like hell. You ask Mr Barber. If you're game.'

Jake wasn't game. And he knew he was beaten. He couldn't think of a way to rid himself of this bastard. Not yet anyway. It was madness for them to be together. One of them would have to go. But at least he now knew that Mrs Horwood had made it to the police. She was safe thank God. He really was sorry that she'd been involved in that mess, and although she didn't have the sense to realise he was on her side, she was one fine lady. He'd found himself taking a good look at her on the beach, wishing things could be different. She was too fair, and too damned shapely to be married to that old goat Horwood.

Jake shrugged. What a waste, he thought, as he turned back to deal with Bartie Lee.

When it was time for him to leave, Raymond couldn't thank Mr Li enough.

'I don't know how I could possibly repay you for your care and your kindness. My leg is almost completely healed. I feel I have overstayed my time, taking advantage of recuperation to enjoy myself here.'

'The pleasure has been mine, Mr Lewis. I will miss our conversations.'

Raymond looked out over the sapphire-blue sea. 'And I'll miss this magnificent view.'

'Ah yes. This small house is temporary. I have been thinking that one day I should build a sturdier house here. It would make a fine retreat looking out to sea through the palms and jungle plants. They have been a great inspiration to me.'

'You might remain here permanently?'

Mr Li nodded. 'It seems many of our people who have either fled the goldfields, or succeeded there, are looking to settle in this area. The land is fertile and well watered, ideal for agriculture. I feel a responsibility to remain with them.' He smiled, his eyes mischievous. 'You could say I would be a missionary looking to their physical welfare.'

Raymond was not surprised by that statement. He had seen many Chinese people troop up the hill to see Mr Li, who often held court under a clump of bamboo trees near the gate. But then there was also the financial side to his host's operations. On several occasions Raymond, from his vantage point, had seen heavily armed Chinese horsemen ride up to the house and disappear into a side entrance, and guessed they were delivering consignments of Li gold. They looked as if they meant business too, he'd thought, definitely military class, a cut above a lot of the slovenly guards employed by the government to guard their premises.

Which had him wondering where Hector had got to.

'Succumbed to the lure of gold too, I suppose,' he told Gooding.

'Must have. Whoever picked him as a deputy was scraping the bottom of the barrel. He hasn't even bothered to report in any more. And by the way, the hospital sent this over, the horse rug. They said you forgot it.'

'Thank you. I thought I'd lost it. A friend gave it to me, and I really appreciated it when I had those fevers.'

He was reminded of Mal Willoughby and wondered where he was, but Gooding was more interested in his leg ulcers.

'Li healed you, by God! I'd never have believed it. Makes you wonder, doesn't it?'

'I'm astonished, and forever grateful to the gentleman. He's a very cultured person.'

'So he might be, but they say the brother's a warlord. Runs his camp like a military unit, got it walled off into a stockade. But I'll give him this: we don't have any problems with him or his men!'

Raymond made no comment on that subject. 'I'm glad you came by, Sergeant. I'll be leaving tomorrow. The *Torrens* has long gone but I've passage on a coastal steamer going to Brisbane.'

Mr Li came down to see Raymond safely aboard, and, having said his farewells, was about to walk away when another Chinese gentleman came striding down the wharf. He cut quite a figure, Raymond thought, trying not to stare. He was much younger and taller, and he wore the elegant, stiffened jacket and trousers of the upper classes, with a beaded pillbox hat, but Raymond was especially taken with the ornate sword hung from his waist.

'Now that's something you don't see very often in this country,' he said to a seaman working nearby, but then he was surprised to see Mr Li turn about and speak to the newcomer. After much bowing they left the wharf together.

Raymond wished he'd stayed a couple more days. That fellow looked so interesting. He would miss these fascinating people now that he was forced to return to everyday life – which was what? He was an ex-politician, and a lawyer with no interest in his city clients and their trivial problems. Nor was he keen to head home, which was why he'd stayed so long at Mr Li's house, and why he was looking forward to at least a day in Cairns *en route*, to catch up with his new friends.

'It's called playing truant,' he said to himself, and wondered what Mr Li would think of that diagnosis.

Chapter Eleven

Rain was coming down in fat dollops, thudding on the iron roof and sucking all the colour from the bay. Steam rose from the street below, thick-scented steam, stuffed with jasmine. Two pelicans glided through the grey mists and skidded to a halt on the grassy foreshore, and three horsemen cloaked in shiny oilskins rode down the street, their sodden hats drooping, as impervious to the downpour as the birds.

Esme perched on a stool on the veranda and stared skywards. 'I could believe I was in Hong Kong with this rain,' she said to her brother, Arthur. 'As long as I don't look down. Because there's nothing down there. No one. No, I lie. Some riders went by. They looked like spooks, grey spooks, and they could well be, for all I know. Ghosts of lost souls who came to this place and died in the middle of the street and no one noticed until market day.'

She giggled, reached over to the bottle and glass she had placed on a small table, and poured herself another whisky.

'Drink up, brother dear. What was the joke we used to tell? Why did the duke duck into the duck pond?'

'Why did he?' Neville was standing in the doorway leading from their bedroom.

She was startled by his sudden appearance. 'I don't know,' she mumbled resentfully.

'Bit early in the day for the hard stuff, wouldn't you say, my love?'

Esme shrugged. 'What difference does it make?'

'None at all, I suppose, if you consider it's night in the other hemisphere. I heard you talking. Were you talking to Arthur again?'

She turned away from him, refusing to reply.

'Well now, sweets,' he said at length, 'that's the thing. I'm a little worried about you. I don't think it's healthy for you to be always talking to Arthur.'

'Why not? I love my brother.'

'Of course. He was a pal of mine too. But it's rather a waste of time. Arthur's dead.'

'I know that,' she mumbled.

'Sometimes I'm not too sure if you do, Es. Sometimes I think you have forgotten he's dead. Yesterday you told me he was coming to lunch.'

'I did not!' she said angrily.

Rather than argue, he took her in his arms. 'Do you know what I'd like you to do, Es? Talk to me.'

'You're jealous of Arthur!'

'That could well be. I'm always jealous of people who take up too much of my darling's time. Like that shopkeeper Hillier. He's been a bit much lately.'

'He likes me,' she smirked, and Neville kissed her, sadly.

'So do I.' He wondered how much she'd had to drink. It was only eleven thirty and she was tiddly.

No, he corrected himself. No fancy euphemisms. She was drunk. He'd allowed this to go on too long. When they first arrived in Cairns, she'd had good reason to be shocked and upset, and it hadn't bothered him that she took the extra drinks to calm her nerves with so many strangers about. The thing with Arthur had unnerved him a little at the start, when he'd found himself in what she believed was a three-sided conversation, but he'd thought that would pass as her bruises healed and her hair began to look presentable.

Poor Es, he thought, as he took her back into the room. She tries so hard to be happy and gay with people, covering up this side of the story. But why? What has happened to her?

He kissed her fondly. 'Why don't you have a little nap, darling, while I read the paper, then we'll walk over to the wharf and have a meal at that fish café where they cook the reef fish just the way you like it.'

She nodded agreement and climbed wearily on to the bed as Neville took off his jacket.

'First round,' he said to himself. The Fish Café wasn't licensed. He'd have to think of ways to keep her entertained, to shake off Arthur, and the liquor. 'Somehow, love,' he said, 'we'll fix this. We'll have to talk a lot more if that's what you need.'

Clive Hillier called at the Alexandra Hotel and peeped in to the dining room, hoping to see Mrs Caporn, but she wasn't around so he slipped away.

As he was leaving he met Lyle Horwood, who informed him that he had bought passage for Brisbane on a coastal steamer that would be arriving shortly in Cairns.

'You're leaving so soon? We shall miss you, sir.'

'I'll be back later on. I have an important meeting with the Governor in Brisbane,' Horwood said with a conspiratorial chuckle. 'I'm not exactly sure when it will take place. Have to await His Excellency's pleasure, so to speak.'

Clive grimaced as he moved on. I was always under the impression, he said to himself, that these matters remained confidential until the Palace made the announcement, but maybe times have changed. Whatever . . . this would have to be the worst kept secret he'd ever come across.

It occurred to him then that it might be a good move, socially, to join the Horwoods on their journey south, a good chance to really get to know them, and he might even wangle an invitation to the investiture. That should be a gala affair, a rare who's who of Queenslanders. And also, he reminded himself, the steamer would be calling in at Maryborough. They never bypassed that important river port . . . shortly to be overtaken by Cairns, he mused happily. I should take ship with the Horwoods, spend the week in their company, and disembark in Maryborough. I have things to do in Maryborough. By God, I have. She needn't think she can rob me and brush me off like that. Bought the house! Like hell she has!

Lyle bustled about the little town; had his hair trimmed, not cut, and the same with his fine grey moustache, prevailed on the hotelier's wife to purchase some black socks for him, since Constance was still behaving like an invalid with a bad attack of the vapours thrown in. Signed some papers as treasurer of Apollo Properties, witnessed by Esme Caporn who was company secretary. In name only, of course. Being a woman, she'd no idea what she was signing. But all was going well there. Had their trunks sent up to the room. Took a quiet spell in the bar for a pre-dinner sherry while he contemplated the problem of a wife who'd become a social misfit.

In a way, he could understand her reticence in not wanting to mix socially since she'd spent so much time with those thugs. She must know she was the hub of gossip, not all of it pleasant, and it must be difficult to have people staring at her, wondering what they all got up to in that jungle. But . . . enough was enough. She'd just have to put up with it. Pull herself together and do her duty. He didn't care that she was not interested in sex; neither was he, given the circumstances and, anyway, he was getting past it. But it was essential that she sharpen up socially. It didn't matter in this backwater, but in Brisbane! In the Governor's set! A new society was being born in the young colony and Lyle was determined to be one of the stalwarts. He doubted there'd be more than one or two men in this year's list, located in Brisbane, so he and Constance would be the centre of attention.

He shuddered. His wife, with the dribble at the side of her mouth, too nervy to face people, too lazy even to dress her own hair, devoid of conversation, was a disaster, and time was running out.

As he'd guessed, she was all aflutter because the trunks were standing in the corner of the room.

'We're leaving?'

'Yes. I told you we're going to Brisbane. We can't stay here for ever. I have the tickets. We'll be boarding the steamer on Sunday so I'm asking you now to pull yourself together. I know you've been very upset, and with good reason, but please, for my sake if not for your own—'

'I'm not going.'

'What?'

'I don't want to go.'

'Don't talk nonsense, woman. Behave yourself! You will board that ship with me on Sunday. Now why don't you tidy up and we'll go down to dinner? We'll dine with Mrs Plummer. She's your friend, she'll be kind to you, so you have nothing to worry about. Not that everyone isn't kind to you. Can't you see that when we go for walks, they smile and bow? Constance, you'll be Lady Horwood. Really somebody! Won't that make up for everything?'

She picked up her needlework basket and took out the damask tray cloth she'd been working on. 'I can't go, Lyle. I just can't. You know that.'

'I don't know anything of the sort. Now are you coming down to dinner?'

'I'm not hungry.'

'But I am, and I wish you to accompany me.'

'I can't.' She wiped moisture from the corner of her mouth, and he turned away in disgust.

Late that night Lyle knocked on the Caporns' door.

'I say, Neville, hate to bother you, old chap, but you wouldn't happen to have seen Constance?'

Neville stood at the door in his pyjamas, bewildered. 'Mrs Horwood? Is she not in the hotel?'

'No. I asked the maid. No she's not.'

'She might be with Mrs Plummer.'

'She's playing cards in the parlour with the Kassels.'

'Then where could she be?'

'That's what I asked you, sir.' He tried to peer around Neville's bulk, but Esme came to the door.

'What's up?'

'Constance must have gone for a walk,' Neville said.

'At this hour?' Esme turned to Lyle. 'Does she often do this?'

'She does go for walks on her own, yes. But never at night.'

'Where does she go? Who does she visit?'

'No one, to my knowledge. I encourage her to go for walks rather than sit about in the room. It's trying, living in a hotel room; you must find it trying too. Nowhere to call your own. I can't wait to have my own home again.'

'Yes,' Neville said. 'But it's only temporary.' He frowned. 'If your wife is not in the hotel then we really ought to have a bit of a look around. Wait until I throw on some duds, I won't be a sec . . .'

'Jolly decent of you,' Lyle muttered as the door shut gently and he was left in the dark passageway, feeling confused and rather angry. Had the woman simply wandered off or was she deliberately doing this to annoy him? Well, she'd succeeded. He'd give her a piece of his mind when she came back. What sort of lunatic game was she playing this time? Lunatic was right: she'd been behaving like a lunatic ever since Lewis brought her home! He should have damned well left her there.

Caporn came out quickly in a loose shirt, trousers and slippers, and together they went quietly down the stairs, checking with the card players before walking out into the street.

'One odd thing about this town,' Neville said. 'No locks anywhere. There are no night staff yet the hotel is never locked.'

'A lot of damned good locks did on the *China Belle*,' Lyle said irritably. 'Can you see her anywhere?'

'No. It's a dark night. We'll walk along the front. It's very hot; she could be just taking the air.'

Lyle nodded. 'Damned stupid thing to do, if you ask me.'

They walked along the Esplanade until they came to the mangroves, crossed over and returned via the bayside path that led to the wharves. Here again, there were no guards so they searched the area before returning to the town and checking the streets, where activities in noisy pubs and gambling dens were in full swing and, further down, the notorious Blue Star bordello was well lit, open for business.

Lyle hung back while Neville asked the ladies politely if they'd seen a tall lady wandering about, lost. They had not, but promised to keep an eye out.

'She'll turn up, mister,' one of the whores called out. 'Why don't you two come on in and have a good time with us?'

'Not tonight,' Neville smiled.

'Cheek of them,' Lyle said indignantly.

'I wouldn't be surprised if Mrs Horwood is back by now. She probably just went round the block.'

'It doesn't take hours to go round the block in this place!'

But Constance hadn't returned, and the Kassels had to be told, and that meant Eleanor Plummer too. Lyle was sick with embarrassment. He ordered a brandy and sat by the door of the parlour, wishing he'd stayed in his room, let Constance return in her own time.

Esme Caporn came down in her dressing gown, worried now. 'Did they have a row?' she whispered to Eleanor.

'I don't know, my dear. And we can hardly ask.'

'I think I'd better go myself,' Franz Kassel said. 'I look in the yard and the stables, then round the town again, if you stay here with my wife, Mr Horwood. Other peoples should retire, thank you. Nothing more to do.'

Lyle found himself siting with Mrs Kassel, who kept making commiserating remarks, angering him even more. He wished they did have locks on the doors. He could lock his lunatic wife out. Let her stay out for the night. She was probably sulking because she didn't want to go to Brisbane, but what lunacy was this? They planned to settle in Brisbane, to live there. He would be honoured with his knighthood there. This place, Cairns, was a frontier town a thousand miles north of Brisbane. A man would invest here, plenty of potential, but never live here. What was she talking about, not going?

Mrs Kassel bought him another brandy and he was dozing by the time Franz returned, shaking his head.

'She couldn't have met with foul play?' his wife whispered.

'Surely not,' he said nervously.

A bronze sun came steaming up from the ocean, warning of yet another hot day, while dark clouds in the west threatened thunder.

Mr Horwood was sleeping in the parlour as the Kassels crept out to the kitchen to get the day underway.

'Something must have happened to her,' Mrs Kassel said. 'Should you get Sergeant Connor?'

'Wait until Mr Horwood wakes up.'

By midday Sergeant Connor was extremely worried about the disappearance of a white woman in his town, particularly this white woman, Mrs Horwood.

He took several men with him and raided the Aboriginal camps. The blacks were always chased out of the town come nightfall but some could have sneaked back in, especially women. But it was the men he interrogated with whips and truncheons, demanding they tell him what they'd done with the woman, who had attacked her, dragged her into the bush. There was no precedent for such an attack in the town, but he and his off-siders figured it could have happened, the best bet so far, since a thorough search of the town hadn't located her.

In the end, with several black men lying bloodied and beaten beside their humpies, Connor came to the conclusion that they didn't know what had happened to her, as far as he could make out, so he then ordered two blacktrackers to search the bush surrounding the town.

He came back in to confer with Mr Horwood, who was in a state of collapse, and had taken to his bed.

'Poor man,' Mr Kassel said. 'He's sick with anxiety for her. He was up all night, hard on a man his age. No need to disturb him unless you've got good news.'

'We think she's lost in the bush. She must have wandered past the town boundaries and into the bush. It doesn't take long for people like her to get all turned around. I've got black trackers on the job.'

'People think she could have drowned, or been kidnapped again. They say wild blacks could have got her if she went too deep in that bush.'

Connor nodded, noticing the way the bar was busy today, everyone wanting to be in on the excitement. 'I've got men searching the waterfront. She might have fallen in, or walked in, but the odds against her getting kidnapped again are long.'

Mrs Kassel, shocked, sucked in a deep breath. 'You don't think she went into the sea herself? I mean, surely she wouldn't!'

'Who knows? She could have. At high tide she'd have gone down like a stone. Anyway, tell Mr Horwood we're searching the bush. We'll find her.'

He turned to leave but Jesse Field waylaid him. 'Any sign of her yet?'

'No.'

'What was she wearing?'

'Ah, for Christ's sake, Jesse, who the hell cares? She's the only woman missing in the district!'

'Our readers want to know. Ladies like to know these things. Have you got blacktrackers on the job?'

'Yes, I have. They'll find her, dead or alive.'

'Why is she missing? I mean, what brought this on?'

'I don't know. Ask her old man.'

He did. Horwood was lying on his bed fully dressed. He had no idea why Constance would wander out of the hotel.

'She had left the room when I came upstairs after dinner.'

'She didn't dine with you?'

'No. She likes to take meals in the room.'

'Why? She's an attractive lady, one would think she'd enjoy dining with you and your friends.'

'My wife doesn't. She's a very private person.'

'What would she have been wearing?'

'I don't know.'

'It's important, sir, in the search. What would she have been wearing when you went down to dinner?'

'Oh well, let me see. A blue dress. Cotton thing, nothing fashionable.' He peered about him. 'I don't see it and she wouldn't have hung it up after wearing. It would have gone to the wash. So she must have it on.'

'Good. Well done. And no hat, I suppose?'

'Ladies wear hats in the street as my wife would have done, unless she has gone quite mad.'

Jesse caught that tone. 'Do you think this is the problem, that she suffering a little with nerves or maybe a hysteria of some sort?'

'Certainly not. How dare you say such a thing about my wife?'

'The ordeal she went through, the kidnapping, that must have had some effect on her. She must have been terrified.'

'Mrs Horwood is young and strong. Lesser women would never have coped at all. It's in the past now and they never hurt her anyway, so we don't dwell on it.'

'I guess not. But can you think why she would take a walk at that late hour in a rough town like this? I mean it's not exactly Park Lane, is it?'

'Ladies don't wander about Park Lane at night on their own either, I can tell you that.'

'Exactly.' Jesse peered out the French doors at the sultry clouds before picking up his hat and preparing to leave. 'It is obviously quite out of character for Mrs Horwood to do this, which is why it has to be important to know why. Do you think she was running away from something?'

'From what?'

Jesse shrugged as if to say: 'You tell me.'

'Running away? Rot! Bloody childish thing to do, to wander off and get lost.' Lyle flapped his hands impatiently. 'Typical of silly women. They don't know when they're well off! Mr Field, would you ask them to send me up fresh tea? And something to eat. I'm starved.'

'Certainly, sir.'

Jesse called on Mrs Plummer before he left the hotel, but she couldn't suggest where Constance Horwood might be.

'I'm very worried about that girl but I really can't help. I've known Lyle for a long time, but I only met Mrs Horwood on the ship, on the day of the mutiny. And then since Mr Lewis brought her back she's been quite withdrawn. We don't see much of her.'

'What about Mrs Caporn? They were both assaulted by the mutineers. Do they socialise?'

'No. Esme Caporn has made several attempts to call on Mrs Horwood but her husband says she's not up to visitors.'

'Do you think he won't allow visitors?'

'I did at first,' she said, 'based on other experiences not relevant here, but the maids tell me that's not the case at all. They say she won't see people, that it's an effort for her even to get dressed. That he tries to get her to cheer up, even to the point of becoming angry with her, but she just sits and concentrates on her needlework.'

Jesse thought about that for a while and then he asked: 'Mrs Plummer, do you think Mrs Horwood is quite well?'

'I think the girl is much troubled from her bad experiences.'

'But the doctor has seen her several times, I believe, and prescribed sedatives.'

She smiled wanly. 'Ah yes. The latest cure-all. Would it were that easy, Mr Field. By the way, I was wondering – would you mind if I go over and have another look at the house?'

'Not at all. I should hear from Kincaid soon.'

'Thank you. I'm praying. And I'm praying for Mrs Horwood too.'

* * *

Saturday and still no sign of Mrs Horwood. Citizens, convinced she'd been abducted by blackfellows, took up arms, threatening to blast local blacks off the face of the earth. This caused a very swift exodus of blacks from their camps along the foreshore. They fled inland to take shelter with tribal blacks, who were incensed that white men should threaten peaceful families, and who gave fair warning that this would not be tolerated by lighting hundreds of campfires in the mountains overlooking Cairns.

That dark night the fires twinkled like stars above the town, stars full of menace.

'How stupid do you have to be to want to bring those bastards down on us?' Sergeant Connor ranted at the would-be vigilantes. 'They're no different from you. There's always someone spoiling for a fight. So you get about your business and let me run mine.'

Having dispersed the posse, Connor had to deal with Mr Horwood, who was accusing him of incompetence, at the same time bewildering the police sergeant by insisting that he had to be on that coastal steamer on Sunday.

'And by God I will be,' he shouted at the door of the police station, banging his walking stick on the wall to emphasise his point. 'And when I get there I'll go straight to the Governor and inform him that my wife has been abducted again, under your damned nose! I shall tell him that you are not fit to be called a sergeant. What are you doing? Nothing! Riding around the place like a tin soldier! The people of this town deserve the protection of the law and I shall see to it. You mark my words . . .'

Not for the first time, Connor let him rant on. It was easier than arguing with him, but when it ended and Horwood went charging back down the street with the Caporns, he turned to Jesse Field.

'Did you hear that? He reckons he's leaving on the steamer. Do you think he'd go without his wife?'

'I hardly think so, but to tell the truth that's what it sounds like.'

'Sounded to me as if he's going gaga. The strain maybe.'

'Maybe. It's been two days. The bet is that she's drowned.'

'I know. I've got people searching the bay, but don't print that, for God's sake. I don't want to make it any worse for the old bloke.'

Esme took her husband aside when they reached the hotel. 'Does he really mean to leave? He asked me to look after her when we find her! He said he'd be back as soon as possible.' She was confused. 'I'm sure that's what he said.'

Neville grinned. 'Well, he's dead set on getting that knighthood, come rain, hail or missing wives. It wouldn't surprise me at all if he leaped on the steamer tomorrow whether we find Constance or not.'

'He wouldn't!' Esme was aghast.

'I believe he would. He has to find out what the arrangements are for the grand ceremony and then make sure he's there to put his hand up when they call his name.'

Neville rather hoped the old chap would go. His plans were working out extraordinarily well. All the money was in from his immediate circle and several other local investors, amounting to more than five thousand pounds, the biggest haul he'd ever achieved. And so simply. He had gradually syphoned off most of the funds from the Apollo Properties Trust account by withdrawing monies, ostensibly to pay for company expenses, which included the services of the builder who agreed to draw up the plans and to order building materials, most of which would have to come from Brisbane. Another large withdrawl was approved by Lyle himself. This was to be payment for the land on which the shopping centre was to be built, newly surveyed blocks that had to be purchased from local authorities. Those funds ended up as cash in Neville's wallet, the one he kept in their cabin trunk. 'Because,' as he told Esme, 'I can't pay them. That's my excuse.'

'But you have to,' she said. 'Won't the shareholders get suspicious?'

'No. I can't pay yet because I haven't come to an agreement with the clerks in the Lands Office over the purchase of the land.'

'Why not?'

'Because I keep presenting impossible requests, and they have to keep reading the regulations to figure out whether I'm right or not. We need a little more time. Once Horwood is out of town we can go, Es. We'll be home free.'

He prayed Constance would be found wandering in the bush, so she and Lyle would leave and the Caporns could depart on the first ship travelling south, their pockets stuffed with lovely money.

'Where's home, Nev?' Esme asked wearily.

'Aha. I think we'd better give Brisbane a miss, with Horwood batting about there, and go on to the big cities, so the next stop will be Sydney. If we can make this sort of money in the backwoods like Cairns, imagine what we can earn in Sydney!'

'I didn't mean a bus stop, Nev, I meant home. Where's home?'

'Home? Wherever you choose. Anywhere you like, after we make enough to retire. We could buy a house in Sydney if you're sick of living in a hotel. It would be our home until I finish our business there.'

'I'd rather buy a house in Hong Kong.'

'Why not? When we have the money we'll do just that. I want you to be happy, I know you're miserable here; when we leave you'll feel better. Let's go up to the room and relax awhile.'

As they climbed the stairs, Esme was quiet. She had nothing to say until he closed the door behind them.

'I've been thinking, Neville. I have been miserable here, because I am so homesick for Hong Kong.'

'Then I'll do my best to deliver you there within a year. How about that for a deal? Just give me a year. We can't go back there broke.'

Esme sat in the armchair and took off her shoes. 'There's more to it, love. You said we should talk so here goes. I feel trapped, trapped like a wounded rabbit.'

'Why on earth—'

'No.' She held up her hand. 'Let me finish. People are nice to us here. They respect us. It's a pleasant change for me but it also embarrasses me. We live on the outer edge, Nev. We're confidence tricksters, cheats. Thieves . . .'

'I say, that's a bit hot.'

'Oh, please, try the truth for once. I realised why I like to be in Hong Kong. It's because I can hide my face. I can walk about and be totally anonymous all day if I like; get lost in the crowds. Because the few friends we do have there are as shady as we are, and I don't want to look at them or me any more.'

She burst into tears and he went down on his knees to try to console her. 'Darling, I hate to see you like this. But what can I do? Please don't be so hard on yourself. On us. I'll make it up to you.'

'Make what up?' she asked angrily. 'You're all waffle. Can't you see I hate our lives? I'm ashamed because I want to be normal like other people.'

'Like who? The mad Horwoods? Do you aspire to society now?'

'Don't try to con me, Nev,' she wept. 'That's a spurious argument and you know it. There are plenty of normal people about, people who work for a living and do their best for their friends. The sort of people we prey on.'

Neville was shocked and upset. 'I don't know what brought this on! Too much gin, perhaps. Mother's ruin.' He climbed to his feet, took a handkerchief from a drawer and handed it to her. 'Time you took the temperance vow, Es, or you'll get worse, feeling sorry for yourself like this.'

'There you go again,' she sobbed. 'Because I tell you how I feel I'm a drunk. You're shifting the blame again.'

He walked to the door. 'There's no one to blame,' he said quietly. 'We are who we are, Es. That's about the guts of it. You have a rest, I'll go back and buy that frilly white sunshade you were admiring.'

Some stockmen came into town from the Kincaid cattle station and were bailed up by Connor for news of the outback.

'Nothing unusual,' he was told. 'We're starting to get some good rains at last, and the rivers are running deep. The blacks are keeping out of the way of the plague—'

'What plague?'

'Plague of bloody gold diggers marching all over the countryside. A couple of them drowned at Jacob's Crossing. One of them a woman.'

'A young woman?' Connor asked anxiously.

'No, an old dear. Should have more sense than to be staggering around out there. Station blacks found their bodies.'

'Hey, Connor,' one of the men called as he dismounted, 'you seen Jesse Field?'

'Yeah. He'll be around later.'

'Good. Tell him Kincaid said the old lady can have the lease on his house.'

'What lady?'

'I don't know. I'm just the parrot.'

'All right.'

The lady, Mrs Plummer, was on her way to visit that lovely house again, believing it might be her last chance to enjoy it before the owner refused her request.

She opened the gate, frowning at the thick undergrowth advancing on the garden, assisted by the heat and the recent heavy rains. She stopped to dislodge thick vines that were choking red grevillea bushes and then wrench weeds from the flower garden until she remembered it wasn't her place to be doing this. Hurriedly she collected the weeds from the path and dropped them in a corner, then, her hands covered in mud, she walked round the back of the house to use the laundry taps.

As she emerged from the laundry, she was startled to see that the kitchen door was ajar.

She worried she was intruding, that possibly someone else was viewing the house – maybe even, sadly, a buyer.

'Is anyone there?' she called. When no one answered she went up the steps and peered into the kitchen. 'Anyone there, please?'

Gingerly she stepped inside, walked through and called again, but with no response, guessed that the last person inspecting the house must have left that door open.

But had they? Eleanor felt a tingling at the nape of her neck, remembering that she thought she had glimpsed someone or something here on her last visit. Nervously, preparing to run at the slightest hint of trouble, she peered into the sitting room and then into a bedroom. Since there was nothing untoward in that room she turned away, but then she changed her mind and turned back, intending to go across the room and look out on to the veranda.

No sooner had she entered the bedroom than she heard a scuffle and realised someone was there, hiding on the floor on the other side of the bed.

'Come out!' she demanded of the fellow, in a voice that carried more strength than she felt. 'What are you doing there, sir?'

The face that emerged shocked her. It wasn't a man, it was a woman! It was Constance Horwood, looking like something the cat had dragged in backwards.

'Good Lord!' Eleanor said. 'What are you doing here?'

She was so appalled at the grubby state of the woman, who was cringing in a nest of blankets on the floor, and by the obvious trespass, that it took Eleanor a few minutes to summon compassion.

'Constance,' she whispered, moving closer. 'My dear. Are you all right?'

When there was no answer, Eleanor dropped down and sat on the blankets with her. 'Goodness me, you gave me such a fright. I thought there must have been a mouse in here. What a relief to find you instead.'

She reached out and brushed tangled hair from Constance's face. 'I've always thought you have such nice fair hair. Didn't you bring a comb with you?'

'No,' Constance said, clasping her hands together and looking away.

'I haven't one either. But never mind. Why are you here in Mr Kincaid's house?'

Constance shook her head, tried to smooth her crushed cotton dress and then looked helplessly at Eleanor. 'I don't know.'

'Ah, I see.' In fact, Eleanor didn't see at all. She tried to think what to do for the best without upsetting the woman any further. Mrs Horwood seemed to be distraught beyond reason.

'Would you like a cup of tea?' she asked brightly.

'Yes, please.'

'Good. That's what we'll do. We'll go and get ourselves a cup of tea.'

Eleanor climbed to her feet, rearranged her skirts and reached out to Constance to help her up, but when the woman pulled away, she asserted her authority. 'Come on now, Constance, hop up.'

That met with some success. She waited patiently while Constance, very slowly, and with obvious reluctance, got to her knees and then just stood, glumly, miserably.

'Where are your shoes?'

'I don't know.'

'Goodness me, shoes? Where could they be?' Eleanor hunted about the room until she found them, made Constance sit on the bed while she slipped them on her feet, and stood her up again, thinking it was like trying to get a sleepy child moving.

'Now we go!'

At the kitchen door, Constance suddenly balked. 'No!' she screamed. 'I'm not going out there!'

The sudden scream made Eleanor jump. 'Good God!' she said crossly. 'Don't do that to me again! You gave me the fright of my life. There's no tea here, and we want a cup of tea, so we have to go and get one.'

'I'd rather stay here.'

'Very well, sit down at the kitchen table and tell me why.'

They sat for a while in silence. Eleanor was able to provide a glass of water from the kitchen tap but there were no other foodstuffs.

'How long have you been here?' she asked, knowing the answer.

'Days.'

'You must be starving. Is it that bad out there that you felt good about starving yourself to death?'

'I didn't feel good about it.'

Eventually she managed to piece together enough of Constance's answers to gather that after her woeful experiences she hated being in the public eye . . . 'People stare at me all the time, and ask awful questions.'

She also hated living in the hotel, for the same reason.

'So you ran off?'

Constance nodded.

'Didn't you realise that the whole town would be looking for you? That they'd have search parties everywhere?' With difficulty, Eleanor managed a good word for her old foe. 'Lyle is very upset, dear. Very upset.'

'Why? I'm all right here.'

'But you're not all right. You'll starve here, remember?'

'Not if you go and get me some tea, and some food. Please, Mrs Plummer, let me stay. I saw you here with Mr Field and would have asked you then but—'

'This isn't my house, Constance. You're trespassing. You can't stay here. Now we both have to leave.'

'No. I won't go back to the hotel. I won't.'

'Oh dear, what am I to do with you then?'

Constance sat pouting while Eleanor racked her brain for a solution. 'What were you doing here anyway?'

'I saw it on my walks, and it looked so nice I sneaked in and had a look a few times, and when that happened and I had to run away, I knew I'd be happy here.'

'Oh Lord, when what happened?'

'Nothing.'

Eleanor would have left her there and gone for help, to the police being her first choice, but she was afraid that Constance would run away again and this time get into more serious bother. There was only deep bush at the rear of this property.

'Very well, I know where we can go to get a cup of tea,' she said. 'An imposition certainly, but he's a kind man. We'll go to Mr Field's house, which is over in the next street. So come on!' She was on her feet again. 'There's no time to waste.'

There certainly is not, she thought to herself as she helped Constance down the steps. Mrs Horwood, the second Mrs Horwood, is weak and light-headed from malnutrition and she should be in hospital.

* * *

Jesse's housekeeper shrieked with joy when she recognised Mrs Horwood, and after serving them tea and cheese buns, which Constance devoured immediately, she dashed away to find her employer.

'Not a word to anyone else just yet,' Eleanor warned, but apparently that request didn't sink in. Not long after Jesse came home, Lyle Horwood arrived with Sergeant Connor and the local doctor, and despite Eleanor's pleas to take her quietly, the three men converged on the woman.

Eleanor groaned, watching as Constance ran screaming to the corner of the room, refusing to talk to her husband, refusing to talk to any of the men.

As they tried to quieten her she called to Eleanor, 'Mrs Plummer, help me!'

'Can she lie down somewhere?' Eleanor asked Jesse, who quickly ushered them in to his bedroom.

'I only have one bedroom,' he apologised. 'But she can rest here. And by the way, I almost forgot. Kincaid has agreed to let you lease the house.'

'Oh! Marvellous!'

Eventually Constance was resting quietly, and Eleanor came out to see what was happening with the men.

'I told you not to frighten her,' she said to them. 'Mrs Horwood should be in hospital.'

'Not possible,' the doctor said. 'She's not that sick. Our bush hospital can't afford the luxury of treating invalids. It's not Switzerland. You might find a sanatorium in Brisbane, Mr Horwood, where your wife can get rest and good food.'

'An asylum; more like it.' Horwood muttered. 'I am so sorry, Sergeant Connor, that she has caused you so much trouble. And I would appreciate as little coverage as possible in your newspaper, Mr Field. Especially, I want no mention of her trespass. You may simply say she has been found fit and well somewhere. Lost in the bush or something.'

When the sergeant left, and the doctor went on his way after prescribing sedatives, Eleanor took Lyle aside.

'I heard what you said about an asylum. I hope you're not serious.'

'You keep out of this. You've interfered enough. You couldn't come quietly down to the hotel and let me know where she was! Oh no! You had to get the press first. Anything to embarrass me. You were always jealous of me with Fannie, as if she were your property.'

'This has nothing to do with Fannie. Your wife is still suffering from the effects of the kidnapping. She can't face people yet, and living in the hotel upsets her.'

'You think I don't know that? Where else would we live here? Now you get out and mind your own business!'

Taken aback, Eleanor collected her handbag and would have gone in to see Constance once more but Horwood stood by the door, barring the way.

When she left, Lyle called to Field, who was in his office, poring over back issues of newspapers.

'Mr Kassel is outside with his gig,' he said stiffly. 'I'll take my wife back to the hotel now. But remember what I told you. I shall speak to the owner of the paper on this matter myself.'

'There is no need, Mr Horwood. I have no intention of embarrassing your wife.'

'Ha! Good! I'm pleased you've got enough sense to listen to me.'

'Not you, sir. Some of us do have principles.'

They went in to his bedroom where Lyle roused his wife. 'Constance . . . Connie. My dear, you can't stay here, this is Mr Field's room. We'll go along to the hotel now where you can have a nice bath and hop into bed, and Mrs Kassel will bring your dinner.'

She managed to sit up. 'I don't want to go back to the hotel.'

'But you must, Connie. It's just for one night. We're leaving for Brisbane tomorrow. I believe the steamship is already in port.'

At that, Constance started yelling at him. 'I won't go! I won't get on that ship. I'll jump overboard if you try to make me.'

With that, she leaped up and ran out of the front door, racing down the street in stockinged feet to catch up with Eleanor.

'I'll drown myself first,' she screamed, throwing herself into Eleanor's arms. 'I will. I swear I will.'

When he saw that Mrs Horwood was safe with Mrs Plummer, Jesse turned back to Lyle, who had only just made it, puffing, to the gate.

'I think I've got an answer to your problem, for tonight at least,' he said. 'They can go back to Kincaid's house. It's very comfortable. I'll get Lulu to air the place and cook something for them.'

'Certainly not—' Horwood began, but Jesse cut him short.

'Listen, you don't have any choice. You can't force her to go to the hotel. You'd embarrass the Kassels. Your wife is not well, that's obvious, so have a care. She'll probably feel better in the morning. Less confused.'

'Less confused? I'm the one who's confused. My wife has been behaving like a prison escapee, hiding out in someone's home, and now you tell me she may sleep there!'

Jesse nodded. 'It's all right. Mrs Plummer will be living there. She's taking out a lease on that house, so Mrs Horwood won't be trespassing.'

'I don't want that Plummer woman interfering.'

Exasperated, Jesse gave up. 'All right, you don't! What's your alternative?'

Horwood paced a few yards up the street to think about the situation and then turned back. 'Very well. She stays tonight. I'll come for her early in the morning to get her ready for travelling and we'll board that ship. You be firm with her, Mr Field. I cannot have any more of this nonsense!'

* * *

In the morning Lyle arrived at the Kincaid house with a doctor and a nurse, and a warning to Eleanor that if she interfered any further the police would be called.

'I am only trying to help your wife,' Eleanor said. 'She is a lot better this morning. She slept well but she's frightened of boarding that ship again . . .'

'Exactly!' Lyle turned to the doctor. 'I told you Mrs Horwood is full of self-pity, dragging up that trouble on the *China Belle* and the rest of it all over again. It's not good for her.'

'It certainly is not,' the doctor said angrily. 'You should not encourage her, madam.'

Eleanor had not liked this plump little man yesterday, when she'd seen him toadying to Horwood, and she liked him less today. 'Who are you?' she snapped, being deliberately obtuse. 'We have not been introduced.'

He was taken aback and Lyle stepped forward, unimpressed. 'Mrs Plummer, this is Dr Fanning. Where is my wife?'

Eleanor had no choice but to remain, unhappily, in the hall while they attended to Constance.

At first there were tears and arguments, then quieter talk and eventually the nurse emerged with Constance, the two men following.

Eleanor was upset. 'Wait. You can't take the poor girl out into the street like that. Let me at least do her hair.'

'We can do that in her cabin,' the sturdy nurse said firmly. 'Come along now, Mrs Horwood, this way. Good girl, I can see we're going to get along just fine.'

At the front door, Dr Fanning turned back with a smirk. 'Good day to you, madam.'

Lyle marched straight out, followed by Constance, who was supported by the doctor and the nurse. Tears were pouring down her cheeks but she was no longer resisting.

After they left, Eleanor stood sadly at the door of the house she was to call home for the time being, and shook her head.

'Not an auspicious start,' she murmured. 'I hope there's not bad joss in this lovely house. I'll have to get some Chinese to perform happy spells to chase off evil spirits.'

Raymond Lewis was on board the steamer *en route* to Brisbane, when it berthed in Cairns. He took advantage of the few hours in port to rush about and catch up with his former shipmates.

The Horwoods were busy packing, prior to joining him on the voyage south, so that was good news. The Caporns were also at the hotel. They invited him to morning tea and he heard all the news about the company Lyle Horwood had formed with them, to build a shopping centre in Cairns – an interesting and probably viable concept Raymond thought, but he declined to take advantage of their kind offer to invest in the remaining available shares.

'Good of you to think of me,' he told Neville amiably, 'but I seem to have lost interest in business affairs. Had a lot of time to sit about and rethink my life, you know. It had become rather boring.'

'Hardly boring since you stepped aboard the *China Belle*,' Neville laughed.

'True. Although I was intrigued with China. During my convalescence in Cooktown with the bad leg, I stayed with a remarkably erudite Chinaman, had a very pleasant time, very pleasant. Too long, according to my sister, so I must get on home before she calls out the military.'

He couldn't bring himself to mention that he'd lost his Parliamentary seat and was relieved that the subject didn't come up. There were too many other matters to talk about, not least the mutineers.

'From what we can make out, all the Chinese from the ship have been arrested, except Ah Koo, but the others have gone to ground.'

'It's such a small place, I don't understand why the police haven't caught them all,' Esme said.

'You have to see those places, Cooktown and the goldfields. Imagine over a thousand people converging on this little town and more pouring through every time a ship berths! Authorities can't catch up, let alone try to organise facilities, and from what I saw, the government doesn't appear keen to proffer much help.'

'Why not?' Esme said.

'Because gold rush towns can quickly turn into ghost towns and facilities are left to rot. So, for now it's chaos. Difficult to find anyone, especially with so many Chinese, and people with bogus names. But I'd better run along. It's been nice to talk to you again, and I'm glad you're finding this town very liveable.'

'Oh yes, we do,' Esme said enthusiastically. 'It would be lovely to just stay here.'

'But I thought you were settling here?'

Neville jumped in on that. 'Of course we are,' he said quickly. 'But Es can't make up her mind. She misses Hong Kong very much.'

'Ah. I suppose you would, my dear. A huge contrast in life styles. Oh well, you'll sort it out, I'm sure. Now I must go and find Mrs Plummer.'

'May we come with you?' Esme said. 'We'd love to see this house.'

'By all means,' said Raymond jovially. 'Let's call on her.'

Later, after hearing of Eleanor's slight misgivings about the presence of bad joss in the Shalimar house, it was Raymond who volunteered to trot over to the Chinese quarter to seek advice, a convenient errand for him. He was able to purchase for himself a small quantity of opium. What had begun as urgent pain relief, issued to him by the Maytown doctor, had become a comfort when he was in hospital, his supplies provided by Joseph. Then Mr Li had shown him the sensual pleasure of opium-taking in tranquil surrounds, and Raymond learned to enjoy the passivity of this self-indulgence without the guilt often attendant upon the use of opium. Before he left, Mr Li had presented him with a small gold pill case for his supply, and taught him what to ask Chinese herbalists for. Raymond was aware that even respectable druggists did sell it, but he had no idea who they might be in Brisbane, and anyway, it would be preferable to obtain his pills from less public sources.

He was a happy man when he returned with the necessary candles, firecrackers and herbs to chase away Eleanor's bogeymen, and they all came down to the ship to see him off.

'I'm very much enamoured of North Queensland,' he told Eleanor. 'All these experiences have widened my outlook. I know I would find my law practice far too tedious now, stuck in dark offices with musty files and the necessity to listen to endless confrontations, which seem trivial to me these days.'

'You may think differently about all these things when you are back in your own home with your pipe and slippers,' she laughed. 'It isn't so easy to throw everything aside and step out into a new life. I'm trying to do that . . .'

'I'm sorry, my dear, I didn't know . . .'

'It's all right. Look at what I walked into! Dreadful trouble. The mutiny! It's bumpy, Raymond, so watch out.'

'I will that. But you take care. Whatever happens I shall certainly return to visit you all one of these days.'

When the steamer sailed across the bay from the Cairns wharf, there was no sign of Constance or her nurse, but three gentlemen stood on the aft deck looking back at the little town nestled in the shadow of the misty green mountains.

'Splendid view,' Raymond said.

Clive Hillier agreed. 'Remarkable. I was impressed with this scenic bay the first time I saw it, and never tire of observing it.'

'I believe you are disembarking in Maryborough?' Raymond said.

'Yes. I have property there that I need to dispose of before we settle permanently in Cairns.'

Lyle Horwood turned abruptly to Clive. 'Why are we stopping there?'

'It's a well-established port, sir. Gateway to the rich inland cattle and sheep stations.'

'Never heard of it!' Horwood said peevishly. 'But see here, I wanted to talk to you, Lewis, now that you're back from your wanderings. When we get to Brisbane I'll need an introduction to the new Premier. And tell me this, with the new government, does the Governor of the colony remain the same?'

'Yes.'

'That's a relief. I say, Hillier, when you get back from this place you're going to, I want you to take a good look at the foundations of the Apollo shops, make sure they're firm. I won't have any shoddy work, and I want the best timbers used. You can see to that too. Come on, Lewis, can you go a game of crib?'

'I suppose so,' Raymond sighed. He hated crib and wondered when he would begin this great reformation of his life. Obviously not yet.

Chapter Twelve

The river port of Maryborough was bustling with pride. The quarter-century anniversary had been a huge success, and country people, having made the effort to travel hundreds of miles to join in the celebrations, stayed on for weeks afterwards, keeping everyone busy.

Clive had a distinct twinge of fear when he stepped ashore in the crowded town, seeing all the buggies and wagons lining the streets, the hotels so busy and so many pedestrians strolling along under the shop awnings. Maryborough made Cairns look what it was: a lowly little settlement on a beautiful bay; a rough frontier town that may not prosper as this town had done. Then where would he be? He shuddered.

'It will,' he muttered to himself. 'It has to. I know I'm right.'

'Ah there, Clive,' a stock agent confronted him in the street. 'What's this I heard about you deserting us?'

'Yes, moving north.'

'To Cairns, they say?'

'Yes.'

'Mad you are. It's too far up. The blacks'll take it back one dark night.'

'I shouldn't think so,' he said stiffly, and marched on, past shoppers inspecting men's shirts in the window of the Hillier's Emporium, past the entrance to the ladies' section where a rack of monstrous evening dresses, all reds and purples, caught his eye. He nearly choked at this aberration, standing there, staring, reminding himself that someone else's taste was now in vogue. He turned to flee, only to be confronted by two ladies, former customers, who gushed with questions, anxious to be the first with news of his movements.

'I believe Mrs Hillier is remaining in our fair town.' One of the ladies slid that remark into the conversation before he could make his escape, but he pretended not to hear, and in return assailed them with a glowing account of the scenic beauty of Cairns and its bay, compared to the muddy Mary River behind them, until they began to fidget, looking about for rescue.

'Good day to you, ladies,' he said at length, raising his hat and marching on.

'Stupid bitches,' he muttered, wondering what sort of a story Emilie was putting about. Wondering what the bank manager had made of her sending him only half of the sale monies. He felt his face redden and pulled the brim of his panama hat down to avoid recognition and further irritating approaches. But then he realised he had outlived this country town, so he didn't have to worry about upsetting customers, or anyone else here for that matter. Maryborough, he decided, now that he was back and could assess it again, had reached its peak. Towns like Cairns had the world at their doorstep. He'd made the right move and had no regrets.

He had a few business calls to make in the town and then it would be time to call on Emilie.

When he turned into the street he could see the house sitting as neatly as ever behind the hibiscus hedge and, looming over it, the big jacaranda tree was in full bloom. That pleased him as he crossed the road. He'd always found the purple jacaranda a spectacular tree. It was one of the reasons he had chosen this house.

When he walked in the front door, he hesitated a moment before dropping his suitcase on the polished floor. It looked different. Furniture had been moved about. The brown drapes that should be hanging in the passage to separate the front hall from the back of the house were gone, the leather chaise from the parlour was now in the hall beside a tall potted palm and the hallstand looked decidedly bare – but the leghorn sunhat hanging there, that was Emilie's.

He added his hat, took off his jacket and hung that too, then, since there seemed to be no one about, he went through to the kitchen where Nellie was at work.

'What's for dinner?' he asked, and she jumped, sending a tin baking dish clattering to the floor.

'Why, Mr Hillier! You gave me such a start!' Then overcome with confusion she managed to stammer: 'Oh, Irish stew, sir, Irish stew, and I'm stewing plums here too . . .'

'Good. I like Irish stew. Where's my wife?'

'In the laundry, sir.' Nellie jerked her head in that direction. 'Do you want me to tell her you're here?'

'Yes. I'll be in the parlour.'

The crystal decanters were still on the sideboard but they were empty, as was the cupboard below. He banged the door shut: not a drop of liquor to be found. Not even a sherry.

Emilie appeared in the doorway, wearing an apron over a cotton dress, all of her dark curls, except for a few strands, caught up in a mobcap, and Clive grinned. 'I say, you look rather fetching in that cap. What are we doing? Spring cleaning?'

'I'm washing the drapes. What are you doing here, Clive?'

He sat in the big leather armchair, his favourite armchair. 'I live here, or hadn't you noticed? I don't suppose there's some sherry in the pantry?'

'No.'

'Oh well, never mind. I thought you would have the house packed up by this.'

She remained in the doorway. 'Why?'

'So that we can ship everything to Cairns. I have to get back as soon as possible.'

Emilie moved in to stand behind the circular table. 'All of your possessions have been shipped to Cairns. This is my house now. You know perfectly well I will not be going to Cairns. I explained everything in my letter, so, Clive, please don't pretend this is not happening. The marriage is over. I'm really sorry about it but I've made my decision and it's final.'

'All right,' he said calmly. 'But do sit down. You'll give me a stiff neck. You have to allow me to have my say. It's only fair.'

She took a deep breath, nodded, and sat primly on the couch by the window. 'If you must,' she said, and Clive could see she was very nervous.

He leaned forward. 'Right then. First things first. You've oversimplified everything, Emilie. In fact, you've been downright foolish. This house, for instance – the deeds are in my name.'

'I know. I'll have them transferred to—'

'Ah, but I'm not selling to you. I did not agree to that arrangement. I will not. The house will be sold to the first taker. I need the money. But you don't have to worry about it because I'll do the organising. That's why I'm here. I've arranged for a shipping firm to pack up our furniture. They're coming tomorrow. And what else? I know . . . I talked to the bank manager. He's sorry we're leaving. I've drawn out the balance of our account—'

'You can't do that! The account was mine!'

'What can't I do?' he smiled. 'This coming from someone who tried to take my house. I'm your husband. What's yours is mine, what's mine is yours. We share, my love.'

Her face was chalk white.

'Now, as for the rest of it, Emilie, no hard feelings, eh? I can understand your nervousness at not wanting to live in a strange new town, but Cairns is really a charming place. You'll love it.'

'I'm not going to Cairns,' she said through clenched teeth.

'Oh, don't be silly. Of course you are.'

'I can't, Clive. I simply can't. The way you treat me is just dreadful. I've warned you before, I can't live like that.'

He stood and went over to her. He sat down beside her, took her hands and held them gently. 'Don't you know how much I love you? That letter you sent me almost broke my heart. Have you forgotten our wedding vows? And our beautiful lovemaking?'

Emilie blushed; tried to draw her hands away but he wouldn't allow it. 'You're so beautiful,' he said, kissing her on the cheek with a lightness he didn't feel. He wanted to take her in his arms, make love to her here, right here on the couch, such was the passion she was arousing in him after the weeks of separation.

She was talking. Arguing. Blathering on. Lecturing him. And all the time he was thinking of nothing else but her warm body. His arm went around her, made her cross, so he withdrew it and, teasing, slid a hand up her dress to caress her thighs.

'Stop it!' she was saying. 'Stop it!' pushing him away, but she was small, and slight. Laughing, ignoring her anger, he lifted up her skirts and then Nellie came in.

'Oh!' she said. And then another 'Oh', this time of irritation. 'Dinner's ready,' she added drily.

He behaved as if nothing had happened – that she hadn't written the letter. That she was only bluffing when she insisted she was leaving him, and required financial support. And he was so nice about everything that Emilie was frustrated at every turn. He simply wouldn't listen to her. And worse, he had trampled her plans. How could she leave him now? He wouldn't hear of a separation and it was obvious not a penny would be forthcoming. She had nothing now. Emilie struggled through the meal, realising she'd made a fool of herself. How could she have been so naïve as to think he'd allow her to buy the house? Why hadn't she taken the money and run away when she could? Before it was too late.

It's because I like it here, where I know people and could easily re-establish my life. With the baby. It's because I was too scared, too much of a coward to run off to a strange place on my own.

Believing there was still a chance they could come to some arrangement for a separation because he was being so nice over dinner, Emilie responded with as much courtesy as she could muster, despite Nellie's frowns. In her heart, though, she knew it was hopeless, and while she worried that he might want to stay the night, he talked about the new poll tax of ten pounds on Chinese immigrants, the colonials defeating the visiting English team in a cricket match, and congratulated Nellie on her stew.

'I know you're still upset with me, Emilie,' he said later, 'though you're keeping a brave face, so I'll sleep in the spare room. Unless you'd rather—'

'No,' she said quickly. 'No.'

'Very well,' he shrugged. 'Now don't be worrying your pretty head any more. I'll be the best husband in the world, you'll see. We'll be all right, Em, off to a wonderful new start.'

That night she wished she had a lock for the bedroom door, but Clive surprised her by not bothering her at all. He was up early, fixing the hinge on the side door and looking about for some paint to 'touch up' the front fence to please prospective buyers.

At breakfast he was all enthusiasm. 'We've no time to waste now, Em. We have to start packing right away. At least you've sent some of my stuff on.' He added without a flicker of resentment. 'That will save some time.'

'Clive,' she said, 'I've told you. I'm not coming with you.'

'Of course you are. You can't sulk for ever, Em. We've got a lovely voyage ahead of us. It'll be like a holiday, and you're going to love Cairns. Now cheer up, and when you've finished your coffee get Nellie into packing up the parlour. The family portraits have to come down. And the wall brackets, we're not leaving them.'

The house was sold. They called on friends to say farewell. Mrs Mooney, proprietor of the Prince of Wales Hotel, gave them a surprise dinner party, which was enjoyed by everyone, but she found time to take Emilie aside.

'Forgive me for being a bit nosy, but we're old friends and I care about you, Missy,' she said, picking up on the nickname bestowed on Emilie by Mr Manningtree. 'Didn't you say you weren't going to Cairns, or was I hearing things?'

Emilie was embarrassed. 'I did think of staying on here. I really didn't want to leave Maryborough, but it wouldn't work. Cairns is too far away.'

'Is that all it is then?' Mrs Mooney said. 'You've not got any worries about going?'

'Oh no,' Emilie sighed. 'Just rather sad, that's all.'

'You can always come back here, you know. Plenty of room upstairs.'

'I know.' Emilie kissed her on the cheek and fled back to the table before Mrs Mooney's kindness, and her obvious suspicions, reduced her to tears.

She hoped Clive had changed, that he would mend his ways. It was possible. And he did love her. He'd never been kinder or more attentive to her than in the last few days, and last night he'd come to her bed, all apologies, his loving self again.

But she still couldn't bring herself to tell him about the baby. Not yet. Not until she was absolutely sure of him. Nellie had said to her straight out that she was a damn fool when she said goodbye, and Emilie was too proud to admit she didn't have any choice.

'We'll see,' she sighed.

The ship ploughed down river and out into the bay. Across the other side was Fraser Island, the great sandy island that she'd tramped over to see Sonny, to find him camping along the great ocean beach at a place he called Orchid Bay. Where they'd talked seriously at last. And she'd broken the news to him that she would be marrying Clive.

She smiled, recalling his sad reaction: 'Oh well, I suppose you could do worse. Like marrying me.' He was hurt but, typically, had to make a joke of it.

Who could tell, she thought. Sonny was different from anyone she'd ever known, a countryman, a bushman. He didn't go looking for adventure, it came to him. Landed on him. Life with him would have been very strange, and unpredictable. Clive's world was hers. Neat. Businesslike. Nice house. Nice friends. Church on Sundays. Safe. That was her choice. Lately, though, she'd been thinking a lot about Sonny, because of the ongoing news of the mutineers. She'd read about the tragedy in the newspapers and felt for him, knowing how dreadfully shattered he would be over the death of his wife. Sonny, who wore his heart on his sleeve.

Emilie turned back and went into the saloon so that she wouldn't have to look at Fraser Island, or think about Sonny. Or Clive. She felt weary now and wanted to try to make the best of this voyage.

Chapter Thirteen

His arrival at Cooktown in the steamer *Morrison*, with several hundred diggers, was observed from the minute he stepped ashore. He was seen to step out into the town, up one street and down the next, as if he needed to learn and understand the layout. Then he went to the big Chinese general store in Charlotte Street where he bought supplies: blankets, an oilskin groundsheet and coat, and a rawhide hat, leaving his purchases there to be collected later.

He bought a newspaper, sat in the bar of the Digger's Rest Hotel to read it while he drank a pint of beer and ate a steak pie. And he asked a lot of questions in a cool, polite voice, surprised to hear that there was now telegraphic communication between Brisbane and Cooktown, and even between Cooktown and the Palmer goldfields.

'Well, I'll be blowed!' he said, and walked outside to watch six horses being harnessed to the regular coach bound for Maytown.

A stranger in a town full of strangers, he didn't seem to be in any hurry. There was nothing to report for the next hour or so, he was just there, sitting on a bench outside the hotel, taking in the town, watching riders and passers-by.

Sergeant Gooding walked past him, in uniform, but there was no communication. None.

The stranger took a room at the hotel and at dusk set off to explore the town all over again. This time, though, he started asking questions in the Chinese section. He was looking for Malayamen. Malay seamen. Malay coolies, who would be more easily spotted by Chinamen. He handed out money, holey dollars and the occasional sovereign everywhere he went, even into gambling dens. Walked right in without a qualm, talking to people, looking around. He sat at street tables, smoking, drinking Chinese wine, smiling his broad, sleepy smile sometimes, but mostly all seriousness, listening intently to every man who came to him with information.

'Aha!' Mr Li thanked the servant who'd followed the stranger until he'd retired to his hotel room. 'You have done well. This is indeed our Mr

Willoughby. Though he appears to be casual about his movements, he does not waste his time. Follow him again tomorrow.'

The next day Mr Li was pleased to be able to send a telegram to his friend Mr Lewis in Brisbane to advise that the person he was expecting had arrived in Cooktown. Tactfully, he did not include the name since Mr Willoughby had not contacted the police or any reporters, but he was extremely surprised when Mr Willoughby himself came tramping up the gravel path, leaving Mr Li's bewildered servant hanging back at the gate.

'Are you Li Weng Kwan?'

'That is correct. What can I do for you?'

'You can tell me why you are having me followed. Your flunky back there has been on my tail ever since I came into town.'

Mr Li stepped back, bowed, and swept an arm out in welcome. 'I am honoured that you should visit my humble house, Mr Willoughby. Will you join me for tea?'

'No, thanks.'

Mr Li noticed his visitor was armed today, a revolver in a holster at his hip, half-hidden by the cotton drill jacket.

'Do not be alarmed,' he said. 'Your friend Mr Lewis asked me to look out for you.'

'Lewis? Mr Lewis the politician? He was here?'

'Yes. He was searching for the mutineers, but fell foul of tropical ulcers so had to go home. He was most grieved that he was unable to locate the ringleaders.'

Willoughby nodded. 'Good of him. But still no reason for you to snoop on me. What are you up to?'

'Curiosity, that's all. I was interested to see if you could make any headway. So far only the Chinese mutineers have been caught.'

'I know that. All except Ah Koo, the cook. Do you happen to know where he is?'

'No.'

'Then I'll be on my way. And call off your heeler. I don't need company. Good day to you, sir.' He lifted his hat and walked back down the hill.

Mal glanced back at the house decorated with the usual lanterns and drapes and soft wind chimes.

'Trust the Chinese to make themselves comfortable,' he murmured amiably, remembering Mr Xiu's fantastic junk moored in the Mary River at the time of the Gympie gold rush. 'Rich ones, I mean.'

He wouldn't have minded the decent cup of tea that Li would certainly have provided, but it wasn't worth getting tangled up with that bloke until he knew more about him.

Talking to several Chinese last night he'd soon identified the man who'd been behind him at every turn, and discovered that his boss was the wealthy Mr Li who lived on the hill. A few more half-sovereigns bought him more information, in that Li's younger brother, Wong Su, owned and managed the huge Moonflower mine and battery at the Palmer, where he employed about three hundred coolies.

Now that he'd met Li the elder, Mal understood the operation. The one he'd met was the business boss, handling the import of coolies and whatever else they needed, and the export of their gold, a tricky business with revenue men hot after every penny of duty. Mal had heard that a lot of Chinese gold was smuggled out, and that didn't surprise or interest him. Not for one minute had he believed that Li was keeping an eye out for him only on Raymond Lewis's behalf. There was more to it than that. Mal wished Lewis hadn't been so trusting of this mob. He could do without complications. They could be friends or enemies of the Xiu family, or even their connections. They could also be smugglers on a heftier scale than just of gold, since opium was no small market. Then again, looking about this town where they had bought up prime land, they could just be putting down roots. Not a bad move with all the civil unrest in their own homeland, but from the point of view of the colony of Queensland, and the Aborigines, a very bad idea. Not that Mal cared one way or another. Just so long as they kept out of his way.

He had a start. Some Chinese had told him of a group of Malays who were working their own mine at the Palmer. And no, they did not have a white man with them. His informants couldn't provide names, but Mal explained they wouldn't have used their own names, so that didn't matter, but he needed the location of their mine.

He discussed this with a few men who had forsaken the goldfields for their own market gardens on the outskirts of town, since food supplies, as Mal had already noted, were bringing outrageous prices. Several of them recalled that one of the Malays was arrested for rape.

That was important news but Mal needed to know where that mine was, and eventually came away with a carefully drawn map showing the exact location of the Malayamen's claim.

The new Cooktown police station, with its four rooms and a veranda, was opened without fanfare. Scowling residents waited in line to air their grievances as Sergeant Gooding and his two constables lugged boxes of papers across the road, and unloaded cheap furniture from a packer's dray.

'These windows have to have shades,' Gooding said, contrasting the glare of the rooms with the soft light of his tent office. 'I'll go bloody blind in here.'

'We could paint them,' a constable offered.

'We could board 'em up too,' the sergeant snapped at him. 'Take those boxes to the back room and unpack them into the cupboard there. I'm going to see Tilly Yeung – she's got bamboo blinds in the front window of her shop. She might get us some.'

As he strode down the street, he pondered a problem that had been nagging at him for some time. Where was that clown Snowbridge? He hadn't been sighted for weeks. Someone said that with the Palmer beginning to peter out, Hector had joined the rush to the new Hodgkinson goldfields, and Gooding wouldn't have put it past him, but for the horse. He'd left his horse outside the Cock and Bull pub in the heart of the Palmer mining district.

The horse had a police brand, fortunately, or it would have disappeared by the first morn, and the saddlebag was intact. It contained some potatoes, tea and salt; a knife and spoon, a blue singlet and some rags; an authority from Cairns police appointing Snowbridge a temporary deputy, application forms for mining claims and several tins of tobacco. Nothing that would give any indication of where he might have got to.

'I'll have to post him missing,' Gooding muttered to himself, knowing that the Cairns police wouldn't take kindly to this news. What did they send a fool like that up here for anyway, he mused. Lewis had said he was 'difficult', a kinder description than others had given. The men at the Palmer station believed he could have gotten into a fight and come off second best.

Gooding stepped off the boardwalk outside China Tilly's shop, taking special interest in her bamboo blinds until he saw a large poster plastered on the wall. It carried sketches of two men, one an Asiatic, the other a white man, both clean-shaven. He peered at them, didn't recognise either of them, but the names were clear enough: Jake Tussup and Bartie Lee. And the reward: one thousand pounds.

'What's going on here?' he asked, bewildered. The smaller print was in Chinese, but down the bottom of the page was another name: 'M. Willoughby'.

'Well, I'll be damned!' he said, and waded through the press of customers in the shop to find Tilly.

'Do you know anything about that sign out there?'

'Oh yes,' she gushed. 'Nice man. He speak Chinese! Good sign, eh? And a tousand pound! Ayiyi!'

'Where is he now?'

'I doan know. Sign say any information on the bad men tell police damn quick and get the money.'

Gooding forgot the blinds. The posters were everywhere, in Chinese and in English. And they were professionally done. There were no facilities in Cooktown for a job like this. Willoughby must have brought them with him. Willoughby! He'd been told that this bloke would turn up sooner or later but had expected him to report in. This was worrying. It meant Gooding had a vigilante on his hands. He hurried back to the station to find two Chinese boys carefully pasting posters on the outer wall of his new building.

'Hey!' he yelled. 'Stop that!'

One of the boys grabbed the bag of posters and raced away, but Gooding collared the other one.

'Who paid you to do this?'

'White boss. No bother, he say. Let me go!'

'When did he pay you?'

'Yesterday.'

'I thought so. Take them down, all but one, savvy? Get them down now or I'll lock you up.'

The homemade paste of flour and water was still damp, so Gooding left the kid to it and stormed inside.

'Did a bloke called Willoughby come in here?'

Constables and people in the queue all looked blank. But then a man broke from the line and called out: 'Hey, mates! Look at this! I'm going after these blokes! Jeez! Wanted for murder!' He turned to Gooding. 'Would it be a thousand each?'

'I don't know,' the sergeant growled. 'Where does it say "for murder"?'

'Right here!'

Gooding went back to study the English version, and shook his head. 'Damn fool! I haven't got time for this!'

He looked down the road and sure enough, men and women were already rushing up towards the police station, most of them with their lies rehearsed, he was sure, and with pictures of pound notes in their eager eyes.

'Bugger Willoughby!' he snarled, and called to Constable Hicks, 'Come inside and I'll brief you on the *China Belle* mutiny. Then I want you to line up that mob, there'll be more yet, and interview them one by one. Make them sit by the fence and if they complain about being kept waiting, all the better; tell them to push off.'

He jerked his head and took Hicks into his office. 'Not that we can expect any of them to give up that easily. Not with Willoughby's reward blotting out the sun.'

Camped deep in the rainforest. Mal was wakened by insistent birdsong, and he lay there listening, trying to identify the songsters. The melodic peals of butcherbirds were easily recognisable and, in the background, the bell-like pipe of king parrots. Lesser beings of the parrot family flashed and screeched through the treetops and the 'tuwhip' of the whipbird lashed the air. One after another he listed more than a dozen familiar members of this bush orchestra, and he gazed at the greenery above him, watching a pair of pink and grey galahs tearing strips of bark from a tree to reveal tasty insects.

Mal sighed. He'd always wanted to explore these misty green mountains and here he was, but not in the circumstances he would have chosen. This rainforest truly was beautiful, with its strange plants and peculiar blooms. He wished Jun Lien were here so he could show it all to her and introduce her to the birds and all the other little bush creatures that skittled about.

'But she's not,' he said finally. 'And Jake Tussup is. He's out there on the other side of the ranges. Keep your mind on the job.'

Soon he was back on the track again, a packhorse roped to his own mount, riding with a group of men who had come all the way from New Zealand, and were now hoping that the gold would hold out long enough for them to find their fortunes.

Mal was aware that Tussup and the others could have left the Palmer by this time, but no matter where they were, he'd track them, starting with the Malayamen, if the posters didn't get results.

The partnership, based on mutual distrust, was working. To their neighbours, Bartie Lee was 'Moore's' coolie, and Bartie was happy with the arrangement. His short stint as a boss had been a monumental failure and, worse, left him with a burden of terror regarding his former companions. He had no sense of guilt over their deaths, none at all, but his superstitious mind kept conjuring up images of them popping up from their grave in that tunnel and pointing at him. And then the white men with their ropes would hang him from one of those high gaunt trees.

He had money, more money than he'd ever seen in his life, one hundred and eighty pounds at last count. Jake had more, a lot more, from his previous partnership with the skinny white feller, and Bartie wanted to go now, but Jake wouldn't quit while there was still gold to be found.

'We rich blokes now, Jake. We go now, eh?'

'No,' Jake had said. 'That money will soon be gone and what then? We have to get as much as we can while we can. If you want to go, you go. I'm not stopping you.'

So Bartie hung on. Truth was, he'd come to rely on Jake to look after all the tricky business involved in mining and gold changing. It was Jake who decided that no more gold would be found in their last mine and moved them to another claim, which was paying steadily. Jake filled in the papers, he signed for their gold at the battery, he bought the equipment they needed, but Bartie was at his side, watching eagerly when their gold was changed into currency. Jake's share went into his bank, but Bartie Lee would have none of that. He took his money and placed it in a leather pouch with the other pieces of gold from his first venture. But there was another thing, which Bartie would never admit to Jake and give him more power over his partner. Bartie was feeling very insecure . . . displaced. Misplaced to be exact. He had no idea where he was. He was never one for maps. He'd come from the rice paddies to work on ships, mainly below decks, and to head ashore in ports, money in his hand, looking for a good time, and eventually stagger back to his ship.

But this place! He would never forget his shock when they trekked to the top of that range on their way to the goldfields and he could see out over the land. He could see to the edge of the earth! He'd been frightened of horizons when he first went to sea, but people had told him they never sail that far. It had come to him then that he didn't know where he was on this earth. Didn't even know which country. Had no idea. He'd heard white fellers laughing that a lot of the China coolies didn't know where they were, they could be on the moon for all they knew, and he was mortified that he shared their ignorance.

Hence, he vowed to himself, he must cling to Jake as long as possible. It had been disappointing to learn that Jake's money was in the bank, but a little reassuring since thus he would not be tempted to kill him and make himself doubly rich. To Bartie, the newly rich, Jake was both his servant and his keeper. He was simply waiting now for Jake to give up and get him out of this place.

But then he saw the poster. He couldn't read English or Chinese but he could see the pictures – by crikey he could.

He stood peering at them, his wide conical hat hiding the shock, as his face reflected the face before him, even to his dark moustache and long hair slicked into a knot. He noticed the artist had missed the scar on his right eyebrow, but was mystified as to how the picture could have been made without him being present. He was about to turn and ask someone what this was about, when it struck him that he'd seen other pictures like this, but where?

Both hands slapped onto his face when he remembered.

At the police station! On the noticeboard outside the Maytown police station! Crikey! Pictures of bad white men. Smaller than this, though.

Bartie glanced quickly about him and tore the picture off the tree, shoved it under his shirt and ran back to the mine. Ran!

Jake had a pot of stew cooking over the campfire ready for the potatoes that Bartie had been sent to fetch, and he frowned when he saw him running back empty-handed.

'What's up?'

'Come here,' Bartie said, diving into Jake's tent. 'Look at this!'

He shoved the poster at Jake, who took one look at it and hissed: 'Jesus! Where did you get this? God Almighty! It's you and me. And he's even taken my beard off.'

Bartie stared at the clean-shaven Tussup. 'You don't have no beard, Jake.'

'I did! Christ, we have to get out of here!'

'Who write this paper, Jake?'

'Willoughby.'

'Who's Willoughby?'

'From the ship. He was a passenger. You tried to kidnap his wife, you idiot. The Chinese girl. If you'd left her alone, he wouldn't be coming after us.'

Bartie was intrigued by the pictures. 'Who draw these, Jake? Who know what you an' me look like? How they draw us?'

'I told you. Willoughby. Never mind how. He's offering a thousand-pound reward for us. A bloody thousand! We have to get out of here.'

'How he comin' after us, Jake? Where is he?'

'This says if you've got any information about him you have to report to the Maytown police station. I'd say he's up here and he's trying to flush us out.'

'Then we find him and kill him quick, before he set the police on us.'

'Don't be bloody stupid. Get going. We'll split up. Lend me some money, Bartie. I can't go to the bank for a while.'

Bartie was frantically trying to assess the sudden situation. 'No, I go with you. You doan leave me here.'

'I'm not leaving you here.' Jake tossed the stew on to the ground and stamped out the fire. 'You have to hide from the police. Now get your swag packed and bring me some cash. Forty pounds. That should hold me for a while.'

'Give you money to run out on me?' Bartie shrieked. 'You so smart go to banks, now you got no money. You a bloody fool, Jake. We get out of here orright, plenty quick smart, but you stick with me, you doan need no money, only that gun of yours.'

Jake pushed past him. 'I'm not running out on you. It's safer for us to separate. Jesus, it's there on the bloody page! The twosome. A bloody pair! We have to split!' He tore up the tent pegs and hauled the canvas down. 'Now give me some money and get the hell out of here!'

'Where I go?'

'Where?' Jake hesitated, trying to subdue his panic. He had to shake off Bartie Lee, but how could he do that when they were both headed in the same direction?

'Where?' he echoed. 'Down to bloody Cooktown, of course.'

'And you meet me down there, eh, Jake? Meet me on the wharf. We get a ship like real passengers? Get away!'

'Yeah, we'll do that.' Jake packed essentials into a blanket and tied it with straps. He rolled the small tent into a tight bundle with his rifle inside, and placed it by his saddle, then he called to Bartie: 'Dump everything we're not taking into the mine. That way it doesn't look as if we've left in a hurry. We don't want to draw . . .'

There was no answer from Bartie so he rushed over to his humpy, only to find it deserted, the usual trash littering the clearing.

He dashed to the rear of the rough shelter, hoping Bartie would be somewhere nearby, but soon realised his partner had gone. With his money.

'Oh God,' he muttered, despairing. 'I won't get far broke. Jesus. I'll have to take a chance on no one recognising me at the bank.'

While he was cleaning up the site, he found the poster and grabbed it, ready to tear it to pieces, but he had to read it one more time.

'Bloody hell!' he spat, but then the wording hit him. Murder! It said murder, wanted for murder!

'I haven't committed any bloody murder!' he said, shocked. 'I didn't! The crew killed Matt Flesser. They can't pin that on me, goddamn it!'

Jake was so distraught, he gave up on the chores and carted his few belongings down to a clump of trees where his horse was hitched. Still thinking of the murder charge, he shook his head, disbelieving. Bartie yes. But not me. Bugger them! I'm not going up for a crime I didn't commit!

As he saddled the horse and rigged it for travel with the tent and swag, a water bottle, frypan and tin billy, he worried about being recognised at the bank. In a frail attempt at disguise, he rubbed mud on his face and let it dry, and pulled his hat down hard on his forehead.

In the crowd at the bank he was just another mud-splattered miner lining up at the counter. The teller was a cranky fellow who hated his job, envied common labourers who dug up fortunes, and was always meaning to have a go at prospecting himself but somehow never got round to it.

Nearing closing time he could see men herding themselves into the bank at the last minute, so he pulled his green eye-shade down and shot the customers through like sheep, calling 'next' with staccato voice, even though next was only a few feet away on the other side of the counter. He counted, stamped, counted, stamped, trying to get them all out of the way so he could shut the bank on time without getting abused by locked-out would-be customers.

Head down, Jake shuffled in his turn, handed over his withdrawal request for all of the contents of his account, and muttered 'the lot' as was the accepted term, and the teller counted, stamped, slapped the money down, counted coins, pushed them forward, called 'next!' and sent him on his way without even raising an eyelid.

Unable to linger, Jake squashed the money into his pocket and rode down the street, right past the turnoff to Cooktown. He went through Maytown and headed west.

Bartie Lee was confused. He didn't think to bring anything from the camp except his treasure. He'd just run away like crazy! But now he had to follow Jake's instructions and go back over the mountains to Cooktown. No foot-walking this time, he told himself, recalling the horrific trek up the range, he had money, plenty money.

He bought a red silk embroidered jacket and shiny black pants, emulating a boss Chinaman, but retained the wide coolie hat to hide his face. Then he purchased the first horse offered to him, along with a fine saddle and bridle, but when he was ready to leave Maytown he began to ponder Jake's instructions, thinking that something didn't sound right. But then he laughed. He'd beaten Jake this time, made him look stupid with no money. Maybe that was it.

Just to make sure, and maybe even to postpone setting out alone on the long and scary journey back to Cooktown, he decided to station himself among some wagons opposite Jake's bank.

The effort paid off. There was Jake, standing in line to get his money. Bartie chuckled. He didn't have no other choice. Only mad men left the Palmer without their money. Or dead men.

He felt better now. Jake was probably right. They shouldn't travel together, but at least he could follow Jake. Keep him in sight. Then he wouldn't feel so jumpy, being on his own. What if he lost the way going through those hills and jungles? What if blackfellows attacked him? Bartie shuddered. He didn't want to think about the savages.

Jake left the bank quickly, mounted up and was off down the road at a fast clip, and Bartie Lee was riding behind him.

But what was this? Jake had missed the turnoff! He was going straight on, back towards the river flats. Bartie was confused. He tapped the horse and followed.

He saw Jake stop and buy provisions, and sighed with relief. He should have bought supplies too, but there were stores further down the track; he would get what he needed down there. Stupid of Jake to be passing other stores to get to this one, when he was supposed to be in a hurry. He'd have to turn back through Maytown now.

But he didn't turn back. He kept on, forded the river, heading west and Bartie could only stare, even more confused. He couldn't make out where Jake was going . . . until it came to him that this must be the track down to that other goldfield. Jake was double-crossing him, the bastard. Telling him to go the busy track way, where he could easy get caught, while he sneaked off the back way. Well, he wasn't gonna get away with it. No fear! No bloody fear. No one double-crosses Bartie Lee!

He rode down to the river, nervous about fording the muddy waters, and the horse agreed, shying away, giving Bartie more time to figure this out. He snarled at the animal, somehow feeling better now, rage at Jake soothing his nerves. Somewhere out in that great empty land – he'd never even seen a house that day on the high-up lookout, not a house or a farm or a fence, nothing but trees scattered about like knobs, and no roads – and somewhere out there, the goldfield. But did he want to enter that landscape alone, just to catch up with Jake? There could be more savages out there or, worse, monsters, evil creatures, out of the nether world. He almost cried out in fright.

As he turned away, urging the horse up banks that had been ploughed over and over by prospectors, a man standing on a loaded wagon called to him: 'Hey, coolie! Yes, you! Get over here!'

Bartie rode over warily. 'What you want?'

'Give me a hand here. I need someone to keep the ropes tight and stop this stuff sliding about while I drive the horses.

'Across the river?'

'Of course across the bloody river. You are going that way, aren't you? Hitch your horse to the wagon!'

'The horse?' Bartie echoed, trying to make up his mind between Jake and the monsters, and maybe not finding Jake anyway, but letting him get away with double-crossing him.

'Yes, the bloody horse, dummy!' the man shouted. But Bartie Lee was a rich man now, and fed up with all this panic and confusion. He snarled abuse at the wagoner and rode away from the river, heading back to Maytown.

Mal sat outside the Maytown police station, satisfied with the reaction to his posters. There was a mob clamouring for police attention, all shouting that they knew these wanted men. He guessed the same clamour would be under way at the Cooktown station, but he had no sympathy for the police, who would have to find time to cope with the sudden barrage. Mal Willoughby was not overly fond of police, not since he'd been arrested and gaoled for a murder he hadn't committed. Though he'd been exonerated, it had taken a long time for him to regain his self-confidence after an ordeal like that, so he still had a lingering resentment of police.

Some people over there were waving pieces of the posters and Mal's face set in a grim smile as he recalled the number of times he'd drawn those two faces, over and over again, to get them right, as soon as he could after they left *China Belle*.

He had the posters printed in Brisbane on his return from China, while he met with the Police Commissioner for an update on the apprehension of the mutineers, disappointed that the fellow had little to tell him. In fact, he recalled, the meeting had been a dud.

'So you only caught a few coolies,' he'd said. 'All this time and no ringleaders. Typical! Oh well, it looks as if I'll have to do your job for you. I'll bloody shake up the system.

He was permitted to visit the Chinese crewmen from the ship and, after talking to them, landed back at the Commissioner's office.

'Did you know,' he said angrily, 'or don't you care, that murderers are loose on the goldfields?'

'We are truly aware of your concerns, sir. Now, as I said before—'

'Then you are aware that the cook from *China Belle*, a Chinaman called Ah Koo, was killed with a machete near the Endeavour River.'

The Commissioner was taken aback. 'Where did you get this story from?'

'The same place you should have looked. In your gaol. Ah Koo was murdered by a fellow called Mushi, who is also in your gaol using the name of Lam Fry. How bloody stupid are your blokes that they didn't pick up on that garbage name? You might have Mushi in gaol for rape, but he's also a murderer, and I'm told the crew boss, Bartie Lee, stood and watched him kill Ah Koo. He's just as dangerous.'

'I see,' the Commissioner said, the voice patronising. 'Perhaps you could give these details to the sergeant at the front desk.'

'What? Weren't you listening? Tell him yourself!'

Mal strode down the corridor, past the front desk and out into the glare of the Brisbane street.

'Next stop Cooktown,' he'd told himself as he bought a newspaper and headed for the Ace Printing Company.

The Chinese diggers he'd met in Cooktown were right. After studying the claims register for that small area, Mal was able to identify the abandoned mine leased by the Malayamen after they'd split up with the Chinese crewmen. He then asked neighbouring miners if they knew where the Malays had gone, but no one seemed to know.

'There were several of them,' he said. 'Surely someone must have noticed them working on new claims somewhere.'

Having come to a stop there, he went back to the registrar and checked the names Bartie Lee and his men had used.

'They are all false names,' he explained, 'but still important. Can you check their next claim? I can track them this way.'

'There are thousands of names in these books, mate. But if you want to go through them, it's all right with me.'

'Thank you, I will, but I only need them from this date on.' He was able to give the registrar the date of Mushi's arrest, gleaned from the butcher, father of the victim, in his travels round that section of mines.

The result of his search was disappointing. They must have used more false names, or even just one false name for their next claim. There was no further record of the mysterious Asiatics or their diggings.

Mal leaned against the fence and lit a smoke. Maybe later in the day he'd call in at that police station and see what information they'd gleaned from the public, but in the meantime it felt good just to let them get on with the work. The queue was even longer now. They'd be kept busy for hours. In the meantime he could do with a meal. His supplies had been sufficient for the three-day journey over what was now referred to as a 'much-improved' track.

'It must have been hell before this,' he said to himself as he set off to walk back to the Shamrock Hotel, where he'd taken a room. It was the first pub he'd come across on the road into the goldfields, and a welcome sight it was too, he recalled, for all weary travellers. The place was perpetually crowded, and noisy as hell, but Mal didn't care as long as he had a bed and somewhere to stable his horses.

As he walked across the road towards the Shamrock, some horsemen passed him, among them a Chinaman in a flash red silk jacket, teamed with a coolie hat.

Mal smiled. Typical, he thought. Anything goes out here. He had almost turned away, still amused by the incongruity of that outfit. He had nearly missed the familiar shape of that squat bulky body. Nearly!

'Hey!' he yelled. 'Stop that bloke. In the coolie hat! Stop him!'

Heads turned every which way. There were several coolie hats in the vicinity. One of them looked back, the one on horseback. Looked back, startled! Looked straight at him. Recognised him. Put his head down and spurred into action.

'In the red shirt!' Mal shouted, but by then his quarry had galloped down the road and disappeared round a corner.

Mal raced over to the hotel and down a side lane to the stables, shoving people out of the way as he tore across the courtyard to claim his horse.

'Where's my saddle?' he shouted angrily at a stablehand. 'I left it here in this corner.'

'So you did, mate,' the elderly workman drawled. 'Don't get yourself all het up. It's not stole. I put your stuff in the storeroom. You don't go leavin' quality gear like that lyin' round here.'

'Where's the bloody storeroom?'

'Over there,' the man pointed, and Mal pushed past him.

He grabbed his gear, unrolled his swag, pulled out ammunition and a rifle and raced out to saddle the horse.

Within minutes he had scattered the men grouped in the courtyard as he galloped out of the open gateway and down the road after Bartie Lee.

As he hurtled after the Malayaman, Mal forced himself to picture him, and his horse. It was a brown stockhorse, not much other colour to be seen except a flush of white around the eyes and above the nose, but the important thing was the overall appearance. There was only the rider. No gear packed on the horse. No weapon on view.

To Mal this meant that the rider wasn't equipped for the trek over the range to Cooktown. Or not yet. Being spotted could force him to make just that move.

Mal's horse was a Thoroughbred. It should easily have overtaken the stockhorse that Bartie Lee was riding, but after he'd travelled several miles, determined to catch him, he knew that the Malay must have pulled off into the scrub. He wouldn't have dared stop at one of the few general stores here on the outskirts of Maytown, not with me on his trail, Mal reasoned, as he turned round. He rode back up the track, investigating side clearings and narrow trails, all the time asking passers-by and road workers and campers if they'd seen an Asiatic in a red silk jacket. No one had, but Mal wouldn't give up. He stopped to talk to some road workers, and one of them did remember Bartie Lee, only because he'd seen him twice.

'What?' Mal cried. 'When?'

'Saw him first bolting down the road, early in the piece, then only a while ago I seen him again, going down that bush track with some other Chinks.'

'Riding or walking?'

'He was walking with them, leading his horse.'

'Thanks,' Mal said. 'If you ever spot him again grab him. He's got a fat reward on his head.'

'Is he one of the pair on that poster?'

'Yes.'

'Ah, Jeez! And we let him past!'

Mal didn't wait to commiserate. He headed down the leafy track, shoving aside overhanging branches, and vines as thick as ropes, until he came to a squalid coolie camp. He dismounted, to stare at the scraps of corrugated iron, canvas and bark that provided shelter in this dilapidated settlement, and then to cover his nose at the smell of the place, where obviously no attempt had been made to provide sewerage of any sort.

Bony coolies wandered listlessly about, taking no notice of him as he led his horse towards the first set of dwellings, but an old woman came out to scream at him, to try to chase him away, yelling: 'You get out! No girls here. You not come here!'

He answered her quietly, in Chinese. 'Pardon, mother. I'm not looking for girls; I'm after a bad man. A Malayaman. If he comes here you tell me and I'll pay.'

Her dark eyes lit up. 'You pay now?'

Mal shook his head and grinned. 'First you say.'

She spat. 'He tries to be Chinese smart man. Wears a red coat . . .'

'That's him!' Mal reached into his jacket pocket and jingled coins, and she was quick with an offer to show him.

'Just a minute,' he said. 'What is this place?' He felt a pang of guilt that he'd guessed it to be a coolie camp, though he hadn't seen one before, suddenly realising that they must be kept hidden in the bush like this. Obviously he'd stumbled down a rarely used back entrance.

'Here coolies live. They work for big Moonflower mines. Come and go all day and night.'

'What are you doing here?'

'Some women here service them. Not me though,' she cackled. 'I mind the women, keep them safe.'

I bet you do, Mal thought, giving her half a sovereign.

He was there. Sitting cross-legged on a mat, playing a dice game with two coolies, his swarthy features unmistakable. The red jacket had been discarded, revealing his bare, sweaty torso, an easy target for a clear shot.

Mal watched them from a slight rise that overlooked the edge of the camp, safely hidden by tangled bush. He listened to their chatter as coins plinked on to the mat and hands grabbed.

His rifle was trained on one of the men who had murdered his wife, but he couldn't press the trigger.

The bush was shrill with insects, a kookaburra hooted, the afternoon sun was liquid heat, and the stink of the camp rose to challenge its surrounds. Leaves wilted around him as Mal wiped sweat from his eyes, ordering himself to do this thing, get it over with, but then he remembered Jake Tussup. This one could lead him to Jake Tussup; he had to know where Tussup was. He began to move forward, to bail up Bartie Lee, arrest him. The coolies would scatter. He would take Bartie Lee in. But first belt the hell out of him, and the information he needed.

Suddenly there was a disturbance coming from the rear track. Mal could hear men running and shouting. He looked back, angry at this interruption, but before he could see them, he heard the shouts of, 'Get him!', 'Quick, lads!', 'You're a bleedin' fool, Davey!', and realised it was the road workers. They were coming after Bartie Lee, and the reward!

Lee hadn't woken up to the reason for the ruckus on the track outside the camp. He and the coolies were staring about them when Mal put his rifle down, slid towards the humpy and burst out of the bush. Bartie was fast, though. He was on his feet and running by the time Mal plunged past the humpy after him, past the bewildered coolies, who began to run too, believing this was yet another unprovoked raid by armed white men.

The uproar was infectious. Camp dwellers went panicking in all directions, but Bartie Lee kept on, dodging madly around the huts, shoving obstacles out of the way and screaming abuse at bystanders hindering him. Mal managed to keep him in sight, despairing when he realised Lee was heading for the bush, where he could lose him, and pushed himself even harder, so that he was right on Bartie Lee's heels when the Malayaman jumped a small gully and slipped on an exposed tree root.

Mal grabbed him as he fell, not in the least surprised when the knife flashed by his face, as Lee sprang to his feet. He caught his arm and twisted it up behind his back until Lee screamed in pain, then he sliced Lee's back with his own knife.

'Drop the knife, Lee, or I'll cut you up.'

Lee began to whimper. 'What is this name? Not me, sir. I no Chinee.'

'I know who you are, you bastard,' Mal said. 'Drop the knife.'

His prisoner obeyed, the knife dropped on to the ground and Mal kicked it away, but at the same time Bartie Lee swung about and delivered a vicious kick to Mal's stomach, winding him. But Mal still wouldn't let go of his grip on Bartie's arm. As he doubled up, he dragged the Malay down with him and jabbed the knife into his neck.

'You stay very still,' he puffed, 'very bloody still.'

Whimpering again, Bartie did lie still, his face in the dirt, and Mal moved swiftly to kneel on him until he caught his breath. He was aware now that Lee was very strong and he'd have difficulty dragging him back to the camp unless he could think of a drastic measure.

'Like cutting the bastard's throat,' he muttered to himself.

Bartie heard him. 'No hurting me, sir. I do no wrong. Please you lissen me.'

'Shut up. You're Bartie Lee, a bloody murderer from *China Belle*. You talk when I say so. Now . . . where's Jake Tussup?'

Bartie Lee brightened up at that. 'I tell you where Jake, you let me go, eh?'

'Yes.'

'Ah, so you go find Jake. He a very bad man.'

'Where is he?' Mal pricked his neck with the knife, and pushed the face back into the damp earth.

'Aaah, I bleeding! Jake gone cross river. Down to other goldmines.'

'When?'

'This day.'

'What? Today? He's only just left!' Mal was angry with himself for missing this pair in his search, and now appreciated the difficulty experienced by Mr Lewis and the local police.

'Gone today, sir. He seen the pictures.'

'Ha! You saw the picture too, didn't you, you bastard? Where were you going?'

Bartie managed a shrug. 'Jake a rich man now. He find plenty gold. I take you to him, eh? You pay me?'

'Yeah. What goldfields? Where?'

'Dunno. Funny name. Over river, all diggers go there now.'

'Where are your mates? The other crewmen?'

Bartie Lee shook his head. 'They bad fellows. Mushi, he took to gaol.'

'I know about him.'

'Then why you call me a killing man. Mushi kill the bosun, not me.'

'Where are the rest of your mates?'

'They bad men too. They run away, steal all my money, make me have to go take coolie job at Midas mines.'

'Right. Now take off your belt.'
'Pants fall down.'
'Take off your belt. We've had enough talk for now.'
Bartie slipped off the thin rawhide belt and Mal used it to bind his hands behind him, unconcerned that the flapping pants fell to the ground, leaving Lee naked.
'You said you let me go.'
'The hell I will! Start walking. I've still got my knife here and it's razor sharp.'
He was marching Lee back into the camp for help in handing the bastard over to the police when a dozen or more astonished coolies came out to watch and giggle at Bartie's predicament, but they stopped instantly when he started shouting at them in heavily accented Chinese.
'Help me. This white man kill me like he kill you. I got plenty money, I pay. You know I rich now. You see my horse. My own horse. I give it to you—'
'No! No!' Mal was trying to shout him down in his own imperfect Chinese. 'Not true, no! No. He's a liar! A murderer!' But Bartie was known to them. His coolie friends began advancing on them with sticks.
Mal kept Bartie in front of him, threatening to cut his throat, at the same time wondering if he could make a run for the rifle he'd left in the bush.
No time, though. He had to shove Bartie aside to defend himself as the coolies rushed at him, but then a shot was fired and everyone ducked for cover, including Mal, though he believed the road workers may have come to his aid. When there were no more shots, the coolies began to climb to their feet but Mal was already tearing through the scrub to grab his loaded rifle and race back to claim his prisoner.
'The odds are bloody better now,' he muttered, shoving his knife back into the leather strap at his ankle.
'Right! All of you,' he shouted. 'Stand back! Where's that bloody Malay?'
None of them seemed concerned with him any more. They pointed to the naked body of Bartie Lee sprawled on the ground, bleeding from a wound in his chest.
'Was that the shot? Was he shot?' he cried, dropping down to check. But Bartie Lee had died instantly.
'Who the hell did this?' he shouted at the coolies, who were now backing away.
'What does it matter, Mr Willoughby?' a familiar voice asked quietly. 'He was but scum.'
Mal blinked as he looked up at a tall Chinaman with a thin moustache and a long heavy pigtail, who, oddly, was wearing Western clothes: neat moleskin trousers, check shirt, and riding boots. What with things happening so fast, it took Mal a few moments to register that he knew the Chinaman.

'God Almighty! It's you! Chang! What the hell are you doing here? Did you shoot him? Bloody hell, I needed to question him . . .'

'Greetings, Mr Willoughby.' Chang bowed. 'I am pleased to see you in good health.' He spoke quickly to men standing nearby and they rushed in to carry off the body.

Mal called to them to stop. 'I want his body taken to the Maytown police station, Chang.'

'As you wish.'

'I'll have to report this,' Mal said, to make his intentions plain.

'Yes. That you shot him in self-defence.'

'What? I didn't shoot him. You did! Didn't you?'

'Why quibble? It was of necessity.'

'It wasn't bloody necessary at all, dammit. But it's too late now. You can tell the police that you were forced to shoot.'

'Very sorry, Mr Willoughby, but that will not do. Dangerous for Chinese to be involved in any shootings. Laws here most unreasonable. For you, no case to answer. And many witnesses. Let us walk; not a pleasant place this.'

As they trudged back up to the road where he'd left his horse, Mal learned that Chang was working for the Moonflower Mining Company, as an overseer.

'And you expect me to believe that?'

'Of course. Your talk of the gold places intrigued me, so I decided to see for myself, but I had no wish to suffer the great discomforts you warned of. Therefore it was necessary to be paid while assessing. You understand?'

'No. I think you are following me.'

'That is not correct. I made enquiries in Tientsin and was referred to the Li family, who were prepared to offer me suitable remuneration for my services. And you were right, the gold digging is only coolie work, however enviable the results might be, at often times.'

'And how did you happen to be here, at *this* time?'

'You mean when you need me, Mr Willoughby?' Chang smiled. 'Because I saw the posters. Because people said that man used to work in the Midas mines. Because I had word you were in the coolie camp, so I came swiftly.'

'Ah, yes?' Mal said suspiciously. 'Then didn't you see the other face on the poster? The face of Jake Tussup? You or your imaginary guard just shot the one person who could tell me where to find that bastard. And the rest of the Malay crewmen. Now I'll have to start all over.'

Chang shrugged. 'Regrettable.'

'Yes, bloody regrettable. I'll have to get back into Maytown now and report his death to the police. I suppose I should thank you for intervening on my behalf . . .'

'Not necessary. Maybe you'd wish to visit the mine. My offices are congenial and we have excellent Chinese wine.'

Mal grinned. 'I'm sure you do, and maybe I'll make a social call one day. When I've got Tussup well and truly locked away.'

Sergeant Gooding looked over his file on the *China Belle* mutineers. They'd finally completed interviewing the hundreds of reward-seekers but gained little helpful information. A young whore claimed she'd shaved off Tussup's beard, and he'd told her his name was Rory Moore. That was followed up, and the Maytown police found there were claims under that name. Very interesting, though, was the fact that on his last two claims, 'Moore' had a coolie working for him. This information came from diggers who didn't actually know 'Moore', a fellow who kept to himself, but they'd mined nearby and seen the pair at work.

'Could be,' Gooding murmured. The last claim had shut down suddenly and both 'Moore' and the coolie had disappeared.

A miner who said he never forgot a face said Tussup had stolen his horse outside a pub, but since he was drunk at the time, as questioning established, that tale was discounted, along with the hundreds who said they saw him. One Theodore Tennent said he'd partnered 'Moore' in a mine. Past tense. A fat lot of good that did. He'd had to be thrown out of the station, demanding his thousand for that useless piece of news. The prostitute Madeline might be entitled to a few pounds.

But there was more interesting news. Two of the Chinese crewmen in the Brisbane gaol had been stabbed to death while awaiting sentence. And, best of all, Willoughby had found and shot the villain Bartie Lee after a serious fight as he was trying to apprehend him in coolie quarters. Apparently Willoughby was distressed that he'd been forced to shoot the Malay, in self-defence, because he'd hoped to learn more of Tussup's whereabouts from his prisoner. All he discovered from Lee was that Tussup had gone on to another goldfield.

'And good riddance,' the sergeant sighed. 'That takes the lot of them out of my territory. If Tussup's gone south to the Hodgkinson goldfields, then the Cairns police will have to find him.'

He wondered, though, about the posters. They'd said murder. Wanted for murder. To his knowledge, Bartie Lee could have been responsible for the murder of the bosun on that ship. But Tussup? Conspiracy maybe. It looked like Willoughby was blaming them all for his wife's death, when from all accounts, she'd drowned trying to escape from them. Jumped overboard and drowned.

'Ah, good luck to him,' he muttered, and closed the file.

The unwritten file was very much open in Chang's mind. He bowed to Mr Willoughby and went on his own way with a wry smile. His friend was entitled to be cranky. No matter. He would recover.

His servant brought Lee's horse to him and Chang was delighted to find a cache of money and small gold nuggets in a leather pouch, hidden under the saddle. A bonus for the day's work.

He had spoken the truth to Mr Willoughby. Through important contacts, he had found suitable employment was available to him in these fabled goldfields. Thus armed, he'd wasted no time in voyaging forth, finally arriving in this strange country to be met by Mr Li Weng Kwan, a charming gentleman who explained his role:

'We have areas of employment in which your knowledge of English will be useful. I have been attending to the bookwork concerning the workers, but it has become too much for me. I was not aware of all the rules and regulations that would attend each coolie. Therefore your immediate duty is to go to the goldfields . . .'

Chang recalled he hadn't so much as blinked an eye at the exciting prospect.

'. . . there to check every one of the coolies, to make certain they are all registered, and the taxes paid. My brother manages the mines. He and his staff handle wages and so forth.'

Chang had bowed his acceptance of the duties.

'Furthermore,' Mr Li said, 'an interesting change is taking place. These goldfields are known as Palmer River. More gold has been discovered in a river far south of here called the Hodgkinson, and so many of the miners have left their claims and rushed down there. We have decided to remain for the time being. The Moonflower mines and several other large mines are still producing well.

'Now, my brother is too busy to be bothered with small claims that have been abandoned by owners rushing off to the other goldfields, but he believes they may still contain gold. Your assignment will be to put men to work reopening abandoned mines, and register them with the authorities. Not all will reveal gold, but my brother believes many will. You will have no shortage of workers and you may select headmen for each mine, who will report to you.'

They discussed this project for a while, and eventually Chang bowed. 'I am honoured to be offered such responsibility. One wonders what extra remuneration might present itself, if one of the resumed mines, one that I might have chosen to reopen, contains gold?'

Mr Li took time to ponder this suggestion. He moved quietly across the room and peered at a lush plant growing nearby.

'Look at the huge leaves on this plant. It grows wild here and is called a *monstera deliciosa*. I am told its fruit smells very sweet and tastes like mixed fruit, but I have yet to be rewarded with the pleasure. Mmm? Perhaps when your resumed mines flower, the rewards might flow. We shall have to see.'

So far Chang had reopened four mines. One was already paying handsomely, and he had received a commission of two per cent, which he considered miserable, but consoled himself that there were hundreds more to be investigated.

And he had discussed another matter with Mr Li.

'I have a letter for you, sir,' Chang had said. 'From the Lady Xiu Ling Lu.'

'Ah yes. A great lady, and a dear friend. Her father, it was, who recommended you to our colleagues in Tientsin, is that not so?'

'That is correct.'

'Be seated. I have ordered refreshments for you.'

Li took the letter and withdrew, as two servants hurried in with a most welcome bowl of chicken and beans and a carafe of wine.

Chang could have told the gentleman of the tragedy that had struck the lady, but considered it ill mannered to pre-empt the letter in any way. He could always answer questions later.

There were many questions from his shocked host.

'Her daughter drowned?' Mr Li cried as he hurried back.

'Yes, sir.'

'What is your connection with the Xiu family and my business interests in Tientsin?'

'Because of the death of Jun Lien.'

'The letter says it is too painful to relate the circumstances, that you can perform that sad task on her behalf.'

'Yes, sir.' Chang told him the story of the mutiny, as he'd heard it from Mr Willoughby, and Mr Li gasped.

'That was here! I know all about that. The young woman who drowned. That was—'

'Mrs Willoughby, these papers would have read. She was Jun Lien, the wife of an Australian.'

Li clasped his hands to his face in horror. 'I am upset that I did not know the young lady was the granddaughter of my friend Mr Xiu! Ah, it is too sad.'

Chang continued his narrative.

'While we were in the vicinity of the Xiu mansions, I took the liberty of informing the Lady Xiu that I intended to travel to this land I had heard so much about, to expand my mind and maybe even my financial situation with so much talk of gold. It was the Xiu family who contacted your people, knowing that you had business interests in this part of the world.'

'I see.'

'Perhaps you might know if Mr Willoughby has arrived here yet.'

'I don't think so. I shall make enquiries. Now the Lady Xiu asks something of you in return for her indulgence. Do you know of her request?'

Chang nodded.

'Very well. If you do as she wishes, payment will be made through our Maytown offices. Is that understood?'

'Yes. When should I leave for the gold town?'

'In the morning. You will have an escort. In the meantime you are welcome to stay here at my humble abode. I have many books pertaining to this land that you may care to peruse.'

'I should be honoured, sir.'

At that time Willoughby had not made it to Cooktown. He'd had to travel via Brisbane, while Chang had voyaged on a steamship owned by Li interests that had come straight down the coast to Cooktown. It had carried many coolies, and was scheduled to return with gold and heavily armed guards for fear of pirates.

Chang instructed his servant to sell Bartie Lee's horse and its trappings, while he had business to attend to. This took him to the office of Mr Li, the younger, where he waited patiently for an audience.

This Mr Li was round and jolly – as he should be with the earth's treasures at his feet, Chang mused, though these surrounds were no reflection of the riches the Li gentlemen were reaping. The office was a corrugated iron shed lacking any semblance of comfort, located a few hundred yards from the huge pounding battery. He supposed the brothers considered the delightful dwelling on the headland at Cooktown enough comfort for temporary residents.

Eventually the great man received him, peppered him with two or three questions about new mines and then asked what, of importance, he had to relate.

Standing, Chang apologised for this intrusion, since his business was normally conducted through Mr Li's accountant.

'When we first met, sir, you were acquainted with the wishes of the Lady Xiu.'

'Ah yes,' his employer said sadly. 'A tragic event, and to have happened in the seas out from here – we are still heartbroken.'

Then he leaned forward and squinted at Chang. 'Have you had any luck? I want to be the one to inform the Lady Xiu. I was always very fond of her. Come on, Chang. What news?'

'The Malay boss, Bartie Lee, who kidnapped Jun Lien, is dead.'

'How? Where?'

'I shot him. Two hours ago.'

'You did, eh? Well done. Did you dispose of the body?'

'No need. Jun Lien's husband, Mr Willoughby, is taking the blame. Self-defence, he says.'

'Why would he do that?' Li asked suspiciously. 'I won't have the lady misled, you know.'

'Because he knows how harsh the authorities are where Chinese people are concerned. I could still be in serious trouble even though the man was less than scum, and a known criminal.'

Li nodded. 'I see. A fine gesture but the least her white husband could do. I will authorise payment to you immediately.'

As he walked away Chang was very happy. The goldfields were proving lucrative for a man of his talents.

His headman was waiting for him down the road. 'Master, we have made the most terrible discovery in a mine we just opened. Dead men! Bodies in there. Ah, so gruesome. Come and see.'

'No, not yet. I will call the police first. In this country we must be exemplary citizens. Always defer to the police and the law.'

Chapter Fourteen

The rains had been poor this season, not enough to carry them through the long dry winter, the cattlemen complained, but now with summer fading into March the big wet rallied, and day after day Cairns was deluged.

No one minded. The wet season was just that, and if it were a little late, then better late than never. Water tanks were filled to overflowing, grasses, people swore, grew a foot a day; houses steamed and women fought mildew on walls and in closets; the streets were a sea of mud and deputations demanded the newly elected council drain them as soon as possible.

Fortunately the roof was on Clive Hillier's building and the four shops were beginning to look interesting with the raised and covered boardwalk in front. Grateful passers-by used the boardwalk, given the state of the streets, and Ted Pask rushed to check with Mr Caporn that the Apollo Properties shops offered similar protection from rain and mud.

'Of course they have,' Neville smiled. 'They'll be wider than the Hillier building. I insisted on a raised timber promenade and corrugated iron awnings. From there the shoppers will be able to lower large canvas blinds to protect pedestrians from glare as well as from weather like this.'

He could easily have added that the boardwalks would have bootscrapers, and receptacles for umbrellas, and hitching rails for horses, to please the bank manager, but decided not to take his fiction too far.

'Just as well we haven't started building yet,' Pask said, as they stood in the lobby of the hotel, staring out at the pouring rain. 'This weather would make a mess of everything.'

'Yes, but we should be able to begin when the ground dries out,' Neville told him, hoping it would rain for a month. Esme was being very difficult, refusing to agree to leave Cairns yet. Trouble was, she didn't know her own mind, one minute wanting to go back to Hong Kong and the next deciding to stay here, both impossible demands.

She had discovered a conscience, he worried, far too late in the day. Though what she expected him to do about that was not clear. He'd tried to explain to her that they weren't criminals. They didn't do any harm. No one got hurt. People bought goods from them, or invested in their projects willingly. No one twisted their arms. And these were people who could afford it. It was simply business. Shopkeepers charged outrageous prices too. And businesses, investments, shares – they were always failing.

'This so-called conscience of yours, my love, has you all mixed up. If you want to feel guilty, look out the window at the poor miserable blackfellows sheltering under those trees. This was their country until just a little while ago. Their homes were here. They were killed, slung aside, robbed of everything and left to starve. And who did this? The people who started this town. Do they care? No fear. So why should you feel bad just because we lift a few pounds from the white folk here? I bet the blacks would cheer.'

She hadn't really swallowed that argument, but it had helped a little.

'I suppose everyone's got a guilt of some sort,' she said sadly.

'No. Only if they go looking for it. To spoil their day. And everyone else's.'

'And am I spoiling your days?'

'As a matter of fact you are. We don't have any fun any more. It's this town. There's nothing to do and the bloody rain is depressing. You'll feel better when we get out of here. What say we stay at the best hotel in Sydney Town? We can afford it.'

For the first time in ages he saw a glint of light in her sorrowing eyes, and kept on. 'We'll buy you a beautiful dress – what colour?'

'Gold!' she said boldly. 'I want a golden dress. Gold satin with layers of gold tulle, sparkling gold tulle, and I'll float in on my golden shoes.'

'You'll look superb. You'll be wearing diamond earrings too, set in gold, of course.'

It was a game they often played when they were down, fantasising about every detail of a brilliant evening – the food, the waiters, the music – and this time Neville played it to the hilt because they could do it; they could have the time of their lives in Sydney.

Esme's mood improved. She even laughed when he sent the fictional champagne back, complaining that it was 'off', then suddenly she stopped. 'You're serious?'

'Right down to the gold dress, my love.'

'Can I tell you something?'

'What?'

'Clive Hillier offered me a job. As his buyer for the ladies' department. He thinks I have excellent taste in clothes. He would pay me to go to Brisbane and Sydney to do the buying. Wouldn't that be the most dreamy job? He says all department stores have buyers, and I suppose they would.'

Neville had to be careful here. Hillier was a smooth piece of work. It would be a long time before women in this bush town needed more than their skirts and blouses and lace-up boots. The bastard's offer was another fantasy, and too close for comfort.

'I wonder what his wife will have to say about that?' he asked. 'No doubt you'd be ideal for the job because you do have excellent taste, but she might prefer to do the buying herself.'

Esme frowned. 'I've seen her, Nev. She's quite pretty in her way, but she's a plain dresser, wears the local uniform of blouse and skirt and long hideous raincoat.'

'Then why don't we invite them to dine with us and we can suss it out?'

'You don't think he means it?' she charged.

'On the contrary, I'd bet he would if he could, because you have good taste. And so does he.'

She looked at him, not understanding for a minute, and then she burst out laughing. 'You're a canny lad, aren't you? All right, invite them to dine. But you mustn't get cross if he flirts with me. I need some fun, you said so yourself.'

That was fine with Neville. At the minute he was finding Hillier's attentions to his wife a godsend.

Ever since they arrived in Cairns, Emilie's life had been a misery. They had temporary residence in a worker's cottage, vacated by surveyors who had completed their town planning assignment and moved on. She wouldn't have minded the tiny two-roomed house, a temporary arrangement, with nothing else available as yet. Nor the incessant rain – Maryborough could turn on the torrent too – but once they landed, Clive changed. Almost from the minute they stepped ashore Emilie experienced his real reaction to her attempted separation. He was livid. Outraged. Determined to punish her for humiliating him. For trying to rob him!

He placed all of the household furnishings and other belongings in a warehouse at the wharf, along with the property that Emilie had already shipped to him.

'We have everything together now, don't we, Emilie? As it should be. And it will stay that way.'

She nodded, standing just inside the door of the warehouse, but he came over to her, gripped her arm and shoved her outside.

'You answer when I speak to you. Do you understand? I'll have no more mutiny in my house. Now answer me!'

She winced as he tightened his grip. 'Yes,' she whispered. 'Yes.'

All the way up from the wharves, across a street and through the rain-sodden town he berated her, threatened her, and reminded her that she'd better not try those tricks again.

Huddled under her umbrella, hurrying to keep up with him, Emilie was sick with fear. She blamed herself for allowing this to happen. For being so stupid as to have come to this place with him. He could hardly have hauled her on to the ship. But then, she reminded herself, how could you have stayed? He had the money and he would have sold the house over your head anyway. And, as often happened to her as she meekly took his harangues, her mind wandered, this time to the use of the word 'mutiny'.

Mutiny. An odd word to use. Was the mutiny on the *China Belle* still in his thoughts? Was Sonny Willoughby still here?

Emilie began to weep, the rain on her face hiding her tears. She thought she would just die if Sonny came upon her now and discovered what a mess she'd made of things. She recalled him saying that she could do worse . . . a joke. But it was no longer a joke. Emilie now believed she couldn't have done much worse.

The house was two blocks from the waterfront, just a bedroom and a kitchen.

'See what you've driven us to!' he shouted, pushing her inside. 'If you'd sent me my money, all of it, I could have had a residence built by now.'

He threw most of their luggage into the bedroom as she peeled off her soaked overcoat and hat and went through to the kitchen. But Clive pulled her back.

'Now you listen to me, Emilie—'

'No,' she said, breaking away from him. 'I've listened to you all the way from the ship, and that has to stop. We're in a new place, we can start again, but you have to settle down, Clive, try to be a bit nicer. I won't allow all that to start again.'

He struck her a stinging blow across the face and she fell back, tried to grab hold of a wooden chair for support but it crashed to the floor with her.

'We can start again all right,' he snapped at her. 'With you waking up to the fact that I could have thrown you out into the streets. What will you allow? Where is this talk coming from? You get up and behave yourself.'

As Emilie climbed unsteadily to her feet, he made no attempt to help her.

'Light the fire,' he said. 'There's dry wood by the stove and a box of supplies in the corner, so get on with it. I want to see how the building works are going.'

She was glad to be rid of him, at least for a while. Her face stung and a tooth felt loose.

'I can't allow this,' she grieved. 'Not with the baby. I'll have to tell him about the baby when he comes back. Surely he won't be so violent then. He's often said he wants a son.'

She lit the fire and hung her wet clothes on hooks in the wall, making the room steamier than ever, then she walked to the back door and gazed out at her dismal surrounds. Nothing but thick grey bush to be seen through the mists.

The next day Clive took Emilie to inspect the building site in Abbot Street, one back from the Esplanade, and though they were only shells as yet, she was impressed. The two main shops, the Hillier's His and Hers, were connected by an open archway, and, in the same style as the Maryborough store, had a mezzanine floor at the rear for offices.

While they were there, men arrived to fit glass in the windows and that meant the rest of the work could be carried on without having to defer to the weather, so Clive was thrilled. He dashed around behind the workmen as they unloaded the glass, anxiously warning them to carry the panes carefully and to watch out that they didn't slip on the floor with so much sawdust lying about, nagging them at every step until one of the men rounded on him:

'Listen, mate, we're not delivering babies. It's only glass. Now get out of the way!'

Surprisingly, Clive did retreat, joining Emilie on the veranda.

'The shops are much larger and airier than I expected,' she said to him.

'That's because I ordered higher ceilings. And windows on the mezzanine floor.'

'What shall we do about curtains?'

'Nothing. Shops are not obliged to have curtains. We can postpone them for a while.'

She thought this rather odd but not a priority. Anyway, it would be difficult to make curtains in their tiny house. Apparently the itinerant life styles of surveyors in newly opened areas only required somewhere to cook and somewhere to rest the head. There were no closets in the house and the bedroom was so small, the bed left little space between it and the walls so it was impossible to unpack. They simply had to climb around their luggage.

'Yes, curtains can wait,' she said. 'But I wanted to ask you if you've picked out a spot for the house?'

'I have, it's a large block further down this street. When the builders finish the shop they can start on the house.'

'That's nice.' Emilie would have liked to know which block, but she was determined to keep the peace. She'd find out where later. They walked over to view the building from across the street, and while he was in his quiet mood she took his arm.

'I'm pleased about the house. We'll be needing more space. I'm having a baby, Clive.'

He looked down at her, surprised, and then nodded. 'About time! I have to find the plasterers and get them here tomorrow, now the windows are in. You might as well go on home.'

With that, he gave the workmen a wave, and walked off.

Emilie sighed. Small mercies, she supposed. Disinterest was better than discontent, or worse.

But she didn't go back to the cottage. She explored the town, pleased that no other clothing stores had materialised since they'd made this decision, bought some groceries, requesting they be delivered to the cottage, and walked back along the foreshore. Emilie had never been so far north before. She'd emigrated from England to the town of Maryborough, which was entirely different from this place in every aspect and, despite the grey misty day, she was fascinated by her first encounter with the real tropics.

When Clive came back for the midday meal, he pushed over the bills for the glass manufacturer, carpenters, timber and roofing merchants and so on, and told her to pay them and keep an account of all expenditure.

'Your own budget included,' he said, 'on a separate sheet.' And then he laughed. 'One thing about living in this hole, it's dirt cheap.'

She was happy to set up an accounting system for the new store. It gave her something to do. It didn't take her long to sort out his papers and, finding few receipts, work out which bills had to be paid. But among the papers was a receipt for five hundred pounds, paid to Apollo Properties, and Emilie couldn't understand what that was about. It couldn't be for their house. Blocks in this town were going for two or three pounds. That was why they were here. The long block in the town centre had cost only fifteen pounds. Five hundred! It must be a mistake. She would have gone to the Apollo offices to enquire but the address was c/o Post Office, like everything here since there was no mail delivery as yet. And, she reminded herself, no water reticulation, no school, no library . . . Emilie remembered how she'd had to learn to cope with an Australian country town after the amenities of London, and realised she'd have to start all over again since this was close to pioneering.

The signature on the receipt was E. Caporn.

Emilie decided she'd have to ask Clive about it. In the meantime, she set it aside.

Clive came home with some news. 'I want you to dig around in your trunk and find a smart dress for Saturday night. We've been invited to dine with the Caporns at the Alexandra Hotel. They're English too, so we'll have that much in common. Wealthy pair, very much à la mode, which is why I want you to try to keep up. What about that silk suit? The blue one with the lace trim. It's only dinner, and the Alexandra dining room is informal to say the least, so you don't want to overdo it.'

'Yes, all right. But how nice of those people to invite us so soon,' Emilie said, genuinely pleased with the invitation. 'I'll wear the silk suit . . .' she smiled, 'while I can. By the way, is Mr Caporn the E. Caporn I saw on a receipt that is puzzling me? You ought to have a look at it. I think he made a mistake.'

She went to the box that had become her temporary filing cabinet and brought out the receipt from Apollo Properties, but before she could show it to him, he dismissed it.

'Leave it. It's correct.'

'But how can it be? What's it a receipt for?'

He sighed. 'It's an investment. I've invested in a construction company headed by Mr Lyle Horwood called Apollo Properties. Everyone of importance in this town is involved, to promote the business centre of Cairns. People are moving here all the time. We have to keep up.'

'But five hundred pounds, Clive! That's a fortune! We shouldn't be spending now, we'll need—'

He slammed a hand down on the table. 'I knew you'd react like that. You're so negative. It's bad enough having you here, so obviously under sufferance, without having to bear your simple sums. I have shares in the company, shares worth five hundred pounds. They can be sold at any time – is this getting through to you? The money is not spent, as you seem to think. Once the building programme is completed they'll be worth double, even triple.'

'I do understand, Clive,' she said quietly, 'but it is a rather large outlay for the present—.'

'That is enough! I won't have you interfering in my business affairs.'

'Family business affairs, Clive.'

'Oh no. You forfeited the right to have anything to do with the business by attempting to ruin my plans for the new stores. You tried to steal the money I needed to get started, and now you have the cheek to call it a family business! So let's get this straight. I'll be running the store – both sections. I don't need you anywhere near it. I don't trust you.'

Emilie was stunned. She had managed the women's department in their last store and had also been bookkeeper.

'Now that you're having a baby you'll want to stay home anyway,' he added. 'It's not seemly for pregnant women to be roaming about in public.'

Emilie realised she had painted herself into this corner by attempting to split the finances, and she certainly didn't mind staying at home from now on, but she was concerned about the business. He had always been hopeless with figures – he lacked the patience for detail, and until she had taken over, his accounts had been riddled with discrepancies. But then, she decided, she might as well leave him to it. For the time being. Knowing he'd be calling on her assistance eventually. They'd been through this scenario before.

'If you're sure you can cope,' she said mildly. 'It will probably be better for me to stay home. I could still do the buying. When the sales representatives call, you could send them on to me.'

'There will be no need,' he said huffily. 'I can manage without you.'

Esme met Clive and his wife at the door of the hotel, rushing to help usher them in out of the rain.

'What an awful night!' she exclaimed. 'I wouldn't have been surprised if you'd cried off. Here, let me take your cloak, Mrs Hillier.'

The cloak and hood were soaked, but they were eminently serviceable for this weather and the visitor looked none the worse for wear. In fact, Esme noticed, she was astonishingly good-looking. Somehow she'd got the impression that his 'little wife', as he'd referred to her, was just that, little, dumpy and plain. Far from it. She wasn't tall but her dark hair, pinned up in Grecian style with a blue band, seemed to draw attention to her deep blue eyes and fair skin. She was wearing a pale blue silk jacket softened by a swathe of white georgette at the neckline and a matching skirt with a short overskirt draped across to a light bustle.

Not the height of fashion, Esme thought – as Mrs Hillier apologised for having to wear boots – but very becoming. Yes. Attractive.

She said: 'Please don't apologise. One would have no choice in these muddy streets. I'd have done the same.'

She thought her own dark blue dress with the choker neckline and slim waist looked rather well beside the lighter blue.

Clive took their wet cloaks and hung them to drip by the door and Neville came dashing out of the bar to join the company.

'So glad you could come, Clive,' he called, 'and we're thrilled to meet you at last, Mrs Hillier. My, she is lovely. Clive, you rascal, keeping a secret like this from us. Now come on through, not too many starters tonight, Mrs Kassel tells me, but she has a fine repast planned for us. Stroke of luck that the hotel was opened just before we got here.'

They settled in well and Esme found Mrs Hillier shy, but quite charming, while Clive rattled on about his store, the one that was nearing completion and what a great boon it would be for the town.

'As will be Apollo Properties too, but I'm in first. Apollo will have to catch up with me.'

'We can learn from you, Clive. The man of experience.'

'What exactly is to be built by Apollo Properties?' Mrs Hillier asked, and Clive spoke up. 'I haven't had time to explain it to my wife as yet, but Neville will explain, my dear.'

'Certainly.' The two men talked enthusiastically about the company – about the non-existent company, Esme thought, while Clive's wife looked troubled, and she sat forcing an interested smile.

As the dinner progressed, with roast pork and plentiful crackling and several of Mrs Kassel's potato specialities to please Neville, the talk eventually came round to *China Belle*, and Mrs Hillier looked up in surprise.

'Oh. Were you on that ship? Oh, you poor things, I didn't know. It must have been dreadful.'

'It was,' Neville said. 'Esme took the worst of it, except for poor—'

Hillier cut in. 'I say, Neville, have you heard from Lyle?'

'We have indeed. We've been invited to the ceremony in Brisbane,' he said with a loving smile at his wife, who simply smiled back. First she'd heard of this.

'What ceremony would this be?' Mrs Hillier asked.

'Our friend Lyle is to be knighted,' Neville told her. 'Arise, Sir Knight – or is it Sir Lyle? Anyway, we will be heading for Brisbane in a couple of days to be present at Government House on the great day. We wouldn't miss it for quids. Sir Lyle and Lady Horwood in their finest hour. I believe there's a reception afterwards. That'll be a jolly affair, nothing but the best! By the way, anyone for a glass of the finest? Mrs Hillier, champagne?'

'Oh, I don't know.' She looked to Esme. 'What do you think?'

Esme was irritated with Neville for plunging them into this new tale. 'I wouldn't like to say. My husband's been clamping down on me lately. Am I permitted champagne?'

'Of course you are, darling. We'll all have champagne with the dessert.'

Hillier was still interested in the Horwoods. He sounded peeved that he'd been left out. 'Anyone else from here invited?'

'Invited where?' Neville asked him innocently, and Esme knew he was teasing the man.

'To Brisbane. To be present when the knighthood is conferred on Lyle?'

'Ah . . . let me see. Lewis is going. He was on the ship with you, the trio, you set off together. Did you have a good trip? I forgot to ask you.'

'Yes, excellent, thank you. Unfortunately I had to disembark at Maryborough, though I was considering taking them up on their invitation to carry on to the capital.'

This time Esme saw Mrs Hillier blink and wondered if this were true, or if Clive's wife had not known about his considerations. She grinned and looked over to Mrs Hillier, as the champagne was being poured.

'Do you know Brisbane well?'

'Not really. When I first came to this colony with my sister we landed in Brisbane, and we were there for a little while. We were governesses.'

Clive laughed. 'Out here looking for husbands. That's all governesses are on about.'

Esme saw Mrs Hillier blush and sized up the marriage. She decided she liked the wife better than the husband. 'I was a governess once,' she lied, enjoying Neville's raised eyebrows. 'Yes, I taught two delightful children but though their fabulously wealthy *père*, who was a widower, begged me to marry him, I preferred single life. Until my Neville came along, of course.'

'Things would be different in Hong Kong, though, I imagine,' Clive was saying, blustering, as Neville raised his champagne glass.

'Here's to good fortune for all!'

They were finishing the dessert when Neville remembered to ask Clive how his shops were progressing.

'Extremely well. If the Apollo constructions proceed as well, we should all be in clover.'

'And when do you expect to open?'

'In a month or so, I'm hoping. The stock I've ordered should be in by then.'

'You've already done all the buying?'

'Not quite,' Clive said cautiously, pushing a strand of lank fair hair back from his face. 'Just enough to get started.'

'That's a relief. Esme was looking forward to her new role. You do still want her to do the buying of the ladies' fashions?'

'Yes,' Clive muttered. 'Yes, of course.'

Mrs Hillier gazed serenely across the table and said not a word.

'Perhaps she could look around and see what's available in Brisbane while we're there?' Neville offered.

But Esme was tiring of it all. She winked at Mrs Hillier. 'Maybe you and I should go to Hong Kong to do the buying and leave the men here with their constructioning.'

'A good idea,' Mrs Hillier said drily. 'I have never been to Hong Kong. Do tell me about it; it sounds a fascinating place.'

The two women found common ground and chatted amiably over Mrs Kassel's excellent coffee, though Neville and Clive were a little at odds, disagreeing every now and then about the designs for the Apollo shops. They were distracting Esme, who knew their whole conversation was pointless, since there would be no Apollo shops. She was about to tell them to give over and find something interesting to discuss when Neville looked up as two men came into the dining room.

He jerked back in his chair. 'Oh God! Look who's here!'

Esme recognised Mr Field, the reporter, and then the other man, Mal Willoughby!

Neville was already standing, his hands outstretched in welcome, as Esme jumped up and ran across the room to Mal.

'Oh,' she cried. 'We're so glad to see you. Are you all right? Did you take your dear wife home? We heard you had. To China . . .' She was weeping, and weeping as if she might never stop, all the pent-up emotions of that terrible day released. She was truly able to cry now, seeing him, crying not for herself but for him, and his ordeal, and for the death of his beautiful wife.

He put his arms round her, and held her to him.

'It's all right now, Esme,' he murmured. 'It's over, thank you. She's home and sleeping.'

His voice sounded so familiar that Esme realised it wasn't her late brother she'd needed to turn to for consolation – it wasn't Arthur at all – it was this man. The suddenness of Jun Lien's death, and his terrible grief had struck her so deeply at a time when she was trying to overcome her own ordeal that she'd taken it all to heart. She'd needed to talk to him, to help him, to have him help her, to tell him how sorry she was. Something like that. But now here he was, telling her that everything was all right, releasing her from the pain.

There was just sadness now, she thought, as Neville came over, so happy to see Mal again.

Gently, very gently, Neville took her aside.

'You got a shock,' he said, 'seeing Mal again. Don't cry, Es, everything is under control.'

She wanted to tell him that her real sufferings had just welled to the surface and flowed from her, that she really was all right now. She looked back to Mal and saw him staring at Mrs Hillier with a lovely smile of recognition.

'For heaven's sake! Emilie! How are you?'

Mrs Hillier beamed. She was pleased to see him; obviously they were old friends.

'And Clive!' Mal held out his hand. 'How're you going?'

Esme saw Clive stand and give his hand, but with none of the pleasure Neville had shown. In fact, when Mal turned back to introduce Jesse Field, Clive's expression was downright unpleasant.

'Mal's staying with me,' Jesse told Neville. 'He wanted to catch up with you again, but let me tell you that two of the three men we've been chasing are no more. The Malay, Mushi, was hanged in Brisbane and the other one, Bartie Lee was . . .' Esme noticed Mal's slight frown and Jesse's hesitation before he continued, '. . . was shot during capture.'

'That's a relief,' Neville said. 'What about the officer, Tussup?'

'He's still out there.'

While the men talked, Esme went back to sit with Mrs Hillier, who was looking quite pale.

'I had no idea you knew Mr Willoughby,' she said.

'Oh yes, he's an old friend.'

Esme was relieved that Mrs Hillier made no effort to enlarge on that response, because she was weary now, not up to any further conversation. She looked at Mal, who was standing talking to the other men, and she could still feel his warmth, but Clive came back and plonked himself down at the table.

'What was it they used to call Mal?' he asked his wife nastily.

She was quiet. Nervous, Esme thought.

'I don't know,' Emilie said to him as if to brush the question aside but he persisted.

'Sonny! They called him Sonny. Because he had such an innocent baby face. Did you know that, Esme?'

'No, I didn't.'

'But my wife does. When he got into strife she went running to his cause. Rescued the poor little innocent, didn't you, my dear?'

Mrs Hillier preferred not to reply, and Esme was wishing Neville would come back.

'Well, let me tell you,' Clive said, draining the last of a table wine into his glass. 'He's not the harmless little gent my wife makes him out to be. Do you know who shot Bartie Lee? He did! The saintly Mal Willoughby.'

Mrs Hillier looked shocked. As if this were hard to believe. But Esme believed him. She turned on him.

'Then bravo, I say. Bravo! I find it rather unelevating of you to talk like that, Clive.'

A few minutes later Clive announced that he and Emilie were leaving. 'We've had a very enjoyable evening,' he said as he was ushering his wife to the door, 'and I'm sure you people have plenty to talk about.'

Jesse offered to drive them home in his buggy, since the rain was still pelting down, but Clive wouldn't hear of it.

'They'll get drowned,' Neville said, and Esme shrugged.

'I think that wouldn't be the worst of it.'

'What do you mean?'

'Nothing.'

She heard Mal telling Jesse he'd only be here for a few days, and was disappointed.

'You're leaving again? So soon? Where are you going?' she asked.

He shrugged, gave her a wry smile, as if he'd prefer not to answer, but relenting, said, 'I'm going bush for a while, Esme. But I'll be back.'

She felt like crying out to him, to tell him that they wouldn't be here. That she and Neville had to leave any day now – the next ship, probably, since that story about going to Brisbane at Lyle's invitation was an excellent excuse for them to leave Cairns without creating suspicion. Neville could have had it in mind even before he came out with it at dinner.

And they'd never see Mal again.

Emilie knew it would happen. She'd even considered asking if they could stay at the hotel for the night, using the rain as an excuse, but Clive would never have agreed to that.

From the minute Mal walked in the door, she'd guessed it would happen, and as Clive became nastier she had no reason to expect a reprieve. She had remained at the table, wondering if she could pluck up the courage quietly to ask Mal for help. Mal, her friend. She would only have to whisper to him and Mal would step in.

You should do it, she kept telling herself, even if it is humiliating. You don't know any of these other people.

In the end, of course, such courage did not materialise, and as the flimsy door shut behind them, and Clive lit the lamp in the kitchen, where the roof was now leaking badly, Emilie stood shivering in the bedroom, afraid to remove her dripping cloak, afraid to remove its protection.

But he tore it from her. He beat her with his razor strop, ignoring her pleas for the child. She screamed for help and he punched her about the face and body to make her stop. No one came. She cringed on the floor, begging him for pity. 'My arm's broken,' she wept.

'And I'll break the other one if I ever see you talking to Willoughby again.'

Emilie stayed on the floor in agony, too frightened to try to get up. She blamed herself for believing in his promises. She blamed herself for not protecting her unborn child by keeping a weapon in the house to ward him off. But then she must have passed out because she awoke to daylight and thudding rain and blood in her mouth. As usual after his violence, Clive was missing so she went about the familiar misery of cleaning herself up. More difficult this time. Her arm was broken between the wrist and the elbow. She knew she'd have to go to the hospital to have it set, but how to do that in this state? She turned a shawl into a sling to rest her arm, and sat down, exhausted, knowing she didn't even have the strength to walk to the hospital. Outside, incessant rain had cleared the streets, and there was an ominous quiet about the little town. With no one to help her, Emilie curled up on the bed and closed her eyes to the world.

'I wonder what Mal Willoughby will do now?' Esme asked Neville as they sat over morning tea in the hotel lounge.

He looked out the window, distracted by the relentless rain and the windswept foliage littering the street. 'I beg your pardon, Es. What did you say?'

'I was wondering what Mal will do now.'

'He said he was going bush. Do you realise what that means? He's after Jake Tussup.'

'Oh no. Why doesn't he leave it to the police? Where does he come from, anyway? Where's his home?'

'Lyle said he grew up in a country town somewhere. Made a heap on the Gympie goldfields and went to explore China with a friend he'd met at Gympie, who just happened to be a bigwig in the Xiu family.' He spread his hands. 'Money meets money. Some people have all the luck.'

'And that's how he met Jun Lien?'

'Yes. Now you stay here, Es. I want to take a look around outside.'

'Why? What's to look at?'

'I'm not sure. But what does all this rain and humidity remind you of?'

Esme looked puzzled. 'I don't know.'

'Yes you do. Think about it. We sat it out in the cellar of the tennis club in Hong Kong.'

'Oh, my God. You don't think there could be a hurricane? Do they have them down here?'

'I believe so. I was getting nervous yesterday, so I asked about. They call them cyclones here. There have been four along this coast in the last ten years. In other towns. But I'm beginning to think Cairns is in for its first.'

'Couldn't it just be monsoonal rain?' Esme asked him hopefully.

'Could be. But I think I'll get my coat and go for a walk along the wharves. See what the seafarers have to say.'

The sea was buffeting the shores of the bay, and high tides were depositing banks of foam on grassy ridges. Gusts of warm wind were bending palms and swirling rain, as Neville stepped on to the sodden timbers of the wharf.

'Storm out there?' he asked an old fisherman, who was gathering up crab pots.

He nodded. 'I reckon.'

'Some people seem to think it could be a cyclone.'

'Some people could be right, mate, but the buggers swing around. It could hit here or fifty miles north or south. Or it could fade off into the ocean. No point worrying about it.'

But it did worry Neville. As he walked along the deserted waterfront he could feel the strength in that wind, he could tell it had accelerated even in that short time. He hung on to an aged mango tree to steady himself and looked out to sea, wondering what dangers lurked beyond the bay, and beyond that huge reef out there in the wilds of the Pacific. Are great winds gathering, coiling themselves into a fury, ready to make a run at us? he wondered.

Despite the fisherman's philosophical approach, Neville felt he had to do something.

He ran back to the hotel and found Mrs Kassel. Her husband, she said, had gone to the butcher's.

'I think there's a bad storm coming,' he told her.

'Coming?' she echoed. 'It's already here. I can't get the washing dry. The stables are flooded. Everything is such a mess. Not even customers today.'

'This will be worse, I'm sure of it. There's a smell in the air, I can't explain it but you must prepare. The stairs are solid. People can shelter under there. The wind will come from the sea, so open the back windows and back door, to release pressure.'

'Goodness me, Mr Caporn, we can't invite the weather in!'

'It will come in. Please, Mrs Kassel, my wife and I have endured several hurricanes in the Far East and a particularly bad one in Hong Kong.'

'A hurricane? You say there's a hurricane coming?'

'I think so.'

'Why aren't we warned? I must warn Franz. I have to go get him . . .'

Neville held her back. 'I'll get him. You take the servants and anyone else in the building, and shelter under the stairs. And what about the creamery in the yard? That's brick. Some should go in there if they can fit.'

He hurried to the parlour door and called Esme. 'I think there is a hurricane moving in. You take shelter under the stairs, I'll go and find Franz. His wife needs him.'

'I need you,' she replied, coming over to him. 'Don't go out in that weather. You can hear it getting worse.'

He kissed her. 'I won't be long. He's not far away.'

The winds were accelerating. A tree across the road crashed down. The hotel seemed to creak and groan its displeasure. One of the housemaids ran to close the back door, but Esme called to her to leave it, insisting that the kitchen staff take shelter.

'It'll blow over, madam,' the cook said. 'No need to worry. Would you like a nice cup of tea?'

'I would not, and you are to come with me immediately!'

It took time for Esme to round them up, with three other guests, and persuade them into the storeroom under the stairs.

'We'll suffocate in here,' someone complained.

'Leave the door open for a while,' Esme told them. 'Where's Mrs Kassel?'

'She went out the front to look for Mr Kassel.'

'Oh no!' Esme rushed out and dragged the protesting woman inside.

Clive had spent the rest of the night in his partly completed shop, stretched out on canvases used by the painters. He awoke stiff and sore, and with the familiar sense of dread that always followed his bouts of rage.

As he climbed to his feet, glaring out at the sodden, windswept street, he told himself it was her fault for provoking him. But he would apologise to her, might as well. Anything for a quiet life. Besides, there was a lot of work to be done here before the store could be opened. He needed her help.

He ran his hands through his hair in an attempt to look presentable, and reached over to pick up his overcoat. It was then he noticed water streaming down the back wall.

With a yelp of surprise, he rushed over to find the cause. It seemed to be coming from the mezzanine floor, so he tore up the stairs and stared at the stain of water across the ceiling and down the wall. Then he heard a clatter above him! A sheet of corrugated iron roofing had come loose and was banging precariously against the timber beams.

Clive was in a panic. It had to be fixed. If it tore away, the whole place would be flooded! He looked frantically about for a ladder and, not finding one, ran back inside for his coat and dashed off to locate the builder.

The fellow was not at home.

'He's gone off to help a mate,' his wife said. 'A tree blew down across their house.'
'But this is urgent. He has to fix my roof!'
'I'll send him over when he gets back.'
'That won't do. Can I borrow his ladder?'
'He's got it with him. On his dray. He be needing it, mister. Do you want to come in and wait?'
'No, I'll find the plasterer. I can borrow one from him.'
He ran six blocks, only to be met with a flat refusal.
'I'm not climbing a ladder, outside, in this gale. Nor should you, mate. If the place is getting a bit of water in, don't worry about it. We can fix it. Better a damaged wall than a damaged head. Tell you what. As soon as the wind drops I'll get over there meself and hammer it down. But for now, come in and have a rum. Nothin' else to do on a miserable day like this.'

As the storm worsened, Jesse and Mal called on Mrs Plummer in her new residence, to make sure she was coping, and she was so thrilled to see Mal, she insisted they stay for coffee. They had intended to press on into the main centre of town to see if the winds were causing any major damage but decided half an hour or so wouldn't make much difference.
They had passed Clive on the way but he'd been head down, pushing into the wind, and hadn't noticed them.
'There's hardly a soul about today,' Jesse told Mrs Plummer. 'The shopkeepers won't be too happy.'
'I don't know about that,' she replied. 'If people are sensible they stock up for storms like this. I always do. But tell me, Mal, how are you, my dear? And if I may ask, how did you get on with your dear one's family?'
Mal sighed. 'I'm well thanks, Mrs Plummer. Quite well. I didn't get on too good with the family, I have to say . . .'
'No,' she murmured. 'I was worried about you.'
'But you see I survived, and Jun Lien is in a beautiful garden in the family estate.'
'Ah, *requiescat in pace*. That is good. Now, you can help me set the table, and, Jesse, on the sideboard is the book you wanted to view, on the growing of Chinese herbs and spices.'
The coffee was brewing, the table set with a formal tea cloth and china setting, cake and biscuits placed on a tray for Mal to take to the dining room, when the noise of the wind raised to a roar.
'I'm glad you're here,' Eleanor said to them. 'This is really quite frightening.'

At 11.30 a.m. that March day, the cyclone that had been prowling malevolently along the coast wound itself into a massive force and headed for land.

It shouldered past the reef, tore across Trinity Bay with its weapons of darkness and destruction, and slammed into the town of Cairns with the suddenness of a sledgehammer.

The buildings along the front took the brunt of the violence. Huge seas whipped up by the cyclonic winds surged across the wharves, as the warehouses and customs offices shattered, the wreckage picked up by thundering waves and cast ashore like tinder.

It struck the hotel with such force that the people cringing under the stairs expected the building to collapse. But it seemed to hold, so they remained in place, listening to the chaos hurtling around them. Neither Neville nor Franz had returned before the storm hit, and Mrs Kassel was distraught. Esme did her best to comfort her, but she was desperately anxious herself, and prayed to God that the men were safe.

Further down the street, palms were flattened, trees uprooted, debris was flying everywhere. The general store, the Fish Café, and several other buildings, including Hillier's new shops, were completely wrecked. All over the town, houses were laid low. Several, tightly locked against the winds, actually imploded, including the little surveyor's cottage where Emilie Hillier was last seen.

The cyclone rampaged for more than an hour, terrorising the populace, before the winds eased to a light blow, rain drifted about almost as an afterthought and people began to emerge to assess the damage.

They were shocked to see the roof had been ripped off the Alexandra Hotel, exposing the first–floor rooms to the rampaging elements, and sending water cascading down to the ground floor. They stood staring at the wreckage of the business centre along the Esplanade and the street at the rear, where only a few chimneys remained upright.

Suddenly there were shots. Two shots. And people ran wildly about, looking for cover where none existed. But Sergeant Dan Connor announced that they'd had to put down two injured horses, and everyone breathed a sigh of relief.

Franz and Neville finally staggered into the hotel, having sheltered in the Bank of Australasia until the storm abated, and then climbed over piles of wreckage to make their way back. At the sight of his hotel, Franz collapsed, and willing hands carried him into the wrecked lobby, where Mrs Kassel was wandering about, dazed.

'I think he only fainted,' Neville told her, as Franz began to recover, hoping he wouldn't pass out again when he saw the inside of the hotel. But then Esme came running out.

'You had me scared,' she told him.

'Me too. I was frantic for you, but we couldn't get back. You all right, Es? No bumps or bruises?'

'Only squashed toes. The cook stood on them. It was damned hot under those stairs. I have to have a wash.'

Just then Sergeant Connor could be heard calling people to attention with a loudhailer that sounded thunderous in the abnormal silence of the main street.

'I want all able-bodied men to gather here, so that we can organise a thorough check of buildings. I am sorry to have to inform you that we have had one fatality. Tom Panhaligan was killed this morning, struck by a flying branch. Our deepest sympathies to Mrs Penhaligan. Several people have been injured, but fortunately the hospital didn't suffer much damage so they are admitting casualties. Now, all of you blokes,' he called to the men gathering in front of him, 'we'll start at the bottom of the street, at the first damaged house. I want every wrecked building to be thoroughly searched by teams of men, in case people are trapped in them, and a report made to me before moving on to the next place. Don't bother about clearing the streets just yet. I want to make sure everyone is accounted for.

'Now, one more thing. Get moving. I want this done as quickly as possible because this isn't the end of it. That storm, the cyclone, will be back.'

'What?' Some people laughed. Others looked about them at the fleecy clouds that were already allowing patches of blue.

'He's right,' Neville called. 'We are in the eye of the storm. It's calm. Too calm. The other side of the circle of wind is yet to strike.'

Voices still murmured disbelief, but Connor had no time for them. 'Mr Caporn has given you the explanation. Believe what you like. But get on with the job.'

Mal and Jesse were already at work with several helpers, sawing branches off the massive tree that had landed on his house.

'You have to admit all that foliage saved the place from being totally blown away, and us with it,' Mal grinned. 'So look on the bright side.'

'And you've got enough firewood to last a century,' another man called, tossing down a heavy branch. The town's a mess,' he added. 'It'll be a helluva job to clean it up and rebuild.'

'Yeah, then you'll all have plenty of firewood,' Jesse told them.

The sky was a curious yellow as the clouds began to drift back and rain started to fall again, but Clive didn't notice. He was in the ruins of his shops, frantically tossing wreckage aside to release pools of water that had collected on his timber floors.

Not one of the shops had survived. All the walls were down, except the archway that had led from the women's to the men's section, and that stood gaping like giant jaws. He stumbled through in disbelief, crunching over glass, glass from the new windows, kicking at lumps of plaster and lifting sheets of corrugated iron in the faint hope that something there, something underneath, had survived. But what had been there before? Nothing, he realised. There weren't any fittings in place.

In a daze, hardly aware of what he was doing, Clive found a shovel and started work in earnest, as if this setback could be overcome by quick action. Shirt off, he was shovelling broken glass into a heap when a group of men came by.

'Everything all right there?' one called to him. 'No casualties?'

Clive stared at them, uncomprehending. 'What do you call this?' he shouted angrily. 'Give me a hand here.'

But they trooped away and for the first time, Clive realised the pub next door was gone, and so was the Stock and Station agent's on the other side. It was difficult to ascertain where his property ended and theirs began, and that worried him. He had become so maddened by the ruination of his splendid shops that he shovelled meticulously along a line that he had drawn in the mud, to make sure he didn't waste any effort on next door's problems. But when the rain started again, and the wind returned, destroying all his hard work, he sat down on the edge of his collapsed veranda, and wept.

Two men saw him there, took him to be a casualty, and marched him off to a shelter in the bank as the big blow began again.

But before that, volunteers came to the wreckage of the surveyor's cottage. They heard a faint voice and searched carefully, removing debris, piece by piece, until they found the lady wedged under the bed. They carried her several blocks to the hospital, where she was placed with other casualties in the safest place that could be offered: nearby brick stables that had been built by John Kinkaid to house his Thoroughbreds.

'I'm sorry, Mrs Hillier,' Matron told her. 'You just lie there and rest, and we'll get to you as soon as we can.'

At first the storm had been a comfort, giving her an excuse to stay in the bed, cocooned in the soft eiderdown. Rain was thundering down, and Emilie didn't mind. She liked listening to rain. Especially when it wasn't accompanied by scary thunder and lightning.

The wind was strong, though, she could hear it whooshing through the surrounding bush, and the occasional crack of branches that had given way under pressure. Then the shingles on the roof of the cottage began rattling and Emilie held her breath, praying that they'd hang on, but the wind was too much for them. As they blew off, rain began pouring into the cottage.

'Oh no!' Still wrapped in her eiderdown, Emilie sat up, wondering what she could possibly do to protect their belongings from the deluge, knowing though, that she was completely helpless, when suddenly the cottage seemed to explode.

Her immediate reaction was to dive under the bed, forgetting about her broken arm, and causing herself excruciating pain. She lay on her side, the eiderdown pulled up over her head to try to shut out the terrifying roar of the storm and the crashing noises as the cottage collapsed around her, burying her beneath the rubble. But the rain kept on. Though one side of the double bed had collapsed, the other side held, providing a narrow refuge, but not from water. It seeped through, soaking her so quickly that soon she was lying trapped in muddy water.

She tried to free herself by pushing at the walls of her small cave with her feet, but that caused a frightening dislodgement of something heavy – she thought it could be a roof beam – and more rubble falling into her precious space.

Emilie took stock. She had only suffered a few extra cuts and bruises. She had air. By the sound of things the walls had caved in so there wasn't much else to fall on her. But the winds were still raging out there so she would just have to stay calm until they abated. Try to stay calm.

She forbade tears. She could not allow self-pity. When the noise of the wind stopped she would call for help. Clive would come. Someone would hear. It wasn't as if she was in some deep dungeon. Then she would have her arm set. Blame the storm to avoid embarrassment. And then what?

A hotel, she supposed. Until she could get back to Maryborough. This time there'd be no reprieve for Clive. She would never make that mistake again. She would demand enough money from him to be able to return to Maryborough. He would have to give it to her. She would be very firm with him. And she'd sue for divorce immediately . . .

Plans kept her mind so busily occupied that she hardly noticed the wind had died down until she heard the men's voices. She took a deep breath and yelled for help, surprised that she was able to raise her voice to such a level. Again and again she yelled until she heard someone respond.

'Hang on, lady, we'll get you out.'

They seemed to take an eternity, moving rubble bit by bit, until there was daylight, wondrous daylight, and a man peering down at her.

'You all right?'

'Yes, but I've got a broken arm.'

'Ah, you poor little thing. Hey, you blokes, we got to be careful here. This poor lady's got a broken arm.'

They were so gentle and kind, those strange men, that she felt weepy, and had to fight off the tears. And then there was a blank, time lost, until the matron told her to rest, and a woman started screaming that the hurricane was coming back, and they'd all be killed.

Emilie thought the woman was simply hysterical, that the storm had passed, but then torrential rain began again, and the winds began building up. The woman screamed and screamed until someone yelled at her to shut up, which she did abruptly, resorting to loud sobs.

The brick stables survived the next onslaught while Emilie lay in the hospital bunk thoroughly confused. She couldn't understand what was happening, and her first question, when a doctor and nurses hurried in to see the patients, was: 'Will the storm come back again?'

'No, it's all over now,' the doctor said. 'We have to get you dry and into a warm bed and then I'll set your arm. The nurse will take your particulars and look after you now. You've been very brave. I'm so sorry we had to desert you before, but we'll make up for it now, I promise you.'

Emilie smiled. 'People are so very kind,' she said to the nurse.

As soon as the cyclone blew itself out once and for all, Jesse Field rushed over to the hospital and found a weary Dr Fanning taking a break in the matron's office.

'Do you want a cup of tea?' Fanning asked him, as he lit a cigarette.

'Surely would.'

'Then help yourself. What can I do for you?'

'Checking the situation here. The second blow was as bad as the first. I couldn't believe it would return with such force.'

'Believe it. We have quite a few new patients. Several people took a battering, some with concussion. Two boys marching around barefoot have their feet badly cut. And Joey Bryant's not too good. His horse panicked, kicked him in the head. There's a seaman missing from the ketch *Jupiter*. They think he fell overboard.' Fanning sniffed. 'They think! I think they were all boozed. They don't know what happened to him.'

'I'll look into it. Where's Joey?'

'Matron's with him. You can't see him yet.'

'All right. I'll come back later. I'd better get over to *Jupiter* and see if they've found that bloke. What's his name?'

'I've no idea. But there is something curious going on. We've got a woman in the casualty ward. They dug her out from under the old surveyor's cottage and brought her here before the second blow. She's rather badly knocked about. She had a broken arm. I set it, and at Matron's request had a good look at her other injuries.'

'Oh yes,' Jesse said, mildly interested. The woman was only one of many.

'But listen here,' Fanning said. 'She didn't get all her injuries from the storm. She'd been beaten, badly beaten. I've seen razor strop injuries plenty of times in my day, and she's a classic example.'

'Who did it?'

'There's the rub. The storm, according to her, which gives the lie to an attack by some unknown lout or mugger. She'd have owned up to that. And for my money, the razor strop points to the husband.'

'Bastard! Who is he?'

'Surprise, surprise,' Fanning smirked, lighting another cigarette. 'Our new upstanding citizen Mr Hillier! Clive Hillier! He was here this morning, all upset for her and lovey-dovey. Fussing about the little woman like a mother hen.' He laughed. 'Matron said someone should whack him with a rolling pin. She got rid of him smartly. But still the wife had nothing to say, any more than that the cottage had collapsed on her.'

Jesse was concerned for Emilie. 'How is she now?'

'Exhausted. Totally exhausted. I told them to keep her here for a few days. But don't you go quoting me on this, Jesse.'

'No, we never write up domestic fights. Now what have we got? How many would you say the hospital has treated in all, because of the cyclone?'

'Twenty-two, I think. One dead, one missing. We got off rather lightly, considering.'

'Thanks. I'll be on my way.' Jesse hurried out, and stood in the hall, trying to make up his mind what to do, more concerned about the plight of Emilie Hillier than the lurid articles about the cyclone that needed to be submitted as soon as possible. He wanted to visit Emilie right away, to see if she needed help, or just some company, but decided against it for the time being. Obviously she needed that rest.

But what about Hillier? Had he really beaten her? Though he did not dispute old Fanning's verdict, it seemed impossible to Jesse that anyone would beat that sweet young woman. She was so gentle, and quietly spoken . . . would Clive do that?

And then he remembered Mal. She had been his sweetheart before Clive married her. Come to think of it, Clive hadn't been overly thrilled to see his old mate at the hotel.

He wondered if Mal ought to be told about Emilie. He was her friend. He could find out what really happened.

'Yes, and make the situation a bloody sight worse,' he muttered. Why was it so hard to work out the best thing to do in these domestic rows?

He was just about to slip out the back door and cut across the paddocks to the newspaper offices, which had survived, except for broken windows and the wreck of the glass front door, when he heard a commotion at the entrance to the hospital. Immediately, he changed his mind and ran through to see what was happening, hard on the heels of the matron.

Someone was shouting for the doctor. Shouting for him to come quick!

They were better organised at the Alexandra Hotel, despite the mess, when the cyclone struck again. The floor of the haven under the stairs had been mopped dry, and rugs covered the damp boards. A pitcher of water and a dipper was placed inside the door to help combat the heat and everyone was rounded up again, when the town fire bell began clanging a warning.

Once they were settled in the darkness, Franz called out: 'Where's my wife?'

'She's in the back,' Esme said. 'I brought her myself.'

'No she's not,' one of the maids said. 'She forgot the chooks. She ran out to lock them up.'

Esme couldn't believe it! She'd had to insist Mrs Kassel stop working in the kitchen and take cover, almost dragging her into the shelter with all the others. 'Are you in here, Mrs Kassel?' she called, certain of an answer.

When there was no response, Franz began pushing to get out, but Neville stopped him. 'No, stay there. I'm closest. I'll get her.'

He was gone before anyone could stop him, shouting back at Esme through the increasing noise to shut the small door.

Neville ran down the passageway into the kitchen, feeling as if he were in the epicentre of an earthquake. The wind velocity was terrifying. It was bad enough in the kitchen, with the whole building shaking, but outside all he could see was this whirlwind of debris and rain. Instinctively he drew back into the small pantry; that seemed to provide a little more shelter than the large open kitchen with its broken windows and dripping ceilings.

He prayed Mrs Kassel had taken shelter in the creamery, even though it would be rather crowded. They'd arranged for several women and children from neighbouring houses to bundle in there when the bell rang. But then he heard her shout, and expected her to come dashing into the kitchen, but that didn't happen so he peered out the pantry window.

'Silly woman, chasing chooks at this stage,' he muttered when there was no sign of her from that aspect. 'They're probably all being tossed about like shuttlecocks. Or learning to fly the hard way,' he grinned, picturing the scene, knowing he ought to find the woman. But the pantry was a good, safe place as it turned out. Why should he risk his neck out there in the mayhem? It'd be like walking unarmed across a battlefield. His eye fell on a heavy leather overcoat, one that Franz had obviously brought from Germany. There'd not be much call for it in this climate. Except now, he mused crossly, as if the thing was beckoning him to grab it, use it for some protection.

He did. He did not want to think about this madness, he just pulled the thing on and plunged into the kitchen, from where he had a better view of the yard. He could see her now – Mrs Kassel, the chook chaser – hanging on to a big bloody tree down by the gate. Nowhere near the brick creamery. The kitchen was closer. The tree was thrashing about like crazy, adding branches to the flying debris, threatening to join the whirlwind itself.

Neville shouted at her to let go. To make a run for it before it was too late, but she had her head down against the torrential rain and he doubted if she had heard him. He shouted again, shouted at her this time!

'Let go for, God's sake, woman! That tree won't hold much longer. Get over here. Quickly!'

Was she deaf? Scared witless? Frozen to the bloody tree? Before he could stop himself, knowing it was stupid, Neville ran. Crouching, ducking, wrestling the winds, knowing now why she couldn't let go. It was like taking on a tidal wave, but he made it. Somehow he made the two-hundred-yard dash across to her, in the slowest time, he thought, ever clocked.

'Come on,' he panted, not about to waste any time out here.

'No,' she shrieked, her arms clasped about the tree trunk. 'I can't. I can't!'

'You have to,' he yelled, using a solid branch for an anchor against the grasping winds. 'You can't stay here, it's too dangerous.'

'It's more dangerous out there,' she cried, through wet hair that was plastered across her face.

'No, it's not,' he argued angrily.

But then the tree made the decision for them. It began to creak and gave a lurch. It managed to remain standing, but for how long? Neville could feel the pressure now, as if the voracious winds had found a victim in this tree and would not now let up. The tree trunk creaked again, and groaned dismally. Mrs Kassel looked up at Neville, and then peered frantically about for a closer refuge.

'Go!' he shouted at her, so, suddenly she began the run towards the kitchen, stumbling on her long wet skirts, battling the wind, but he kept behind her, pushing her on until she was able to break free and make the rest of the way on her own.

With a sigh of relief he straightened up and ploughed on.

He saw it coming. The sheet of corrugated iron, scooping up air in a magic carpet sort of way, first this way and then that, making it difficult to judge exactly where it was going. He put an arm up to defend himself in case it did swoop on him, the bloody dangerous sheet of metal, but it was too late. It came so fast upon him. He felt the thump across his back and then he was lying on the ground in the soft wet mud. The rain was cooling, he thought, and it was a damn sight safer down here than trying to battle the unfair odds of a storm like that. He was glad he was wearing Kassel's greatcoat to protect him. Good move that. He hoped Es was safe in the cubbyhole under the stairs. She'd rope Mrs Kassel in there pretty quick smart. Good old Es. A real champion she was. He smiled. Yes. He'd buy her that gold dress. Es . . .

When they didn't return there was anxiety, but Esme thought they probably couldn't make it all the way through the hotel to the stairs, and had grabbed what shelter they could elsewhere.

'Like you and Neville did last time,' she told Franz, who agreed it was probable.

Nevertheless, Esme was worried. 'That storm sounds worse now.'

'No it's not,' the cook said. 'The first blow was ten times worse. Frightened the hell out of me. And am I imagining in it or is the floor getting wetter?'

'Yes, water's seeping under the door,' Esme said with a cheerfulness she didn't feel. 'Just enough to make us even more uncomfortable.'

So they waited – nervous, worried, irritated – until eventually the winds eased and the building stopped creaking, and they could creep out to stretch their limbs and look about at even more damage to the hotel.

Franz and Esme pushed wreckage aside to hurry on to the rear of the hotel, as the hotel staff took stock.

'They'll have to rebuild this place stick by stick,' the cook said, 'to make it safe. And get all new furniture. This lot's shot, well and truly.'

'The linen's all mud-stained,' a housemaid said miserably. 'Even the good stuff in the linen press. We'll have to wash the lot and even then I don't think . . .'

They heard Franz shout and rushed down the passage to the kitchen, fearing the worst, but it turned out that Mrs Kassel had been sheltering on the pantry floor. She looked a mess, covered in mud, but Franz and Mrs Caporn got her to her feet and he hugged her to him, telling how scared they'd been for her, and kissing her, while Mrs Caporn was trying to find out where her husband was.

'He's safe,' Mrs Kassel said, leaning on Franz for support. 'Such a good man. He brought me in. Helped me. He was right behind me.'

'Then where is he now?' Esme asked, relieved.

'I couldn't go any further. I just collapsed in here. Mr Caporn, he must have gone on. To the stairs.'

They all looked about them. 'No, he didn't,' Esme said.

Mrs Kassel glanced out the window and screamed. 'See. The tree has fallen down! The one that was protecting me.' She blessed herself. 'Oh, Franz, thank God for Mr Caporn. If he hadn't come for me, I'd be under it. Oh dear God, I've never been so frightened in my life. It was a nightmare! I must sit down, I feel faint.'

'I'll get her a brandy,' the cook said. 'I could do with a nip myself.'

Esme had rushed through to the front of the hotel, looking for Neville. She peered out into the street, saw a few people wandering about, and two men already picking up debris from the street. She jumped back as half a dozen huge, horned cattle came stampeding around the corner and hurtled wildly past her.

She searched the battered parlour and bar, looked in the hotel office and then the dining room and from there, pushed the swing door into the kitchen.

'Find him?' Franz asked. Then he doubled back as he passed the kitchen window. 'What's that? What's my coat doing out there?'

He strode out the door to pick it up. No one took much notice. A coat left out in the rain was low on the damage scale.

'He's not in the hotel,' Esme was saying to Mrs Kassel. 'Why would he go out again? Where could he be?'

Esme felt a chill in the room, in the big roomy kitchen where they were all gathered by the long, scrubbed table with the marble chopping block on the end, the stove end, where the cook worked, and a silence was in the room, hand in hand with the stillness. A tableau. It was a tableau that she hadn't yet understood, hadn't grasped the significance of it, and she glided through it slowly, so as not to disturb the symmetry, stepping outside into sudden warmth and down the broken steps to where Franz was kneeling, by a coat that seemed so important to him that she had to know what was underneath. Needed to know.

'My dear . . .' Franz tried to tell her. Convince her. But she wouldn't have it.

'He is not!' she screamed. 'He is not!' She turned to scream at the girl behind her. 'He is not. Get a doctor. Go! Now! Get the doctor.'

Before anyone could stop her, the young housemaid took off, sprinting across the yard and out the gate to do exactly as she was told in this emergency! To save Mr Caporn! She'd never had such a responsibility in her whole life, so now she was glad she was a good runner. Her dad always said she could run like the wind. And with poor Mr Caporn lying there in Mr Kassel's leather coat, which was split across the back now and soaked in blood, never a better time to prove it. She hurdled a fallen log, her black skirt hitched up like a hussy, and raced on, thinking of Mr Caporn's white face, or the half she could see – with the bruise spread across his nose and forehead, like as if he'd been in a fight, but he had a little smile on the side of his lips, and that gave her heart. He was relying on her to get help before it was too late. She tore up the carriageway of the hospital, past an overturned wagon and jumped up on to the veranda, ignoring the skewed awning by the front door and began shouting for Dr Fanning.

Mal knew the Alexandra Hotel had taken a battering, so he walked there by way of the waterfront, to see how they all were and offer assistance.

The town smelled mouldy, a suffocating smell, old and mouldy, as if the winds and fallen trees had laid bare ancient caves. And everything looked askew. Everything that was still standing, that is. But the muddy ground was already beginning to harden into slabs, and the same heat that was cooking the mud bore down on soggy trees as if punishing them for their wretched state.

'But it's an ill wind,' he grinned, picking up a large ripe mango from among the dozens lying beneath a tree.

He peeled the skin back and bit into the succulent fruit, not caring that the juice was dripping on his torn shirt. Mal had never tasted mangoes until his travels had brought him north, and now he loved them. It occurred to him that he should get a bucket from the hotel and collect all of this fruit instead of allowing it to rot on the ground, but just as he went to cross the street to the hotel, a herd of cattle came pounding round the corner and raced madly past him, a whip-cracking rider in full pursuit.

Mal leaped out of their way, at the same time glimpsing Esme Caporn at the front of the hotel. But by the time the stampeding cattle had thundered past, she had gone back inside.

She was looking woeful, he thought, and well she might be, amid the wreckage of a hotel stripped of its roof.

He finished the mango, sucking the stone for its last morsel, grabbed another one and crossed the road.

The inside of the hotel was a sad sight, all care and proud efforts spoiled. There wasn't a soul about now, so he peered into the bar, where everything was drenched and already gathering mould, and slabs of ceiling plaster were cast about like discarded platters. The once-colourful array of bottles had disappeared from the mirror-backed shelves, hopefully as intact as the mirrors that now reflected only broken windows.

Absently he righted a fallen chair and stepped back into the lobby, looking up at the sturdy staircase, now relieved of its carpet runners and brass fittings, wondering what all this destruction would cost the owners, when he heard the screams. A woman screaming.

With the utmost care, he and Franz carried Neville inside, to place him on a daybed in the small sitting room off the kitchen, but it was a difficult task.

Mrs Kassel was trying to manoeuvre Esme away, for those few minutes, but she wouldn't, couldn't let him go. She clung to Neville, telling him he'd be all right. That the doctor would be here soon – kissing him, begging him to wake up. She took the damp cloth Mrs Kassel handed her and washed the dirt from his face, talking to him all the while, insisting he must wake up. She cried out that Franz was wrong, that Neville was only unconscious and, after an age, with everyone standing helplessly by, Dr Fanning appeared at the door.

'Oh, thank God you're here!' she cried. 'He's very bad. He's lost a lot of blood.'

Fanning managed to slide past her to examine her husband, kindly taking more time than was necessary, Mal thought, to console the woman, but eventually he took off his stethoscope and shook his head.

'I'm sorry, Mrs Caporn, he's gone. He took a terrible blow. Across his back and neck . . . But he wouldn't have felt a thing, God rest his soul.'

Mal had to persuade Esme to release the body. To allow it to be taken to the mortuary. When, eventually, she did agree, she insisted on walking behind the wagon.

'I can't leave him yet. It's too soon,' she sobbed. 'He's not ready, Mal. He needs more time.'

'That's true. It was sudden for both of you. I'll walk with you to where they are taking him. It's not much of a place, believe me, but we could just sit under the trees across the road from there, for a while, until you get used to the idea.'

'The idea of him gone?' she whispered.

He nodded. 'Something like that.'

There was so much to do, and everyone was so busy that Esme, left to mourn on her own, felt shut out. They moved her things to a downstairs bedroom, and took it for granted that she'd sort out her own clothes – rescue what she could from the soaked and mouldy heaps – but Esme could only sit and stare at them. What did it matter now? Who cared? And, anyway, she wasn't a laundress, she had no idea how to go about fixing them.

On the second night, Mal came to see her and found her squatting on the bed, smoking Neville's pipe.

He didn't seem to notice the mess, or the mouldy smell, or even the pipe. 'How are you?'

'As you would expect,' she said dully. 'Bloody awful.'

He nodded. 'Yes,' and peered out the window. 'They've just about cleared all the wreckage from upstairs, and they'll be starting on this floor tomorrow. The place is shaky. Not fit for habitation.'

'They want me to move out?'

'The Kassels have to go too. But Mrs Plummer wants you to come and stay with her. What do you think about that?'

Esme couldn't think. She didn't know what to think about that. And what's more, she didn't care. She shrugged.

'Good, that's settled.' He shoved bunched clothes from a chair onto the floor so that he could sit down, and Esme blinked. Startled.

'I don't know what to do about those clothes,' she said – felt she had to say. 'They're all ruined, I think.'

'Mrs Plummer will help you sort them out. Do you mind if I have a smoke?'

'Hardly.'

They talked in short gaps, neither trying very hard. It wasn't the time, Esme thought, for conversation, and he was a quiet man. He allowed silences, didn't make any attempt to fill them, and neither did she.

'I was wondering,' he said eventually, 'if you would do me a favour.'

'What sort of favour?'

'Do you remember Mrs Hillier? Clive's wife? You met her the other night.'

'Yes.'

'She's in hospital. Had a battering . . . had to be rescued from a house that collapsed around her.'

'I'm sorry. She seemed a nice person.'

'Yes. Trouble is she's very downhearted, miserable . . .'

Esme sucked angrily on the pipe. 'She's still got a husband, hasn't she?'

Mal nodded thoughtfully. 'Yes, that's true. Don't worry about it. We'll talk about that later. What we ought to talk about is Neville's funeral.'

'No!' She switched her feet off the bed and planted them firmly on the floor. 'No.'

He sighed. 'It has to be done, Esme. Do you want me to see to it?'

'No,' she sobbed, and the tears she'd been trying to control began all over again, while he sat patiently. Like a sentry she thought. On guard. And when she eventually blotted the tears from her eyes, she changed her mind.

'I'm sorry. I mean, yes, I wish you would do the funeral thing for me. I couldn't, I just couldn't.'

'All right, I'll arrange it. Tomorrow, Esme? Can we make it tomorrow?'

'Oh God . . .' She was sobbing again. 'So soon?'

'It's best.'

Esme looked up. 'Neville was my best friend, Mal,' she said in a small voice. 'My only friend. I can't imagine what I will do without him.'

As she spoke, she saw Neville's document bag lying beside the open cabin trunk, and she almost passed out in fright! It was full of money. Or was last time he'd opened it. Money that belonged to Apollo Properties.

'Oh God,' she said again, and Mal was concerned.

'You've gone very white, Esme. Are you feeling sick?'

She certainly was, but she had to hang on. 'Just a little,' she said, handing him the pipe. 'It's gone out. But it doesn't matter. I think I'll lie down, Mal, if you don't mind.'

'Not at all. I'll be off. I'm really sorry about Neville. He's a hero to everyone, you know, for saving Mrs Kassel.'

'Is he?' she said weakly. 'He'd like that.'

Yes he would, Esme said to herself when Mal left.

She was off the bed in seconds, to open the bag and find the money was still there. All that damned money! And what a bloody awful position that placed her in.

'Why did you have to be a damned hero now?' she wailed.

Chapter Fifteen

The matron was watching out for that husband, and caught him as he was on his way into the hospital on the second day.

'A word with you, Mr Hillier,' she called.

'If it's about paying, I might have to—'

'It's not about paying. No one has to pay in an emergency like this, so you can rest easy on that score. It's about your wife.'

'Yes, I'm taking her out today. The house we were renting was destroyed but I've managed to find digs at the Cable Company's hostel, for the time being.'

'She won't be going home today,' Matron said, folding her arms. 'There's no hurry. I wanted to ask you, who gave her that beating?'

'What beating? Who beat my wife?'

'That's what we'd like to know.'

He stepped away from her. 'What sort of story has my wife been telling you? She was hurt in the storm. No one beat her. I'm surprised you'd even imagine such a thing. Now excuse me . . .'

He pushed past her and the Matron let him go. She wasn't a court of law. He may have denied it but at least now he knew full well that he'd been caught. But, in her experience, it was as well to follow this up while the wife was still in the hospital. There was nothing she could do for the woman after that.

Sure enough, there he was at her bedside, his face grim and menacing. Not a sign of concern for a woman who had been assaulted by someone.

I thought so, she mused, as she joined them. 'I hope you aren't accusing Mrs Hillier of telling stories, sir. She hasn't said a word about it. The marks on her back and legs tell their own tale.'

She saw the woman on the bed cringe in fright. 'Now, Mrs Hillier, you're having a baby. You have a responsibility to the child . . .'

'I know that, Matron,' she whispered.

'Then don't be afeared or humiliated into keeping his violence a secret. Tell the world and you'll find he's not so smart.'

'How dare you?' Hillier exploded, but the matron turned on him.

'And how dare *you*, sir! You ought to be ashamed of yourself. Now here's Dr Fanning, so best you run along.'

Enraged, Clive rushed out into the street, his heart pounding. Hadn't he enough trouble with his shops wrecked and no insurance? Their belongings in the cottage ruined, as well as their furnishings that were stored in the wrecked warehouse? And on top of all that, Emilie had the audacity to sit comfortably in a hospital playing the waif. Whining to them about her so-called injuries. Telling lies that the whole town would soon hear about. It's a pity that cottage didn't break her neck instead of just collapsing around her.

But . . . forget about her. What now? Where would he find the money to rebuild and stock his shops? He'd have to take out a considerable loan. Maybe he could open only one, not two shops, mixed clothing, to get started. Rent all the others. He would have to get on to it right away.

'Not a chance Clive,' the builder said. 'You'll have to get in line. We've got a contract to rebuild the Alexandra Hotel, which we constructed in the first place. Fair broke my heart to see it wrecked like that. And then we have to give priority to government buildings, like warehouses and the customs house. There's so much work here after that cyclone, this town will be short of good tradesmen for a year or more, so you'd better get a team lined up as soon as possible.'

Easier said than done. Everyone he asked was already contracted. Thoroughly frustrated, Clive gave up and marched into a makeshift bar, set up beside the ruins of the York Hotel. It wasn't until the third whisky that he realised he wasn't entirely ruined. He had his shares in Apollo Properties! He would sell them. Five hundred pounds! That would build his shops and leave plenty of change. Marvellous! He was saved.

The long, low hospital had sat out the storm with only minor damage to the verandas and the roof, and workers were already on the job.

The morning was humid, and the streets were still covered with a mouldy carpet of strewn leaves, but the sun was making an effort to atone by shining weakly through a ceiling of drab clouds.

Mal was on his way to the undertakers but he slowed his steps as he passed the hospital. He was feeling depressed and generally dispirited. He knew he ought to load up a couple of horses and get going, but he couldn't muster the energy. It wasn't as if anyone here really needed him. People coped, no matter the trials and tribulation heaped on them. Maybe, he thought, it was just this dismal, overcast weather, the aftermath of the cyclone, the slowing down of the senses.

'A bloody paralysis, more like it,' he muttered. 'If you don't get going, you'll lose Tussup's trail altogether.'

'No I won't,' an inner voice objected. 'I'll find the bastard.'

And then? He couldn't think past that point. Wouldn't.

And try as he might he couldn't walk away from the hospital. Ignore her. Jesse Field had told him about her. Said he'd have heard anyway. Hospitals were often a source of news in a small town – or gossip. Call it what you like. Told him on condition he didn't rush out and give Clive a taste of what he'd given Emilie.

Mal was still shocked. He couldn't imagine Clive beating her. Not Emilie! He must have been drunk. Off his head.

Mal had loved her, a long time ago it seemed now, because she was so sweet and gentle, the cultured little English girl who'd stolen his heart at first glance. He remembered how stuffy she'd been when he'd spoken to her in a Brisbane street. Letting him know, very firmly, that she did not like to be addressed by strangers. Even if the stranger were trying to redirect her, to warn her that there was a riot in full swing down the way she was headed.

But the meeting was meant to be, because later, he met her again in the street – in Maryborough. That was his Emilie. The only person who believed in him when he was framed for robbing the gold consignment and killing the guards. Mal still shuddered at that nightmare.

She showed she had steel in her though, by hiring a lawyer to defend him – a good lawyer, thank God, who stood by him until the police woke up and realised that it was the Gold Commissioner himself who'd planned the whole thing, with a partner. They were both hanged in the end, but the police never found the gold.

Emilie heard his voice; he had a deep, resonant voice, with a country twang. She was watching the door when she saw the tousled blond hair, the tanned face, and that smile, turned on her full blast now, in an effort to be cheerful. He had a shyness about him, too; it was still there when he stood at the end of the bed, clutching his hat.

'How are you, Em?' he asked nervously.

'I'm quite well now, thank you, Mal.'

'Then how come you're still in hospital?'

'Just resting.'

'Ah. Resting. I suppose so. They said a house fell on you that night. That'd be a shock to the system, I bet.'

'Yes. It was.'

'So where was Clive?'

She felt the blush. 'He'd gone out.'

'Ah. The town's a real mess. I grew up in New South Wales. I'd never seen a cyclone before. Had you?'

'No. It was quite an experience.'

'And how's your sister? Ruth. Isn't that her name?'

'Yes. She went back home. To England.'

'You ever think of going home?'
Emilie was surprised. 'No. Not really.'
'Perhaps you should,' he said softly.
He reached over and touched her hand. 'Listen, Em, I've got some things to do right now, but I'll come back in an hour or so. Can I get you anything? I think the store is still standing.'
She shook her head, tears stinging. He knew. He was giving her time to think that over.

The only undertaker in town had a pine coffin ready for Mr Caporn.
'I just need someone to choose the trimmings. Would that be you, Mr Willoughby?'
'Yes, I can try.'
'Let's see then. You can have silver fittings, or brass, or these painted lead ones, nobody would know the difference. Depends on what the bereaved wishes to pay.'
'Just use the best you've got, and I'll cover the cost.' He thought of Chang, and remembered the flowers. He'd never let on that he'd known many of the exquisite flowers surrounding Jun Lien's ashes had been artificial. Some of the country they'd passed through at that time of the year would have been lucky to produce weeds.
'Mrs Caporn would like flowers too,' he said.
'That could be difficult. Tropical flowers don't last, and the storm has blown so many blooms away, but we've got wreaths here. They're made of artificial leaves, and quite reasonable.'
'No, the lady requires flowers. Is that the hearse over there?'
'Yes. I was thinking we could have the burial tomorrow. Say at three o'clock?'
'No, make it six, it will be cooler. Now, about the flowers. I want you to fill up your hearse with flowers. I'm sure you can find a lady to arrange them nicely.'
'But we haven't any flowers, sir.'
'Oh, hang on,' Mal said crankily. He marched out into the street where children were playing.
'Hey, kids. We need flowers here. Even flowers that have blown off the trees. Two bob for every bucketful you bring in.'
'What sort of flowers?' a girl asked.
'All sorts. Frangipani, daisies, wildflowers, whatever you can find.' He clapped his hands. 'Chop chop! Away you go!'
Back inside he emptied his pockets of change. 'The kids will find you flowers. I'd appreciate it if you'd pay them. If it costs more put it on the bill. Now what's the routine for the funeral? I have to explain it to Mrs Caporn.'
'What religion is she?'
'I forgot to ask her! I'm sorry, I'll go back and find out.'

* * *

Everyone seemed to be looking for Mrs Caporn.

She'd come into the kitchen early this morning and eaten a little breakfast, much to Mrs Kassel's relief, but then she'd gone out. No one saw her leave.

The housemaids were concerned. 'Mr Kassel said we had to clear that room out this morning,' they told his wife.

'I know,' she worried. The workmen had already begun stripping back the ground-floor rooms. 'You'll just have to pack her bags and get the men to carry them out to the shed.'

Next thing, Mrs Plummer appeared on the scene to collect her. 'I have a nice room aired and ready for her, Mrs Kassel. So I'll just sit and wait until she returns, then if Mr Kassel would be so kind . . .'

'Oh yes, he'll drive you home, my dear. That's no trouble. We're just so glad you have come for her, poor thing. I'm still badly shocked myself. And eternally grateful to her late husband, God rest his soul. Do you know when the funeral is to be?'

'I'm afraid I do not. Perhaps Mrs Caporn is arranging these matters. That's probably where she is.'

'Yes. That's probable. I'll have the girls put a chair out there across the yard for you, Mrs Plummer, while you wait. There's too much dust and dirt flying about here.'

She sighed, and wiped away sudden tears. 'Our lovely hotel! They're pulling it down . . .'

Then there was Mr Willoughby, also looking for Mrs Caporn.

'The funeral's at six o'clock this evening,' he told her. 'I'll let you know about the details later.'

The front entrance to the hotel was closed down, so he retraced his steps to the gate just as Clive Hillier was entering the yard.

'What are you doing here?' Mal asked angrily.

'I've come to see Mrs Caporn. Not that it's any of your business. And I'll thank you to keep away from my wife. I heard you were at the hospital a while ago. You can't let go, can you, Mal? I knew you'd come looking for Emilie as soon as you found out she was here.'

Mal couldn't be bothered arguing with him. He'd noticed, and been surprised by Clive's cold stare, hardly a greeting, when he'd met him at the hotel for the first time in years. They'd been old friends. He'd introduced him to *his* girlfriend, Emilie. And lost her to him. He hadn't carried a grudge, and Clive had no reason to. But whatever he was on about right now, he was bloody annoying as well as everything else. Mal reminded himself that he had promised Jesse not to retaliate against Clive for being the bastard, for beating Emilie.

But he wasn't about to stand here and argue with him.

'Sorry, Jesse,' he said, and punched Clive on the jaw. Hard. Very hard. Set him flat on his back.

'Good gracious!' Mrs Plummer called when she saw Mal Willoughby strike Mr Hillier and then just stride away.

Mrs Kassel saw Mr Hillier trying to climb to his feet in a rather drunken manner. 'What happened to him?' she asked.

'I've no idea,' Mrs Plummer said primly.

Emilie wanted Mal to come back but yet she was afraid that he would.

She'd been wrong about those shares, she admitted to Clive, though she would have felt better had the money been in the bank all the time. He'd gone off to sell them now, claiming they'd be worth a darn sight more than the five hundred pounds he'd paid for them. None of which solved her problem. She wasn't going back to him.

He'd found 'digs' for them at the Cable Company hostel, used to house men who maintained the telegraph lines – admitting they weren't up to much, but the wrecked town had little else to offer. He'd talked to her, once again, as if nothing had happened, almost making her believe that the weals on her back, and the broken arm were caused by the collapse of the cottage. Almost.

Emilie had been dreadfully embarrassed by the matron, who had recognised the cause of some of her injuries – but not that Clive had also broken her arm – and yet the plain-talking woman had given her some heart. There was at least some satisfaction in watching Clive bluster under Matron's tirade. She must have dozed, trying to think all this, because when she opened her eyes, Mal was there, leaning against the windowsill.

'You had a very good sleep,' he said, as she struggled to sit up. 'You must have been very tired. Here, let me help you. That arm must be a real load to cart around. How long will it have to stay in plaster?'

'Weeks, I believe.' Emilie pulled her shawl across to hide the nightdress, as he lifted her higher in the bed and plumped the thin pillow behind her back.

'You still don't look too comfortable, Em.'

'I'm all right, thank you.'

'The name's Mal,' he grinned, 'in case you've forgotten. And some years ago you got me out of one helluva spot, hiring that lawyer. He said I was fortunate to have a friend like you.'

'Mal, he proved you were innocent. He was the friend.'

'Yes, he was a clever bloke. Lanfield, that was his name. Lanfield.' He stepped over to the corner and picked up a chair, placing it beside her bed. Once he was seated he spoke very quietly. 'Now, Em, a friend's a friend. We've got to talk about this business with Clive.'

'Oh, please, no.'

'Yes, we do. Was this the first time? The beating? Now you tell me the truth, Missy or I'll see the black line on your tongue.'

When she couldn't reply, Mal groaned. 'Bloody hell! Why didn't you leave him?'

She found her tongue then. Why couldn't people understand it wasn't so easy? The promises kept her there. The fear of public humiliation. A lot of things, including . . .

'With what?' she snapped. 'In a marriage, men control the money. I couldn't get away from him.'

Mal was genuinely startled. 'Good Lord, I never knew that. Least I never thought about it much. It's a bit of a trap, isn't it?'

Emilie frowned at him. 'It's not a bit of a trap, Mal. It's a prison, if you want to know.'

They sat awhile, digesting the situation. Emilie knew he was waiting for her to speak, to make some decision, because he was there to help where he could. So, in the end she took the plunge.

'Mal, I wouldn't ask if I weren't desperate, and don't worry if you can't, but please, could you lend me a little money?'

'Yes, of course. Whatever you want. What's the plan?'

'I'm reminded of Mr Lanfield. I'll go to Brisbane and ask him to arrange a divorce for me.'

Mal whistled. 'That bad? You don't think you ought to talk this over with Clive?'

'He broke my arm this time,' she said bitterly.

'For God's sake, why?'

'It doesn't matter now.'

He stood up and kissed her on the cheek. 'Don't be worrying, Em. You stay here and I'll check on the shipping. I'm sorry about this, I really am.'

She watched as he walked away, looking slightly dazed, as if he couldn't imagine how her marriage could have come to this.

For that matter, she thought, neither can I.

Mal wasn't so much dazed as furious. He had a few words with the matron, ensuring that Mrs Hillier be kept in the hospital for her own safety.

'Can you keep Hillier away from her?' he asked.

'Not without a police order signed by her.'

'She wouldn't do that.

'No, I wouldn't think so. It would involve too many people, be too public, and she's a very private person, I realise. But we'll keep an eye on her, Mr Willoughby. She's not going back to that brute, is she?'

'No, I'll try to get her on a ship to Brisbane before he wakes up to the fact that she's gone.'

'Oh, well done,' Matron beamed.

* * *

Esme was hiding in the park by the bank, clutching Neville's document bag, nursing it to her chest as if afraid someone might dash past and wrench it from her. All the trees around her had sprung into bloom again and the bushes had about six inches of baby green growth, thanks to the heat and tumultuous rain, reminding her of their Singapore days. Carefree days.

Tired of lurking about as if she were up to no good, she found a shaded park bench and sat there, looking as serene as any young lady would, quietly enjoying the view. She had dressed in her very best – the large black hat with its satin bows, and the black silk tea gown, embroidered with rosebuds. She'd had to ask one of the maids to iron it for her, ignoring the clucking noises the girl made when she saw the skirt was watermarked.

'It doesn't matter,' Esme had said impatiently. 'Just iron it. People will think it's supposed to be like that.'

As if people think anything at all, she murmured to herself, when she finally pushed the girl out of the room with the dress.

But now, she had to rethink that remark. She was very much aware now that she had to be careful of the impression she gave, because people did have opinions and they could be disastrous. Especially now.

She mulled over her options for the umpteenth time. She could take the money and run. Board the first ship north, south or anywhere. It was a huge haul, she could settle comfortably with that much cash while she worked out what to do next.

'And really,' she told herself, 'it's the only sensible option. There is no company called Apollo Properties. Someone will wake up soon, and you'd better not be here when it happens. Neville put you down as secretary.'

But what if someone twigged if she bolted and they used the telegraph to notify the police. What could she say? She was in Brisbane temporarily to attend the Horwood jubilations, given the chosen ship took her there.

But with company money?

Damn! The ship would have to be sailing north, out of Australian waters. Headed for the Far East. It could take a while to find such a ship. Maybe she should go down to the port this very minute and make enquiries. But Neville's funeral was today. People would recognise her. They'd be wondering what on earth she was doing.

Esme rocked back and forth on the hard bench, still clutching the bag. Neville's funeral! Tears racked her whole being. She couldn't bear a funeral. She couldn't allow them to bury him, put him in the ground just like that. No, not Neville.

'Jesus, Lord! Neville wasn't ready to die!' she sobbed. 'He was full of plans. For us. What am I to do now?'

She let the bag slide to her lap. She didn't want any part of the thing. It spelled serious trouble whichever way she looked at it. And she was tired of the whole business. Sick of it.

Esme Caporn, widow, stood up, straightened her hat, pulled the dark veil down over her face and took a deep breath. She had made up her mind what to do, but it would take real cheek. She prayed that Neville would be listening and stand by her. She was on her way to meet with the bank manager. What was his name? Oh God, she had to keep focused. Ted something. Ted Pask.

He was only too pleased to receive the young widow in his office, gushing with condolences and praise for her heroic, late husband.

'Thank you, Mr Pask, you are kindness itself. I've come here today to seek your advice on a business matter. Regarding Apollo Properties, actually.'

'Oh yes. How fortunate were we that our construction work hadn't been under way. It would have been splintered apart just like Hillier's'

Esme blinked. She didn't know that Clive's shops had been blown down. But it was certainly a bonus for her story.

'They say we ought to consider anchoring roofs more securely, to protect buildings from cyclonic winds,' he was saying, 'and I think that is an excellent idea.'

'I'm sure it is,' she said sadly. 'You must do that. In fact with Lyle Horwood away you're the only person I can talk to.'

She dabbed at her eyes with a lace handkerchief. 'I'm secretary of the company, as you know, and I'm left on my own now that my dear husband has gone.' Tears were flowing now. 'I suppose I have to pay the tradesmen this money,' she said, dumping the wads of notes on his desk, 'but I don't know who. I remember Mr Caporn being very cross that he'd drawn the money to get the tradesmen moving but the Land Office was holding everyone up. I think that's what it was . . .' She was talking in a rush, breathless. Confused.

Pask stared. He picked up the wads and put them down again. Fluttered them through to make sure they all contained bank notes.

'What do you want me to do with them?' he asked, bewildered.

'Put them back in Apollo's box,' she said, adding a touch of simpleton.

'You mean the Apollo account?'

'I suppose so. I don't want the responsibility of minding that money. What if it had blown away in the storm? Goodness me, Mr Pask, it's too much to ask of me. You can be secretary now.'

He began to count the money.

'It's all there,' she wailed. 'I hope you don't think I would touch a penny of it.'

'Oh no, dear lady. I'm only counting it to give you a receipt. I won't be a moment. I'll have a teller write it out immediately.'

He dashed out of his office and, through the missing louvres on the outer window, she saw Clive Hillier walking past. She wondered how his wife was. Mal had said she was injured in the storm.

Mr Pask hurried back, gave her the receipt, and coughed delicately. 'I know it isn't the best time to be bringing up such matters, but Mrs Caporn, about the loan your husband took out. He was rather overdue on the repayments. Perhaps you could come and have a talk with me in a day or so, hmm?'

Oh ye Gods! Esme knew she should have escaped from here on the first available ship. With all that lovely money. She'd totally forgotten that damn loan. And there were only about forty pounds left. They owed sixty.

'Yes of course,' she said calmly as she picked up the receipt. 'When I'm feeling a little better we'll attend to it. In the meantime, should I write to Lyle and tell him you'll be taking over as secretary?'

'No, Mrs Caporn, tell him director. I'll be his co-director. My wife can be the secretary.'

'Very well,' she said, and glided out, her heart beating furiously, and hurried down the battered street to take refuge in her room, but the room no longer existed.

'Don't worry,' Mrs Kassel said. 'You're going to a much nicer room now. With Mrs Plummer. I'll drive you there.'

Esme thought they could easily be driving her to prison for all she knew. She really had made a mess of things this time. And then Mal was waiting at Mrs Plummer's lovely house to talk to her about the funeral, and the religious service. Next came a minister, Pastor Lawder, to discuss the service, and his wife, who wanted to pray with her, but Mrs Plummer eased them out when the details were settled. Esme thought there was to be no end to this awful day.

'Would you cancel all that?' she called to Mrs Plummer from her latest bedroom. 'I'm not going. He wouldn't want a bloody funeral. He hated all that stuff.'

'I'm making you some lunch. Then you have a little sleep. Then a nice cool bath and get looking nice for him, for Mr Caporn.'

'I haven't got anything to wear.'

'Yes you have. I've cleaned your black dress, the one with the jet beading. I always admired that dress. And the hat you were wearing today is just beautiful. There are only three of us from the ship now. We have to look our best. Mal is escorting us. I told him, nice white shirt, stiff collar . . .'

Mrs Plummer smiled. The poor girl had fallen asleep in the pretty four-poster bed with its muslin mosquito netting. She had news of her own today, but she hadn't bothered anyone with it. First, her lawyer in Hong Kong had won an uncontested divorce for her on the grounds of deliberate misrepresentation of identity with intent to defraud. In three months, he advised, she'd be legally single again.

Not the most tactful of men, he wrote: 'By that time the talk and gossip about this will have died down, so you can come back, Eleanor, and resume your life among your friends. I think you were rather hasty in selling your house, but we'll find one equally suitable for you.'

Eleanor decided she would reply on the morrow, thanking him for his excellent service and asking how to change her name back to her maiden name, Von Leibinger. And then there was the letter from Lyle Horwood, advising her that, thanks to his position in the Oriental Company, and because of his insistence that passengers from the *China Belle* be properly compensated . . .

'Including yourself,' she'd commented cynically.

'. . . all claims for loss of jewellery will be met in full, immediately. And no other compensatory claims will be considered.'

Esme did manage to make it through the church service, and the agony of the pastor's funeral oration, and the eulogies given by local dignitaries who felt the need to step up and praise the hero, the man who'd given his life to save a lady in distress. She was amazed that so many people had attended. The little church was packed to overflowing, and the hymns, the old favourites that she'd learned back home, sung with such fervour in this little bush town on the other side of the world, touched her heart. She hoped Neville could hear it.

The coffin was elegant, covered in gorgeous flowers, and as people arrived they brought even more. They were all placed in the church as if to lessen the sadness of the occasion with colour. Esme concentrated on them to keep from falling apart with emotion.

At the graveside it was all too much though. She wept her farewells to Nev, but Mrs Plummer was there by her side, being motherly, and Mal stood with them, seemingly impassive, probably feeling as awful as she did. But at last it was over.

The next morning Esme slept late. When she awoke she found three letters on her bedside table. Two were condolences from local people and the third was from Lyle Horwood. That gave her heart a bump. Why was the co-director of Apollo Properties writing to her?

But when she opened the letter, her heart missed a beat. Esme gasped! The jewellery! That impossible list of 'stolen' jewellery, that she'd invented! Had she finished it? Or had Neville? She couldn't remember. But he must have handed it to Lyle for the insurance claim.

And they had agreed to pay it?

'Oh my God! I claimed my jewellery was worth a thousand pounds, I think.'

She shuddered. Not knowing whether to laugh or cry. And picked up a small silver-framed photograph of Neville that Mrs Plummer had kindly placed on her dressing table.

'So much for honest Es,' she said to him. 'I can't give this lot back.'

* * *

The ship was bound for Brisbane.

'Will you stay there or go back to Maryborough?' Mal asked Mrs Hillier.

'I'll stay in Brisbane until I get the divorce, thanks to your help. I can't believe your generosity, Mal. I'll never be able to repay you.

'You already have, Emilie. So we're quits. What then?'

'I think I'll go home. To England. My sister is still in our old house.'

'All right. But you keep in touch now. You let me know where you are and how you are. Write to me care of Jesse. That'll find me until I settle somewhere.'

Emilie laughed. 'You settling?'

'Yes. Don't you think it's about time?'

'I suppose so. What will you do?'

'Who knows? I sold my business in China . . .'

They talked, chatted. A little uneasily, knowing he would have to go ashore any minute. Emilie was distant. She wanted to throw her arms about him and thank him for everything, but she couldn't intrude on his emotions in such a manner. He was still mourning the loss of his wife.

That was where he differed from most people. Mal always spoke so openly, you always knew where you stood. And yet here she was, holding back on him already. She hadn't told him she was pregnant, for fear he'd worry about her even more. And she'd be even more obligated to him. Or he might have second thoughts about spiriting her away from the child's father.

This morning she'd been surprised by a visit from Mrs Caporn, who brought her a small suitcase containing some clothes and a few necessities for travel, explaining that Mal had sent her. She didn't stay long, pointing out that she wasn't much company these days, and Emilie understood.

After she left, Emilie had tears in her eyes for Mrs Caporn's loss and Mal's kindness.

As she was looking through the contents of the case again, impressed by Mrs Caporn's sure eye for size, even in button-up shoes, Emilie found an envelope in a side pocket. It contained a ticket for passage on a ship *en route* to Brisbane this very afternoon, some banknotes and a very important-looking certificate that turned out to be a letter of credit to the Bank of Australasia in Brisbane, made out in her name, to the amount of a thousand pounds.

Emilie was shocked. This was outrageous! But then Mal was outrageous. He was larger than life in everything he did. Like suddenly taking off for China!

And then there was the gold. She'd always been curious about the gold from that robbery. Mal hadn't stolen it. That was certain. The two men involved had confessed. But the gold was never found. One man hanged himself, the other went to the gallows boasting he'd die a rich man, refusing to give up his treasure.

Somehow, Emilie mused, it would not have surprised her if Mal had worked out where they'd hidden it. But maybe not . . . it was simply government property. Never found. A fortune in gold.

When Clive came to visit, the suitcase was well hidden. He was pleased to hear she could leave the hospital that afternoon, if the doctor approved.

'I'll come back later,' he said.

'No need. It's not far, I can walk from here.'

'Good. I'm busy. I'm trying to sell those shares.'

'Why don't you keep them and let the company build the shops so that you can rent one, without all the trouble of building?'

'Oh, I see. You mean build a house for you first? That's your priority? Well, it isn't mine.'

He gave her two shillings to buy some groceries on the way home, asked how long the cast would have to stay on, ate the bun on her lunch tray and strode down the ward, wishing the other ladies a good morning as he passed them by.

Emilie had no feeling for him at all. She was concerned about taking so much from Mal, but determined to repay him, even though such a staggering amount could take years. She dressed quickly, signed out of the hospital and walked with her suitcase towards the wharves and SS *Mangalore*.

Always less inhibited than her, it was Mal who reached out and gave her a hug.

'I have to go, and you listen to me, Missy. The money was not a loan. I don't want it to be a burden. Just be happy and forget about old Clive. I ought to feel guilty for introducing you.'

'But you don't,' she smiled. 'And tell me this, Mal. Do you think anyone ever found that gold?'

'What gold?' he asked as they strolled along the deck.

'You know. Did you happen to find it?'

He pushed the thatch of blond hair back from his face. 'Me? If I'd found it you'd have made me give it up to the police.'

'If I'd married you, don't you mean?'

'Ah.' He paused at the gangway, standing back to let others go ashore. 'But you didn't marry me.' He grinned. 'You enjoy the voyage. It looks a nice ship.'

He was sad when the ship pulled away with its story of what might have been, but reality was now. He had to begin all over again by finding a couple of good horses and ordering supplies from stores that weren't overstocked at the minute.

Jesse found him at the saleyards, looking over a few horses for sale, obviously unimpressed by what was on offer.

'Saturday,' Jesse told him. 'The stockmen bring them in on Saturdays so that they can have a booze-up over Sunday. You'll see some good mounts then.'

'I can't wait till Saturday. I've been held up here too long as it is.'

'Where are you going?'

'To the goldfields west of here. I'm still ahead of Tussup. I jumped on a ship. He'd need more than a month to ride this far south from Cooktown, if he's lucky. If he's got good horses. And if he doesn't drop dead on the track. There's nothing in between, is there?'

'No. Only a few cattle stations, and they don't welcome diggers of any colour tramping over their land.'

'That land? You could send the British Army marching across any one of those big stations and the bosses wouldn't notice.'

Jesse looked up at the heavily wooded ranges looming over Cairns, and frowned. 'It'll be tough going, but I'm willing. I wouldn't miss this hunt.'

'What hunt? You're not coming.'

'Of course I am! You're news, Sonny! You'll be headlines again if you capture the boss mutineer. The *China Belle* story is far from dead.'

Mal patted a horse that was standing dejectedly by the gate. 'This fella's the only one that comes near to what I want in a packhorse, but he's a bit old. Same goes for you, Jesse. You stay home and do your reporting, but leave me out of it. I don't want to be news. And stop calling me Sonny. You'd think I was only ten or something.'

'I'm a lot tougher than you think,' Jesse argued, as they turned to leave the saleyards.

'You're not coming. If he's not on the goldfields I'll be going up the track, and by all accounts it's rough country to tackle.' His face was grim as he joked. 'I hope Tussup's enjoying the ride.'

'Let me come as far as the goldfields then. I have to go. I can't let someone else grab the story.'

They were headed for Jesse's house when he remembered Mrs Plummer had invited them to dinner.

'No,' Mal said automatically. 'Leave me out.'

'Why? She really wants you to come.'

'Because I don't want to. Some other time.'

'She's a great cook, Esme says. And she's making a real effort for you with roast beef and potatoes and pudding . . .'

'I'll be there.'

Mrs Plummer was delighted that her first little dinner party was such a success. She hadn't cooked for herself for many years, but as she told them: 'One can't forget how to cook a simple meal like this.'

'It's English fare,' Esme said. 'Though I must admit you've improved on the potatoes. It's a nice change after Asian food, isn't it, Mal?'

'Yes. I always thought rice was only for custard, but I got used to it.'

Eleanor was sad for them. Who'd have thought, as they boarded the *China Belle*, that they'd both have lost their spouses by this time? Looking at them now, the fair-haired, blue-eyed widower and the widow with her rich red hair and soft brown eyes, she thought they made a lovely couple. Lord knows, she mused, as she ushered them all out on to the veranda for coffee, and made sure Mal and Esme were side by side on the sofa, they have much in common. Hurt and loss and shared experience. A formidable combination.

She was glad Esme had come to stay with her; she was welcome to stay as long as she wished. Eleanor liked company. But a girl like Esme needed a good strong husband to look after her. The right man was already looking out for her. Hadn't he arranged the funeral and all those wonderful flowers? And paid for everything! And was known by Jesse Field to be a person of integrity.

Mal Willoughby might be mourning now, as Esme was, but grief dims in the passage of time. Then they should reach out to each other.

She was greatly disappointed when Mal told them he was leaving for the outback on Saturday.

'So soon?'

Esme was surprised too. 'You're not going after Tussup, are you?'

He shrugged, unwilling to discuss his plans.

'You've done enough,' she said. 'Why don't you let the police get him now? They'll find him. His picture has been in all the papers.'

When Mal simply shook his head at her, Jesse spoke up.

'Don't worry, he'll be in safe hands. I'm going with him.'

Mal raised his eyebrows in resignation. 'I hope you can swim,' he retorted. 'Those rivers out there will be running like steam trains after that big wet.'

The next day Esme had reason to call on Mal. She really didn't want him to leave; she felt she might fall down without him to lean on. No one knew how worried she was that her Apollo story might blow up in her face and have the police on her doorstep. Not that Mal could help if that happened, but he wasn't the type to be shocked or offended if the real Caporn story came out.

'I had to come and see you,' she explained. 'I met Clive Hillier in town and he's distraught. He can't find his wife. He found out I was at the hospital and he actually accused me—'

'Oh God, I forgot about him,' Mal said. 'I'd better get into town and tell Jesse, so he can stop a flap. Mrs Hillier left town yesterday on SS *Mangalore*.'

'Without telling him?'

'For her own safety,' he said. 'But that's between us. We'll just have to leave it at that. She's gone. Clive can make up his own story.'

'Is that why I took her the clothes?'

'Yes,' he grinned. 'But you're innocent of any part in the conspiracy.'

'How intriguing! Will you tell me the rest one day?'

'I might. If you're good. Come on, I'll walk you back to town.'

Esme put up her parasol and walked with him. 'When you're finished all that chasing about out there, wherever it is you're going, what will you do then? Will you come back here?'

He nodded. 'Yes, I'll be back. So you be good and take care of Mrs Plummer. If you need a friend, Esme, you'd be hard put to find a better one than that lady. She's seen a lot more of the world than most.'

'Yes. I guess you're right. Sorry to be a misery.'

'Don't be sorry. You're never a misery.' He smiled at her. 'Mrs Plummer isn't the only one who appreciates your company. We all do. You just have to take one day at a time.'

'All right.'

He noticed how nice her hair was looking now, with its coppery red glow and remembered the shocking treatment she'd suffered on the ship, and instinctively drew her to him.

'You've had a bad time of it, love,' he said. 'A bloody awful time. I wish I could say it'll be easy putting away the past, but worth the effort.'

He looked down at her. 'So, come on. Give me a smile now, and we'll go and break the news that old Clive's wife has flown the coop. That'll really spoil his day.'

'With pleasure,' Esme said, wondering what it was about Mal that could make her feel much better, even happy, at the same time as she learned he was going away indefinitely. She hoped he'd meant it when he said he was coming back. That he wouldn't go off on his travels and forget to return.

Chapter Sixteen

Young Mr Li was vastly impressed by the new fellow, Chang, and would have promoted him to his own staff were he not involved in the sideline duty on behalf of the noble Lady Xiu Ling Lu. His work in reopening those mines had been commendable, but it wasn't difficult. Any one of Mr Li's headmen could have carried out those instructions. Chang's value was more in the line of people handling. He was intelligent, charming in the right circles, and yet he was a tough boss who could keep the coolies and their headmen working to well-organised rosters. And in the case of the bodies found in a mine, he sorted that out with the police without having to bother his master, for which young Mr Li was grateful. He was always nervous of the hulking white policemen, with their loud voices and their power. His own number one major-domo would come out in a rash whenever any of them came by the offices. But not Chang. They didn't bother him one speck. And he could even talk their dialect.

So it was that young Mr Li was not surprised to be informed that Chang wished to see him on personal business.

'Mr Willoughby, son-in-law of the noble lady, has left here, Mr Li,' he explained. 'This means that the leader of the murderers, one known as Jake Tussup, has gone.'

'I see. So it is your duty to go after him?'

'Yes, sir. I have come to humbly request your permission.'

'Do you know where he has gone?'

'I think so. I believe he has followed the inland route to the new goldfields far to the south. The ones with the unpronounceable name, known as the Hod.'

'Ah,' young Mr Li pondered this while inspecting a crusted nugget of gold that had been handed to him only this morning. 'You will, of course, report to me of developments?'

'Certainly, sir. I have observed preparations to take some coolie gangs down to the Hod fields.'

'That is so.'

'Would it be presumptuous of me to request permission to travel with them? I believe it is a long, arduous journey.'

'Yes, it would be presumptuous. I do not want my coolie bosses observing your activities. You keep away from them. And tell me, is that Mr Willoughby on the same road now?'

'No, sir, he went by ship.'

'As I shall have to do,' young Mr Li sighed, as if this were even more of a trial than overlanding. 'So he will catch your man first?'

'Maybe not. I may come upon him before the Hod river.'

Young Mr Li nodded sagely. 'I received your message regarding the bodies. You say they were Malayamen?'

'Yes. And the police were satisfied this was so. They say they were seafarers and no doubt of the *China Belle* crew.'

'That is good news. I may inform the noble lady this is definite?'

'Yes, sir. Only the officer Tussup left.'

They discussed this and other matters, including arrangements for Chang to collect his payments. Then Mr Li dismissed him.

He saw Chang hesitate before he bowed and withdrew from the dusty office, and smiled. Payments are made for work done, he mused. I do not spend the noble lady's money on accidents. The mine caved in. Mr Chang was not responsible for those demises. Let him find the white man. There's a worthwhile challenge.

The wagon track was drying out after the rains, setting gouged mud into hard wedges, so most horsemen avoided it, leaving vehicular traffic to grind it back to dust. Instead they spread out into open grasslands that were dotted with enough trees to provide shelter, until the flat country deteriorated into rough hills and flooded gullies. The inland route wasn't as hazardous as the steamy jungles that shrouded the ranges, but by the time Jake had reached this section, only a week into his journey, there was no actual track to follow and concern for the horses had him travelling a lot slower than he'd planned.

There weren't as many diggers on the track as he'd expected. Sometimes he didn't see a soul for days, but that suited him. This was a world Jake understood. Lone travellers in the bush were not seen to require company or conversation – a man was entitled to his own space – and this right gave Jake a breather. He liked to ride, and after all that hard work on the goldfields, he felt he'd earned a little pleasure.

Willoughby had been too clever, guessing that he would have shaved off his beard and publishing a picture of him clean-shaven. Now that a dark beard had blurred that image, he was a little safer but still wary. Jake was very much aware that a real danger out here was injury or loss of a horse; no one would get far walking in this heat, and vehicles were few and far between. This being so, he rode steadily along, taking in the countryside, interested in everything about him, the flat-top mountains that sprouted in the distance, the abundant wildlife, mobs of emus and kangaroos, massive flocks of birds and, surprisingly, the newcomers in this endless paddock – cattle! He kept an eye on them, though, realising that there'd have to be a home base for them somewhere out here, even if it were only an outstation hut. Good to know in case of an emergency.

During the second week of his trek he came across several dead cattle, newly killed animals. He stared at them, wondering who would be mad enough to butcher animals in this manner, instead of using the tried and true slaughtering techniques. Then he saw some dingos loping towards him and realised they'd got the scent at the same time, so he wheeled his horse, and jerked the packhorse, into a swift retreat. Obviously Aborigines had speared the cattle from sheer perversity, a warning to whitefellers, so it was no place for him. He galloped away, regretting leaving fresh meat behind, but he knew that if even the blacks hadn't bothered to carve up the spoils, the dingos would never let him near their feast unless he shot them all.

By the third week he was out of supplies, reduced to living on fowl and wallabies, stunned that there were no roadside shacks selling provisions. He had seen a team of packhorses hauling a loaded wagon but there were several riders travelling with them, ready to assist over difficult terrain, and he would have approached to try to buy some supplies, if only flour and tea, but he was not inclined to take a risk. Willoughby could have been with them.

Eventually he found himself descending into a valley, past ancient rock formations, and huge trees that soared into the blue. In the distance he could see a long line of coolies trotting down the track towards a river and considered catching up to them to see if he could buy some rice, but once again had to fight off the temptation. If he were silly enough to appear among the Chinese, he'd stick out like a sore toe. Right where Willoughby could spot him or hear of him. He'd have known that once his picture was plastered all over the place, Jake Tussup would have been out of the area in a flash. And he wouldn't be stupid enough to go down the coast road where police and troopers would be on the watch. He wondered if they'd caught Bartie Lee by this time. It had been sheer bloody heaven to be rid of that bastard, who'd been on his back like the old man of the sea. Willoughby had done him a favour there. What he ought to be doing was endeavouring to waylay Willoughby, not letting it happen the other way around.

It was Willoughby who had set the police, and most probably the populace as well, dead against him for murder. He ought to shoot the bastard himself; put a stop to that tale. But it was too late. The damage was done. He figured he had three aims now. Keep out of sight. Get to the Hodgkinson and find more gold. Money could buy him safety. And somehow shake off that murder charge. The mutiny charge was maritime law, too hard for these bushies; he could beat that by claiming he was forced to leave the ship by the Asians. But with Willoughby blaming him and Bartie Lee for the murder of the bosun, he was in real trouble. Bush police could spell murder. That was an easy charge in their land of murder and mayhem. He shuddered. Their idea of justice was swift. He'd seen a horse thief hanging from a tree outside a settlement on the outskirts of the Palmer goldfields, and, as for the Aborigines, well that was just plain war, Jake had observed, no matter what anyone said.

For a while now he'd heard the rush of the river in the distance and the horses, smelling water, picked up their pace, but when they finally emerged from the bush, Jake shook his head in despair because there was one hell of a river, in flood! Squinting against the glare from the watery expanse, he peered downstream to where a ferry was hauling travellers across to the far bank.

'Now what?' he asked himself as he took the horses to drink at the water's edge. 'How do I get across here without joining that mob and running the risk of being recognised?'

There was no other way, of course, so he decided to make camp and wait until dusk to ride quietly down to the ferry without hanging about the busy riverbank.

On the goldfields he'd relearned the old cooking recipes used by his mother, unheard of on his Asian travels. She'd made damper, a common bush substitute for bread, of flour and water, a pinch of salt, a dab of butter, and a handful of currants. On this trek, butter was only a memory, the currants soon ran out, and by now he'd used the last of the flour that had cost him an exorbitant ten pounds a half-bag as he was leaving Maytown. Now he chewed on stale damper dipped in tinned golden syrup, not even bothering to light a campfire in the gathering dusk because he'd also run out of tea, and sat by the river thinking how bloody stupid life was . . . considering that he had savings of five hundred pounds on his person and nowhere to spend it. He recalled an incident on the Palmer goldfields where a digger had drowned fording a river with his pockets full of gold.

A fish jumped briefly from the silvery river surface and sped on its way. A hawk dropped out of the blue like a stone and caught the next one cavorting from the water, winging speedily up and over the deep forest on the far bank.

Envy-ridden, his mouth watering, Jake turned away to consider the situation downstream. Though he could see only the ferry toiling across the river, he could hear an axeman at work, smell food cooking and see the curls of campfire smoke, so he knew this had to be a main junction, all trails converging on the crossing.

Maybe that's not so bad, he mused. If there are a mob of folk about I'll be better off, less conspicuous than if I turn up as a lone traveller.

'You waitin' to feed the crocs?' a voice asked, and Jake jerked back in surprise to find a tall, leather-faced man standing behind him.

'Crocs?'

'Yeah. Big blokes. Monsters, in these waters. Take a gent like you in a snap.' He extended a grimy hand. 'The name's Auguste. You coming or going, mister?'

'Waiting to cross. I'm Tom Smith. Just resting for the minute. It's been a long trek down from the Palmer.'

'Do any good?'

'No,' Jake lied, 'but I was too late there. I'll do better at the Hodgkinson. Are you a prospector?'

'Not me. I believe the Good Lord provides. No need to be tearing His earth apart. I'm working for the ferrymen.'

Jake was still cautious. 'I've still got a few shillings left – is there anywhere I can buy some grub?'

'Buy? Forget it. There's scroungers down there would sell you baked snake for a quid, and blokes coming through here starved enough to fall for it. But that ain't in my nature. If I can't feed a hungry traveller then my name's not Auguste. Come with me, mate,' he said, as he dipped a bucket in the river. 'You got a pretty poor camp here I can't help to be seeing.'

Jake packed up and, leading the horses, followed his new friend through the bush to a camp beside the track that ran down to the ferry. It was a bit too close to civilisation for his comfort but he kept to the trees, his back to the straggle of passers-by, watching hungrily as Auguste threw potatoes and a slab of beef into a pan.

'Isn't there anywhere here I can buy some food to take me on?' he asked.

'Not that you'd notice,' Auguste said nonchalantly.

'Where do the ferrymen get their supplies from?'

'Mostly Kincaid Station.'

'And they won't sell them?'

'No fear. But once a week a pedlar comes up from the goldfields with a conglomeration of edibles, and sells them at a price would make the devil blush. He oughta be here tomorrow, mate, but don't get your hopes up if you've only got a few shillings. If I had some spare coin I'd gladly help you, but I'm light on meself.'

'You think he'll be here tomorrow?'

'Considering he's already two days late, I'd reckon he's either not coming or he'll be here tomorrow.'

'Then it looks like I'd better wait. I can't go on without supplies.' Realising that he, apparently, had no means to afford supplies, he added: 'I'll figure something out. See if I can sell the packhorse.'

'You won't have any trouble there. Half the loons tramping past here have done in their mounts.'

For days Chang had searched Maytown for some clue to the whereabouts of Jake Tussup, beginning with the mine Tussup had worked with the scum,

Lee. It was Lee's coolie friends who directed him to the mine and, under his instructions, collected every scrap of their belongings left lying about.

Chang poked at the ungainly heap in the humpy that Lee had used.

'Miserable livings,' he muttered to himself as he kicked a mattress aside. 'This gold mining, a foul life without your own coolies.'

He noted that they must have taken off in a hurry to leave so much stuff behind, even cooking pots and clothing. The heavy spades and picks needed for their work were left in the excavations. Bartie had had no equipment of any sort with him, and he'd been caught on the other side of Maytown, so it was evident he'd been heading down to Cooktown, there to escape by ship.

'No doubt the white man also went that way,' Chang's servant, Wu Tin, said, but Chang was not so sure.

'Terrible though this vast empty land is,' he said, 'I would not hold any fears for a native like Tussup.'

Chang had voiced his opinion of this country before. He hated the jungles on the eastern side of the ranges, and was terrified of the black savages with their painted faces and sharp spears. The Palmer goldfields were a confusion that he could cope with, and the view from the high country out over the western lands meant little to him, except that it was empty. Apart from the few savages lurking in the forest, this whole damned country seemed empty to a man accustomed to a populace rushing by him. He'd been told too, he recalled, awed, that when the gold ran out even these villages like Maytown and Cooktown would empty and die. He was convinced that this barbaric land was no place for a gentleman, and the sooner his mission was completed the better. He had earned a considerable sum, one way and another, with more to come, and that would do. He could afford to live in Hong Kong now. An exciting prospect.

Having decided that Tussup had taken the inland route that led south to more goldfields and then on to a coastal village called Cairns, he began to enquire at the stores. For surely Tussup would have needed considerable supplies to take on that empty countryside.

At a store by a river crossing, Chang's persistence paid off. As did the generous incentive he promised the storekeeper for more detail. He learned that the man in the picture he proffered had bought supplies to get him through to the goldfields and, more importantly, he had two horses.

'Description?' Chang urged.

'Let me see. One was a chestnut, can't remember much else there. The packhorse was a grey, a patchy blurred grey with a whitish rump.'

'What else?'

'Not much else, mate.'

'What was he wearing?'

'A checked shirt. Couldn't say the colour. I sell hundreds of them. Everyone wears them round here. Except you blokes, of course.'

'And you think he forded the river?'

'Didn't actually see him but it's a fair bet he joined the great south march.'

So did Chang and his servant.

They kept to the well-travelled track, asking after the man with the two horses, one a patchy grey, but without success for the first few days. They then rode faster, hoping to catch up with Tussup until, on the fourth day, a man in a light dray said he'd seen him a couple of times.

'How can that be?' Chang asked. 'He would be riding, making quicker travel than you, sir.'

'That's true. But I seen him all right. Once riding down a gully, off to the right he was. Might have been going down to water the horses. Big bloke he was, noticed him because the first time I seen him, he was camped in the scrub, off the track. I spotted him because I thought it was early in the day to be pulling up. Reckon he's taking his time. You fellers,' he grinned, 'you're probably passing him all the time.'

Chang thought about that as he set off again. Taking his time? Why not? A pursuer would race after him, as he had done.

Off the track? Chang nodded. Ah yes. Fear would keep him meandering through this open forest like a shy deer keeping well away from enemies. From man. Any man who might have seen a picture of Jake Tussup.

Now that he knew where to look, Chang instructed his servant to keep to the track at a steady pace while he patrolled the areas adjacent to the route.

They followed that plan for a few more days, and Chang met folk in slow vehicles several times, but there were no more sightings.

One man gave him good advice. 'There's a ferry a day's ride on from here. It's the only way to get across the big river at this time of year. The ferryman will be able to tell you what's what. If he's crossed over, they'll know.'

The plain meal of meat and potatoes and boiled onions was manna to Jake, who insisted on placing some shillings by Auguste's tent, despite his protests. He could see that his host was getting on in years and, judging by his patched clothes and poor camping equipment, he was by no means flush with cash, but he was a genial sort, good for a yarn.

'Time to move on,' Jake said at length. 'I can't thank you enough for that meal.'

'Think nothing of it, Tom. I'll leave you to get set now; I have to get back to work. Just chuck them plates into that tin dish over there. I'll fix them up later. See you down at the ferry.'

He picked up a heavy walking stick. 'Getting old, I am,' he added. 'Broke my leg a while back and it's still a bit shy.'

It occurred to Jake that the leg hadn't seemed to be troubling Auguste prior to this, but he grinned as the fellow limped away. In his day he'd met his share of workmates who found excuses not to pull their weight – bad backs, gammy legs, cramps – they invented all sorts of reasons to slack off. But then he dismissed the thought. Not his problem. Auguste had been kind to him, unreservedly kind.

Rather than go walkabout and risk recognition, he decided he might as well get some rest, so he tramped further into the bush and lay down in the long grass, his swag for a pillow, listening to the mellow bird calls, feeling content at the close of this balmy afternoon. Hopefully the pedlar would arrive in the morning so that he could buy provisions and head on south. Lately he'd begun to think of the farm in Goulburn. It would be good to go home. To have a home. The threat posed by Mal Willoughby disturbed that reverie, so he turned on his side and thrust it away.

The attack was so sudden Jake couldn't grasp what was happening for a few precious moments though knew something had struck him on the head. He managed to climb to his knees, blood streaming down his face, but then the second blow came and though he tried to strike out at his attacker, he felt himself falling into a pit, and trying to fight his way out of it.

Forcing himself into consciousness, Jake butted his head against strong hands that were forcing a cloth into his mouth, thinking maybe this was a nightmare because he was feeling so helpless, but then he realised he was on the ground, his hands and feet tied. And there was Auguste, binding his mouth. No longer genial talkative Auguste, but a silent, grim-faced menace.

To Jake's amazement, when he was expertly roped into a crouch, unable to call for help, Auguste simply kicked him away and walked off! Jake couldn't believe he was still wearing his boots. The boots that contained his money!

The fool must have believed his story about having failed in his search for gold. He must have believed he was broke, so what was this all about? Jake tried to free the gag from his mouth, at the same time writhing about, hoping to break free of the ropes, but the excruciating pain from the wounds on his head was wearing him down, and he just let go for a while to gather his strength.

'Oh Jesus no!' he could only mumble when he awoke, as he began to force out the gag, knowing the binding rag would loosen if he kept at it. Auguste had missed his money, and the only other possessions worth anything were his horses. Had the bastard taken his horses? Left him to walk the rest of the way? Hadn't he said men were forced to walk when they lost their mounts? In other words, no replacements were available.

Jake swore and spat and practically frothed at the mouth until finally, after at least a half-hour the binding fell down to his neck and he spat the gag. He shouted for help again and again, but no one came so he began inching himself through the scrub towards the track, feeling like a caterpillar, commiserating with caterpillars forced to travel at this pace, but determined to get his horses back.

The day beat him – the time of day. It was dusk when he fell down that gully. It took an age to drag himself up the other side without impaling himself on sharp eucalypt saplings beginning their reach for the heights. Two snakes slid by him, one a harmless green tree snake but the other a deadly brown, and Jake lay very still for a long while, his heart pounding. His face was scratched and bloody by the time he tumbled out on to the track, still shouting for help, and even then it seemed to take an age for two men to loom up and ask what the hell had happened to him.

As soon as he was freed, Jake ran down the hill. Ran, stumbled, fell, picked himself up and ran on to the jetty, shouting his outrage. Forgetting his fear of recognition.

No! No one called Auguste worked on the ferry. Yes, a hefty middle-aged bloke had gone across with two horses. And you've missed the last ferry. Come back in the morning.

'What pedlar?' a ferryman laughed. 'No one brings supplies up here. We're only three days' march from the goldfields.'

Later, as the ferryman joined a mate for a pint, he asked, 'Did I hear you say that two Chinks were looking for a bloke riding a chestnut and leading a grey packhorse?'

'Yes. I told them they were only an hour or so behind a bloke who sounded like their man.'

The ferryman nodded. 'Popular character that one. Can you spare me some tobacco?'

He was riding as fast as he could, with a grey packhorse galloping along beside him, but Chang and his servant followed him with ease. They kept well back, biding their time, waiting for the right circumstances.

Chang was excited. He'd been correct in his assumption that Tussup would try to keep out of sight during this journey, the spectre of that poster picture hanging over his head. He guessed the ferry would force him out into the open and thus it had.

The narrow road detoured round a rocky outcrop and then plunged into a forest – conveniently, Chang thought, because Tussup had slowed down after the initial burst of speed, allowing his horses to trot sedately along the lonely track. They hadn't seen a soul for miles and this area was isolated enough for Chang's business, so he kneed his horse and went after his quarry.

As he rounded the bend he called cheerily: 'Hah! Tussup!'

The man was guilt personified! Instead of waiting to find out who was approaching, he only jerked a glance over his shoulder as he set his horses to the gallop, racing down the track.

Chang was surprised by the speedy exit, though he knew he should not be if he'd had his senses about him. He took off after Tussup, needing to catch him before they ran into company.

When he realised Chang was catching him, Tussup cut the packhorse loose and hurtled on, causing Chang's horse to swerve in order to avoid the grey as it dropped back. He picked up again, though, and Chang was determined to end this now. He had intended to use a knife – quieter – but it was too late. Tussup couldn't be allowed to get away from him. It was a matter of disposal of the body – and his own safety, of course.

He took his rifle from its holster, slowing his horse so that he could load it, now feeling nervous, with sweat dripping from his forehead as he kicked his horse on again, because he wasn't sure he could do this, and was afraid Tussup would turn and fire at him.

Unsteadily he raised the gun and fired at Tussup, who hunched over and raced on, so Chang fired again, skidding to a halt as Tussup slid from the saddle. Instead of falling cleanly he caught his foot in the stirrup and was dragged along until the panicky horse stopped abruptly, and stood shivering by the side of the road.

Chang approached cautiously, but Tussup was dead, his whiskered face gouged and bloodied by the stony ground. Fortunately Chang's servant caught up then, leading Tussup's packhorse.

'Quickly, cut him loose,' he said. 'Take him into the forest and bury him, then get back out here and cover any traces of blood on the road.'

As his servant went to work, Chang dismounted, took the saddle and bridle from the packhorse, and dumped them in the bush. Once his servant had removed the body, he did the same thing with the other saddle and bridle, returning to chase off Tussup's horses. Both of them, still spooked, clattered madly away, charging into the scrub at the next bend in the road.

A pity to have to do that, he thought. They'd be worth a bit, but they'd also lead folk to me. Better to let them go. He wondered if Tussup had any money on him, and raced into the bush, wading through high grass to check.

'Yes, sir,' Wu Tin told him. 'He had this.' Chang found himself looking at a few coins.

'Is that all?' he asked, incredulous.

'Yes, sir. I searched most carefully.'

Chang turned away. 'Very well. Get on with it.'

He had been of the opinion that Tussup had done well on the goldfields. So where was his money?

As he tramped back to their horses, he slapped his forehead. 'Of course! Banks! There were banks at Maytown. He must have banked his money rather than risk it on this wilderness journey. Now no one has it. A small fortune lost to the bankers.

'Enough to make a cat spit!' Chang said as he waited.

They rode on to the outskirts of the next goldfields, sold their tired horses and bought two new mounts before seeking temporary shelter in a Chinese dosshouse. Wu Tin went off to find a suitable eating-place, and hopefully a clean campsite, while Chang pondered the problem he'd been struggling with ever since he left young Mr Li's office. He had one more duty to perform.

'Am I to understand that you do not welcome this particular undertaking?' Mr Li had snapped at him. 'Do you think to pick and choose of your obligations to your benefactor?'

'No, sir. Except this person is known to me and therefore—'

'Therefore,' Mr Li interrupted, 'therefore, your job is easier. You did not know the other criminals, you had to ferret them out yourself. You know this person.'

'Forgive me, sir. This undertaking would be most difficult for me. I was not aware the Lady Xiu Ling Lu had sanctioned this action. I am nervous that she may not approve.'

'Are you so? You insignificant sod! It is not your place to query the decision of any members of the Xiu family, let alone Xiu Tan Lan, her father. He has given this order and you will carry it out or I will find someone who will.' Li slammed his hand on the desk and leaned forward menacingly. 'Do you not know you cannot pick and choose, you dolt? Your reluctance smells of disloyalty! You give me an answer fast! Fast! It will be done anyhow . . . will you do as ordered?'

Chang bowed to the threat. He nodded his head and mumbled acceptance.

'Get out of here,' Mr Li snarled. 'Get the job done and report back to Mr Li in Cooktown! If you renege on me, your replacement will have *you* on his contract.'

He snapped his fingers and waved Chang out as one of his menials came dashing in with a pot of fragrant tea.

Moodily, recalling the humiliation, Chang gave a halfpenny to a coolie to mind their possessions, and strolled from the dosshouse to a wayside stall where he barked instructions at a young Chinese woman and was promptly brought a canvas chair, a bottle of wine and a long cheroot. Once settled, he took stock of his situation as his eyes scanned the faces of every passer-by. Now he had to find Mr Willoughby. What a surprise he would get to learn that his man, Chang, had eliminated his sworn enemy, none other than the notorious mutineer, kidnapper and murderer Jake Tussup. Scum. He had beaten Willoughby to the punch once again. He wondered if Willoughby knew that several of the mutineers had been wiped off the list also, found dead in a collapsed mine. It would be fun to tell him that his great odyssey was over now. All of the mutineers were accounted for.

This location was different from the Palmer area. It was much more heavily wooded and the terrain was uneven, with river valleys broken by rocky hills and spurs. Chang had studied a map in the Maytown Claims Registry and learned that these goldfields had a coastal outlet, a small village called Cairns. After that, he was astonished to learn there was very little in the way of towns for thousands of miles until one came to a city, and that confirmed his disdain for this uncivilised land. Born and bred in Tientsin, Chang loved the constant voice of cities and the rush and surge that surrounded him. Out here, even with the determined activity trudging by, it was still quiet. You could hear the peal of songbirds at any time of the day and night – a pleasure, he had to admit, since these birds were incredibly musical – but that accentuated the quiet, which Chang equated with loneliness. Normally. Maybe, he reasoned, I am experiencing homesickness, a malaise new to me.

But that was only a minor concern. He drew on the cheroot, released the smoke evenly and gazed at four white men who were sauntering by. A burly, ginger-haired man noticed him and turned back angrily. 'What are you looking at, Chink?'

Chang looked bewildered, thrust his hands apart and jabbered helplessly, apologetically, in Chinese, though he was actually mouthing what he considered to be fitting obscenities.

'Leave him be,' one of the man's companions called, and the ginger-head shrugged, spat on Chang's boot and slouched away.

As soon as they had gone, the girl servant rushed out with a bucket and cloth and washed Chang's boots, apologising to the esteemed customer for that miserable incident. He nodded his appreciation and looked up to see Wu Tin hurrying back with the news that there were no suitable eating-places here, so he instructed him to set up camp nearby, and make arrangements with this servant girl for meals.

'But, Master, this is a liquor shop.'

'She wouldn't be here alone. She'll have family around. Tell her I require cooked meals in my camp and will pay well.'

That sorted out, he called for his horse and left to explore the place, interested to note that the roads were well defined and the population more diverse. He saw cowboys riding by, treating pedestrians as arrogantly as the ginger-head had treated him; gentlemen in neat attire with wide clean hats, and families in covered wagons riding westwards from the goldfields, waving cheerfully, he thought acidly, as they rode into nothingness.

There were attempts at villages scattered about, as the scenery, unlike the dreary Palmer landscape, became more robust and colourful. Huge trees soared from the rich soil and ahead of him rocky ramparts jutted stubbornly over the narrow road.

Chang saw a sign pointing to the Barron River and another to Barron Falls, but neither meant anything to him except as possible barriers for his exit to the coast. He supposed he'd better return on the morrow and reconnoitre that route, so that he could travel directly to the port without delay, when the time came.

When the time came! He shuddered. Though not officially recognised as such, Chang considered himself a gentleman. He had taken pains to learn the speech, demeanour and conduct of a gentleman. In fact, he rather believed that he was more of a gentleman than some he had met. Though not born to their cloth, he sighed. That, to his mind, was the pinnacle, never attainable for his likes. However – and this was important, he mused – one should not go around killing innocent people. Heroic gentlemen rid the world of scum, by various socially acceptable means, but they did not kill to order. That was left to scum. The very thought made him want to scream. Did the Li family and Mr Xiu see him only as scum? Chang turned his face away from that depressing thought, but was confronted by the other image. That of a man, gentleman or not, who disobeyed his lord and master, thereby inviting his own destruction.

Trying to keep calm, though his inner voice was wailing, 'Oh, oh, oh!', Chang rode down by the river and dismounted. There were hundreds of people, young and old, of many races, diligently panning for gold in the shallows, so he sat on his haunches to watch a few of them. He'd always found this work fascinating and so he was soon distracted by the excitement generated.

So distracted was he by the solid gold pebbles in one wide sieve, that he didn't notice the man moving closer to him, threading his way among the crowds on the bank. He still hadn't seen Mr Willoughby until he touched him on the shoulder.

'Where did you spring from?' he asked, catching Chang unawares.

'Look at that,' Chang said coolly. 'I think he has a few gold pebbles in that pan. Almost makes one want to start panning oneself. Have you tried it, Mr Willoughby?'

'Once. Did better underground. But what are you up to?' He glanced at Chang's neat black shirt, more a Russian style than Chinese, and black trousers. 'Doesn't look as if you've joined the diggers.'

'No, I'm not reduced to that yet.' He shook off his fascination with the gold and turned his full attention to Mal. 'I'm pleased to see you, we've got a lot to talk about.'

'Like what?' Mal asked sourly.

'Many things. But this is no place. Would you care to visit my camp?'

'Not particularly. There's a pub up there by that clump of bamboo. That will do.'

He was still angry with Chang for shooting Bartie Lee, and for his crafty alibi, but he was more than curious to know what the Chinaman was up to now. 'How did you get here?' he asked as they trudged up the high riverbank.

'Horseback. An interesting journey, but I am not keen on your bush.'

* * *

When he collapsed at the ferry, Jake was taken in by the timbermen who had found him trussed up by the road. They dressed his wounds and bound his head, commiserating with him on his bad luck, what with the horses and all, and consoled him with whisky.

In the morning, he rose at dawn, having laboured through a night burdened with cares, and stumbled out of the tent to find the men lining up for breakfast at a long communal table. Kindly, they made him welcome and offered suggestions for his next move.

Some said he ought to 'leg it' out to Kincaid Station and buy a horse if he could afford it. Another said it would be easier to wait and buy or beg a ride on the next vehicle to come along, if it had space on board.

'Most wagons do,' he said, 'but they don't like strangers.'

'I can see their point,' Jake said glumly.

'Personally, mate, if you're headed for the goldfields on the upper Hodgkinson, I'd hang out for a horse,' another man advised. 'The terrain can get hairy between here and Cairns. That is, if you're going after the gold. Are you?'

'No.' Jake was surprised by the firmness of his answer. 'No,' he said again. 'I've had enough. I'm heading out. Cairns is the port, isn't it?'

'Yes, a good little town. But if you're headed in that direction, why don't you wait a couple of days? A mob of us are going down to Cairns for a break while we arrange supplies and pick up our pay. You can come with us. We'll be taking shortcuts down the mountains.' He laughed. 'Quicker down than up, believe me.'

'I'd be obliged,' Jake said, 'but what about a horse?'

'We'll lend you a horse. We can use it as a packhorse on the way back.'

Over the next two days Jake was able to make himself useful doing odd jobs round the camp. He knew he couldn't even attempt to match their prowess with the axes, but he enjoyed watching the loggers at work, felling giant cedar trees, and all too soon, after a pleasant sojourn in the camp, he was on his way back to the coast. Had he known what a hazardous journey this would be, putting the trek over the ranges to the Palmer River to shame, Jake would never have agreed to accompany them. They battled their way through closed-canopy forests, over ravines and swift-flowing creeks, often forced to lead the horses for miles, and several times Jake, the incompetent, held them up or had to be roped or hauled along with them as they scaled slippery jungle tracks.

His new friends weren't concerned, though. They simply retaliated by teasing him mercilessly, laughing when he fell off his horse, landed in a deep stream, and found it surprisingly cold.

In all, though an endurance test, the journey was an interesting adventure with the best of company, Jake concluded, when they finally sighted the blue of the ocean in the distance. These men, who lived isolated lives working in the forests for months on end, were more concerned about the attitudes of blackfellows in their region than the goings-on of the outside world. They probably had never heard of the *China Belle*. Anyway, Jake was accepted in their midst, even offered a job as a logger – 'we'll toughen you up, mate' – but he had defined his priorities now and needed to move quickly. He rode into town with his eight companions as just another of the heavily bearded men who came in occasionally from the logging camps scattered about the region.

They made straight for a small pub, watered their tired horses, and settled down at a table covered in frothing pints, to watch the world go by.

At another pub, on the Hodgkinson goldfields, Chang had related his version of events.

'You what?' Mal couldn't believe his ears. 'You found Jake Tussup and shot him? I don't believe you! That's bloody ridiculous. How could *you* have found him? And then you *shot* him? Jesus, Chang! What the hell are you talking about?'

Mal began to realise that running into Chang a second time was no accident.

'Did you come down here from Maytown to find me?' he asked.

'Yes, I wanted to tell you about Tussup.'

'No, wait. Back up. First you went after Tussup, then you came looking for me?'

'Yes.'

'You left your job and took it upon yourself to find Tussup. Why?'

'To help you. You knew he'd be headed this way, so you took ship. I simply followed his route, so that we could catch him in a trap. Extremely simple, do you not agree?' Chang opened a tin of small cheroots and offered one to Mal, who took it absently.

'You're all heart,' he muttered as he lit the rare treat, tobacco and the papers being the best available in this district.

'Exactly. I knew the pain that scum caused you, and having found him on the track down there, I couldn't let him get away. Had I raised a hue and cry about the man being a murderer, who would have believed me? White men would rather have strung me up.'

'I see,' Mal nodded. 'Now tell me who's paying you?'

Chang was taken aback. 'You must appreciate that your story touched me deeply. And quite probably I have saved your life for a second time. Had Tussup seen you here, he wouldn't have run like Bartie Lee. He was armed. Tussup would have shot you on sight. It is fortunate I saw him first.'

'Who is paying you?' Mal grated, as he hurried Chang past the drinkers in the bar and into a back room. 'Is it those Li brothers?'

Chang sulked as if a favour had been rejected. 'Oh well. If you must!

The Li brothers pay me for the work I do for them. But I was initially employed by the Lady Xiu Ling Lu, to dispose of the men who kidnapped her daughter.'

'Oh Christ. So Bartie Lee was on the list too?'

'Of course.'

'All right.' Mal slumped down in a chair beside a card table. 'Now, start again. Jun's mother suddenly emerged from the mansion to find you and send you on this errand?'

Chang nodded calmly, as he peered out of the window.

'Or was it the other way round?'

'Why all these questions?' Chang asked angrily. 'I expected you to be relieved. So what if I did a little negotiating? You it was told me about the goldfields. I had to see for myself, I merely mentioned to Xiu people that I would be travelling to these parts, and offered my services.'

'As a bloody killer? Are you mad?'

'I merely offered my services, I said.'

'Oh Christ!'

Mal stuck his head out the door and called to the barman for two whiskies, remaining at the doors, as if guarding it, until the order was delivered.

'I won't run away,' Chang grinned as he took his drink.

'You can bet on that. So let's start again. I want to hear the whole story from beginning to end.'

Chang sighed. 'Why? It's not your business. The matter is now closed. Tussup is dead, believe me, and buried by the road out there. Someone will find the body soon enough, if wild animals don't carry it off. They'll have trouble identifying him because he has no papers and no money.'

'Why? Did you rob him as well?'

'Certainly not! There's nothing about his person to assist them, but *you* know it's Tussup and your quest is over. It's in your interests to keep out of it, in case they think you shot him! How else would you know about the body?'

'I know because you told me, you maniac,'

Chang shook his head with a smile. 'Told you what? My servant, who is travelling with me, can attest that I am down here to liaise with Mr Li's miners, before I carry on to the coast. We know nothing of the man you mention. You were the one searching openly for him. But don't worry, there's no need for you to fuss. We are turning back now. Returning to China as fast as the winds will carry us.'

Outraged, Mal stared at the tall figure with a face as calm as if he'd been reciting a Sunday school prayer.

'How did you know it was Tussup if he had no identification?'

'Because I tracked him all the way, from the time he bought his provisions in Maytown. He was travelling with a packhorse, the horses described to me by a storekeeper grateful for an extra pound. And when I confronted him I called him by name. It was Tussup, you may be sure. The beard couldn't disguise him.'

Mal was shocked. 'You really did shoot him!' he gasped.

'I told you, yes! And don't look so woebegone. He was scum, a murderer. The world is well rid of him.'

Mal drank his whisky with a gulp. Tussup a murderer?

What have I done? he asked himself frantically. I was so obsessed with my revenge I lumped them all together, the crew and Tussup. We know Tussup didn't kill the bosun; it was either Bartie Lee or Mushi Rana. Tussup had Jun in the boat. She jumped. He didn't push her. She jumped.

'By the way,' Chang said, 'they found several of the Malay crewmen buried in a collapsed mine—'

'Shut up!' Mal shouted savagely.

All along he'd seen Tussup as party to Jun's death, part of the cause, therefore guilty, but now he was confronted with the word he had used to describe him, in a rage, the word he'd put out to the world: murderer. Bartie Lee and Jake Tussup. Murderers. Now he was confronted with the awful effect of his charge, his own madness. What had he done? Abruptly he shoved the chair aside and stormed out of the room.

Chapter Seventeen

Word of the cyclone that had devastated Cairns stunned Raymond Lewis. Fearing for his friends, he rushed out to buy a newspaper, and there he read that three people had lost their lives, one of them being Mr Neville Caporn, gentleman, of Hong Kong.

His partner, Gordon McLeish, looked up as he hurried back into the lobby of their offices. 'What's wrong?'

'The cyclone in Cairns. A friend of mine was killed.'

'So sorry, old chap.'

'God knows how they'll cope there now. He was a nice chap, left a young wife. Lovely girl. I don't know how she's placed. It says here most of the town has been flattened. I feel quite faint, it's such a shock.'

'I'll have the girl bring you tea.'

'No, don't bother. I think I'll go home. No, on second thoughts I'll go and see Sir Lyle . . .'

Irritated, Gordon turned back before he stepped into his own office. 'Raymond, you have a client coming at ten. Mr Mortensen.'

'Oh Lord, yes, so I have. You see him, Gordon. You know the story. I really must go.'

He set off down the short corridor but Gordon called him back.

'Wait. This won't do at all. When you said you wanted to wind down your practice, with a view to retiring, I agreed, but I didn't realise that winding down to you meant missing appointments and wandering off when it suits you. It's totally unprofessional, Raymond; puts me in a bad light as well. I won't put up with it. You name a day and go, and stop this shillyshallying. I don't know what's got into you, man!'

Raymond nodded. 'I am sorry, Gordon. You are quite right. I just can't seem to raise any enthusiasm for the law these days.'

'It seems to me you were much more affected by that dreadful experience on the *China Belle* than you realise. You haven't been the same since you got home. You're not getting any younger, you know.'

'Ah, but that is it! Not the mutiny, Gordon, or my troubles on the goldfields, just the feeling that I was becoming a dull fellow. Do you know what I mean?'

Gordon shrugged. 'I can't say that I understand your attitude. As gentlemen we do what we have to do. We have our responsibilities and if we acquit them well, then that is hardly dull.'

'But I feel that my life is slipping away on me . . .'

'All of our lives are. Eluding responsibilities is hardly a remedy – more like a slip into second childhood. I require an answer, Raymond.'

'Very well, I will try to conclude by the end of the month . . . week.'

'And Mortensen?'

'All right, I'll see him.'

Raymond suffered a twinge of guilt. He knew his habit was causing inconsistencies in his affairs, so he'd tried to stick to the daily ration he'd set for himself, of twenty grains of opium per day, but it was difficult. His routine of five grains four times a day was soon broken by temptation, with most taken by mid-afternoon, and a necessity to find more for the evening. At heart a shy man, he found the dreamily pleasant powers of opium irresistible . . . a bulwark against the insecurities that had always dogged him. It was common knowledge that his father had arranged the seat in Parliament for him, and that he'd never stood out in that theatre of ambition, nor in the courts, but those concerns were behind him now. Light-heartedly he recalled a few lines from the Chester Cathedral prayer: 'Don't let me worry too much, about that fussy thing called I.'

He was bemused that this 'medicine' had come into his life as a result of those dreadful tropical ulcers.

'Every cloud has a silver lining,' he told himself solemnly. 'The good Lord came to my aid.'

As soon as he could, Raymond called on Sir Lyle at his new home in Fortitude Valley, a large, nondescript residence with a sizeable garden given over to ornate fountains and chichi statues. Raymond had expected that the Horwoods would rid the garden of the angels and cupids, but instead more were added, along with Lyle's pride and joy, a stone armchair that looked suspiciously like a throne. Unkindly, Lavinia had remarked that the grounds were beginning to resemble a cemetery.

He found Horwood, who now insisted on being called Sir Lyle, and would correct any regress without compunction, in the library, surrounded by crates of books.

'Just in time, Lewis,' he called. 'I'm in a mess here. I've no one to sort these books. The bloody servants started placing them under colours, so I had to put a stop to that. I want them set up alphabetically, but these fools don't know their ABCs. And I want the readable on that side of the room behind my sofa, and the unreadable on the other, so that I don't waste time. Now see this,' he tapped a leather-bound book, '*The Perfumed Garden*. Now that can go over there under B for Burton, on the unreadable side. I can't be bothered with those flowery poetries, milksop stuff.'

He handed the book to Raymond, who grinned and dutifully placed it on a high shelf on the unreadable side.

'Now this is more like it,' he cried, pulling up a pile of books. 'Read these? By William Kingston? Great adventure stories. *Peter the Whaler* was my favourite. Put them on my side. I'll end up calling the shelves "my side" and "her side". The books in that crate are all hers. Byron, and the Brontë women – all that stuff – they're my wife's choice. Put them over in the unreadables.' He laughed. 'The Bs, eh? The Bs. Get it?'

'Yes,' Raymond smiled, taking off his hat and placing it on a credenza with his cane. 'Actually, Sir Lyle, I came to tell you about the cyclone.'

'In Cairns,' Horwood puffed, hauling up more leather-bound books and dumping them on the polished table. 'I know about that. Listen here, I'll call the servants back. They can put them all out on the table and I'll try to sort them from there. It's my wife's job really, but now that she's away I have to do it.' He pulled a long cord and a few minutes later a manservant returned.

'Unpack this lot and sort them on the table. I'll break my back getting into those crates. Now where were we, Raymond? Oh yes, Cairns. Would you take a glass with me?'

When finally they were placed in the parlour with their whiskies, Raymond volunteered his sister's name to take on the book sorting, so that he wouldn't be recalled for the chore.

'I know Lavinia would be delighted, Sir Lyle.'

'Jolly good. I accept enthusiastically. I'm quite fond of Lavinia. Can she come tomorrow?'

'Possibly. Did you say Constance was away? Might I enquire . . .?'

'In a sanatorium, old chap. Chest, you know. Not to be bandied about, that information. She is in St Clement's Hospital.'

'Oh, I am so sorry. I had no idea. Should we call on her? Lavinia and I? Take her some sweets, or flowers perhaps . . .'

'No, no. Not at this time. Not until she's feeling better.'

Raymond was appalled. 'My goodness. What must she think of us? Not a word of commiseration from us.'

He was genuinely upset to think that Constance had succumbed to what he gathered was consumption, but annoyed with Horwood for not advising him. Too many people spoke in whispers about consumption, just as Horwood was doing now, and he considered the attitude unenlightened and unfair. And very cruel to the patients.

'Is she that bad?' he asked then, an edge in his voice, but Horwood assured him that she wasn't in dire straits, but under doctor's orders she needed complete rest.

'But surely visitors would cheer her up.'

'The doctor says they would only excite her. So do leave well enough alone, there's a good chap. Now, as for that cyclone . . . a lot of wind and rain I'm told. They'll survive. Fortunately, the building of our planned brace of shops in the centre of the town hadn't commenced, but they can get moving on it now. Especially now. Did you know the new shops erected by Clive Hillier got razed to the ground, totally destroyed.' He raised his glass. 'It's an ill wind, eh?'

'And Neville Caporn was killed,' Raymond said tersely.

'Eh?' Horwood sat up with a jerk. 'By Jove! Is that right? Poor fellow. How do you know this?'

'It was in today's paper.'

'Good God! I wondered why it was Ted Pask, the bank manager, who sent me the telegram regarding Apollo Properties. Good man, he must have taken the reins—'

'Upon the untimely death of your chairman, I suppose. Who was also a friend. Did he say anything about Mrs Caporn?'

'In a telegram? Of course not. We'll hear in due time. I believe the Alexandra Hotel, the only decent accommodation in town, was also destroyed, so I won't be visiting there for a while.'

'Of course not,' Raymond snapped. 'I think I'll be running along now.'

'I shall be dining shortly. Care to join me?'

'No, thank you. Lavinia is expecting me.'

Raymond fumed as he strode out to his waiting gig. He wondered why he had to call on the fellow at all. Needing kindred souls to join with him in mourning for Neville Caporn, he supposed, the Horwoods being the only other people in this town who'd known Neville.

He sighed, as he snapped the reins and the horse trotted quietly down the street. 'Poor choice,' he muttered. 'Damn poor choice.'

Lavinia, though, was sympathetic. 'How dreadful,' she said. 'The poor fellow, having to endure the mutiny, only to meet his death once safely ashore.'

'His wife fared very badly on the ship,' Raymond recalled. 'Those wretches actually beat her, dragged her about and even chopped at her hair. Nice red hair she has too.'

'Was she the one? Oh, the poor woman!'

Over their pre-dinner sherries, they discussed the town of Cairns and the impact such damage would have on the populace, but Raymond was still peeved with Horwood.

'The man is so self-centred,' he said, 'it's practically impossible to have a conversation with him. I couldn't get out of the place fast enough.'

'Goodness me, Raymond, how you do go on. We're all self-centred to a certain extent. We have to be to survive. I like Sir Lyle. I think he's quite charming.'

'I'm glad you do because I just remembered I offered your services in setting up his library. I said you'd help him.'

'I'm quite happy to assist. It'll be most interesting. But where's Constance?'

'Mmm. I'm not supposed to say, according to him. She's in that new sanatorium, St Clement's. Suffering from consumption, I gather, poor girl.'

'She's where?'

'St Clement's?'

'That's not a sanatorium, Raymond. Where did you get that idea? It's an asylum for the mentally disturbed.'

Raymond was shocked. 'It can't be. He said she had chest problems. That to me sounded like consumption, because he was so mysterious about it.'

'Well, it is. And that's probably why he said no visitors. I'm shocked at him for lying to you. The man would know full well what the place is. And making a pretence about consumption! Maybe he was covering up for her sake.'

'For his own, more likely,' Raymond said bitterly. 'His lack of concern for his wife, or anyone else bar himself, is quite disgraceful. He didn't even bat an eye when I told him that Neville Caporn had been killed. And what's more, I don't think Constance is mad. She was troubled. That's all. Got the fright of her life at being kidnapped by those fellows.'

'Who wouldn't? I shudder at the thought, the poor girl.'

Later, having worried about Constance all evening, Raymond came to a decision. 'I'm going to see Lady Horwood.'

'You can't just turn up at those places. It's government-run. They won't let you in.'

'Oh yes, they will. I will be her lawyer, with papers for her to sign. Civil servants respect paperwork, and I'll have a pile of it.'

'That's outrageous! Not to mention offensive. Sir Lyle will never forgive you.' She gathered up her skirts and walked along the wide veranda. 'It's so much cooler now. I do love our autumn,' she said absently, and then she turned back to her brother:

'I am concerned for that girl, though, Raymond. And I'd have a better chance of getting in there than you.'

'How?'

'I am the president of the Ladies' Health and Welfare Auxiliary. We do raise a lot of money for charity, as you well know. Nothing opens doors faster than the whiff of money. I shall write a note to the matron, requesting an appointment to view the premises. I can say we're considering an annual grant for St Clement's.'

'An excellent idea. Now you may introduce yourself as the president of a charitable concern, but you can only say you are *considering* bestowing funds on them. You must not pretend to be speaking for the Auxiliary.'

'Very well. Leave it with me. I won't get myself arrested.'

* * *

The response came in the affirmative. Miss Lewis was invited to attend on Thursday during visiting hours.

'Good. I'll come too,' said Raymond. 'We'll take the carriage; it's a long way out of town.'

'They'd hardly have an asylum in Queen Street!'

'I suppose not,' Raymond murmured. He was relieved that Lavinia was taking the initiative. She was better at getting her own way than he was. Very practised at it, in fact, he reflected gloomily.

But it was just as well.

St Clement's, as it turned out, was a former military barracks surrounded by a high paling fence. It was a cheerless place. No attempt had been made to replace the dusty grounds with gardens, or to plant a few trees for shade. The few visitors they saw were walking the length of the former parade ground with pyjama-clad patients, as if for their health also. They all seemed so intent on the exercise that Raymond felt they should be telling beads as well.

'Why are the patients wearing pyjamas?' Lavinia asked him, as they followed directions to Administration, among the long timber buildings.

'Because they're sick. Why would they not? This is a hospital.'

'Like a military hospital! Besides, one would think mentally ill patients were not necessarily bed-patients.'

'I don't know,' Raymond said irritably. 'Where's the damn front entrance to this place?'

'As you can see, there is no front entrance, so Administration is probably the sum of it. Here we are. Up these steps. In here.'

They were met at the counter of a bare lobby by a young woman who, gushingly, took them through to 'meet Matron! She's been so looking forward to meeting you, Miss Lewis.'

Matron Bassani was a sturdy woman with a wide smile and, disconcertingly, a missing front tooth. Obviously aiming to please, she ushered them into a small, sad, sitting room adjacent to her office, where she served them tea and fruitcake.

'I am so pleased you came, Miss Lewis,' she said as she poured. 'I've heard about your auxiliary and the splendid charity work that you perform. Let me tell you, we need every penny we can find here. One can't complain about a government doing its best, but there is so much more we could do for our poor patients if we could afford more staff.'

She turned to Raymond. 'And is your wife a member of the auxiliary, Mr Lewis?'

'My brother is a widower,' Lavinia said. 'Tell me, Matron, why are the patients out there still in their night attire at this hour?'

The Matron looked at her, blinked, and gave a patronising laugh. 'Because they are patients, my dear. But tell me, Mr Lewis, what is your field of endeavour?'

'Legal practice, madam. Legal.'

The laugh gushed. 'Oh dear. A gentleman of your importance, I hope we don't take too much of your precious time. I do so admire legal folk, and their great courage in protecting us against the criminal element.'

'I rather thought that was the job of the police,' Lavinia sniffed.

'Ah, but once arrested, it takes clever legal minds to make sure the villains don't squirm out of it. I often go to the courts to watch the dramas unfold. I must watch for you, Mr Lewis. It will be exciting to see someone one knows, in action, up there before judge and jury.'

'Hmm, yes,' Raymond said, under his sister's scowl. 'I wonder if we might have a look around, Matron?'

'Certainly, Mr Lewis. I have to warn you, though that some of our patients are in "states", so to speak.' She turned to Lavinia. 'Miss Lewis, you might find them upsetting. Would you rather stay in here while I take Mr Lewis—'

Lavinia finished her tea. 'Do not be concerned on my behalf, Matron. I shall be pleased to accompany you.'

When they set off, the matron strode forward, bringing Raymond along with her and leaving a fuming Lavinia to trot along behind.

First they saw a common room where listless patients in their night attire were congregated, some standing about, some sitting on drab chairs and sofas, and others on the floor, lolling against the wall. They were a wretched lot, unkempt and dirty, faces wreathed in confusion, and they seemed not to notice the visitors.

'They're very quiet,' Lavinia whispered, and the matron beamed.

'Yes, aren't they? As you see, they're well looked after, and hence content.'

Amazing what little doses of laudanum can do, Raymond pondered as he scanned the room for Constance.

Next door was a long, empty refectory, so they marched down a few steps to observe a remarkably clean kitchen where women were working, and moved on to the next building, which was a large, deserted dormitory of unmade bunks and an overpowering smell of tobacco and urine.

'That's the men's dormitory,' Matron said, seemingly unaware of Lavinia's obvious disapproval. 'It's hard enough to teach boys to be tidy, let alone these demented fellows. They're not good at making their beds. In fact they actively dislike the chore. But then, what gentleman makes his own bed? I'm sure you don't, Mr Lewis.'

'No,' he agreed.

They progressed to the female dormitory, which was even worse. The foul smell hit them as the door opened to more mess, with bedding thrown everywhere.

'As you can see,' Matron said blithely, 'they do have adequate lodgings, a roof over their heads and three meals a day, better than being flung on to the streets. But come on, we do have private rooms, I can show you them. Further down there, as you can see, two buildings are set apart, behind the wire fence. There we hold the dangerous patients, people who are raving mad. I can't take you in there.'

Lavinia shuddered as two wardsmen came towards them, hauling an elderly man, who suddenly screamed abuse at the visitors.

'Don't mind him,' Matron smiled. 'That's Mr Hannerly. It's his weekly bath time and he hates it. Thinks someone is trying to drown him.'

'Then why not sponge him down instead?' Lavinia asked.

'This is not a health spa,' Matron retorted, 'but we do our best. I consider a plunge bath beneficial and soothing. In many hospitals, patients are lucky if they get so much as a wipe over with a damp sponge. Of course there are still people in the community who cling to the old ways, rejecting baths, and there's no excuse for that in this lovely warm climate. Is there, Mr Lewis?'

'Eh? What?' Raymond had been scrutinising a group of women gathered on a veranda, engaged in the serious business of eating apples, which a nurse was peeling and slicing, handing the fruit to them piece by piece. Constance wasn't there either.

'Excellent climate, yes. You are not a native of Brisbane?'

'No, I'm from the cold country. From down there in Tasmania. I fear, Mr Lewis, we are far more advanced in the treatment of mental cases than folk are here.'

'Then we are fortunate that you have chosen to come here,' Raymond bowed, and she clucked her delight.

The private rooms, in another long timber building, all led off a veranda, but like everywhere else in this compound, the windows were barred. Neither Lavinia nor Raymond commented, though. They were too busy with surreptitious glances in those windows, while they strolled along with the matron, listening to her outlining the latest treatment available to ladies in this block.

'You do what?' Lavinia exploded.

'It's very beneficial, Miss Lewis. They are mentally unbalanced so I have them held upside-down for a half-hour each day. They—'

'Excuse me,' Raymond said. 'I hope you don't find me out of order Matron, but I thought I saw Lady Horwood in that room.'

'Who?' Lavinia cried, feigning surprise. 'Lady Horwood?'

'It is,' Matron beamed, not disposed to sacrifice a social plum for the sake of a patient's privacy. 'As I said before, we have many well-placed ladies and gentlemen in our care.'

'Might I have a word with her, bid her good day?' Raymond asked, but the Matron frowned.

'I'm not too sure. I don't think—'

Lavinia leaned forward to speak quietly to her. 'My brother was a passenger on the *China Belle* at the time of that dreadful mutiny. He shared those difficult times with Constance and Lyle Horwood. He is a close friend – surely you wouldn't begrudge him.'

'Very well, a few minutes, Mr Lewis, though I really shouldn't. Not in private, though. You might give her a relapse.'

She unlocked the door and called to Constance, who was lying on the bed. 'You have a visitor, dear. I've got a visitor for you.'

'I don't have visitors,' Constance replied wearily.

'But this gentleman knows you. It's Mr Lewis.'

'Who?'

'It's me, Raymond Lewis,' he said and with that she came rushing to the door, a blue silk housecoat billowing over a long nightdress.

'Raymond. It is you! Where have you been? I've been waiting to see you. I have to talk to you. Come in, there's a chair behind the door there. Sit down, I'll sit here on the bed.'

'You may go,' she called to the matron, oblivious of the other visitor standing in the doorway. 'I wish to have a private conversation with Mr Lewis.'

'I'm afraid we can't do that, dear. The rules, you know . . .'

'Get out!' Constance shouted, and bundled the two women aside, closing the door.

'I'm sorry, Raymond,' she said. 'They think I'm mad, so they might as well go on thinking it. Do you mind being stuck here with a madwoman?'

'Not at all.' Out of the corner of his eyes he could see the matron peering in the window. 'In fact, I'm pleasantly surprised to see you looking so well.'

'Better than when you found me in Cooktown, eh?'

'You were in a state then. Understandably, I'd say.'

'Yes, I was in an awful mess, quite ill and disoriented.' She gathered her gown about her, tightened the sash and settled herself on the end of the low bed. 'Not much of a room, is it?'

'Rather bare.'

'Couldn't be more bare. But it does. You really think I'm looking better?'

'Indeed I do. But I am concerned. They don't make you stand on your head?'

Constance sighed. 'Suddenly gaining a title has its advantages, I've discovered. When Lady Horwood yells, they jump. I do not stand on my head, nor do I have breakfast before nine. But forget about them. As you can see, I still dribble, and I have a tic at that side of my mouth that I can't control. Lyle hates all that. It embarrasses him. I embarrass him.'

'Oh, surely—'

'No, don't worry about that now. I need to talk to you.'

Raymond listened patiently as she explained her situation, wondering why the woman was in an asylum in the first place. But never being one for snap judgements, he placed that thought aside.

It seemed that she had been drugged by a doctor in Cairns before being taken on to the ship bound for Brisbane. They'd drugged her because she'd refused to set foot on a ship again after her terrifying experiences on *China Belle*.

'You were on board too,' she said.

'I know. I had my suspicions about that, but you were in the hands of a nurse.'

'Never mind. I kept getting these attacks of panic that turn me into jelly, even though the danger was gone. I thought that if I got on another ship I would go off my head altogether, but lo and behold, I survived that sea trip. I didn't get seasick and the world didn't fall in on me. Then we stayed in a hotel until Lyle's investiture – you were there – and that was a nightmare for me. I didn't want to attend but he insisted, also insisting that I wore that hat with the veil to cover the dribbles.

'A doctor here tells me I'm suffering from a variety of ailments including hysteria. That one I'll allow. I'm terrified of going out in public. You might recall I managed to get through the investiture at Government House, but I'd clutched my hands closed so tightly, they were bleeding; the nails had cut into them. That was why I couldn't make the reception.'

'I'm sorry.'

'A minor matter. After that he bought the house in Fortitude Valley, but things got worse between us. Lyle still believes I was raped or had sexual relations of some sort with my captors.'

'Oh no, surely not! That didn't enter anyone's head.'

'You're a nice man, Raymond. Thank you for that, but he does believe so and, worse than that, I have people actually ask me point-blank what *really* happened. Our new housekeeper had only been with us one week when she had the gall to ask me – solicitously, of course – was it true that I'd been "interfered with" by those Asians. I fired her on the spot.'

'Well, of course,' Raymond said indignantly.

Another sigh. 'Yes, but Lyle didn't think so. He said I should have sat her down and sworn on the bible that the rumour was not true . . . and so on and so forth until I got into such a state I was screaming at him. Threatening to leave. Anyway, to cut a long story short, Lyle called in a doctor for my nerves, and I ended up in here.'

'Of your own accord? I mean did you come here willingly?'

'Into a madhouse? No. I knew I wasn't mad; I just couldn't cope with things. But they signed me in, and Lyle told me if I didn't go willingly, he could have the police take me away.'

'Oh, my dear!'

Matron Bassani put her nose in the door. 'Visiting hours are up, Mr Lewis.'

Raymond stood and walked to the door. 'Matron, I'd appreciate more time if you please. Lady Horwood has just appointed me as her legal representative. I am therefore entitled to discuss her incarceration,' he frowned darkly on the woman as he leaned on that word, 'in this establishment when and as I wish.'

'Well done,' Constance smiled. 'I'd forgotten you were a lawyer.'

'At your service, milady.'

'Excellent, but that's not what I wanted to talk about. I didn't want to come here but I'm really not minding it. To be honest, getting away from Horwood is a good start. You see, in here I can concentrate, the better to work out what is wrong with me, because I'm damn sure the doctors are as confused as I am. Sometimes, like today, I'm quite lucid, but at other times I am not, and I have found that coincides with my fits of the miseries and none of . . . none of any of this happened before the horrors I suffered during and after the mutiny. You see, Raymond,' she said breathlessly, 'I have to solve this. I am a healthy person and—'

'Whoa,' he cried. 'Hang on now. I fear this is too much for me to take in all at once.'

Her face crumpled. 'You think I am mad?'

'No, no, no! On the contrary, you're doing well. It's me. I have to keep up. So let's try this: are you willing to engage me as your legal representative?' Raymond was aware that in her situation, she couldn't reliably engage his services, since she was probably registered as 'of unsound mind' before she was lodged at St Clement's, but at least he was giving her confidence.

'Indeed yes, please do.'

'Then what about I come back tomorrow at three? That will give you time to work out what you want to do. I rather surprised you today.'

'Yes, you did. A very pleasant surprise, believe me. Are you thinking it best to observe me over a few days yourself, Raymond? To see if my story holds up?'

Raymond nodded. It pained him to be truthful. 'Since you are not being ill-treated here, as far as I can see, it will be best to take our time. I see no point in rushing things. All the same, I will be here at three tomorrow. Is there anything I can bring you?'

'I'd love some fruit. They never have fruit here. And some books.'

As he stood, she shook his hand. 'I have come to the conclusion that there are only two people in this world who can help me. You're one of them. What a happy chance that you came by.'

Raymond smiled. 'Not happy chance, my dear. Lavinia and I were concerned about you.'

Her eyes filled with tears, and, as he walked away, he regretted that remark, realising she was in a vulnerable state, her emotions close to the surface. He sighed, wondering why he hadn't just let it pass. Have her think it had been a coincidence finding her.

'But no,' he murmured. 'You had to boast of your good works. Stroking your ego. The hero to the rescue, who was also curious as to her situation and not a little peeved with her husband.'

On the way home he mentioned that *faux pas* to Lavinia, who was not surprised.

'You're too hard on yourself, Raymond. You've taken to self-examination like an Inquisition bishop, ever since you came home. And it sounds to me as if that girl is doing the same thing. Preferring to stay in an asylum! I never heard the like. Does she realise what she's doing to her reputation? You ought to go and see Horwood and demand he gets his wife out of that place.'

'I can't do that. I'm not even sure I can get her out without his approval.'

'That's the last straw!' Gordon said, when his partner advised him that he needed the afternoon off to see a client in hospital. 'I require you to set a time, Raymond, so that we can settle our affairs once and for all. Set a time, and be there!'

'Yes, very well. I'm sorry to be inconveniencing you, Gordon, but my heart's not in office work these days. I'd like to travel, see more of the world. I shouldn't put it off any longer. What about tomorrow morning at nine? Are you clear?'

'Yes, nine. I'll have the books ready. I will continue the practice in these rooms on my own, so I'll just need a pro rata on the rent.'

'Don't worry if there are a few months left on my rent. You keep it. With this short notice I wouldn't want a rebate.'

Gordon shook his head. 'Raymond, you owe me.'

The firm of Lewis and McLeish wound up at noon, and Raymond hurried home for lunch before setting out for St Clement's. He had made an appointment to see Matron Bussani, in company with one of Lady Horwood's doctors, at two, so that he could introduce himself officially and seek their advice.

Matron gave him tea again, this time thin sandwiches and an orange sponge cake were added to the table, but there was no sign of any doctor.

In answer to his questions, she was of the opinion that Lady Horwood was suffering from recurrent madness caused by hysteria.

'. . . a state not unknown among highborn women. They're hothouse flowers, Mr Lewis, absolutely unable to handle the slightest setback. One woman I heard of went completely off her head when confronted with a bee.'

'Is that documented or hearsay?'

'Oh, documented somewhere, I should think.'

'And you think Lady Horwood is a hothouse flower?'

Warned by his tone of voice, she backed off. 'Oh, heavens, I wouldn't exactly say that of her, but she does like her own way. Then again, the treatments she chooses to avoid are not mandatory.'

'Lady Horwood did have dreadful experiences because of that mutiny,' he said, and the Matron agreed.

'I know. I have it all here. But her husband said her experiences were no worse than those of the other two women.' She opened a folder, turned a page or two, and read the names. 'Mrs Caporn and, an elderly lady even, a Mrs Plummer.'

'That's not correct. I fear you only have half the story,' Raymond was beginning to explain, when a tall man with grey thinning hair and a wispy beard entered the room, and without so much as a nod to Matron Bassani, rounded on the visitor.

'Are you Mr Lewis?'

'Yes.' Raymond stood, ready to extend his hand at the introductions, but the niceties were ignored.

'I am Dr Shakell, Chief Medical Officer here, and you, sir, are trespassing. I require you to remove yourself.'

'But, Doctor, this gentleman did have an appointment with me,' Matron tried.

'Then keep your private arrangements private, and off these premises!'

She blushed scarlet, as Raymond stepped in.

'Such discourtesies do not help matters, Doctor. I am a lawyer and a personal friend of Sir Lyle and Lady Horwood. I have a right to be here.'

'You do not. Lady Horwood is not permitted visitors. Her husband and I are quite clear about this.'

They argued for a while and, in the end, Raymond agreed to leave, on one condition. That he see the section of Constance's admitting papers that the Matron had just mentioned.

As expected, Dr Shakell flatly refused.

'In that case, I shall inform the health authorities that I intend to take legal action against you, Dr Shakell. Not against this establishment but against you, for dereliction of duty.'

'What the hell are you talking about?'

'You heard me clearly, sir. I simply wish to see those notes.'

'Which will prove what?'

'Quite possibly that my surmise is incorrect and you are innocent of any wrongdoing.'

'I don't need you to tell me that, sir. You may not view our records, so kindly leave. And your request to see Lady Horwood is denied. Should you wish to see the lady at another time, you may do so with written approval from her husband. Is that understood?'

'Yes. I'm sorry if I have inadvertently caused you vexation,' Raymond said quickly, changing tack, 'but my concern is for my dear friend Lady Horwood. I was much relieved to be able to speak with her yesterday and have her tell me she is content here.'

Shakell warmed to the compliment. 'Sometimes our work is appreciated,' he murmured.

'Then answer me just one question. I know about Lady Horwood's suffering at the hands of brutes on the ship *China Belle*. I was there. You have a record in your notes, or part of the story. I presume you have the rest notated elsewhere. The part about her abduction.'

The doctor shook his head, exasperated. 'What abduction?'

'She was kidnapped by the crew. Taken ashore with them. From the glimpse I saw I had the impression this was not mentioned.'

'I don't know anything about this.'

'Then, as her doctor, don't you think you should?'

Shakell quickly ushered him into the matron's office, where he commandeered her desk, allowed her to sit in a corner of the room and instructed Raymond to take the chair before him.

'Now what's all this about, Lewis? You have seen Lady Horwood, you can see she's in good hands, why are you intent on causing problems? And what's this about an abduction?'

He was dumbfounded when Raymond told him, at length, about his patient's terrifying experience, and rifled through his notes as if he had mislaid that information.

'I'm sure I was never informed of any of this,' he said. 'I can't understand it.'

'It was in the papers,' the matron said. 'But I didn't know it was Lady Horwood who was abducted by the white slavers, it was Mrs . . . someone. I can't recall her name now.'

'They were not white slavers, madam,' Raymond said crankily, 'and there, Doctor, is probably one of the reasons both Sir Lyle and Lady Horwood have shut up about that episode. I'm no physician but it seems to me that you need to know.'

Shakell was agitated. 'I have been practising in Western Australia until recently. We rarely have any news of the East. I had never heard of the *China Belle* until it was mentioned in this case. And I certainly did not know there was a great deal more to it. The poor woman! She must have felt hideously degraded.'

'Exactly.'

'I'll have to give this a great deal of thought now, especially since the lady herself has avoided mention of the abduction, or even of you finding her in that hellhole of a village in the Far North. I'm afraid I misjudged you, Mr Lewis.'

'Then couldn't I see Lady Horwood for a few minutes?'
'A few minutes. I'll accompany you.'

Constance was amiable in the company of the doctor, but wary. Raymond delivered his fruit, and several books by Dickens, which she rejected as being too full of misery, but she welcomed the light romance novels that Lavinia had added to the basket.

Obviously, she would not open up to Raymond as she'd done the previous day, so all three sat on the veranda and talked of the weather, and of the necessity to landscape the grounds so as to provide pleasant gardens for the patients, there being any amount of space for such a programme. Raymond even found himself donating a hundred pounds to start the ball rolling, much to her ladyship's delight.

'You're in good spirits today,' Shakell said to her, as he rose to end the visit.

'It's Mr. Lewis, he's a tonic,' she said, managing to hold Raymond back as the doctor was leaving.

'There's someone else I have to see. You have to find him.'

'Who is that?'

She clutched his sleeve. 'Please, Raymond, I have to talk to him. He's the only person who can prove I never had any physical contact with any of those men. Jake Tussup will speak for me – he has to. I beg you, Raymond, if I'm ever to hold my head up again, you have to find him.'

'What was that about?' Shakell asked.

'Tell me, do you stand mental patients on their heads?' Lewis asked him.

'I put a stop to that idiocy, but it takes time to make changes in these institutions. Why?'

'Because my friend's life is in your hands. I need to know you care about logically seeking a solution to her problems as she is trying to do.'

'She's a headstrong woman in a maze. She's barging about trying to find her own way out. I think I can help if I'm allowed to see the full picture. And to be honest, I am rather shaken that Sir Lyle expects me to treat his wife but withholds vital information.'

'Maybe he's the one should be in here.'

'Shame,' Lavinia said when he told her of Constance's request.

'What's a shame? That Tussup's a wanted criminal?'

'No. That people, including that wretch of a husband, have put such shame on an innocent woman that she can't face the world until someone who was there can attest to her good name. And as for Horwood, he can sort out his own library!'

'Oh well, it's up to Dr Shakell now. There's no chance of her seeing Tussup.'

'Why not?'

'Because he's on the run, still up in the goldfields last heard, and dodging them all rather skilfully.'

'Then you go and find him!'

'What?'

She sighed. 'Raymond. They'll get him in the end. They always do. Let's hope they don't shoot him first. He is her only chance, fantasy though it is, because who'll listen, or care to accept the boring truth? When they catch him, he'll need a lawyer. You can be Johnny-on-the-spot.'

'Constance is not the only one believing in fantasies,' he growled.

'What did he actually do? He deserted ship. He didn't kidnap the women. And he got Constance away from the brutes. Saw her safely into Cooktown.'

'Safely? You should have seen her. She was half demented.'

'What was he supposed to do? Escort her to the police?'

'Leave it, please! You don't know what you're talking about.'

That night, though, he did give thought to returning to Cairns. Going back, finding out how they were all coping after the cyclone. How Mrs Plummer was. A fine woman, that. And, of course, poor little widowed Mrs Caporn. And Mal Willoughby. A wild card there.

He had a worrying thought. He hoped Mal had settled down, given up on seeking revenge. There was always the danger that he might shoot Tussup and end up in gaol himself. Then *he'd* need legal representation.

Chapter Eighteen

Miners travelling to and from the Upper Hodgkinson still used the large base camp at the splendid Barron River, giving Jesse Field enough stories to keep his editor happy, and make a sojourn in this picturesque spot a downright pleasure. He saw men come through on the return journey to Cairns wild with joy, and others dejected, broken in health and pocket by the heat and the harsh conditions. He watched wagons, drawn by teams of horses or bullocks, hauling impossible loads inland, and others making for the port with wool and skins. Daily, the dead and dying were brought back and Jesse chronicled the deeds of violence and of diseases, drownings and despair. He interviewed the newly rich, the 'delirious', as he called them, wading through a feast of friends and well-wishers; and the secretive winners who wanted only to escape with every hard-earned speck of gold still in their pockets.

On this day, a group of important gentlemen led by the Queensland Governor, Sir Arthur Kennedy, and his official photographer, arrived at the camp prior to setting off on an expedition to view the mighty cataract the Aborigines called Dinden but which was charted as Barron Falls.

While the party was preparing to begin the climb, Jesse saw Mal Willoughby riding down the road in company with two Chinamen. The first one, a big fellow with a shoestring moustache, was nattily dressed – for these parts – and the other, bringing up the rear, was obviously his servant.

'Halloo there! Mal!' he called. 'I'm with the Governor's party. We're going up to see the falls. Do you want to come with us?'

Mal dismounted. 'Sorry, I can't. We're going on to Cairns. But I did want to talk to you. It's urgent.'

'Why? What happened? Did you find Tussup?'

'Not exactly.'

Jesse laughed. 'How do you figure not exactly?' But then he saw a warning glance from Mal. 'Is everything all right with you, mate?'

'Yes. Fine. More or less.'

'Then why don't you wait for me? That's the Governor over there, and his entourage. I'm travelling with them, a golden chance to quiz him about a lot of things.'

Mal turned back to the first Chinaman with a grin. 'See over there, Chang? That's our Governor, the one standing by the tent eating a sandwich.'

'No!' The Chinaman was amazed. Impressed by the title but stunned at the informality of the scene. He gazed at the group, giving Mal a chance to whisper: 'Something's up. I'll tell you when you get back.'

Without bothering to introduce his friends, he swung back on to his horse and they rode away.

For a few minutes Jesse contemplated going after them, to find out what was troubling Mal, but the opportunity to meet Kennedy was too good to miss. There were so many questions he needed to ask, not the least being the request to speed up public works in Cairns, to help the town climb back on to its feet after the cyclone.

Chang was bursting with curiosity. 'Your friend knows the Governor?'

'Yes,' Mal said.

'Where are his servants?'

'They'll be around somewhere. There is little formality in bush expeditions.'

'Where will the Governor sleep?'

'In a tent.'

'Ayiyiyi! This is too much. And no female servants at all?'

'No.'

Chang wanted to ride by the Governor's camp again, crowing that when he went home he'd be able to say he met the lord of the whole country, and Mal obliged, not bothering to explain the difference between colony and country. He was only too glad to have this diversion. He wished he could have talked to Jesse, talked over this latest state of affairs.

Chang's arrogance was something to see. He rode right by two mounted police without batting an eye, confident that Mal would not turn him in.

'Don't be so bloody sure,' Mal muttered to himself.

While Wu Tin was setting up their camp, Mal started to question Chang again. 'Who gives you your money?'

'I will be paid by Mr Li when I go back to Cooktown, on my way home. The family pay Mr Li. Very simply done.'

'How can you prove to them that you killed Tussup?'

'I told you. Wu Tin will witness.'

'You could be making it up. Both of you. For the money.'

'And get my throat cut? No, no.'

Mal's stomach churned. He desperately wanted Chang to admit he was lying, but no matter how often he brought up various aspects of their story on the ride down to this camp, the facts remained the same.

He'd thought to ask Jesse to make some enquiries about the possibility of a body being found in the bush near Merthyr's Ferry, but that wouldn't work.

Besides, it was probably too soon. There was no telegraph out here. Anyway, what did it matter? He would have to turn Chang in, and Wu Tin as his accomplice. The police would investigate. If they couldn't find the body, or there was no body, the charge would be dismissed. On the other hand, if they found Tussup, this pair would swing for murder.

'I'm going over to the pub,' he said, and strode away from them, wishing they would disappear out of his life.

The pub was only a shanty on the other side of the road. Mal could see them from his position by the open door. Wu Tin was boiling the billy over the campfire to make tea, and Chang was lazing against a tree, smoking.

Mal had to make a decision. Turn them in, he decided, as he bought another beer. I'll definitely turn them in. But not yet. As soon as I hear that they really did kill Tussup and this isn't just some drama Chang has invented to ingratiate himself. As soon as the body is found and word filters down to Cairns.

By which time they could have left. Jumped on the first available ship.

And, he argued with himself, you really don't believe that Chang has invented this tale. You know he has killed Tussup. You're the one inventing excuses. And why is that?

Because you don't want to go to gaol! He almost shouted. He's got you by the throat! You're scared that you'll be shoved into gaol again for something you didn't do. You're scared witless at the thought of gaol, that's why you're frozen to the spot. Can't make a move. Can't bring yourself to go to the police and have these two bastards back one another up as innocents. So why are you going over and over the same ground? Tussup's dead. It's not your fault. Forget it.

A man walked over to speak to him. 'G'day, mate. Aren't you Sonny Willoughby? Nearly got done over in the gold raid a few years back?'

'No,' Mal snapped, and pushed past him to stride out back into the harsh glare of the day. His head ached as he walked down the road, hoping the Governor's party was still in the clearing by the river, but it was deserted, only the shiny new tents remaining, with a few attendants wandering about. He watched some wallabies nibbling grass at the edge of the rainforest as birds squabbled in the press of palm trees above them, and he was suddenly tired of these places. Of jungles and sweaty nights and rain at the wrong time of the year . . . 'and bloody insects,' he groaned as he slapped at mosquitoes. He missed the rolling hills of the south, the crisp air and the feeling of space, and a cool breeze!

'It's time to go home,' he murmured. 'Get on with things.'

He had hoped to buy a sheep station on the Condamine River, in country that he knew well, and take Jun Lien to live there, 'happily ever after,' he intoned bitterly. Since her death he'd dismissed that idea out of hand, but what else was there for him, other than to roam around the country aimlessly?

He had no family to call on – his sister had turned her back on him when he was in trouble, and his own uncle had given him up to the police for the reward. For the last few years it had been a dream of his to own a fine property and stock it with the best-bred sheep available. Maybe begin a stud . . . breed merinos . . . that would be something.

'It would,' he told himself. 'So you'd better get on with it.'

When he went back to their camp he found Chang and Wu Tin arguing viciously.

'What's going on?' he asked.

'The fool wants to remain in this country,' Chang said. 'He does not wish to come down to the coast and return to China with me. He wants to go gold searching on his own. I tell him he is owned by the Misters Li and he has to do as he's told.'

'I thought he was your servant?'

'Assigned to me by the Misters Li.'

'You must be highly thought of.'

'As you see,' Chang acknowledged with a grin.

'Tell him we're all going down to Cairns first thing in the morning.'

Jesse was concerned for Mal. He hadn't liked the look of the tall Chink travelling with him; he'd had an arrogant glint in his eye as he'd gazed down at them, as if neither he nor Mal counted in this world. Jesse wondered if the Chinamen had anything to do with Mal's troubles, and the more he thought about the trio the more worried he became. And what did Mal want to discuss with him?

He was able to have several short conversations with the Governor by the time they arrived at the falls, and he was looking forward to continuing their talks, when he heard the party had decided to move on to the goldfields.

'But I thought this was just an overnight camping trip,' Jessie said to an aide. 'There was no mention of the Hodgkinson.'

'Change of plan. The boss has decided since we've come this far we might as well push on. He's game for the climb so we have to look lively too.'

Jesse wasn't looking forward to the 'climb' now that there was an easier route to the goldfields, and he still had a nagging feeling that Mal was in trouble. In the morning he decided to forego travels with the Governor and asked an Aborigine guide to take him back down to the base camp.

As he expected, Mal and his companions had already left, so he wasted no time riding after them, knowing he'd soon locate Mal in Cairns if he missed him on the coastal track.

Wu Tin was disturbed. His horse was lame, and Chang was angry with him for not looking after it. Though Wu Tin knew not what he could have done.

'Leave it then,' Chang said. 'Get down and walk. You can give me the saddle to carry.'

But Mr Willoughby intervened, shouting at Chang – they had been arguing ever since they met by the second gold river – and he took all three horses to a nearby rocky stream to water them.

'What did he say?' Wu Tin asked Chang.

'He said you're a lump of turd, a burden on us now.'

'You lie. His face said different. He said two on your horse, I think. And you lie about him too. All the time. Your friend, he's taking us to the police, straight down the hill to hang for killing that man.'

Chang looked about him. Willoughby was wading in the stream himself. Cooling off. 'I told you ten times that he would not do that. He hated Tussup; he's pleased we shot him.'

'Then why has he the face of rage every time I hear the word Tussup? And why are you now saying *we* shot him? You did. Not me.'

Wu Tin was becoming hysterical. They had met mounted police in black uniforms with silver buttons on this road and Willoughby had stopped to talk to them. Though Chang kept trying to tell him their arguments were only over trivial matters, Wu Tin knew that was lies. He'd watched them both, and come to the conclusion that Chang had lying eyes. Willoughby, though a white man, had honest eyes. They were troubled; it was plain to see, and Wu Tin was convinced that Willoughby did not want to give his friend Chang to the police for murder. But he would. He didn't believe for one minute Chang's story that this white man was afraid he'd get the blame if he reported them. How could that be? He was a member of the ruling class! Hadn't they just seen evidence of that? With the great lord Governor only a few steps away.

The more he worried the problem, the more terrified he became. Chang was too full of himself lately. Overconfident. Showing off his great friendship with Willoughby, who was only biding his time. But why? Then it dawned on him. Why arrest him and Chang now, and have to drag them down to the coast? Willoughby, the cunning fellow, was letting them ride to their doom.

Wu Tin was sweating as he gathered twigs to make a fire for Chang's interminable tea. Willoughby was content with water during the day. He watched Chang take off his jacket and shirt and hang them on a tree branch before he also went down the bush track to the stream. Suddenly, a great black bird swooped right across Wu Tin's face! It landed close by and cawed at him, a mournful horrible sound. Petrified, Wu Tin saw it as a bad omen. They were only a day away from the port now, a day away from prison, so was the black bird telling him this was the last day of his life? He shivered and shook in terror, grasping his sharp cutting knife, peering around him for more bad joss in this lonely place, and then Willoughby appeared, as if from nowhere, standing right where the black bird had been. Wu Tin lunged.

'What the hell?' Willoughby roared as the knife slashed the side of his throat, and he lashed out with his boot, sending Wu Tin flying, but though he was a small man, he was agile and he hurled himself back to finish off the man who would see him hanged.

Chang heard the fight. He heard Willoughby yell and Wu Tin scream so he slipped into the bush, got a glimpse of the fight and went back to the stream. They could kill each other for all he cared. Then there'd be no one to witness against him for killing a white man.

When the noise stopped he strolled up past the horses, to see Wu Tin lying in a heap on the ground.

'He tried to kill me!' Willoughby, a handkerchief to his neck to stop the blood, was astonished.

'Is he dead?'

'No, but I had to fight him off with a lump of wood. He's out cold. What the hell is that all about?'

'He's mad,' Chang shrugged. 'You ought to finish him off while you can, otherwise he'll come after you again.'

'Why?'

'Because he thinks you're taking him to prison,' Chang said casually. 'I told him you wouldn't do that, but he doesn't believe me.'

'So you let him attack me.'

'I knew you'd win.'

Willoughby threw water over Wu Tin to wake him, then he bound him with rope.

'What are you going to do with him?' Chang asked.

'Probably hand him over to the authorities.'

'Where? His horse is lame.'

'It's not too bad. If we go quietly, give it rests, it can carry him.'

'I don't think that's a good idea. It'll be better to get rid of him here. He'll talk. About Tussup. And we can't have that.'

'You mean *you* can't have that.' Willoughby turned back to Chang as he spoke. He saw the revolver that Chang had thought to take from his pack as he passed the horses.

'It's loaded,' Chang said sorrowfully. And he really was sorry. It was just that Wu Tin could be right after all. His friend Mr Willoughby might just take his chances with the police and spill the whole story before he was safely away . . . *en route* to China with a comforting purse of gold, his duty done, and so no need to fear the Xiu family. But then he saw a horseman coming towards them.

'Too late now,' he said quickly. 'I can't shoot him. We have company.'

'I had the impression you intended to shoot me, you bastard.'

'Then you are sadly mistaken, and I am deeply hurt.'

'Give me the gun.'

Chang shrugged and handed it over. One weapon was as good as another. But he was relieved. Deep down he didn't want to have to obey Mr Xiu. His contract was with the mourning lady. And Willoughby had done no wrong. Even now he was being fair. Stupidly fair.

The horseman was Jesse Field. He'd met some mounted police on the road and they'd told him Mal wasn't too far ahead with his Chinese mates, so he'd ridden fast to catch up with them.

'What's going on here?' He was amazed to see one of the Chinese tied up and the other holding a revolver, which he suddenly handed to Mal. And Mal with a bloody gash on his neck.

'We had a little disagreement,' Mal said. 'Have a look at this cut for me.'

Jesse swung down from his horse to examine the wound as Mal picked up a billy of water. 'You can swab it with some with this.'

'It's only a surface cut,' Jesse said as he cleaned it, 'but hang on while I get some tea tree oil to disinfect it.'

That done, Mal introduced the men, explaining who Chang was, and pointing out the other fellow as Chang's servant.

Jesse was intrigued to meet the man who had been such a help to Mal in China, and relieved that he was Mal's friend, putting the lie to his first impression of this very self-assured Chinaman.

They shared their provisions and had a meal of vegetable cakes with rice, and corned beef buns, washed down by black tea and a bottle of the Governor's fine wine. Jesse quizzed Chang about his impressions of the country, pleased to hear that Chang thought it was a wonderful place, so beautiful and grand. He was only sorry that he had to return to China now that his work was finished, and so would be prevented from visiting the other cities.

'What work do you do?'

'I have been mine manager, sir. For the esteemed Li brothers, who have many mines and many coolies, but the gold is not much now on the Palmer goldfields and running out at the goldfields we just left.'

Soon they were on the road again. Mal had untied his attacker, who was still groggy, sporting a large lump on his forehead, and stuck him on his horse, his hand tied to the saddle. They travelled steadily, favouring the lame horse, and all this time Jesse had been waiting for Mal to tell him what it was they had to discuss so urgently. But nothing was said, so Jesse assumed the problem was not for the ears of their companions.

'Are you going to charge that character?' he asked, jerking his head at Wu Tin.

'No,' Mal said.

'But he tried to kill you.'

'No he didn't. It was a fight, that's all.'

* * *

The road through the lowlands into Cairns wound through waist-high grass, ancient ferns and exhausted-looking palm trees. They passed farms with flattened maize crops and muddied vegetable patches, but the lonely farmhouses seemed to have survived. Further on they saw some battered houses, and in Cairns, tangled ruins still littered town blocks right next to buildings that had managed to survive the storm, and others already under reconstruction. People seemed to be limping about, dragging about their business, as if they too had suffered damage.

Jesse was amused by Chang's description of the battered town as they rode in. He said it was an 'invalid town, in need of much treatment'.

'You can say that again,' Jesse laughed, but he noticed both men were watching Mal warily.

Wu Tin called out to Chang. He sounded scared.

'What did he say?' Jesse asked Mal.

'I don't know.'

'I thought you could speak Chinese?'

'Some, but I don't know his dialect.'

'He wants to know if you're taking him to prison,' Chang said.

'Tell him no. I am taking him straight to where you can get tickets to leave the country.'

'Ah, good,' Chang settled back with a self-satisfied smile, and Jesse, not knowing enough about the situation to make any comment, quietly observed them all.

They headed for the wharves, where one warehouse had been rebuilt, and a long corrugated-iron shed now housed Customs and Immigration as well as the shipping offices.

Mal looked to Jesse. 'Are they all lumped in together now?'

'Yes. They've had plans for bigger and better premises on the table for ages. Thanks to the storm they'll be built now. Or so says the Governor.'

'Good!' Mal nodded to the Chinamen. 'There you are, Chang. That's where you get your tickets. Have you got enough money?'

'Yes.' He jumped down from his horse and marched over to Wu Tin. 'You apologise to Mr Willoughby. You're lucky he didn't have you arrested. He's a kind man. He understood your concern.'

Wu Tin groaned, dismounted, gave a shivery bow to Mal before hitching their horses to a rail and running after Chang, who had shouldered a small leather bag and was already striding into the building.

'Here, take this,' Mal said, and slid some papers over to Jesse.

'What are they?'

'Chang's papers.'

'But he'll need them.'

Mal winked. 'I know. Now I have to go.'

'Where?'

'I'm going back.'

'You're what?'

'I have to go back to the Hodgkinson. I have to check on something.'

'Now?'

'Right now. You'd be wise to move off now too, but while I'm gone, and I won't be long, do me a favour and keep tabs on that pair. I need to know where they are.'

'They won't be far without papers.'

'Come on. Let's get out of here.'

He rode his horse right up to the open door, and shouted to Chang: 'I'll see you later.'

Chang waved back. Royally. To show the two clerks at the trestle table desk facing the door that he was in the company of local gentlemen, one in particular who was a friend of their Governor.

'Wasn't that Willoughby?' one asked the other, but it was Chang who responded.

'Yes, that is my friend Mr Willoughby.'

'And who might you be?'

'I am Chang Soong and this is my servant, Wu Tin. When is the next ship leaving for Cooktown?'

'Papers, please?'

'I wish to buy two tickets of passage, sir.'

'Papers,' the clerk said drily. 'The shipping people are down there,' he pointed down the dimly lit shed, 'but we have to see your papers first.'

'My papers are here but my servant, Wu Tin, does not have papers, unfortunately. He entered your country under Mr Li's coolie quota.'

'Who's Mr Li?'

As the interrogation went on Chang searched his bag for his papers. There were his two purses, bulging with banknotes, and Chinese papers, reading matter, the treasured introduction from the Lady Xiu, his work journals and occasional notes of his travels, neat summaries of his finances and expectations, writing papers and parchments, ink and brushes and other bits and pieces including some gold rings he'd bought from poverty-stricken diggers, but he couldn't find his entry papers – two pages, in English, signed by the authorities and allowing him twelve months' temporary residence. What had he done with them?

'Any gold?' the clerk asked as he waited.

'No.'

'Looks like you got plenty of dosh. Where did you get that?'

'My pay, sir. I was a mine manager.'

'What are we to do with your mate here? No papers, no go no place, savvy?'

Chang went on searching, setting his personal belongings out on the concrete floor, trying to think where else he might have put them.

He thought he might have left them in a pocket of one of his garments, it had been so long since he'd seen them, right back in Cooktown when he'd first arrived. He hadn't seen them since. He turned on Wu Tin, bellowing at him that he must have removed them, or seen them in a pocket and thrown them out, not being able to read or write in Chinese or in English.

'I'm sorry, sir, I can't find them now. Can I buy more?' he asked.

The clerk didn't seem concerned. He sighed. 'Another pair. Listen, Mr Chang, you can't buy more but we can write to Immigration in Cooktown, they'll have your details, and they'll find his. As soon as we get your number from them, proving you're not illegals, you'll be free to go. In the meantime . . .' He put two fingers to his lips and sent forth a shrill whistle, alerting two burly immigration guards, who ambled over.

Chang argued, complained, demanded to be permitted to seek Mr Willoughby's advice.

'He can't help, he can't produce papers out of thin air.'

'Where are you taking us?' Chang screamed as the guards began searching them for weapons.

'You're going to the stockade with the rest of your clan until we see what's going on. You wouldn't get back into Cooktown without papers anyway.'

Wu Tin was certain he was going to prison now, and he started shrieking at Chang, telling all and sundry that it was Chang who killed Tussup, not him, but Chang simply stared him down and none of the onlookers understood a word he said.

'What about our horses?' he asked civilly, certain that his important friends or, as a last resort, bribes, would get them out of whatever this stockade place was.

'If you're leaving the country you might as well sell them,' one of the guards told Chang as they were being led away. 'My name's Wiley; I can arrange the sale for a quid, if you want. In the meantime they'll be in the police paddock. They can always do with a few spare nags.'

Carrying their belongings, they were marched several blocks away from the town and admitted past armed guards into a high-fenced stockade, inhabited by hundreds of their countrymen. Wu Tin immediately disappeared into the throng while Chang patrolled the fence line looking for a safe corner. He had no weapons and a lot of money, a very dangerous situation. Grimly, he thought he would have been better off in a real prison. He had to get word to Willoughby as soon as possible. He understood this was only a temporary, though disgustingly bare, holding yard, and there was a possibility that Willoughby could not help. At least he could mind his money for him. Willoughby was his friend; he could trust him.

He squatted by the fence to sort his belongings, at the same time searching for those precious papers. He still couldn't find them, so cursing this misfortune, he began to divest himself of everything but bare essentials, tossing aside the large leather pack and most of the extra clothing and blankets he'd needed for travel. Then he moved away.

Within minutes they were snatched up by other inmates. He knew he could have sold them, but in this hungry company it was best not to be seen receiving money.

He strolled down to the heavy timber gate and called to a guard.

'Excuse me, sir.'

His polite tone bought attention.

'What do you want?'

'Please to tell Mr Wiley I want to sell my horse.'

One horse, he'd mentioned, one horse only, so that Wiley would come back to persuade him to sell both and then he would tell him to pay the money to Mr Willoughby, therefore guaranteeing it would not stay in Wiley's pocket.

His chores complete, Chang retreated to the position he'd chosen by the fence, opposite a roofed section of the yard that was obviously primitive sleeping quarters. Time enough to have to share his dreams with coolies. He could smell the sea. A gentle breeze was wafting over this monkey cage from the brilliant blue/green bay he'd seen from the wharves, and he wished he'd taken more time to appreciate the view, and thus sustain himself in his miserable condition. But the glimpse of beauty would have to do for now. At least it was something new to contemplate. As for the temporary imprisonment, he shrugged, it wasn't too bad. Chang had been in far worse situations than this.

Under half-closed eyes he watched two coolies sidle past him for the second time, interested no doubt in the belongings he had not discarded. One was carrying a short, stout stick.

When they came by a third time, one kicked dirt in his face and the other man lunged for the belongings he'd been guarding.

His response was swift and cruel. Two fingers with hard nails stabbed at eyes and tore down a leathery face; his foot found the crotch of the other man and lifted him, flailing, out of the argument.

Later that day, Wiley came, wanting to know why he wasn't selling both horses.

'But I am, sir. The message was wrong. Do you know Mr Willoughby?'

'No.'

'Then do you know Mr Jesse Field?'

'Writes for the local paper? Yeah, I know him.'

'Then please to give him the money for the horses and saddles. Safe-keeping, sir. No safe pockets in here, eh?'

'Yeah,' Wiley agreed reluctantly. 'Two horses. That'll be two quid I take off the sale price before I give the cash to Field.'

Chang nodded. 'And tell my friend Mr Field I am here and in need of urgent assistance.'

The journalist did answer the summons the following day, feigning surprise that Chang and Wu Tin were being held by Immigration.

'Wiley gave me forty pounds,' he said, 'for the horses. What do you want me to do with the money?'

'Give it to Mr Willoughby. Tell him I'm here and ask him to arrange my release.'

'Willoughby has left town.'

Chang was taken aback. 'Left? Where did he go?'

'I've no idea.' Truthful enough, Jesse thought. For some reason Mal wanted these characters held awhile.

'When will he be back?'

Jesse shook his head. 'Well now, I couldn't say. This isn't his hometown. He just took off. Maybe he's gone home for a while.'

Bewildered, Chang looked about him. 'I shouldn't be in here. My papers are in order, but I've lost them. I think Wu Tin stole them to drag me down. He's the one without papers, but I was taking him back to Cooktown where his employers will speak for him. You have to help me, Mr Field. I can pay . . .'

Jesse listened patiently and promised to do what he could. He knew it would take weeks for Immigration to receive an answer from Cooktown with proof of these men's identities, and felt guilty to be in possession of Chang's papers. In reparation, he offered to see what he could do.

'Thank you, sir. And please to hold this bundle with my horse money for safe-keeping.'

'There's no gold here, is there? Gold has to be declared.'

'No. Only my earnings and a few valuables. Not safe in here, you understand. But Mr Field, could you not speak to your friend the Governor? Tell him I am a man of good character. This is a harsh place for an innocent man.'

'I'll see what I can do,' Jesse said again. He wished he knew what Mal was up to. He still couldn't figure out what on earth would cause him to be dashing back up there, especially since he'd travelled down to Cairns at a leisurely pace, with no hint of any urgency.

'Oh well, time will tell,' he shrugged as he set off to cover the commencement of the building of the new shopping block. Ted Pask, Director of Apollo Properties, had collared the mayor to turn the first sod, and the widow Mrs Caporn was to be guest of honour at a slap-up luncheon to mark the occasion. There was talk that Sir Lyle Horwood and Lady Horwood would be in attendance but they hadn't arrived on the scene, so that left Pask and the mayor vying for the limelight. The reception, catered by Hilda Kassel, was to be held in the Community Hall, which still lacked a roof, but the sun was back full blast again. Jesse never enjoyed these functions but he was looking forward to Hilda's food.

And the company, of course, he corrected himself when he came across Eleanor Plummer and Esme Caporn standing shyly by the door, allowing others to press on into the bedecked hall.

'Ladies, you do look elegant. May I have the pleasure of escorting you to the banquet?'

'Oh, Jesse, thank goodness you're here,' Esme whispered. 'Eleanor didn't want to have to go in on her own and I don't want to sit at the official table and have people staring at me.'

'Then don't,' Jesse said. 'Come in with me and I'll find seats for the three of us. By the way, for the record, are you still secretary of the company, Esme?'

'Oh no. Mr Pask has taken that over. I'm much relieved not to have to worry about it any more. When did you get back, Jesse?'

'Yesterday.'

'And is Mal staying with you?'

'No. We no sooner got back to town than he up and left again.'

'He left?' Eleanor cried. 'Without even coming to see us?'

'I don't think he's far away. To be honest, I don't know what he's up to at the minute.'

'Did he find Tussup?' Esme asked nervously.

'That I don't know either. He wasn't saying much at all.'

Just then the mayor swept up, looking hot and bothered in a dark suit and bowler hat. 'Come along, my dear,' he said, grasping Esme by the arm. 'Sorry I'm late. In we go!'

'But I'd rather not sit up there . . .' Esme tried, but he wouldn't have it.

'Nonsense. If it weren't for your dear departed husband's foresight we wouldn't be here today.'

As he whisked Esme away, Eleanor turned back to Jesse. 'She won't enjoy herself up there.'

'It won't be for long. Besides, there is more fuss coming for her yet. They've taken up a collection in the town to present Neville's widow with a small token of their appreciation. She's to receive an engraved silver rose bowl which will contain an envelope,' he grinned, 'which will contain fifty pounds!'

'How very nice.' Eleanor gathered up her skirts. 'We'd better go in now and you can tell me what you and Mal have been doing.'

Jake shared the bunkhouse behind the pub with the timbermen. He bought a ticket on a coastal steamer leaving for Brisbane in two days, and returned to the pub where he feigned exhaustion and spent most of the day on his bunk. He emerged that night to join his friends for a meal and a few drinks under the stars, but disappeared when the booze was flowing freely enough to bring on arguments with other drinkers.

The next morning he learned that police had been called to restore order, but no one had been arrested. His mates sat around the bunkhouse with a bottle of rum for the cure, and someone tossed him a newspaper.

Jake found himself staring at a photograph of Mrs Plummer and Mrs Caporn – two women from the ship – taken at a local function. He read where the *late* Mr Neville Caporn had set up a company to build shops in the town, backed by Sir Lyle Horwood . . .

God Almighty! he muttered under his breath. Are they all here? What are they doing here? I'd never have set foot in this bloody tin-pot town if I'd known they were here.

'I think I'll have a swig of that rum after all,' he said, and the bottle was passed on to him.

Jake Tussup had plenty of sleep that day, and at nightfall he farewelled his friends, walked quietly over to the wharves and boarded the ship that was due to sail on the early tide. He had taken a first-class cabin, where he could keep out of sight until he reached Brisbane. Then it would be time to make serious decisions. He couldn't go back to sea and he had no wish to remain on the run for the rest of his life. As it was, he had to pray that he was not already acquainted with any of this crew.

Jesse was in his office, busy with a plethora of news items, but at his editor's request he began another piece about the severe storm damage to the town, and yet another human interest story – about the small boy who'd lost his pet carpet snake in the storm and, to his parents' horror, had brought home a venomous roughscale to replace it.

Soon, though, his pen was flowing with news of a successful telephone line between Sydney and Maitland; the game of tennis first played in Australia at the Melbourne cricket ground; many Chinese killed in a fight between miners in Maytown; seamen threatening a six-week strike in protest against employment of Chinese crews; and the Kelly gang declared outlaws with rewards of five hundred pounds for the capture, alive or dead, of each.

'Phew,' he said. 'That's hot!' Jesse had a soft spot for the battling Kelly lads.

He sat back and was rereading the background to that saga, sent to this paper by a stringer in Melbourne, when Mal walked into his office.

'Can you spare a minute?'

'Yes. Sure. Come on in. Have a seat.' He jumped up and moved a bundle of papers from a chair, relegating them to the top of a heap on the floor. 'Now, when did you get back?'

'I got back just now,' Mal said, taking off a dusty jacket. 'Have you still got Chang's papers?'

'Yes, do you want them? I've got them in this drawer here somewhere . . .' He bent over to check, but Mal told him to leave them for a minute.

'I have to talk to you. I've been back to the Hodgkinson. Not all the way to the upper river – I didn't have to. I got talking to police along the way and finally got what I was looking for.'

'Which was?'

'The news that a man's body was found in the forest on the way to Merthyr's Ferry.'

Jesse grabbed the pencil from behind his ear. 'A body? Who? What happened to him?'

'The body,' Mal said wearily, 'was Jake Tussup. He'd been shot in the back.'

'What? God help us! You didn't shoot him, did you?'

'No. I heard a whisper about a murder out on that road, and it was worrying me. That's why I went back. To see if there was any truth in it.'

Jesse took his time lighting his pipe. He stared at Mal, and nodded. 'I see. There *was* truth in this whisper, there *was* a body and it just happened to be Jake Tussup.'

'Yes.'

'And is that all there is to it, this instant investigation of yours?'

'No, there's a lot more to it.'

'I would bloody hope so,' Jesse growled. He ran his hand through a thatch of steel-grey hair. 'Can you hang about a while? I've got stuff to finish here but I won't be long.'

'Suits me. I'll wash up and grab a meal somewhere, and come back.'

'See you do. I'll have the desk cleared for this one.'

When Mal returned he bought Jesse a beef bun, some pickled onions and a bottle of beer.

'This might take a while,' he explained, 'so go on, eat up.'

As Jesse munched on the bun, Mal began explaining his latest meeting with Chang and the information Chang had given him.

'He told me this happily,' Mal almost wailed. 'He thought I'd be pleased that he'd saved me the trouble. Said Wu Tin could back him up. They'd tracked Tussup all the way down from the Palmer River. Caught him. Shot him!'

Mal slapped his hands together and then threw them apart, palms wide, in exasperation. 'Just like that!'

'They murdered him?'

'Right first go! That's why I went back. To find out if they were telling the truth.'

'So you manoeuvred them down here into the stockade to give yourself time.'

'Yes. But now we come to the tricky part. Chang's no fool. He has already warned me that if I hand them over to the police, they'll deny it. Claim it was the other way round: that I killed Tussup and boasted that I'd finally got him. You see . . . he claims he'd have no reason to kill Tussup, but, Jesse, he does. He was being paid to find Tussup and kill him, paid by Jun Lien's family in China.'

'Whoa! Where did all this come from?' Jesse reached for the bottle and a pewter mug. 'Do you want a drink?'

'No. I had a couple at the pub.'

They went over the details of Tussup's murder and Jesse was surprised to hear Mal blaming himself. 'When I came back from China, I was in such a rage I called them all murderers. And I had those posters printed, advertising Bartie Lee and Jake Tussup as murderers. To my mind, at that time, they were. I blamed the lot of them for Jun Lien's death.'

'Understandable,' Jesse sighed. 'But what's done is done. Nothing you can do about that now.'

'How can you say that? I set the dogs on the man. Basically I'm responsible for his death. Don't you remember what Constance Horwood said? That Tussup risked his life by sneaking her out of Bartie Lee's camp, finding her some clothes and getting her across the river into Cooktown? When I heard that, I wasn't impressed, I was so hardened against them all. I wouldn't have cared if Tussup had delivered her safely to Cairns.'

'Ah, you're too hard on yourself. Allow remorse if you must, Mal, but not guilt. Tussup was on the run from the law, not from you. It's tough times up north; he could have been shot by the police.'

'It's no use, Jesse. I just can't wipe the slate like that. I'm going to hand Chang and Wu Tin over to the police and make a statement regarding mitigating circumstances – see, I learned a bit about the law in prison,' he smiled. 'I'll explain that I'm to blame for the whole thing.'

'No!' Jesse shouted, almost toppling from his chair. 'No. That's what Chang wants you to do! Jesus. Mal, you don't want to go through all that legal madness again, do you? You're the obvious suspect. The Chinamen at best could go down as your partners in crime, at worst as only carrying out your dirty work. Can't you see what Chang's saying? Not just that he'll shift the blame to you. No. He's saying that if they go down you go down with them!'

'I know.'

'Well, know this, chum. If you turn up in the courts again, people will start wondering if you really were innocent of robbery and murder over that gold assignment. I know you didn't do it and you were given a pardon, but mud sticks, Mal. And it will land solidly on you this time if you stick your neck out.'

Despite the persuasiveness of this viewpoint, Jesse felt he might still lose the argument, so he stalled for time. 'I don't want you to do anything until that body is identified.'

'It's Jake Tussup.'

'What if it isn't? What if that pair are stringing you along?'

'They're not.'

Jesse cleared his throat. 'You asked about and the police up there told you a body had been found. Did you offer to identify it?'

'No. I just said I'd heard in the pub that a body had been found.'

'Who identified it then?'

'No one.'

'So how do they know it's Tussup?'

'They don't. But I do. They don't know who it is . . . was.'

'All right. That does it. You can leave those birds in the cage until I find out who the dead man is, and in the meantime, Sonny, for God's sake do nothing. Don't go making a damn fool of yourself claiming to be able to identify a body you haven't set eyes on.'

Jesse felt worn out by the argument. 'I've got more work to do. You go on home and get some rest. I'll see you later. On second thoughts, why don't you go and visit the ladies, Eleanor and Esme? You're their blue-eyed boy!'

'Me? Since when? I thought you were the Romeo around here.'

Jesse walked to the main entrance of the Cairns *Post* with Mal and watched him ride off. Made sure he rode off, before he slipped down the street to have a serious talk with his friend Sergeant Connor.

'I've got some news for you. There's been a murder out near Merthyr's Ferry.'

'Who says so?'

'Bush telegraph. Your troopers haven't identified the body yet, but I thought you ought to know before they bury it and lose their memories.'

'They better bloody not do that again,' Connor muttered. 'I'll get someone up there right off.'

'Yes, we have to try to look dignified,' Jesse declared, 'and give the murdered man a decent burial.'

'And you a better story! Who did it, do you know?'

'No. I only heard he was shot in the back. But I want to ask a favour. I've got a little Chinese bloke in the stockade. His name's Wu Tin. He's only a servant, brought in by the Li brothers. If you don't object, I'd like to telegraph Sergeant Gooding in Cooktown and ask him if he'd confirm this with the Li people, and get me the number of the entry permit.'

'Sure, go ahead. It'll save me the trouble and the telegraph fees can go on the *Post*'s bill.'

Jesse raced over to the post office to send his carefully composed telegram, reply paid, to keep Gooding on side, and then he tramped back to his desk.

He pulled out Chang's immigration papers and copied out the details before replacing the original papers.

He gave a sigh of satisfaction for his efforts so far. 'You told me to mind his papers, Mal,' he murmured. 'So they can stay right here. You didn't say anything about copying them, though.'

After that he stepped out of the office and marched around the front to the shipping office where he purchased two third-class tickets on a Japanese ship. It was the only northbound ship in the port and was scheduled for departure on Saturday morning; first stop Cooktown, then Singapore.

This will please Chang and his mate, he thought. It won't please Mal, but it's for his own good. I can't bring back Tussup, but if I get this pair out of the country they can't implicate him in the murder. I just have to keep hoping that Mal doesn't break and dob them in, and that the accusing eye of the law doesn't look in their direction before I can get rid of them.

To keep Chang quiet, he went round to the stockade and let him know that with luck he should have him and Wu Tin out of there by Friday.

Chang was delighted, most grateful for his kindness. 'Is Mr Willoughby back yet?' he asked.

'Yes. He sent me to get all this fixed up. He's at home. Not well. He has a fever.'

'I thought you said his home was elsewhere.'

'Indeed it is, Chang. But when he is here for short times, he stays at my home.'

'Ah. The home is yours, sir? Does the Governor come to visit?'

'No, I'm afraid not. I'm a newspaperman. Not important enough.'

'You are a very kind man, sir.'

'You don't know how kind, you bastard,' Jesse growled as he strode away.

Gooding sent back the information he needed regarding Wu Tin's papers, so all was in order. Jesse planned to get the Chinese out and on to that ship on Friday night. This being Thursday, on the wane, he knew he'd have to sweat out the next twenty-four hours. If Mal decided to visit them at the stockade in that time, they wouldn't be going anyplace. Maybe he could think of something for Mal to do in the meantime. Keep him busy.

When he arrived home he found his friend down the back of his block with Lulu, trying to rejuvenate her vegetable garden.

'The rain really pounded it,' he said to Jesse, 'but some of the cabbages could survive.'

'They're full of dirt!' Lulu grumbled. 'All ruination here.'

'It will wash out,' Mal said cheerfully.

'I was talking to Franz Kassel,' Jesse said. 'They've started rebuilding the hotel but they're shorthanded. Do you reckon you could give them a hand for a couple of days?'

Mal straightened up. 'Yes, I suppose so. Any news from Sergeant Connor?'

'Not yet. It's too soon. Saturday night might see some activity.'

Busily organising Mal's time, he announced that he'd invited Eleanor and Esme to dinner that evening, sending Lulu into a panic. She rushed off to the kitchen, unimpressed when the two men, following her, offered to help.

'You help?' she screeched. 'No fear. You get away!'

Jesse laughed. 'That leaves us with time to fill in. You set up the card table on the veranda, Mal, and I'll get the drinks. It was fortunate I invited them, Eleanor said she had something to celebrate this evening.'

'Like what?'

'She said she'd tell us later.'

After an excellent dinner, served by a calm and smiling Lulu, Eleanor made her announcement.

'I am now a single woman again, having extricated myself from a disastrous marriage. Wouldn't you say that's something to celebrate?'

They all agreed.

'So what now?' Mal said. 'Will you go back to Hong Kong, or on to Brisbane as you originally planned?'

'Oh, I'll be staying here. I have a year's lease on Mr Kincaid's house. That will give me time to make up my mind. And next month, my dear friend Gertrude will be coming to visit. I believe the winters here are most pleasant.'

'They are,' Jesse said. 'A joy to behold. You ought to stay on, Mal.'

'No, I'm heading south. I like a chill in the air, and log fires.'

Listening to them, Esme smiled; she couldn't think of anything to say. It was pleasant here. Safe. But it was such a small town, and everywhere she went, people treated her kindly. Too kindly. Almost addressing her in whispers. The widow. She supposed it would wear off.

She'd done some extricating too, she mused. Neville had been wrong, telling her that they were who they were – in other words they were a couple of spivs – and that was that. He could not see, nor did he wish to see, any way that they might alter their paths, try going straight. He was a risk-taker, stimulated by roguery. Probably, she thought sadly, he'd have found earning the honest quid damn boring. And in the end, the risk he took was one too many. He had risked his life to pull in that damned woman.

My Neville was a hero in the end, she pondered. Who would have thought it? He never had a lot of time for heroes.

And in the end I got myself out of this building scam, by the skin of my teeth. But for me it's not the end, it's the beginning. Of what? I'll have to get a job of some sort. Dammit! I don't know if I'm ready for this.

'You're very quiet tonight,' Jesse said to her, and she lit up her face with a practised smile.

'Not really. I was wondering when Mal is going to tell us if he managed to locate Tussup.'

'No, Es,' Mal said, unaware that he'd shortened her name, as Neville used to. Neville hadn't ever liked her name, and neither had she, but to be contrary she'd refused to change it. 'We're following leads, nothing yet. But the scenery up there was worth the trip. It's magnificent, isn't it, Jesse?'

'Yes, I saw the falls in style, part of Kennedy's entourage.'

Esme was startled when Jesse suggested they play cards. 'Do you play, Eleanor?'

'Oh yes, I enjoy cards. What about you, my dear, do you play?' she asked Esme, who gulped and nodded.

'What will we play?' Mal asked. 'What about euchre? We have a four. Do you ladies know euchre?'

Esme managed a weak 'yes', thinking she knew every card game known to man. Even the new one beginning to do the rounds . . . whist. She was an expert card player and she knew how to win.

Oh Lord, she worried. I really have to watch myself now; try to make sure I don't cheat.

Esme took this new foray into cards very seriously, ignoring the opportunities presented in this friendly game but, nevertheless, Mal was ecstatic.

'We wiped the floor with them, partner,' he crowed after the game, giving her a hug, and Jesse felt relieved that his plans were proceeding on schedule.

Chapter Nineteen

Jake Tussup yearned for the day when he could stop looking over his shoulder. As he stepped ashore in Brisbane he was thinking that if he hadn't been lumbered with Bartie Lee and his mob, he'd be a rich man by this time, guilty only of deserting his ship, a common occurrence in ports with access to goldfields. If he'd been able to move about normally, he'd have kept prospecting in the Palmer with proper equipment and advice, and invested in a syndicate that would provide the resources to dig deeper. Then he'd have moved on to new fields, with his bank balance multiplying by the day and . . . He sighed – no use going over all that again – and trudged into the town.

He checked into a hotel in the wide main street, and then took himself off to a gentlemen's outfitters where he purchased a decent wardrobe and a fine pigskin suitcase. Next door, he had his beard trimmed, rejecting the barber's advice that whiskers were going out of fashion.

Back in his hotel room, he dressed in his new finery and paraded before the wardrobe mirror.

'I have to look my best today,' he said to his image. 'I'm mixing with class this day, I hope. That is, if I don't get chucked out on my head.'

Locked in his cabin, claiming seasickness, he'd had time to work on a plan. A bold plan, which would be 'Sydney or the bush', as a betting man would say. But definitely worth a try. 'And where to start?' he asked himself, more with bravado than courage, 'but the top.'

He enquired and learned that Parliament House was only three blocks away. It was a long stone building on the riverfront, and the sandstone was sheer beauty. It had a gentleness about it, surrounded as it was by palms and plush green trees, the trademark of this colony, he thought, as he strode manfully in the gate.

'I wish to see a Member of the Parliament,' he asked a liveried gentleman in the foyer.

'Yes, sir. And which gentleman might that be?'

'Mr Raymond Lewis,' Jake said, his heart thumping.

'I'm very sorry sir, but Mr Lewis is no longer a Member of the Parliament.

But his rooms are not far from here, in Charlotte Street. Do you have his address?'

'No.' Jake lost the wind from his sails. He stood mutely while the polite fellow wrote the address on a card and handed it to him.

'Good day to you, sir.'

There were the rooms all right, Jake pondered, and there were the names on a gold shingle outside the door. 'LEWIS & McLEISH, Solicitors.'

He hadn't banked on Mr Lewis being a lawyer. On the passenger list he'd been listed as an MP, not as a lawyer. This put a different complexion on things. What if Lewis had him arrested before he'd even opened his mouth? And he got thrown into the nearest lockup? In these new clothes, and with a sweet-smelling new leather wallet fat with notes? Jesus! His legs almost gave way under him.

This time it took real effort to push in the glass door, follow the long panelled corridor with its clacking red and brown tiled floor, past other equally intimidating doors with their gold lettering and 'please knock,' until he was confronted by the name again, and forced himself to obey the instruction and knock. Timidly.

'Enter,' a woman called, and he did, closing the door quietly behind him.

'What can we do for you, sir?' she enquired, from behind a high desk.

'Mr Lewis,' he croaked. 'Can I see Mr Lewis?'

She was very attractive, with neat blonde hair and a sweet smile. 'I'm sorry, sir. Mr Lewis is not taking any more appointments. He has resigned this office, but would you like to see Mr McLeish?'

'No, thank you.' Jake's hand, the one holding his new felt hat, was sweating. He felt claustrophobic in here, as if McLeish might dash out and arrest him. 'I'm a friend of Mr Lewis. An old friend. Where can I find him then?'

Swiftly she did her duty. She wrote the address and handed it to him. 'This will find Mr Lewis, sir.'

'Thank you,' he said, trying to produce a smile in gratitude for hers, and blundered out.

He walked to Lewis's house, high on a hill in a leafy suburban street. Even though it already had a lofty view, the large white house with a wraparound veranda was built on stilts, the more to catch the breezes below and above.

He pushed the gate open and began to walk up the path, but a tall woman coming from the side of the house approached him.

'I'm looking for Mr Lewis,' he said quickly.

'Oh yes. Very well. Go on up those steps.' As he headed for the steps he heard her call out, 'Raymond, you have a visitor!'

'Righto!'

Jake knew the voice. It was Mr Lewis all right. No backing out now. Jake was actually puffing as he laboured up to the veranda of that house, despite being in fit condition, his invisible burdens weighing as heavily as any load.

Raymond saw him coming up the steps, taking them two at a time – a fine stamp of a fellow, neatly dressed, no fripperies. Raymond abhorred the current fashion for jewelled cufflinks and tiepins, worn during daylight hours.

He walked through from the parlour to meet the stranger at the front door, wondering who it might be. He seemed slightly familiar but Raymond was dashed if he could put a name to him.

The door to the veranda was open, and the visitor stood a way back from the coir doormat as Raymond approached.

'Good day to you,' he said, still puzzling. 'Did you wish to see me?'

'Yes, sir.' The stranger looked behind him, peering out over the railing as if he might take a short cut down that way in a single leap.

'Then come on in,' Raymond said cheerily, stepping back, ushering, but his visitor hesitated.

'Don't you recognise me, Mr Lewis?' The voice was more incredulous than plaintive.

'Should I?' Raymond leaned forward. 'I seem to think I should . . .' And then he stiffened. 'Good God! It's not? It's . . . it's Tussup. You're First Officer Tussup! What are you doing here? I trusted you'd be in a lockup by this.'

Tussup shrugged. 'I need your help. I had nowhere else to turn.'

'Why me, man? I would have thought I'd be the last person you'd want to have any parley with.'

'Mr Lewis, I thought since you were in the parliament you'd know all about laws, but then I found out you were a solicitor and that's even better.'

'Are you saying you want me to act for you, after what you did?' Raymond was outraged. 'You've got a damn cheek, you have. I should send for the police right now.'

Tussup flushed. 'What are you, judge and jury? I am not a murderer. I am not! Yet when I read about me in the papers and see my face in posters they say I am. I want you to tell me, Mr Lewis, who did I murder?'

'You haven't been charged with murder,' Raymond said uneasily.

'That's a cop-out, that is. What's to stop some hillbilly policeman bailing me up on the charge? Or some cowboy making a name for himself by plugging the outlaw Tussup? Hounding me like the Kelly brothers are being hounded!'

'You could have given yourself up.'

'That's what I'm trying to do, but I need your protection.'

'Why should I protect you?'

'Because you know I didn't kill anyone and yet you never lifted a finger to set the record straight. To give me sporting chance!' Tussup was shouting. 'A man in your position, you could have spoken up, told the papers they were wrong, they would have listened to you, but no, you didn't care. So much for you and the law! You're a humbug, Lewis!'

Raymond was shocked by this accusation. He could see his sister had stopped halfway up the front steps, undecided as to whether she should go on or go back. Tussup had turned on his heel and was storming away.

'Wait,' he called. 'Wait a minute!'

'Why? So you can send for the police to remove me from your conscience?'

'No. Just stop a minute! You come to my door out of the blue, asking for help and the next thing I know I'm the villain.'

Tussup stopped. Lavinia hurried up the steps. He stood back with a polite, 'ma'am' as she scuttled past him and hurried away from them to enter the house through the French doors at the end of the veranda.

'Come on in,' Raymond said, with an exaggerated sigh, as if he were wondering why he was allowing this, but in truth he was rehashing Tussup's accusation. Was he a humbug? Should he have contacted the editors and pointed out their error? Should he have remonstrated with Mal Willoughby over those posters, when he'd known full well they were not correct? He supposed he should have, come to think of it, but it hadn't entered his head. It simply had not.

He led the fellow into his study, rather than to the parlour, to keep this visit on a business-like basis, offered him a chair by the desk and took his place behind it. 'Now am I to understand you wish to engage my services as a solicitor, Mr Tussup?'

'If you will.'

Raymond's heart sank. He could still send the fellow away. He should. Imagine what his fellow passengers would have to say about this. Especially Mal and Esme. And Constance.

'Good heavens,' he muttered, jerking out of his ruminations. Constance! There'd be no complaints from her. She wanted to see him. Desperately.

'Mr Tussup, tell me about the abduction of the two women, right from the word go. I need to know every detail truthfully, including the manner of Mrs Horwood's escape from you people . . . from her captors, as it were.'

He took up a pad and pencil and began making notes as Tussup gave his statement, a long and carefully worded report, which Raymond accepted as being true to Constance's story, except for a few minor differences. She'd said she had no idea where her rough clothing had come from, but Tussup cleared that up, explaining he'd bought them from a woman in a camp. Constance said she'd escaped from him in Cooktown but Tussup claimed she was becoming hard to cope with, so he'd let her go. But only for a few minutes. He then worried about leaving her alone at night in a rough town like that, but when he turned to take her in hand again she was gone. He couldn't find her.

'I suppose you thought you were well rid of her anyway,' Raymond snapped.

Tussup was frank. 'In a way, yes. I was in enough trouble. What happened to her then? I saw her name in the paper a few times after that so I knew she was all right.'

'I'll let her tell you herself,' Raymond said sourly.

'Mrs Horwood?' Tussup was confused.

'Never mind about that now. I want you to go back to the very beginning. How this whole dreadful business came about.'

This time Raymond interrupted the narrative several times, to get the full picture. He had Tussup explain how Bartie Lee had ended up his partner in a gold mining venture, when they'd been enemies in Cooktown.

'Partner?' Tussup said savagely. 'Blackmailer more like it. His Chinese had run off on him, and by the sounds of things the Malay crew had run off too, so he leeched on to me. I had to watch my back with him around, believe me.'

Lavinia knocked. 'Your visitor has been here quite a while, Raymond. Would you like some afternoon tea?'

'Yes, we would.' Raymond rose from his chair, excused himself and followed Lavinia out of the room, wheeling her by the arm into the dining room.

'Do you know who that is in there?'

'No. Who?'

'Tussup,' he hissed.

'Who is Tussup?'

'The officer from the *China Belle*. The mutineer.' He checked himself, with Tussup's defence beginning to take shape. 'I mean the deserter.'

'What's he doing here?' she whispered, with due concern for the situation.

'He wants me to represent him. He's tired of being on the run.'

'Well, I never. And I thought he looked such a nice fellow.'

It was a long and tiring afternoon, but Raymond put together as much information as he thought he'd need, sitting back in his leather chair and mulling over his options.

'What should I do now?' Tussup asked.

'I want you to go back to your hotel. What hotel was it again?'

'The Treasury.'

'Ah yes, I know it. Excellent food. Yes, stay there, and tomorrow I'll take you to meet the Police Commissioner, Mr Salter, and we'll get this sorted out.'

'Will I go to gaol?'

'There is every possibility that you will, Mr Tussup, but I'll do my best.'

'Thank you, sir. That's all I can ask for. I just want this all over with and, believe me, no one is sorrier than I am about everything that happened. My plan got totally out of control. I had no idea that it would turn out so bad.'

Raymond changed his mind. The following day he called on his friend Jasper Salter, and invited him to lunch at the Queensland Hotel, where a new Italian chef was said to be serving magnificent meals.

'Are you celebrating your retirement?' Jasper asked as they took their places at a quiet table by the window, overlooking the Botanic Gardens.

'Oh no, I haven't quite retired yet, I have one more case and I need your advice. My client is First Officer Tussup from the *China Belle*.'

'The ship you were on? Wasn't Tussup the leader of the mutineers?'

'No. And there wasn't a mutiny. They didn't take over the ship, they deserted. A different thing altogether, wouldn't you agree?'

'Pack of thugs whatever way you look at it. I'm surprised you, of all people, should want to defend that bloke! God stone the crows, Raymond. After what happened on that ship! Two dead. Women beaten, abducted, other passengers roughed up. I read every word about it because you were on that ship. My wife and I were worried sick about you.'

They had an excellent lunch and Raymond walked back to the Commissioner's office with him, still debating the issue.

'He wants to give himself up, Raymond, so for God's sake go and get him.'

'It would help if I knew what he was to be charged with, because there's not a lot here, Jasper. In fact he's only a deserter. Hundreds and hundreds of men deserted ships for the goldfields in Melbourne; the owners were desperate for crews. Were they arrested and charged?'

'I suppose not. Let me think about this.'

'What's worrying Tussup is that he has been branded a murderer, far and wide, when in fact he didn't kill anyone and he rescued Lady Horwood from those thugs the first chance he got.'

Jasper slumped into his chair. 'I think I ate too much. That was a bloody good feed. I understand what you're saying and, what's more, Tussup's got strong support with Lady Horwood to speak on his behalf.'

Raymond didn't bother to disavow him on that score, given Constance's delicate health. The last thing she'd do was appear in court over the very subject she and Lyle were trying to make disappear.

'Come to think of it,' Jasper pondered, 'if any papers called him a murderer – and Willoughby stated categorically in the posters he distributed that Tussup was a murderer – well, the fellow would be within his rights to sue for libel.'

'Don't put ideas in his head,' Raymond groaned.

'It's a point, though.'

'What happened to the other fellow? The second officer, Tom Ingleby? He was one of the party leaving the ship but his longboat overturned. He was taken into custody in Cairns and sent on to Brisbane. His case would have a bearing on Tussup's situation.'

'Ah, yes. A peculiar situation there, come to think of it. He was here in the watch house, on remand—'

'Charged with what? I don't recall, there was so much confusion at the time.'

'Mutiny,' Jasper grinned. 'The Cairns police decided that would do, but his father is on the Brisbane Town Council and he made a helluva ruckus about it, on much the same grounds you've mentioned. But then Sir Lyle Horwood arrived on the scene and had the charges dismissed! That was a surprise, I can tell you. Instead, they charged Ingleby with theft of a longboat!'

'Theft? He was charged with theft?'

'Yes, true as I stand here. He was fined, the months he'd spent on remand taken into account, and he was let go. I had the impression that poor old Horwood was sick of the whole business. He told me he just wasn't up to court cases after the ordeals he'd already suffered.'

'I can imagine,' Raymond said bleakly.

'But of course your fellow's situation is much more complicated. The death of one woman and the abduction of another. The deaths of crew members on the goldfields. There should be an official inquiry now to sort out the whole mess. You surely wouldn't have any objections?'

'No, but I don't think Sir Lyle and Lady Horwood will co-operate.'

'Why not?'

'For the same reason you've already stated. They're both fed up with the whole thing, they just want to put it behind them. The Attorney General would be better advised to put a couple of his people on to it, to draw up a full report for him. The Horwoods would see his investigators in private without a fuss. And he wouldn't have the expense of bringing all the players down here from as far afield as Cooktown.'

Jasper nodded. 'I suppose you're right.'

Raymond didn't press the point. Tussup, he knew, came from Goulburn in New South Wales. He even had a property there. If he decided he wouldn't co-operate with a judicial inquiry he only needed to cross the border from the Colony of Queensland into his home colony and there'd be a devil of a job to get him back. And besides, as Tussup's solicitor, he dreaded bringing his client face to face with Willoughby, whose misguided but understandable accusations could stir up trouble. No, an open inquiry had to be avoided. Tussup would have a much better chance one to one with an investigator from the Attorney General's office.

'Also,' he said, 'I doubt if the widow, Mrs Caporn, would appreciate having to appear at an inquiry when the brutes who assaulted her are all dead. I mean, what's the point, Jasper? When you come down to it, all the real villains have gone to meet their Maker.'

'So what do I do now?' Tussup asked, when Lewis explained the situation.

'Just wait. You can't leave town. It might take some time. These things do drag on, so you might wish to move to cheaper lodgings.'

'I don't think so. I like it here.'

'Then I gather you had some success on the goldfields.'

'You could say that. But I'd have done better if I hadn't been hounded.'

'Is that so?' Raymond snapped, resisting the urge to rub his badly scarred leg. 'You caused dreadful havoc in people's lives. I am concerned that you don't appear to suffer any remorse at all. Your friend Bartie Lee nearly killed Mal Willoughby.'

'Nearly? What happened?'

'There was a fight. Mal Willoughby killed him.'

'Hah!' Tussup was jubilant. 'So that bastard's dead? Good riddance! But you stop and think, Mr Lewis. The bush boy, Willoughby, was on the warpath. Had that been me and not Bartie Lee, I could be turning up my toes now. So don't tell me I wasn't being hounded! For my very life!'

Raymond gave up. 'Don't move from here without advising me, or you could be hounded again. This time by a police force, not by a couple of overworked country police.'

When he left, Jake was jubilant. Lewis was a cranky old gent but he'd shown him things weren't so bad after all. It was obvious that the solicitor didn't like him, and that was to be expected. But who cared?

He walked out into the busy street, gazing fondly at all the trappings of civilisation after the sickening privations of the wilderness, and eventually called a horse-cab, for the sheer delight of exploring this river port in comfort. Compared to that other river port, Cooktown, he shuddered, this place is heaven.

After they'd been round the town a couple of times and through the riverside gardens, he told the driver to take him to the offices of the *Brisbane Courier*, where he asked to see the editor.

'He's rather busy. Was it important, sir?' a young fellow enquired, and Jake announced that he had very important news for the *Courier*.

'What would that be?' the editor asked impatiently as he was steered into his cluttered office.

'My name is Mr Jake Tussup and I intend to sue this paper for the sum of ten thousand pounds.'

'Ah yes. Why is that?'

'Because you called me a murderer on your front page some time back, and I am not a murderer. Never was. Never will be. So you're looking at a very serious libel case.'

'When was this?'

'Weeks back. The name again, Jake Tussup, formerly first officer on the *China Belle*.'

The editor nodded slowly. 'Oh yes, I remember you. The mutineer. You've got a cheek coming in here!'

'Watch yourself. I'm not a mutineer either. That's libellous. I think I'll just sit down here and have a smoke while you do a little checking.'

He cast an eye about and saw the name James J. Boddy on some sort of citation on the wall and guessed he was in the presence of the same, who hesitated a few seconds before leaving the office without a word.

Curiosity itself came past several times in the form of newspaper workers – reporters or clerks, Jake couldn't tell – but they all peered in at him and hurried away.

Mr James J. Boddy took his time. He returned with another gentleman from, as he was told, their legal department, though no names were exchanged.

'Which exact page are you referring to?' he asked.

'All of the pages in which you mentioned me.' Jake guessed there could be more than that one page he'd sighted in an old paper, when he was leaving Mayfield. At the time he didn't dare ask if he could have the paper. Besides, it hadn't bothered him as much as Willoughby's posters, there being no photos, and he'd almost forgotten the incident until his enforced quiet time on the ship to Brisbane.

'I'm afraid I don't recall any mention of you,' James Boddy said.

'That's all right, gentlemen. You have until this time tomorrow to find them.'

His cab was waiting.

'Is there a library in this town?' he asked the driver.

'Sure is. Would you be wanting to go there?'

'Indeed I do,' Jake grinned.

The librarian was helpful. Yes, they did have copies of the newspapers. The current copies of the *Courier* were available if the gentleman wished to read them.

'What about older ones?' he asked, and learned they were in the archival section but were certainly available also.

Jake requested papers from the date they'd left the ship, and settled down to acquaint himself with everything about the subject from that day, but he was not prepared for the shock of reading that Mrs Willoughby had drowned! All this time he'd thought that her husband had rescued her from the sea. Hadn't he seen Willoughby in the water with her? Seen him begin the swim back to the ship with her, before the longboat ploughed away, making for the shore?

She'd jumped overboard. No one could have stopped her. She was only a little thing; she'd slipped away from them. Drowned? Christ Almighty! To this minute he hadn't known she'd drowned. He could feel his face go cold, and he shuddered at the thought of the lovely woman lost in the waters, and the pain Willoughby must have experienced, frantically trying to save her life.

Jake leaned back in his chair, taking gulps of breath as if he too needed life-giving air.

'Are you all right, sir?' the librarian asked him. 'Your face has lost its colour. You look ill. Was it something you read there, sir?'

He rose slowly from the chair, feeling faint. 'Can I come back tomorrow and read the rest here?'

'Of course, I'll put them aside for you.'

He stumbled out of the library and walked shakily down the street, knowing now what Lewis had meant about remorse. Knowing now why Willoughby was hunting him. Lewis and Willoughby were friends. How long would it be before Lewis gave him up to the bereaved husband? He'd probably already done so.

Jake decided he'd better get his business in this town over and done with as soon as possible.

He went back to the library and read every single shred of information he could find about the *China Belle* débâcle, amazed to learn that it had been Lewis who'd found Mrs Horwood in Cooktown. He learned that several of the Chinese crew had been captured, and that some of Bartie Lee's gang had died in a mine collapse, finding it curious that Bartie hadn't mentioned that.

The story had drifted to the back pages and faded out altogether. *China Belle* was now history. Jake closed the last page of this day's *Courier* and placed all the papers together again in a neat pile. He had what he'd been looking for, that front page: 'Two mutineers from the doomed ship *China Belle* are known to be on the Palmer goldfields. Both of these murderers, Jake Tussup and Bartie Lee, are armed and are said to be in the company of several Malay and Chinese coolies.'

On two other pages there were small articles with news of Maytown. One stated that a Malay rapist had been captured and there had been sightings of both Jake Tussup and Bartie Lee, wanted for murder. In another instance, two days later, that was repeated.

Jake was punctual for his appointment, gave James Boddy the dates of these entries, and asked if they were willing to settle his libel claims out of court.

'My solicitor, Mr Raymond Lewis, suggests we have a cordial discussion on this matter,' he lied, 'before I make a formal claim of libel against your paper.'

Boddy wasn't convinced. 'We made those statements in good faith, Mr Tussup, and you haven't given us any reason to retract.'

'Is that so? Then I demand here and now that you call in two witnesses and state who it is I murdered.'

The discussions that followed were far from cordial. The argument became so heated Boddy ordered Jake out of his office.

'You're just a cheapskate out to make a quick quid, mister, but you won't get away with it here. You can't blackmail me.'

'This isn't blackmail. It's about my reputation,' Jake snarled.

'Your reputation? That's a laugh, First Officer Tussup. Where's your ship now? I'll tell you where it is. At the bottom of the ocean. Now get out!'

Jake refused to move and there was a mild commotion in the outer office as the legal man, who introduced himself as William Perriman, hurried in.

'I'm sure this can be settled without getting heated,' he said.

'Yes it can,' Boddy retorted. 'Get this shyster out of here.'

Jake shook his head. 'He's just a bag of wind. He can't name anyone I'm supposed to have murdered, so he thinks he can save the day by shunting me out. But it won't work, Mr Perriman. I'll try you then. Who did I murder? That's the crux of this argument.'

When Perriman finally discovered that it was true that Boddy didn't have a name to offer, he was aghast.

'As I tried to tell your mate here,' Jake said, 'my solicitor, Mr Lewis—'

'Raymond Lewis?'

'Yes. He said we should have a cordial discussion about this before resorting to the law.'

'I agree,' Perriman said. He turned to the editor. 'I think I can take this from here, James. Mr Tussup and I will have a little chat.'

Eventually it was agreed that an apology would be printed in the *Courier* and, after some haggling, the sum of two hundred and fifty pounds was agreed upon.

Jake had hoped for a great deal more, but he found that Perriman was no pushover.

'Let's get this straight, Mr Tussup,' he'd said. 'You're accusing us of besmirching your reputation, and I agree that we were misinformed and mistaken by referring to you as a murderer. However, you yourself have besmirched your reputation considerably, as I'm sure Mr Lewis would have pointed out, when he advised discussion. He's a wise man, is Mr Lewis; he would have known that a libel case could shred what remains of that reputation. Two hundred and fifty pounds, take it or leave it.'

'If you put that retraction on the front page, using the word innocent, I'll take three hundred. I'm not a bloody murderer! I want it on the front page of tomorrow's newspaper.'

'Done,' Perriman said, shaking hands with Jake, and escorting him to the door. 'Give my regards to Mr Lewis.'

Dear Mr Lewis,

This is to tell you that I was not to know until yesterday that Mrs Willoughby had drowned. I thought her husband had rescued her when she jumped from the longboat and he swum her to the ship. Tomorrow the *Courier* will print an apology for calling me a murderer and say that I am innocent and I need you to show that page to Mal Willoughby. I know now why he was after me and I'm not hanging around for him to kill me, since he blames me it's plain to see. I do not think the Brisbane police have got anything on me or they would have run me in by this. And that is thanks to you. You can send your bill to me c/o the Sydney GPO.

I remain,
Your obedient servant,
J. Tussup

Raymond threw the letter down on the desk. 'Damn the man! He's made a bloody fool of me. I never should have listened to him!'

He snatched up the letter and marched out to the breakfast room. 'Where's the paper, Lavinia?'

'I was just about to bring it to you. Look at this, it's quite extraordinary. Did you arrange it?'

Raymond peered over her shoulder at a few lines down the very bottom of the page, which read: 'The *Courier* apologises to Mr Jake Tussup for mistakenly referring to him as a murderer. Our writer was misinformed. Mr Tussup is innocent of any such misdeed.'

'No I did not arrange it! Tussup must have leaned on them. But the wretch has run off on me, after Commissioner Salter specifically told me to see he didn't leave town.'

'Why would he do that? You have everything under control.'

Raymond handed her the letter.

'Oh my!' she clucked. 'Oh Lord. Do you really think Mr Willoughby is so hellbent on revenge?'

'It has been worrying me, I must say.'

'And Tussup too now. He must have the wind up, to flee just when you're so close to settling his problems. And what about Constance? Didn't you say you planned to take him to see her? She asked for him.'

He picked up the silver coffee pot from the sideboard and poured himself a cup.

'That'll be cold now,' she said. 'Do you want a fresh pot?'

'No, this will do. I intended to tell him about her today. Obviously he doesn't know that she's had a breakdown. Few people do, for that matter. I can't be worried about Tussup. He can look after himself, but I'm dreadfully disappointed to be letting Constance down. If I'd told Tussup she needed to talk to him he might have stayed a little while longer.'

'I don't think so, Raymond. He seems to me to be a thoroughly irresponsible person. Lord knows how he got to be an officer.'

'Because he's intelligent and he looks the part. And I'm inclined to agree with you, the wretch has been ducking his responsibilities right from the start.' He gulped down cold coffee. 'I suppose I'd best go into town and see Jasper. And get a bawling-out for my troubles.'

Lavinia took back her newspaper. 'If I were you I'd find out what Jasper has to say first, before you tell him the bad news.'

'That Tussup has run for his life? Not from the police but from Willoughby? And open another can of worms? The cad has left me with no explanation for his behaviour. I'll send him a bill, all right. I hadn't intended to, but he'll get a stiff one now. I suppose the best thing I can do is keep him informed of the situation by mail, and demand he returns if necessary.'

He strode back to his study and sat staring out of his window at the creamy blooms on a magnolia tree. 'Sydney, eh?' he muttered. 'Going home, are we?

When the investigations were first begun in Cairns, the police had wanted to know the backgrounds of all *China Belle*'s crew and Captain Loveridge had obliged. He'd said, as Raymond now recalled, that Tussup had come from New South Wales. From Goulburn. If I heard that, he mused, Mal would have too. He was in the room at the time. But would he recall the conversation?

Raymond planned his day. He would see Jasper, come home for lunch, and this afternoon he and Lavinia would visit Constance again. Lavinia wanted to bring her home, to this house, since she wasn't happy about going back to Lyle. She still couldn't accept that Constance did not wish to leave, insisting that the invitation hadn't even been issued yet. She couldn't conceive that the woman would resist being taken under her protective wing. Nor would she stop nagging her brother about taking legal steps to have Constance released. A daunting prospect.

'I thought I could take a holiday, visit Cairns when I retired, but now I'm busier than ever,' he complained to Lavinia as he was leaving.

'Stuff and nonsense,' she said. 'You've very little to do now, and you take all day to do it.'

Mrs Plummer organised a street fête on this day, selling cakes, pies and preserves to aid the victims of the storm, and setting up a long table with second-hand and storm-damaged goods and clothing for sale, at a penny an article. Esme was serving behind the counter when Jesse came along.

'How's business?' he asked her.

'Jolly good. Do you want to buy a sponge cake?'

'Good God, no. Lulu would have a fit. She makes the cakes in my house.'

'Then take this one back to the office with you. Have it for morning tea.'

So, laden with a cake covered in pink icing, he continued on his way to the police station, where he enquired about six horses stolen from Murnane's stables.

'No sign of them yet,' Sergeant Connor told him. 'But what hope have we got with hundreds of itinerants tramping through the town and bands of Chinese setting up camp here? I don't know who's a local and who isn't any more.'

'Chinese don't steal horses.'

'Why not?' Connor asked, genuinely surprised, and Jesse laughed.

'Yeah. What's wrong with our horses? Have you heard any more about the body in the bush? Was it true? And who was he?'

'It was true all right. I dunno when that report would have reached me if you hadn't given me the tip. The stupid constable up there had buried the victim, so I sent orders for him to unbury the body, get a new coffin and bring it down. And no, they couldn't say who it was, but I'll find out. They might get it down tonight. Do you want me to give you a hoy?'

Jesse didn't want Connor alerting Mal before he got that pair of Chinamen on their way. 'No, I won't be home. I'll be working late. I'll call in at the station myself.'

'What's that you've got there?' Connor, famed for his love of food, asked.

'A cake, as if you didn't know. Here, you have it.'

'You're a fine man, Field,' Connor said with a grin, as he took the cake. 'A fine man, if ever there was one.'

A man who's about to let Tussup's murderers leave the country, Jesse worried. Not a lot fine about that.

He left it to the last minute, arriving at the stockade gates just as the guards were shutting down for the night.

Chang and Wu Tin were waiting anxiously for him, and the relief on their faces broadened into nervous smiles as a side gate was opened to allow them to exit.

'We have to hurry,' Jesse said in a whisper, giving the distinct impression that these arrangements were not necessarily legal, which, as he expected, didn't bother them. 'Here are your belongings and Wu Tin's swag. Here's your money for the horses, Chang. And your purses. These are your new papers and two tickets. Now come with me.'

He hurried them down the road to the wharves in the gathering dusk, thankful for the lack of twilight in these northern lands, and by the time they reached the ship it was dark.

Jesse ran up the gangway ahead of them, spoke to the officer of the watch, and handed over the papers. 'They're all in order,' he said cheerily. 'They're happy to be going home and we've got two less for the unions to worry about.'

He went back and sent them on to the ship with a dire warning. 'The ship leaves at first light. So far so good. Just stay on board. Whatever you do don't leave the ship. I don't want you rounded up by overzealous Immigration men.'

Wu Tin scurried about and Chang thanked him cordially. 'Please give my farewells to Mr Willoughby,' he added. 'I am sorry to depart without a chance to speak with him. Is he still sick with the fever?'

'Yes, very ill. Mosquitoes, they say, cause the fevers, and we have plenty.'

'Then I wish him well.'

Jesse watched as Chang walked sedately on to the ship, and the Japanese officer nodded his approval.

'Thank God that's the end of them,' he sighed as he strode back to his office.

Wu Tin was still suspicious. They were, it seemed, safely aboard a ship that would sail in the morning. Or so the white boss said, according to Chang. But it was a Jappie ship, and who could trust Jappies? They might throw us overboard, he fretted. He had been born into servitude. His family had served the awesome Li family for generations, accepting their lowly status without question. When Wu Tin was chosen to go to a foreign land, he was petrified, dreaming, night after night of slathering monsters bent on vile torture, and evil dragons waiting to pounce, to tear him apart.

His wife had no sympathy for him or his nightmares. Instead she shrieked her shame at him, threatening to change her name, for hundreds of coolies were being massed outside of the Li mansions, and she was convinced that her husband had been demoted to coolie status. It was only when his mother used bribes to elicit more information that it was learned that forty family retainers, from squires and stewards and cooks down to the dogsbodies like Wu Tin, would be joining the entourage.

But she learned more from that foray into the corridors of secrets. She learned that the foreign country was far over the seas, so far that the ship (of which the very mention caused piteous wails) that would be carrying them into the unknown could even fall off the ends of the earth.

There was no question of complaint by any of those called up, or even asking the why. They simply went about their preparations as instructed. Wu Tin's swarthy face, with its lantern jaw and drooping eyes, always looked downcast, but now he was even more so. For days his wife had been berating him with her shrill voice and straw broom, for having no money to leave her, causing him great embarrassment; and his mother, already convinced he was destined to fall off the side of the earth, wept loudly, lit candles and donned mourning garments as she prayed for his swift acceptance into the next and better life.

Wu Tin's fears remained. The voyage was sheer terror. The new land was alien, and definitely close to the end of the world. In a jungle town he was assigned to serve Chang, a nobody who thought he was somebody, and forced to walk over mountains inhabited by savages. At the goldfields he was given a horse and expected to know how to ride. He soon learned, and by doing so gained confidence. Never before had he been permitted to ride a horse, and now he knew why. Mounted up there (upon a slow-plodding horse) above heads, servants could get ideas above their station. Wu Tin certainly did. Though outwardly he kept his lowly demeanour, he really saw himself an officer of the Li guard, brave and fearless. A dashing picture that allowed him the courage to raise his eyes slightly, all the better to see the world more clearly.

He became accustomed to his master's needs and served him well, gaining approval from one of young Mr Li's stewards, who, Wu Tin had already observed, was jealous of Chang and was afraid the outsider could replace him. And that steward soon slipped Wu Tin coins to spy on his master, warning him that Chang was not to be trusted. He was up to mischief that could be blamed on his servant, who would then be hanged in a white man's prison and never see his homeland again.

And Wu Tin soon found out Chang did need watching. He saw him kill the Malay seaman and, to his surprise, soon realised that young Mr Li paid for the killing. Next came the man Jake Tussup, and the bewildering news that he, Wu Tin, was expected to be witness to the deed, ordered by young Mr Li. And he had to be sure to witness, so that Chang would be paid for carrying out orders.

But matters had taken a dangerous turn when Chang, obviously stirred by blood lust, had boasted of the killing of Tussup to a white man, his friend Willoughby! And worse, he had implicated his servant!

In Wu Tin's wary eyes, this sudden release from the port prison was too easy. If it were all above board and lawful, why all this stealth? And why did that man hurry them on board after dark? He wondered what Chang was up to this time.

Trembling with fear, Wu Tin hid on the deck near the gangway, watching the comings and goings of the Jappie crew. Chang had shot the man they called Tussup, and Willoughby was shocked and angry with him for that crime. He wanted to tell the police, that much was obvious. Had Chang talked him out of it? Or paid him? Chang was so friendly with these white men, what was to stop them from agreeing to dispose of the only witness? Money had changed hands between them; he'd seen that with his own eyes, at the stockade gate.

Only an hour later, he saw Chang slip across the deck and slink down the gangway.

He knew it! Wu Tin leaped up! Maybe Chang had left him to the Jappies. Paid them to kill him while he disappeared (clean hands, known to be elsewhere). He ran from the ship, swiftly and silently, across the heavy timbers of the wharf and on to the sandy road, keeping Chang in sight.

When Chang approached a group of men standing outside a noisy grog shop, Wu Tin sucked in his breath at his cheek. But the men didn't attack him; he saw them offering directions, pointing the way, and Chang set off again at a leisurely pace. As if he owned the world, Wu Tin thought jealously.

The night was clear, star-spangled and very still. Flying foxes, feeding on fruits and blossoms provided by the tall trees in Jesse's garden, chattered and flapped across the dark sky, upsetting Lulu, who emerged from the house with an umbrella.

'It's not going to rain,' Mal laughed.

'Not rain, it's them damn bats, they get in your hair!'

'No they don't. They're only flying foxes; a fox wouldn't jump in your hair. He's got better things to do.'

'They're still bats!' Lulu sniffed, eyes searching the sky. 'I have to run to get away from them.'

'Not tonight then. Come on, I'll walk you to the gate. The least I can do after that fish you cooked for me.'

She nodded and took his arm. 'All right, we go quick!'

'What time does Jesse come home from work?' he asked as he closed the gate.

'He work late getting paper ready. Maybe nine if he don't go to the pub.'

'Good-oh,' he said. 'I'll wait up a while.'

He walked back up to the house and took the front steps in a bound, brushing aside the horde of insects massed around the hanging lantern. He was surprised then, to hear a voice behind him, since the house was empty and Lulu hadn't come back.

He whirled about and was amazed to see Chang standing on the path outside the pool of light.

Mal was about to say 'How did you get out?' but checked himself. He wasn't supposed to know that the two Chinamen had been temporarily detained in the stockade. Jesse had told him the scheme worked.

'What are you doing here?' he asked. How had they managed this?

'I came to wish you farewell, Mr Willoughby. I am leaving the invalid town on the morrow. Sailing to the north and thence home to China via Singapore, for it is a happier home for me than this country. I do not claim to understand your ways.'

'You can say that again,' Mal growled.

'For instance, you wanted Tussup dead and then you did not, after the deed is done. You disappoint me.'

'What do you want, Chang?' He dropped back down the steps to confront him.

'I have another errand yet. My mission is incomplete.'

Mal saw the gun he'd drawn from under his shirt, and looked at it in surprise. 'Is that for me?'

'Unfortunately. You see, my patrons require more than I was aware of when I first undertook this mission. Lady Xiu, I was given to understand, could not forgive you, but she wished you no harm. Her orders were to see to the crewmen who had abducted her daughter. Her husband, though, your father-in-law, he is very much different, I am told. A hard man. After we disposed of Bartie Lee, I learned he had insisted that your name be added to the list for failing to protect his daughter.'

'So?'

'Do not make this difficult,' Chang said, keeping to the shadows, but Mal could see the gleam of the gun. 'I find it distressing, and I must tell you, as a friend I was not pleased with this order. Believe me when I say I did protest.'

'I'll bet you did,' Mal said bitterly.

'Yes. But I have meditated on this and have two thoughts to share with you. One is obvious. If I don't do as I am ordered, my own life would be in danger. The second is that ever since your beloved wife drowned, you have been living on borrowed time. It may help for you to understand that, Mr Willoughby. At least you know you have been avenged. All the criminals have gone before you. To a different place.'

'And you think you can kill me, go down and get on a ship and leave the country.'

'That's the easy part.'

Mal's eyes had become accustomed to looking into darkness by now, and when he saw movement in the bushes behind Chang, he glanced down and was able to make out Wu Tin's shiny black slippers. He didn't know whether Chang knew he was there or not. Maybe he was backup, but worth a try.

'And is Wu Tin going with you?'

'Only as far as Cooktown. I will have no further need of him from there.'

Mal grinned and spoke in Chinese, praying that Wu Tin, who only spoke a country dialect, could at least understand some of what he was saying. Surely, he thought, he must have picked up some of the prevailing Chinese by now, even if English was still beyond him.

'You mean Wu Tin will know too much about you after that?'

Chang replied in Chinese, amused by the switch. 'Exactly. I am an efficient man. He can come with me to Cooktown, be my witness, after that . . .' he shrugged.

'He's going to kill you, Wu Tin,' Mal shouted in Chinese. 'Did you hear that?'

Wu Tin charged out of the bushes, but Chang had moved so swiftly, still with the gun trained on Mal, that his servant blundered on past and would have fallen had Chang not grasped him and steadied him.

'What are you doing?' Chang said crossly, speaking to Wu Tin in his own dialect, as if he were addressing a child. 'Why are you interfering in my business?'

'You are going to kill me!' Wu Tin screamed. 'I heard! I knew you would. I was warned never to trust you.'

'You heard no such thing. How dare you accuse me? Now you are here in my way. I have business here for the Lord Xiu, and you, you termite, interfere! If I report this—'

'You are making deals with this man behind my back!'

'Making deals with a gun, you fool! I am here to kill him on the orders of Mr Xiu and Mr Li, and now you barge in!'

Mal saw Wu Tin was furious, so he must have understood something he'd said, but Chang was calming him down. The lantern jaw was gaping as he tried to grasp what was going on.

'He'll kill you too,' Mal called to him. A mistake.

'Ha! Did you hear that?' Chang challenged Wu Tin. 'He said "too". Like he knows I have to kill him and he's trying to squirm out of it. Now you go back to the ship. Go!'

Wu Tin couldn't work all this out but, as bidden, he went to leave, to go, but suddenly he turned back and confronted Chang. 'If that's true about your orders, do it. Then I know you are not making deals with this man. Or maybe he will pay you more than Mr Li, eh? Maybe I get some this time?'

'No, it's nothing to do with money. I have to kill him.'

'Then do it quick. Why you waste all this time? We should not be off the ship. Our true friend said that. This one is no friend. Do it and get it over with.'

'I am,' Chang said, and Mal desperately wished he could figure out what they were talking about, but he heard the uncertainty in Chang's voice. Uncertain? Chang? Since when? Mal worried as the gun wavered.

'Is it loaded?' he asked, seeing Chang's finger on the trigger, feeling the sweat dripping down inside his shirt, poised to jump any second. Now, he thought. Now!

But Wu Tin took them both by surprise.

He lunged at the gun but only Chang understood him. 'If you won't kill him I will!' Wu Tin yelled frantically.

'No, no!' Chang cried.

There was no struggle; Wu Tin had been too fast. He had the gun in the second that Mal had thrown himself sideways, had a small, strong finger curled around the trigger, pointing it at Mal, who was already moving away, and fired. He fired as Chang tried to grab the gun back. He fired as Chang's body came between him and the white man, and Chang fell to the ground. Willoughby had gone, disappeared into the darkness.

Wu Tin squealed, pushed at Chang with his foot. 'Get up!' But he could see the blood, black on the pale blue shirt. Spreading. He turned then and fired into the bushes, anxious to succeed where Chang had failed. To win the approval of Mr Li, and the bounty money.

The magnificent revolver with the silver trim, that Wu Tin had long admired, was empty, so he shoved it into his pocket and ran. Ran all the way back to the ship, but walked back aboard, slowly, like tired. Which he was.

An officer spoke to him, a Jappie officer, so he spoke a greeting and went below, to check on their belongings, pleased to find the large sea box allotted to them still locked. Chang had the key but that didn't matter, Wu Tin knew what was inside. He could break it open when he pleased. Things hadn't turned out bad after all. He was a rich man, with all Chang's money and no one to say him nay. He smiled and curled up on the nearby bunk. If the Jappies asked, he could say Chang changed his mind. Didn't want to go. And what would they care?

Mal cared. He'd seen Wu Tin bolt after missing him with a wild shot, and had come running back to Chang, shocked to see blood welling from his chest. He dragged off his shirt and pressed the bundle on to the wound to try to staunch the blood, at the same time shouting for help.

'Too late,' Chang whispered. 'I think I am your real friend perhaps.'

'You are. Yes. Hang on, I can hear people coming.' Surely he thought, the gunshots would have brought someone out, as he took Chang into his arms to give him the warmth he knew shock would be draining away.

Chang coughed. 'You know I am a gentleman,' he said drowsily.

'Yes, and I am honoured,' Mal said in Chinese. 'Deeply honoured to have a gentleman like you as my friend. Deeply honoured . . .' He didn't know how much Chang had heard as his body went limp and the light disappeared from his eyes.

Mal was distressed. 'God dammit!' he cried. 'Is there no bloody end to all this? Why didn't you stay home, Chang?'

'What's happening in there?' a man shouted from the gate. 'Are you there, Jesse? Is everything all right?'

'No it's not,' Mal called.

Wu Tin was taken from the Japanese ship that night and charged with murder, but Jesse was appalled that his interference had almost cost Mal his life. He felt he had no choice but to explain to Mal, privately, that he'd tried to get the two Chinamen out of the country so they couldn't cause him any more trouble.

'How could you do that, Jesse?' Mal was furious. 'They murdered Tussup. I had them held in the stockade for a bloody good reason, and now that the police have found the body they were headed for the gallows, not a jaunt back to China.'

'I'm sorry, I really am, but I felt they had you in a nasty spot. And Tussup was dead anyway. Nothing you could have done about that. And if they'd made up that tale, and they hadn't killed anyone—'

'Don't go on, Jesse, please. In future don't do me any favours.'

Another time, Jesse thought, he'd take the opportunity to remark to Mal that what goes around comes around. Chang had escaped the gallows but lost his life anyway and the rope was waiting for his servant Wu Tin. But in the meantime, as he remarked to Eleanor, he was surprised that Mal was so upset about the whole business, especially since Chang had come to kill him.

'But in the end he couldn't do it,' Eleanor told him.

'Who said so?'

'Mal. He didn't want that side of the story in the papers, so don't you go writing this. He was very sad, he said they were really friends, he and Chang, and . . . oh, I don't know, Jesse. It's just the pity of it all.'

Two days later the body of a murdered man was brought down to the Cairns morgue.

'We still haven't identified him,' Connor told Jesse, 'and I'd surely like to know where you picked up on that rumour.'

'You know me; it was in the pub at the Barron River. I keep my ears open. Heard talk, asked about, no one knew anything. I thought I should keep it in mind though, keep digging. That's why I asked you. I'll go and have a look; I might recognise him. And I'll take Willoughby with me. He's been hanging about the goldfields for months.'

'All right,' Connor said. Then he looked at Jesse cautiously. 'Ay! Your mate Willoughby – is he accident prone or something? Always something happening to him.'

'Yeah,' Jesse nodded, wondering what Connor would make of things when Mal identified the body as Tussup. Maybe, he thought, I should tell Mal to shut up. Pretend he doesn't know him and put a stop to any more questions. Just leave well enough alone.

'I don't think he'd appreciate that advice,' he muttered. 'I'm not doing any more interfering. He's on his own.'

But he did go with Mal to the mortuary, waiting outside for the verdict.

After a few minutes he had it.

'It's not Tussup,' Mal sounded edgy and frustrated. 'The man . . . the body . . . far too old. But he was shot in the back. Now I don't know what to make of Chang's claim. Is this the bloke he shot, do you reckon?'

'I'm not keen on coincidences. It has to be. So where's Tussup?'

'Bloody Tussup!' Mal looked up at the mortuary. 'This is where I brought Jun Lien, and you helped me. I never thanked you, Jesse.'

'You can buy me a drink then. And then we'll tell Connor, truthfully, we can't identify the body.'

'Truthfully? Why wouldn't we have told him the truth?'

'Never mind.' His words were reminiscent of the youthful Sonny Willoughby he'd met years ago, but who was long gone now. Jesse stole a glance at him as they walked back to the police station. Strands of blond hair still dipped untidily over the tanned face but the blue eyes were more aware now; the soft almost feminine mouth had firmed, and the jaw seemed to have squared.

'What's Mal short for?' he asked suddenly.

'You don't want to know,' Mal growled.

Eleanor had news for them. News that Esme hoped she'd keep to herself, but no chance of that, she lamented. Eleanor insisted they go straight into town and tell Jesse.

'It's about Jake Tussup,' she cried, bustling into his office with Esme following. 'I know where he is!'

'What! Where?' Eleanor's bombshell had the desired effect. Jesse was up and placing chairs for them. 'Tell me! I'm sorry, Esme, how are you, my dear? Now calm down, Eleanor and tell me.'

'You calm down,' she laughed. 'So I say what happened. Today I have a letter from Raymond Lewis. He is retiring, and soon coming to visit us. He says Lady Horwood is not well, she is still suffering seriously, as well she might, I tell you. That girl is high-strung, and Lyle, he rides roughshod over her as if only he has a say in anything. He did the same with his former wife, my dear cousin and friend, and then when she became ill he wouldn't let her friends visit and he himself ignored her—'

'Oh yes . . .' Jesse, eager for news of Tussup, tried to interrupt.

'He's one of those men can't abide illness, people said,' Eleanor continued, 'making allowances for him, but why should that be allowed? If Constance is ill they should watch out that he doesn't flick her out of his way,' she threw her hands up dramatically, 'like he did to poor Fannie. I'll be writing to Raymond to warn him. I don't care if he's a "sir" or whatever—'

'Did you say Mr Lewis mentioned Jake Tussup?' Jesse nudged.

'I'm coming to that. I have the letter right here.' She began fishing in her large handbag, but Esme touched her on the arm. 'Your own words will do, Eleanor.'

'Yes, well exactly.' She looked up. 'Tussup is in Brisbane. He is Raymond Lewis's client. He has engaged Lewis as his legal protector so to speak, and I am very surprised that Raymond should sink to such a level, accepting a fellow like that as a client, and I will tell him so. I will.'

'And will you tell Mal?' Esme asked Jesse.

'I'll have to.'

Just then the editor of Jesse's paper knocked at his door. 'Good morning, ladies,' he said. 'I hope you'll forgive this interruption but I thought you'd like to see this, Jesse. Look here, the *Brisbane Courier*, front page. An apology to Jake Tussup for calling him a murderer! I'll bet they had to pay him for that blunder. You'd better be careful what you say about Tussup from now on. I hope you didn't call him a murderer?'

'No. Only that the police were looking for him. No exact charges.'

'Just as well. Lovely day for an outing, ladies. If you'll excuse me . . .'

Jesse studied the paper. 'I might as well tell him now,' he said to Esme.

'Mal is going to Brisbane,' Esme told her friend when the older woman rose from her afternoon nap. 'Lulu dropped in with the news. And some eggs.'

'I thought he would. But I've been thinking about Constance. And Raymond. And my friend Gertrude, who is in Brisbane, and I've decided that there is no better time than this to visit the capital. We must prepare.'

'We?'

'Of course. You must come too. You could talk to Constance, better than I.'

'Eleanor, I couldn't. Mal might think I'm following him.'

'He's not that sort. He'll be pleased that we're going to do all this visiting and have a vacation as well. Do we not deserve a vacation? Come along now and stop seeing worries behind trees. What would the climate be in that town of Brisbane? And woo-woo! Now we have to pack our tropic dresses away and get out the finery, eh?'

Mal felt he was becoming an authority on this Queensland coast. 'I've been up and down like a Jack-in-the-box,' he told Esme as the steamer headed across Trinity Bay.

'I want you to know,' she said, 'you're not obligated to mind us. I mean, just because we're on board doesn't mean—'

'Who else will I talk to but you and Eleanor? I don't want to talk to strangers. I was sort of hoping you'd protect me.'

She laughed. 'Protect you? I just heard you agreeing to a game of cards with that Smith couple before the ship even left port.'

'I thought it would amuse you.'

'Euchre, I suppose?'

'Yes.'

'You like to win, don't you, Mal Willoughby?'

'Oh yes,' his eyes twinkled, 'with a little help from my friends.' She was a good card player, had plenty of practice, by the looks of it, and nothing wrong with that.

Which reminded him he'd been accosted by Clive Hillier before he boarded the ship.

'I hear you're off to Brisbane. Running after my wife, eh?'

He'd looked at Hillier and whispered: 'No,' though he'd been tempted to push him off the wharf.

The short voyage was uneventful. Pleasant. They all carefully avoided mention of *China Belle*. And many times Mal had considered having a serious talk with Eleanor, because she was a wise and worldly woman, on the subject of Jake Tussup. But he'd held back. Eleanor would probably give him sound advice, like letting go – she'd hinted it several times – and he wouldn't be able to accept her advice, so what was the point?

And Esme? Could he talk it over with her? Probably not. She was already confused. She hated Tussup, really hated him, that was abundantly clear. But she didn't want him confronting Tussup, for the obvious reason. Trouble.

Mal spent a lot of time alone in his cabin, trying to work out what he'd do when he did see Tussup in Brisbane. He was still shaken by Chang's claim that he had shot him, but understood now that he'd had no control over the Chinese vendettas.

Since Raymond was defending Tussup – an inexplicable decision – they'd taken it for granted that the brute must be in gaol, but Raymond's letter hadn't said that. He'd said he was in Brisbane. Mal hoped he was in gaol. Then he couldn't be tempted to horsewhip him. Or worse.

The women were excited as the steamer headed across Moreton Bay for the mouth of the Brisbane River, but Mal was scowling as they passed the infamous St Helena island, the maximum security goal, where he'd been imprisoned awaiting trial. He had to turn away, to try to obliterate memories of the horrors he'd endured in that vicious hole.

'Never mind,' he insisted to himself. 'Stop this. Forget it! You made them pay for the months you spent in there. The bloody government never got their gold back!'

'But I was so young,' an inner voice argued. 'Never been in trouble before. Wondered what struck me. And I'd just met Emilie. Fallen head over heels in love with Emilie. And all this strife fell on me like a ton of rocks.'

'No!' he shouted, a silent shout, as the blue sea brushing past, reminded him of the horror of Jun Lien's death. The pain was back, the agony, and desolation, and he felt like throwing himself into the cool, crystal-clear water, and ending it the same way she'd died.

Esme was walking towards him. She saw the tears and abruptly turned away.

A blustery wind plucked at their fashionably large hats as Eleanor and Esme emerged at Wharf Street for their first look at the colonial capital, finding it much smaller and more countrified than they'd imagined.

'After the hordes of people in the Far Eastern cities,' Esme said, 'it's hard to get used to so few people in the streets. I feel we stand out like a couple of turkeys.'

Mal caught up with them and heard that remark. 'Turkeys? Lord, no, you both look so lovely people ought to stare. I've sent the luggage on to the Treasury Hotel. It's very posh and not far to walk.'

'You know the town well?' Eleanor asked him.

'Yes. I met a famous bushranger here once. I was most impressed.' He kept looking about him, hoping that with luck he might spot Tussup, but that was not to be, so they were soon at the hotel, and rooms duly allotted.

'I'll leave you for a little while ladies, I have things to do.'

'You're going to see Raymond!' Eleanor accused him. 'But I suppose we can't all land on his doorstep. He lives in Paddington – is that very far out of town?'

'No, but too far for you to walk. Let me see if I can find him. He's sure to be in a rush to see you both when he hears you're in town.'

'In the meantime,' Esme said, 'why don't we unpack and then go into the parlour for afternoon tea? It'll be fun.'

'Very well, but don't be long, Mal. I'm so curious about Tussup and poor Constance, my patience will be wearing thin.'

As he was about to walk past the reception desk, Mal detoured on a whim and asked the clerk if a Mr Tussup was staying in the house, not surprised when the answer was 'No, sir.'

But he did stop in his tracks when the clerk went on to say: 'But he was here some weeks ago. Mr Jake Tussup?'

'Yes!' Mal could hardly breathe. 'He was here? Staying in this hotel?'

The clerk looked a little confused. 'That's right, sir.'

Mal strode away, swearing under his breath. Why was he always a couple of lengths behind the bastard?

But then he was cheered by the thought that Tussup had probably been taken from here to prison. To the Brisbane Gaol. A rotten, miserable heap of stones and sweat. Mal could testify to that. He certainly could.

Miss Lewis came to the door. 'Goodness me! It's Mr Willoughby, isn't it? I recognised you from the pictures in the paper. Do come in. Raymond will be delighted to see you. I'm his sister.'

She took him through the glassed-in lobby to a large parlour with brown carpets, stout leather furnishings and portraits of stern antecedents. Ferns and small palms in brass jardinières stood in a corner, almost swallowed up by the dark panelling. Choking for air they were, giving off a musty smell to signal their distress.

'Raymond's out the back giving instructions to the gardeners. I'll get him for you. I was so sorry to hear of the loss of your dear wife. Please accept my most sincere condolences. It was all a terrible shock. We first heard of the *China Belle* tragedy by telegraph from Cairns, and you can imagine my fright . . .'

She heard her brother enter the house and called to him. 'Raymond. Look who's here! Would you like tea, Mr Willoughby? Or something stronger?'

'Tea will be fine, thank you, Miss Lewis.'

She jumped up and rang for a maid, obviously with no intention of leaving the room and missing out on a most interesting conversation that this meeting foretold.

Raymond wasn't as enthusiastic about the visitor as she was, but as Mal noted, he made a good show of it, welcoming him grandly.

'Tea, Raymond?' his sister asked when the maid popped her head in.

'No,' he said bluntly. 'No. What brings you to the capital, Mal?'

'Eleanor's letter. Where's Tussup? In prison I hope?'

'Afraid not.' Raymond settled himself into a large armchair.

'You're defending him, Raymond?' Mal asked quietly

'Not exactly. He hasn't been charged with anything actually.' He took off his spectacles and began to polish the lenses with a large handkerchief.

'You must understand that Mr Tussup simply arrived at our door,' Miss Lewis said, 'much as you have. Raymond only did what was best. You see, Mr Tussup wanted to clear his name.'

'He'd need plenty of soap and water for that,' Mal remarked.

'I imagine so, in the long run,' Raymond said. 'But he was primarily concerned with being called a murderer.' He leaned forward. 'He was upset, Mal.'

'You don't say! Was it you who got him the apology in the *Courier*?'

'No. He organised that himself. I went to see the Police Commissioner to find out what charges would be laid against him, once he was prepared to give himself up. He was tired of running. But it seems his main problem is you, Mal.'

'Why me? And why didn't they lock him up?'

'Because of Sir Lyle Horwood,' Miss Lewis said angrily. 'He pulled strings behind the scenes. Even mentioned to the Police Commissioner that he'd be in line for the Queen's Honours or the like—'

'Lavinia! Jasper told me that in confidence,' Raymond objected.

'And he ought to be ashamed of himself for even considering such a despicable offer,' she snapped.

'What's it got to do with Lyle?' Mal asked.

'A great deal,' Raymond said slowly, 'a great deal. Let me tell you about Constance.'

'Oh yes, Eleanor and Esme are concerned for her,' Mal said. 'They're anxious to see her as soon as possible.'

'They're in town? Here? When did they arrive?' Raymond was bewildered and not a little pleased. From that point, Mal had a hard time pinning Raymond down to telling him the whole, miserable, unfair story of Tussup wandering off free as a bird, and of Constance in real trouble. Fortunately, Miss Lewis had found an outlet for her anger, and Mal was soon filled in on details that Raymond was scudding over in his eagerness to end the conversation. He was more interested in calling on the ladies. Eleanor in particular, Mal thought.

In the end, Raymond's patience ran out. 'I'll get out the gig and drive you back to town,' he told Mal, who was pleased to accept the ride but still angry that he'd missed Tussup again.

Though Raymond had been looking forward to seeing Eleanor and Esme, their meeting in the hotel lounge was far from joyful. The women were outraged that no charges had been laid against Jake Tussup, and very upset when they learned of Constance's whereabouts. But, as Raymond explained, there was little to be done in either case.

'Nothing at all?' Eleanor asked crossly. 'Is that because Tussup is your client or because you can't be bothered, Raymond?'

'That's hardly fair,' he said. 'One does one's best for all concerned. I have gone out of my way to look out for Constance. We had a job even getting in to see her, and having achieved that, we visit her as often as possible. I must tell you, though, Lyle Horwood is unaware of our visits. Were he to find out we'd be barred.'

'And you haven't taken legal measures to challenge Horwood on the treatment of his wife.'

'Because Constance wants to stay there. She feels safe there.'

'In an asylum?' Esme cried. 'I'd be petrified in an asylum! What are you thinking of, Raymond? If doctors say she's mad and you say she's not all there at present, why the hell would you accept her assessment of the situation? If you're her lawyer, it's up to you to make the decisions, not just go along with it.'

'Try to understand, Esme, I'm on shaky ground legally. By rights I shouldn't even be there. I have no legal right to visit Constance.'

'Then have you challenged Lyle Horwood?'

'There's no point, given the fact that Constance wants to stay there. But my dear, what about a glass of wine? Or champagne would be even better. What do you say?'

Their acceptance was rather listless. Raymond, trying to inject some enthusiasm into the party, clapped his hands cheerily to the waiter, while Eleanor nudged Mal and whispered: 'I think his little habit is slowing him down, dear.'

'What . . .?' Mal looked at her, astonished, but she simply shrugged. He turned to peer at Raymond but of course there was no way of telling whether he had an opium habit or not, by merely looking at the man.

Despite his anger at the way this conversation was going Mal had to smile. Who would have thought it of Raymond? He recalled that smooth customer in Cooktown, old Mr Li . . . Raymond had said he'd stayed there, rescued from the horrors of a field hospital by the gentleman. Mal guessed that Li had soothed his furrowed brow with the delights of the house, as well as ointments for the leg ulcers.

The champagne arrived, and Raymond toasted happy days, but Esme was still on Tussup's case.

'I can't get over it,' she said. 'I can't believe that he was here, right here! Mal said he was even staying at this hotel, and yet you and the police let him get away! What were you thinking of, Raymond?'

'Firstly let me point out,' he said huffily, 'that I am not the police and I am not in control of their decisions. Secondly, Tussup was extremely concerned that Mal had branded him a murderer. I know Mal was upset at the time—'

'That's an understatement,' Mal snapped.

'Let me finish. But it was a foolish thing to do. I always disapproved of those posters you distributed. He could have sued you for every penny you own.'

Mal shook his head, disbelieving this plaintive excuse. 'Good. Did you tell him to go right ahead?'

'I didn't apprise him of his rights in that direction, if you must know, though I probably should have, being his counsel. But he knew anyway, since he knew enough to take on the *Courier* and force an apology.'

'Which comes back to the thing that's worrying me,' Esme said. 'Why did you take him on in the first place? Why didn't you send for the police first up?'

'Because I was taken aback by his sudden arrival at my house.'

'Not able to quite grasp the situation?' Eleanor said archly, raising an eyebrow for Mal's benefit.

'Exactly. He'd come to engage me as his lawyer, since I'd been on the spot and could understand how his plan had been overtaken by Bartie Lee and the other thugs.

'So you talked the Police Commissioner into letting him off.'

'Not quite, Eleanor. I knew there'd have to be a charge of some sort. I was trying to find out exactly what. Then I heard that the file was closed, thanks to Lyle Horwood. And anyway, by then, Tussup had left town.'

'What a surprise,' Eleanor said acidly.

It was a surprise to Raymond that they were being so unkind to him over all this, and he was upset with the attitude of these people whom he considered dear friends. After all they'd been through together! He ordered more champagne to bolster everyone's spirits and changed the subject.

'I had thought that after dinner you might care for an evening at the theatre. I have a box at the Playhouse.'

'That would be nice,' Eleanor said. 'It's so long since I've been to the theatre. What's playing?'

'J. C. Williamson and his wife, Maggie Moore, in a comedy, *Struck Oil*. I hear it's excellent.'

'Count me out,' Mal said moodily, but Esme couldn't resist the invitation either, so it was agreed, and Raymond breathed a sigh of relief. He reminded the ladies of the other invitation he'd issued when he'd first greeted them at the Treasury Hotel.

'My sister would be delighted to have you over for dinner, ladies. She's looking forward to meeting you.'

'Ah yes,' Eleanor said. 'Thank you so much. We are certainly looking forward to meeting Miss Lewis.'

Raymond was feeling more comfortable now. Although he did not say so, he blamed Mal for encouraging the ladies to question his decisions. None of them seemed to understand that he'd done the right thing. He'd been fair with Tussup and it wasn't his fault that the wretch had run off on him. He was extremely hurt that even Eleanor had been cross with him. Eleanor, such a wonderful, elegant lady! He'd been very much taken with her right from the start, and it was only her presence in Cairns that had prompted his proposed visit. He'd hoped to see a lot more of her there, in quieter surrounds and with no obligations to draw him away. And, in time, have a serious conversation with her about their futures.

But, all was not lost, he told himself as he escorted the ladies into the dining room. Eleanor had been first to accept the invitation to the play. So perhaps the little upsets were over and done with.

Mal didn't join them for dinner. Instead he walked down George Street to Parliament House, looking back into the orange and pink swathes of sunset that were colouring the sandstone building. Old timers had told him that not so long ago, this area was dense rainforest and beyond, to the hills, were grassy fields, idyllic country for the Aborigine clans that resided here.

Deep in thought, he followed the Botanic Gardens across the small peninsula to face the river again, and stood looking at the Edward Street sign, wondering why that rang a bell with him.

As he turned into that street he heard singing coming from St Stephen's Cathedral, and slowed his steps to listen to the soaring voices of a boys' choir. He had almost decided to go in and enjoy this rare pleasure, when a name struck him. A name! Just one word: Lanfield!

He clapped a hand to his forehead. Have I lost my wits? What's the matter with me that I hang around sulking over Raymond's pathetic efforts, when Lanfield is just up the street? In Edward Street, for God's sake!

Mal began to run. It was late, shops were closing. Office workers were stepping out on to the street. Horses clopped by, hauling an empty wagon, and a horse-cab driver shouted at him as he dashed across to Victoria Chambers, another imposing sandstone building which, once upon a time, had intimidated him just as much as his lawyer, Mr Lanfield.

Lanfield, he grinned as he pulled open a heavy glass door. Short-tempered. Sour. Snooty. But a brain! You couldn't call Lanfield smart, he thought, standing aside to allow a top-hatted gentleman to come down the stairs before he headed up, that would probably offend him. He was just very good at the law. Who else could have got me off? Mal asked himself, when I'd been framed by the Gold Commissioner himself.

'Mr Willoughby! What are you doing here?' a stern voice addressed him, and Mal looked up to see Lanfield descending the stairs with his colleagues.

Mal gulped. Already intimidated. 'I was coming to see you, sir.'

'My office closes at six thirty on the dot.'

It would, yes it would, Mal thought. On the dot. But then Lanfield stopped beside him. 'I've been reading about you, Mr Willoughby,' he said in that high-toned voice. 'I was most distressed to hear of the tragedy that befell you. Might I extend to you my most sincere condolences on the death of your wife? Dreadful! Now, you wished to see me?'

'Yes sir.'

'Then be here at nine in the morning, sharp.' With that, the tall, gaunt lawyer tipped his hat and strode to the door that another gentleman was holding open for him.

Mal smiled. The condolences were unexpected. A peep into Lanfield's human side. And a very nice gesture.

'I'll thank him tomorrow,' he said to himself as he followed them outside.

They found the play comical. They were enjoying it immensely. Raymond offered to bring them refreshments at the interval but Eleanor wanted to stretch her legs, so they walked out into the plush foyer, neither Esme nor Raymond aware that Eleanor had an ulterior motive.

'Excuse me,' she said to them. 'There's someone I wish to speak to.'

'Who would that be?' Raymond said to Esme as he asked a waiter to deliver a jug of iced lemonade to his box, with three glasses.

'Oh Lord!' Esme stood on tiptoe to peer through the crowd. 'It's Lyle Horwood!'

Eleanor hadn't wanted them with her. She'd spotted Lyle in the theatre and was waiting for this opportunity to have a few words with him. In public!

She tapped him on the shoulder, and then he turned, a smile of anticipation on his face at being addressed by this attractive woman. The smile faded.

'Mr Horwood, I do declare!' she said, deliberately ignoring his new title.

He nodded curtly. 'Mrs Plummer.'

'How are you, Lyle?' she said, before he could get away.

'Very well, thank you.'

'And Constance?' she urged. 'How is your dear wife?'

'She's well also.'

'I'm pleased to hear that, Lyle, because I have it on good authority that your wife is not well. I heard you had her put away.'

His face crimsoned under his thick white hair. 'That is not true, Eleanor, and you know it,' he whispered. 'And kindly lower your voice.'

'Either you lie or others lie,' she said loudly. 'Is Constance to be shut away in her illness the way you shut away your first wife?'

'She is not shut away. And I did not come here to discuss my wife or anything else with you, madam.'

'But I did!' she insisted. 'It's very fortunate that I should find you here this evening, Lyle, because I need an answer. Where is Constance?'

People were turning, looking, listening to this exchange. Raymond shook his head in despair that Eleanor should make a scene like this, but Esme decided to invent a part for herself.

She pushed through the curious crowd. 'Excuse me, Lyle, were you discussing Constance? Where is she? I'm told she's not at home any more, so where is she?'

'How dare you two accost me like this? Don't you realise who I am?'

'My dear chap, we know exactly who you are,' Eleanor said with a flick of her fan. 'You're the husband of our friend, Constance, Lady Horwood, who appears to be missing.'

'She's not missing,' he blurted desperately. 'She's at home.'

'Then we shall call on her tomorrow.'

'You may not, madam!' He shouldered away from them and dashed towards the staircase.

'Eleanor!' Raymond whispered as the crowd thinned out. 'What on earth possessed you?'

'The need to embarrass him into some decent behaviour,' she said calmly. 'He's a dreadful little man and a horrible snob.'

'But did you have to make a spectacle of yourself at the same time?'

'We can't all sit around and hope problems will go up in smoke, Raymond. Come on, we have to get back, the second act has commenced.'

Later that evening she outlined her plan to Esme. 'Tomorrow we pay a call on Lyle. We tell him we know she's in the asylum, and we need his permission to visit her. If he refuses, we simply threaten him. Are you on for that?'

'Good show! Threaten him with what?'

'Lots of things. That we will expose the fact that he has put his wife away, which I hope is the English polite term. That we could place an advertisement in the paper asking for information as to her whereabouts. He'll have kittens at that. I am thinking, though, that he'll be already sorely punctured after the contretemps at the theatre, with so many people listening. They'll have him the talk of the town by noon tomorrow.'

'Do you think it will work?'

'Oh yes. Sooner or later.'

As it happened, after an angry exchange at his front door, Lyle gave them permission to visit his wife. Written permission, as requested by Eleanor.

'I believe the asylum is a long way out of town,' she said. 'We wouldn't want to travel there and be turned away.'

'This is Raymond's fault,' he turned. 'I told him where she was, in confidence. He's done nothing but stir up trouble lately. Poor Constance, it would be the end of her if she got dragged into court to give evidence about her sojourn with all those men. They drove her mad, you know. You'll see. Then you'll leave the poor woman alone.'

'Like you have,' Eleanor snapped, but Esme wasn't so sure.

As they drove back into town in the horse-cab, with their letter of introduction to the matron at St Clement's, she worried.

'Didn't Raymond say that Constance wanted to stay there? That she's desolated by what she thinks people are saying about her? In which case Lyle could be right. She couldn't face having the humiliations discussed in open court, even if it meant Tussup got what he deserved.'

Eleanor sighed. 'My dear, I don't know. Let's just take one step at a time.'

'Now, Mr Willoughby, take a seat. What can I do for you?'

Mal clutched his hat and sat obediently in front of Lanfield's desk. 'I wanted to thank you for your kind words, sir . . .'

'About the loss of your wife?'

'Yes, sir.'

'I doubt anything I could say would come anywhere near to consoling the excruciating grief that a young man like you must have endured. So forgive me, Mr Willoughby, if I blunder on. Now what is it?'

Mal looked at the wispy grey hair and the puffy sideburns that were so strangely at odds with this man's cold green eyes and thin lips. 'It's about Tussup, sir. He was—'

'First Officer of the *China Belle*? Yes, I read all the newspaper reports. Avidly, I must say. Personal interest in one's former client perhaps. But you're not in trouble this time, surely?'

'No, sir. It's Tussup. So far he's got off scot-free and I think that's wrong. The Police Commissioner here was looking to charge him I'm told, but someone waved a knighthood or whatever in front of him—'

'Enough of that Willoughby. Not our business. Stick to the point.'

'The point is he got off scot-free!' Mal retorted.

'And what do you want me to do about it?'

'I don't know. Think of something to charge him with.'

'Like what?'

'Conspiracy. I'm not allowed to say he's a murderer, and I actually had a moment of regret, thinking I may have unfairly labelled him as such, but if my wife hadn't been in that boat—'

'You're right.' Lanfield's Adam's apple twitched over the stiff collar and bow tie. 'According to reports, even recent reports, you can't accuse him of murder. Conspiracy maybe,' he mused, 'but his fellow conspirators are all dead. Difficult to sustain. We'll pass on that ridiculous charge that allowed the other bird, Ingleby, to fly. Robbery? We have no evidence that Tussup stole anything. Except the aforementioned longboat. So you see the difficulty the police faced. Desertion of a ship in these gold-mad times isn't worth the effort, and mutiny wouldn't hold up.'

'What about causing a murder? He ordered the bosun locked up so that he couldn't raise the alarm, and while he was there Mushi or Lee cut his throat. Surely Tussup has to bear some responsibility for that?'

'Who is there to go to court to give witness to that order? Ingleby? An officer himself and in on the plot? Not likely. The order would hardly be written in the log. But that does lead us to another similar charge that I have been contemplating.'

He twiddled a curved brass letter-opener. 'I don't think abduction would hold, since – and I don't want this to be more painful to you than necessary, Mr Willoughby – it is established that the Malays abducted the two ladies, took them to the boat, and that Tussup objected, and was overruled.'

Mal's control broke. 'He objected?' he shouted. 'The bastard had a gun! He could have refused to take my wife and Constance. He could have called off the whole business when he saw the women were involved. But do you know what drove him on? Greed! Drove him past any thought of the women. Any care for them! He was at the helm or whatever you call it in a bloody longboat. That bastard was in charge.'

'And there you have it,' Lanfield said quietly, placing the letter-opener carefully on the desk, in line with a leather-covered blotter.

He sat up, elbow on the desk, hand on his chin. 'Unlawful detention. Do you see? He was in charge of that boat. The crew acknowledged that. The ladies knew. Your poor wife leaped from the boat to escape his clutches, but Mrs Horwood, Lady Horwood, stayed. She's your witness.'

Mal was excited. 'What do we do now? Ask the police to charge him?'

'I'm afraid not. The case is closed. And even if we did manage the impossible, it's well known that Sir Lyle wouldn't want to have to endure a court appearance.'

Mal brushed that setback aside. He was aware that Constance herself would be another hurdle, but that would keep for now. He could see a glimmer of hope and had no intention of letting go.

'If the police won't charge him then I want to. Can I do that? I don't care what it costs. I have to get him, Mr Lanfield.'

Lanfield shrugged. 'You could bring a tort – a tortious action.'

'What's that?'

'A civil suit.'

Mal leaped up. 'I can? Then I'll do it. How do I go about it?'

'Firstly, where is he now? I heard he left town.'

'That he has. But I'm damn sure I can find him this time. I reckon he's in Goulburn.'

'Isn't that in New South Wales?'

'Yes.'

'Then he's out of our Queensland jurisdiction, I'm afraid.'

'Oh, no!'

'Never mind. I agree the scoundrel shouldn't get off scot-free, Mr Willoughby, if only for your sake. I believe you need to do this last thing before you can put down your crying, as the Aborigines call the end of the time of mourning.'

'Yes, I know about that, Mr Lanfield, but I never sort of . . . applied it to myself.'

Lanfield nodded. 'It was worth mentioning. Let us go over Tussup's part in the *China Belle* events again.'

They talked for a while, until Lanfield tapped the desk. 'Very well. Now I want you to leave this with me for a couple of days. Don't go rushing out of here to find Tussup. I have a gentleman in Sydney who will do that for me. A Mr Fred Watkins, an excellent investigator. He can find out, for a start, if Tussup really has gone to ground in his home town as suggested.'

'It wouldn't surprise me, if he thinks he's safe leaving this colony.'

'Probably is, as far as our police are concerned. He has seen how lackadaisical they are here, and would take it as given that the New South Wales police would be even less interested. But first we find him. And in the meantime I shall write to a colleague in Sydney, a barrister. The law may differ there. All being well, he'll be the one for you to see.'

'Good,' Mal said. 'I think I've got Tussup this time.'

'You may have. Come back on Friday morning. Same time. I will contact Mr Watkins by telegraph and he may have some news by then, so don't go haring off on your own, Mr Willoughby. Leave this to me.'

Mal was so pleased with Lanfield's advice he almost did a jig as he hurried up Edward Street. He felt he could see a light at the end of the tunnel at last. There was one problem, and that was Constance. From the way Raymond had spoken, she was still a nervous wreck from her ordeals, unable to face people. Even accepting being locked up in an asylum. Mal thought that was weird. How did they expect her to get over her fear of facing people if they kept her caged up? Rum sort of cure, it seemed to him. But it didn't augur too well for Lanfield's plan, which would require her to give evidence in court.

And Mal was almost unable to contemplate another worry that had entered his head. Jake Tussup might have gone along with the abduction of the women in his mad obsession to get to that shore, but he had helped Constance escape. She'd said so herself. Many times.

He decided not to mention Lanfield to any of the others for the time being, in case Raymond came up with something useful for a change.

The following evening they were invited to dinner by Raymond and Lavinia Lewis, at their home in Paddington, and Mal agreed to go only when Esme insisted.

'It will be a dismal affair,' she said. 'Like a bloody wake for you and me, but we have to go.'

'I don't,' he said.

'Yes you do, or I won't go.'

'All right,' he said. 'I suppose it will be better than the hotel food. They're mean with their serves here. I can get better grub at the pub on the corner.'

In the end, it wasn't so bad, Mal had to admit. The Lewises did serve good hearty meals and he got along famously with Lavinia.

There was a lot of discussion about Constance. And distress. Eleanor and Esme had visited her, tears all round, and come away even more furious with Lyle.

'You have to get her out of there!' Eleanor demanded of Raymond.

'What can I do? She is being treated there. Those doctors won't sign her out. And where can I find two doctors to challenge their opinions? You know doctors won't contradict each other. They consider it unethical.'

'Smuggle her out,' Mal suggested, and Lavinia laughed.

'Now there's a forthright proposal. Anyone got a better idea?'

'Yes. We go back to Lyle, in a group,' Eleanor was very serious, 'including you, Lavinia, and we demand he have her released. That's how we got his permission in the first place. We have to embarrass him.'

'I won't have any part of such harassment,' Raymond said. 'I wouldn't dream of it.'

Mal was enjoying the argument. 'Then we won't harass him, we'll break his fingers instead.'

'Please don't joke,' Eleanor said stiffly.

'All right. Didn't you say earlier that another of her reasons for staying there, which makes more sense than that she just doesn't want to leave the loony house, was that she won't go back to Lyle?'

'That's right. He's ashamed of her and lets her know, apparently.'

'Apparently?' Esme put in. 'Locking her away seems damned obvious to me.'

'For treatment,' Raymond said. 'For treatment. That is his reason.'

'What's the use of making him release her when she has made up her mind not to go back to him?' Mal asked them. 'That will embarrass him even more, and where will she go? Constance had never set foot in this country before *China Belle*. We're the only people she knows.'

Lavinia spoke up. 'She can come here. She's welcome to come here and stay as long as she wishes.'

'Or she could come back to Cairns with us,' Eleanor added.

The next day Mal had himself added to the list of visitors, thanks to Esme, who forged an exact copy of Lyle's letter to the Matron at St Clement's, and began his daily visits.

At first he went with Eleanor and Esme. The high walls and barred windows upset him, but he fought against their claustrophobic effect.

Constance was embarrassed that he should see how badly her mouth dribbled at one side, and tried to turn away from him when he first arrived, but he took her in his arms and kissed her on the forehead. 'You're looking gorgeous as usual, Constance,' he said. 'But then she always was a stunner, wasn't she, ladies?'

They walked about the grounds with her, talking about the play and what a riot it was, about a picnic Eleanor was organising, about what a fine town Brisbane was, even slyly mentioning Raymond's beautiful house and how Lavinia would love her to stay with them some time, but Constance wasn't interested.

At one stage she complained about the meals, and immediately Eleanor told her she didn't have to stay in this place.

'But I do,' Constance said sadly. 'You don't understand. I have to. I wish you would try to understand.'

'We do, dear. It's just that a lovely girl like you should be out in the world.'

With that Constance shut down, and wouldn't speak at all, until she suddenly asked after Raymond.

'Where is he? I'm disappointed in Raymond, he's let me down.'

'In what way?' Mal asked.

'He promised to bring Jake Tussup to see me. I have to see Jake Tussup.'

'What's this about Constance wanting to see Tussup?' Mal had gone in search of Raymond as soon as they returned to town.

'Oh Lord, sit down here, Mal, here on the veranda. There's a nice breeze. She wants to see him so that he can speak up for her, tell people that she didn't have any physical contact with any of her abductors.'

'What on earth for?'

'Because she thinks no one believes her. I think Lyle doesn't believe her either.'

'Her own husband? The dirty-minded little bugger. And you promised to arrange it?

'Not exactly. When Tussup was here I was trying to work out if that could be accomplished, keeping in mind that I would have needed Dr Shakell's permission to take Jake out to St Clement's. I was only there myself under sufferance. It's a complicated matter all round. You've been there, she's not being ill-treated . . .'

Mal let him meander on. Now, it seemed, someone needed Tussup. Really needed him. Having suffered ignominy and suspicion himself, he understood Constance's misery. Embarrassed, she would have picked up on the sly looks and the whispering in the aftermath of her ordeal, and she would feel that she had to keep convincing people that she was telling the truth. And wonder if they believed her. 'Where there's smoke there's fire?' he muttered bitterly. 'Mud sticks!'

And her solution: hide yourself away in this place until Tussup himself, who was there, tells everyone she's speaking the truth.

'What was my solution?' Mal asked himself.

Run away to China.

Oh yes, he understood Constance's problems very clearly.

Abruptly, he took his leave of Raymond and walked all the way back to the hotel, plunged in thought. But at the entrance he turned away again, not wanting to discuss this subject with the two women. It was too close to home. They'd heard Constance ask for Jake Tussup and were flabbergasted. They'd be bound to bring it up again.

But Constance was living in a dream world, and so was Raymond. Even if, by some miracle, Tussup were able to visit her, what was the use of him confirming her statement in a barred room in an institution? How would that help? Or had they envisaged a written statement from Tussup that she could flutter about in some pathetic plea for approval?

Mal came to livery stables and looked with envy at a magnificent bay stallion being led in at the gate. He missed horses. It was hard to know how to fill in a day in a big town. He wondered if Esme liked to ride.

The next day, he declined Eleanor's offer to go out to St Clement's in the cab, preferring to ride.

'Ride what?' Eleanor asked.

'I've hired a horse. I feel dopey sitting in a cab.'

He noticed Esme looking a bit miffed, but it couldn't be helped. Now he was able to visit Constance on his own.

She was pleased to see him. She was looking forward to their visits now, which was a good sign, and he explained that the ladies would be along later.

After he shared tea and biscuits with her, he drew her into the harrowing story of his arrest and imprisonment, and of his eventual release.

'So there you go,' he said. 'One day, suddenly, it was all over.'

'Thank God for that,' she said.

'I had a good lawyer.'

'Just the same, it must have been a shocking experience.'

'Nearly as bad as the terrifying experience you had with that damned crew.'

She blushed, looked away. Wrung her hands.

'But you survived,' he said bluntly. 'Jun Lien died. So you have to count your blessings. I have to also. Two men guarding that gold consignment were shot. I was the other guard. I was lucky to survive, Constance. I think we have to count our blessings together, don't you?

'I suppose so, Mal. It's all so unfair, isn't it?'

'Yes, I'll agree with you on that. Tell me, do you like horses?' he asked, changing the subject so as not to lead her into depression.

'Yes, I used to ride a lot at home, but never in Hong Kong.'

Mal was surprised. 'Home? Where's home?'

'England. My father lives there. I'd love to see him again. I don't want to live in Brisbane. I hate the place.'

Bit by bit Mal was gaining her confidence and every little piece of information helped. Gradually he began to realise that there was a way out of this, for both of them.

'If Lanfield comes through,' he muttered.

The next day he asked her about Jake Tussup. 'Is it true you want to see him?'

'Yes. I know you hate him, everyone does, but I have to talk to him. Do you know where he is?'

'Give me a day or so, I might be able to pin him down.'

Constance looked at him earnestly. 'Do you mean that, Mal?'

'I'll do my best, Constance.' He felt so sorry for her. A beautiful woman like that should be out in the world, enjoying herself. She was only in her early thirties. He wondered how she'd come to marry Lyle. He was a tall, dignified sort of fellow, and because she was a willowy blonde, they looked well together, but he had to be twice her age.

As he rode back to town, Mal was even more determined to find Tussup. Had that bastard ever stopped to think of the appalling and far-reaching consequences of his actions? Mal wished he could rub them in his face with a handful of mud.

That afternoon Mal took Esme for a walk in the Botanic Gardens, and she was relieved that at last he remembered she was a person, and not just Eleanor's off-sider. While she was fond of Eleanor and greatly appreciated her kindness, Esme knew she had to move on, no matter what difficulties might be ahead. She had settled into this genteel existence as, more or less, companion to the older woman, and it bothered her. She'd seen too much of it. Single women and widows often fell into this trap and turned into what Esme had always called 'wallpaper'. She was determined that this was not about to happen to her.

Mal wandered around the paths of the beautiful riverside gardens, pointing out native trees and plants, and, noticing a koala high in a eucalypt, tried to coax it down.

'Nothing doing,' Esme laughed. 'But isn't he beautiful? Are you allowed to keep them as pets?'

'No. It'd be too hard to feed them, anyway. They only eat the leaves of these trees.'

'How are you getting along with Constance?' she asked him, unable to resist a tinge of irritation. 'You seem to be spending a lot of time with her.'

'I know, but we have to. The more people she sees, the better, despite the frowns of Dr Shake-All.'

'You shouldn't be too hard on him. If you consider the sort of people that normally run asylums, he's all right.'

'Yeah but I think he likes hanging on to his customers. They don't die of their ailments and they don't get better. Damn cushy job, if you ask me, sitting around talking up the cure. You might as well give a parrot the job. She has to get out of there.'

'Easier said than done.'

'I know. How long are you staying in Brisbane, Es?'

The question took her by surprise so she plunged in. 'I'm not going back to Cairns. Everyone is nice and it'll be a lovely little town again soon, but it's not for me.'

'Do you prefer cities?'

'Not necessarily. I haven't got an answer yet. I'm feeling aimless. There wasn't anything for me to do in Cairns but wander around playing ladies.'

He put his arms round her. 'Don't you like playing ladies?'

'Not all the time.'

'What would you like to do?'

Esme smiled up at him. 'This will do for now,' and kissed him lightly, on the lips. Taking a chance. Expecting . . . what? Embarrassment? Rejection? Too late now; she'd played her hand . . .

He was kissing her! Firmly. Lovingly. Without the slightest concern that two women passing by hissed disapproval! He looked over to them, grinned, and wished them good day.

'Bang goes your reputation, Es,' he laughed.

'Let me worry about that.'

They walked to the end of the gardens and back, arms linked like a courting couple, but talking amiably of this and that, of the hotel, of Constance, and finally Esme had to ask: 'You're very quiet about Jake Tussup. Why is that?'

'Because I haven't anything to say. Yet. By the way, when is Eleanor going back?'

'Another week or so. I think she'd like to do more for Constance.'

'I don't know why she doesn't take up Lavinia's invitation and go to stay with the Lewises.'

There was amusement in his voice and Esme knew full well why he wanted Eleanor, alone, to accept the invitation and leave their shared hotel room.

'Because Raymond is keen on her and she doesn't want to offend him,' she said, as if she hadn't noticed. 'She's not interested.'

'She isn't?' Mal was genuinely surprised. 'I must tell Jesse. He's been mooning over her ever since he met her, but he's convinced Raymond's the one.'

'Well, you can tell him the coast's clear. That would be nice – Eleanor and Jesse; they're both interested in writers and poets. And if that works out, there's another reason for me to move on. I don't want to be the gooseberry.'

They reached the gate and he kissed her on the cheek. 'Come on, you don't want to be late for dinner either.'

That night they played cards in the parlour with other guests, and Mal thought Esme looked wonderful with her hair softly waved at the front and swept up into burnished coils on the crown. She had little pink rosebuds tucked in around the crown, which to him seemed very romantic, especially since they drew his eye to the pink rose between her breasts on that low-cut dress.

He knew he'd been too offhand earlier, only being chummy after she'd kissed him. After he'd responded with the greatest of pleasure. But he'd been stalling. He hadn't known what to say. Couldn't decide what to say, more like it. There was a mutual attraction, he knew that, and he'd known it would only be a matter of time before they'd come together – like today – if only for a few minutes. But he wondered if they were simply a comfort to each other. And if, when the pain of the deaths receded, so too would the need for comfort. Keeping in mind that Neville's death was more recent.

Personally, he could see nothing wrong with a little comfort, but with Esme? He wouldn't want to take advantage of her. Maybe, he decided, I'd better have a real talk with her and sort this out. Or sort myself out, he added as he dealt the cards.

The next day he made an early morning visit to St Clement's, putting the horse to the gallop across the flat country for the sheer joy of it. He arrived in high spirits, only to find a new matron in charge, one who was stricter with the rules when it came to visiting hours, and he was sent away. Told to come back at three o'clock.

This didn't suit Mal, but he retreated politely, riding down the road until he came to the end of St Clement's long front fence. Then he turned inland and followed the fence into the bush that surrounded the complex.

As soon as he worked out where Constance's room was located, he hitched the horse to a tree, took off his jacket and tie, and rolled up his sleeves so that he'd fit in with several workmen he'd seen in the grounds. He took off his waistcoat too, exposing his braces, and nodded approval at that extra effort.

In minutes Mal was over the fence and walking casually between the buildings.

When he arrived outside Constance's door, he heard her arguing with a nurse, and even though the exchange became heated, he kept out of it, walking round the block and back again in time to see the nurse slam the door and storm away along the veranda.

'What was that all about?' he asked as he knocked and stuck his head in the door.

'Oh, Mal!' she cried. 'I'm so pleased to see you. They've sacked Matron Bassani, and the new person has taken away my privileges. She says that just because I am who I am, I don't get any special treatment. But I told the nurse I don't get any special treatment because of that. I simply pay more! They say I can't have meals in my room any more, and I have to take part in the stupid exercises, and they've even taken away my books! I won't have it!'

'And you shouldn't,' he told her. 'Definitely not. If that's the way they're going to treat you now, it's time you left here. I've never seen you so upset.'

'I know. I look terrible. I haven't even done my hair yet. It's early, isn't it?'

'Yes. Do you want me to arrange for you to leave here? I can do that.' How, he wasn't sure.

But Constance drew back. 'Leave here? No, I couldn't do that. No.'

He sat with her, holding a hand mirror while she brushed her hair, trying to persuade her to agree to leave, and eventually she relented a little.

'I can't leave, Mal. I've nowhere to go. I won't go back to Lyle and his taunts. I won't.'

'Don't worry. I've suddenly got a very good idea. Why don't you go home to your father?'

'To England? He'd never let me. Lyle wouldn't allow it.'

'He just might. Would you like me to ask him?'

'What's the use? I have to stay here.'

'Not any more.' The conversation reminded him of Emilie, who was escaping physical abuse, but a lot of Constance's problems were in her own mind. He doubted if England would make any difference in the long run. Again he wondered what help Tussup could be to her. But the main thing, he thought, was to get her out of this madhouse.

Eventually, she admitted she might leave if the matron didn't understand her situation, and Mal decided, on his return journey, that he might as well see Lyle himself.

'How are you, Lyle?' he asked when he was shown into a sunny sitting room.

'*Sir* Lyle now, dear boy. Didn't you hear?'

'Oh yes, sorry, I forgot. How have things been going for you?'

'Not so well. There are still repercussions from the loss of *China Belle*. And we're having problems at Oriental Shipping. One of our directors died suddenly, and there's a lot of confusion so I'll have to go back to Hong Kong for a while, just when I was getting this house in order. Nice place, don't you think? I was surprised to find a house of this standard here; thought I'd have to build. Come and I'll show you round. Then we might have a bite of lunch, eh? I don't get many visitors. New to the town, you know how it is.'

Lyle was querulous, and more frail than Mal remembered him, so he went out of his way to be kind to the old chap as they trailed through the house with its drawing room and imposing dining room, comfortable parlour and library, all the while listening to Lyle's woes with the Oriental Shipping Line.

The tour didn't include upstairs, for which Mal was grateful, but Lyle ushered him along the passage to another door:

'Now this is my pride and joy. There's another one exactly the same upstairs. What do you think?'

Mal gazed at a white-tiled bathroom with a huge tub, running water and a water closet. 'That's really something, isn't it?' he said. 'I'd like all this in my house!'

'You're going to build? Then, my dear fellow, look no further. There's a vacant block next door. A beautiful block. You should snap it up.'

'Thank you, sir, but I'm going bush. I'll be looking for a special property. A sheep run that might be coming on the market. That'll keep me busy.'

Lyle seemed disappointed. 'I dare say,' he mumbled. 'I'll show you the garden now.'

Before they stepped out on to a side terrace Lyle issued lunch instructions to a woman who was coming along the passage.

'She's my housekeeper,' he told Mal. 'Ugly as sin but a good worker. Constance never got along with her at all.'

By this time Mal had almost given up hope that Lyle would introduce his wife into the conversation, but at last here was a chance.

'Lady Horwood's in St Clement's,' he said, for want of a more tactful approach.

'Who told you that? Oh, no need to say! That Plummer woman, I'll bet. Telling the world I had my wife put away! She's a dreadful woman. She's started shocking rumours and people have been downright rude to me.'

Agitated, he changed his mind about the garden and dropped into a wide cane chair on the terrace, waving at Mal to do likewise. 'I'm doing the best for my wife,' he groaned. 'It's costing me plenty to have her there, and what thanks do I get for it? Nothing but complaints. Even Raymond turned on me.'

'What will happen to Lady Horwood when you go back to China?'

'Nothing. She'll be all right there. And her father is coming out from England. He should be here shortly.'

'Her father? Here?' Mal almost laughed with relief.

'Yes, he's arriving in Sydney on the SS *Liverpool* in a week or so.'

'That is good news. But he mightn't be too happy to find Lady Horwood in an asylum.'

'What?' Lyle roared. 'How dare you call it an asylum?'

'Because it is, sir,' Mal said gently. 'It's an asylum all right. People know that, and people talk. Especially the asylum administrators,' he lied, 'who are boasting that your wife is their star boarder, so to speak.'

'Star boarder!' Lyle gasped. 'My wife?'

'Yes. And why wouldn't they? But, Sir Lyle, listen to me . . . you know that of all the people connected with *China Belle*, I was the one who suffered the most.'

'Good God! Don't tell me you're going to sue! Oriental Shipping is in enough trouble . . .'

Mal shook his head. 'No, I'm not. No amount of money will bring my dear wife back. But I do care about everyone else. You included. We've all been seriously affected one way and another.'

'You can say that again,' Lyle grumbled. 'There's no bloody end to it. I'm even having to drag back to Hong Kong. Serious problems with the insurers as well, you know.'

'The next in line is your wife. She needs help, but she's very unhappy in the . . . you know. That place. Well . . . Lavinia Lewis, you know her?'

'Yes, nice woman. She's supposed to assist me with my library but she hasn't turned up.'

'Lavinia thinks people here have let you down. That you needed help with Lady Horwood and you didn't get it, so you did the best you could.'

'That's true . . .' Lyle said plaintively.

'So she has volunteered to look after Constance at her lovely home. What a weight off your shoulders if the good lady does that! Her father couldn't complain and you'll be able to return to Hong Kong without having to worry. Unless . . . I'm sorry . . . jumping the gun a bit. Unless of course, Lady Horwood is travelling with you?'

'No, no, no!' He looked at Mal suspiciously. 'Are you trying to manipulate me?'

'I'm trying to make things better for everyone. That's all. And nothing will improve for the Horwoods as long as Lady Horwood stays in a madhouse. You know that, Lyle, as well as I do. And when do we get lunch?'

Chapter Twenty

Friday at last. Mal was at Lanfield's office on time, to hear that Mr Watkins had located Jake Tussup in Goulburn. According to his report, Tussup owned an acreage on the outskirts of Goulburn and had recently taken up residence in a disused cottage on that property. It appeared he was now in the process of renovating that cottage.

'Watkins is a very efficient fellow,' Lanfield said. 'He telegraphed the information yesterday.'

He leafed through some papers on his desk and handed them to Mal one by one. 'This is his address in Sydney, should you require further assistance from him, Mr Willoughby. This is the name and address of a barrister in Sydney who will guide you if you decide to go ahead and charge Tussup with unlawful detention. And this is my account.'

Mal took the papers. 'Thank you, Mr Lanfield. I knew you'd have an answer. I'll pay this bill straight away. I can't thank you enough – for the second time.'

Lanfield stood, and straightened his starched collar. He coughed, rubbed his nose. 'It is not usual for me to discuss another client of mine, but in this case I'll make allowances. Mrs Hillier was here.'

'I thought so. Is she going ahead with the divorce?'

'Yes. And I think you did quite the right thing in giving her the amount of money you did, though she was mortified at having to take it.'

Mal shrugged. 'She shouldn't be. I told her I owed her.'

'Exactly. You did owe her,' Lanfield said primly. 'She went to great lengths to help you when you were in serious trouble.'

'And now she's gone home to England?'

'No. She wanted you to think that to avoid any further embarrassment. She's here in Brisbane.'

'Where is she living, Mr Lanfield?'

'I couldn't possibly reveal a client's address. But when you pay my clerk, you might mention the matter to him. He's been known to tattle occasionally.'

* * *

When Willoughby left, Robert Lanfield stood at the window of his office, looking across at the cathedral. He'd been shocked when Emilie Hillier had come to see him, with a cast on her arm, seeking a divorce.

Willoughby had been madly in love with her. And well he should be, Robert had thought at the time. Emilie Tissington was a lovely young English girl, well educated, and she had the sweetest nature. But what was Willoughby? A young bushman, handsome but barely educated, and of no fixed address. And when she'd come to beg Robert to help Willoughby, he'd been in St Helena prison!

Taking a fatherly interest in the girl, Robert had accepted the case, but right from the start he'd disapproved of the friendship. Willoughby wasn't right for her. He'd considered the man beneath Emilie's station in life, and more or less let her know. When she'd chosen Hillier, of the two men courting her, he'd been relieved that the girl had enough sense to make the right choice.

Now he wished he could take that back. He'd been wrong. Who'd have thought Hillier would turn out such a blackguard, and Willoughby the better man?

Even so, he mused, you just never knew with men like Willoughby. Their lives had a way of going awry. He wondered if Willoughby would try to pick up the pieces. He hoped not; the Hillier marriage wasn't over yet. But this time he had to give him a sporting chance; take his finger off the scale, so to speak.

He called to his clerk. 'Did Mr Willoughby settle his account?'

'Yes, sir.'

'And . . .'

'No. He didn't ask.'

'Good.'

After she was persuaded to be sweet instead of stern with Lyle Horwood, for Constance's sake, Lavinia went into action. She was a whirlwind of an organiser and gloried in it.

Their guest room was prepared, a nurse engaged to care for Lady Horwood during the day, and the latest magazines were placed by the window seat. Then at the appointed time she set out with Raymond, in their gig, to collect the patient, lecturing him all the way on how best Lady Horwood was to be treated. Reminding him also that everyone must respect Lady Horwood's title at all times and no one was to call her Constance.

'I'm quite firm about that,' she said. 'Proper respect will work wonders for her confidence. And we'll have set visiting hours. I told Sir Lyle that, so that the household isn't disrupted. Three to four in the afternoon. And your friend Mrs Plummer – see to it that she doesn't turn up at the same time as Sir Lyle. I can understand her attitude to Sir Lyle when she heard about Lady

Horwood, but I would never condone her bad manners. Attacking the man at the theatre, and embarrassing everyone. Quite uncalled for.'

'Yes, dear,' he muttered again, as the gig skidded along the sandy road, and Lavinia hoped he was paying attention. He'd been very tense ever since those women turned up, and she was sure that Mrs Plummer had her sights set on Raymond. After all, she was no spring chicken and he was a good catch. And despite the fact that Mrs Plummer was a smart dresser and a cultivated conversationalist, she was still a divorced woman, and that wouldn't do at all. Not that, as far as she knew, Raymond was considering remarriage. Why would he, at his age?

She swept into St Clement's, instructed the new matron to bring Lady Horwood and her belongings to reception, brushed aside the matron's insistence that Lady Horwood had changed her mind, and marched down to her room, where indeed she found Constance had gone back to bed.

'Good Lord, girl! Get up this minute. You can't drag me all the way out here for nothing. We had an arrangement, so stop your nonsense.'

As she dressed Constance, she lectured her. 'We have a lovely room for you. Private. No one will bother you. And stop hiding your face. You've got a tic – it's only nerves, it will go away. Consider yourself lucky you're still alive. Did you spare any tears for Mr Willoughby's wife? A beautiful young woman. She died. You're still alive. Count your blessings . . .'

'Mal said that,' Constance offered.

'But obviously you didn't listen to him.'

'I did so.'

'Good for you. Now come along, here's your hat. The nurse will bring up your luggage. I've got some good news for you, but I won't tell you until we are on our way home.'

'Have they found Jake Tussup?'

'Yes, but that's not the news.'

Lavinia breathed a sigh of relief as Raymond slapped the reins and the horses trotted down the drive and out of the gates of St Clement's.

'Now,' she said to Constance, 'you won't be running off on me the way you ran off in Cairns, will you?'

'No,' Constance said. 'But, Miss Lewis, I don't want to be a burden on you.'

'You won't be a burden. I'm very happy to have you come and stay with us. You'll have a nice time. We'll take walks around the block to get you used to being part of the human race again.'

'It's just that I feel I'm not up to facing people.'

'So you say, but you'd better stop feeling sorry for yourself or you'll end up back in there. Mal Willoughby was right. Your poor father would have a heart attack if he arrived to find his daughter in a lunatic asylum.'

'My father?'

'Yes, he's on his way to Sydney.'

'On the high seas right now,' Raymond added.

Constance burst into tears. She threw her arms around Lavinia, who blustered free of the spontaneous embrace and instructed Raymond to slow down 'before this girl tips us all out'.

Once she'd settled into the house, there wasn't much improvement in Lady Horwood's behaviour. When she did venture out she wore a veil on her hat and no one could convince her to remove it. But having made it into the world again, as Lavinia said, she surprised them by making an announcement.

'I'm going to Sydney to meet my father when his ship comes in. I have to do that. He would expect me to. How do I get there, Raymond? Preferably not by ship. Is there a train?'

'No. It's a long way, my dear. You'd have to go halfway by coach and then catch a train from Tamworth.'

'How far in all?'

'About five hundred miles, I think. Too far. You'd have to go by ship.'

'All right,' she said. 'If I have to I will.'

And I'll take all my meals in my cabin, like last time, she told herself. At least I'm feeling stronger now, having to keep up with Lavinia. And it is very pleasant here, I'm really grateful to them. I know Lavinia means well. I am trying not to feel sorry for myself, though I don't think I do. I just seem to have become shockingly shy. And my face is only part of it, I think. I don't know. Raymond says we should get a new doctor but Lavinia says I'm not sick. And I'm not. I feel well. Really well. Except I don't like visitors, not even Eleanor and Esme. Though I endure them, I don't have anything to say. Don't know what to talk about. Everyone avoids talking about *China Belle*. See. I'm back where I started. Except Mal, that is. But they avoid the subject when he's around too. I don't think he notices. I heard him telling them that Jake is in a town called Goulburn. His hometown. I looked it up on a map in Raymond's study. It's west of Sydney. I can't wait to see my father but he'll be shocked. He should have let me come home for a visit when I asked him, last time he was in Hong Kong. I was miserable then, so what's new about things with me these days? He'll want to hear all about the drama of *China Belle* too – and – oh God, what will he think about me being with all those brutes of men? Just as well none of them know my evening dress was hanging off me. Daddy might take Lyle's side in this, be ashamed of me. She felt the familiar blush spread across her face and neck.

Lyle came to say goodbye. He was on his way back to Hong Kong. Didn't know exactly when he would get back. The house was there for Constance and her father, she heard him tell Lavinia and Raymond, and the housekeeper is staying on.

'Not if I have to go back there,' Constance muttered to herself. With Lyle away though, she would have a chance to get all her things out of the house.

And take them where? Tears of frustration welled in her eyes as she sat at the dressing table buffing her nails. She looked up and adjusted the linen cloth that covered the dressing table mirror, and then turned to check the cheval glass. The sheet covering that mirror was still in place. Lady Horwood nodded, satisfied, and turned her attention to her nails, all bitten to the quick.

Jake had cleared the thick undergrowth that had all but hidden the cottage on the side of the hill. He chopped down trees and hauled away the roots to add to the pile of firewood by the back door. He used a machete to slash the high grass and thorny bushes that had taken over the former gardens, and burned them along with the musty furniture he dragged out of the house. Then he thought about burning down the cottage and starting again, but decided against that. Instead, he pulled down the back wall and set about preparing the foundations for a much bigger house. And all the while he marvelled at how small this cottage was. He'd been shocked on his return to find it had shrunk to no more than a tiny shack with a pint-sized timber veranda at front, and barely enough room for the two chairs his parents had used. Their son Jake had always sat on the step.

The day had started out warm and sunny, but now it was turning cold. He remembered people used to say that Goulburn could have several seasons in one day, and he'd swear to that now. He tramped down to the dilapidated fence where he'd hung his shirt, and just as he reached for it he heard a shot, a deafening shot as a bullet ploughed into a nearby fence post.

There was a horseman down by the gate. He was wearing a sheepskin jacket and had a rawhide hat jammed on his head. He also had a rifle. He raised it and trained it on Jake, who shook his head. He'd known Willoughby would turn up sooner or later. Just a matter of time. But all along he'd been banking on his own estimation of the bugger, as he remembered him. Willoughby, the big quiet bushie, wouldn't shoot a man in cold blood.

'All right, Willoughby,' he yelled. 'You've had your fun, now get out of here.'

That was only bravado, Willoughby hadn't come all this way to turn about and ride off with only a warning shot. Jake sensed he'd have a fight on his hands and was glad he'd spent the last six months roughing it on the goldfields. He'd found muscles he hadn't known he owned, and was grateful for them these days. Land clearing was a tougher job than he'd reckoned on.

'Listen here, Willoughby . . .' he called, striding forward.

He saw the rifle, the barrel like a single glittering eye, and he saw the finger tighten on the trigger before that familiar bang shocked him. It blew him back into the woodheap like a piece of old junk.

Mal had a talk with Esme the night before he left for Sydney on the same ship as Lavinia and Lady Horwood.

He let her talk; encouraged her to talk about every little thing. About herself. About Neville. About them. And she told him as much as she could; explaining that the Caporns were actually broke and had come to this country to start a new life. They'd invested in various business ventures in the East, she'd explained, when Neville wasn't working in the public service, but they hadn't done all that well. In fact, Esme told him all she could without lying.

She knew a lot about Mal, she told him, from Jesse, and from the book of clippings the reporter had, all about the gold robbery.

'And the murders,' Mal added. 'No need to slide over them. I was accused of the murder of the guards as well.'

'I know,' she said gently. 'It must have been a bad time.'

'I've had worse.'

Esme gulped. 'And now you're going to find Tussup?'

'I've found him.'

'I know that. I mean, are you leaving again?'

'Yes.'

'What about us? I'll miss you. Dammit, I love you. What am I going to do about that?'

'There's the trouble, Es. I don't know. I love you too in my way. I keep saying I want to settle, to get that sheep property, but I'm still not sure I do any more. I might be kidding myself. And you, Es? Am I the one you need just now, a friend? I could turn out to be no more than that.'

'Are you saying it's too soon for us?'

'It could be . . . I think so . . . why don't we let things ride for a while?'

She was angry. 'Oh very well. If that's the way you want it. But I may not be available when you do decide to come a-calling. I didn't say I'd sit on the stoop and wait for you. But you go and chase your revenge, Mal Willoughby, and when you've run Tussup down, you'll be looking about to find someone else to hate! And it bloody doesn't become you! Now get going and leave me alone!'

When she turned on her heel and stormed away, Mal was shocked. He'd expected her to understand what he was trying to say, not a tirade like that, and he didn't know what he should do. He thought of running after her, but maybe that would only annoy her more. Besides . . . did she really think he was full of hate? Was he?

Mal shuddered. Where had all the love gone now? Was there none left for Esme? If so, she deserved better.

Miserably he tramped back along the deserted streets, irritated by the mournful call of a curlew.

Mrs Plummer, in a long white shantung coat and a large burnished straw hat, was carrying a colourful Japanese umbrella when she came down to see them off on the Sydney-bound ship, but there was no sign of Esme, and Mal was disappointed.

'I thought you and Esme made such a nice couple,' she said to him. 'But Esme says it's not in the cards. I'm thrilled, though, that she's coming back to Cairns with me, after all.'

Mal groaned. 'To Cairns? I hoped she'd wait here in Brisbane.'

'What for?'

'For me to come back.'

'I see.' She raised her eyebrows and peered at him. 'Why would you come back?'

Mal sighed. Exasperated. 'For Esme, of course. If that's what she wants . . .'

'Well, why didn't you tell her that?'

'I don't know, Mrs Plummer. I tried to. It's very hard to know what to do for the best. What's best in the long run, I mean. I have to go south now, not just to have a word with Tussup. It's to find out more about a property I'm thinking of buying.'

'And where is that? Further away still? No wonder Esme's confused. You're always dashing off into the wilds.'

Mal took her hands. 'This time it isn't out in the wilds. Trust me. It's not all that far from Brisbane.' He grinned. 'As the crow flies. Will you tell Esme I'll write and tell her all about it?'

'You'll have to do better than that.'

'How?'

She shut down the parasol. 'I don't think this thing is any good against the sun.'

'Because it's made of paper,' he said. 'The sun would more likely burn a hole in the thing.'

'Well then, I'd better be off. Time for you to go aboard, Mal.'

'Wait, don't go, Mrs Plummer, please. Tell Esme I do love her. Will you do that?'

'And?'

'And what? Oh, all right. I promise I'll be back as soon as I can. As soon as I can find the right property, and become one of the landed gentry. I'll have a home to offer her then. I think that's what we both need.'

She beamed. 'That's more like it, dear boy.'

Lavinia was having the time of her life in Sydney. She and Lady Horwood were staying with Mr and Mrs Somerville in their mansion overlooking Rose Bay – the Somervilles being the parents of Raymond's late wife. They were in Sydney for a week before SS *Liverpool* sailed up the harbour, but what a week it had been! Julia Somerville certainly knew how to entertain her guests. Every day something was arranged, be it luncheons or sight-seeing trips, even one to the zoo – or visits to the most interesting museums and galleries, and of an evening there were dinner parties, or suppers after the theatre.

As expected, Lady Horwood refused to accompany them, but that didn't bother Lavinia. She'd accompanied Lady Horwood to Sydney as chaperone, and she would see to it that the girl met her father's ship. There ended her duties.

She smiled wryly now, remembering she'd had to insist Lyle leave some money for his wife.

'The old villain,' she told Raymond. 'Constance hasn't got a penny. Don't let him get away.'

'Does she need money? I mean, she's all right here.'

'That's nothing to do with it. She needs money, and not a few pounds. You make Lyle give her a bank account. We're going to Sydney, remember. Will you pay for her? And don't forget all her jewellery was stolen on that ship. She can't socialise in Sydney without a speck of jewellery, for heaven's sake! And she needs new clothes, a lot of new clothes. Now see to it right away!'

Raymond had seen to it. Eventually. After a lot of argument. And Lavinia had ordered travel outfits, evening dresses and a selection of jewellery to be brought to the house for Lady Horwood's approval. Such as it was. She'd been grateful to Lavinia for her efforts, agreeing with Lavinia's preferences, but was disappointingly listless about the whole business. At the time, Lavinia had been irritated by her attitude; she'd believed that surely the sight of these lovely new clothes would put some life in her, but they had no effect at all.

In fact, not much here in Sydney either. Most of the outfits and none of the jewellery had seen the light of day.

Mal Willoughby had stayed in town and twice he'd persuaded her to walk with him around a nearby bay, but she wouldn't budge without the veiled hat.

'Protection from mosquitoes,' he'd laughed, unconcerned.

Then came the great day and they all went down to welcome Lady Horwood's father, a portly fellow with charming manners. His daughter dissolved into a flood of tears and clung to him, near to hysteria, and when they eventually set down from the carriage at the Rose Bay house, it was left to Lavinia to explain his daughter's behaviour to Percy Feltham.

The poor fellow was distraught, and outraged to hear that Constance had been in a mental institute. He was equally upset that Lyle had gone back to Hong Kong, leaving his sick wife in a strange land.

Lavinia smiled. 'It's not strange to us, and as you see, Lady Horwood has good friends in this country.'

But the arrival of Feltham made a difference. Constance came down to breakfast, without a hat and veil. Everyone was delighted to see her, but after a warning glance from Lavinia, they pretended to take her presence for granted, as if this were normal for her.

Feltham spent the day talking to Constance. He listened, chastened, he told Lavinia, to everything she said, because he blamed himself for allowing the situation with Horwood to get out of hand.

'Mainly it's the *China Belle* disaster that has caused Lady Horwood to be in such a state,' Lavinia told him.

'I know that now. Horwood wrote to me after they arrived in Cairns, telling me not to worry if the *China Belle* saga was mentioned in our papers, as it was. He said he and Constance had emerged unhurt from the débâcle.'

'The wretch! He lied!'

'I am so sorry.' Feltham shook his head. 'I had no idea that Constance was abducted! My God! What the poor girl went through! I believe an officer, Mr Tussup, rescued her from the Asian thugs. I'd like to see him and thank him.'

'Careful there, Mr Feltham. He was the one who organised that wholesale desertion of the crew.'

'He what? She didn't tell me that. I would appreciate your help, Miss Lewis, in piecing this frightful story together.'

His business in Sydney complete, Mal had come to say goodbye. He had bought a new horse, a Thoroughbred, which Mr Somerville greatly admired, and while he waited for Constance and her father to come up from their walk along the seashore, he mentioned that he was on his way to Goulburn.

'Great country there,' Somerville had told him. 'I believe you're looking for a property; you could do worse than that area.'

'So I've heard, but I've been hankering to get back out to the Darling Downs, just over the border into Queensland. I know that area well. Temperate climate. Good sheep country. There's one up there would suit me fine. But first I've got business in Goulburn, and then I'll ride back north. I've had enough of ships.'

He had a long talk with poor Percy Feltham, who seemed exhausted already, after the long sea voyage, and his worries with Constance.

'I'd like to take my daughter back to England with me,' he told Mal. 'Lyle can keep his house in Brisbane, and servants who treat Constance like dirt. She wants a divorce and I'll see she gets it, and an appropriate settlement. I think it's the best thing to do,' he said wearily. 'Any woman would be a bundle of nerves after what happened to her, being dragged ashore by thugs.'

'Her main problem is shame. She thinks people don't believe that the crew didn't molest her, though she spent nights with them in the bush. Get her over that and I reckon she'll see the light on the horizon.'

The lad chasing rabbits heard the shots and ran down the hill to the old farmhouse. He saw the rider gallop away down the road! He ran into the yard and found a man slumped at the foot of the woodheap. Boysie Hume thought the man was dead. He looked dead with all that blood all over him, and his eyes, burrowed in dark shadows, were closed.

Boysie thought he'd better go tell somebody about the dead man, shot down by an outlaw, by the looks of things, when the dead man moaned, and Boysie jumped nearly a foot in the air.

He ran. Out of there. Down the road. Yelling.

Neighbours came and Boysie watched, spellbound, as they produced torn sheets to try to stop the blood pouring out of the feller, and then they wrapped him in a blanket and put him gently on to a cart and took him to the Goulburn Hospital in Sloane Street. Boysie rode in the back with him, and when the wardsmen came out with a litter to carry the feller inside, Boysie was right there beside him.

Doc Flaherty hurried out to examine him, shoving Boysie out of the way.

'Who did this?' he yelled as he dipped into the blood and gore.

'Willoughby,' Boysie said. 'He told me on the way in.'

'Who did it?' the doc asked the victim, ignoring Boysie.

'Willoughby,' he whispered, his voice fading.

'See, I told you so,' Boysie exclaimed. 'It was Willoughby done it.'

'Who's Willoughby?' a nurse asked, and they all looked blank.

'Never heard of no Willoughby round here,' Boysie said. 'I reckon he's an outlaw.'

'Boysie,' the doc said. 'Get out of here. If you want to make yourself useful, go get the police. But wait a tick. What's this bloke's name?'

'I dunno,' the lad said, and spun away.

He didn't have far to run. Constable Jackson was already hitching his horse to the picket fence out front of the hospital.

'That's not allowed,' Boysie told him. 'You can't hitch your horse there. Matron goes crook.'

The horse stayed. The constable opened the gate and strode up the path, Boysie after him.

'You come to see about the shooting, eh?'

'Yes.' Jackson was at the open front door, there being not much space between the fence and the building, which Boysie always thought looked like a dark old haystack.

'I know who did it.'

'You do?'

Boysie smirked. The copper wasn't so smart now. 'Yes. It was Willoughby done it. And I seen him. Seen him ride off like the hobs of hell.'

They both waited outside the operating theatre. No one seemed to know who the victim was, but Boysie was able to say he'd been working at the old farmhouse up on Dangar Road. A nurse gave Boysie a cake; sent them both off. She said it wasn't much help them taking up space in the corridor when the victim wouldn't be out of surgery for ages and then there'd be no talking to him. He'd been shot in the chest and was in a real bad way.

The constable let Boysie ride with him to the farmhouse where they searched his belongings. They found cash in a drawer, a fair whack of cash.

'I'd say he must have bought the old farm,' Jackson said. 'And he's giving it a good clean up. I'll have to get someone out here to hang some hessian where he's taken the wall down, to protect what's in here from dust and dirt. Reckon the owner won't be back in a hurry. Can you ride a horse, son?'

'Too right!'

'Saddle up his horse then. You can ride it into town.'

By the time they reached the police station the town was abuzz with excitement over the cold-blooded shooting of a newcomer to the town.

Constable Jackson wrote up his report and the sergeant sent two men out to scour the town for someone called Willoughby, and bring him in.

He didn't hold that someone could be living and working in this town and not be known, so he headed for the real estate sales office down the road.

'Has someone bought the old Tussup farm?' he asked the staff.

Not to their knowledge.

He then headed for the Shire Council Offices, where he found that the land was registered in the name of J. Tussup, and recently someone had paid outstanding registration fees.

'They don't amount to much,' the shire clerk told him, 'but when they bring in the land tax they're talking about, we're all going to be hit where it hurts. How is that bloke, anyway?'

'Hurt bad, I hear. I'm going over there now.'

The sergeant didn't go straight to the hospital, though. He went to a house in Lorne Street to visit Carl Muller, a retired police officer.

'I think Jake Tussup's come home,' he said. 'But he didn't get much of a welcome. Someone called Willoughby shot him this morning. He's still alive, but not too good. Could you spare a minute to come over to the hospital and identify him? I'm only guessing. I wasn't here at the time your Sergeant Hawthorne got shot by Tussup Senior.'

'Yes, I remember,' Muller said. 'You were Hawthorne's replacement. I haven't seen young Tussup in years, of course. He'd be a grown man now. Sad about that whole business. She never married again, Mrs Hawthorne. Brought up those boys on her own.'

The two men found Dr Flaherty cleaning up after delivering twins.

'Your man's low,' he told them. 'Took a bullet in the chest, he did, and that had to be dug out. He lost a lot of blood and has a high fever, gentlemen. With a punctured lung and all, but we've sewn him up and asked the Lord God to give us a hand with him.'

'Can we see him?' Muller asked.

'Sure, Carl, but you'll not get any sense out of him. He's only just come out of the ether.'

They went quietly into the recovery ward and a nurse took them to the victim's bedside.

'Dark hair like the father,' Carl said. 'And the same-shaped face. It could be him. I'm not sure. Didn't they find any identification at the cottage?'

'No. Money and provisions, that's all. And the horse.'

The patient opened his eyes suddenly and groaned. He tried to sit up. 'Where am I?' he cried, and the nurse rushed forward to settle him down.

'That's him all right,' Carl whispered as the nurse waved at them to leave. 'It's Jake Tussup come home after all this time! It must be fifteen years since they hanged his dad. The kid took off, went to sea, they say. You wouldn't want to stay around after that, would you?'

The ride from Sydney out to the Goulburn plains was much more to Mal's liking than the hazardous northern journeys. He had a good horse, and a good road through open country, but he'd been warned that there were pickings in this area for outlaws, so he still had a rifle in its holster by the saddle. It seemed all his life on horseback he'd travelled with a trusty gun, he mused, as he reined in the horse at a roadside inn, but at least he'd dumped the knife.

'How much further to Goulburn?' he asked when he walked into the bar and ordered a pint.

'Only about forty miles,' the innkeeper said. 'You want a bed for the night?'

'Yes, I might as well. Get an early start tomorrow.'

In his room Mal checked the papers the barrister had given him, setting aside the thin file he'd been instructed to hand to the Goulburn police. This could have been arranged by the Sydney police but he preferred to do it himself. He wanted to accompany the bailiff when the summons was issued to Tussup, to make sure there was no slip-up. He would be there to point the bastard out himself. To have Tussup see him when he was summonsed to appear on a charge of abduction, or whatever it was in legalese. To know Mal Willoughby had him at last.

He had talked to Constance about the changes he intended to lay against Tussup, and, as he expected, she almost fainted at the idea of having to appear in court.

'No, no, I couldn't do that, Mal! How could you suggest such a thing?'

'But this is what you need. When Tussup is in court on all of these charges, he can tell the world that none of the men put a finger on you. He'll be under oath. You say people think the worst, even your husband, but you can prove it now. The truth will be on record for ever.'

She was confused. 'Why would Jake Tussup say that in court?'

'Because I'll have my barrister ask him. He'll tell the truth. No reason not to.'

Constance thought about that. 'It would also be in his interest to say he got me away from them, wouldn't it?'

'Yes.'

'And what exactly would I have to do?'

'I'm charging him with unlawful detention. He and those other men held you against your will. The few Malays in prison are also liable, but Tussup's the ringleader.'

'Oh yes, I see.'

'Good. And thank you, Constance. I'm really grateful to you for this. Tussup has to be punished. He caused Jun Lien's death and poor Flesser's, and—'

She clapped her hands to her ears. 'No, don't. Please, Mal, I don't want to hear any more about it. I can't . . .'

'All right,' he soothed. 'All right. We won't talk about it again. But take heart now, Constance. Once the court case is over, that will be he end of it. And thank God for that.'

She nodded, dabbing at her eyes with her handkerchief, but he had the distinct feeling that she was avoiding his gaze. Then rather slyly she commented: 'I heard a whisper that you were courting Esme Caporn. Is it true?'

He smiled. 'I hope to. I hope she doesn't give up on me.'

'She won't,' Constance sighed. 'How fortunate she is to have someone so understanding to lean on after all of our travails. But, of course, my husband, Lyle, has always been a selfish man.'

'And your father?' Mal persisted. 'Do I have your permission to tell him what we propose to do?'

'Oh no, I wouldn't spring it on him just yet. I'll tell him quietly myself.'

Not the most stable of situations, Mal knew, but it was as close as he could get to introducing Tussup to prison. He'd heard there was a mighty old gaol in Goulburn. That would do.

The next evening he rode into Goulburn's lamplit streets as the shops were closing and people were retreating to their homes. He took time for a look around the town centre, with its churches and hotels and courthouse, past shops and factories and the offices of a newspaper, the *Evening Post*, and felt that he could have been in any one of these country towns. He'd seen so many of them in his wanderings they'd all begun to look alike to him.

Mal was tired, but before he took a room at a hotel he wanted to get the legal work underway, so he turned back and made for the large stone building that housed the constabulary.

Constable Jackson was on duty at the front counter. He liked this shift. The nights were cold now and it was warm in here, and you got dinner sent in from the pub next door.

'And,' he told himself, 'it's always interesting. You never know what's going to walk in the door of a police station.'

He looked up when a tall man in a pricey winter jacket pushed through the front door, and guessed this'd be someone from the squatter families with their big properties to the west.

The stranger placed some papers on the counter. 'I am advised by my barrister to ask your boss to have a look at these documents and arrange for a bailiff to issue a summons as a result, as soon as possible.'

'All right sir,' Jackson said, and he picked up a pen, licked the nib, dipped it in ink and hovered over the daily logbook. 'Let me make an entry here. Your name?'

'Willoughby. Malachi Willoughby.'

The constable gulped. 'Address?'

'Royal Hotel, Goulburn will do for the time being.'

It was too much for the constable. 'All right,' he croaked. 'Hang on a minute, I'll get the sergeant.'

He ducked away from the counter and sped down the passage to the common room where the sergeant was reading his paper.

'It's Willoughby!' he burst out. 'I've got him out the front there. It's him! What do I do now?'

The sergeant was on his feet, ambling up the passage towards the front entrance of the police station, his tread ominous.

'Your name's Willoughby?' he asked slowly. No need to panic.

'Yes.'

'Do you know a feller called Tussup? Jake Tussup?'

'Yes I do. This is why I'm here.'

Quick as a flash the sergeant whipped handcuffs from the hook under the counter, and tossed them to Jackson. 'Put them on him. You're under arrest, Willoughby, for the attempted murder of Jake Tussup.'

'What?'

No matter how much Willoughby roared – 'and he could roar!' Jackson told people later – the sergeant wasn't letting him go. It look the two of them to drag and shove him down the back to the lockup.

Then the sergeant went off to tell the inspector that they had Willoughby in custody, and when they brought in Jackson's dinner from next door, of course he told them, and soon the whole pub knew and there was no stopping the news now.

A reporter from the *Evening News* dashed in the door.

'Can I have an interview with Willoughby?' he asked urgently. 'There's a bottle of whisky in it for you, Jackson.'

'What size?'

The reporter grinned. 'Pint.'

'All right. But don't hang about too long, the sergeant'll be back soon.'

Mal Willoughby recognised a reporter as soon as he appeared on the other side of the bars.

'Not again,' he sighed angrily. 'Bloody hell! Not again!'

The reporter peered into his cage. 'Haven't I seen you somewhere before?'

'No!' Mal shouted. 'No, you bloody haven't! Go and get me a lawyer.'

Within days, news of the Goulburn shooting was in the Sydney papers, and Lavinia was the first to spot it.

'Good heavens. Jake Tussup has been shot!' she cried, rushing outside to tell Constance. 'He's fighting for his life in the Goulburn Hospital! Mal must have shot him! Lord help us, what a world we live in. I must write to Raymond straight away.'

Constance was far more distressed than Lavinia had expected. 'Show me the paper.' she cried. 'That can't be right. Why would Mal shoot him? He only wanted him arrested, and brought to trial.'

'I think that young man might have been pushed too far, what with his wife's death,' her father said. 'It's understandable that rage finally overtook him after all he's been through.'

'We have to go there, and see what's going on for ourselves,' Constance said. 'We can go by train.'

'You?' Lavinia was astonished. 'You want to go out there? Why on earth?'

'Because I have to, that's all. Father will accompany me, won't you?'

'I certainly will not. And I've decided that on no account will you be appearing in any court case to do with that fellow.'

'But I must! Mal's barrister will be asking Tussup certain questions regarding my situation.' She blushed. 'I explained that to you, Father.'

'So you did,' he said impatiently. 'But I don't believe it is necessary for you to be present during mention of such a graceless subject.'

Mr Somerville interrupted them. 'There's no mention of Mal shooting that fellow, in the paper. It says this happened two days ago. Mal couldn't have been anywhere near Goulburn that day. We mustn't jump to conclusions.'

'Quite right, sir,' Percy Feltham said. 'Now if you would excuse us, a word with you on the terrace, Constance, if you please.' Adding: 'Now, Constance, right now!'

She followed him anxiously through the French doors and out on to the high terrace, overlooking the bay. 'What is it?'

'I've had enough of this Tussup business. I want the subject closed once and for all.'

'After the court case, you mean?'

'No. Now. I understand Mr Willoughby needs you to give evidence, and I too would like to see the villain punished, but not at your expense. You are not to be demeaning yourself by appearing in court.'

'But I am a witness.'

'That's unfortunate, but I've been listening to you, and you don't seem to be able to make up your own mind about Tussup, let alone face court questioning. Time and again I've heard you say that he rescued you from the Malayamen.'

'He did. And I will thank him when I see him.'

'Really. While you're giving evidence that he kidnapped you! And waiting about for him to oblige you and tell the world you were in safe hands with those seamen. It will be scandal enough for you to obtain a divorce from Horwood, becoming involved in a criminal court case is worse. I'll write to Mr Willoughby and apologise on your behalf, and that will be the end of it. We're sailing on the next ship bound for London, and as far as I'm concerned, the sooner the better.'

'But . . .'

'No buts, girl! I've already discussed this with Lavinia. She will arrange for all your effects in the Brisbane house to be sent on. Now you go and make up a list for her, while I go down to the shipping office and book passages.'

Constance hurried through to her room and sat on the bed with a thump. She felt a vague sense of loss, and found herself thinking of Jake Tussup. Even then she hardly dared admit that her father had come very close to the truth, that she had so readily agreed to go to court at Mal's request, because she had hoped to see Tussup again. She'd known her feelings about him were at odds with allowing herself to be his accuser, and was nervous of letting her thoughts about Jake go a step further. Into confusion.

Confusion! She took a deep breath. 'Father's right,' she told herself. 'He is right. I'll be glad to be back home in England and put all this behind me, once and for all.' And strangely, she recalled, wasn't that what Mal suggested when I was in St Clement's? 'Why don't you go home to London?' he'd said. 'You can't stay in this madhouse!'

She smiled. Madhouse! Trust Mal to come right out and use a word like that! I can't imagine what I was thinking of, to have stayed there. I really had lost my way, and if it hadn't been for good friends like Mal and Raymond, I might still be there.

'You'll pay, Lyle Horwood,' she said as she stood up and took the covers off the mirrors. 'Oh, my word, this divorce will cost you a pretty penny. Then, back in London, I'll be the wealthy Lady Horwood.'

Mal was out of prison and holed up at the Imperial Hotel, to avoid reporters, who hoped his alibi wouldn't stand up to police checks.

Fortunately, he'd had the foresight to demand his private documents be returned to him, unread, while he was still in the cell, afraid that mention of his charges against Jake Tussup would send the police off into another frenzy of accusations. His connection with the shooting victim too close for comfort.

His lawyer warned him to keep away from the hospital, which suited Mal. He could hardly serve the summons at this stage. If anything, he thought angrily, forget the summons for a minute, why did the bastard have to claim I shot him? For a while he imagined the whole thing was a put-up job, that Tussup was malingering, but the local lawyer insisted he was not.

'He's seriously ill, Mal. No doubt about that.'

'Then who did shoot him?'

'I've no idea. You stay put and I'll see what I can find out.'

Thoroughly frustrated, Mal went down to the dining room, took a table in a far corner and attacked a large steak with all the trimmings. He'd have to wait now for Tussup to recover. Deep in his heart Mal had a sinking feeling that Tussup was about to slip away from him – that everything was grinding to a halt, and somehow he didn't much care. Maybe because someone else had beaten him to the punch.

He thought about Jun Lien.

And considered going round to that hospital and inflicting more pain on Tussup. Chucking him out of the goddamn sick bed.

'But you won't,' Jun Lien whispered to him, as sweet as she ever was.

'No.'

'So it's over,' she said.

'Yes,' he admitted dully.

'I'm glad, my love. You can take your life back now, find new mountains to climb, and take joy in every sunrise.'

Mal noticed a secluded fernery outside the windows and walked out there to smoke a cigarette and begin to treasure her memory instead of battling the past. She had released him, allowed him to put down his grief, and he felt calmer now than he had been in a very long time. The rage had spun itself out, and he truly could look to new days with the same eagerness that had always amused Jun Lien. And the last person he wanted to think about was Tussup.

But when the lawyer came back, he told Mal that the police still hadn't found the shooter. 'Obviously someone in the town had it in for Mr Tussup.'

'Good. Do me a favour. When the victim recovers, tell him that whoever it was saved me the trouble. I have to be on my way now. I've got a long ride ahead of me.'

'Where are you going?'

'North. To a sheep station in Queensland, on the Condamine River, southwest of Brisbane.'

'That's hundreds of miles from here.'

Mal shrugged. 'I've ridden it before. I'm looking forward to it.'

'Then God speed, Mr Willoughby.'

Once Mr Tussup was deemed well enough to be interviewed, the sergeant took Carl Muller with him to the hospital, and Muller walked quietly over to the patient.

'How are you, Jake?'

'Bloody horrible. How would you think I am?' With an effort, he took a closer look at his visitor. 'It's you, Muller?' he wheezed. 'Did you get him?'

'Get who?'

'Willoughby! The bastard shot me.'

'No he didn't. The sergeant here had him in for questioning . . .'

'See! I told you so! He's here! He's been tracking me for more than a year. I knew it was him! I saw him at the farm. The bastard gave me no warning, he just raised his gun . . .' Jake's head fell back with the exertion. 'Next thing I know I'm in here with my chest on fire. He shot me!'

'You're wrong there, mate. He couldn't have. At the time you were shot he was forty miles away. The police have checked. He was nowhere near your farm.'

'It was him, I tell you. He's lying. He blames me for his wife's death.'

'He does?' Muller asked amiably. 'How did that come about, Jake?'

'An accident at sea. Unfortunate. Plenty of people saw what happened. She drowned, I couldn't help her, and neither could he. But that didn't stop him blaming me. He had to blame someone. So what does he do? Comes gunning for me. You have to lock him up.'

'We can't do that . . .'

'You have to,' Jake raged. 'I'm not safe with him out there. He's likely to hang around and finish the job!'

'There's no need to worry about Willoughby! He's gone.'

'What?' Jake screamed. 'You let him get away!'

An elderly nurse came running! 'Mr Muller, please. You'll have to leave, you and the sergeant. You're upsetting the patient! Look at him! The fever's on him again.' She bustled them to the door. 'Out! Out!'

'Could it have been Willoughby?' the retired police officer asked as they left the hospital.

'Not a chance. But the solicitor who sprung him from the lockup, said he was here to prefer charges against Tussup on another matter. But then when he heard Jake had been shot, he didn't bother. Apparently he said it saved him the trouble.'

At that, Muller stopped suddenly. 'That doesn't sound too good.'

'I know. If he *had* been in town at the time, a remark like that would have seen him roped in quick smart. But he couldn't have been in two places at once, no matter what Tussup says.'

The following day a tall grey-haired woman slipped in to see Mr Tussup, and bring him a box of iced cup cakes.

'You remember me, don't you, Jake?' she said, and he nodded, by no means pleased to see this visitor.

'I thought you might have called on us when you came back, Jake. To see how we were getting along? After all, you went to school with my lads. It's a hard thing to lose a husband.'

'What do you want, Mrs Hawthorne?' he asked tightly.

'I've come to have a little chat with you.'

'About what?'

She took a deep breath, took her spectacles from a leather handbag that had seen better days, put them on and peered at him.

'Looks like you'll live. Are you still claiming that bloke Willoughby shot you?'

'Yes. What's it got to do with you?'

'Plenty. You listen to me, Jake Tussup,' she hissed in his ear. 'And you listen good. I'm not sorry you've been shot but I won't allow the wrong man to take the blame. It's not the first time that's happened around here, is it?'

'I asked you what you wanted!'

'I'm coming to that. Someone shot you. It wasn't Willoughby. And you didn't die. My poor husband, a good and kind man, wasn't so lucky, was he?'

Jake twisted in his bed and pain flamed in his chest. He groaned but she ignored him.

'Trouble is,' she went on, 'my boys never did believe your dad killed their father. They always reckoned your dad was covering for someone. And they've always been very bitter about it.'

'Who shot me? Charlie?'

'No use looking at my lads, not Charlie, or Alec, or Bobs or even Billy . . . Billy's a policeman now, you know. I'm just telling you their opinion. It's a free country; they're entitled to their opinion. They think your dad was a saint and you're a rat. But me, I just want peace and quiet. Can you understand that?'

Jake glared at her, his mouth set hard.

'Yes, it's all long over for me,' she said quietly. 'I never married again, you know. Too busy trying to bring up four sons. It's a hard thing to lose your husband.'

'You already said that.'

'So I did,' she snapped. 'And I said I like the quiet life too, but that's something you'll never find in this town. If I was you I'd be worrying that whoever shot you would get it right next time . . .'

'Are you threatening me?'

'Jake, your poor dear mum and me were great mates. Why would I do that? She'd be pleased I've come to see you. To see you're all right.'

She took off the spectacles, and placed them carefully in her bag. And when she looked up at him he saw the hatred in her eyes.

Had she shot him herself? She could have. The Hawthorne clan were all hunters, he recalled. They were known, even back then to be good shots.

Mrs Hawthorne patted him on the arm as a nurse whisked past the open door.

'You'll be all right now, Jake,' she said kindly. And with a thin smile on her weather-beaten face, she whispered: 'In here. I just needed to tell you I don't think it's safe out there for you. Not safe at all. The sooner you get out of this town the better. Now see here, you lie quiet and get better.'

He watched angrily as she glided out of the room and chatted cheerfully in the corridor with the nurse. For all the world the benevolent neighbour.

When the sergeant came back he was babbling that one of the Hawthornes had shot him. That Mrs Hawthorne had been in, threatening him.

'I heard she was very kind to you, Jake. She brought you some cakes.'

'You don't know her like I do,' he protested.

'And how would that be?' the sergeant said acidly, 'since you haven't seen her in fifteen years, and seen how hard she has worked, not only for her family but for the Church.'

But later, since no suspects had been rounded up, he did mention Jake's latest claim to Carl Muller.

'It's a possibility,' Carl said. 'There was a rumour at the time that it was actually Jake who had shot Sergeant Hawthorne, but he was only a lad, and in the end he admitted it was his old man.' He sighed. 'You never know what sort of angers families chew on behind closed doors. Maybe one of the Hawthorne lads did have a go at Jake, but which one? It'd be hell trying to pin one of them down, and Billy's in the force! Far from threatening him, I think Mrs Hawthorne would have been trying to keep the peace, afraid Jake'd go out looking for payback.'

Muller pondered that problem. 'Any other strangers seen in the town at that time.'

'No.' The sergeant shook his head. 'I think I'll just wait and see what Tussup does. His background's murky anyway, by the sound of things. It wouldn't hurt to see what we can find out about him.'

As it turned out, from the sergeant's point of view, nothing happened. The sleepy town went about its business, the incident having faded into obscurity before the amazing sight of a gentleman riding down its main street on the first penny-farthing bicycle ever seen in the district.

Jake had never seen a bicycle, nor was he interested in such a one-day wonder, the talk of the hospital. He had finally persuaded the doctor to allow him to return home.

'You're still pretty weak on it,' that gentleman said. 'You'll have to take care. Keep warm. No activities, keep to three good meals a day to put some pepper back in you and have a rum and hot milk every night. Now how're you gonna do that out there in that hut on your own?'

'I'll manage. I'll feel better when I get home.'

'All right then. I'll think about it.'

He did more than think. Days later, he took Jake home in his gig, arranged for Boysie's mum to cook his meals, and sent Boysie to bring back Mr Tussup's horse.

When the lad came to his door, Jake was moving quietly about his house, grateful that someone had been kind enough to nail canvas over the hole in the wall that he himself had made, more than two weeks back.

'So it wasn't Willoughby who shot you,' Boysie said.

'No. I was wrong,' Jake muttered.

'So who did?'

'I don't know.'

'They reckon in town 'twas an outlaw, mister.'

'Yeah, they would. What else are they saying?'

'They're saying you used to live here once, and you're only here to fix the house then you're going back to sea.'

'Who said that?'

'Mrs Hawthorne told my mum.'

'She did, did she?'

'Yeah. But you can't go until you can ride, can you? So I was thinking, while you're still here can I come over and ride your horse, give him some exercise?'

'I'd appreciate that, Boysie. Maybe you could go a few messages for me too. Earn a bit of savings money, eh?'

'Yeah,' Boysie said enthusiastically, his freckles twinkling on his small round face.

Late that afternoon, Jake sat in an old armchair by the stove to keep warm, his mug of hot milk heavily laced with rum, and thanked God that he'd escaped the hospital and the gruel they called food.

Boysie had bought the supplies for him. His mother, Clara, had cooked him a hotpot of lamb and vegetables and Jake had bogged into it as if he'd never had a decent meal before in his life. He felt a little better now. He was just a bit short of breath and rather wobbly on his legs, but that would pass. Then he had to get on with fixing this house. It couldn't be allowed to fall into complete ruin.

When he climbed from the chair to stoke the fire, the injured muscles in his chest complained and he lifted the poker with a gasp of pain, recalling the doctor's constant counsel that 'these things take time'. Unimpressed, he sank back into the chair and wrapped the blanket round his knees, realising that darkness was fast approaching, and the night held dangers. The Hawthornes would know he had left the hospital so this would be a good time for them, or one of them, to make good her threat. Jake was in no doubt now that the shooting had been a revenge attack, a settlement of old scores, so he had to be on guard. This time, as he pushed up from the chair, he forced himself to ignore the creaking pains and walked through to the bedroom to retrieve a handgun and ammunition from under a floor board. Returning to the kitchen he positioned the chair away from the window, with his back to the stove, and there he sat through the long, long night, jumping at every sound, until he heard the kookaburras, their loud hooting cackles always the first to welcome the dawn.

When Clara, a gaunt no-nonsense country woman, cast in the same mould as Mrs Hawthorne, found him asleep in his bed that midday, she was pleased to see him taking it easy, and he was too embarrassed to admit he'd not slept a wink all night, having kept a vigil against enemies.

'This can't go on,' he muttered, cutting off a slice of the corned beef she'd left for him. 'I won't let them terrorise me like this.' It occurred to him that they could simply be waiting for him to leave. After all, there was no rush.

'Ah! Who knows?' he asked himself angrily. 'I'm not sitting up all night again, that's for sure. I'll just see the gun's handy.' Not that the gun would be much use, he eventually had to admit, since he was so weary at night, he slept like a log.

He determined then, to get himself fit as soon as possible and began by taking a walk down to the back fence to put his muscles into the work force again. Eat, walk a little further each day, and then rest, became his regimen for recovery, until he had gained enough strength to begin light tasks around the house, but as his work progressed, Jake realised that even if he were completely fit, he didn't have the expertise to do this job properly, so he hired a carpenter.

From that day, Jake's life took a turn for the better. The carpenter was a knowledgeable fellow who pointed out that Jake was getting it all wrong. He insisted on sitting down and asking, first up, how much Jake could afford to pay for these renovations, and on finding that money wasn't a great problem, drew a plan of a larger farmhouse that delighted Jake. Having little imagination in these matters, he hadn't envisaged much more than making the old place habitable again, but this now, was a place to be proud of.

When solitude allowed that thought to revisit, and for him to think how thrilled his parents would have been to see such a fine cottage, he found himself weeping. Massive regrets swept over him for the misery he had caused his parents, who had so loved him they'd . . . he couldn't bear to think of his father's sacrifice, so he turned away and saw himself in the mirror, so much like his father it shocked him. And reminded him that it was time to face what had happened here, face it properly and clearly. He had shot the police officer, it had been a terrible accident. An accident. His father had insisted on taking the blame. Insisted. He blamed himself because he'd had an outlaw in his house. A crime in itself. If that man had not been present, he'd kept telling Jake, with his permission, his son would not have had that loaded gun in his hand.

'You do as I tell you,' Ted Tussup had ordered, 'and say what I tell you to say.'

'And so I did,' Jake wept. 'But I knew better. It was my responsibility. I should have spoken up. Taken the consequences. And the same with the *China Belle*. All I wanted to do was to jump ship and go prospecting, because the ship was so close to the goldfields. I didn't know I would be bringing an avalanche down on all of our heads.'

But an inner voice reproached him: 'You should have known. You had responsibilities. For that ship. For those women. Mrs Willoughby and Mrs Horwood. It's too late now for regrets.'

Only the hard work that he set himself, assisting the carpenter and bringing the farm back to life, staved off the depression that engulfed his soul. He no longer needed Clara to prepare his meals, and Boysie lost interest in him. When the carpenter left, rightly pleased with his work, Jake stood back and looked at his fine house and wept again, because he did, so much, wish his mother and his father could see how their home had grown. No one else mattered. And he no longer cared whether the Hawthornes came after him or not. He was tired of running.

Eventually it became evident that the Hawthornes had lost interest in him too, but by then he'd acquired more responsibilities . . . a mongrel dog that had taken up residence on his back porch, two cows, a plough horse, his own mount, and a screeching white cockatoo. And every evening, he sat on his veranda until sunset, looking down the long road, and thinking he might move on. There was another big gold strike at Mount Morgan, not too far north of Brisbane, and he thought about that, about how it might be worth a go, as the months drifted into years.

Mal rode steadily north, travelling inland through country towns and eventually climbing into the ranges and crossing the border into Queensland. He took a couple of days off at a small town called Warwick, to give himself and his horse a rest, and then he set off again for Willowvale sheep station on the Condamine River, forty miles ahead.

'It surely is a honey of a property,' he smiled as he followed a road that cut through Willowvale land. In the distance he could see the familiar red roof of the homestead, and beyond that, he knew, were the woolsheds where thousands of sheep were shorn every year.

His thoughts now turned back to Esme. Willowvale was everything he'd dreamed of. A man would be proud to bring a wife here. He wished she was with him now, so that he could talk things over with her. She was easy to talk to . . . 'when she doesn't get cranky with you', he murmured with a grin. But he hadn't explained the situation very well to her, and only because he hadn't got it right in his own head. Now, looking at the tranquil countryside, he felt reassured. They could both do with a steady, regular base after all the upheavals, and time to sit and look at the stars. He understood that the fondness they had for each other was in itself a kind of love, a different sort of love from the passion he'd shared with Jun Lien, and it had to be different from the relationship Esme had shared with Neville. But that didn't lessen its intensity, nor did it make it less enduring. They should wed, he agreed with himself. They could have a fine marriage and a good life here.

'I should write and ask her to come to Willowvale,' he pondered, but a warning voice objected.

'No you won't. You have to do the gentlemanly thing. Go and ask her, formally. Bring her to her new home in style.'

Two stockmen were riding towards him, their dogs darting ahead to yap at the stranger.

'I'm Willoughby,' he said, extending a hand.

'Ah yes,' the older man said. 'I'm Mac, and this here is Russ. We've been expecting you. Come on up to the house. You come far?'

'From Goulburn.'

'Ah, good on you,' Mac said. 'Fair sort of a ride. The boss says you bought the place.'

'That's right.'

'You been here before? I mean to say, you didn't just stick a pin in a map didja?'

'No,' Mal laughed. 'I was brought here to have a look around when I was a little kid. My granddad opened up this run. He overlanded sheep from Sydney.'

He shrugged and looked around him. 'The family fell on hard times, and they lost the place. I always hoped to get it back one day.'

'Well, the boss'll be rightly pleased to meet you mate. He's too sick to carry on and he's been hoping Willowvale would go to someone with a feel for it.'

'Reckon Mr Willoughby'll fill his boots all right,' the other stockman said. 'But let me tell you for the start, boss, there ain't no willow trees here. Umpteen square miles we got here and not none of us ever found a willow. People are always looking for them.'

Mal laughed. 'Keep looking.'

All three of them rode up to the large, rambling homestead and around the carriage drive to the front steps. An elderly man made his way down as they dismounted.

'You must be, Mr Willoughby,' he said, reaching out to Mal. 'I did a bit of checking when I heard your name. I hope you'll be very happy here. Welcome home.'

When all was signed and sealed, when Willowvale was finally his and he had waved farewell to the former owner, Mal breathed a sigh of relief and turned his attention to matters of urgency. He strode across the home paddock, past all the work sheds and the men's living quarters, past the stables and over a low bridge to the shearing sheds, presently deserted. Then he followed a narrow path up to the small cemetery that sat sentinel on a windy hill. There were about twenty graves beyond the wrought-iron fence, but Malachi Willoughby's plain white headstone still held pride of place by the gate.

Mal walked in and knocked on the headstone. 'Are you there, Malachi?' he called, jubilation in his voice. 'Do you remember me? I never met you, but my dad and I snuck in here years ago, when I was a kid. We were riding past, along that very road down there, and he said he'd show me Grandpa's grave. And here I am again, with the best news in the world for you. I've got your land back, Grandpa. It's ours. And let me tell you, I'll see to it that the family holds on to it this time.'

He looked out over the pastureland at the flocks of sheep grazing on the hillsides. 'Of course, the family might take a little time. I have a lady in mind. If she'll have me. We'll have a grand wedding in Willowvale's own chapel over there. You'll like her, she's a feisty redhead, the prettiest redhead you ever did see. And she's one heck of a card player . . .'